ALSO FROM JOE BOOKS

Disney Frozen Cinestory Comic
Disney Cinderella Cinestory Comic
Disney 101 Dalmatians Cinestory Comic
Disney Princess Comics Treasury
Disney • Pixar Comics Treasury
Disney's Darkwing Duck: The Definitively Dangerous Edition
Disney Frozen: The Story of the Movie in Comics
Disney Big Hero 6 Cinestory Comic
Disney • Pixar Inside Out Cinestory Comic
Disney • Pixar Inside Out Fun Book
Disney Gravity Falls Cinestory Comic Volume One
Disney • Pixar The Good Dinosaur Cinestory Comic
Disney • Pixar The Good Dinosaur Fun Book
Disney Zootopia Cinestory Comic
Disney Winnie the Pooh Cinestory Comic
Disney Descendants Wicked World Cinestory Comic Volume One
Disney Alice in Wonderland Cinestory Comic
Disney • Pixar Finding Nemo Cinestory Comic
Disney Star vs the Forces of Evil Cinestory Comic
Disney • Pixar Cars Cinestory Comic
Thor: Dueling with Giants
DreamWorks Kung Fu Panda 3 Cinestory Comic

Don't miss our monthly comics…

Disney Princess
Disney Darkwing Duck
Disney • Pixar Finding Dory
DreamWorks Madagascar
DreamWorks Shrek

And Disney Frozen, launching in July!

Disney · PIXAR

FINDING DORY

CINESTORY COMIC

JOE BOOKS LTD

Published in the United States and Canada by Joe Books, Ltd.
567 Queen St W, Toronto, ON M5V 2B6
www.joebooks.com

Library and Archives Canada Cataloguing in Publication information is available upon request.
ISBN 978-1-98803-247-4 (Joe Books US edition)
ISBN 978-1-77275-298-4 (Joe Books ebook edition)
ISBN 978-1-44345-080-5 (HarperCollins Canadian edition)
ISBN 978-1-78585-786-7 (Titan UK edition)

First Joe Books, Ltd. edition: June 2016

Disney · PIXAR
FINDING DORY

CINESTORY COMIC

ADAPTATION, DESIGN, LETTERING, LAYOUT AND EDITING:
For Readhead Books:
Alberto Garrido, Ernesto Lovera, Ester Salguero, Salvador Navarro,
Rocío Salguero, Eduardo Alpuente, Heidi Roux, Aaron Sparrow,
Heather Penner and Carolynn Prior.

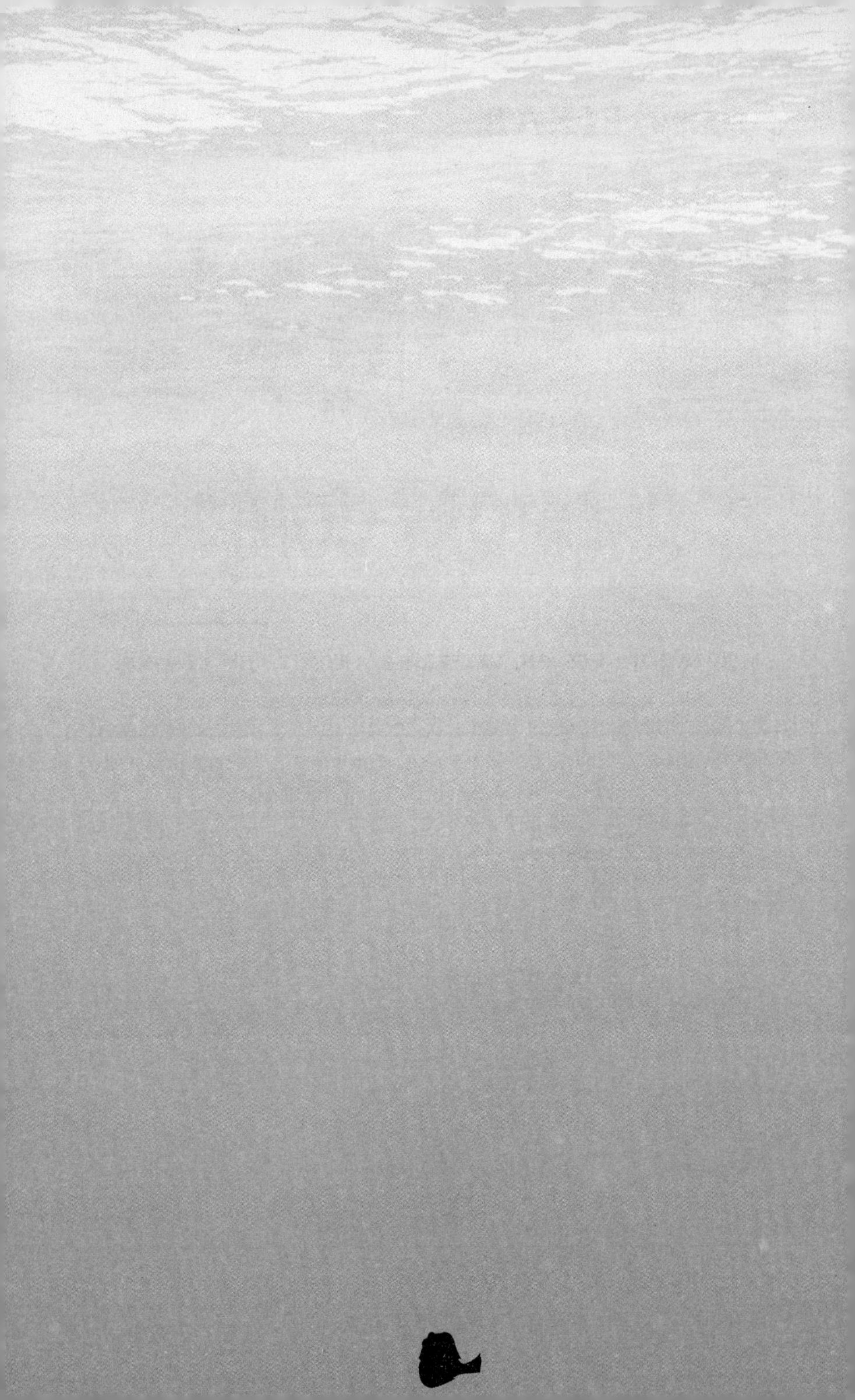

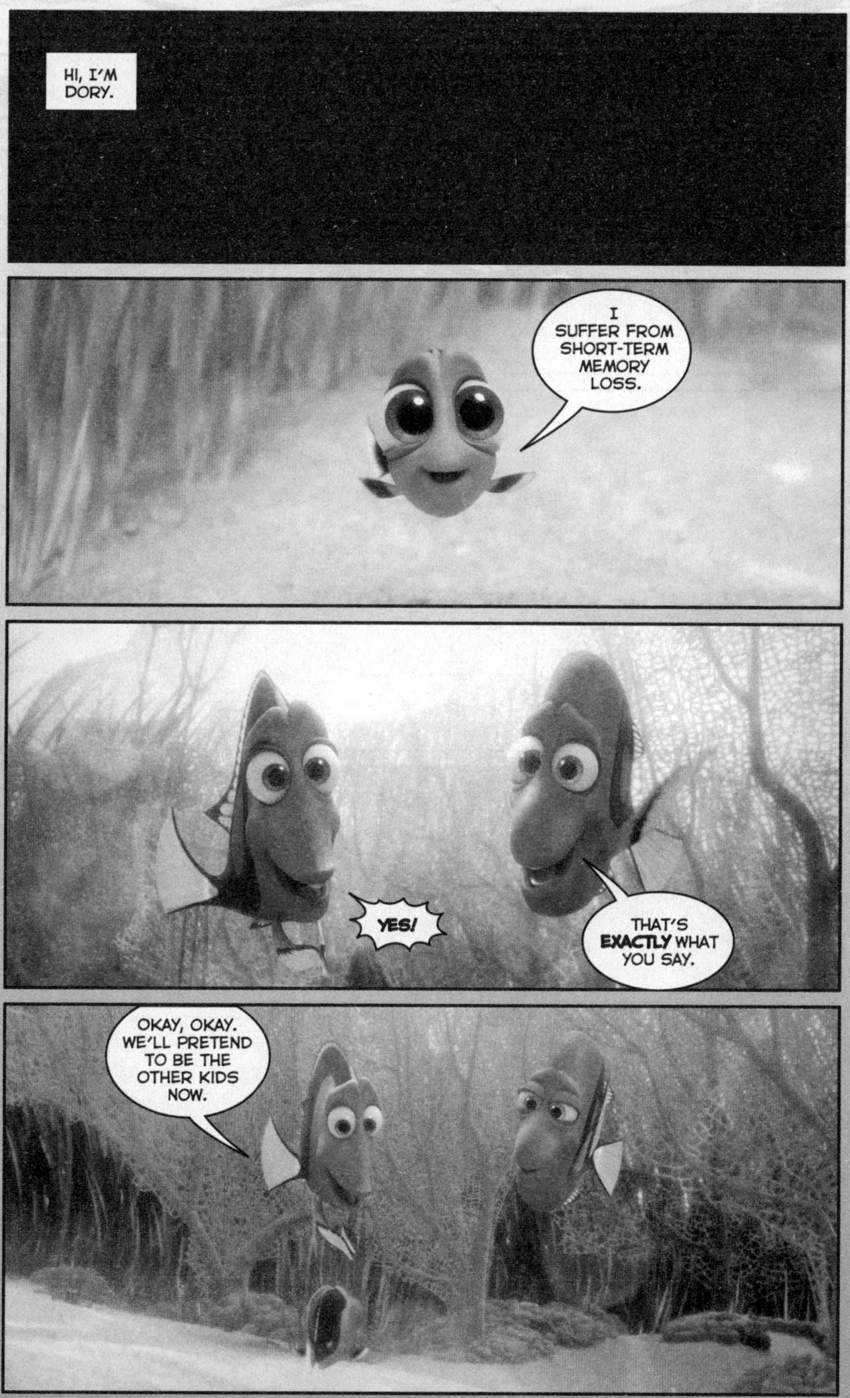
HI, I'M DORY.
I SUFFER FROM SHORT-TERM MEMORY LOSS.
YES!
THAT'S **EXACTLY** WHAT YOU SAY.
OKAY, OKAY. WE'LL PRETEND TO BE THE OTHER KIDS NOW.

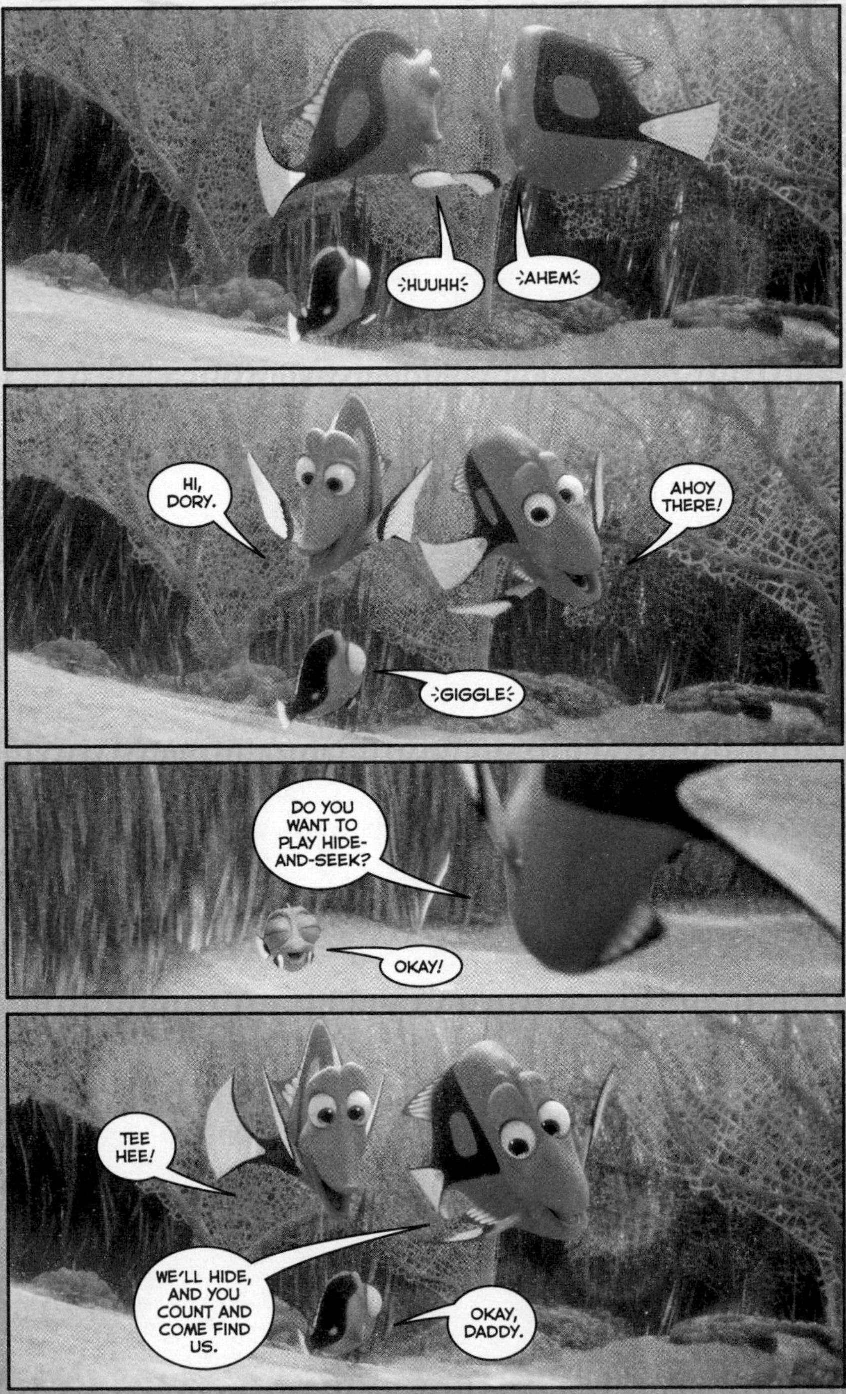
HUUHH
AHEM
HI, DORY.
AHOY THERE!
GIGGLE
DO YOU WANT TO PLAY HIDE-AND-SEEK?
OKAY!
TEE HEE!
WE'LL HIDE, AND YOU COUNT AND COME FIND US.
OKAY, DADDY.

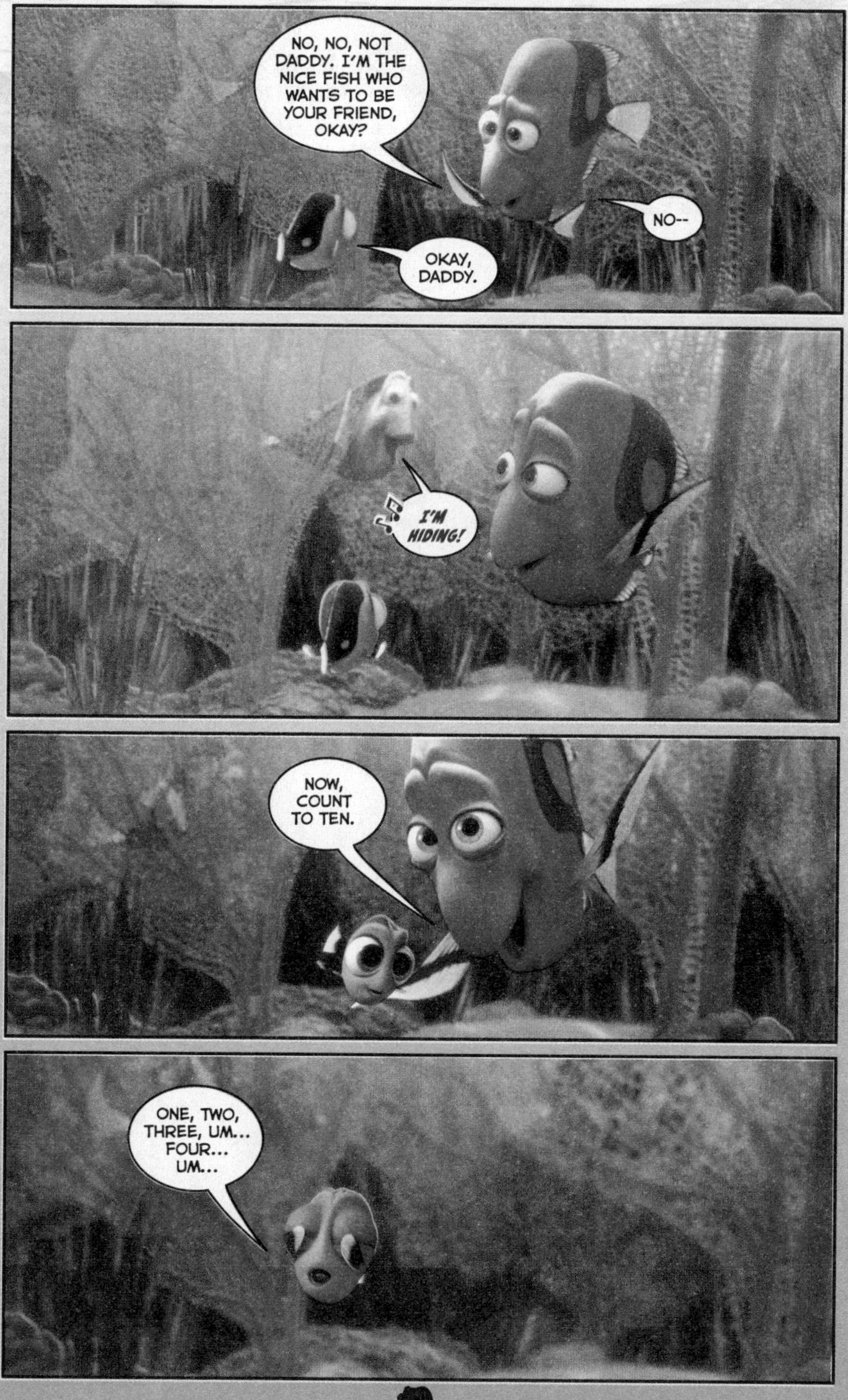
NO, NO, NOT DADDY. I'M THE NICE FISH WHO WANTS TO BE YOUR FRIEND, OKAY?
OKAY, DADDY.
NO--
I'M HIDING!
NOW, COUNT TO TEN.
ONE, TWO, THREE, UM... FOUR... UM...

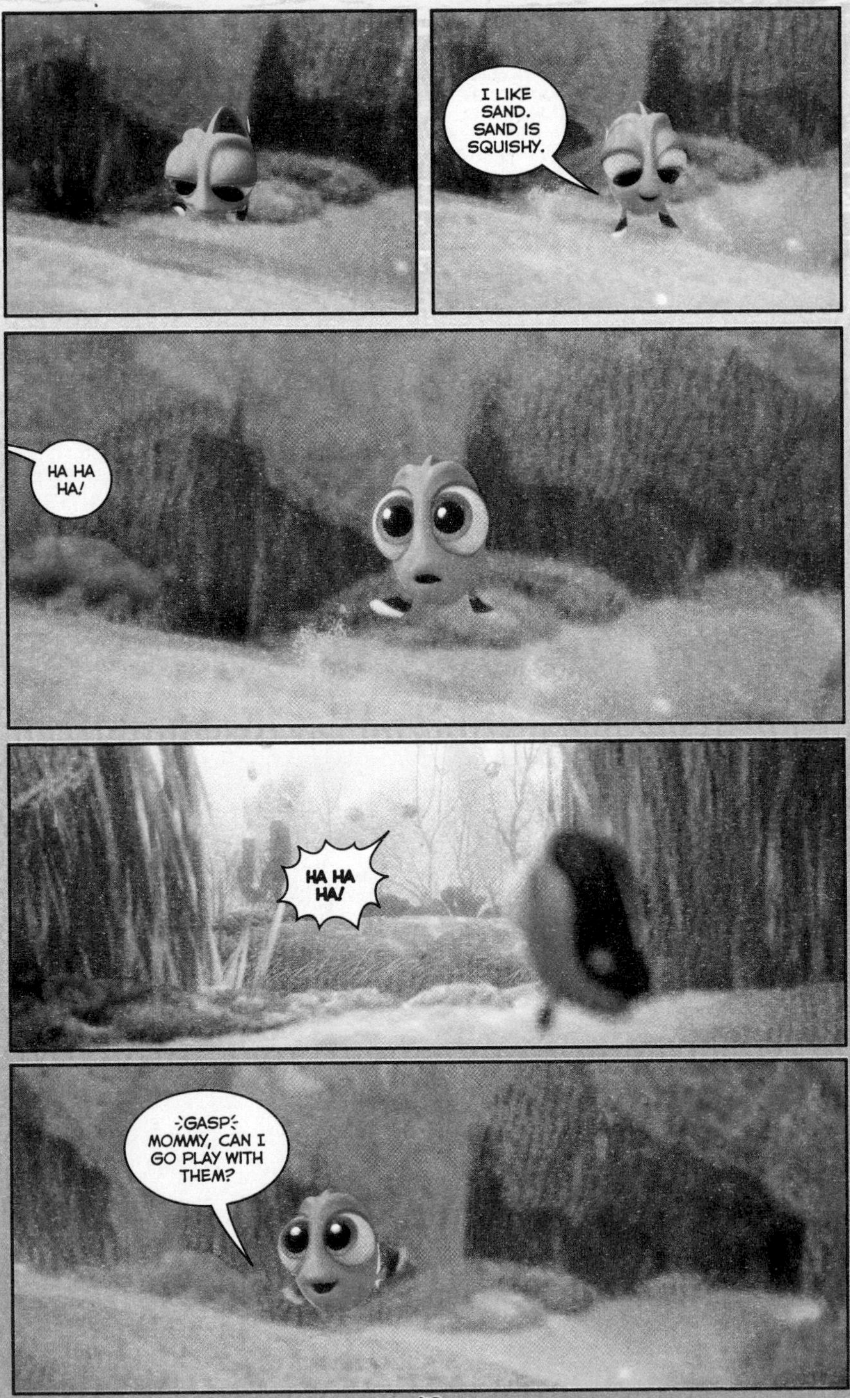
I LIKE SAND. SAND IS SQUISHY.
HA HA HA!
HA HA HA!
GASP MOMMY, CAN I GO PLAY WITH THEM?

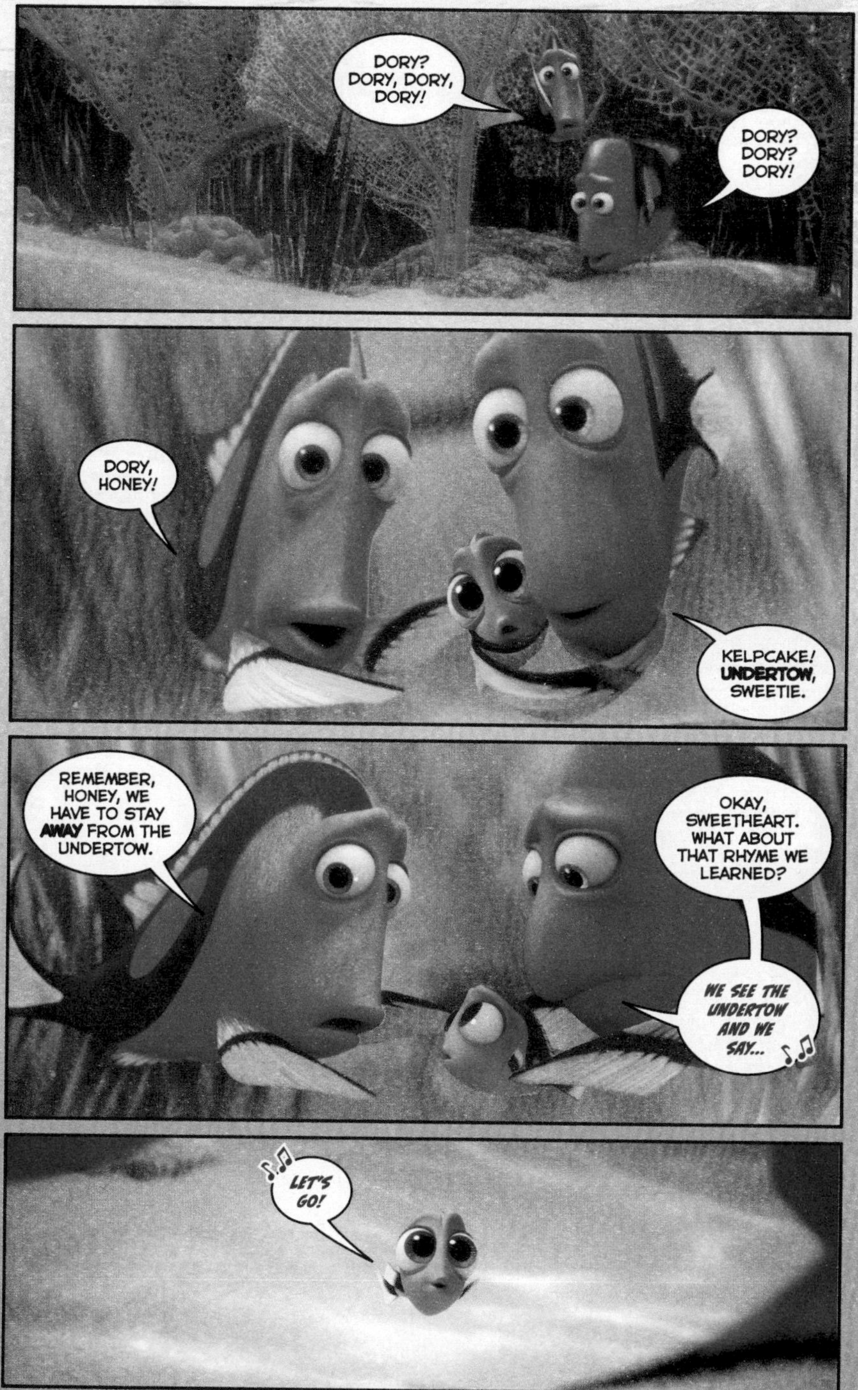
DORY? DORY, DORY, DORY!
DORY? DORY? DORY!
DORY, HONEY!
KELPCAKE! UNDERTOW, SWEETIE.
REMEMBER, HONEY, WE HAVE TO STAY AWAY FROM THE UNDERTOW.
OKAY, SWEETHEART. WHAT ABOUT THAT RHYME WE LEARNED?
WE SEE THE UNDERTOW AND WE SAY...
LET'S GO!

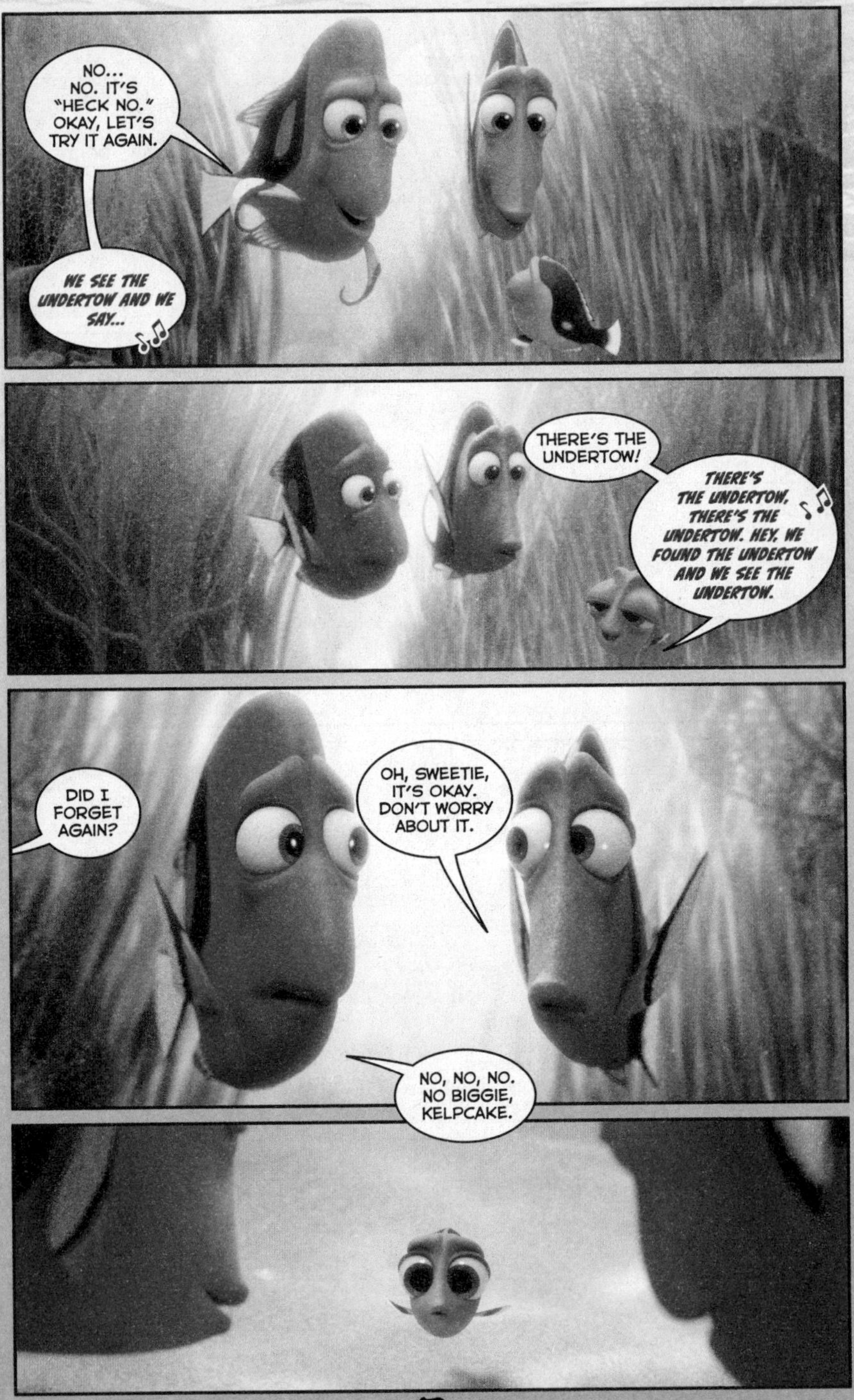
NO... NO. IT'S "HECK NO." OKAY, LET'S TRY IT AGAIN.
WE SEE THE UNDERTOW AND WE SAY...
THERE'S THE UNDERTOW!
THERE'S THE UNDERTOW, THERE'S THE UNDERTOW. HEY, WE FOUND THE UNDERTOW AND WE SEE THE UNDERTOW.
DID I FORGET AGAIN?
OH, SWEETIE, IT'S OKAY. DON'T WORRY ABOUT IT.
NO, NO, NO. NO BIGGIE, KELPCAKE.

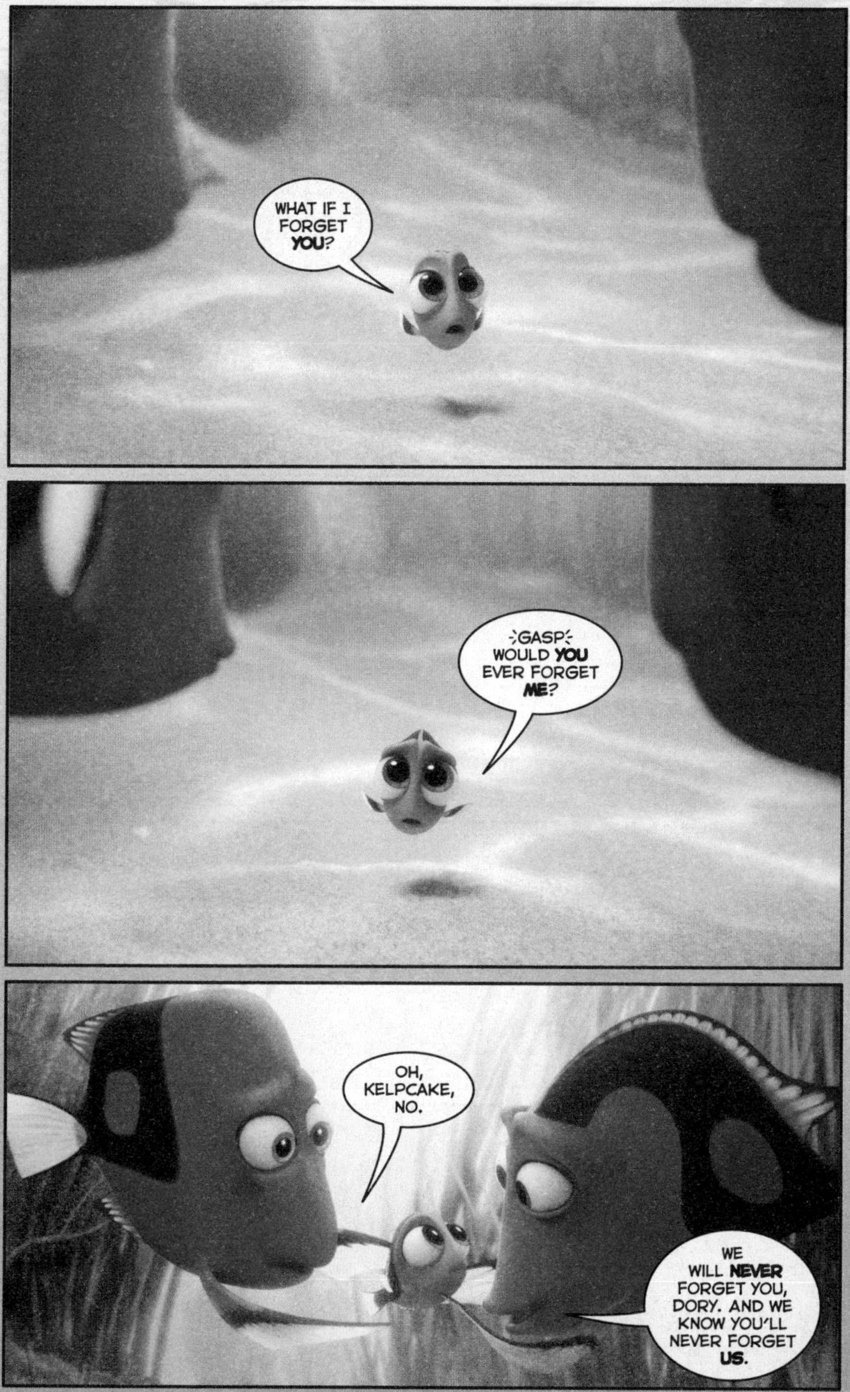
WHAT IF I FORGET **YOU**?
GASP WOULD **YOU** EVER FORGET **ME**?
OH, KELPCAKE, NO.
WE WILL **NEVER** FORGET YOU, DORY. AND WE KNOW YOU'LL NEVER FORGET **US**.

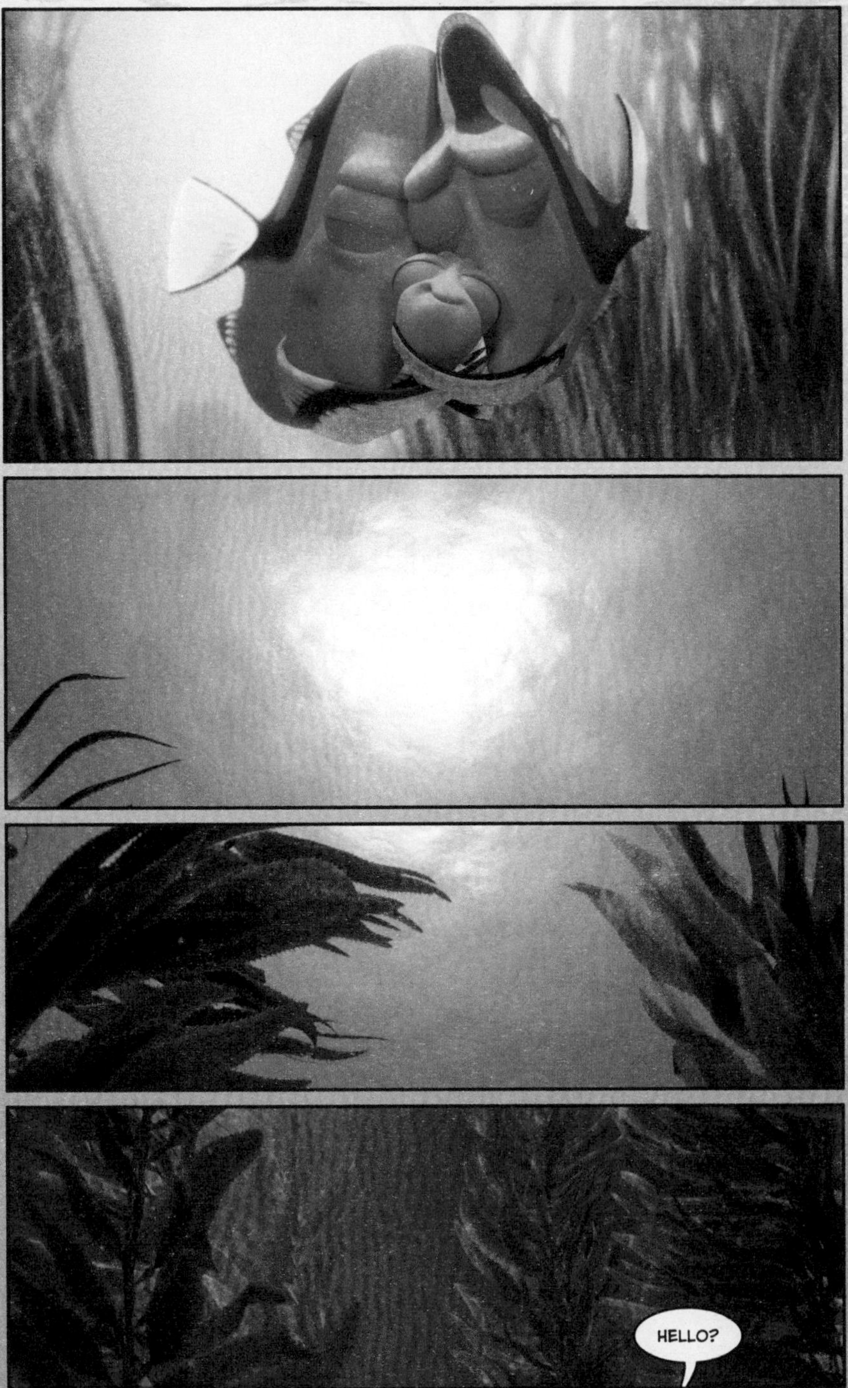
HELLO?

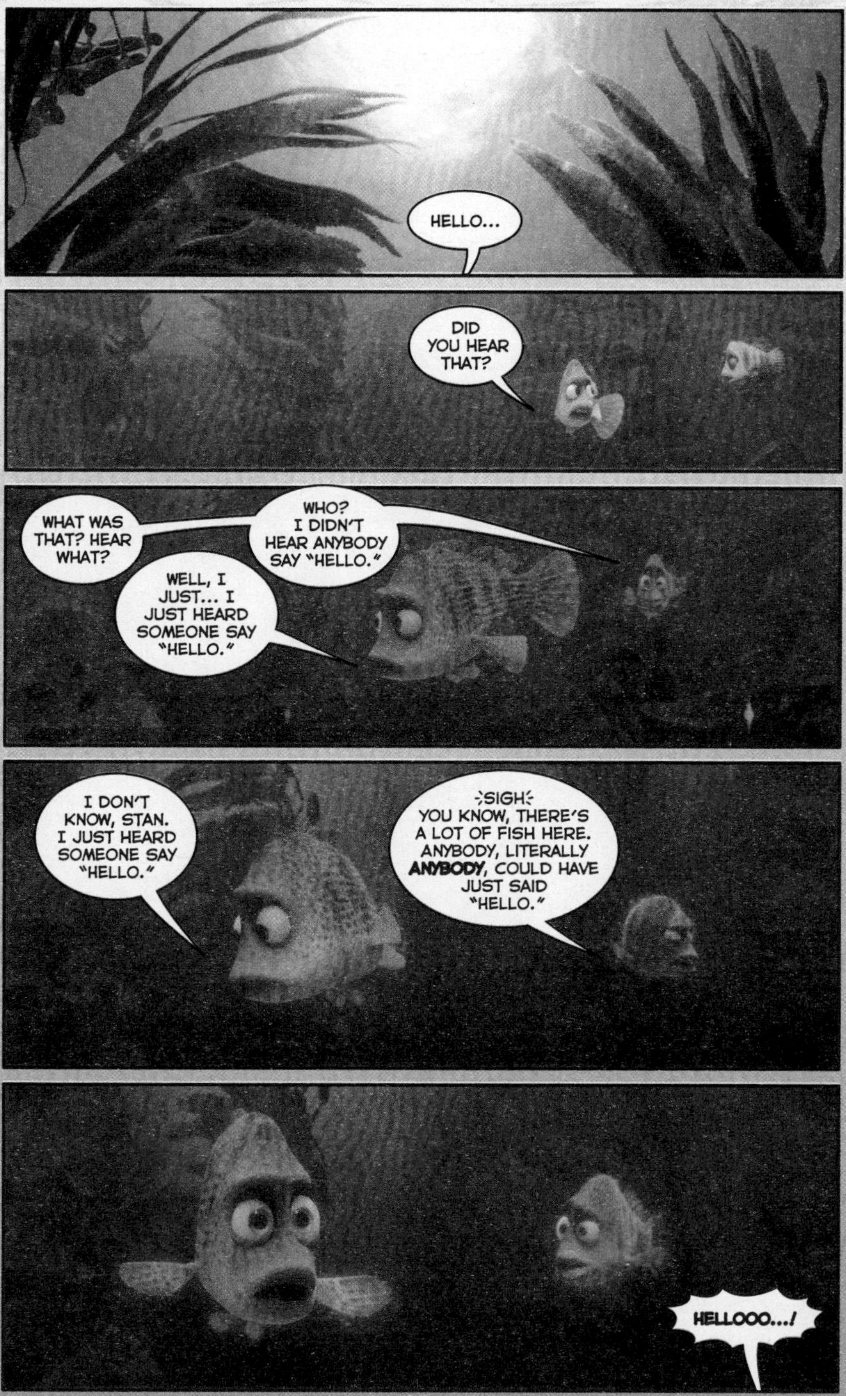
HELLO...
DID YOU HEAR THAT?
WHAT WAS THAT? HEAR WHAT?
WHO? I DIDN'T HEAR ANYBODY SAY "HELLO."
WELL, I JUST... I JUST HEARD SOMEONE SAY "HELLO."
I DON'T KNOW, STAN. I JUST HEARD SOMEONE SAY "HELLO."
-SIGH- YOU KNOW, THERE'S A LOT OF FISH HERE. ANYBODY, LITERALLY **ANYBODY**, COULD HAVE JUST SAID "HELLO."
HELLOOO...!

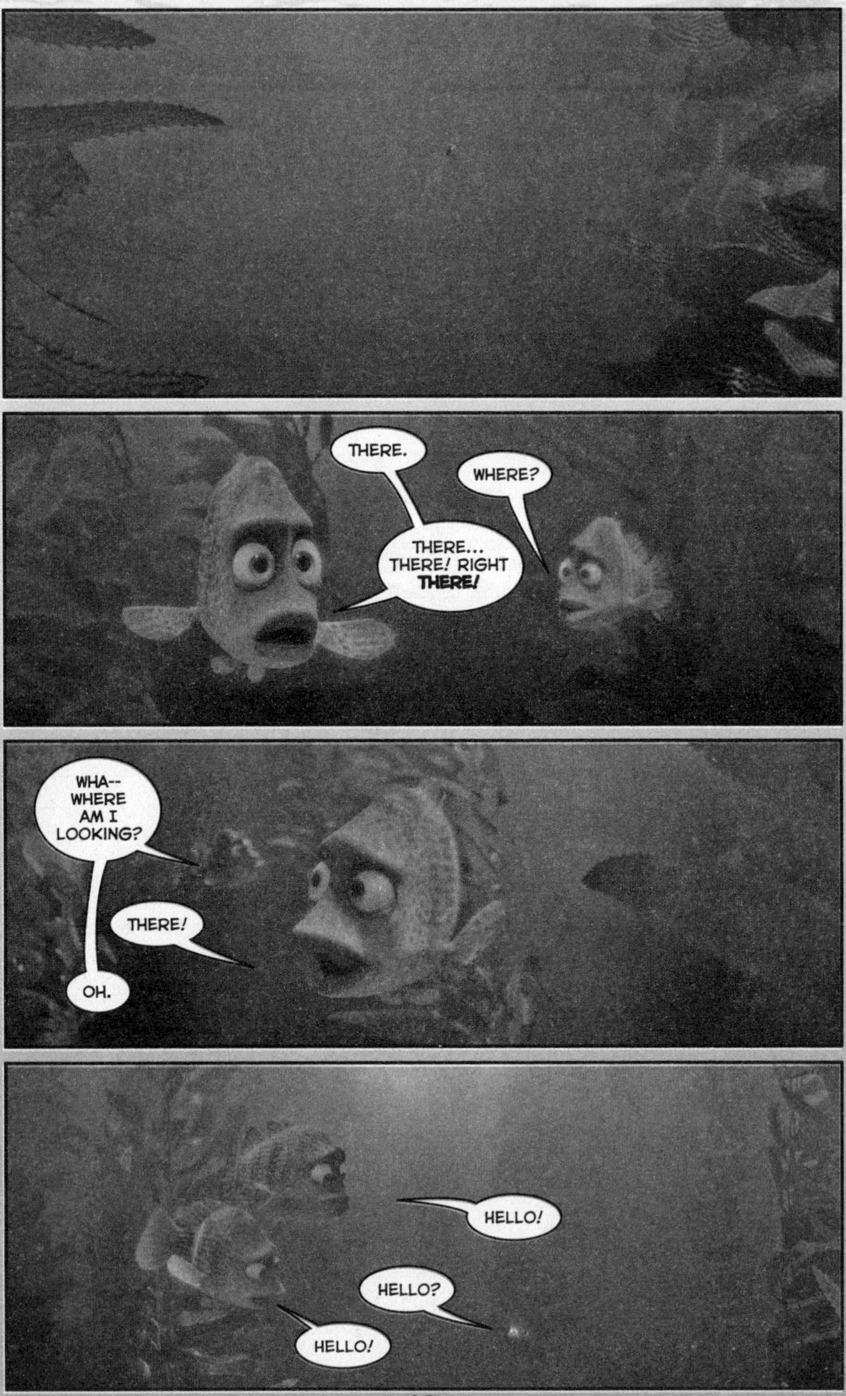
THERE.
WHERE?
THERE... THERE! RIGHT THERE!
WHA-- WHERE AM I LOOKING?
THERE!
OH.
HELLO!
HELLO?
HELLO!

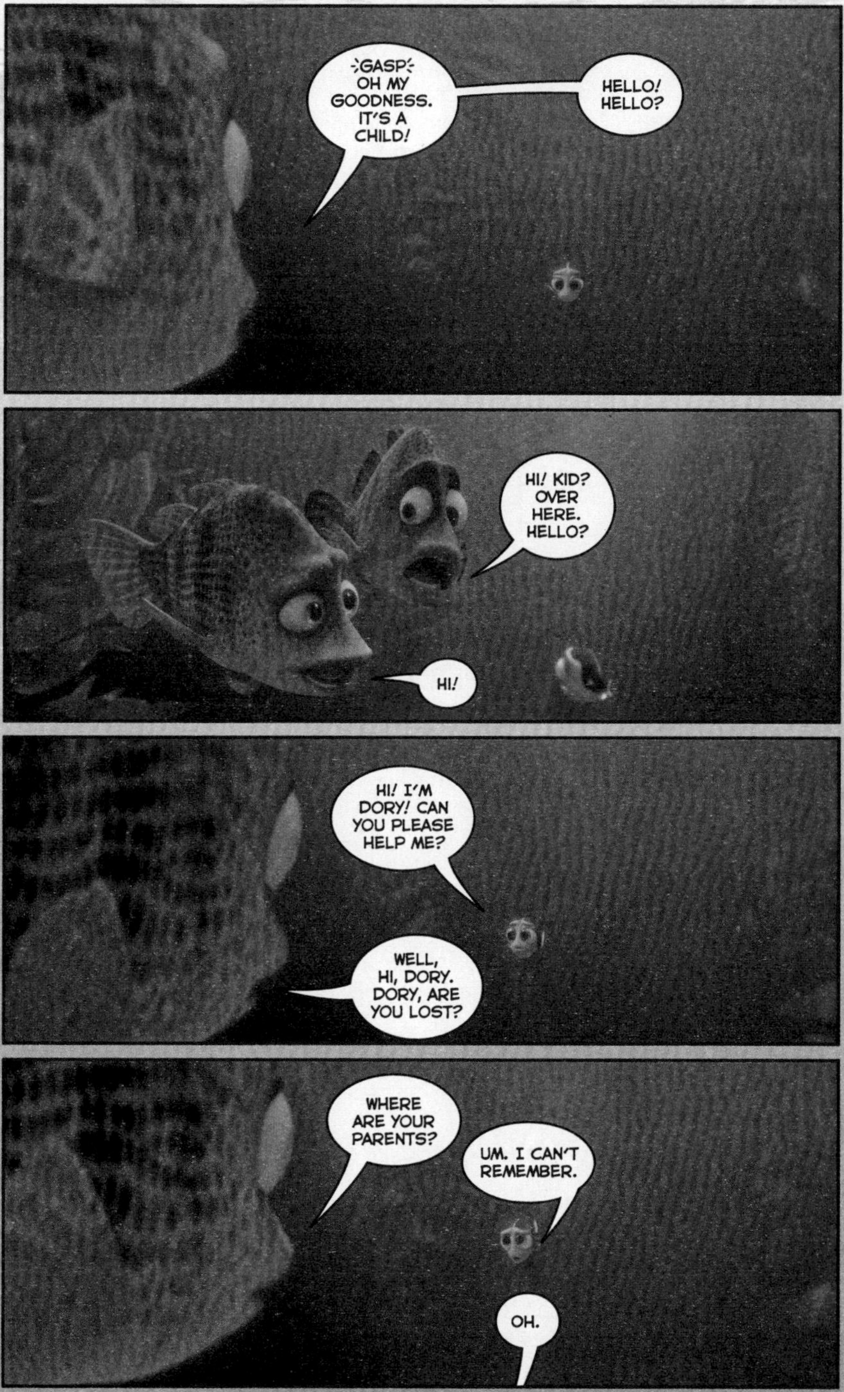
GASP
OH MY GOODNESS. IT'S A CHILD!
HELLO! HELLO?
HI! KID? OVER HERE. HELLO?
HI!
HI! I'M DORY! CAN YOU PLEASE HELP ME?
WELL, HI, DORY. DORY, ARE YOU LOST?
WHERE ARE YOUR PARENTS?
UM. I CAN'T REMEMBER.
OH.

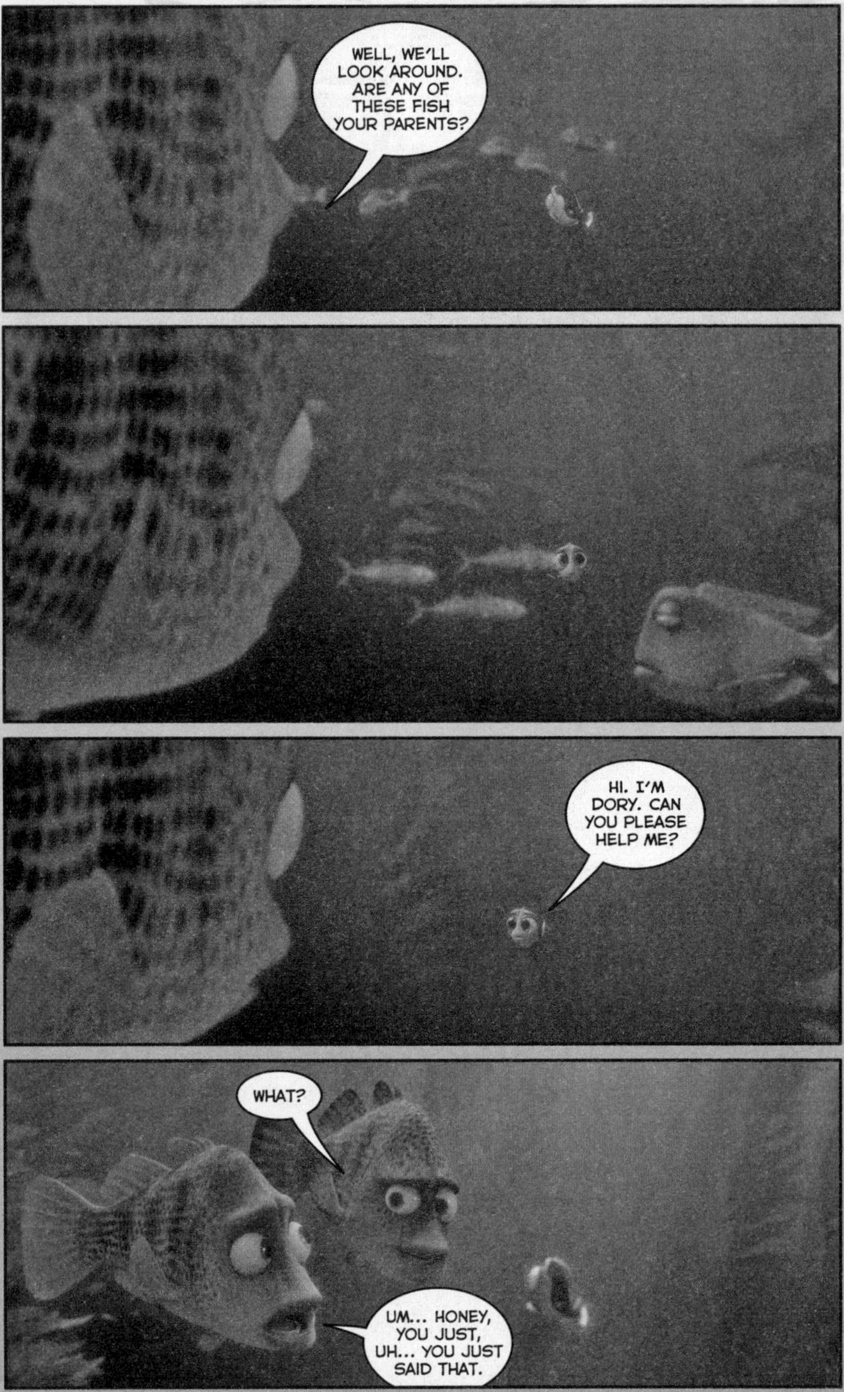
WELL, WE'LL LOOK AROUND. ARE ANY OF THESE FISH YOUR PARENTS?
HI. I'M DORY. CAN YOU PLEASE HELP ME?
WHAT?
UM... HONEY, YOU JUST, UH... YOU JUST SAID THAT.

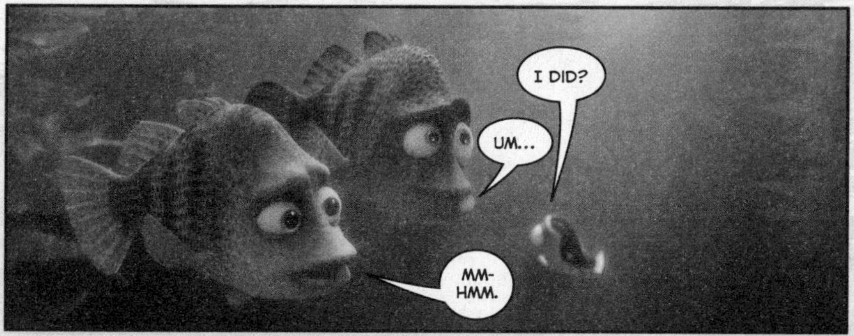
I DID?
UM...
MM-HMM.

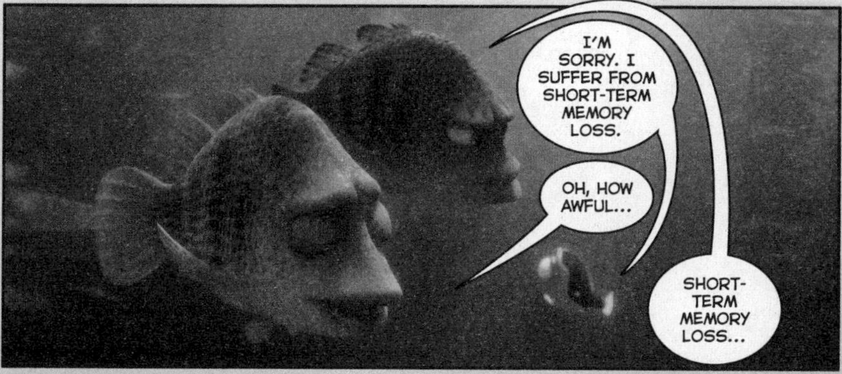
I'M SORRY. I SUFFER FROM SHORT-TERM MEMORY LOSS.
OH, HOW AWFUL...
SHORT-TERM MEMORY LOSS...

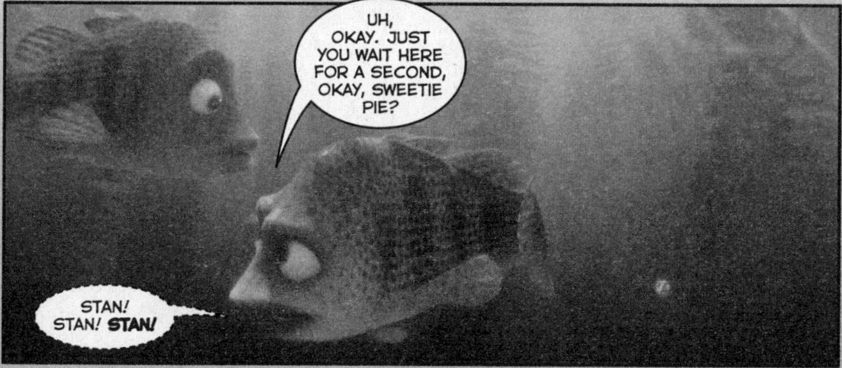
UH, OKAY. JUST YOU WAIT HERE FOR A SECOND, OKAY, SWEETIE PIE?
STAN! STAN! **STAN!**

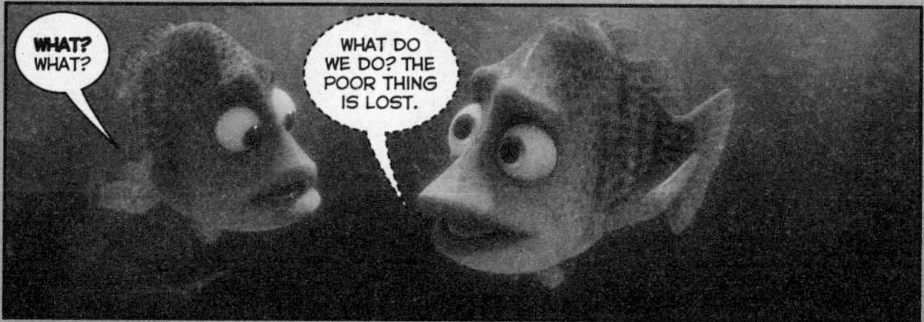
WHAT? WHAT?
WHAT DO WE DO? THE POOR THING IS LOST.

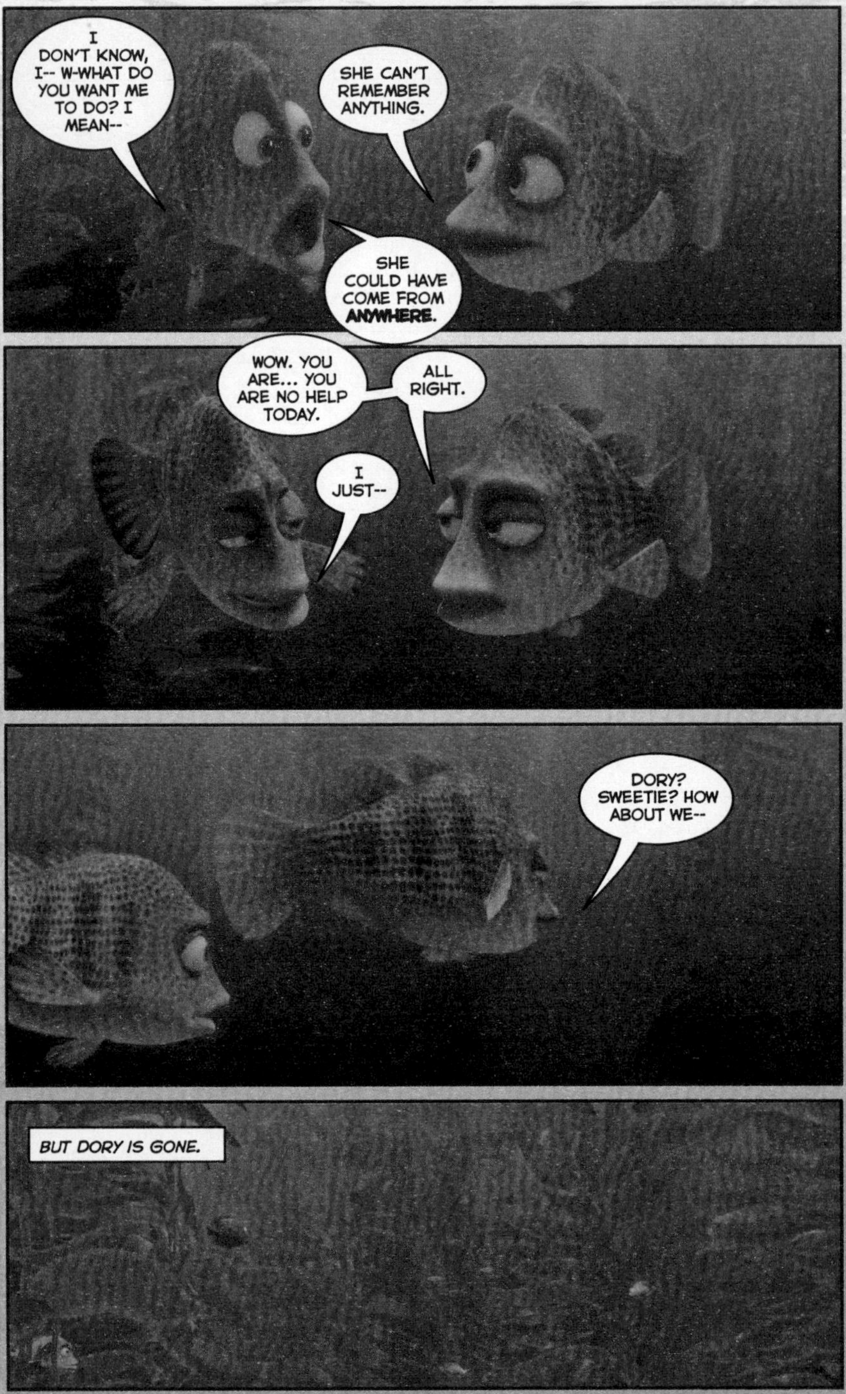
I DON'T KNOW, I-- W-WHAT DO YOU WANT ME TO DO? I MEAN--
SHE CAN'T REMEMBER ANYTHING.
SHE COULD HAVE COME FROM **ANYWHERE**.
WOW. YOU ARE... YOU ARE NO HELP TODAY.
ALL RIGHT.
I JUST--
DORY? SWEETIE? HOW ABOUT WE--
BUT DORY IS GONE.

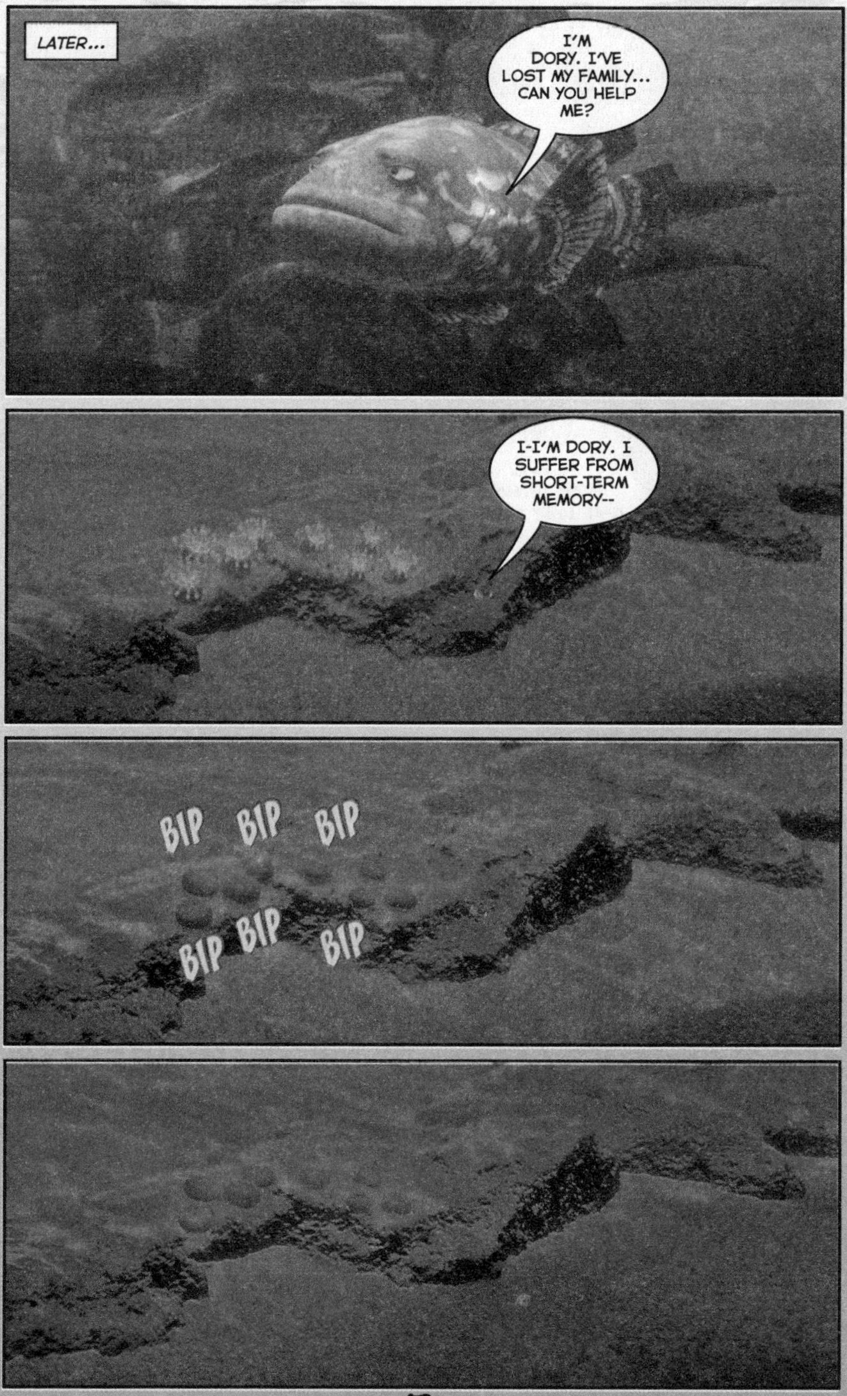
LATER...
I'M DORY. I'VE LOST MY FAMILY... CAN YOU HELP ME?
I-I'M DORY. I SUFFER FROM SHORT-TERM MEMORY--
BIP BIP BIP
BIP BIP BIP

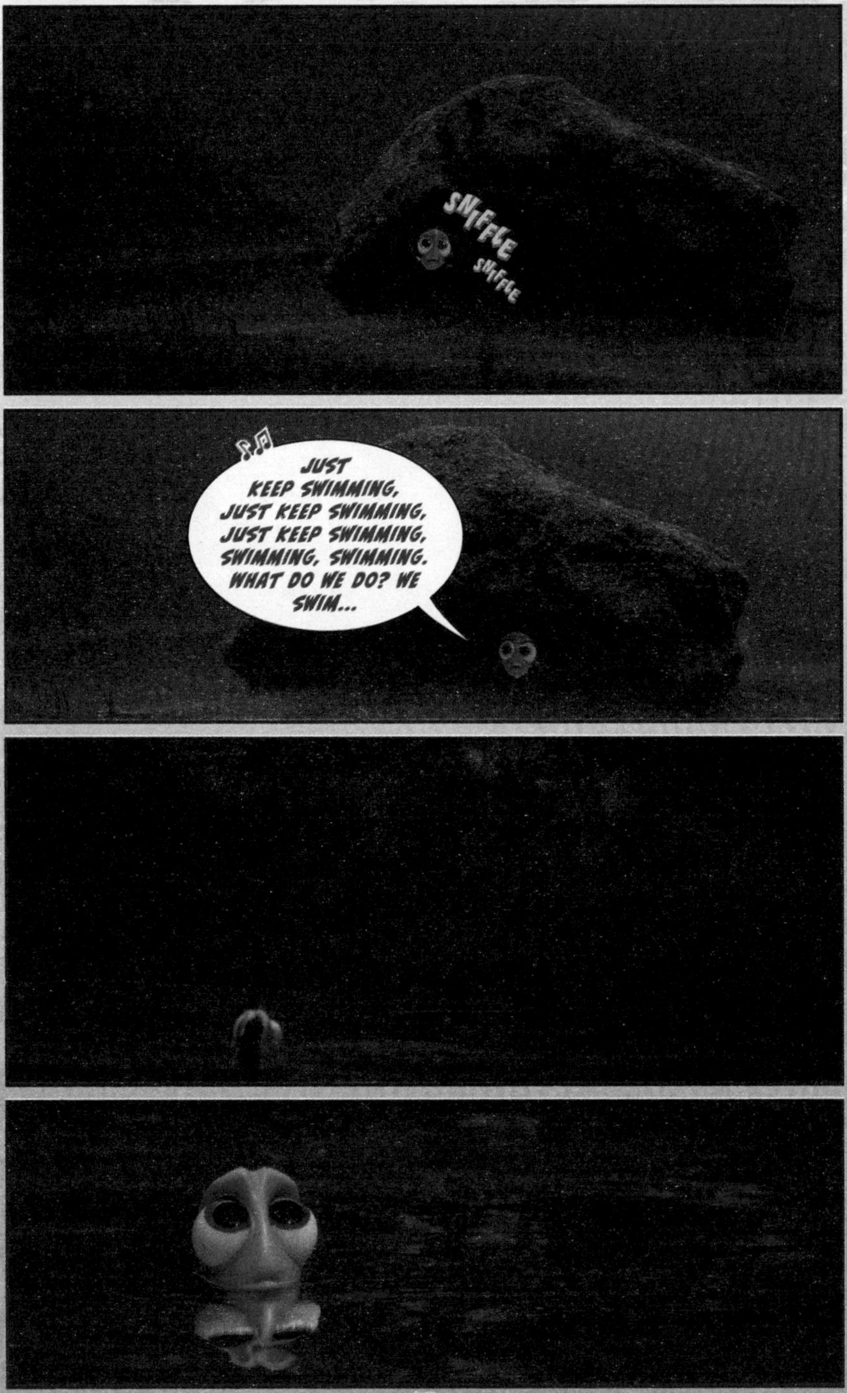
SNIFFLE
SNIFFLE
JUST KEEP SWIMMING, JUST KEEP SWIMMING, JUST KEEP SWIMMING, SWIMMING, SWIMMING. WHAT DO WE DO? WE SWIM...

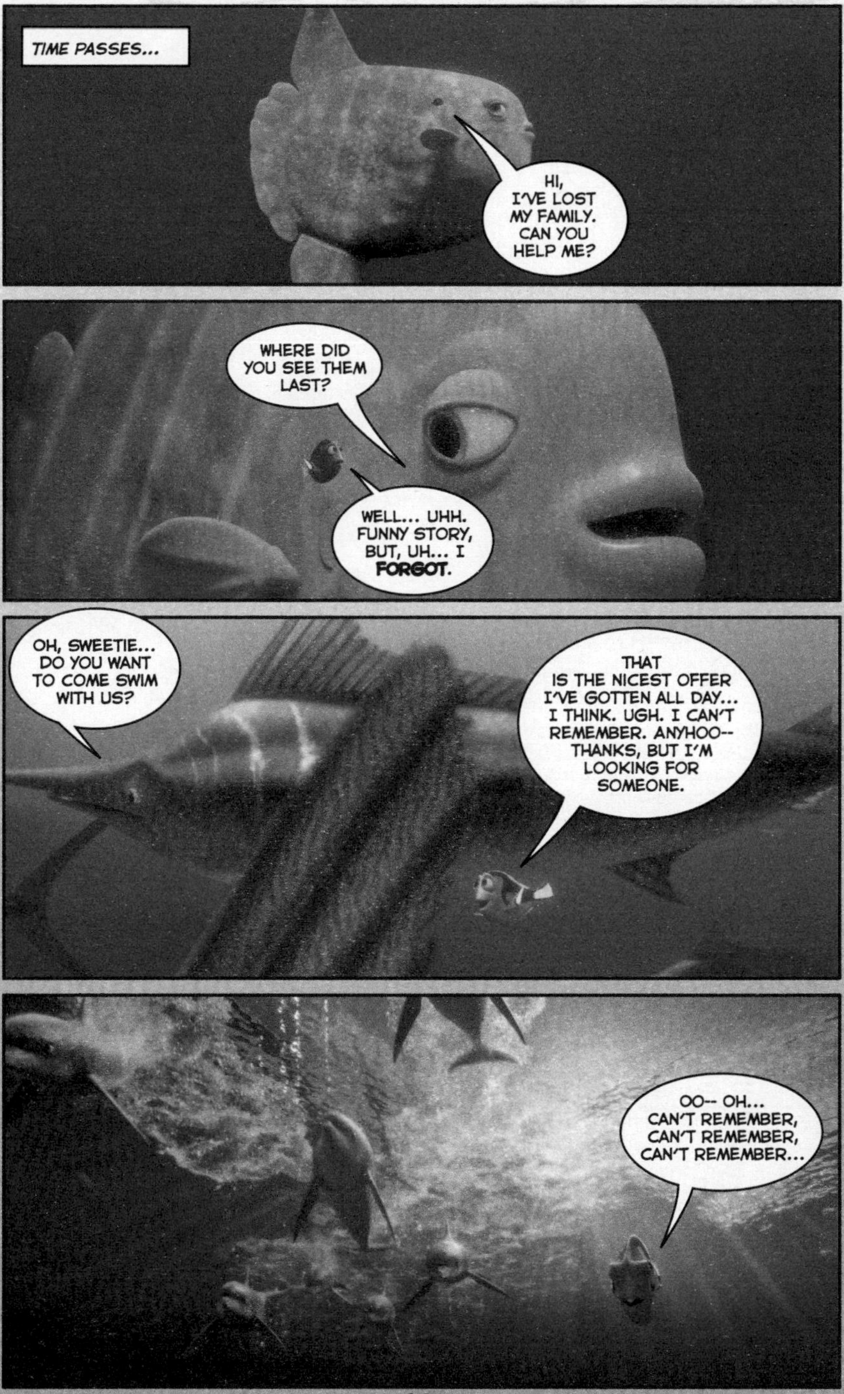
TIME PASSES...
HI, I'VE LOST MY FAMILY. CAN YOU HELP ME?
WHERE DID YOU SEE THEM LAST?
WELL... UHH. FUNNY STORY, BUT, UH... I **FORGOT**.
OH, SWEETIE... DO YOU WANT TO COME SWIM WITH US?
THAT IS THE NICEST OFFER I'VE GOTTEN ALL DAY... I THINK. UGH. I CAN'T REMEMBER. ANYHOO-- THANKS, BUT I'M LOOKING FOR SOMEONE.
OO-- OH... CAN'T REMEMBER, CAN'T REMEMBER, CAN'T REMEMBER...

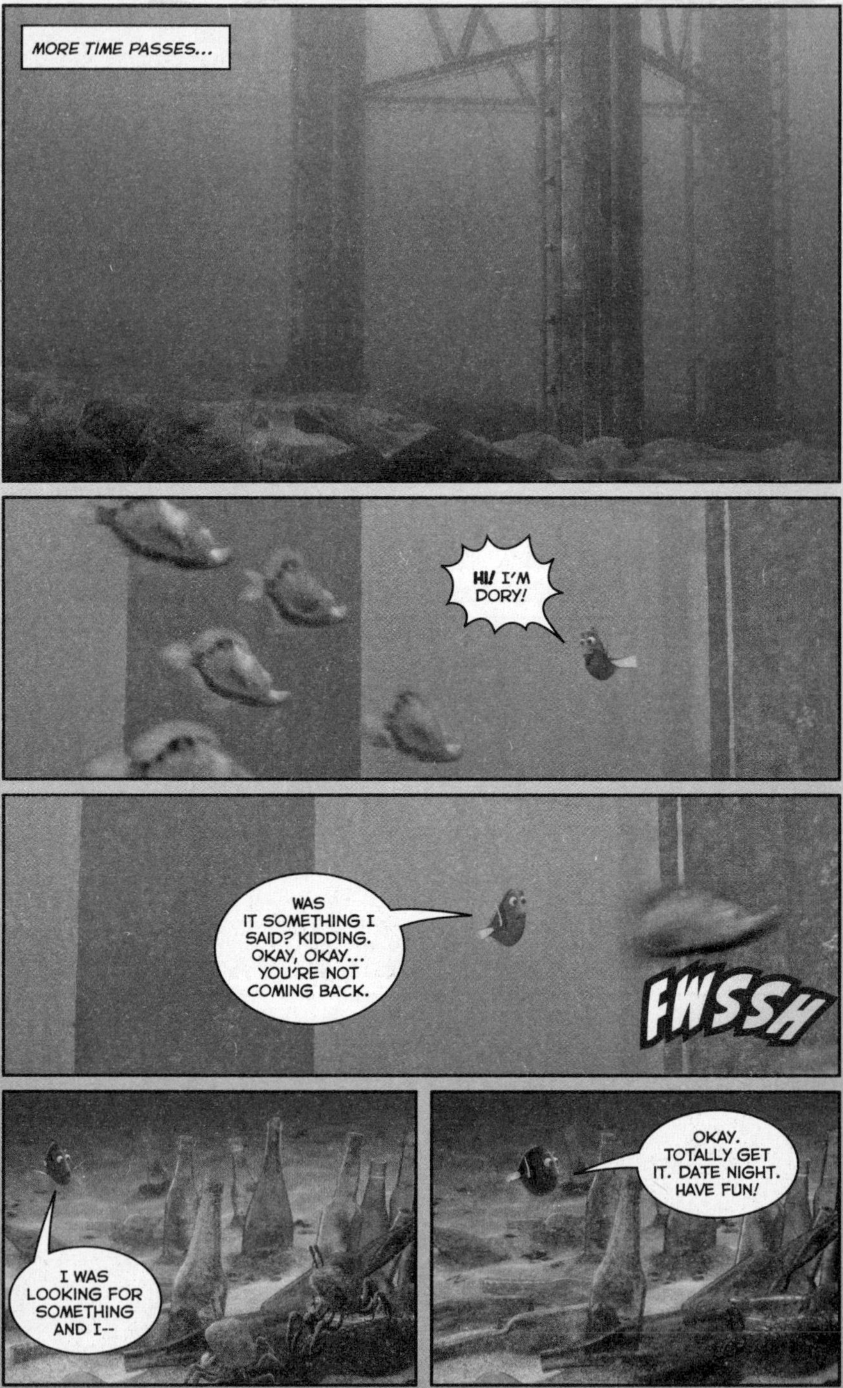
MORE TIME PASSES...
HI! I'M DORY!
WAS IT SOMETHING I SAID? KIDDING. OKAY, OKAY... YOU'RE NOT COMING BACK.
FWSSH
I WAS LOOKING FOR SOMETHING AND I--
OKAY. TOTALLY GET IT. DATE NIGHT. HAVE FUN!

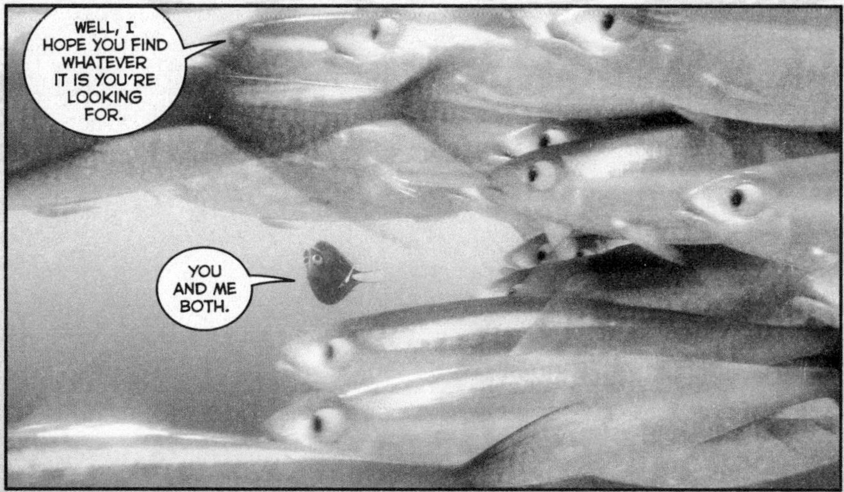
WELL, I HOPE YOU FIND WHATEVER IT IS YOU'RE LOOKING FOR.
YOU AND ME BOTH.

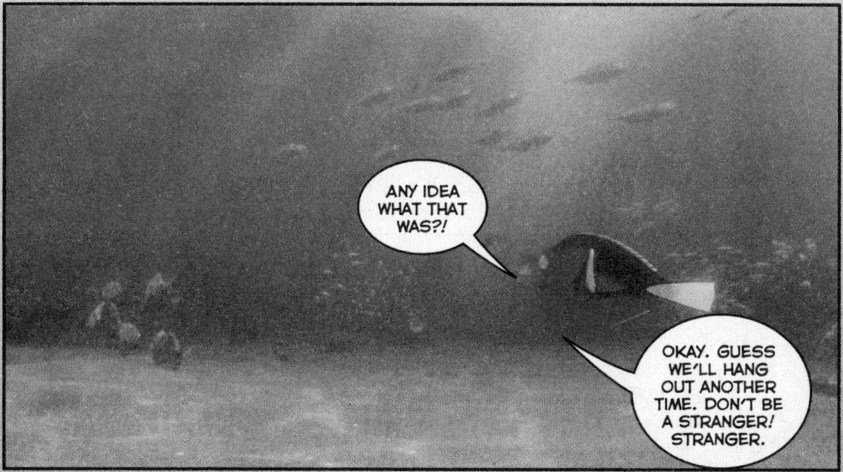
ANY IDEA WHAT THAT WAS?!
OKAY. GUESS WE'LL HANG OUT ANOTHER TIME. DON'T BE A STRANGER! STRANGER.

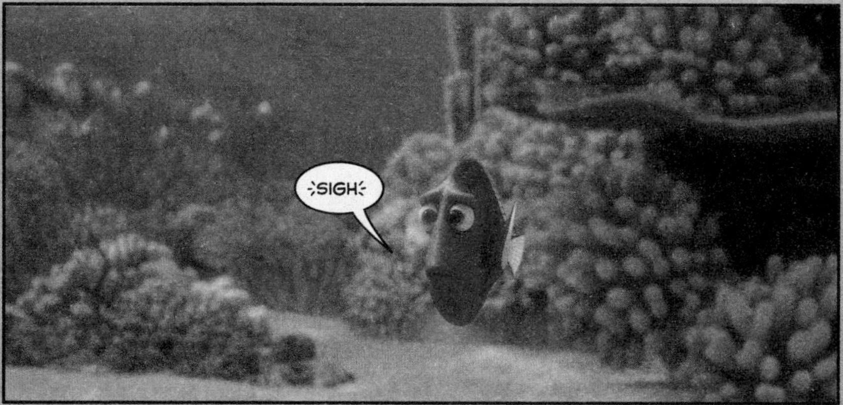
SIGH

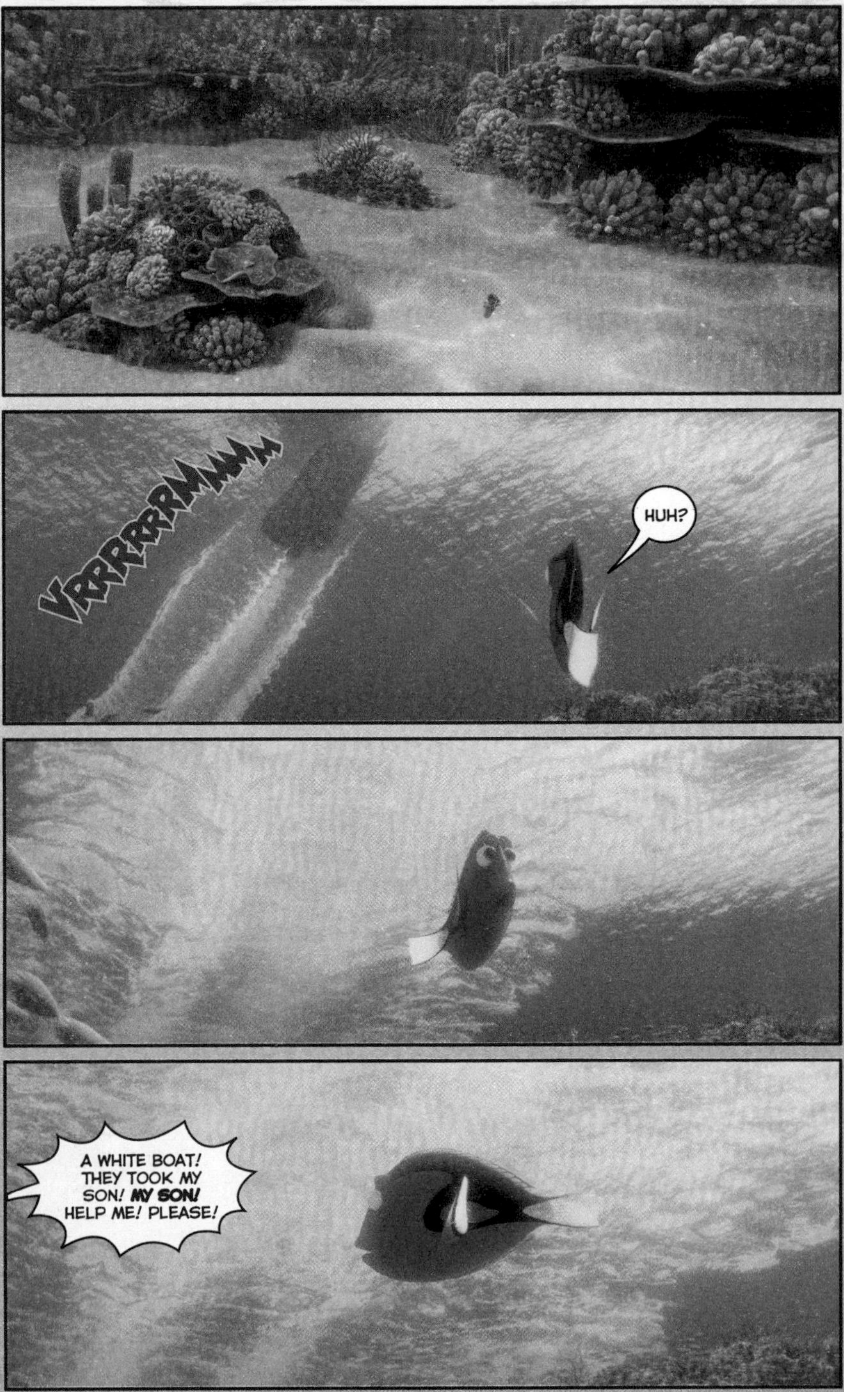
VRRRRRRMMMM
HUH?
A WHITE BOAT! THEY TOOK MY SON! **MY SON!** HELP ME! PLEASE!

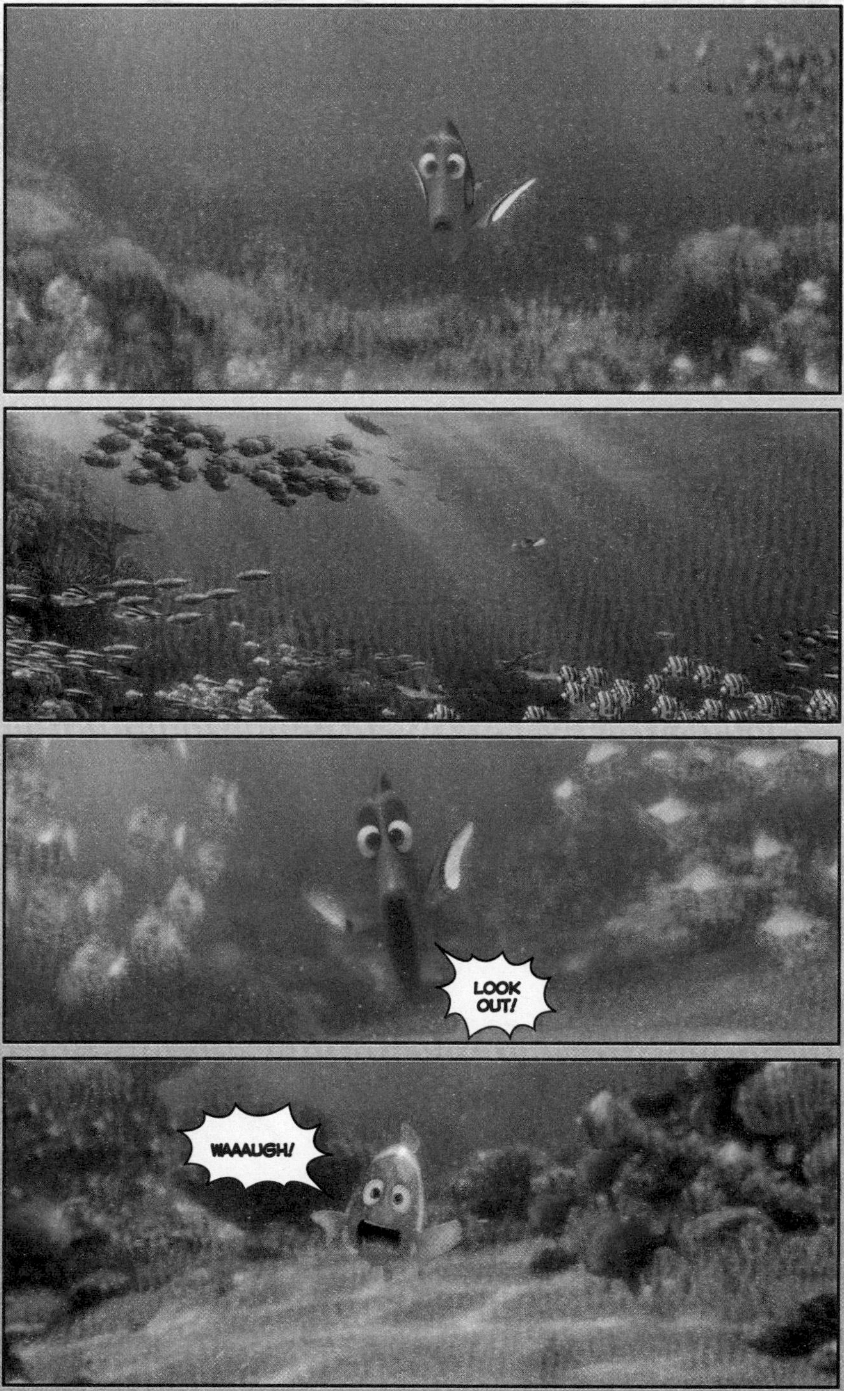
LOOK OUT!
WAAAUGH!

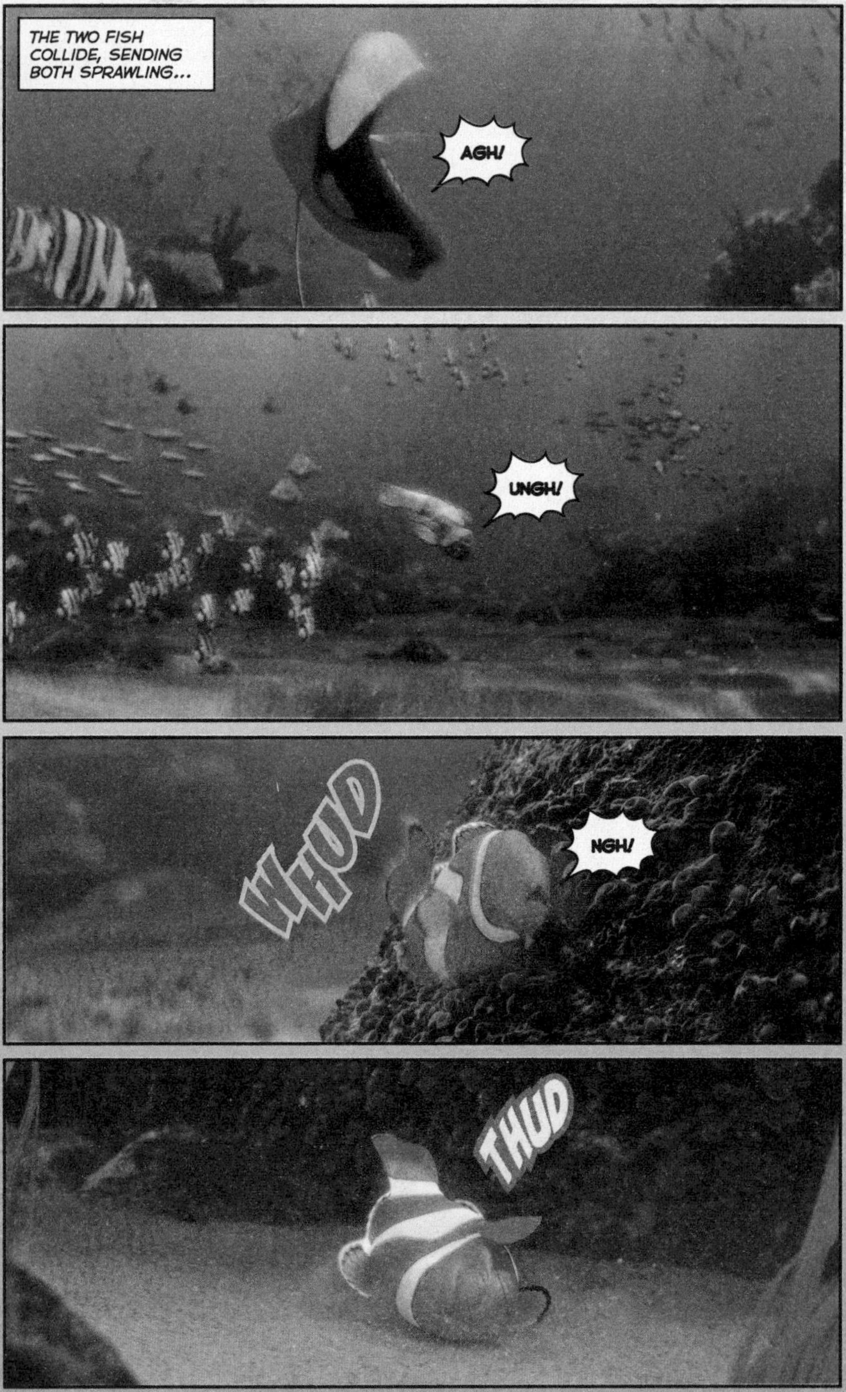
THE TWO FISH COLLIDE, SENDING BOTH SPRAWLING...
AGH!
UNGH!
WHUD
NGH!
THUD

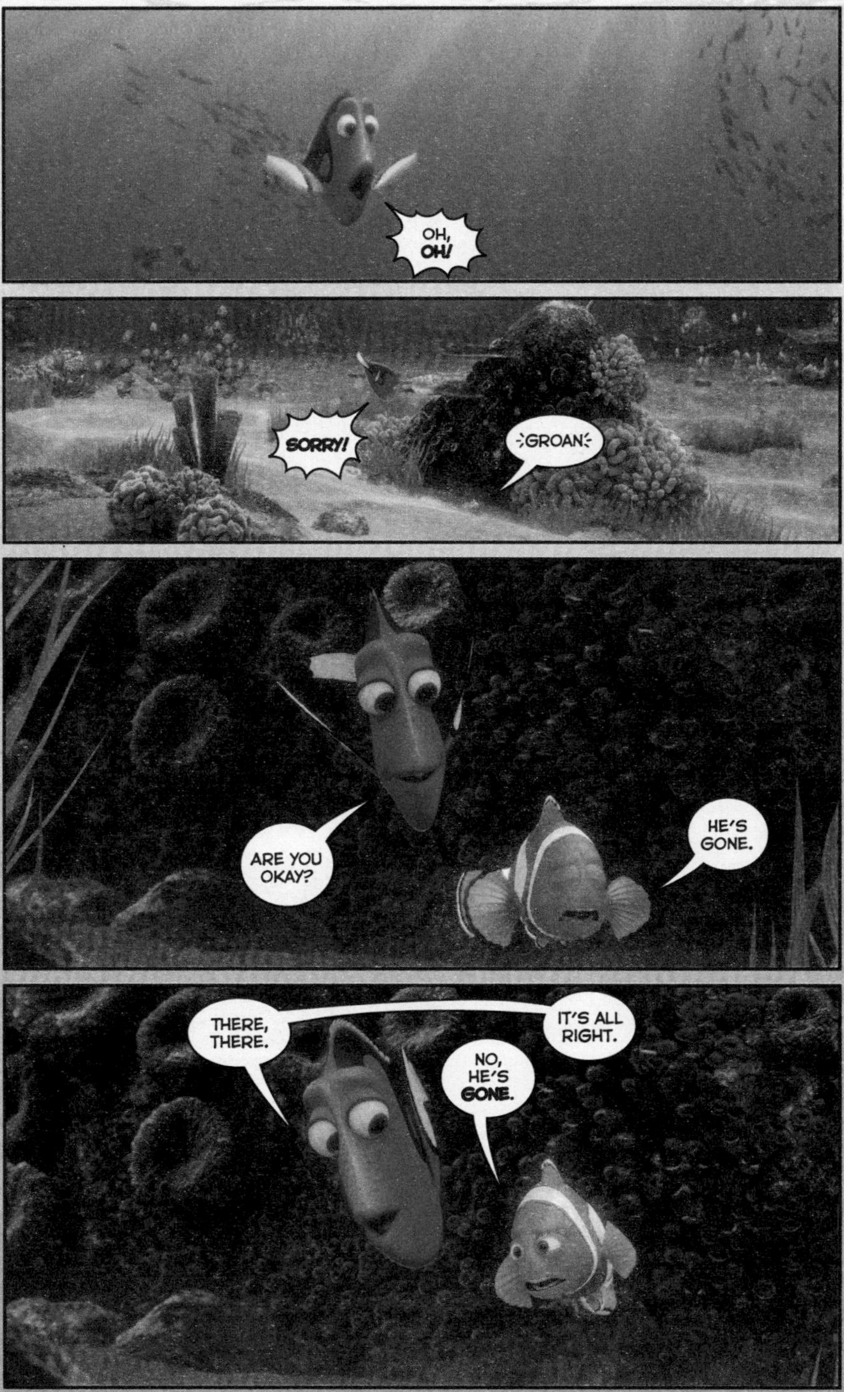
OH, OH!
SORRY!
GROAN
ARE YOU OKAY?
HE'S GONE.
THERE, THERE.
IT'S ALL RIGHT.
NO, HE'S GONE.

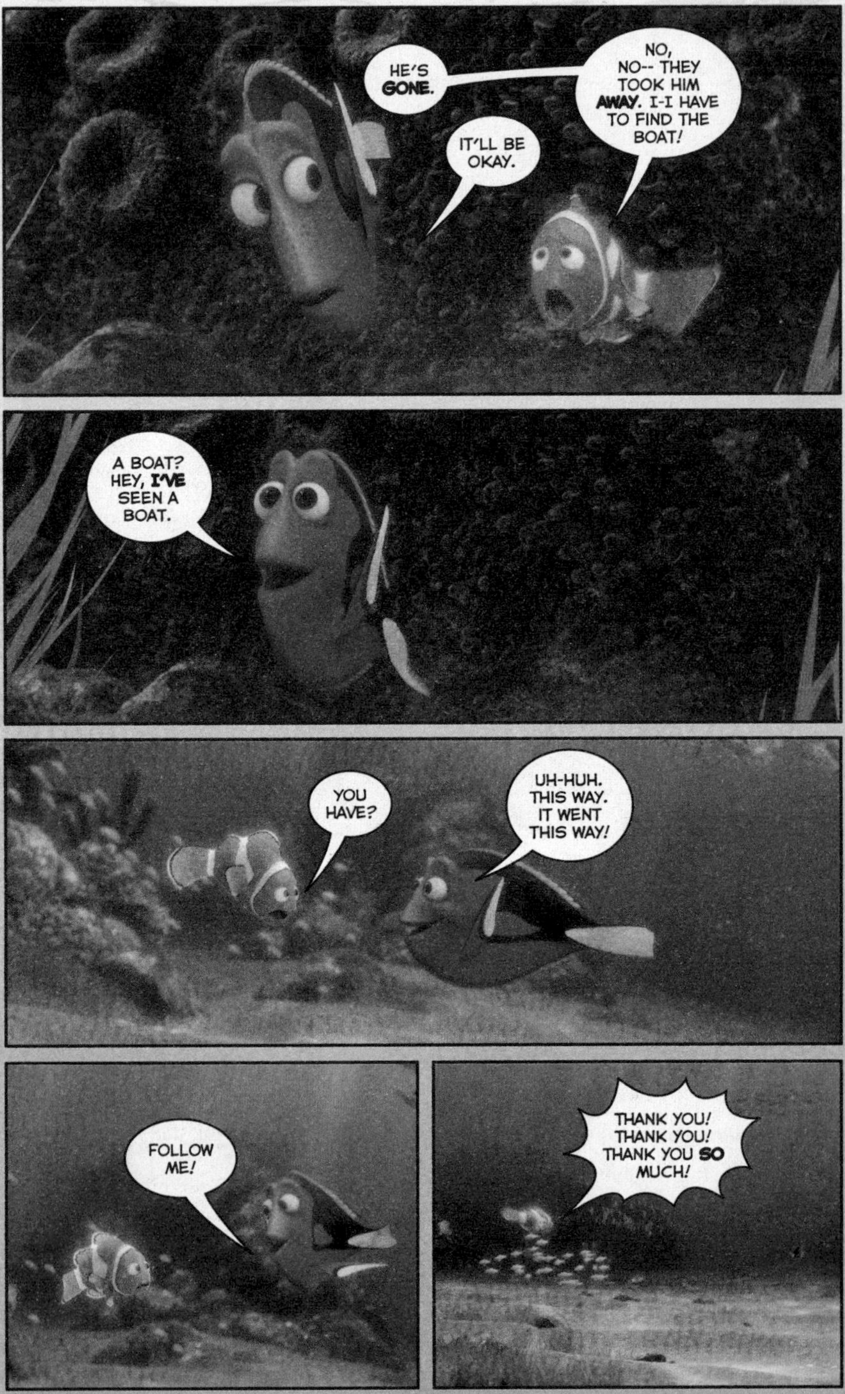
HE'S GONE.
NO, NO-- THEY TOOK HIM AWAY. I-I HAVE TO FIND THE BOAT!
IT'LL BE OKAY.
A BOAT? HEY, I'VE SEEN A BOAT.
YOU HAVE?
UH-HUH. THIS WAY. IT WENT THIS WAY!
FOLLOW ME!
THANK YOU! THANK YOU! THANK YOU SO MUCH!

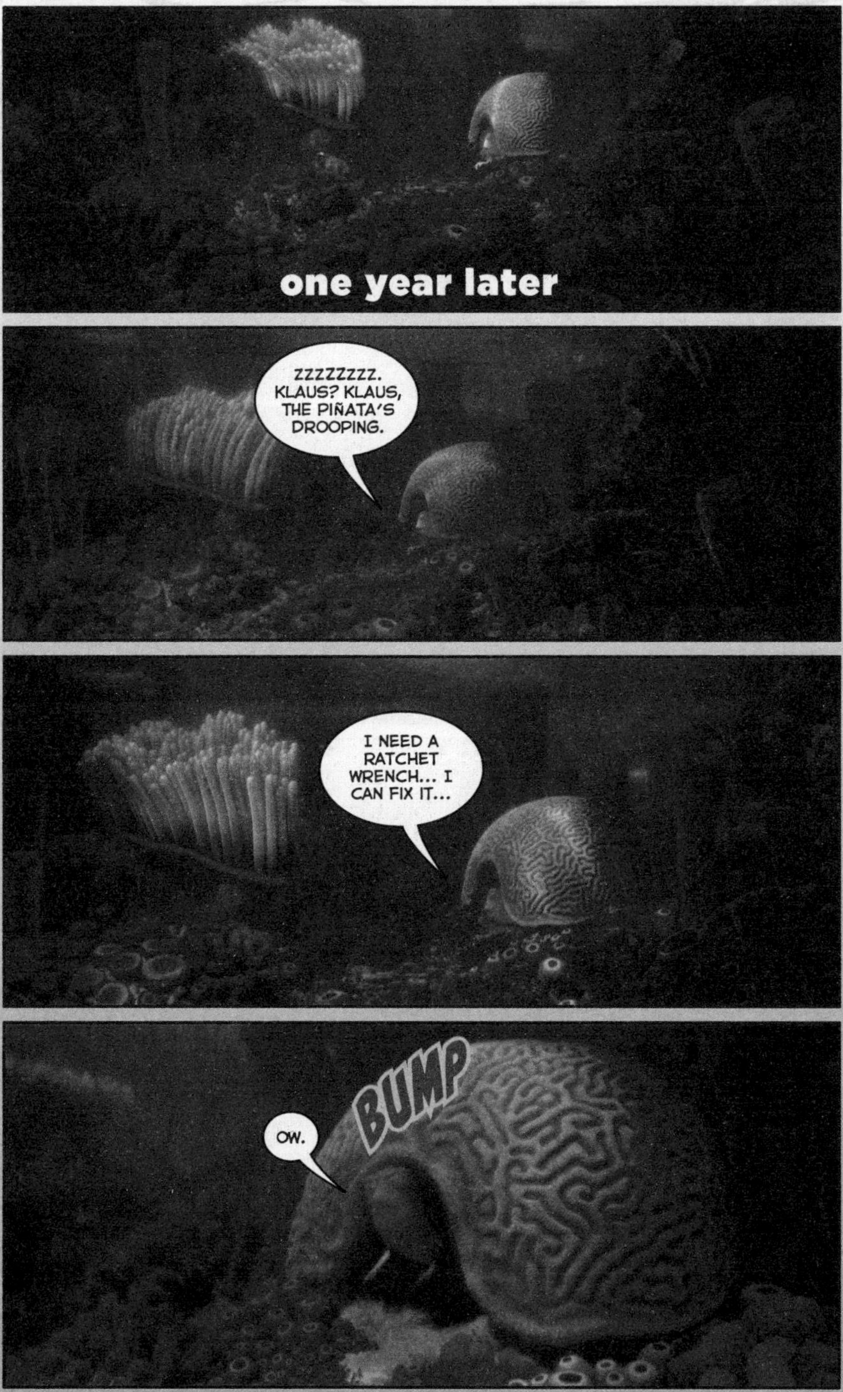
one year later
ZZZZZZZZ. KLAUS? KLAUS, THE PIÑATA'S DROOPING.
I NEED A RATCHET WRENCH... I CAN FIX IT...
BUMP
OW.

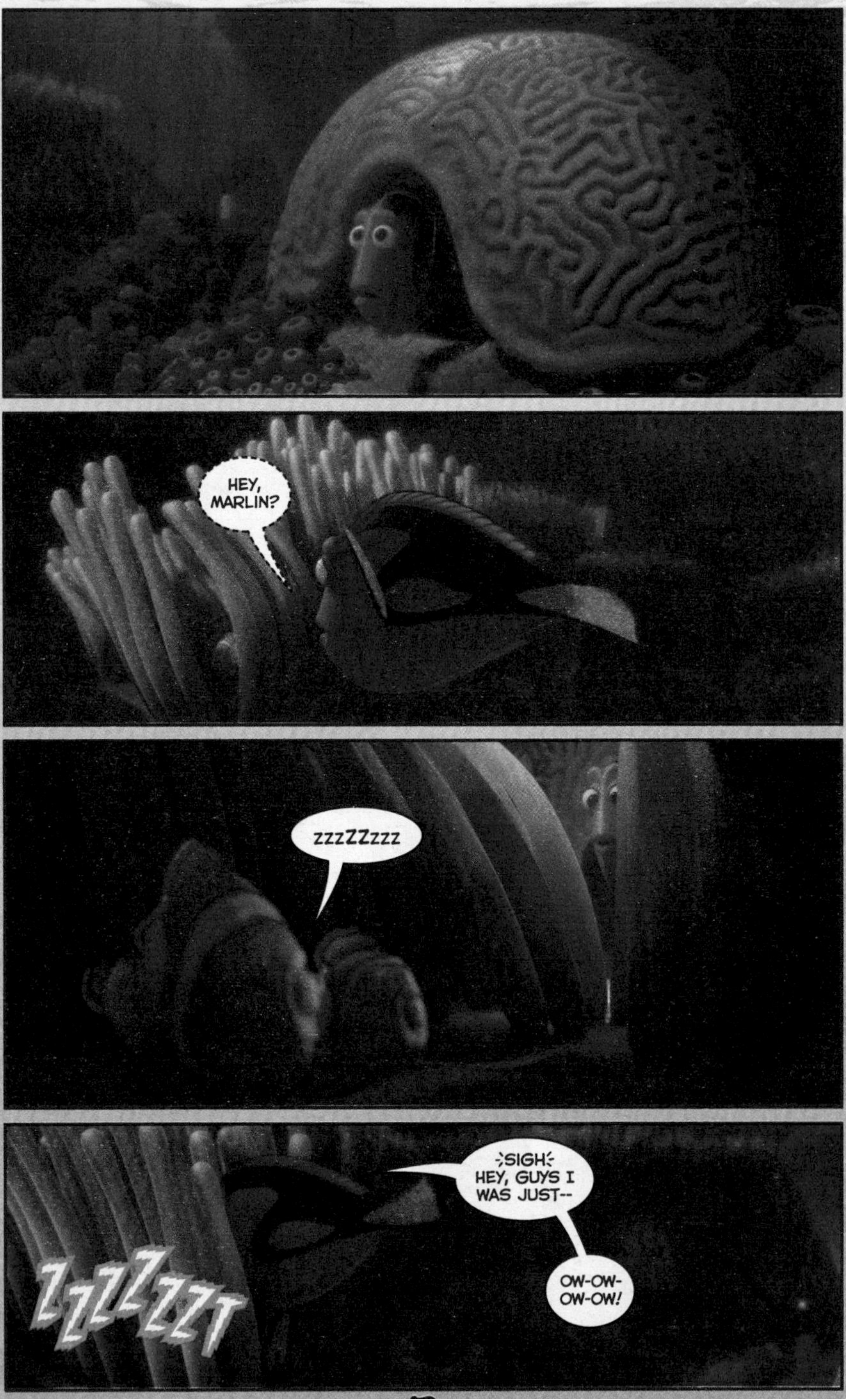
HEY, MARLIN?
zzzZZzzz
SIGH HEY, GUYS I WAS JUST--
OW-OW-OW-OW!
ZZZZZZT

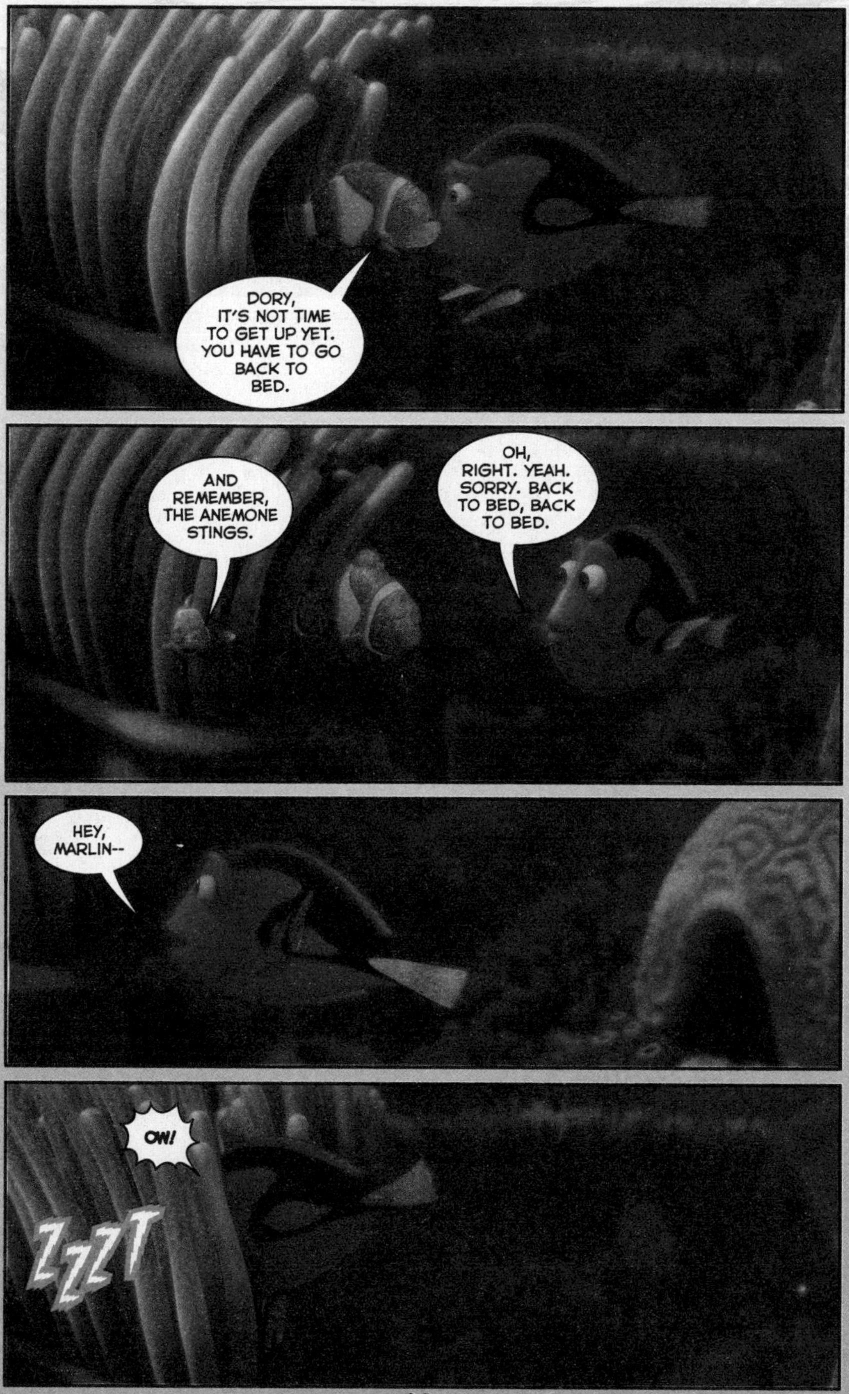
DORY, IT'S NOT TIME TO GET UP YET. YOU HAVE TO GO BACK TO BED.
AND REMEMBER, THE ANEMONE STINGS.
OH, RIGHT. YEAH. SORRY. BACK TO BED, BACK TO BED.
HEY, MARLIN--
OW!
ZZZT

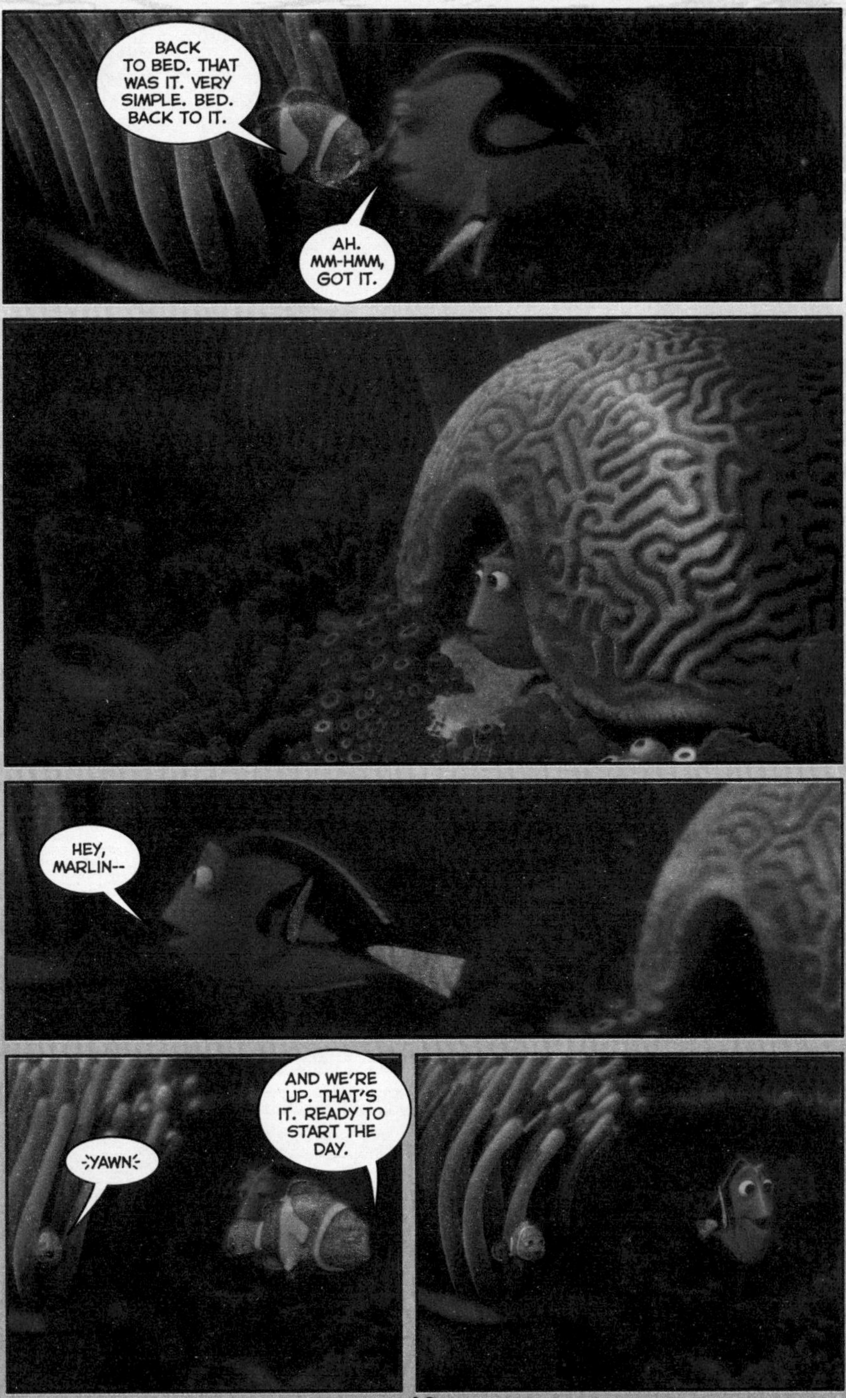
BACK TO BED. THAT WAS IT. VERY SIMPLE. BED. BACK TO IT.
AH. MM-HMM, GOT IT.
HEY, MARLIN--
YAWN
AND WE'RE UP. THAT'S IT. READY TO START THE DAY.

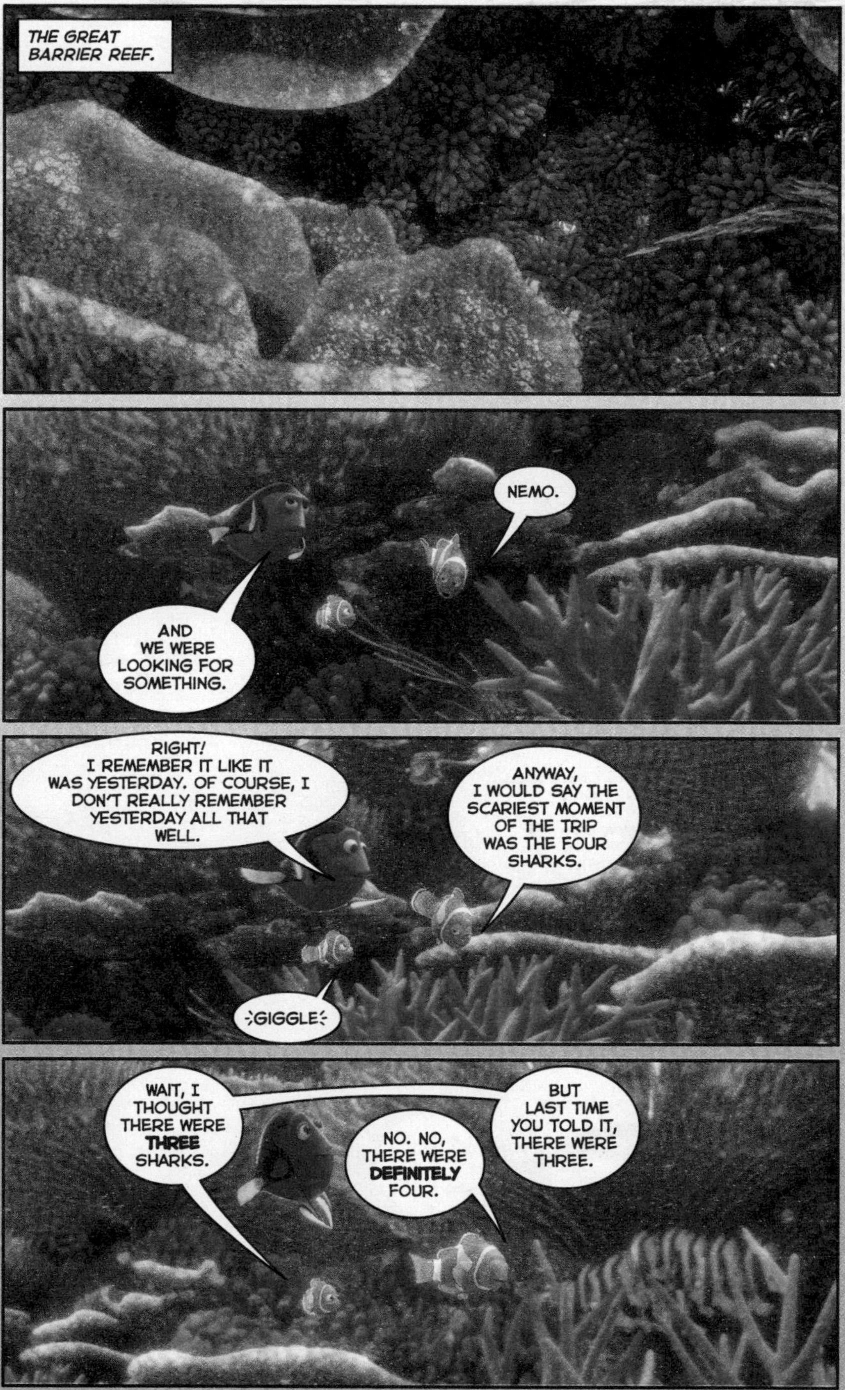
THE GREAT BARRIER REEF.
NEMO.
AND WE WERE LOOKING FOR SOMETHING.
RIGHT! I REMEMBER IT LIKE IT WAS YESTERDAY. OF COURSE, I DON'T REALLY REMEMBER YESTERDAY ALL THAT WELL.
ANYWAY, I WOULD SAY THE SCARIEST MOMENT OF THE TRIP WAS THE FOUR SHARKS.
GIGGLE
WAIT, I THOUGHT THERE WERE **THREE** SHARKS.
NO. NO, THERE WERE **DEFINITELY** FOUR.
BUT LAST TIME YOU TOLD IT, THERE WERE THREE.

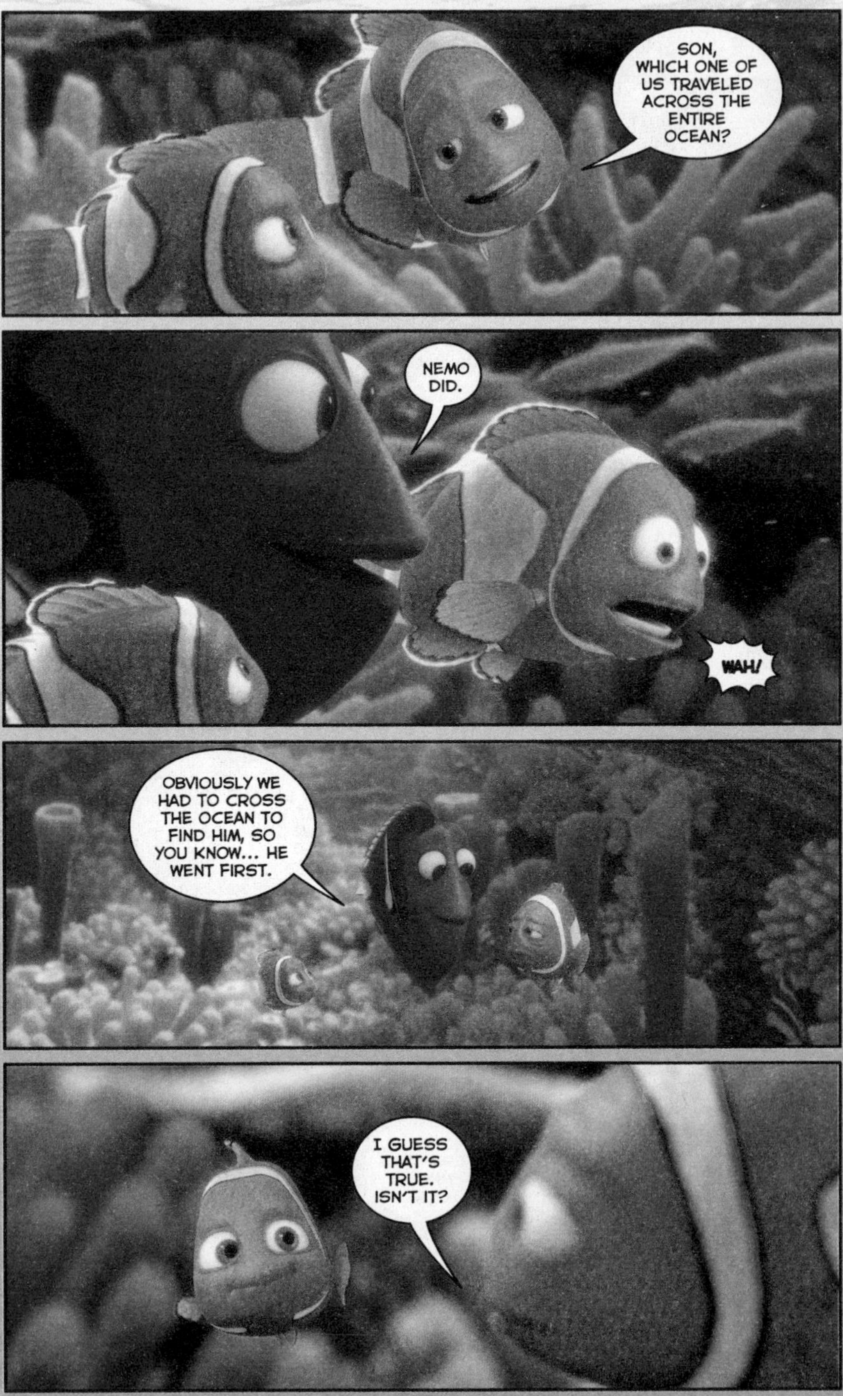
SON, WHICH ONE OF US TRAVELED ACROSS THE ENTIRE OCEAN?
NEMO DID.
WAH!
OBVIOUSLY WE HAD TO CROSS THE OCEAN TO FIND HIM, SO YOU KNOW... HE WENT FIRST.
I GUESS THAT'S TRUE. ISN'T IT?

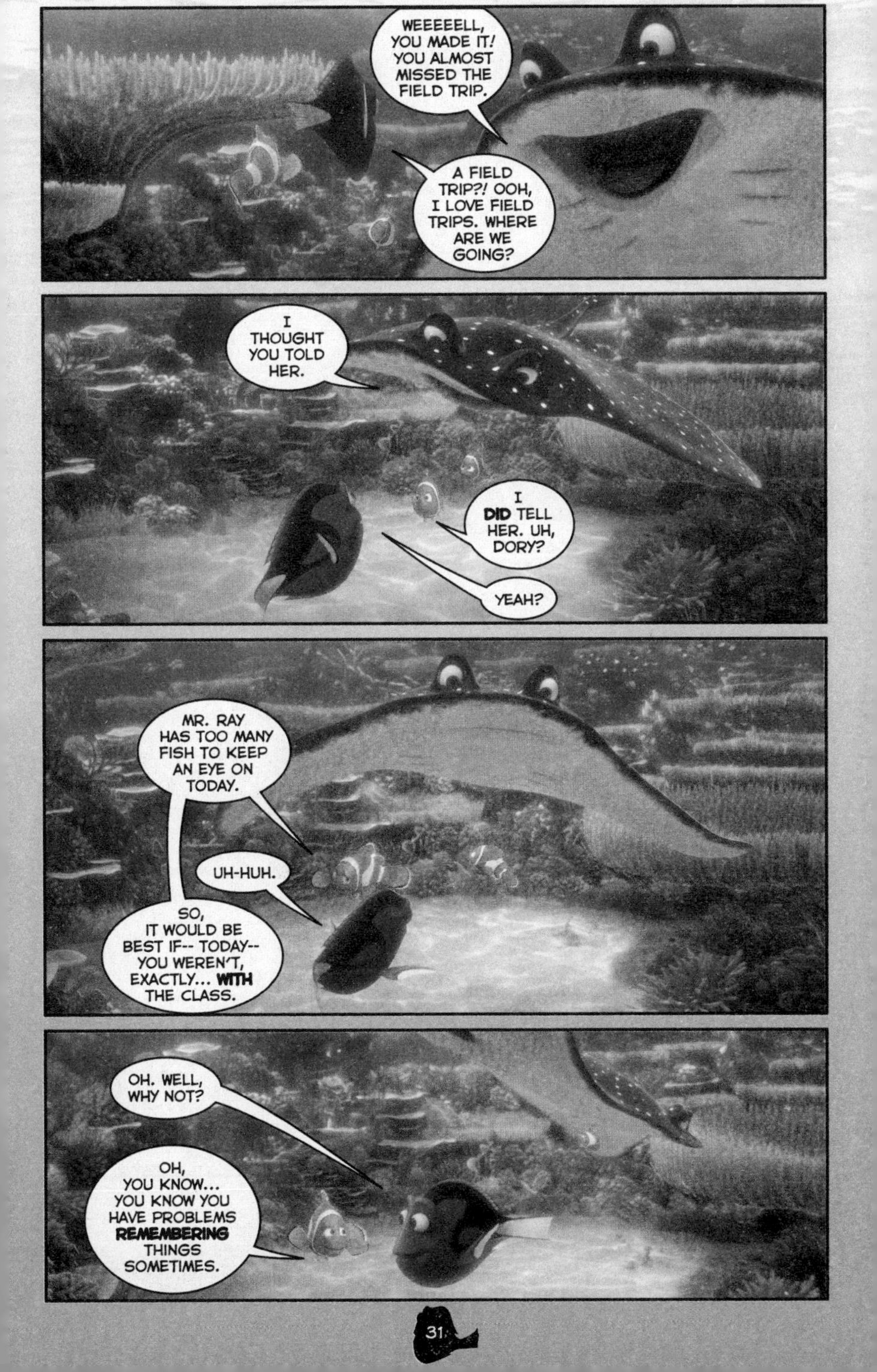
WEEEEELL, YOU MADE IT! YOU ALMOST MISSED THE FIELD TRIP.
A FIELD TRIP?! OOH, I LOVE FIELD TRIPS. WHERE ARE WE GOING?
I THOUGHT YOU TOLD HER.
I DID TELL HER. UH, DORY?
YEAH?
MR. RAY HAS TOO MANY FISH TO KEEP AN EYE ON TODAY.
UH-HUH.
SO, IT WOULD BE BEST IF-- TODAY-- YOU WEREN'T, EXACTLY... WITH THE CLASS.
OH. WELL, WHY NOT?
OH, YOU KNOW... YOU KNOW YOU HAVE PROBLEMS REMEMBERING THINGS SOMETIMES.

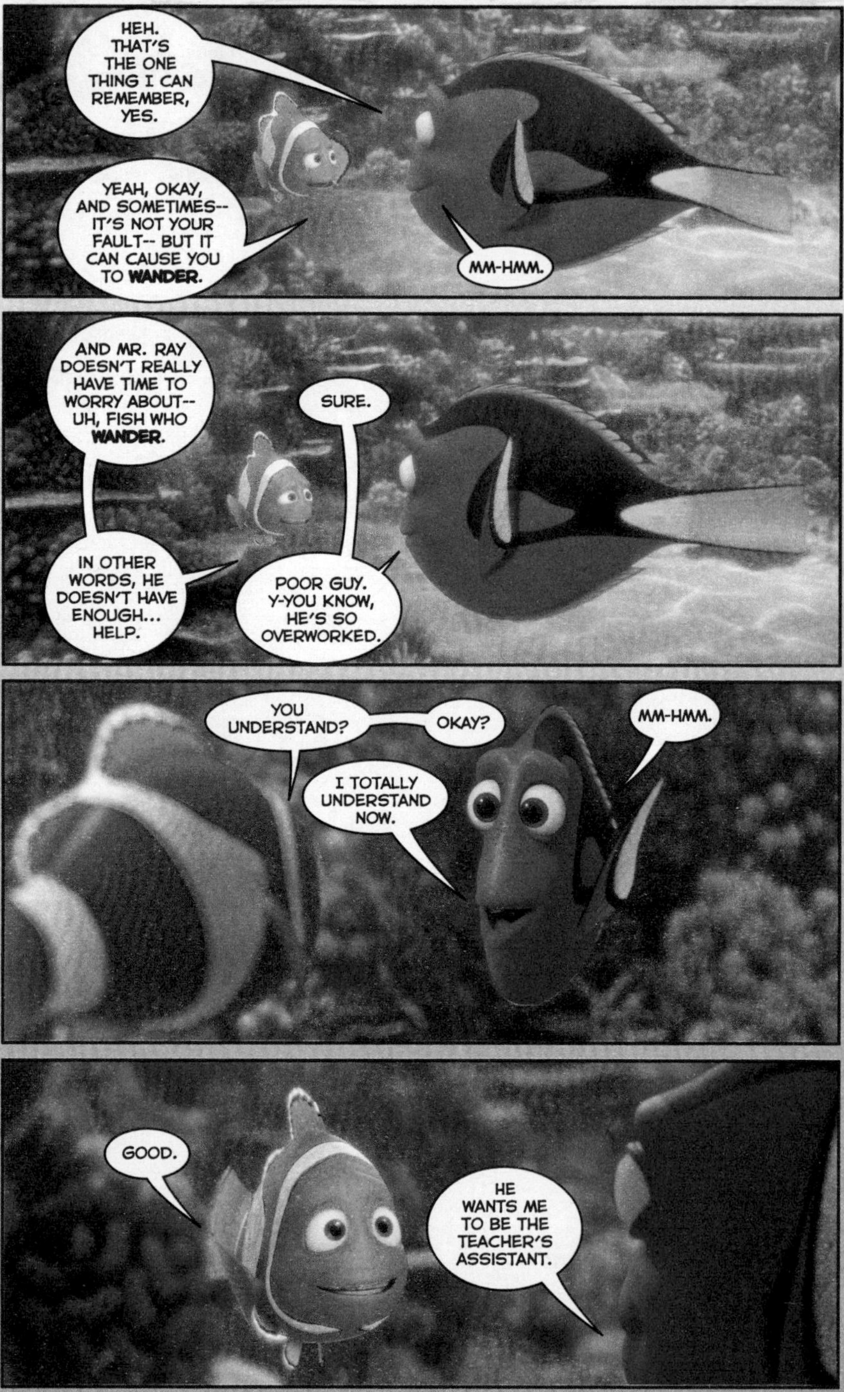
HEH. THAT'S THE ONE THING I CAN REMEMBER, YES.
YEAH, OKAY, AND SOMETIMES-- IT'S NOT YOUR FAULT-- BUT IT CAN CAUSE YOU TO **WANDER**.
MM-HMM.
AND MR. RAY DOESN'T REALLY HAVE TIME TO WORRY ABOUT-- UH, FISH WHO **WANDER**.
SURE.
IN OTHER WORDS, HE DOESN'T HAVE ENOUGH... HELP.
POOR GUY. Y-YOU KNOW, HE'S SO OVERWORKED.
YOU UNDERSTAND?
OKAY?
MM-HMM.
I TOTALLY UNDERSTAND NOW.
GOOD.
HE WANTS ME TO BE THE TEACHER'S ASSISTANT.

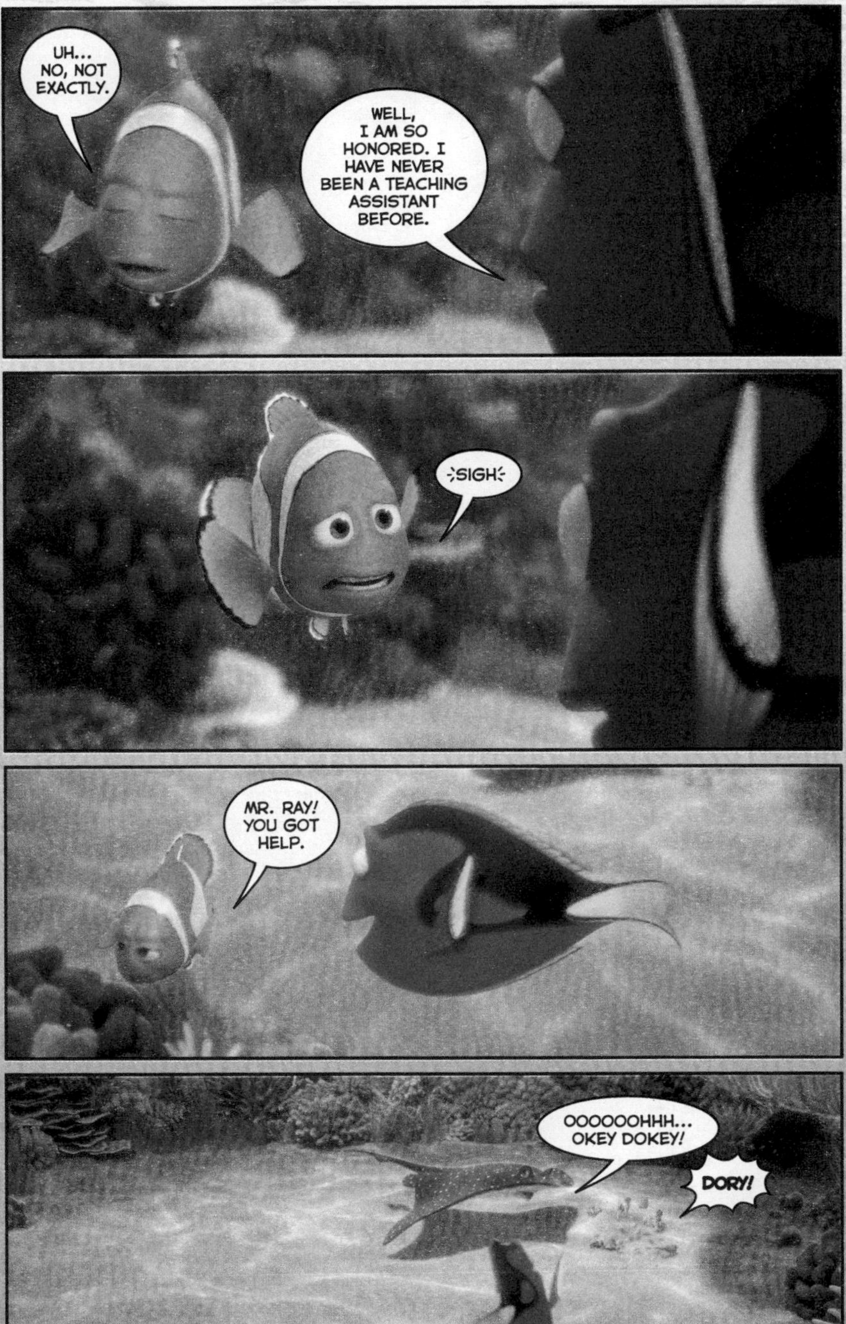
UH... NO, NOT EXACTLY.
WELL, I AM SO HONORED. I HAVE NEVER BEEN A TEACHING ASSISTANT BEFORE.
SIGH
MR. RAY! YOU GOT HELP.
OOOOOOHHH... OKEY DOKEY!
DORY!

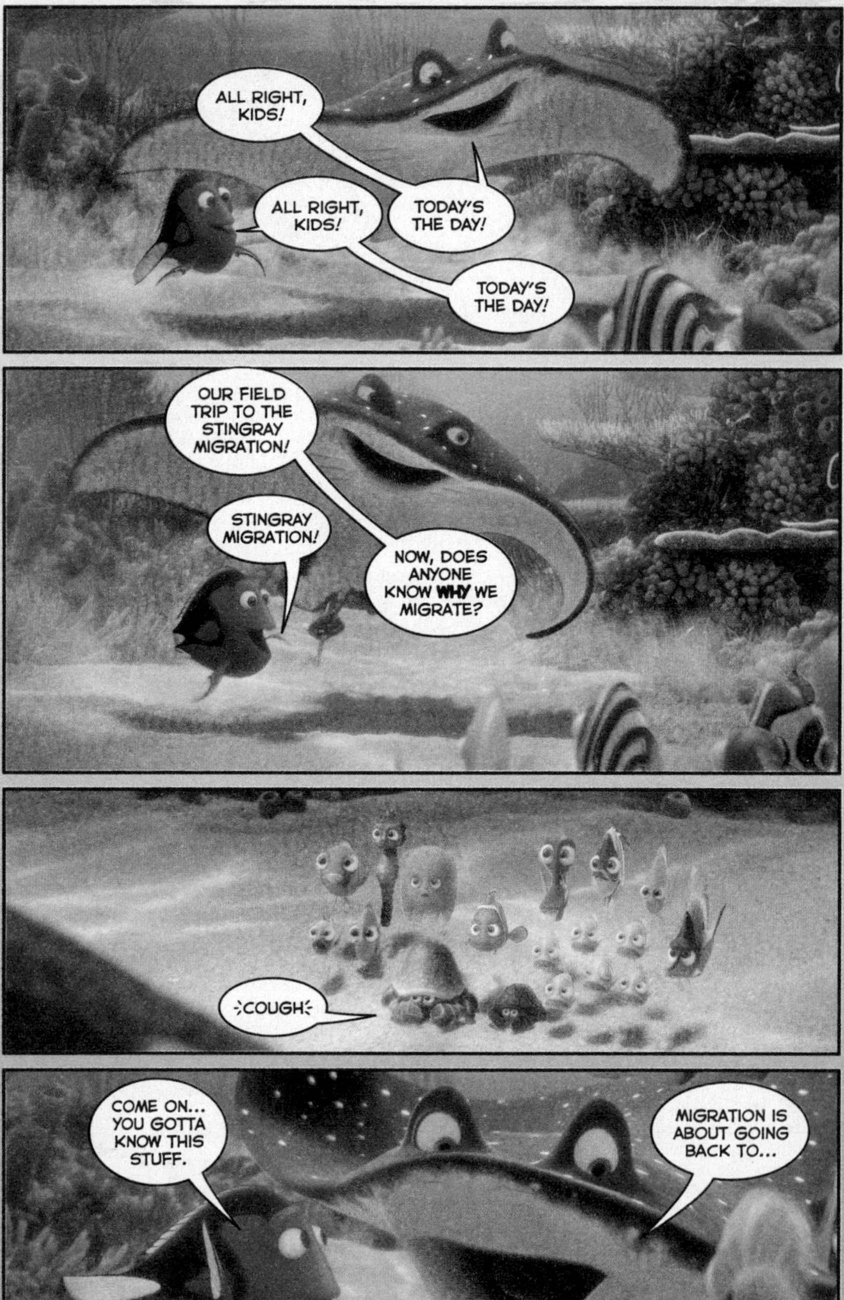
ALL RIGHT, KIDS!
ALL RIGHT, KIDS!
TODAY'S THE DAY!
TODAY'S THE DAY!
OUR FIELD TRIP TO THE STINGRAY MIGRATION!
STINGRAY MIGRATION!
NOW, DOES ANYONE KNOW **WHY** WE MIGRATE?
COUGH
COME ON... YOU GOTTA KNOW THIS STUFF.
MIGRATION IS ABOUT GOING BACK TO...

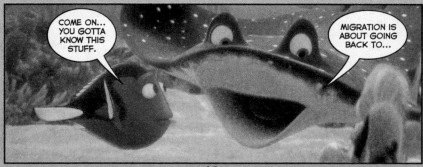

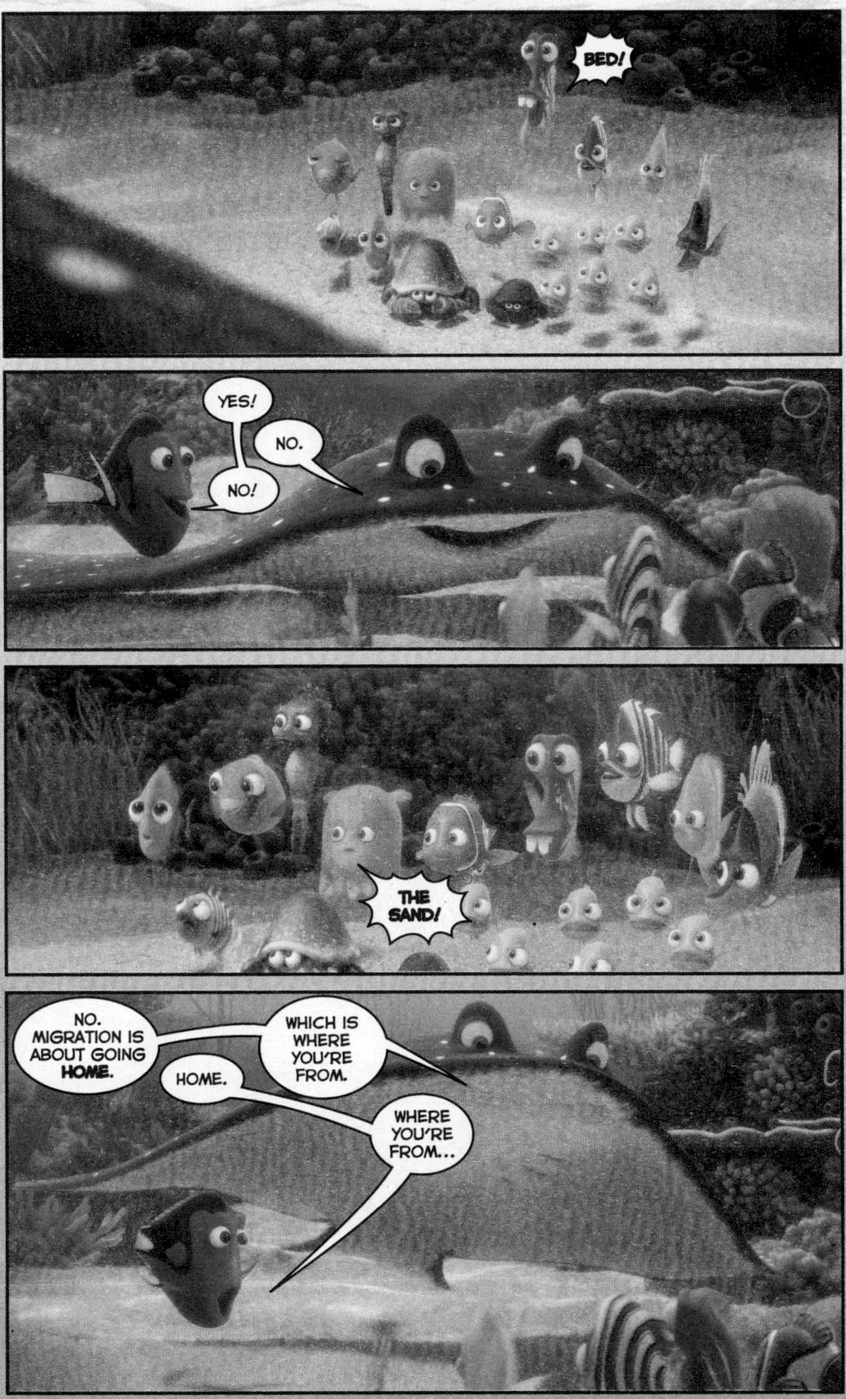
BED!
YES!
NO.
NO!
THE SAND!
NO. MIGRATION IS ABOUT GOING HOME.
WHICH IS WHERE YOU'RE FROM.
HOME.
WHERE YOU'RE FROM...

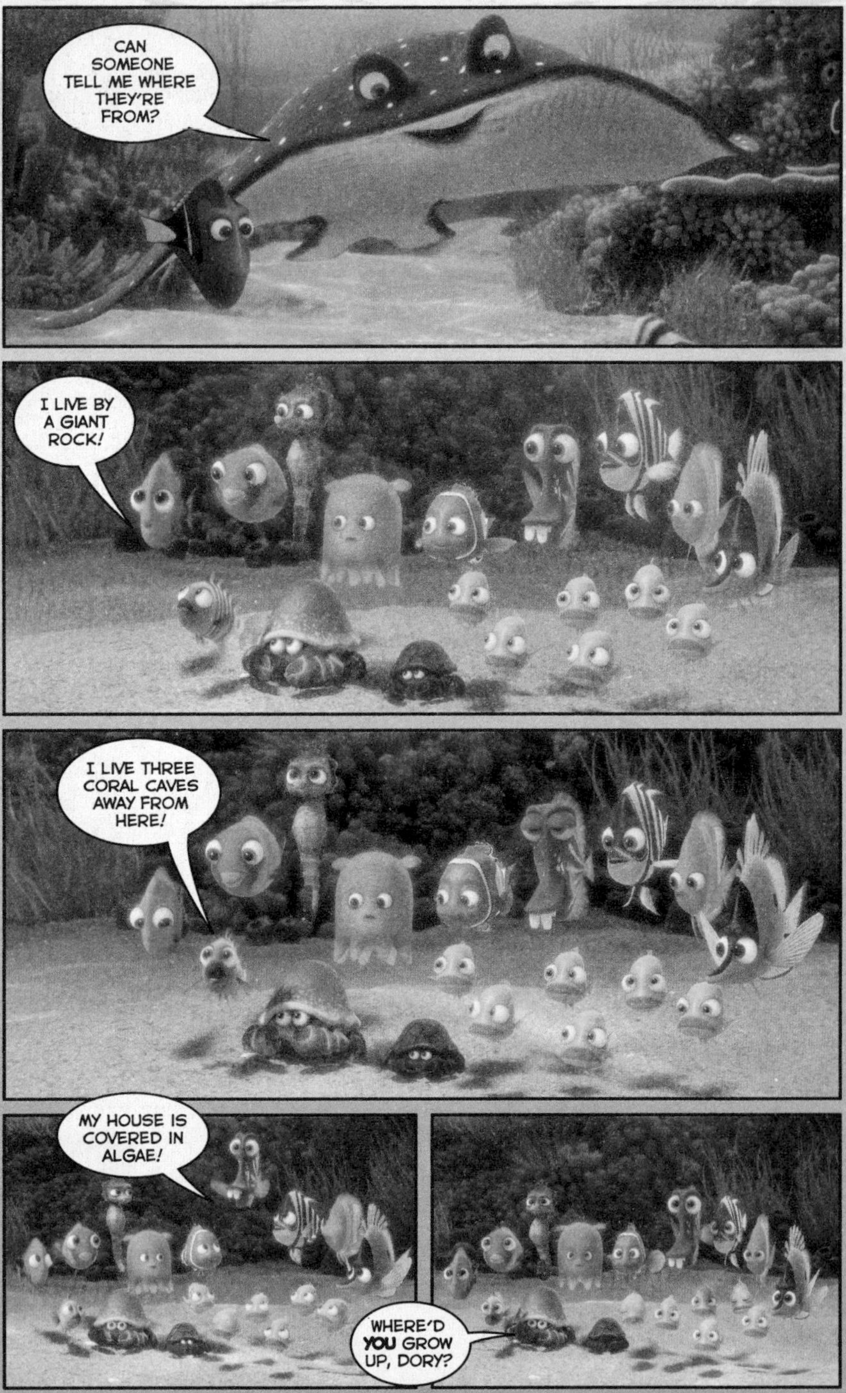
CAN SOMEONE TELL ME WHERE THEY'RE FROM?
I LIVE BY A GIANT ROCK!
I LIVE THREE CORAL CAVES AWAY FROM HERE!
MY HOUSE IS COVERED IN ALGAE!
WHERE'D **YOU** GROW UP, DORY?

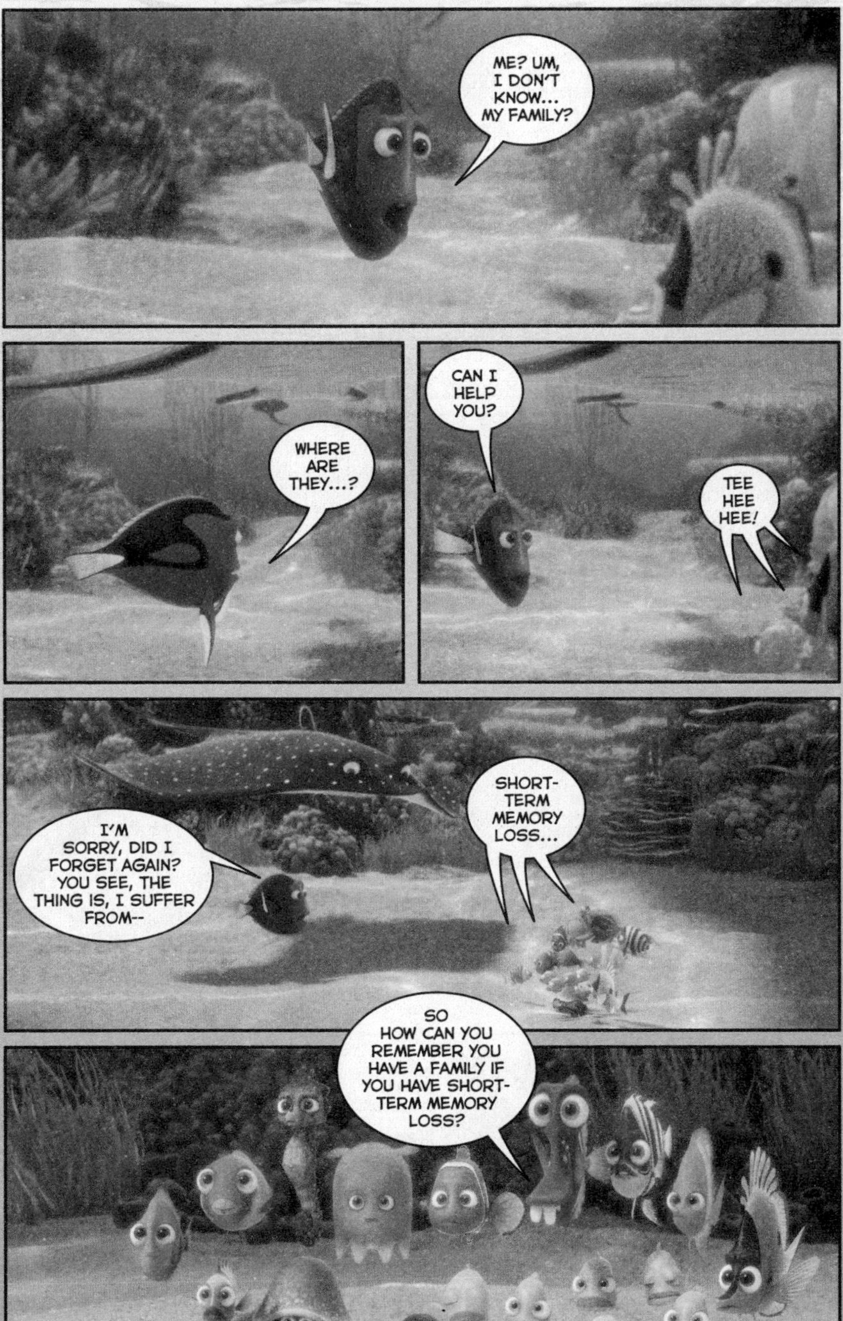
ME? UM, I DON'T KNOW... MY FAMILY?
WHERE ARE THEY...?
CAN I HELP YOU?
TEE HEE HEE!
I'M SORRY, DID I FORGET AGAIN? YOU SEE, THE THING IS, I SUFFER FROM--
SHORT-TERM MEMORY LOSS...
SO HOW CAN YOU REMEMBER YOU HAVE A FAMILY IF YOU HAVE SHORT-TERM MEMORY LOSS?

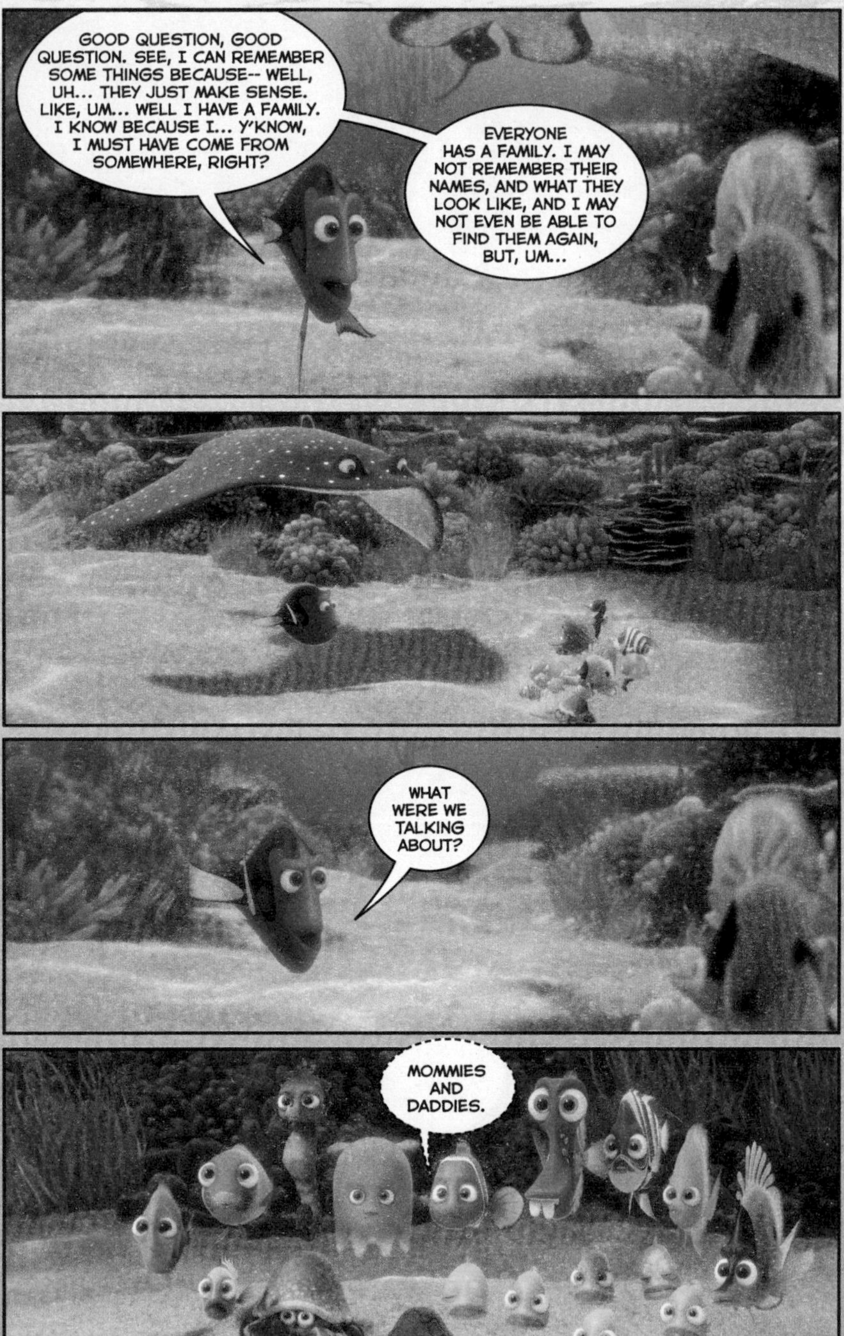
GOOD QUESTION, GOOD QUESTION. SEE, I CAN REMEMBER SOME THINGS BECAUSE-- WELL, UH... THEY JUST MAKE SENSE. LIKE, UM... WELL I HAVE A FAMILY. I KNOW BECAUSE I... Y'KNOW, I MUST HAVE COME FROM SOMEWHERE, RIGHT?
EVERYONE HAS A FAMILY. I MAY NOT REMEMBER THEIR NAMES, AND WHAT THEY LOOK LIKE, AND I MAY NOT EVEN BE ABLE TO FIND THEM AGAIN, BUT, UM...
WHAT WERE WE TALKING ABOUT?
MOMMIES AND DADDIES.

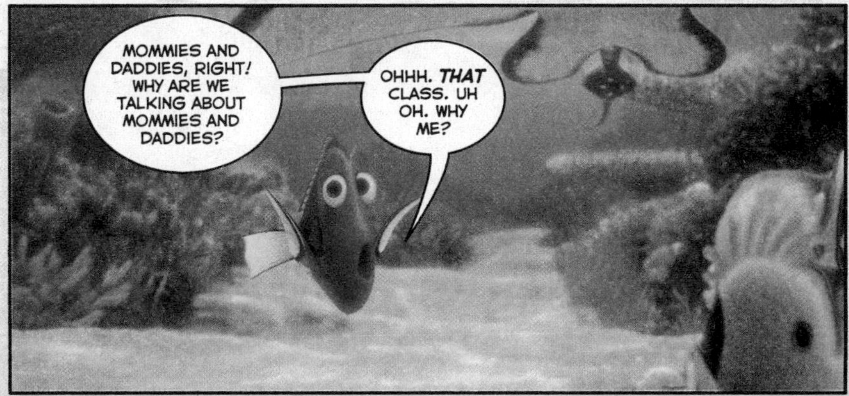
MOMMIES AND DADDIES, RIGHT! WHY ARE WE TALKING ABOUT MOMMIES AND DADDIES?
OHHH. *THAT* CLASS. UH OH. WHY ME?

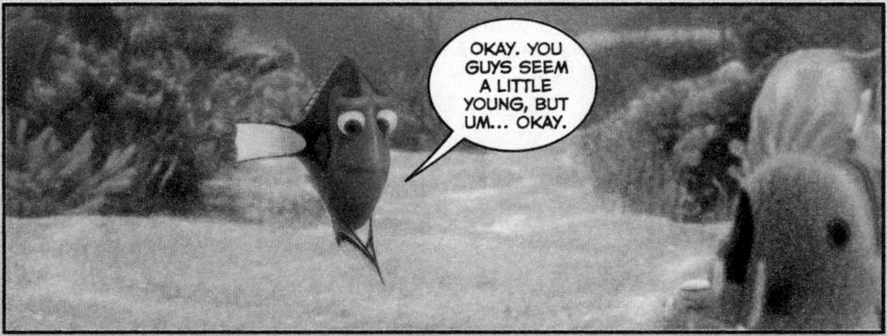
OKAY. YOU GUYS SEEM A LITTLE YOUNG, BUT UM... OKAY.

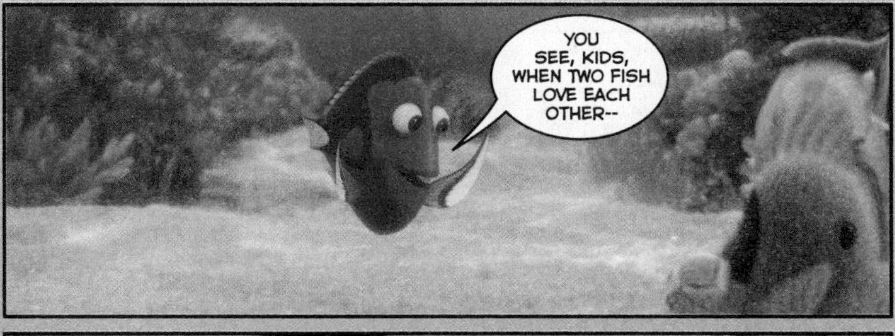
YOU SEE, KIDS, WHEN TWO FISH LOVE EACH OTHER--

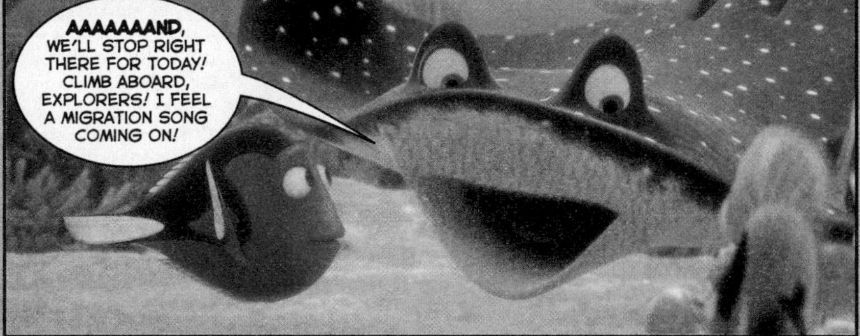
AAAAAAAND, WE'LL STOP RIGHT THERE FOR TODAY! CLIMB ABOARD, EXPLORERS! I FEEL A MIGRATION SONG COMING ON!

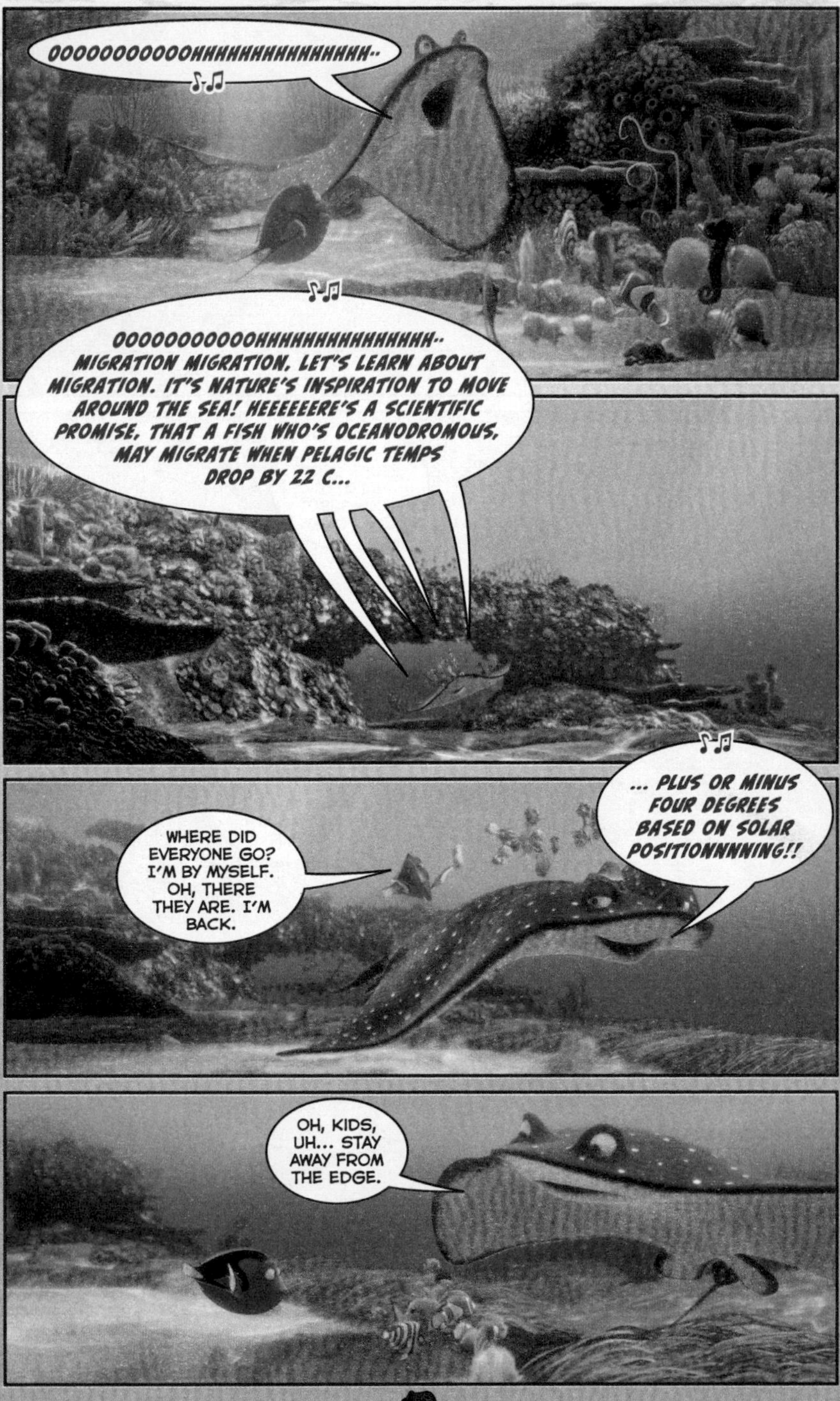
OOOOOOOOOOOHHHHHHHHHHHHHHHH..
OOOOOOOOOOOHHHHHHHHHHHHHHH.. MIGRATION MIGRATION, LET'S LEARN ABOUT MIGRATION. IT'S NATURE'S INSPIRATION TO MOVE AROUND THE SEA! HEEEEEERE'S A SCIENTIFIC PROMISE, THAT A FISH WHO'S OCEANODROMOUS, MAY MIGRATE WHEN PELAGIC TEMPS DROP BY 22 C...
WHERE DID EVERYONE GO? I'M BY MYSELF. OH, THERE THEY ARE. I'M BACK.
... PLUS OR MINUS FOUR DEGREES BASED ON SOLAR POSITIONNNNING!!
OH, KIDS, UH... STAY AWAY FROM THE EDGE.

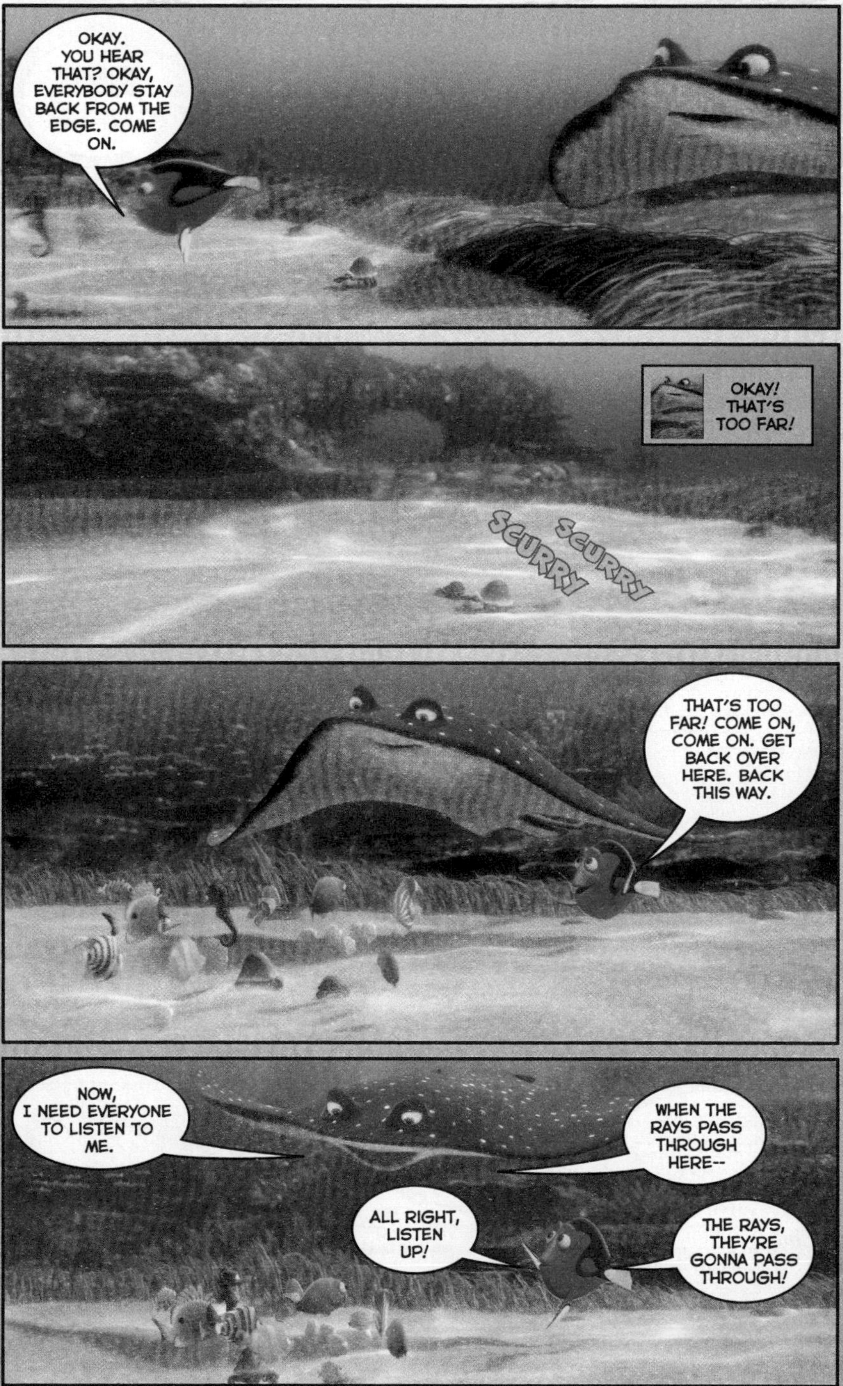
OKAY. YOU HEAR THAT? OKAY, EVERYBODY STAY BACK FROM THE EDGE. COME ON.
OKAY! THAT'S TOO FAR!
SCURRY SCURRY
THAT'S TOO FAR! COME ON, COME ON. GET BACK OVER HERE. BACK THIS WAY.
NOW, I NEED EVERYONE TO LISTEN TO ME.
WHEN THE RAYS PASS THROUGH HERE--
ALL RIGHT, LISTEN UP!
THE RAYS, THEY'RE GONNA PASS THROUGH!

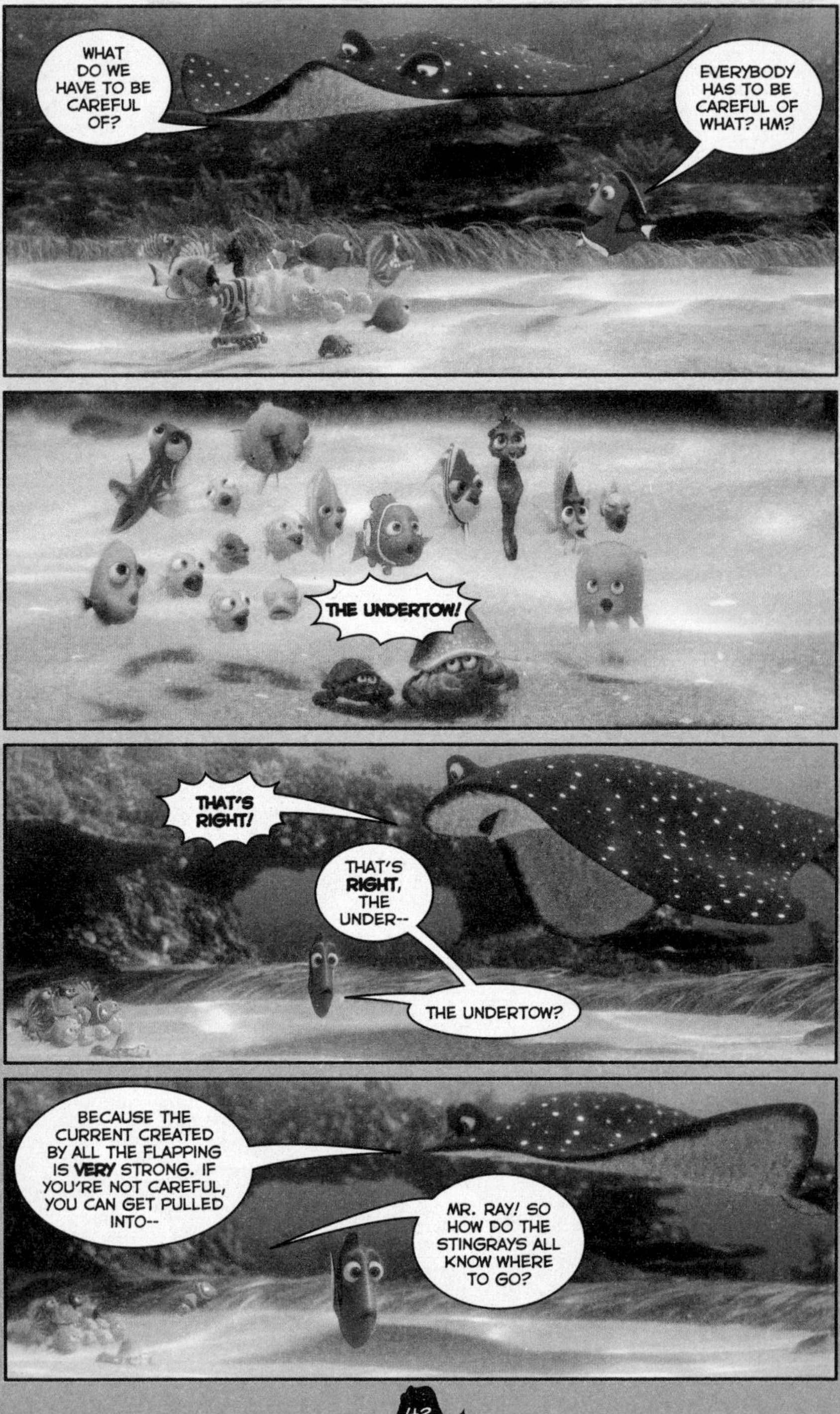
WHAT DO WE HAVE TO BE CAREFUL OF?
EVERYBODY HAS TO BE CAREFUL OF WHAT? HM?
THE UNDERTOW!
THAT'S RIGHT!
THAT'S RIGHT, THE UNDER--
THE UNDERTOW?
BECAUSE THE CURRENT CREATED BY ALL THE FLAPPING IS VERY STRONG. IF YOU'RE NOT CAREFUL, YOU CAN GET PULLED INTO--
MR. RAY! SO HOW DO THE STINGRAYS ALL KNOW WHERE TO GO?

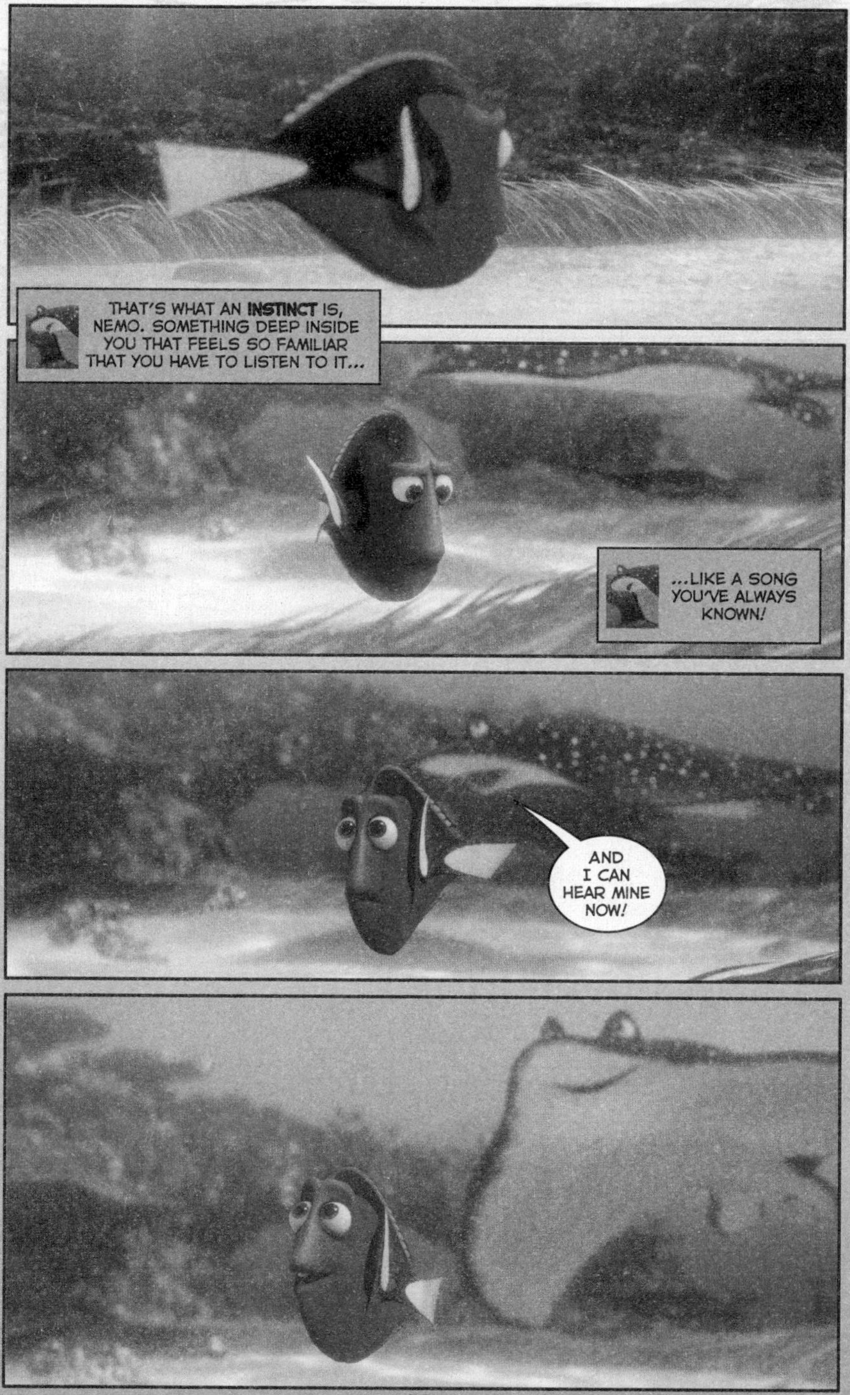
THAT'S WHAT AN INSTINCT IS, NEMO. SOMETHING DEEP INSIDE YOU THAT FEELS SO FAMILIAR THAT YOU HAVE TO LISTEN TO IT...
...LIKE A SONG YOU'VE ALWAYS KNOWN!
AND I CAN HEAR MINE NOW!

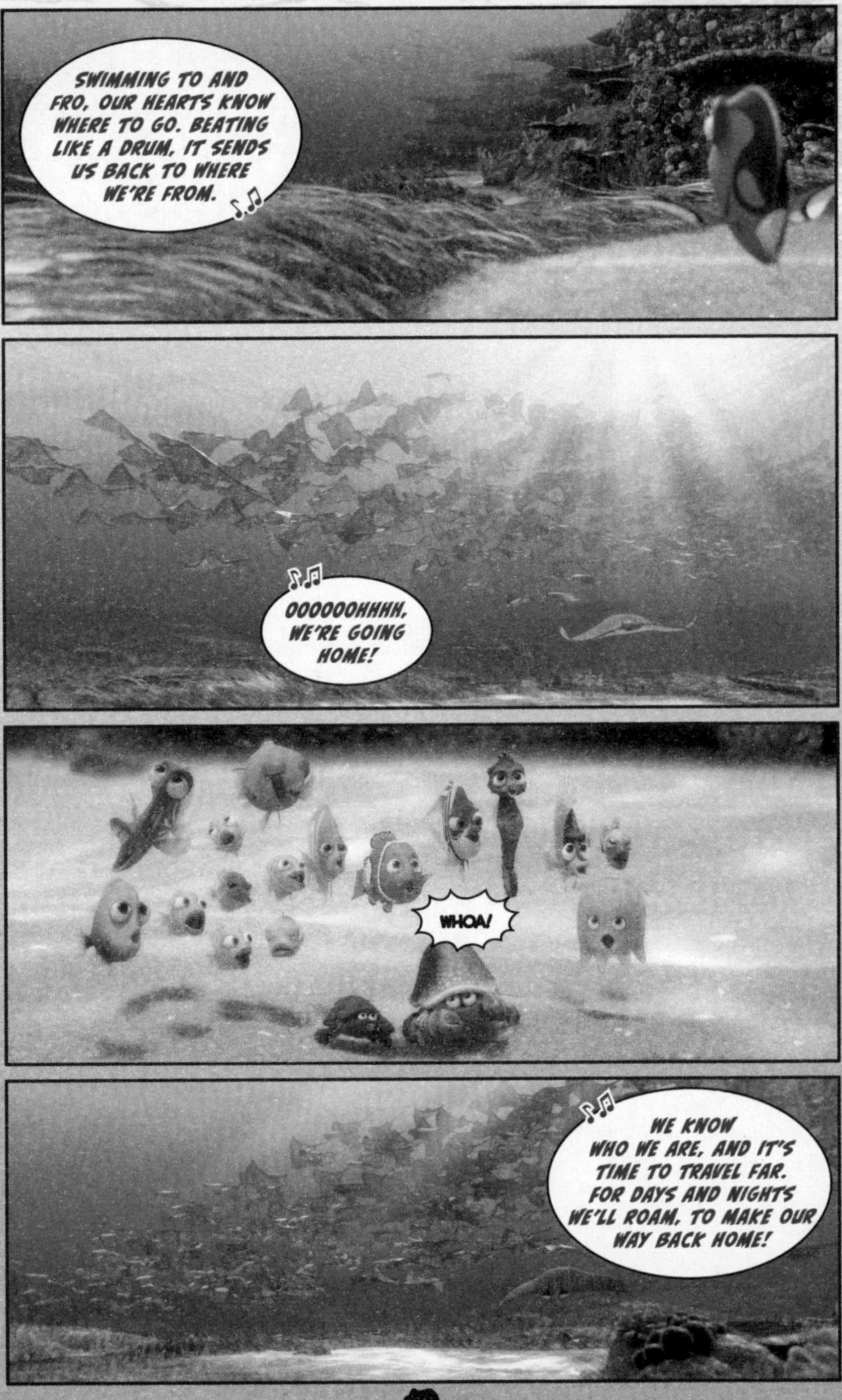
SWIMMING TO AND FRO, OUR HEARTS KNOW WHERE TO GO. BEATING LIKE A DRUM, IT SENDS US BACK TO WHERE WE'RE FROM.
OOOOOOHHHH, WE'RE GOING HOME!
WHOA!
WE KNOW WHO WE ARE, AND IT'S TIME TO TRAVEL FAR. FOR DAYS AND NIGHTS WE'LL ROAM, TO MAKE OUR WAY BACK HOME!

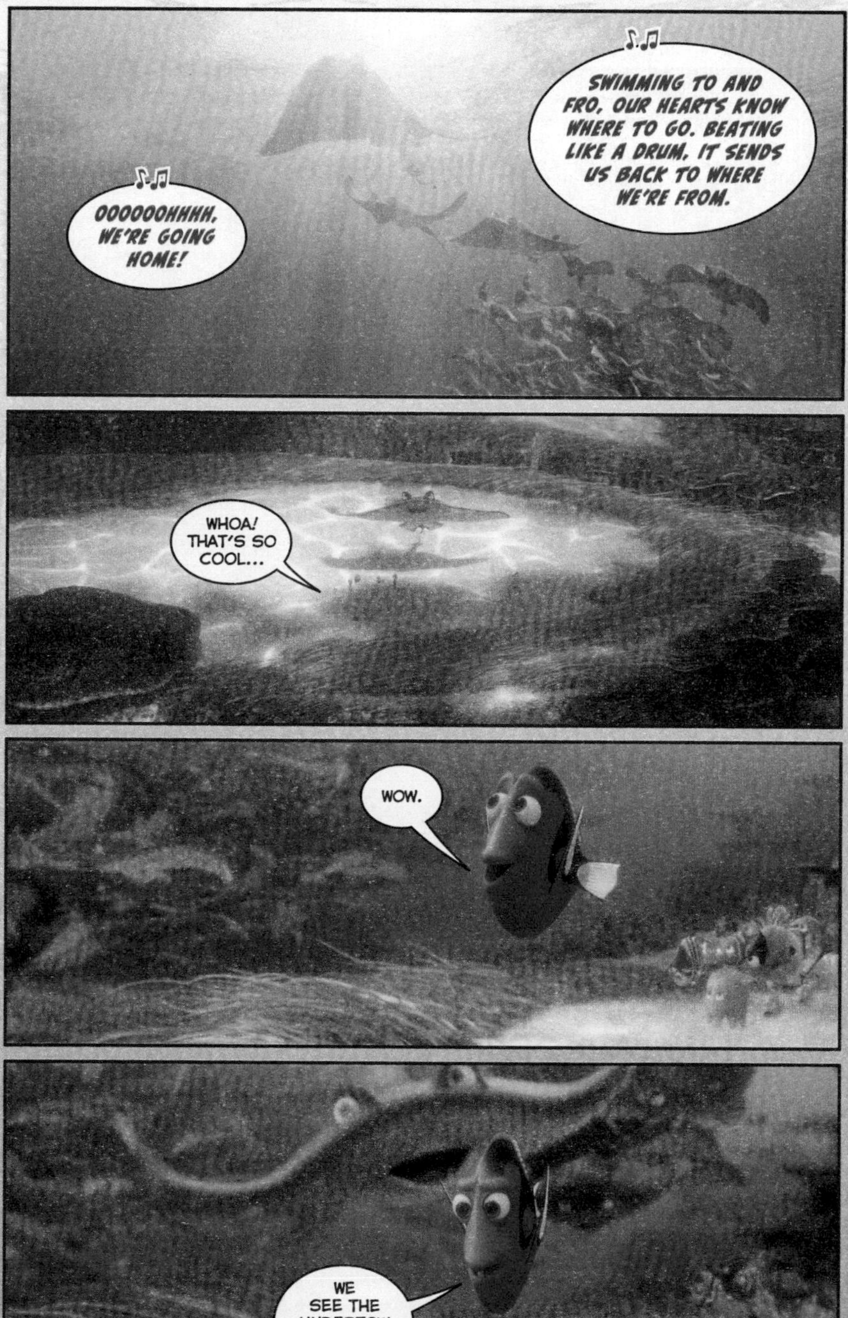
♪♫ OOOOOOHHHH, WE'RE GOING HOME!
♪♫ SWIMMING TO AND FRO, OUR HEARTS KNOW WHERE TO GO. BEATING LIKE A DRUM, IT SENDS US BACK TO WHERE WE'RE FROM.
WHOA! THAT'S SO COOL...
WOW.
WE SEE THE UNDERTOW AND WE SAY...

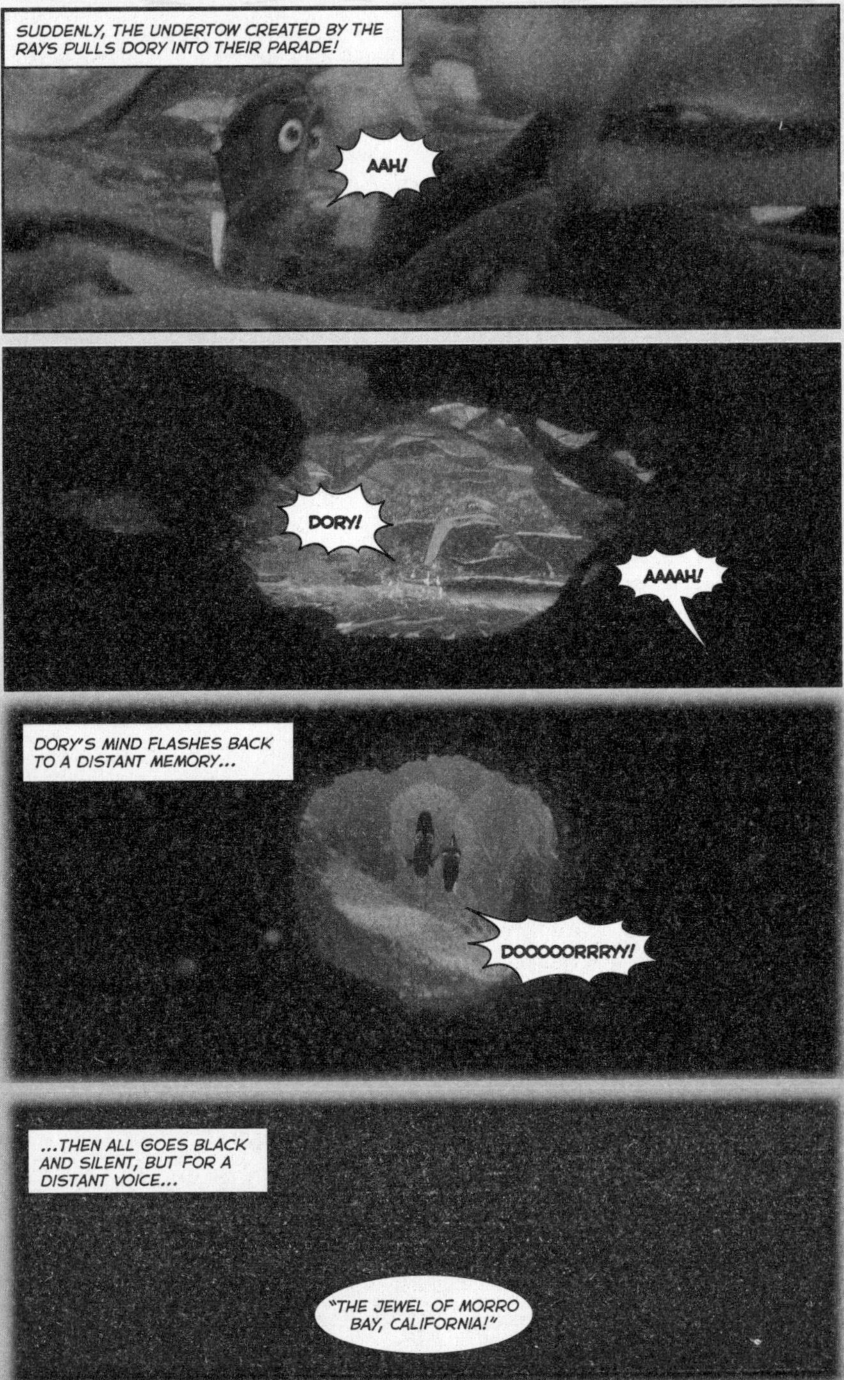
SUDDENLY, THE UNDERTOW CREATED BY THE RAYS PULLS DORY INTO THEIR PARADE!
AAH!
DORY!
AAAAH!
DORY'S MIND FLASHES BACK TO A DISTANT MEMORY...
DOOOOORRRYY!
...THEN ALL GOES BLACK AND SILENT, BUT FOR A DISTANT VOICE...
"THE JEWEL OF MORRO BAY, CALIFORNIA!"

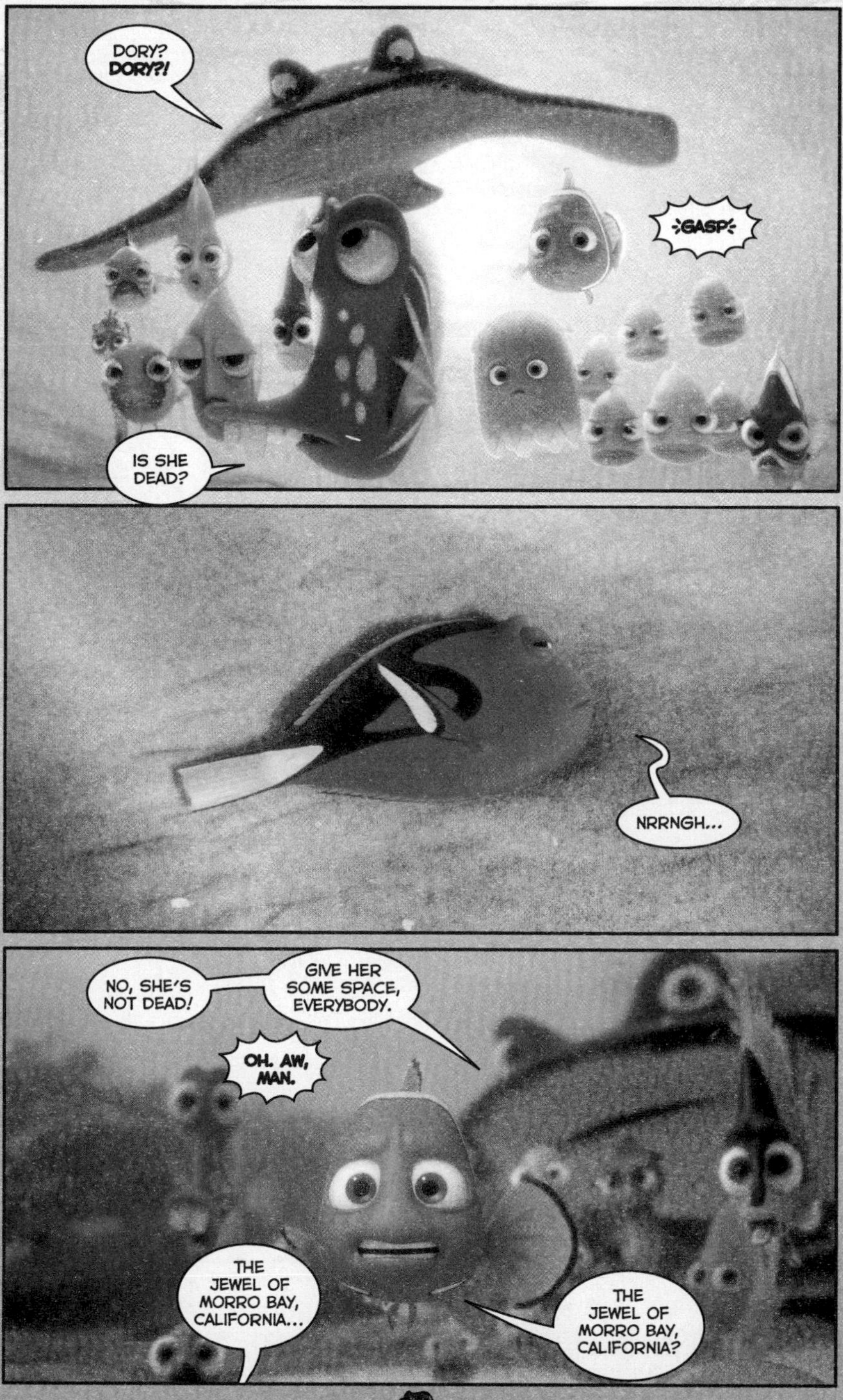
DORY? DORY?!
GASP
IS SHE DEAD?
NRRNGH...
NO, SHE'S NOT DEAD!
GIVE HER SOME SPACE, EVERYBODY.
OH. AW, MAN.
THE JEWEL OF MORRO BAY, CALIFORNIA...
THE JEWEL OF MORRO BAY, CALIFORNIA?

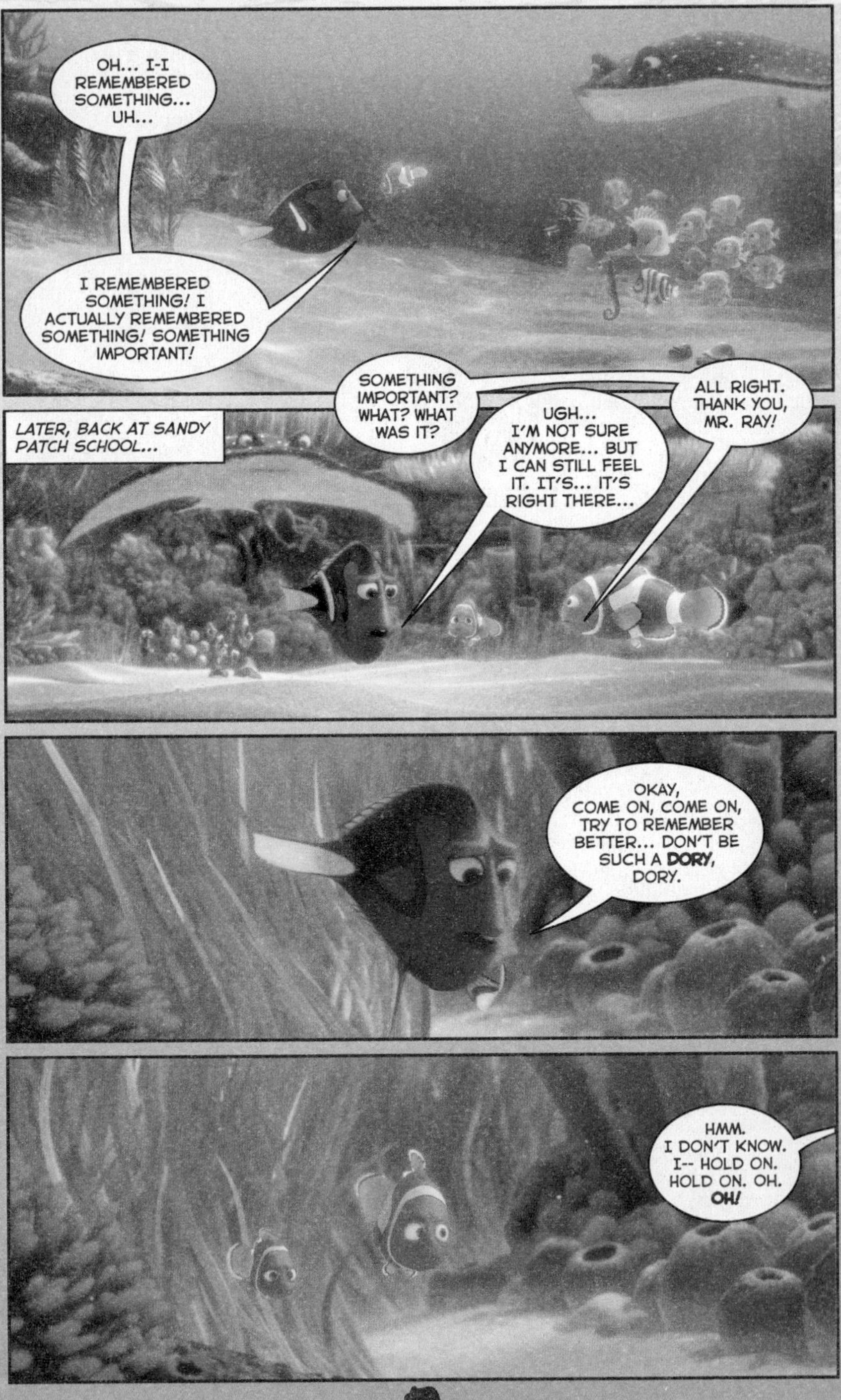

OH... I-I REMEMBERED SOMETHING... UH...
I REMEMBERED SOMETHING! I ACTUALLY REMEMBERED SOMETHING! SOMETHING IMPORTANT!
SOMETHING IMPORTANT? WHAT? WHAT WAS IT?
LATER, BACK AT SANDY PATCH SCHOOL...
UGH... I'M NOT SURE ANYMORE... BUT I CAN STILL FEEL IT. IT'S... IT'S RIGHT THERE...
ALL RIGHT. THANK YOU, MR. RAY!
OKAY, COME ON, COME ON, TRY TO REMEMBER BETTER... DON'T BE SUCH A **DORY**, DORY.
HMM. I DON'T KNOW. I-- HOLD ON. HOLD ON. OH. **OH!**

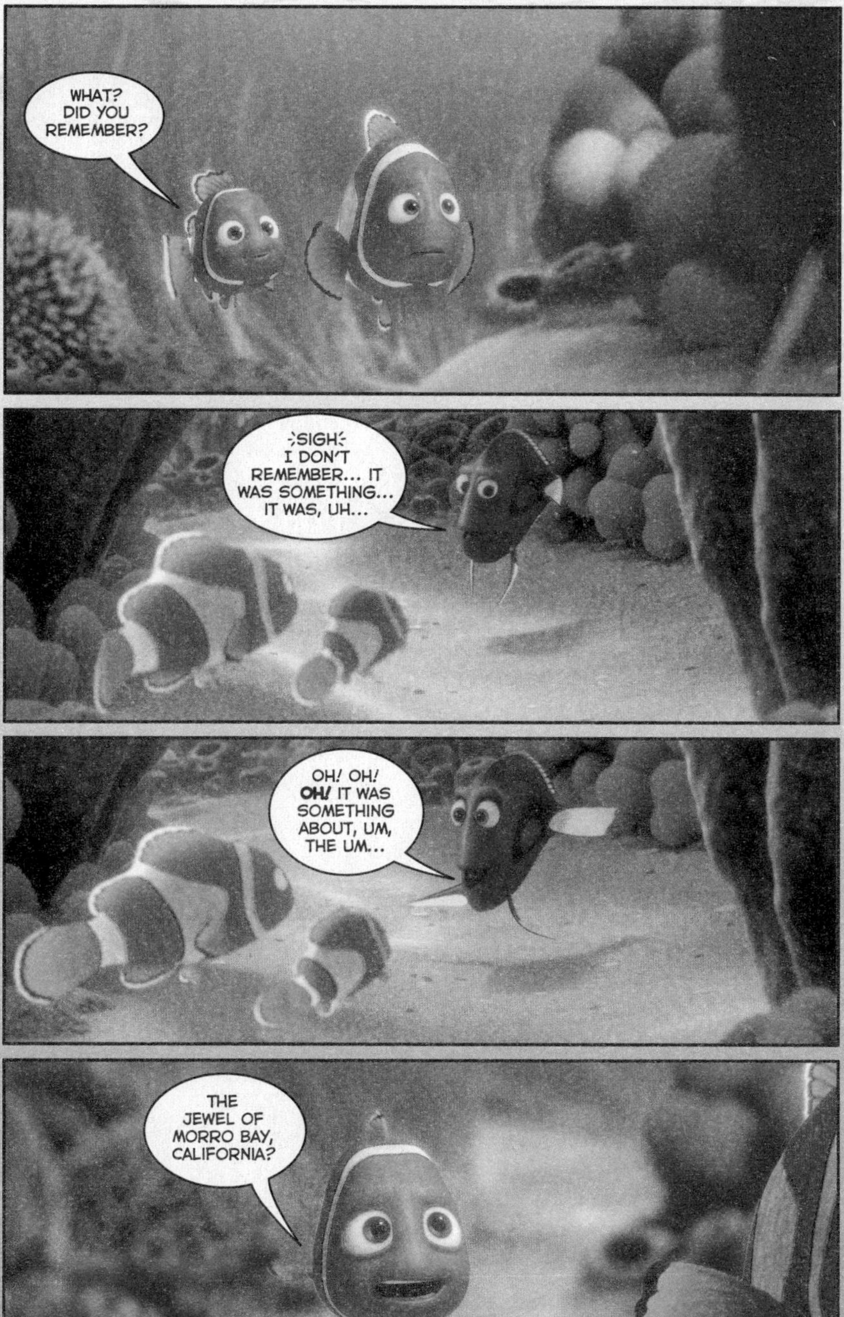
WHAT? DID YOU REMEMBER?
SIGH I DON'T REMEMBER... IT WAS SOMETHING... IT WAS, UH...
OH! OH! OH! IT WAS SOMETHING ABOUT, UM, THE UM...
THE JEWEL OF MORRO BAY, CALIFORNIA?

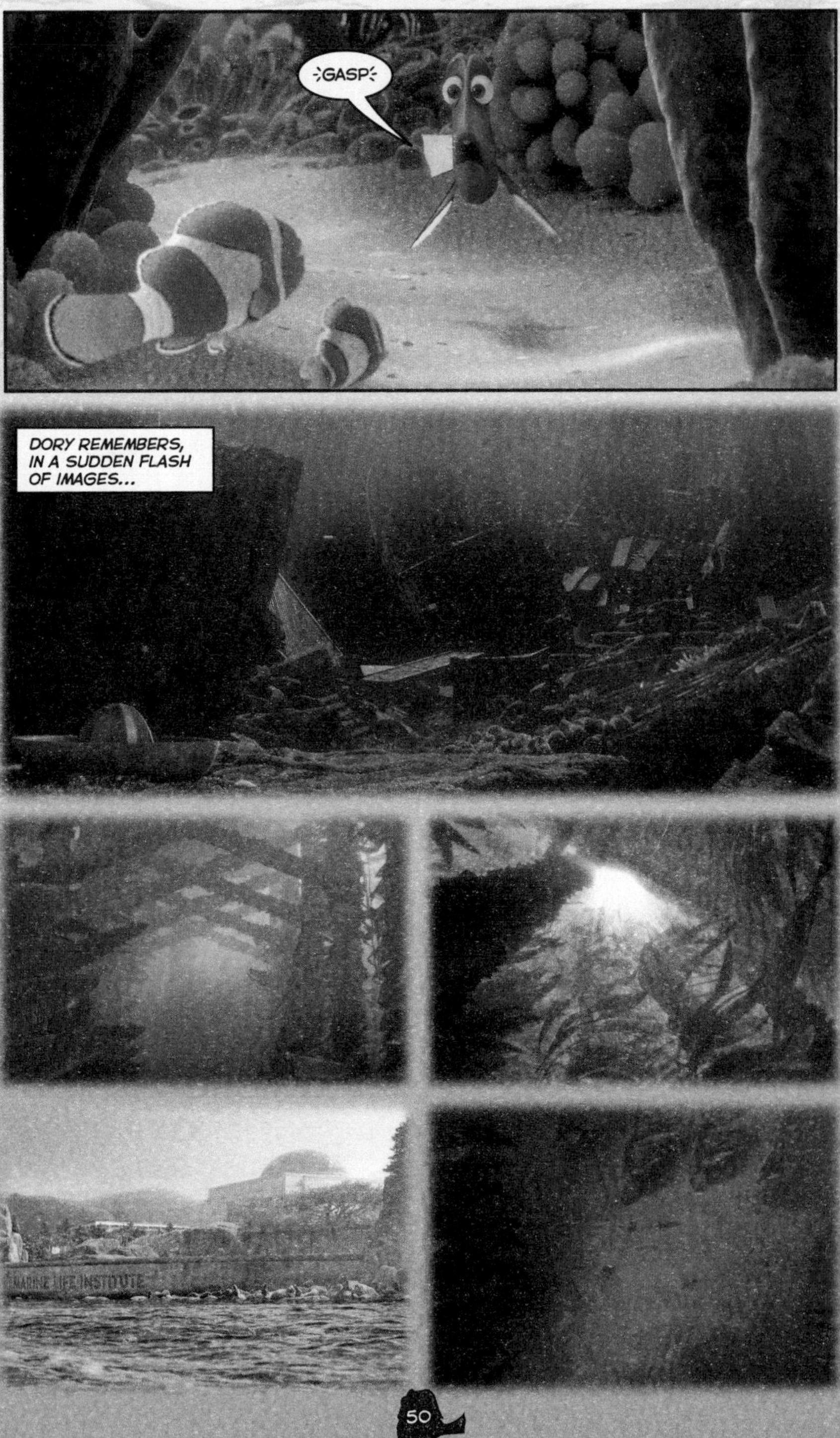
GASP
DORY REMEMBERS, IN A SUDDEN FLASH OF IMAGES...
MARINE LIFE INSTITUTE

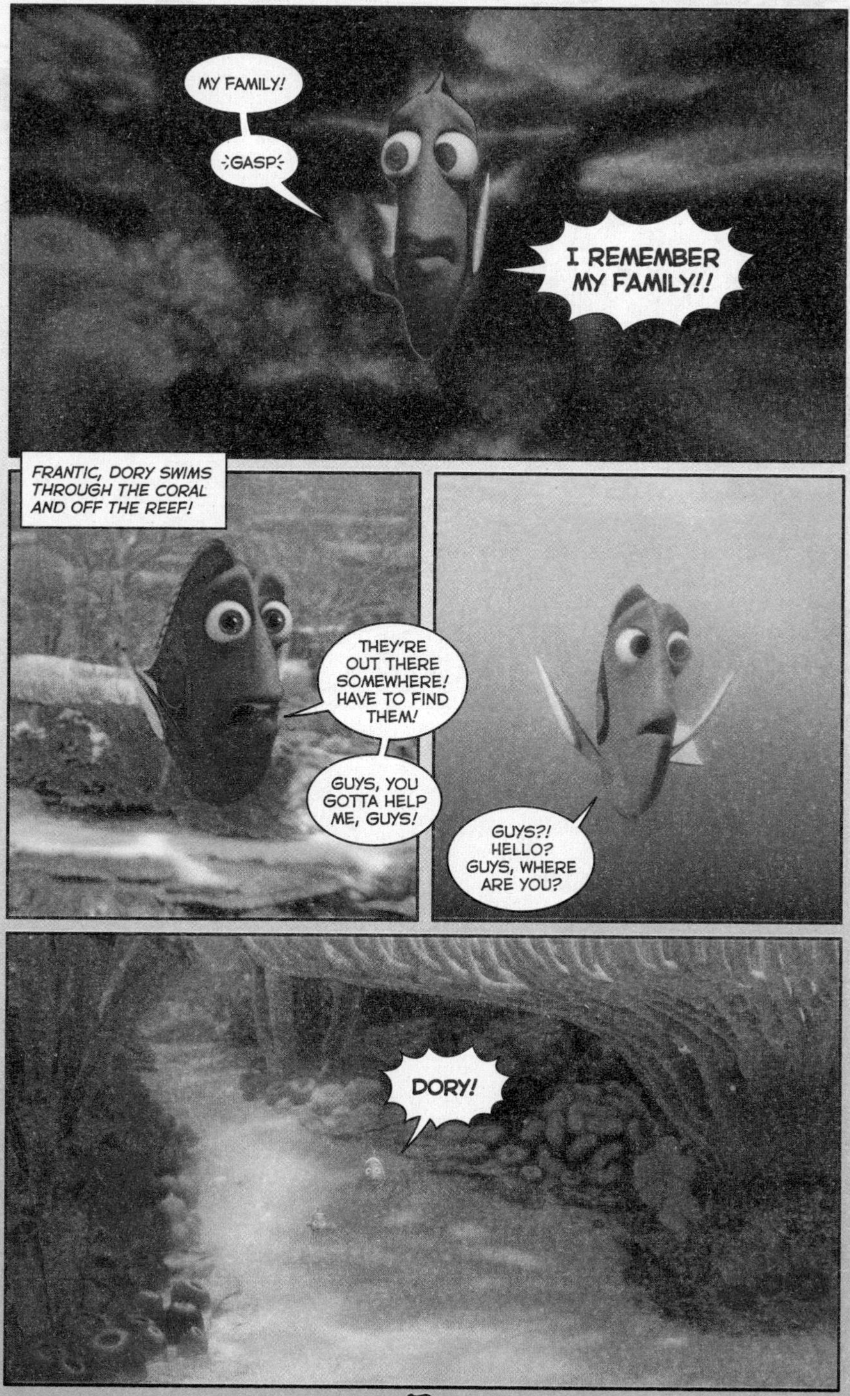
MY FAMILY!
GASP
I REMEMBER MY FAMILY!!
FRANTIC, DORY SWIMS THROUGH THE CORAL AND OFF THE REEF!
THEY'RE OUT THERE SOMEWHERE! HAVE TO FIND THEM!
GUYS, YOU GOTTA HELP ME, GUYS!
GUYS?! HELLO? GUYS, WHERE ARE YOU?
DORY!

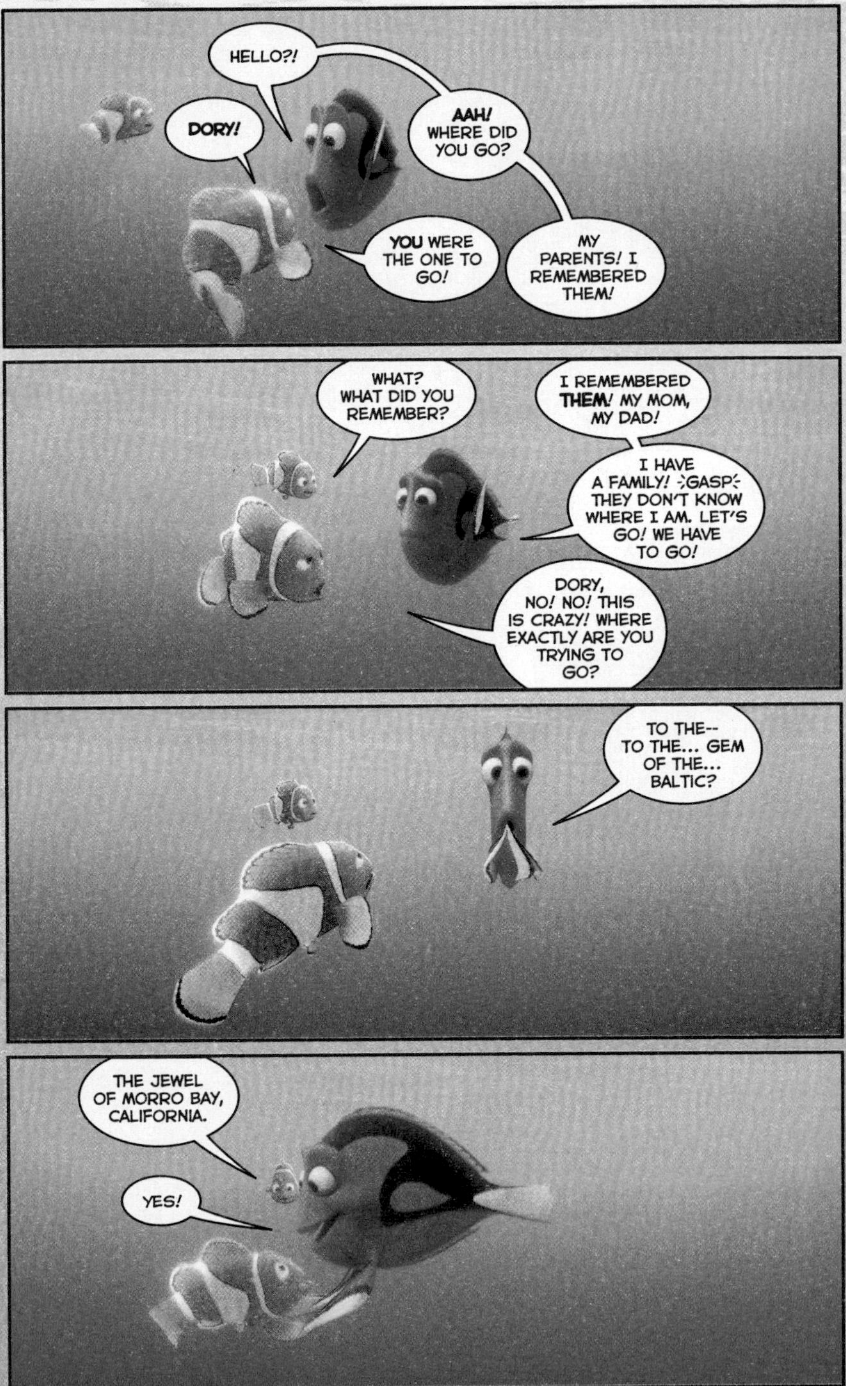
HELLO?!
DORY!
AAH! WHERE DID YOU GO?
YOU WERE THE ONE TO GO!
MY PARENTS! I REMEMBERED THEM!
WHAT? WHAT DID YOU REMEMBER?
I REMEMBERED THEM! MY MOM, MY DAD!
I HAVE A FAMILY! GASP THEY DON'T KNOW WHERE I AM. LET'S GO! WE HAVE TO GO!
DORY, NO! NO! THIS IS CRAZY! WHERE EXACTLY ARE YOU TRYING TO GO?
TO THE-- TO THE... GEM OF THE... BALTIC?
THE JEWEL OF MORRO BAY, CALIFORNIA.
YES!

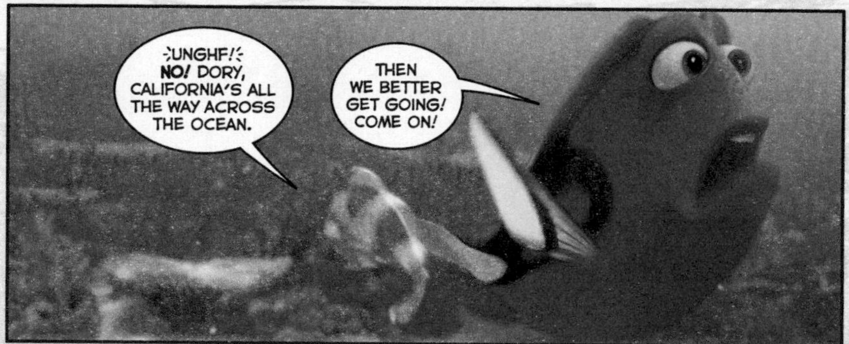
UNGHF! NO! DORY, CALIFORNIA'S ALL THE WAY ACROSS THE OCEAN.
THEN WE BETTER GET GOING! COME ON!

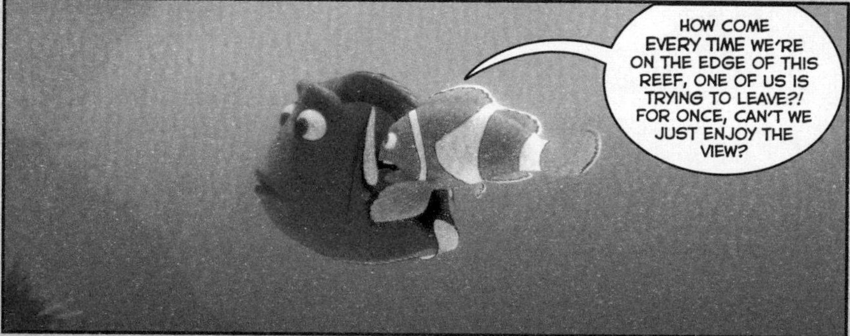
HOW COME EVERY TIME WE'RE ON THE EDGE OF THIS REEF, ONE OF US IS TRYING TO LEAVE?! FOR ONCE, CAN'T WE JUST ENJOY THE VIEW?

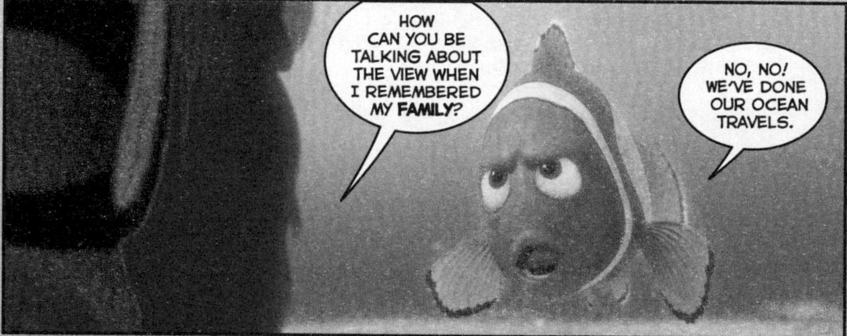
HOW CAN YOU BE TALKING ABOUT THE VIEW WHEN I REMEMBERED MY FAMILY?
NO, NO! WE'VE DONE OUR OCEAN TRAVELS.

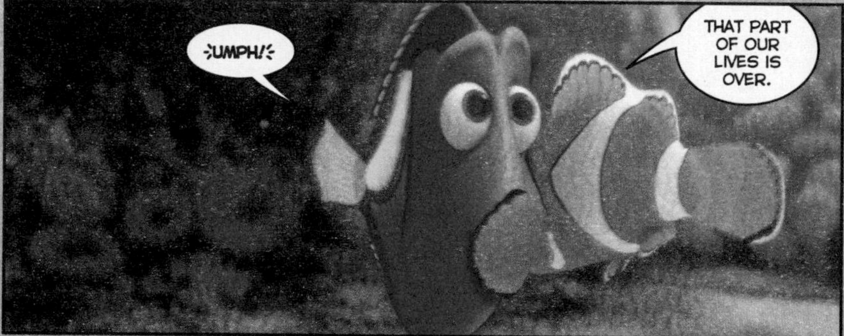
UMPH!
THAT PART OF OUR LIVES IS OVER.

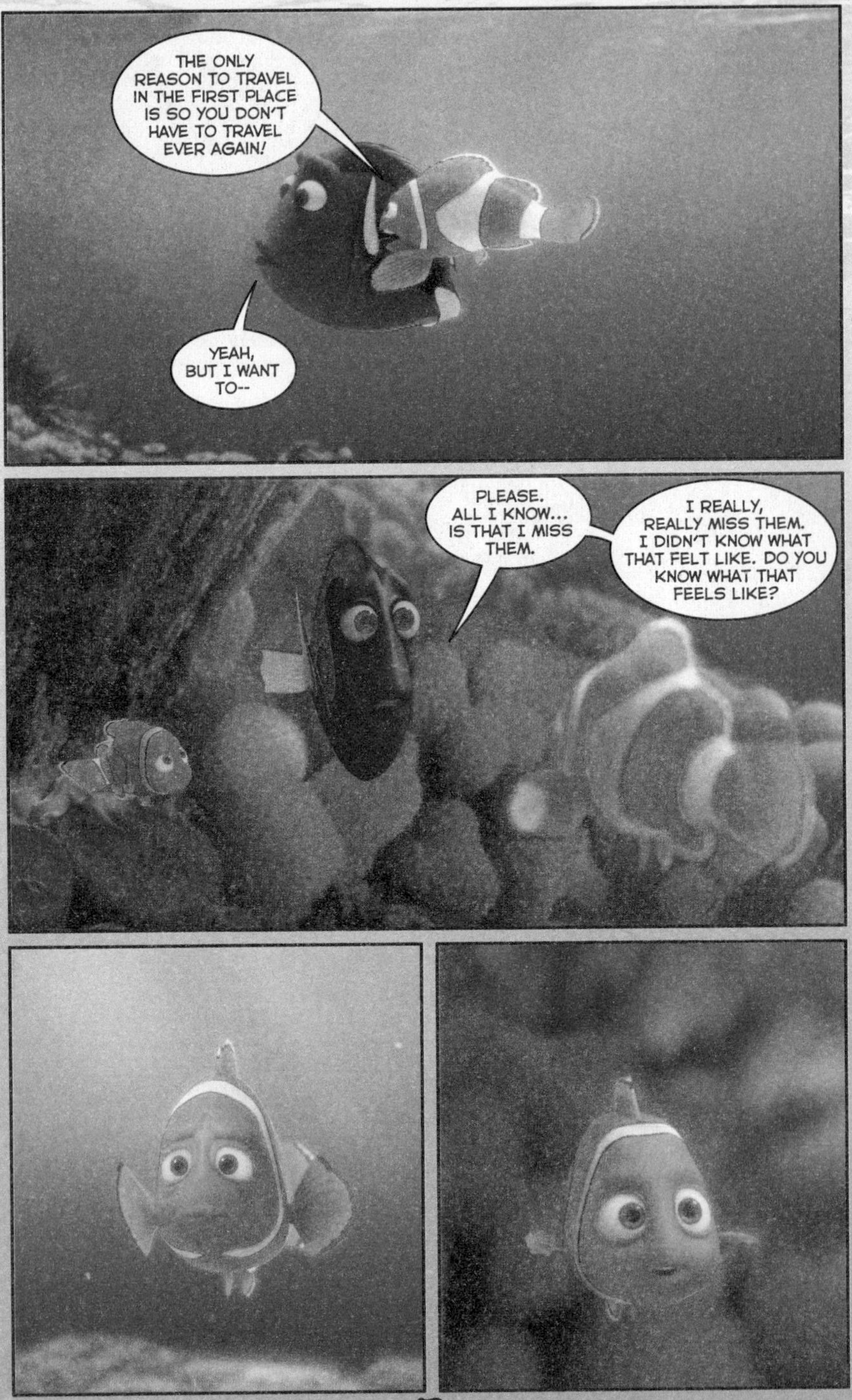
THE ONLY REASON TO TRAVEL IN THE FIRST PLACE IS SO YOU DON'T HAVE TO TRAVEL EVER AGAIN!
YEAH, BUT I WANT TO--
PLEASE. ALL I KNOW... IS THAT I MISS THEM.
I REALLY, REALLY MISS THEM. I DIDN'T KNOW WHAT THAT FELT LIKE. DO YOU KNOW WHAT THAT FEELS LIKE?

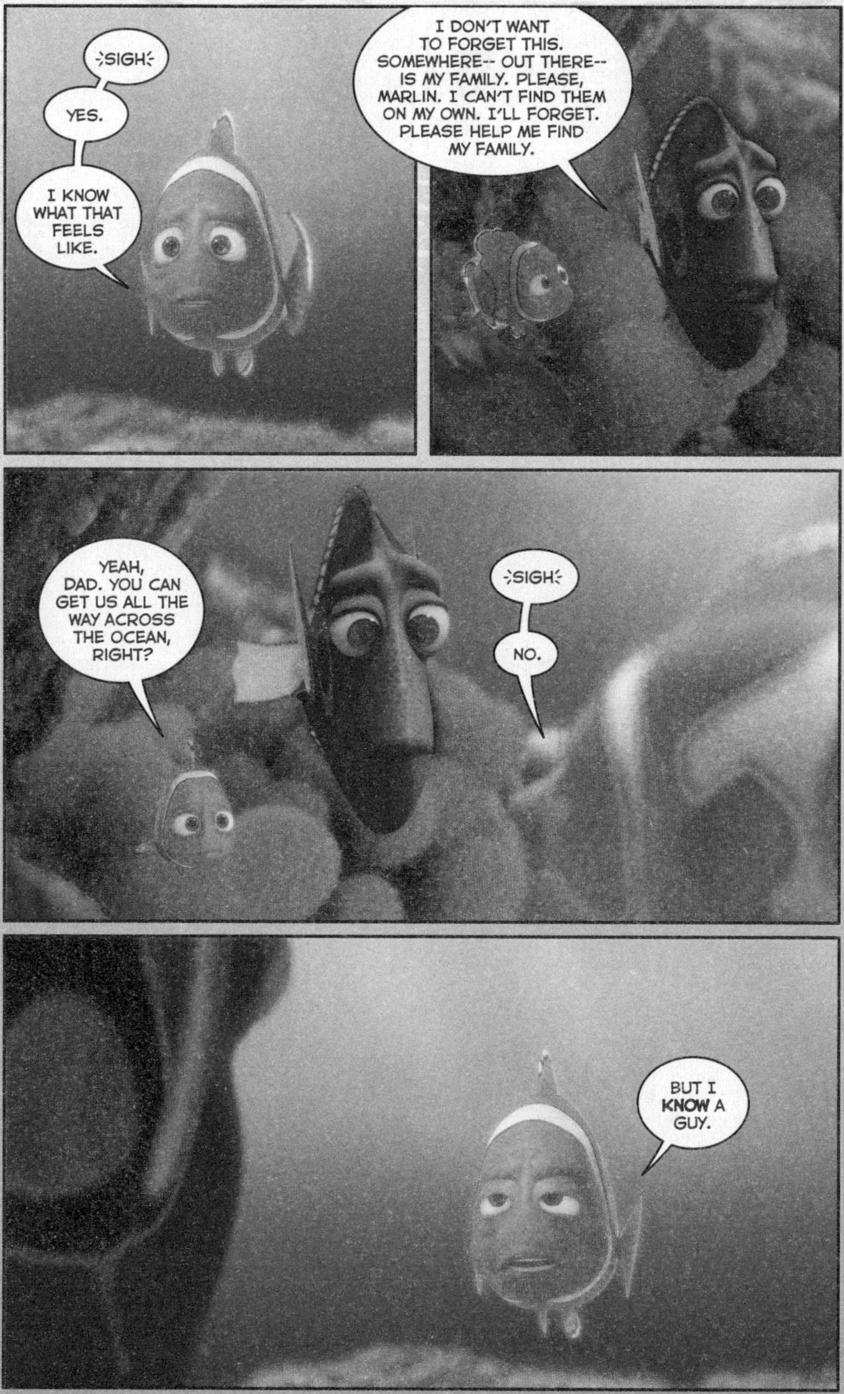
SIGH
YES.
I KNOW WHAT THAT FEELS LIKE.
I DON'T WANT TO FORGET THIS. SOMEWHERE-- OUT THERE-- IS MY FAMILY. PLEASE, MARLIN. I CAN'T FIND THEM ON MY OWN. I'LL FORGET. PLEASE HELP ME FIND MY FAMILY.
YEAH, DAD. YOU CAN GET US ALL THE WAY ACROSS THE OCEAN, RIGHT?
SIGH
NO.
BUT I **KNOW** A GUY.

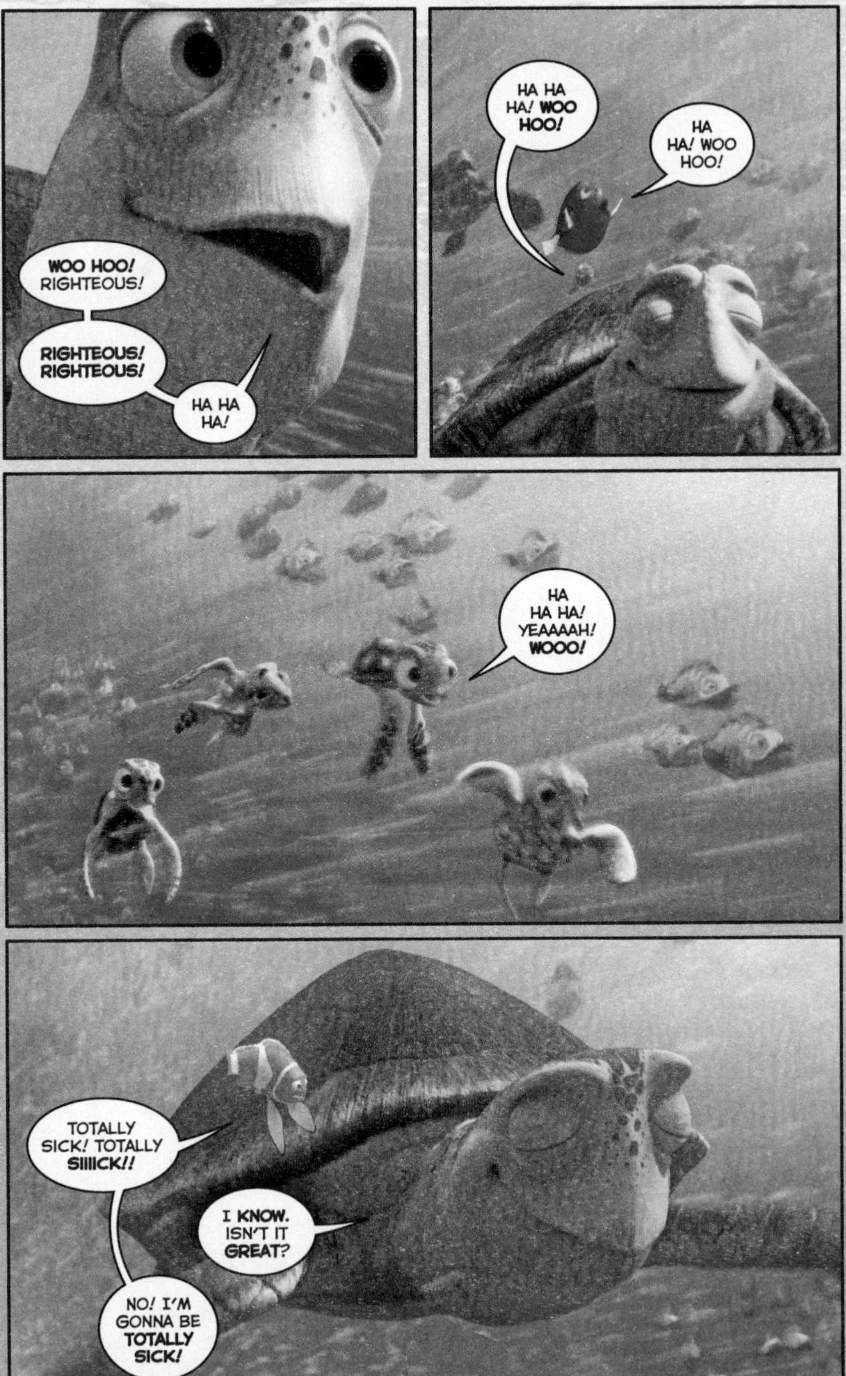
WOO HOO! RIGHTEOUS!
RIGHTEOUS! RIGHTEOUS!
HA HA HA!
HA HA HA! WOO HOO!
HA HA! WOO HOO!
HA HA HA! YEAAAAH! WOOO!
TOTALLY SICK! TOTALLY SIIIICK!!
I KNOW. ISN'T IT GREAT?
NO! I'M GONNA BE TOTALLY SICK!

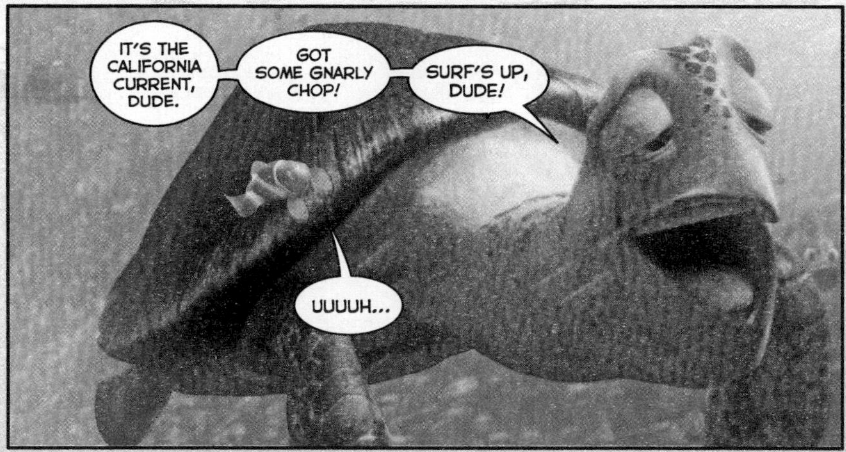
IT'S THE CALIFORNIA CURRENT, DUDE.
GOT SOME GNARLY CHOP!
SURF'S UP, DUDE!
UUUUH...

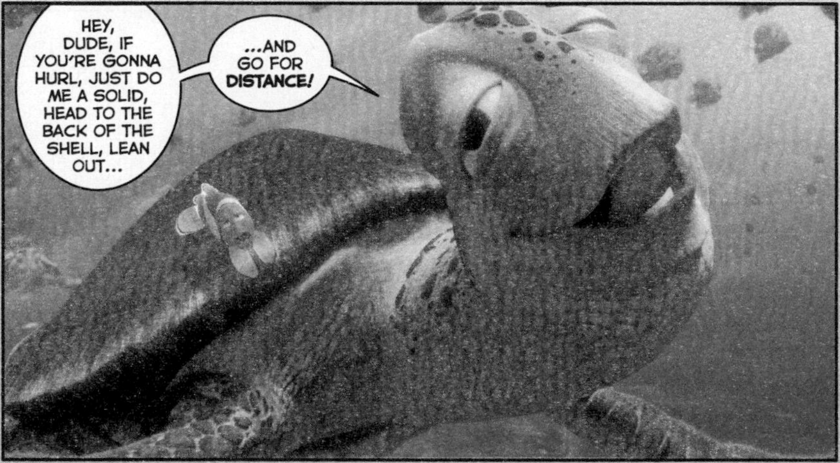
HEY, DUDE, IF YOU'RE GONNA HURL, JUST DO ME A SOLID, HEAD TO THE BACK OF THE SHELL, LEAN OUT...
...AND GO FOR **DISTANCE!**

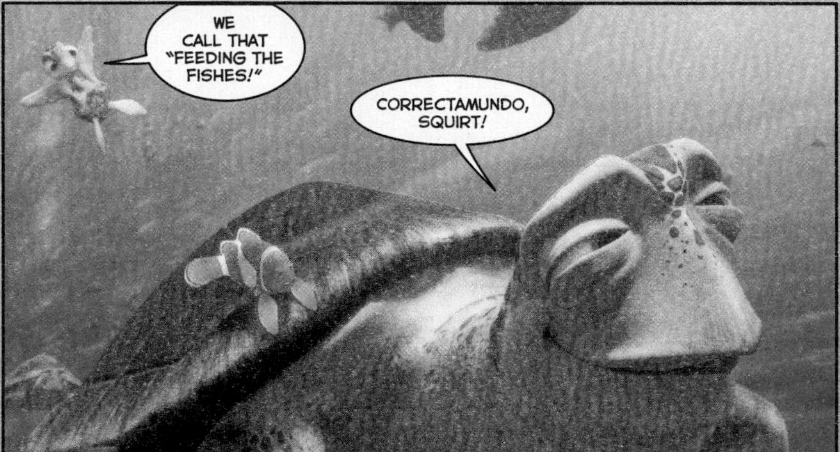
WE CALL THAT "FEEDING THE FISHES!"
CORRECTAMUNDO, SQUIRT!

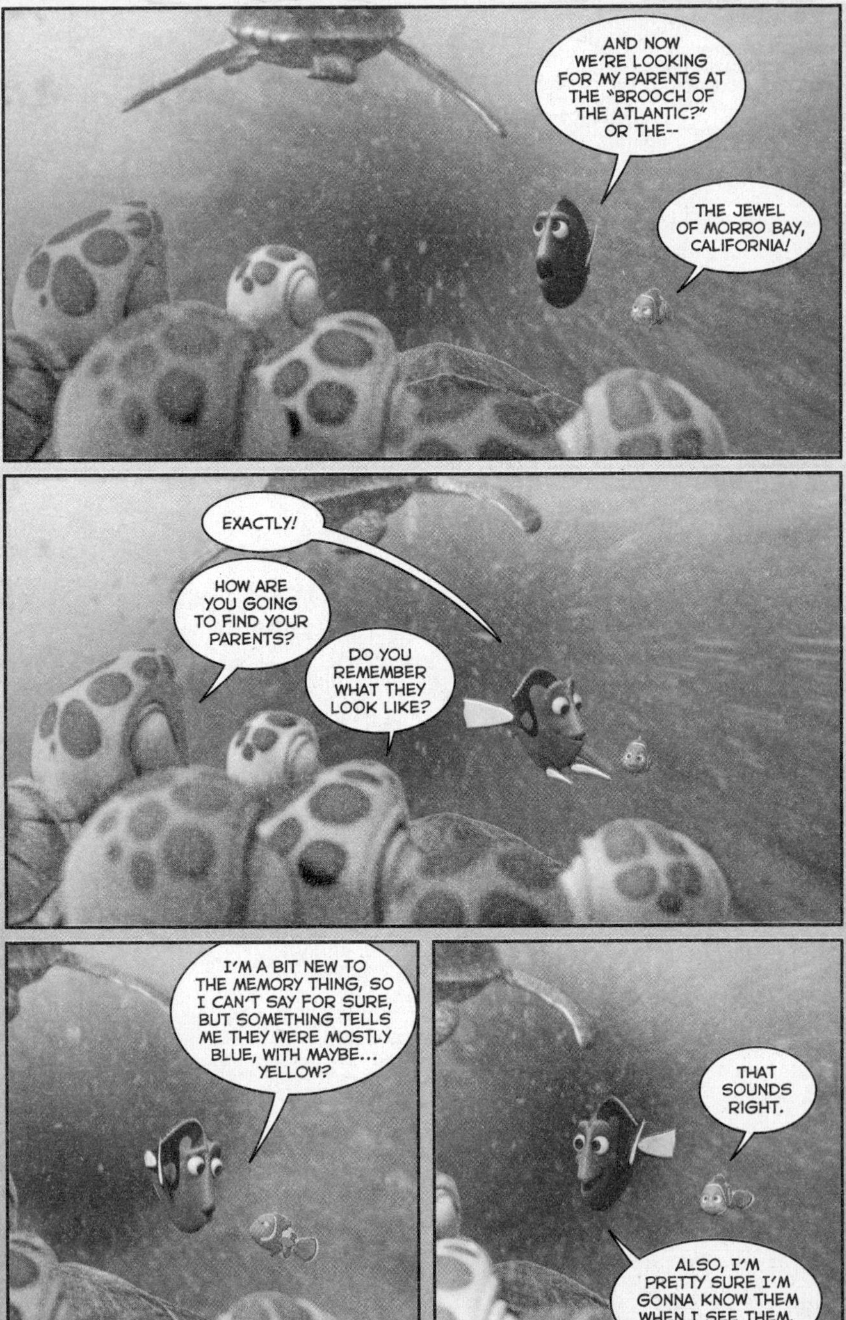
AND NOW WE'RE LOOKING FOR MY PARENTS AT THE "BROOCH OF THE ATLANTIC?" OR THE--
THE JEWEL OF MORRO BAY, CALIFORNIA!
EXACTLY!
HOW ARE YOU GOING TO FIND YOUR PARENTS?
DO YOU REMEMBER WHAT THEY LOOK LIKE?
I'M A BIT NEW TO THE MEMORY THING, SO I CAN'T SAY FOR SURE, BUT SOMETHING TELLS ME THEY WERE MOSTLY BLUE, WITH MAYBE... YELLOW?
THAT SOUNDS RIGHT.
ALSO, I'M PRETTY SURE I'M GONNA KNOW THEM WHEN I SEE THEM. WE'RE **FAMILY.**

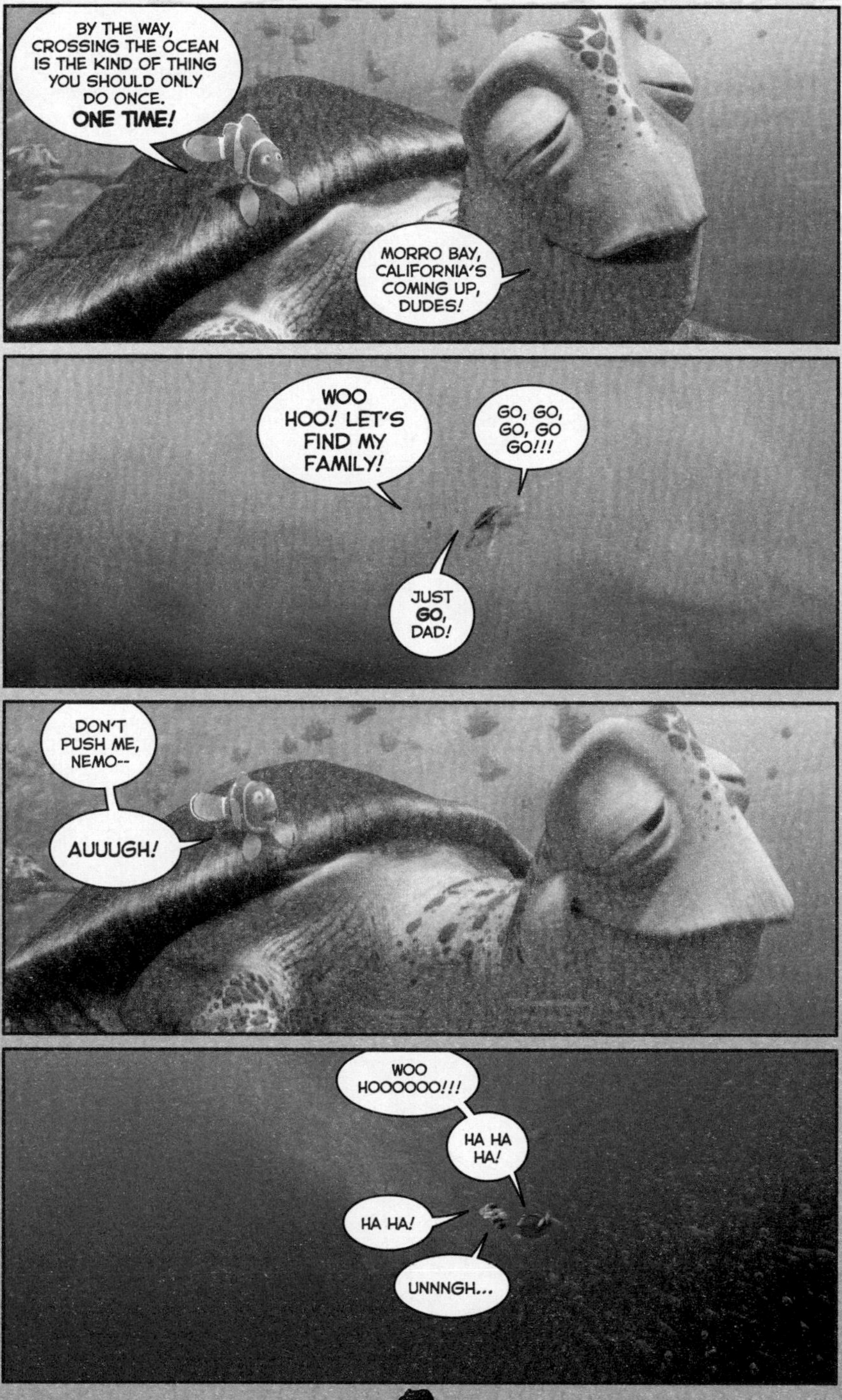
BY THE WAY, CROSSING THE OCEAN IS THE KIND OF THING YOU SHOULD ONLY DO ONCE. ONE TIME!
MORRO BAY, CALIFORNIA'S COMING UP, DUDES!
WOO HOO! LET'S FIND MY FAMILY!
GO, GO, GO, GO GO!!!
JUST GO, DAD!
DON'T PUSH ME, NEMO--
AUUUGH!
WOO HOOOOOO!!!
HA HA HA!
HA HA!
UNNNGH...

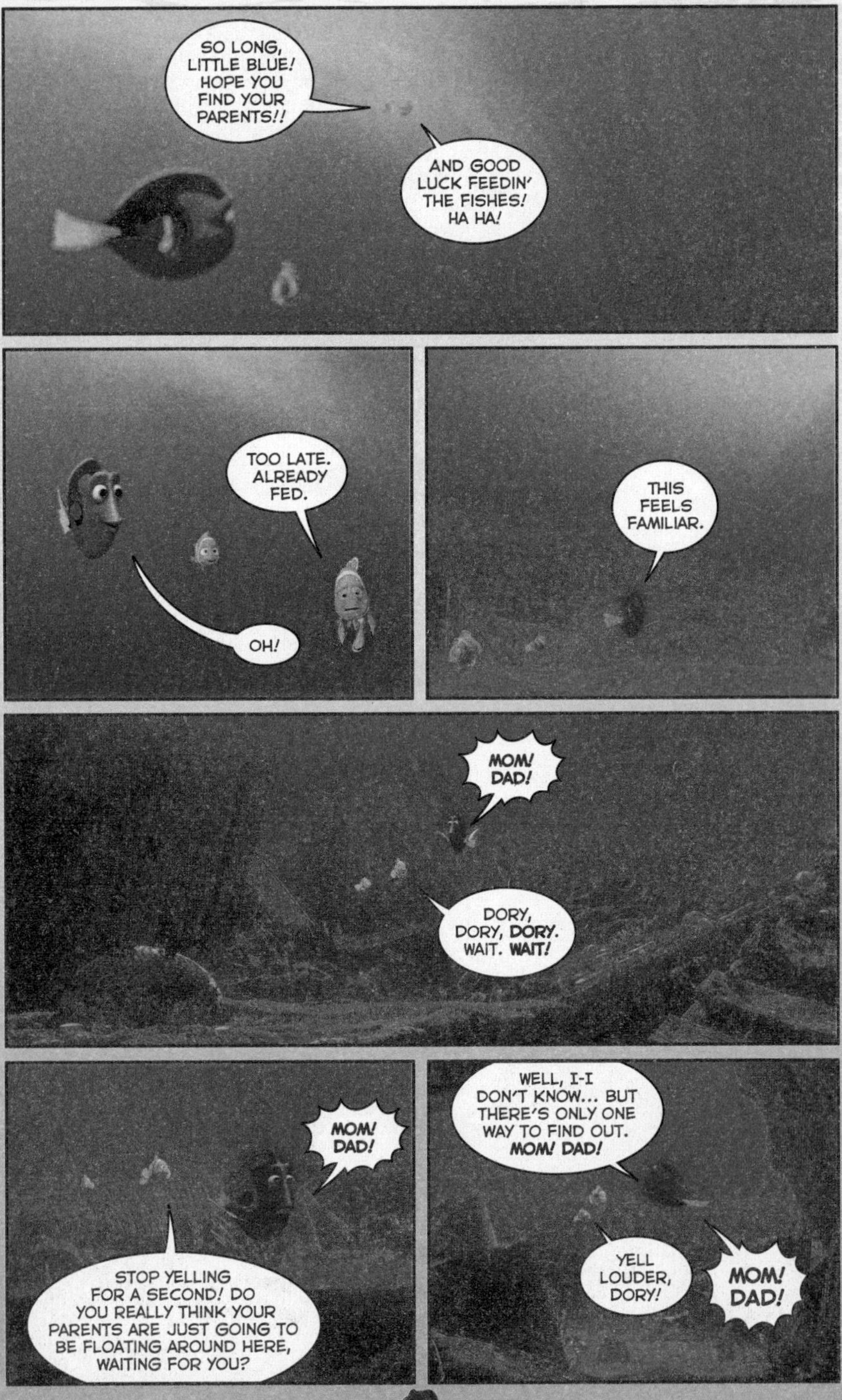
SO LONG, LITTLE BLUE! HOPE YOU FIND YOUR PARENTS!!
AND GOOD LUCK FEEDIN' THE FISHES! HA HA!
TOO LATE. ALREADY FED.
OH!
THIS FEELS FAMILIAR.
MOM! DAD!
DORY, DORY, DORY. WAIT. WAIT!
MOM! DAD!
STOP YELLING FOR A SECOND! DO YOU REALLY THINK YOUR PARENTS ARE JUST GOING TO BE FLOATING AROUND HERE, WAITING FOR YOU?
WELL, I-I DON'T KNOW... BUT THERE'S ONLY ONE WAY TO FIND OUT. MOM! DAD!
YELL LOUDER, DORY!
MOM! DAD!

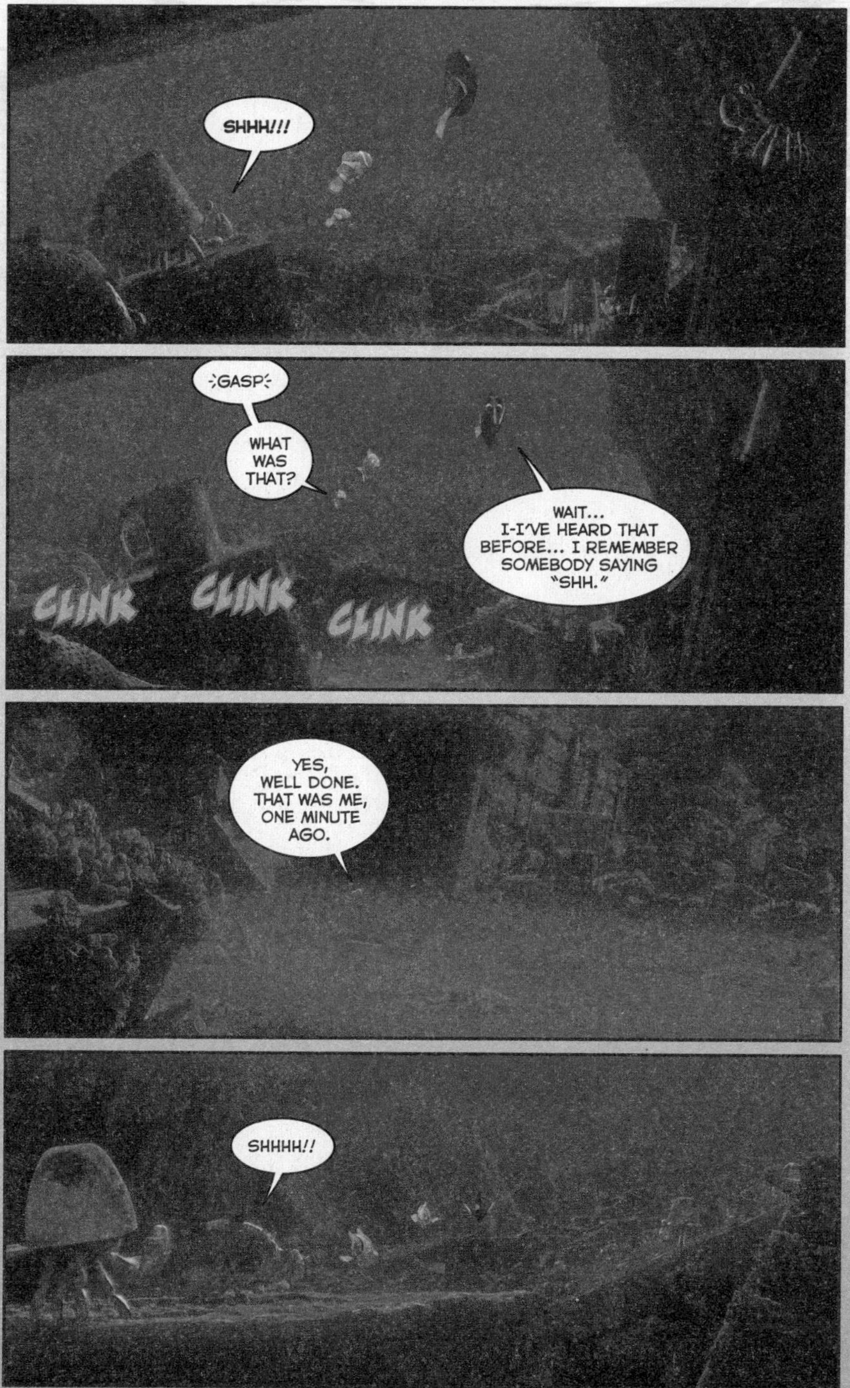
SHHH!!!
GASP
WHAT WAS THAT?
CLINK CLINK CLINK
WAIT... I-I'VE HEARD THAT BEFORE... I REMEMBER SOMEBODY SAYING "SHH."
YES, WELL DONE. THAT WAS ME, ONE MINUTE AGO.
SHHHH!!

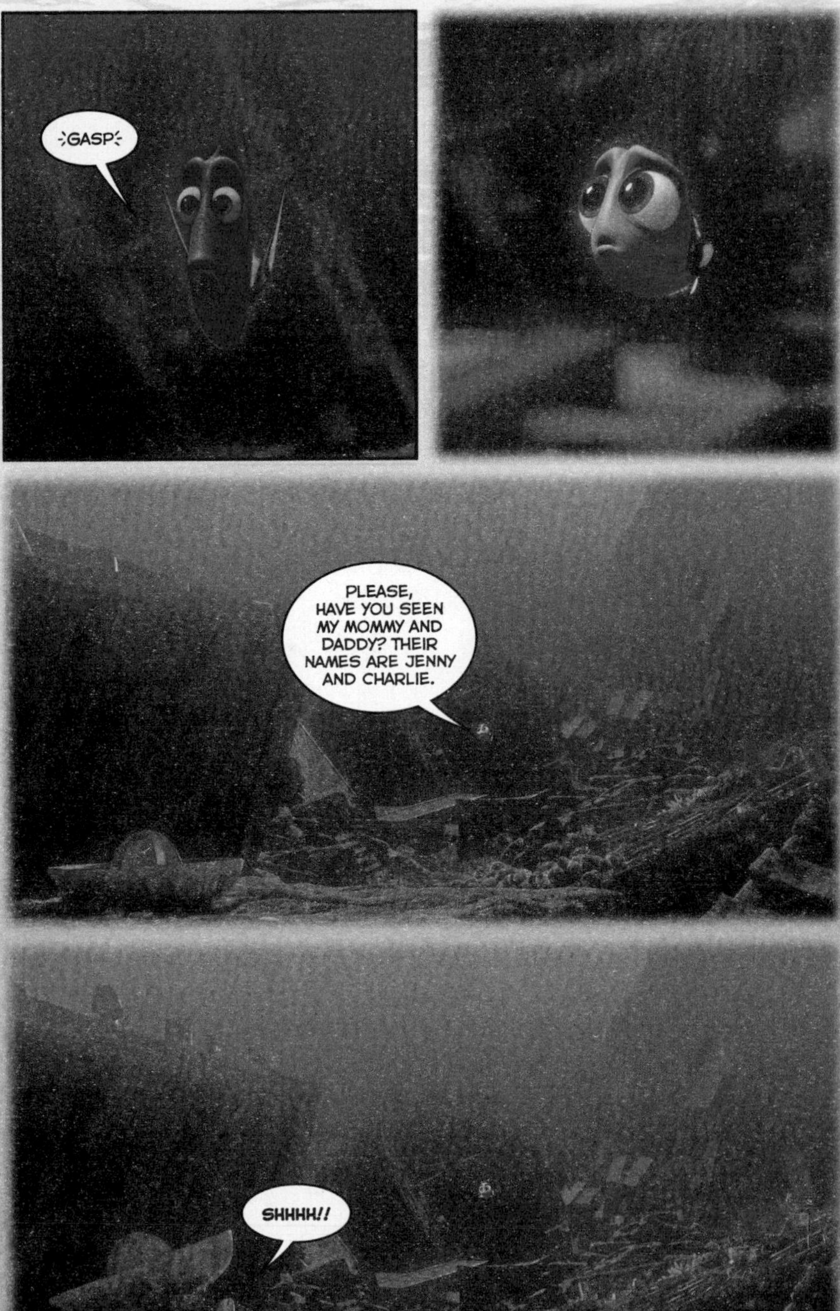
GASP
PLEASE, HAVE YOU SEEN MY MOMMY AND DADDY? THEIR NAMES ARE JENNY AND CHARLIE.
SHHHH!!

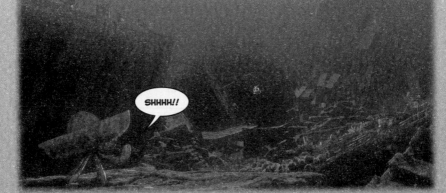

:GASP:

JENNY AND CHARLIE.

WHAT? JENNY AND WHAT...?

THOSE ARE THEIR NAMES. MY PARENTS ARE **JENNY AND CHARLIE!!**

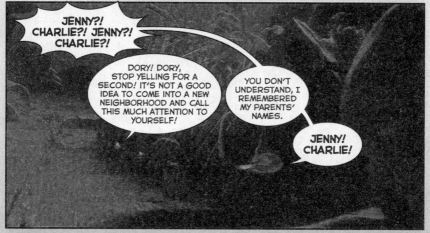

JENNY?! CHARLIE?! JENNY?! CHARLIE?!

DORY! DORY, STOP YELLING FOR A SECOND! IT'S NOT A GOOD IDEA TO COME INTO A NEW NEIGHBORHOOD AND CALL THIS MUCH ATTENTION TO YOURSELF!

YOU DON'T UNDERSTAND, I REMEMBERED MY PARENTS' NAMES.

JENNY! CHARLIE!

SHHHH!

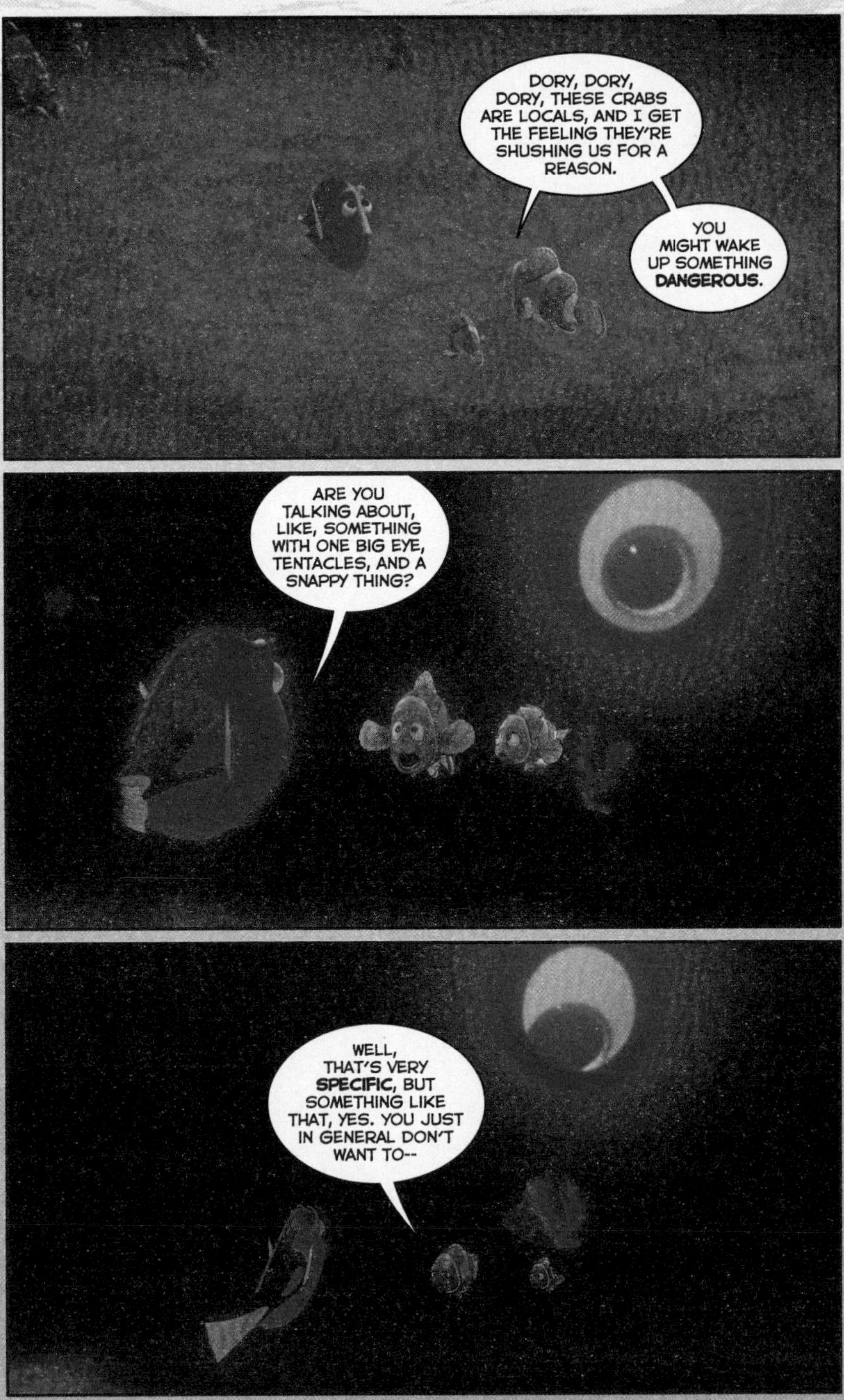
DORY, DORY, DORY, THESE CRABS ARE LOCALS, AND I GET THE FEELING THEY'RE SHUSHING US FOR A REASON.
YOU MIGHT WAKE UP SOMETHING **DANGEROUS.**
ARE YOU TALKING ABOUT, LIKE, SOMETHING WITH ONE BIG EYE, TENTACLES, AND A SNAPPY THING?
WELL, THAT'S VERY **SPECIFIC**, BUT SOMETHING LIKE THAT, YES. YOU JUST IN GENERAL DON'T WANT TO--

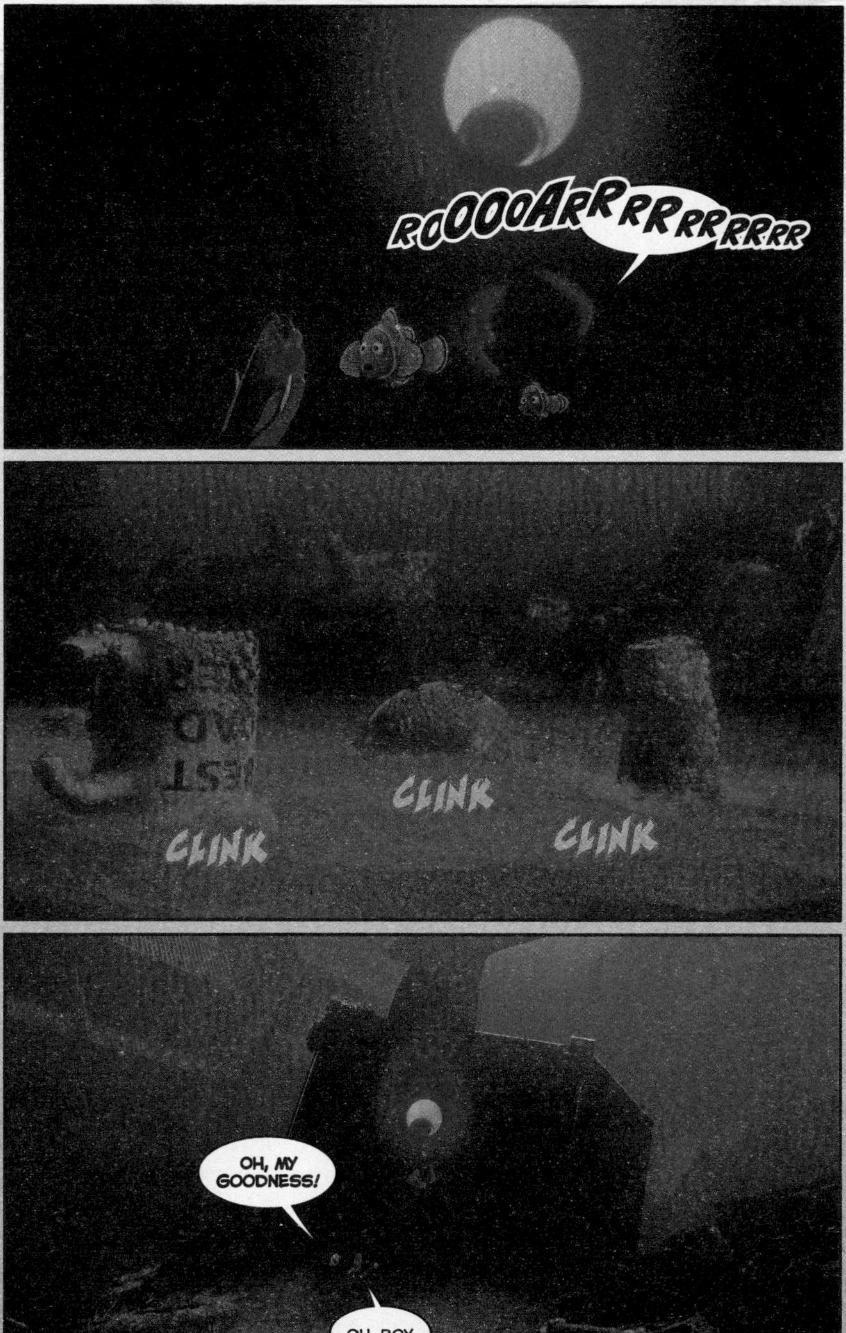
ROOOOARRRRRRRRRRR
CLINK
CLINK
CLINK
OH, MY GOODNESS!
OH, BOY.

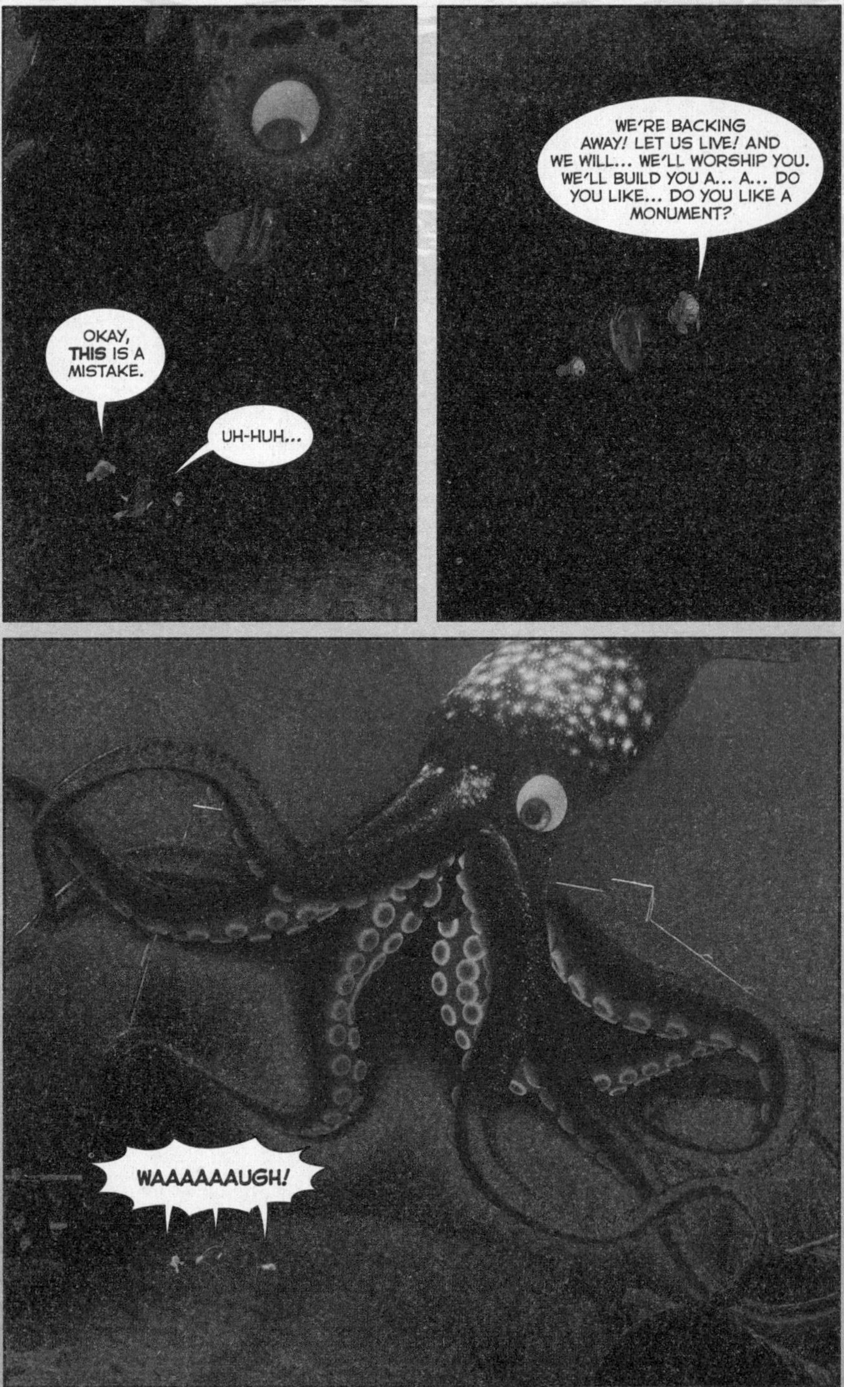
OKAY, THIS IS A MISTAKE.
UH-HUH...
WE'RE BACKING AWAY! LET US LIVE! AND WE WILL... WE'LL WORSHIP YOU. WE'LL BUILD YOU A... A... DO YOU LIKE... DO YOU LIKE A MONUMENT?
WAAAAAAUGH!

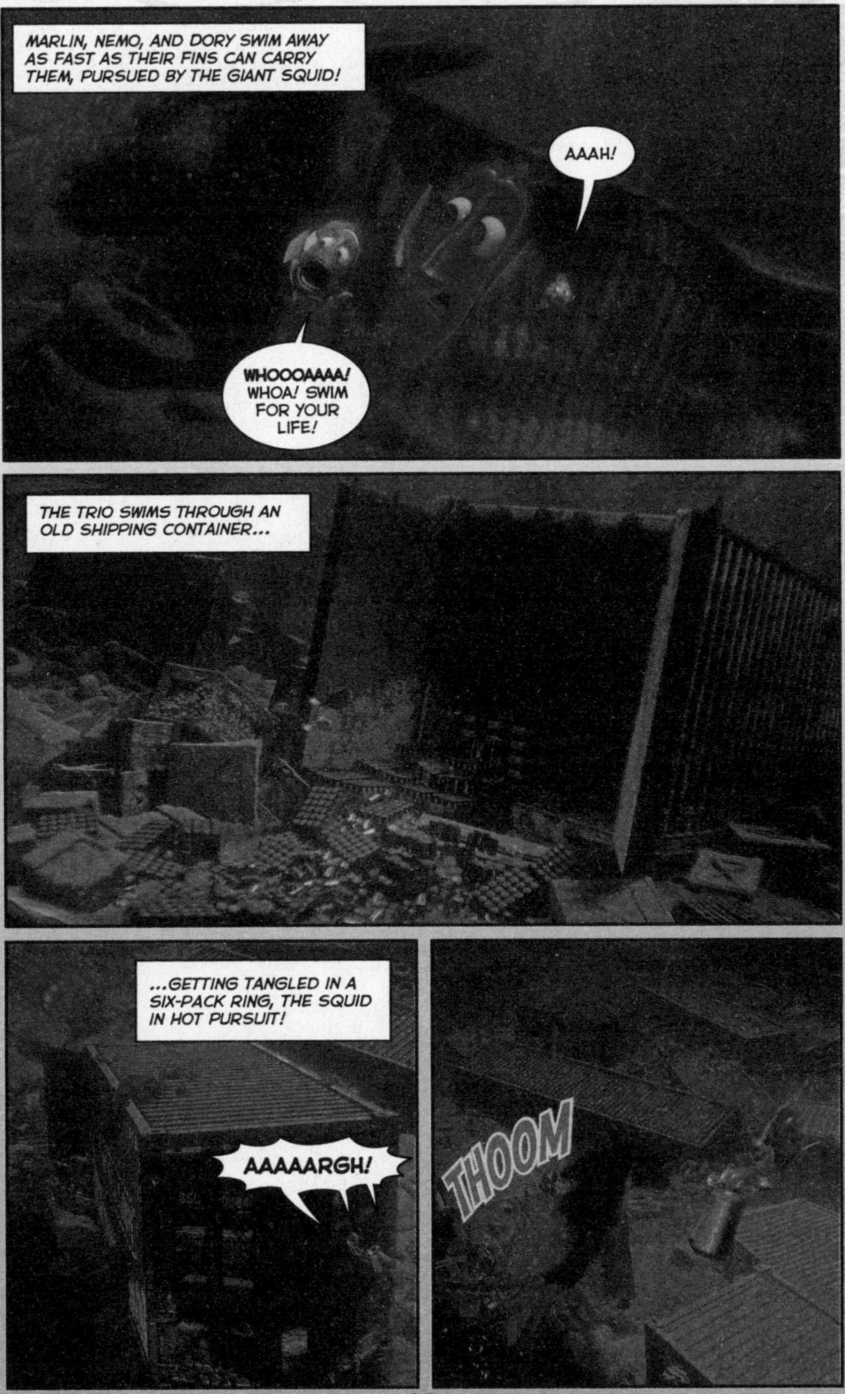
MARLIN, NEMO, AND DORY SWIM AWAY AS FAST AS THEIR FINS CAN CARRY THEM, PURSUED BY THE GIANT SQUID!
AAAH!
WHOOOAAAA! WHOA! SWIM FOR YOUR LIFE!
THE TRIO SWIMS THROUGH AN OLD SHIPPING CONTAINER...
...GETTING TANGLED IN A SIX-PACK RING, THE SQUID IN HOT PURSUIT!
AAAAARGH!
THOOM

DORY, MARLIN AND NEMO RACE AHEAD, TOWARD THE SUNKEN SHIP AND ITS SHIPPING-CONTAINER CARGO...

AAAAAH!

AAAAH!

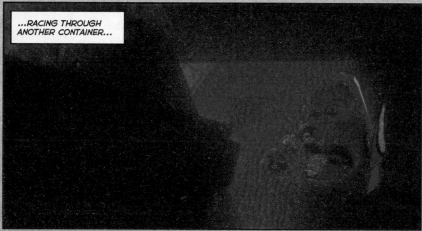

...RACING THROUGH ANOTHER CONTAINER...

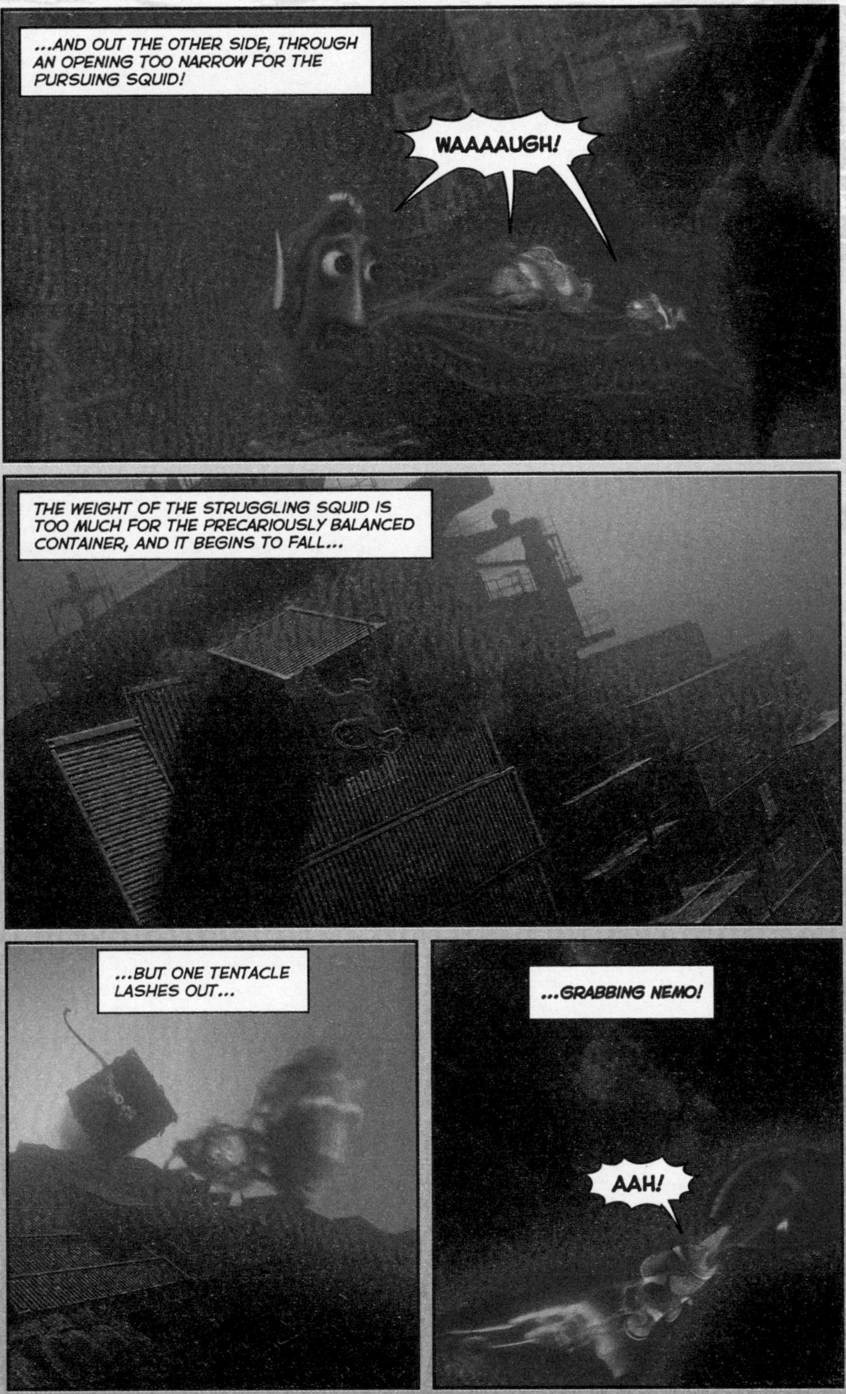
...AND OUT THE OTHER SIDE, THROUGH AN OPENING TOO NARROW FOR THE PURSUING SQUID!
WAAAAUGH!
THE WEIGHT OF THE STRUGGLING SQUID IS TOO MUCH FOR THE PRECARIOUSLY BALANCED CONTAINER, AND IT BEGINS TO FALL...
...BUT ONE TENTACLE LASHES OUT...
...GRABBING NEMO!
AAH!

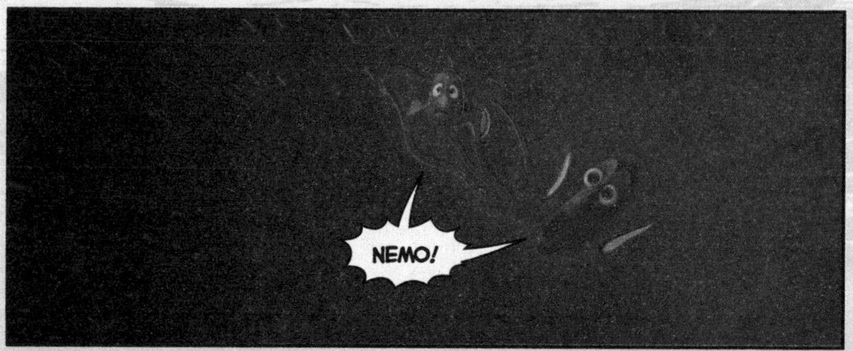
NEMO!

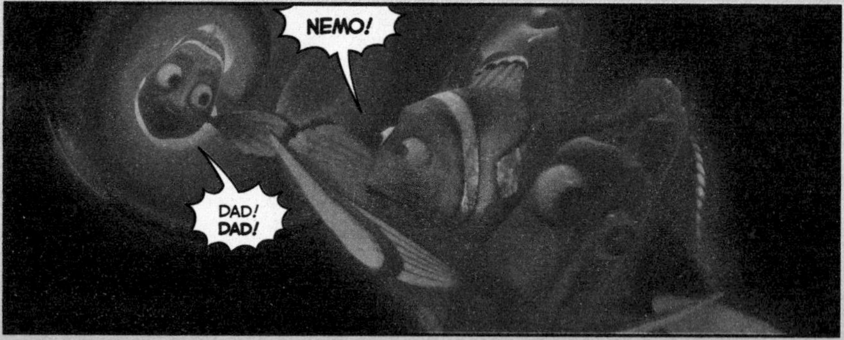
NEMO!
DAD! DAD!

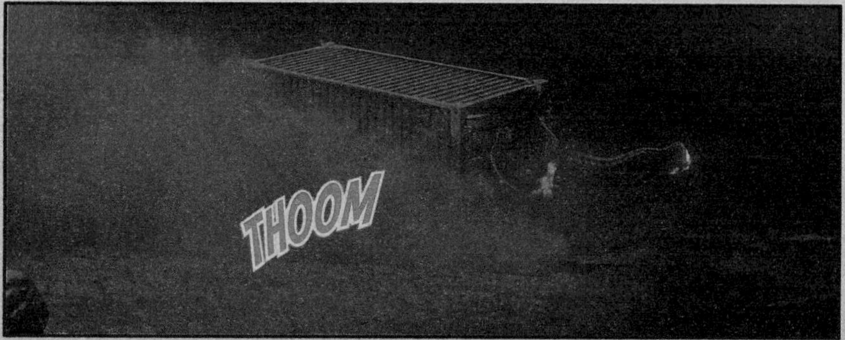
THOOM

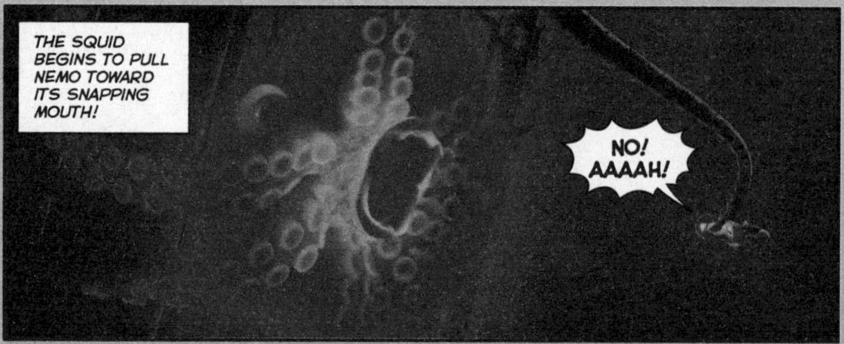
THE SQUID BEGINS TO PULL NEMO TOWARD ITS SNAPPING MOUTH!
NO! AAAAH!

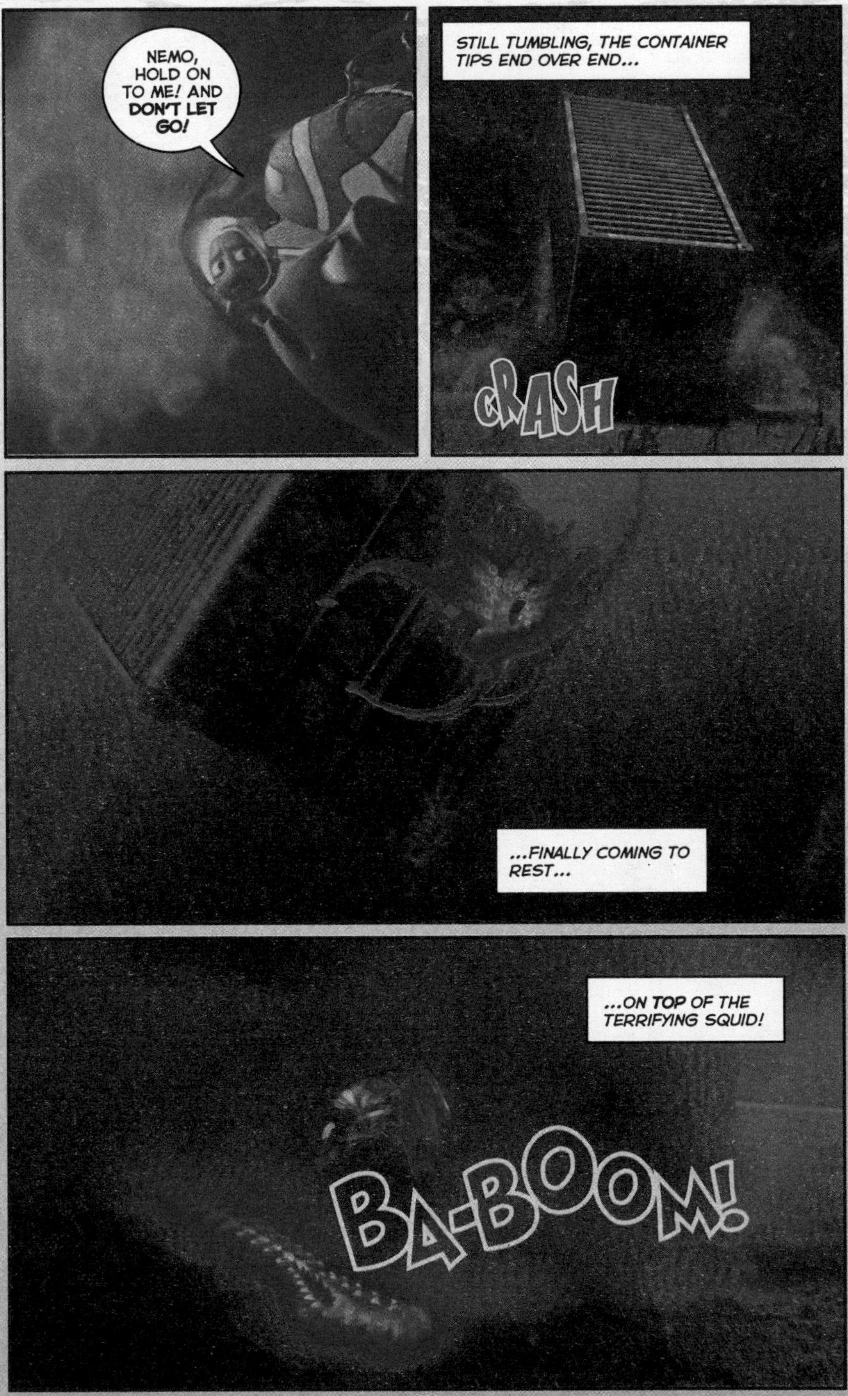
NEMO, HOLD ON TO ME! AND DON'T LET GO!
STILL TUMBLING, THE CONTAINER TIPS END OVER END...
CRASH
...FINALLY COMING TO REST...
...ON TOP OF THE TERRIFYING SQUID!
BA-BOOM!

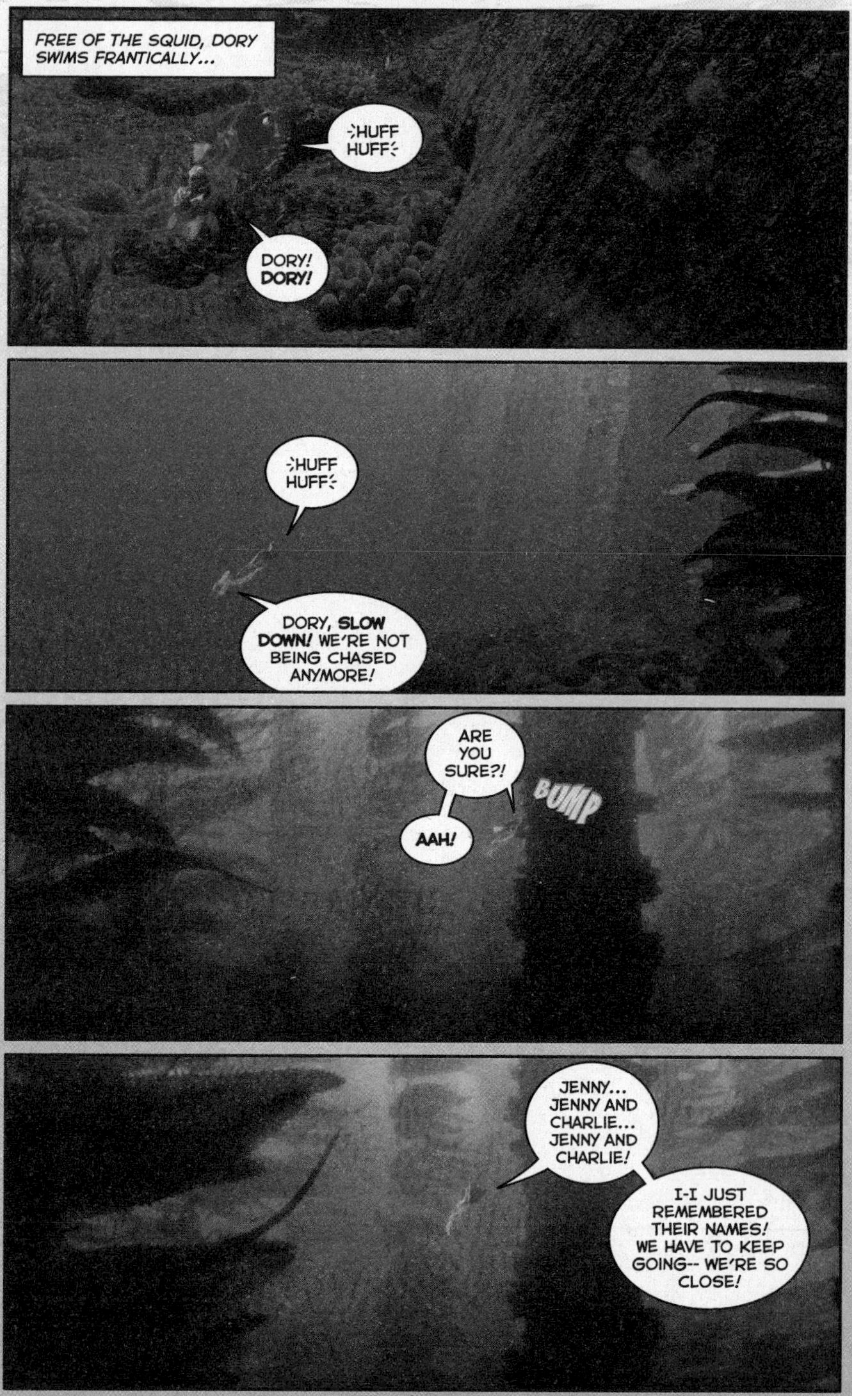
FREE OF THE SQUID, DORY SWIMS FRANTICALLY...
HUFF HUFF
DORY! DORY!
HUFF HUFF
DORY, SLOW DOWN! WE'RE NOT BEING CHASED ANYMORE!
ARE YOU SURE?!
BUMP
AAH!
JENNY... JENNY AND CHARLIE... JENNY AND CHARLIE!
I-I JUST REMEMBERED THEIR NAMES! WE HAVE TO KEEP GOING-- WE'RE SO CLOSE!

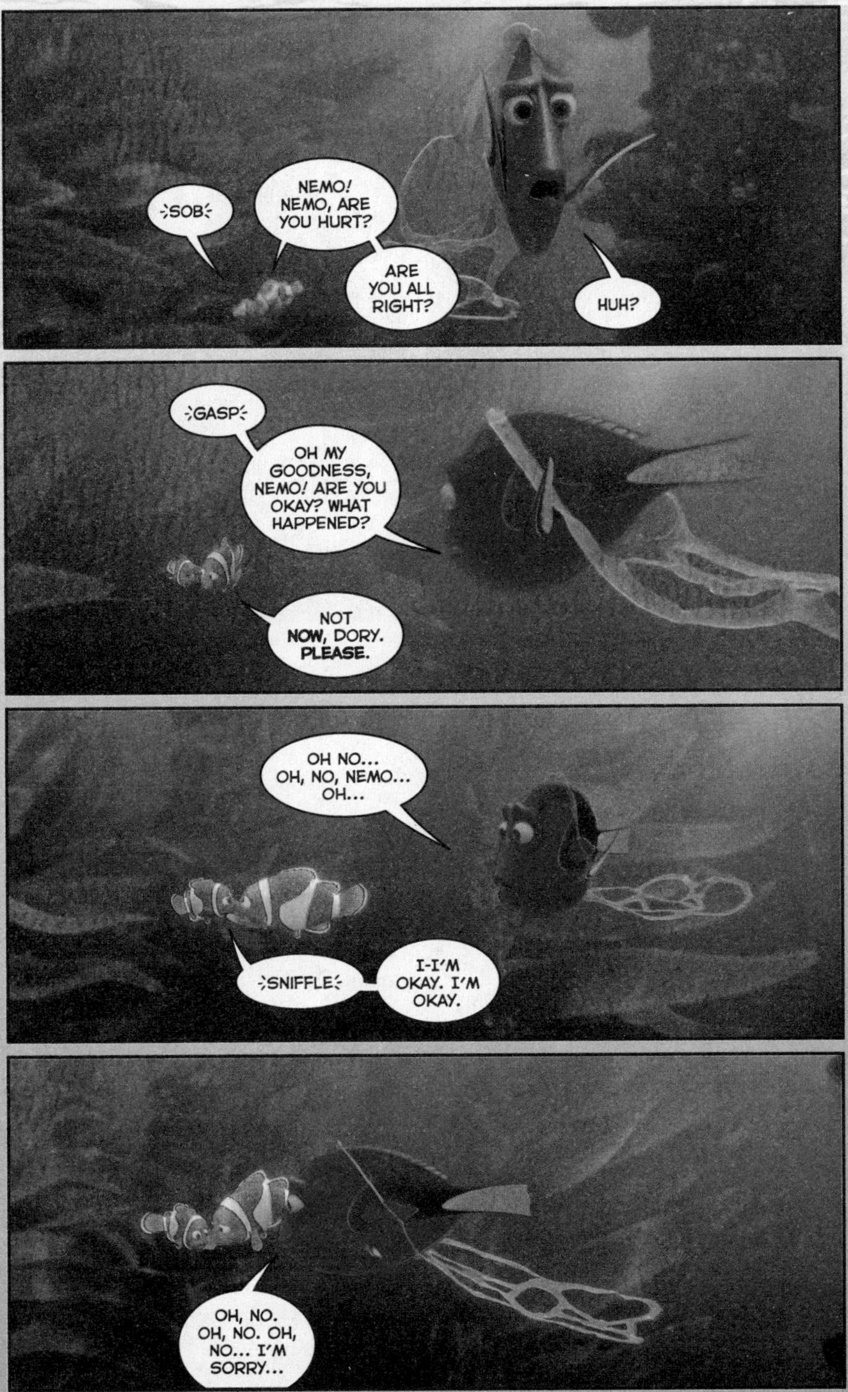
NEMO! NEMO, ARE YOU HURT?
SOB
ARE YOU ALL RIGHT?
HUH?
GASP
OH MY GOODNESS, NEMO! ARE YOU OKAY? WHAT HAPPENED?
NOT NOW, DORY. PLEASE.
OH NO... OH, NO, NEMO... OH...
SNIFFLE
I-I'M OKAY. I'M OKAY.
OH, NO. OH, NO. OH, NO... I'M SORRY...

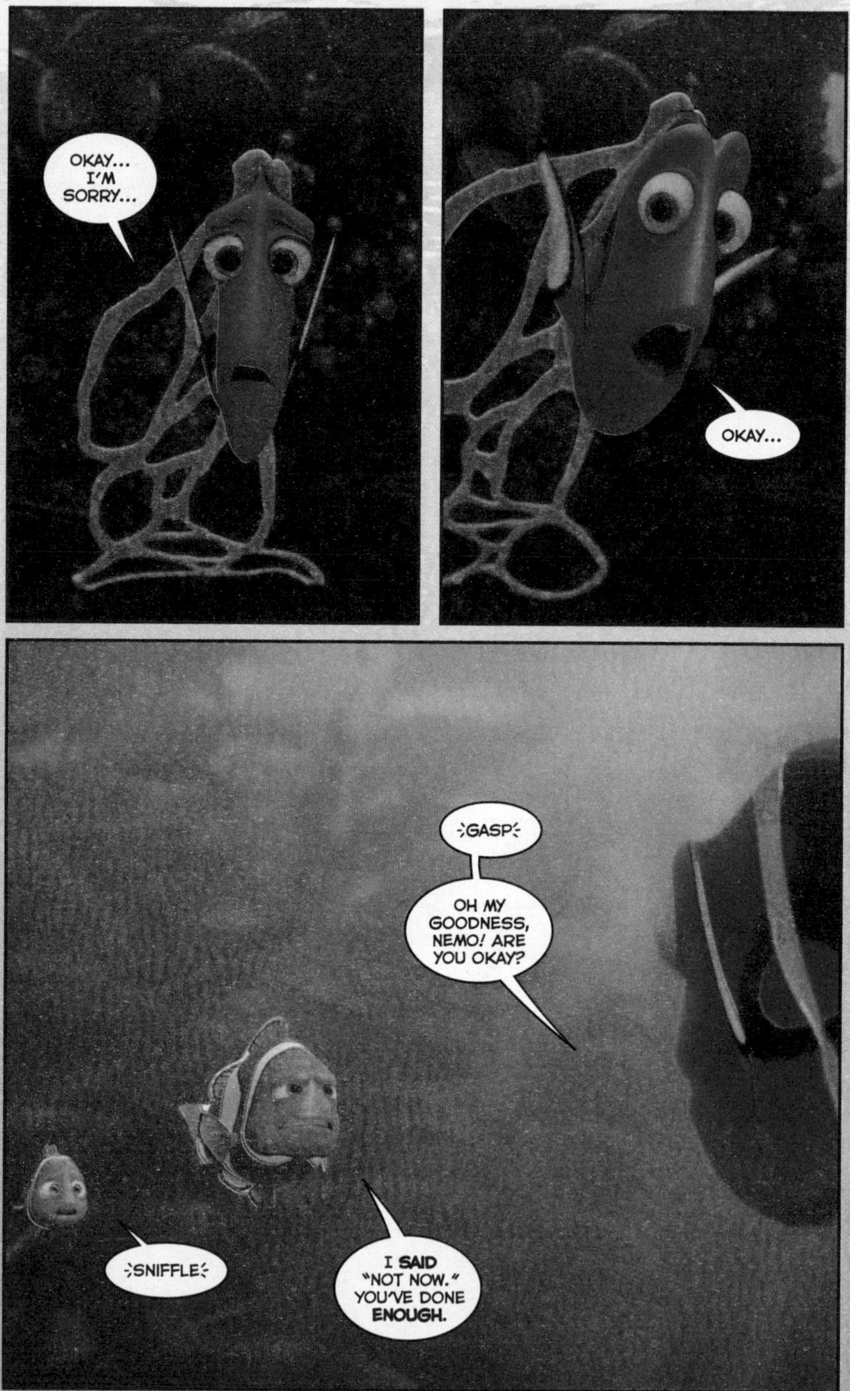
OKAY... I'M SORRY...
OKAY...
GASP
OH MY GOODNESS, NEMO! ARE YOU OKAY?
SNIFFLE
I SAID "NOT NOW." YOU'VE DONE ENOUGH.

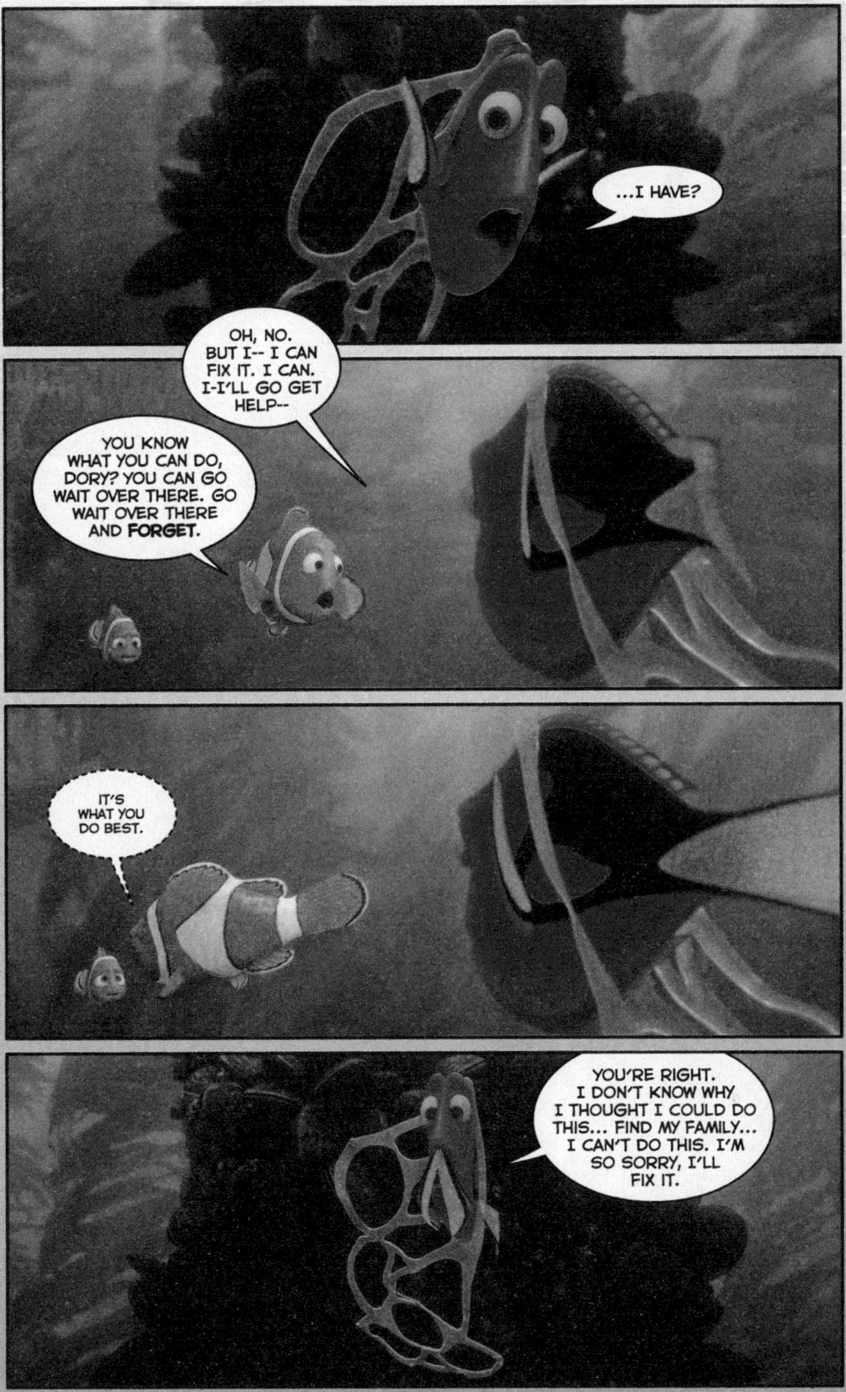
...I HAVE?
OH, NO. BUT I-- I CAN FIX IT. I CAN. I-I'LL GO GET HELP--
YOU KNOW WHAT YOU CAN DO, DORY? YOU CAN GO WAIT OVER THERE. GO WAIT OVER THERE AND FORGET.
IT'S WHAT YOU DO BEST.
YOU'RE RIGHT. I DON'T KNOW WHY I THOUGHT I COULD DO THIS... FIND MY FAMILY... I CAN'T DO THIS. I'M SO SORRY, I'LL FIX IT.

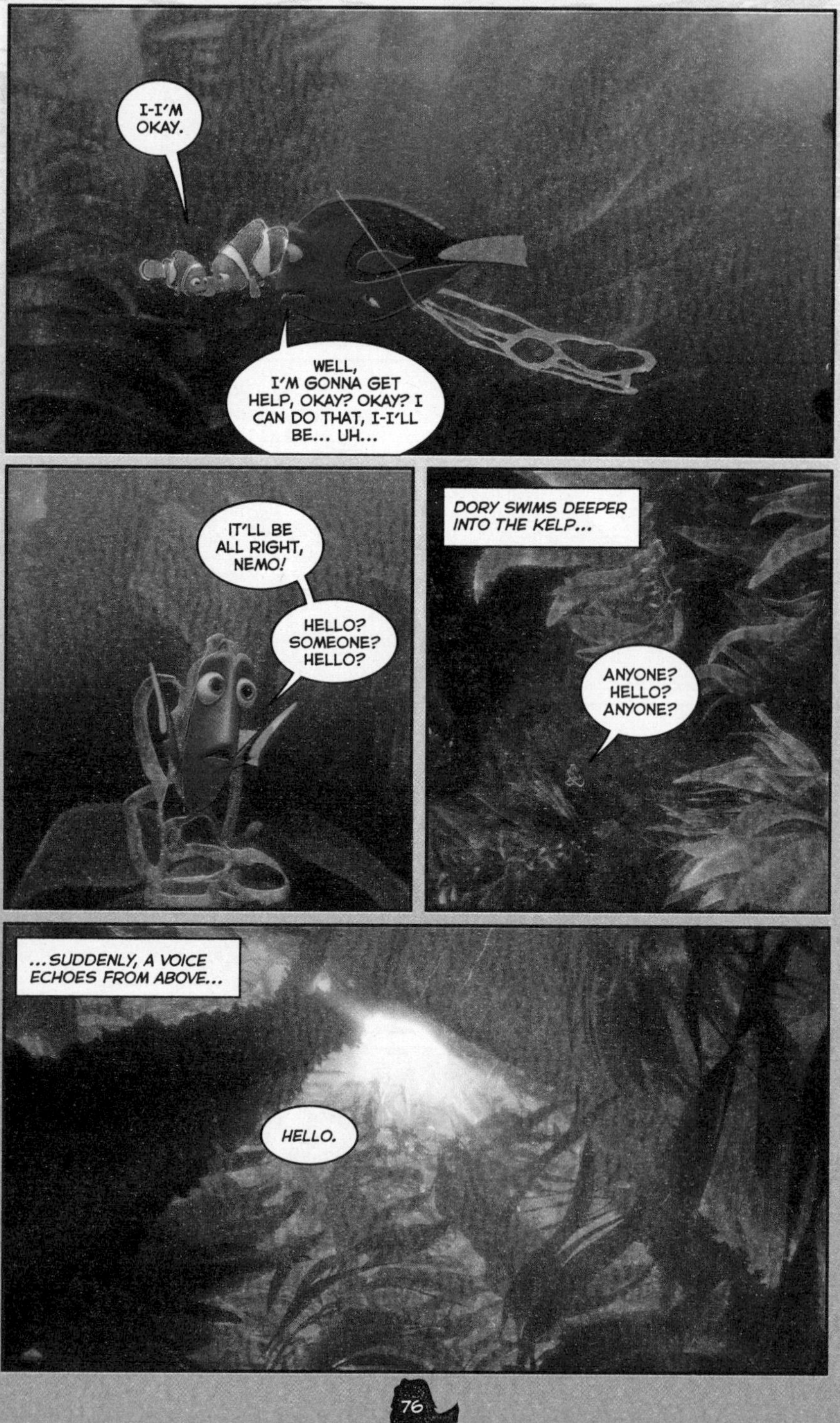
I-I'M OKAY.
WELL, I'M GONNA GET HELP, OKAY? OKAY? I CAN DO THAT, I-I'LL BE... UH...
IT'LL BE ALL RIGHT, NEMO!
HELLO? SOMEONE? HELLO?
DORY SWIMS DEEPER INTO THE KELP...
ANYONE? HELLO? ANYONE?
...SUDDENLY, A VOICE ECHOES FROM ABOVE...
HELLO.

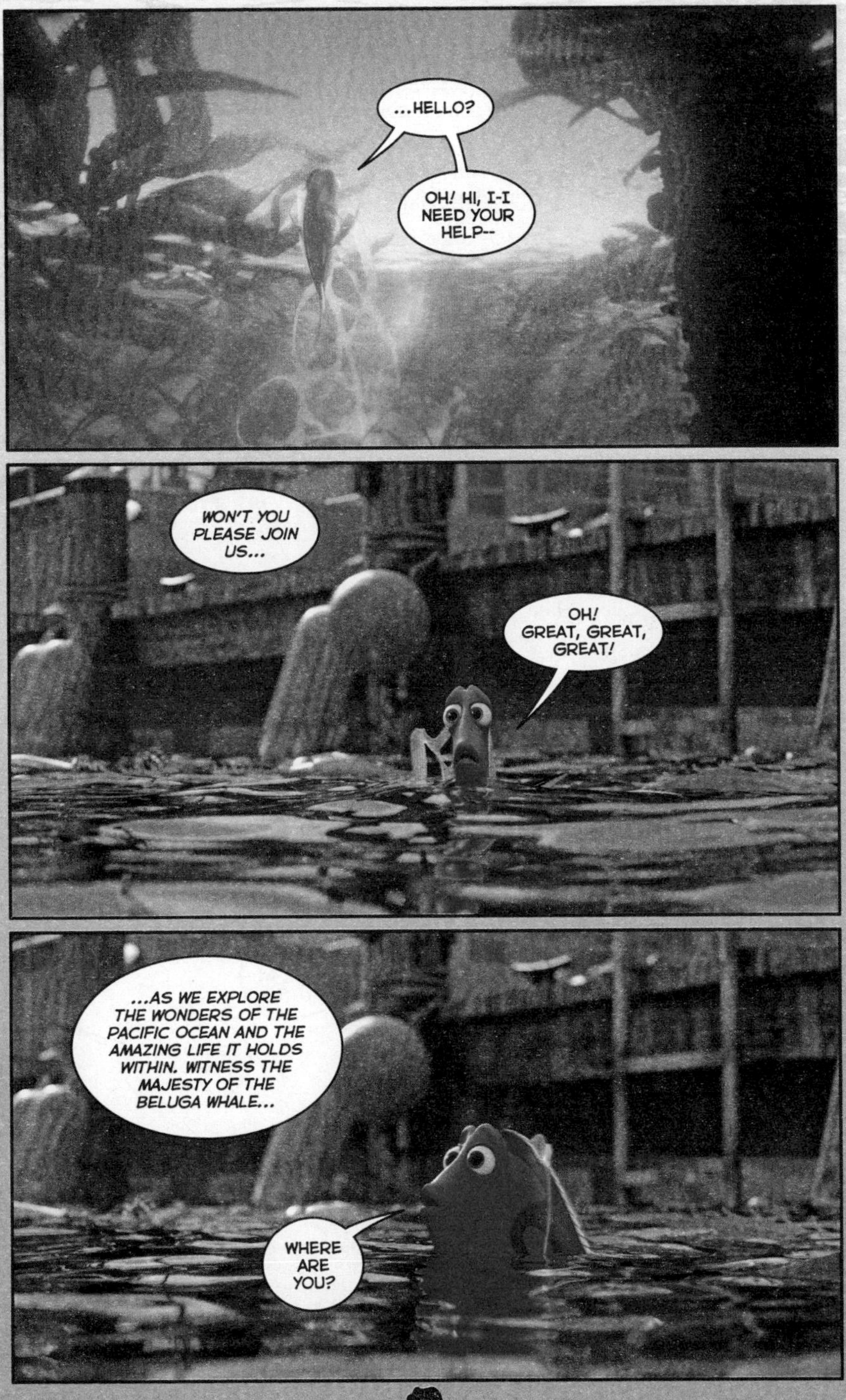
...HELLO?
OH! HI, I-I NEED YOUR HELP--
WON'T YOU PLEASE JOIN US...
OH! GREAT, GREAT, GREAT!
...AS WE EXPLORE THE WONDERS OF THE PACIFIC OCEAN AND THE AMAZING LIFE IT HOLDS WITHIN. WITNESS THE MAJESTY OF THE BELUGA WHALE...
WHERE ARE YOU?

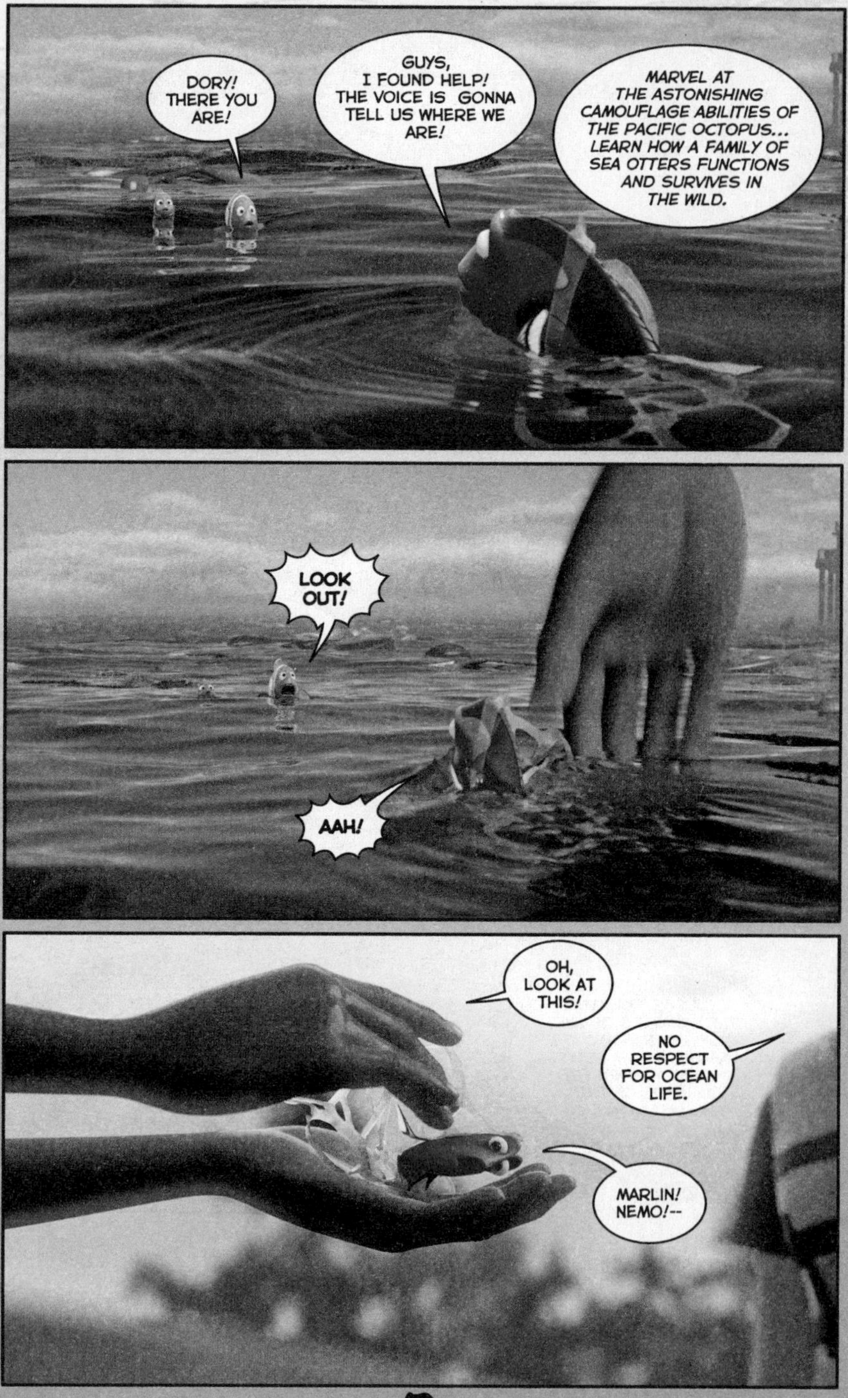
DORY! THERE YOU ARE!
GUYS, I FOUND HELP! THE VOICE IS GONNA TELL US WHERE WE ARE!
MARVEL AT THE ASTONISHING CAMOUFLAGE ABILITIES OF THE PACIFIC OCTOPUS... LEARN HOW A FAMILY OF SEA OTTERS FUNCTIONS AND SURVIVES IN THE WILD.
LOOK OUT!
AAH!
OH, LOOK AT THIS!
NO RESPECT FOR OCEAN LIFE.
MARLIN! NEMO!--

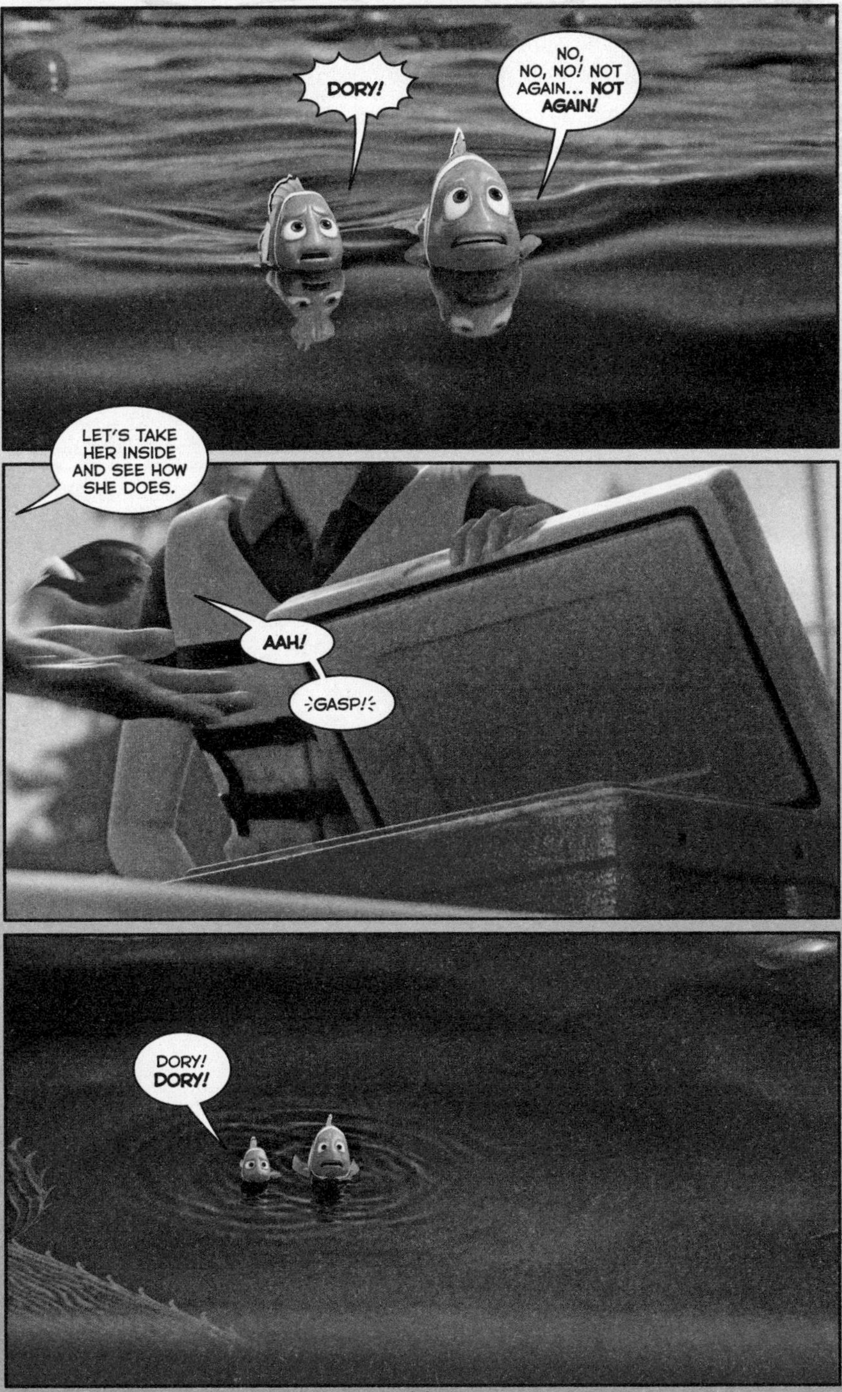
DORY!
NO, NO, NO! NOT AGAIN... NOT AGAIN!
LET'S TAKE HER INSIDE AND SEE HOW SHE DOES.
AAH!
GASP!
DORY! DORY!

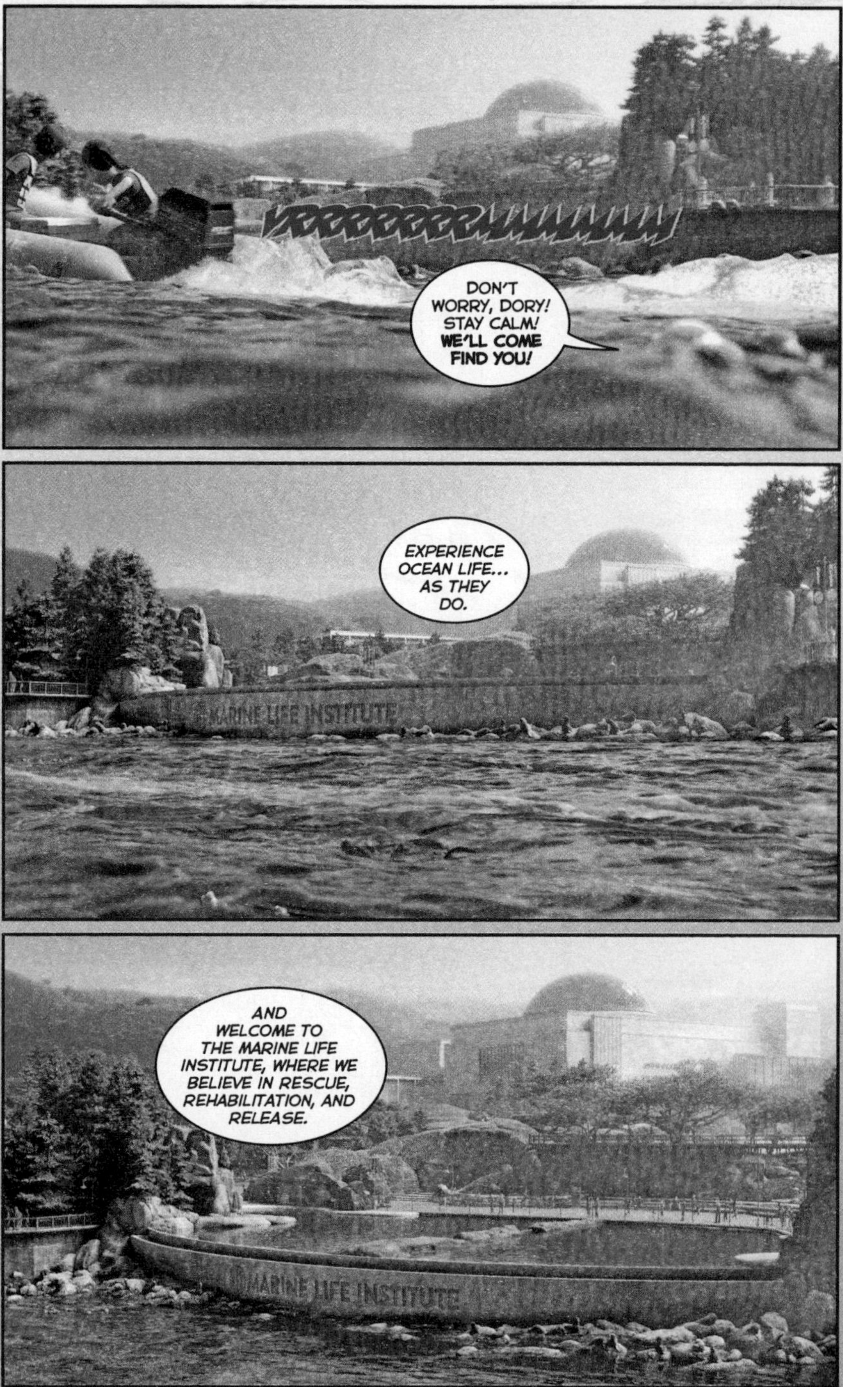
DON'T WORRY, DORY! STAY CALM! WE'LL COME FIND YOU!
EXPERIENCE OCEAN LIFE... AS THEY DO.
MARINE LIFE INSTITUTE
AND WELCOME TO THE MARINE LIFE INSTITUTE, WHERE WE BELIEVE IN RESCUE, REHABILITATION, AND RELEASE.
MARINE LIFE INSTITUTE

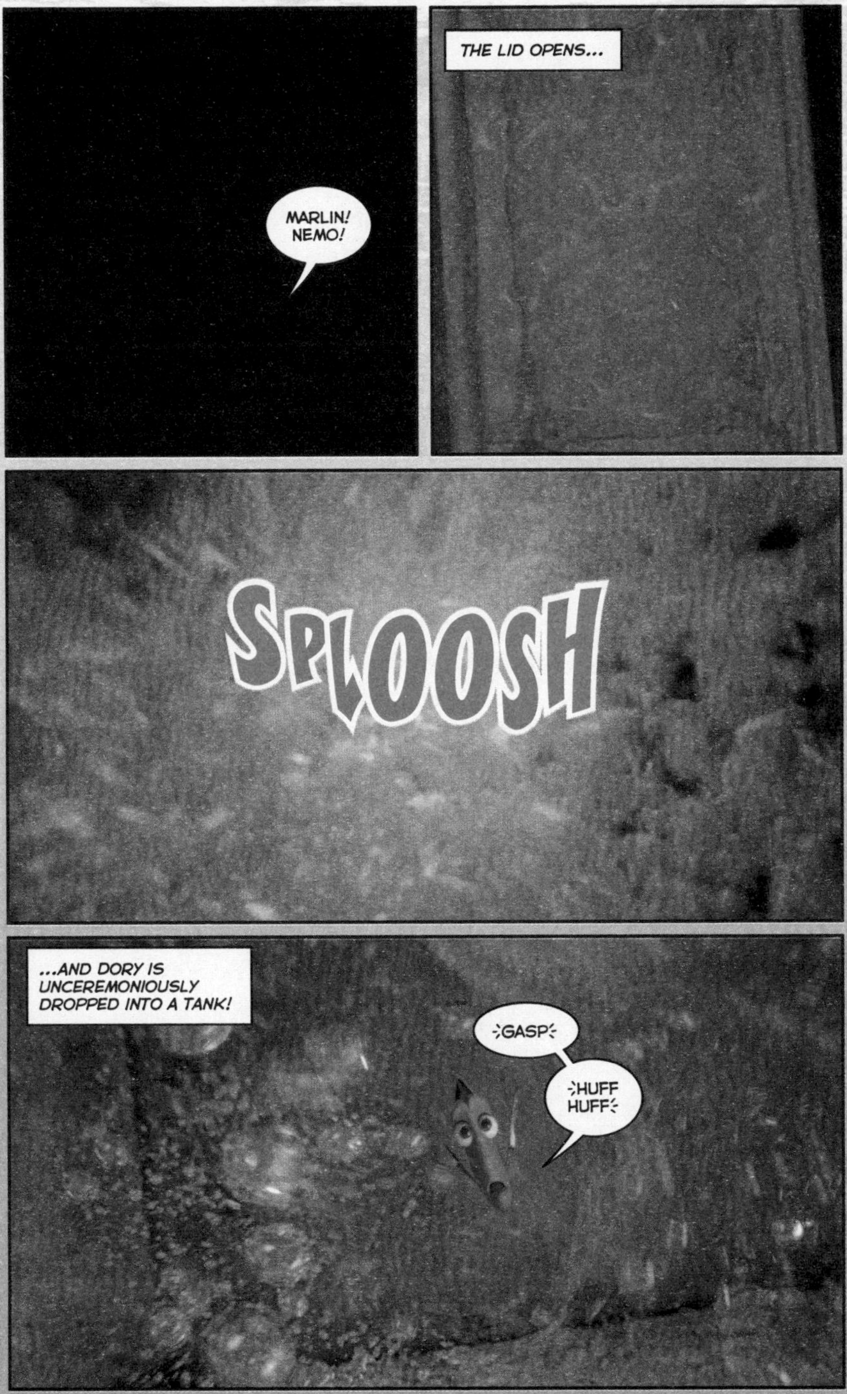
MARLIN! NEMO!
THE LID OPENS...
SPLOOSH
...AND DORY IS UNCEREMONIOUSLY DROPPED INTO A TANK!
GASP
HUFF HUFF

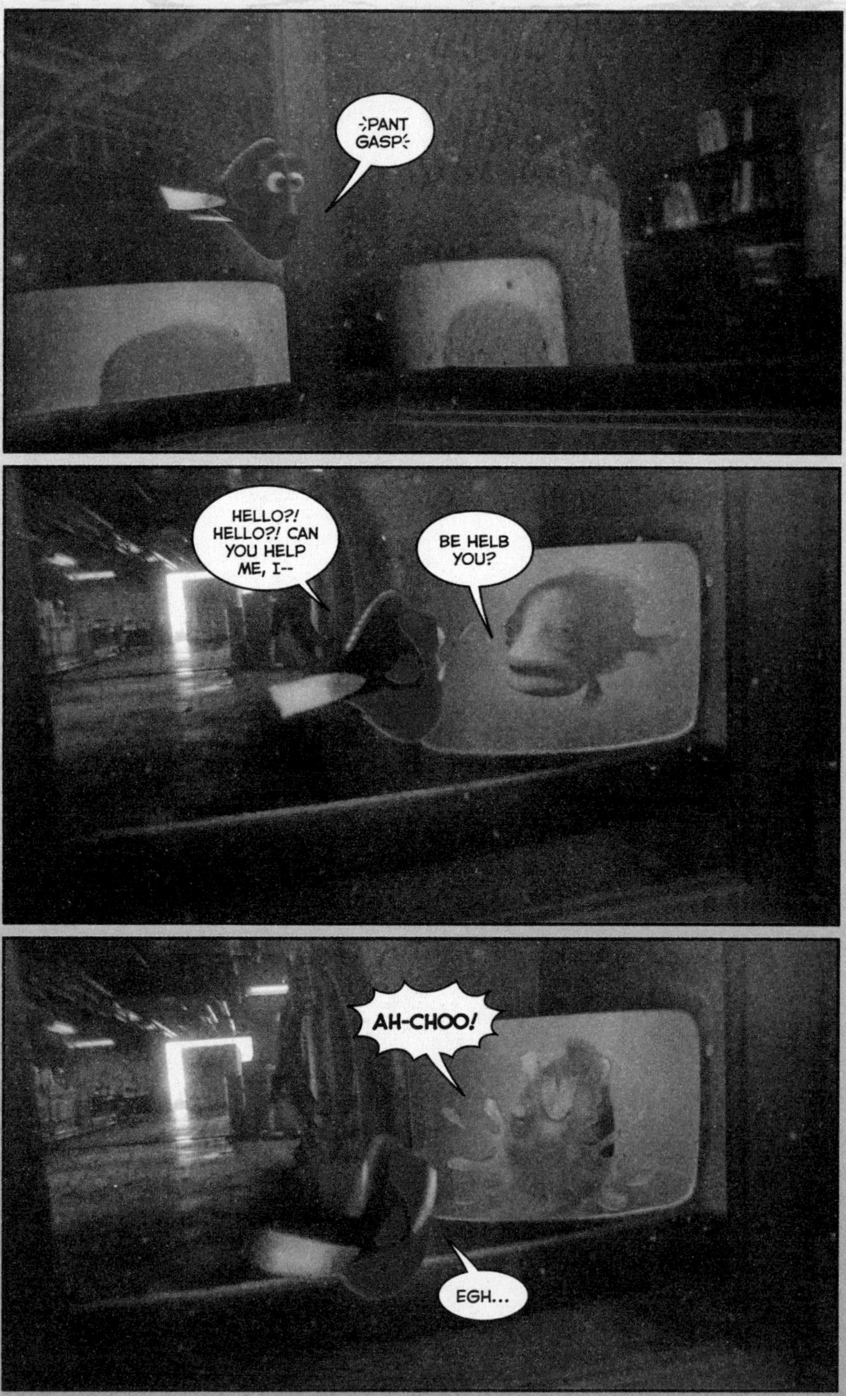
PANT GASP
HELLO?! HELLO?! CAN YOU HELP ME, I--
BE HELB YOU?
AH-CHOO!
EGH...

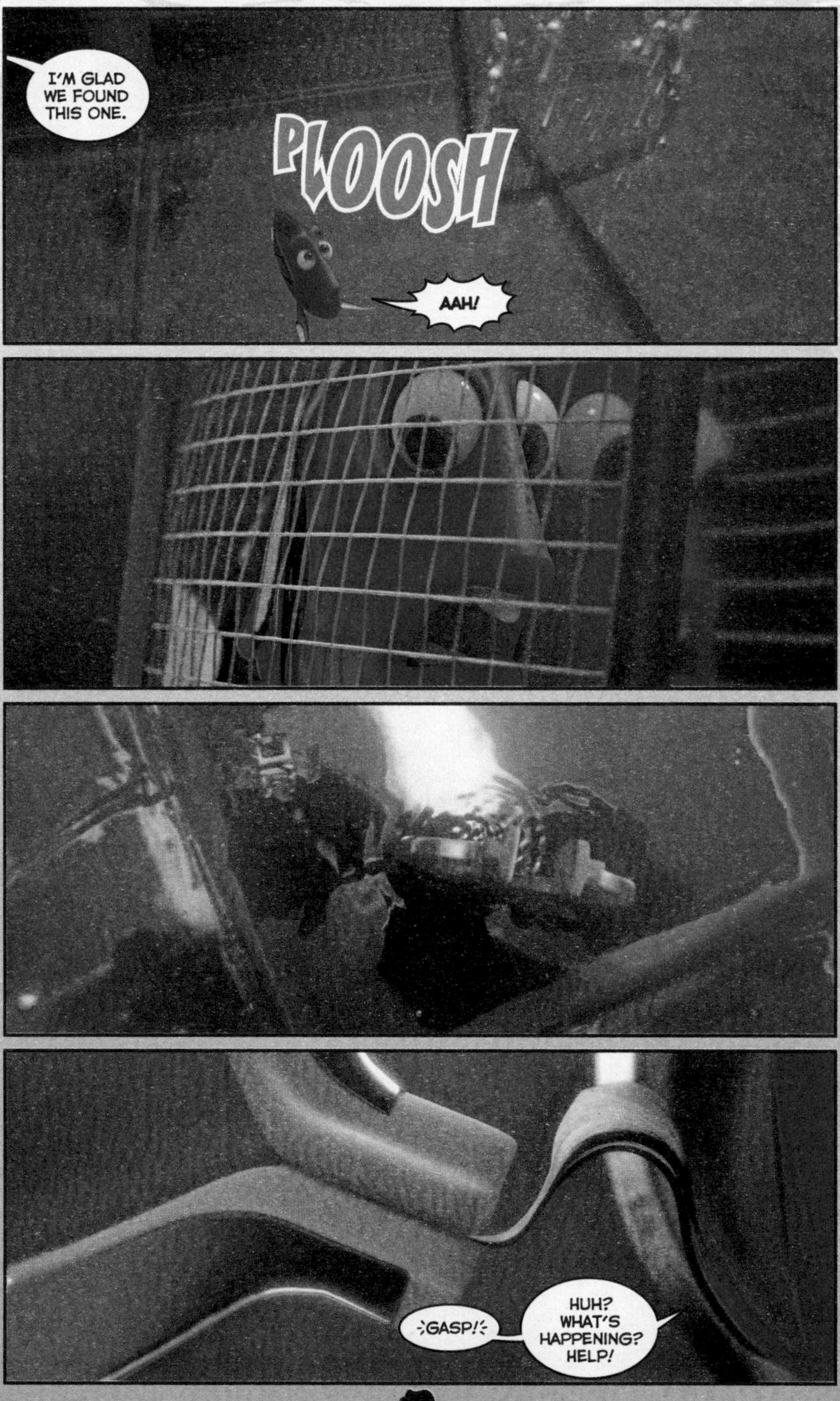
I'M GLAD WE FOUND THIS ONE.
PLOOSH
AAH!
GASP!
HUH? WHAT'S HAPPENING? HELP!

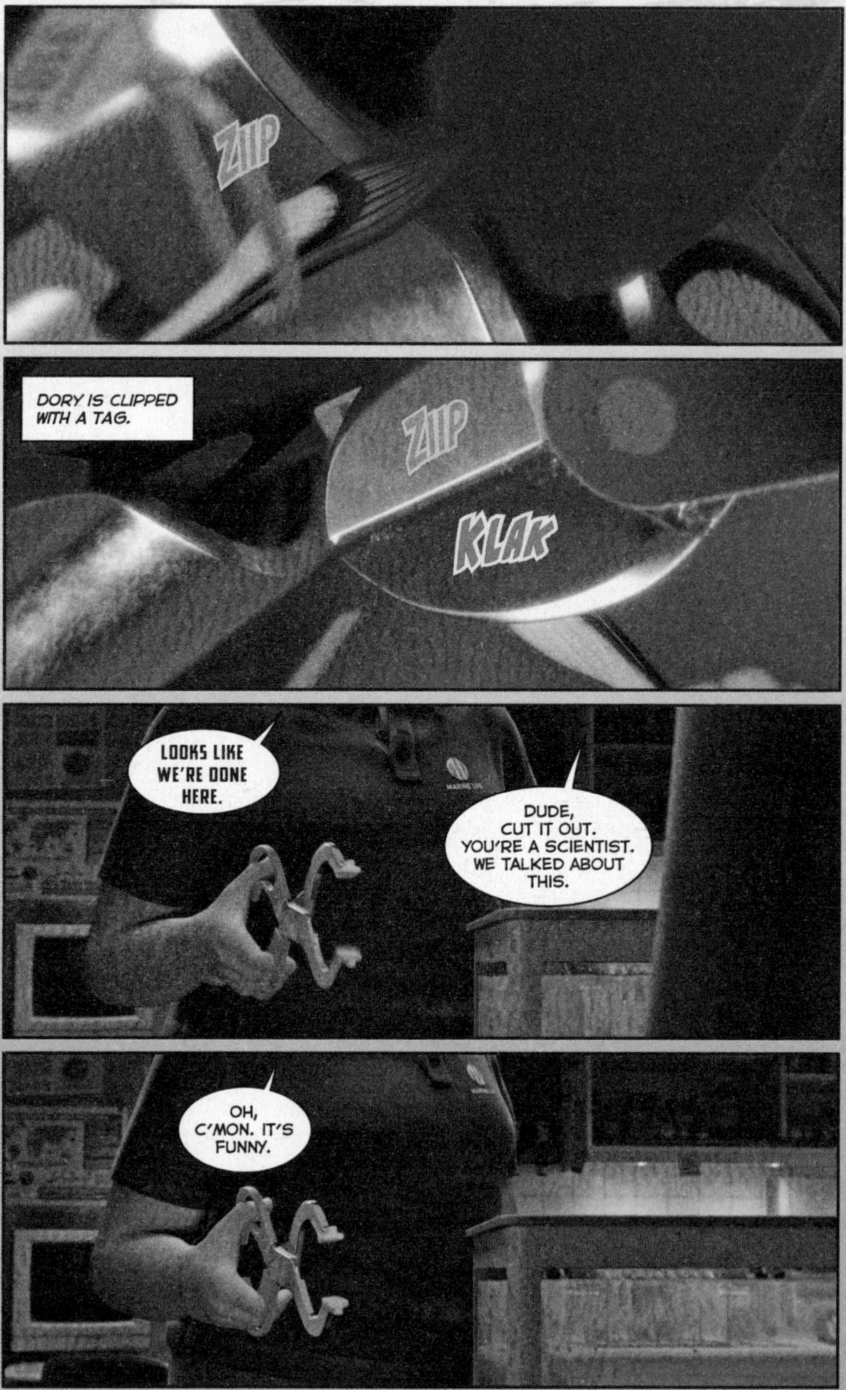
ZIIP
DORY IS CLIPPED WITH A TAG.
ZIIP
KLAK
LOOKS LIKE WE'RE DONE HERE.
DUDE, CUT IT OUT. YOU'RE A SCIENTIST. WE TALKED ABOUT THIS.
OH, C'MON. IT'S FUNNY.

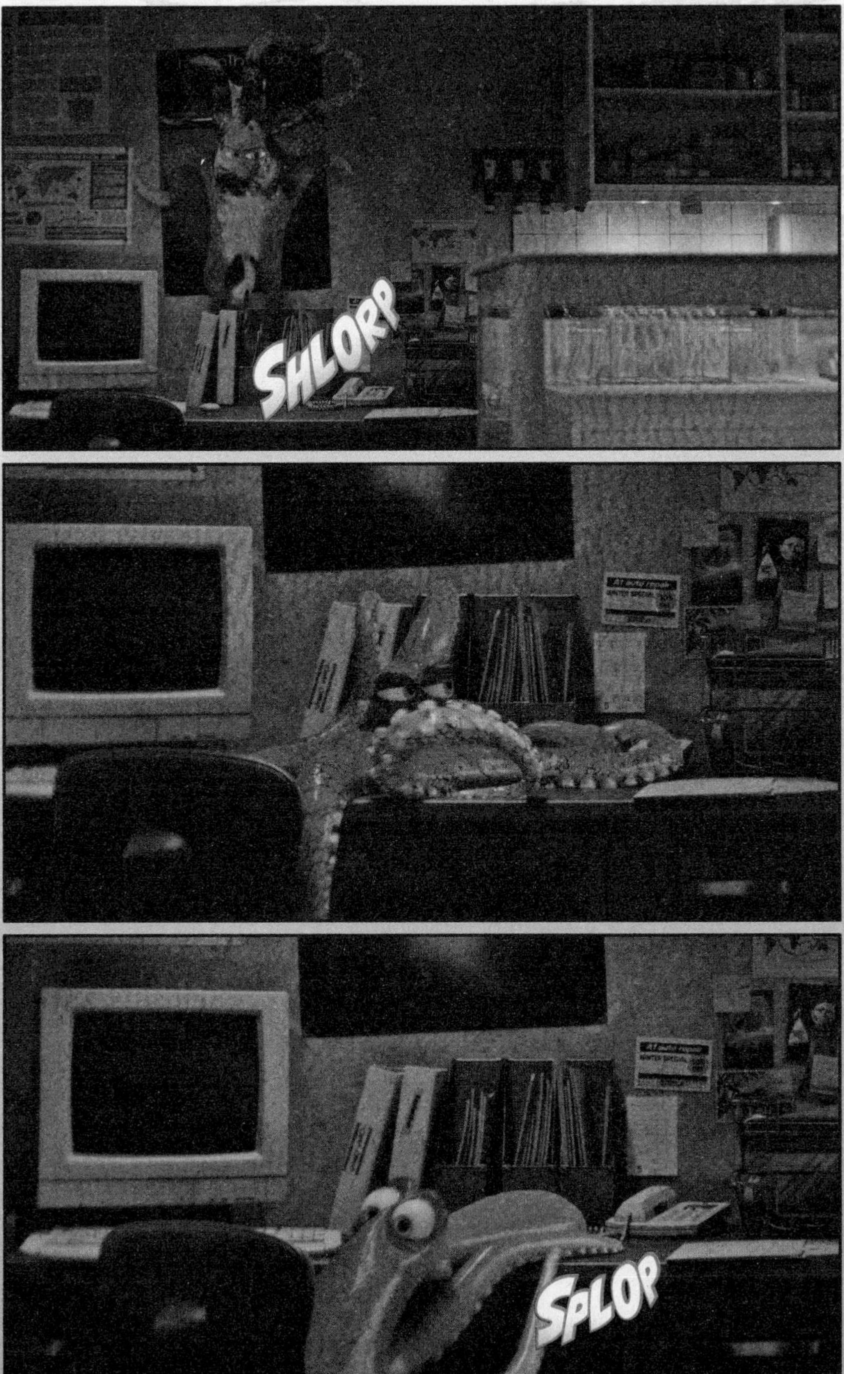
SHLORP
SPLOP

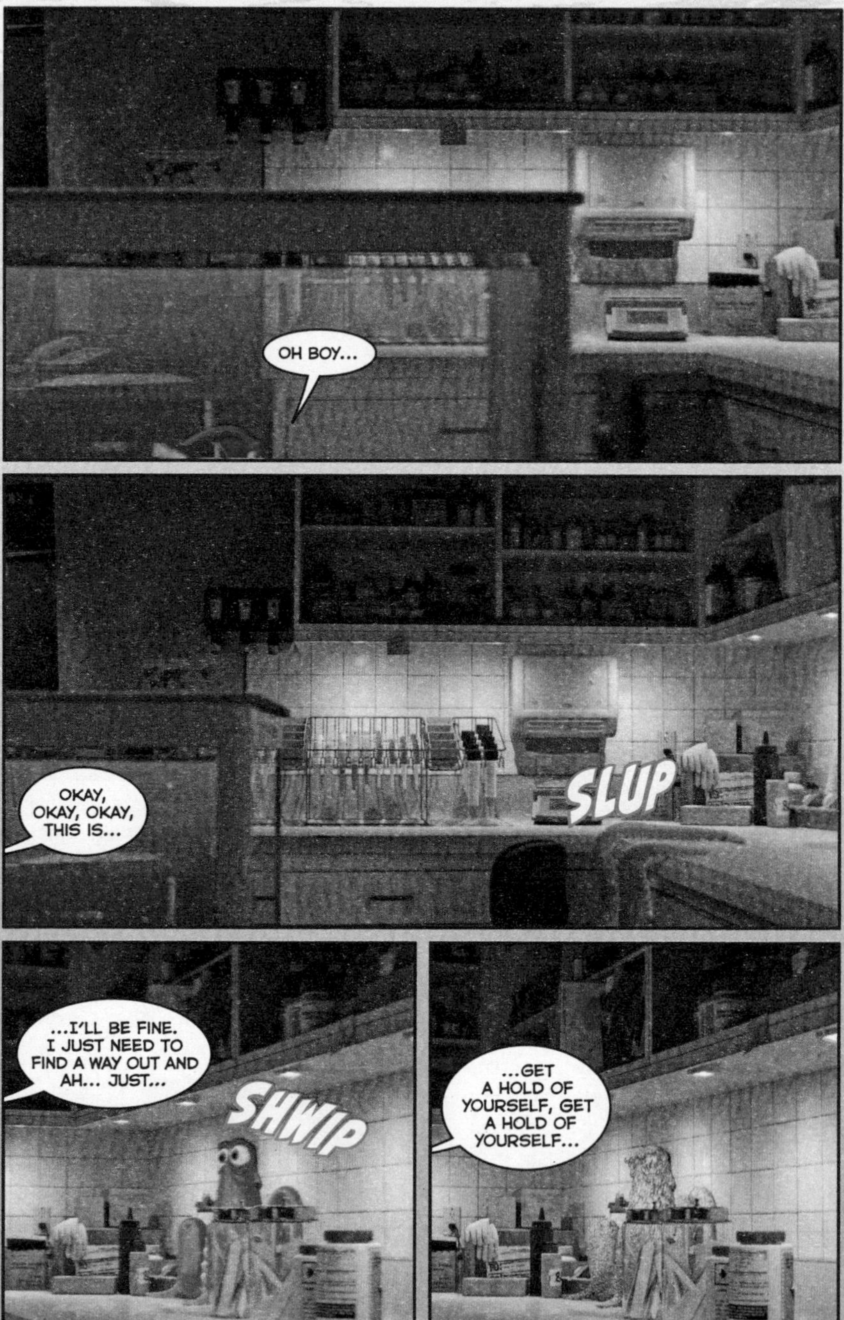
OH BOY...
OKAY, OKAY, OKAY, THIS IS...
SLUP
...I'LL BE FINE. I JUST NEED TO FIND A WAY OUT AND AH... JUST...
SHWIP
...GET A HOLD OF YOURSELF, GET A HOLD OF YOURSELF...

YOU'LL BE FINE, EVERYTHING'S FINE, THINK POSITIVELY...

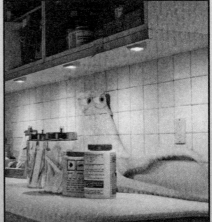

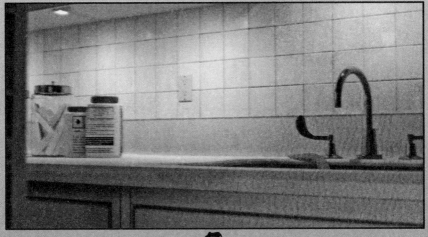

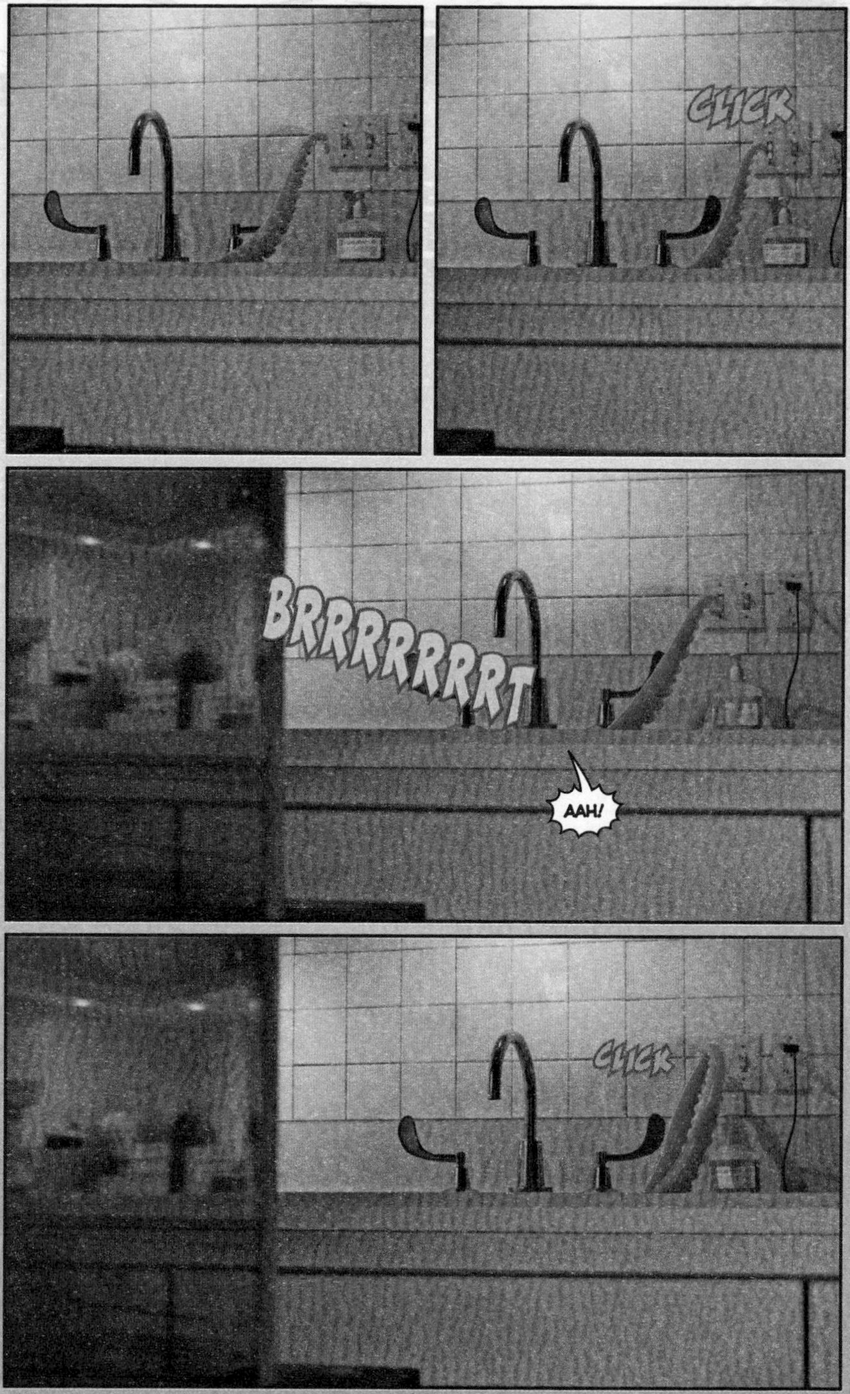
CLICK
BRRRRRRRRT
AAH!
CLICK

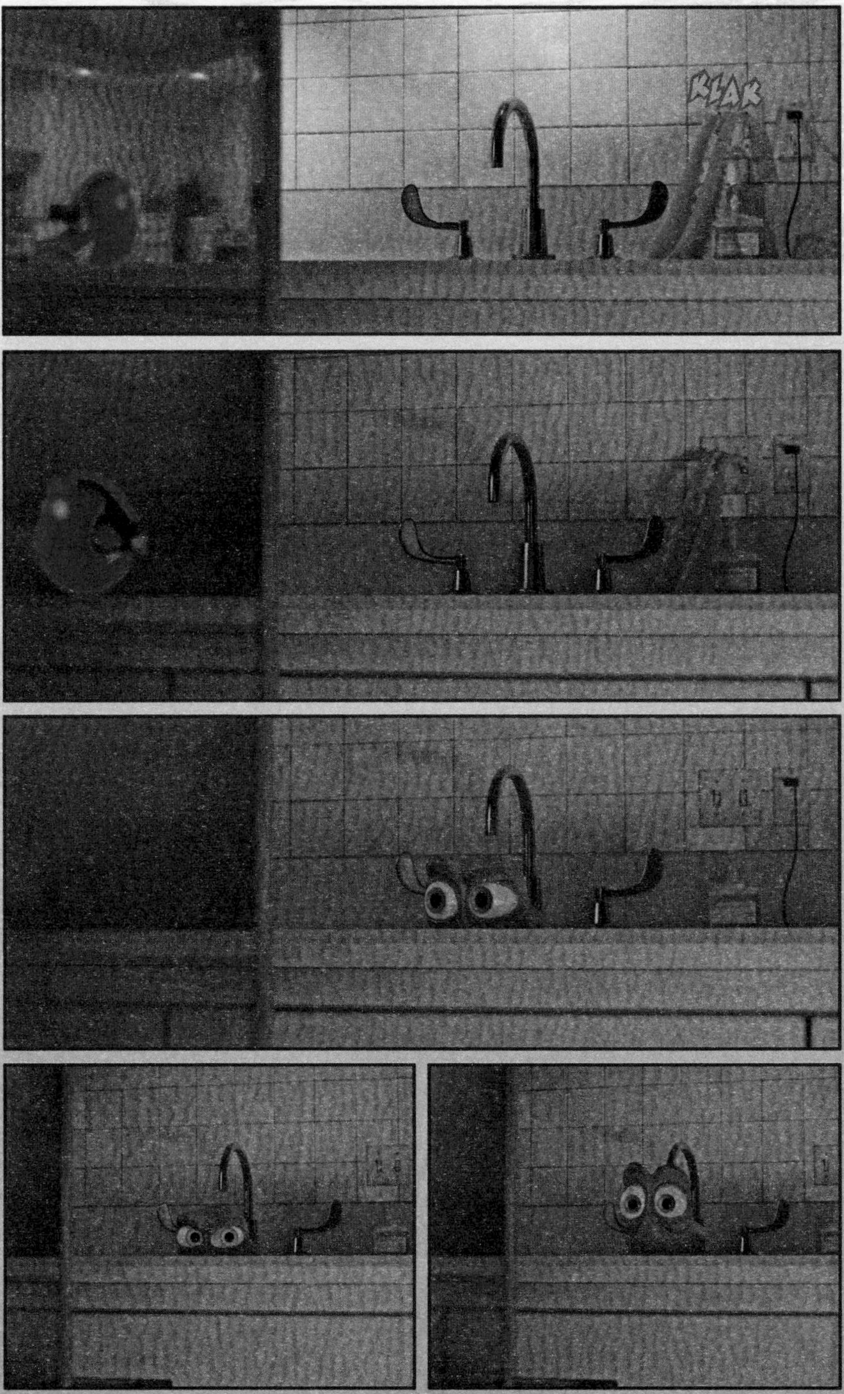
KLAK

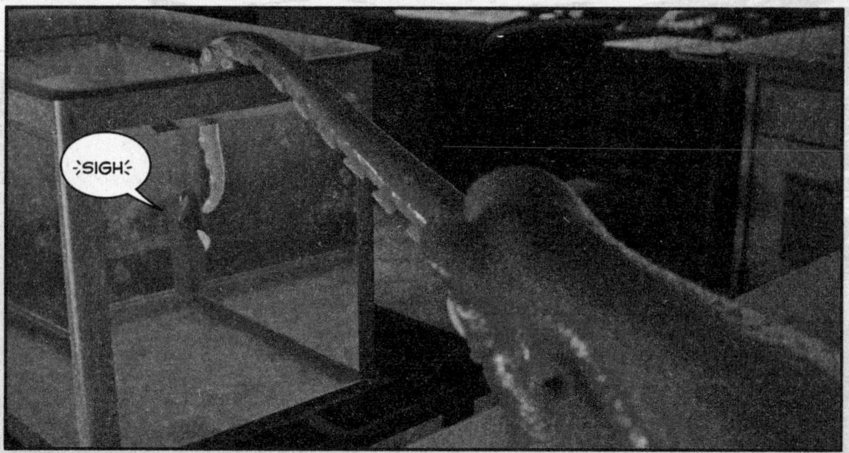
SIGH

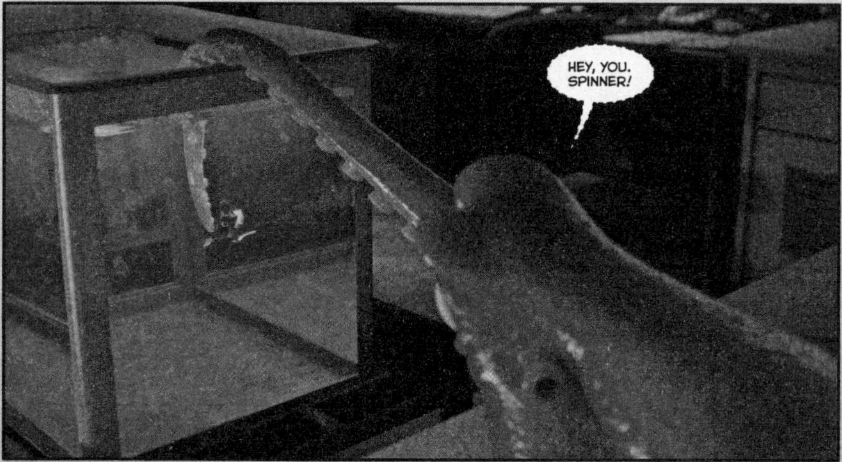
HEY, YOU. SPINNER!

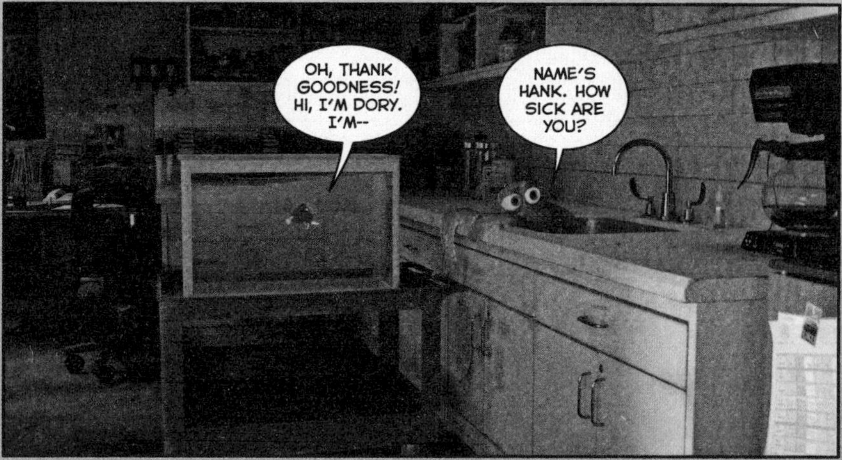
OH, THANK GOODNESS! HI, I'M DORY. I'M--
NAME'S HANK. HOW SICK ARE YOU?

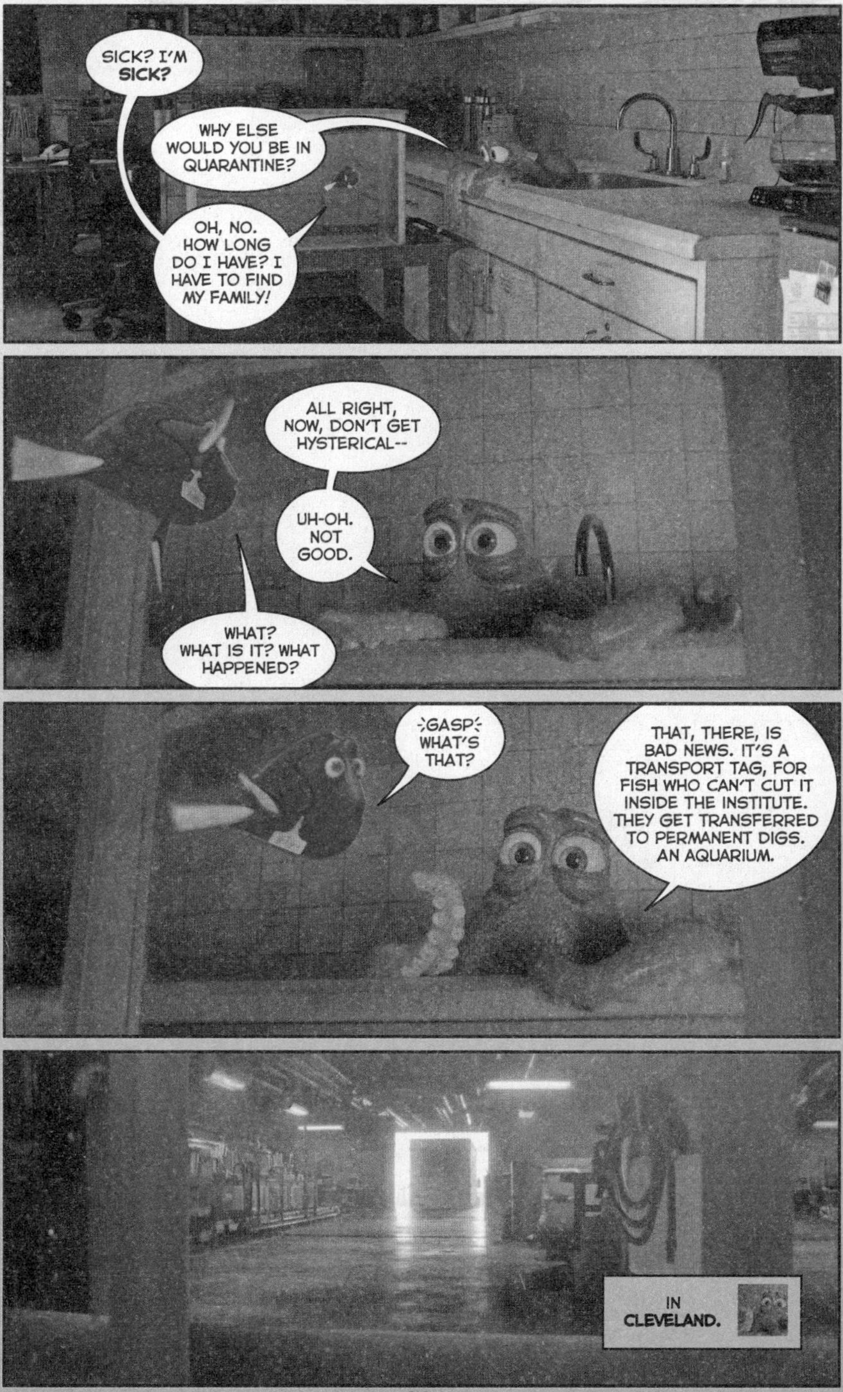
SICK? I'M **SICK?**
WHY ELSE WOULD YOU BE IN QUARANTINE?
OH, NO. HOW LONG DO I HAVE? I HAVE TO FIND MY FAMILY!
ALL RIGHT, NOW, DON'T GET HYSTERICAL--
UH-OH. NOT GOOD.
WHAT? WHAT IS IT? WHAT HAPPENED?
GASP WHAT'S THAT?
THAT, THERE, IS BAD NEWS. IT'S A TRANSPORT TAG, FOR FISH WHO CAN'T CUT IT INSIDE THE INSTITUTE. THEY GET TRANSFERRED TO PERMANENT DIGS. AN AQUARIUM.
IN **CLEVELAND.**

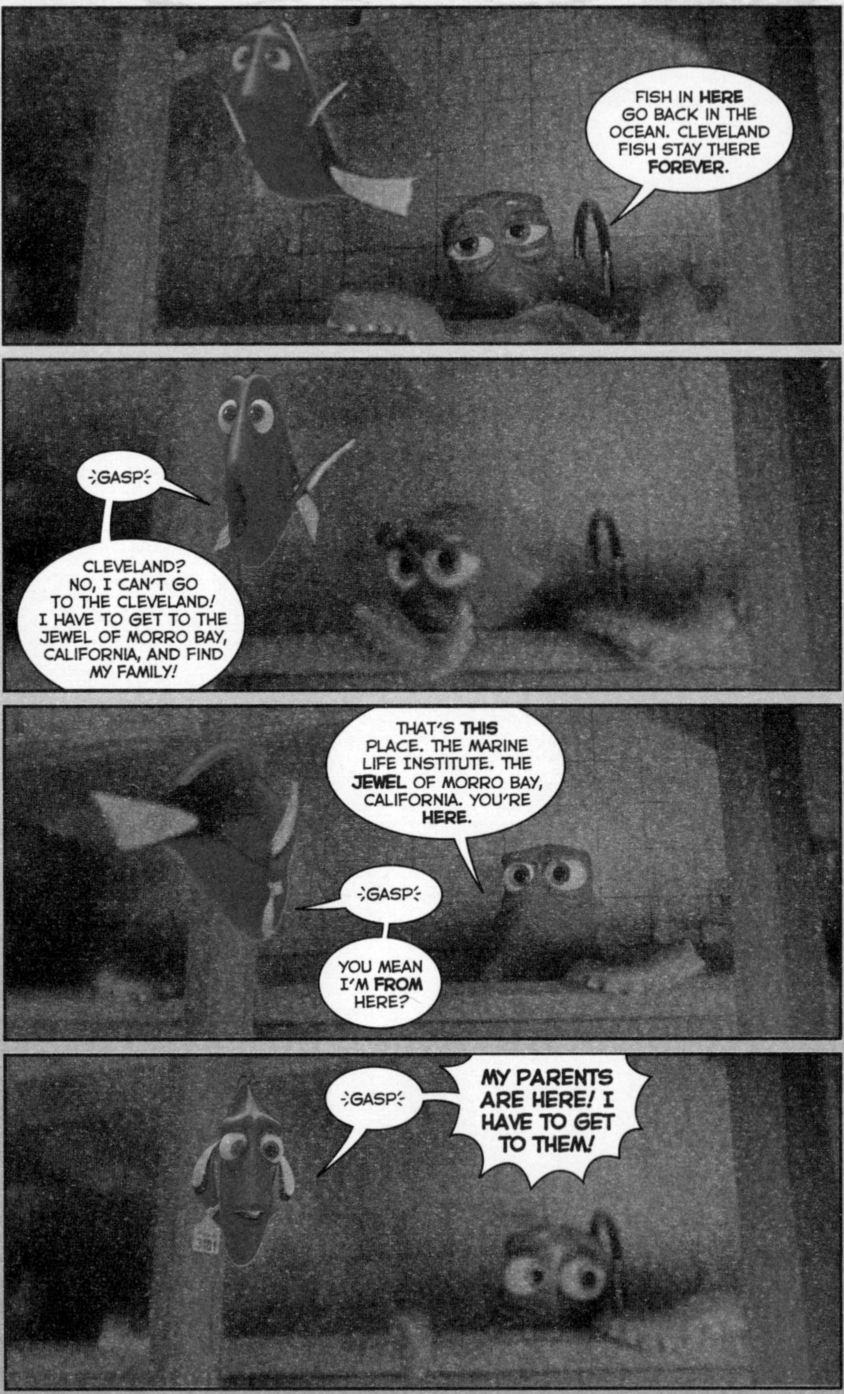
FISH IN HERE GO BACK IN THE OCEAN. CLEVELAND FISH STAY THERE FOREVER.
GASP
CLEVELAND? NO, I CAN'T GO TO THE CLEVELAND! I HAVE TO GET TO THE JEWEL OF MORRO BAY, CALIFORNIA, AND FIND MY FAMILY!
THAT'S THIS PLACE. THE MARINE LIFE INSTITUTE. THE JEWEL OF MORRO BAY, CALIFORNIA. YOU'RE HERE.
GASP
YOU MEAN I'M FROM HERE?
GASP
MY PARENTS ARE HERE! I HAVE TO GET TO THEM!

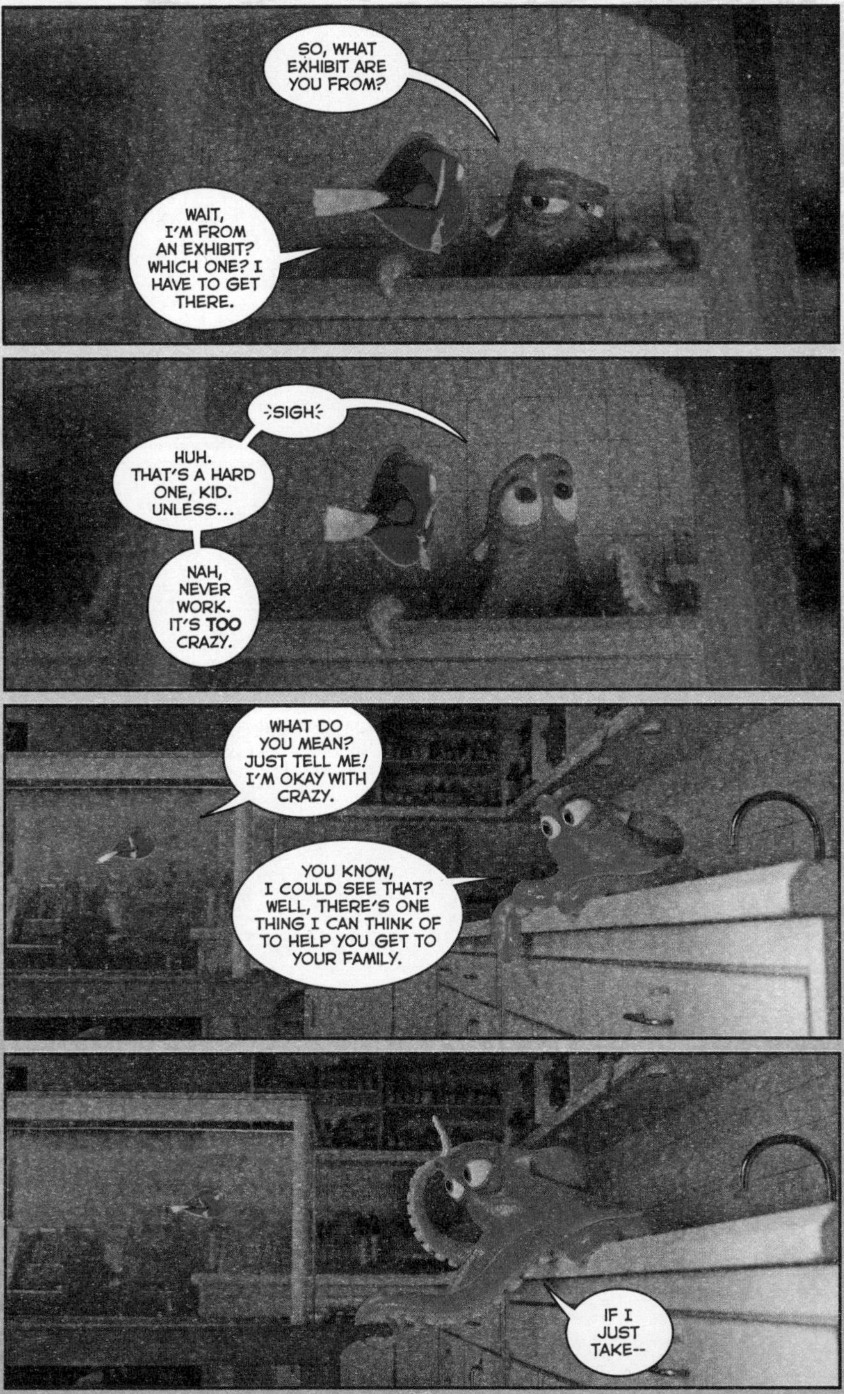
SO, WHAT EXHIBIT ARE YOU FROM?
WAIT, I'M FROM AN EXHIBIT? WHICH ONE? I HAVE TO GET THERE.
SIGH
HUH. THAT'S A HARD ONE, KID. UNLESS...
NAH, NEVER WORK. IT'S **TOO** CRAZY.
WHAT DO YOU MEAN? JUST TELL ME! I'M OKAY WITH CRAZY.
YOU KNOW, I COULD SEE THAT? WELL, THERE'S ONE THING I CAN THINK OF TO HELP YOU GET TO YOUR FAMILY.
IF I JUST TAKE--

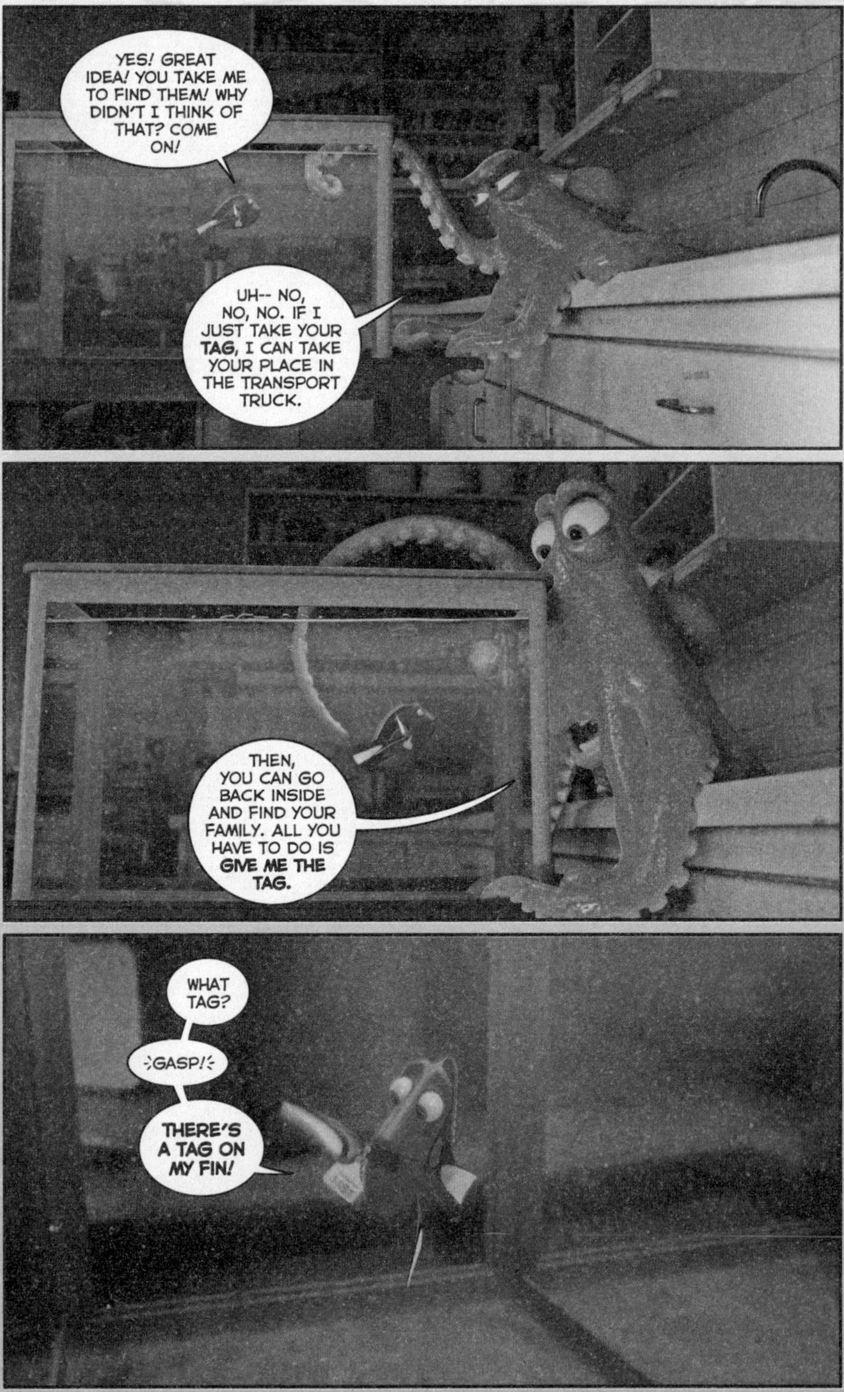
YES! GREAT IDEA! YOU TAKE ME TO FIND THEM! WHY DIDN'T I THINK OF THAT? COME ON!
UH-- NO, NO, NO. IF I JUST TAKE YOUR TAG, I CAN TAKE YOUR PLACE IN THE TRANSPORT TRUCK.
THEN, YOU CAN GO BACK INSIDE AND FIND YOUR FAMILY. ALL YOU HAVE TO DO IS GIVE ME THE TAG.
WHAT TAG?
GASP!
THERE'S A TAG ON MY FIN!

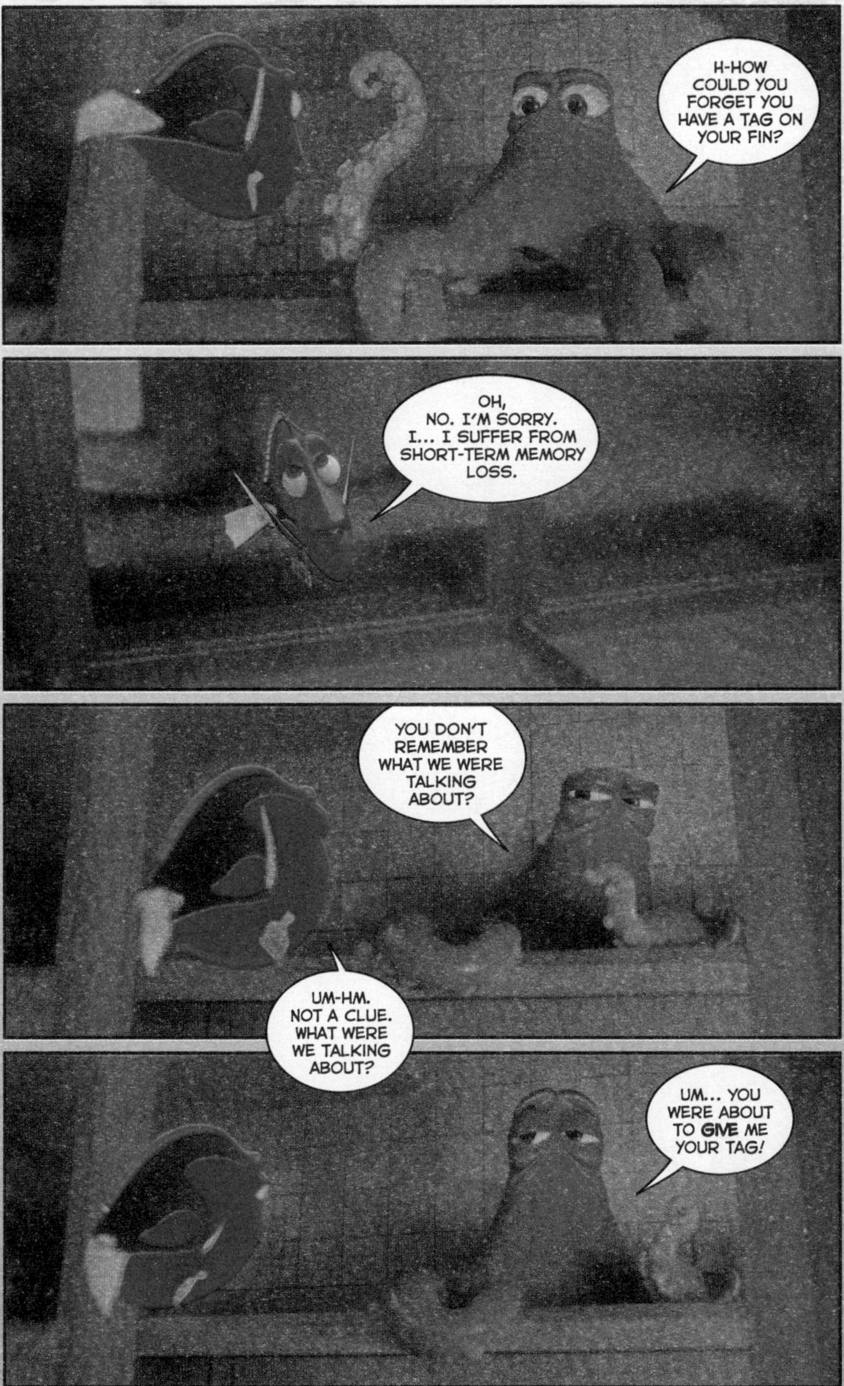
H-HOW COULD YOU FORGET YOU HAVE A TAG ON YOUR FIN?
OH, NO. I'M SORRY. I... I SUFFER FROM SHORT-TERM MEMORY LOSS.
YOU DON'T REMEMBER WHAT WE WERE TALKING ABOUT?
UM-HM. NOT A CLUE. WHAT WERE WE TALKING ABOUT?
UM... YOU WERE ABOUT TO GIVE ME YOUR TAG!

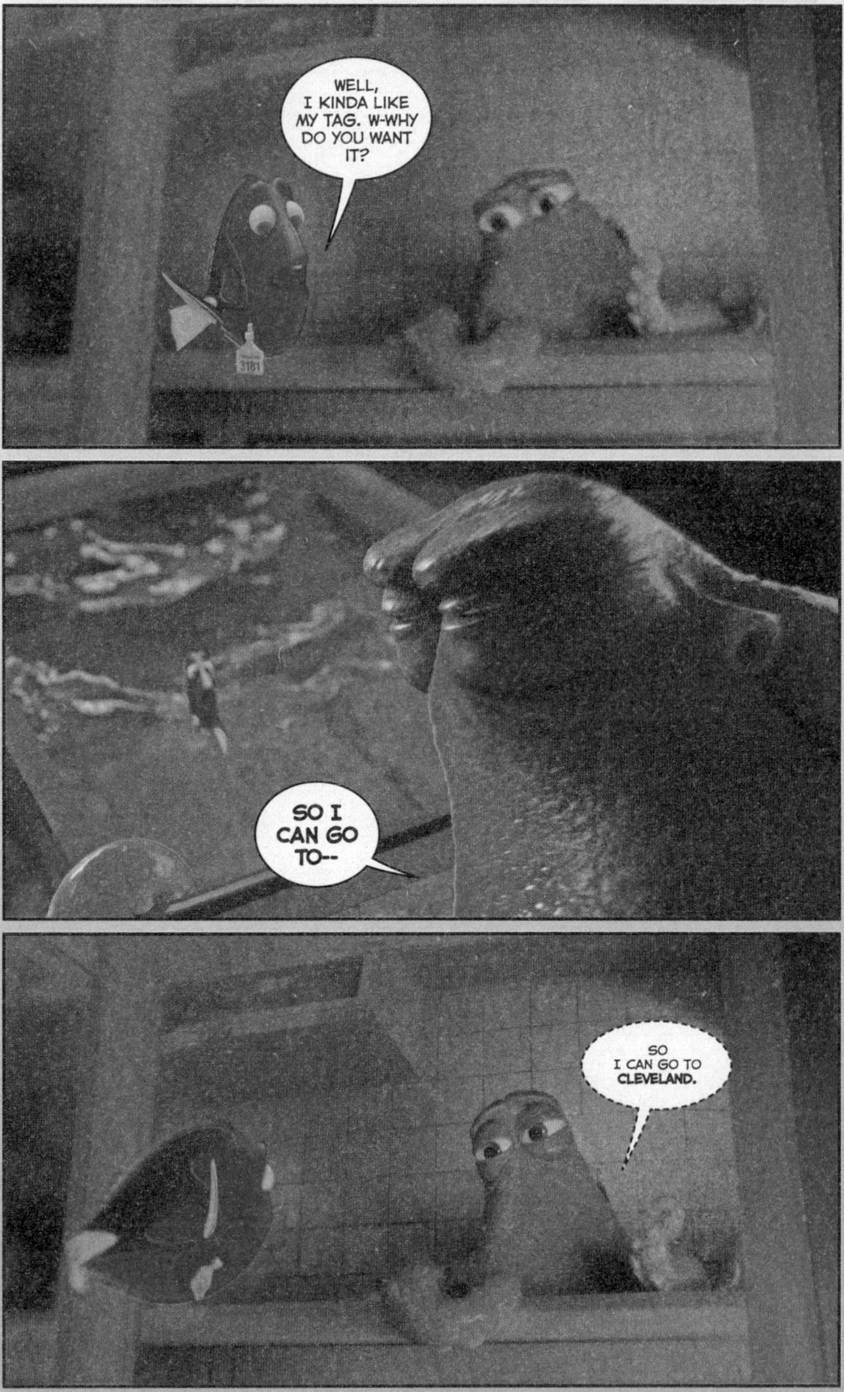
WELL, I KINDA LIKE MY TAG. W-WHY DO YOU WANT IT?
SO I CAN GO TO--
SO I CAN GO TO CLEVELAND.

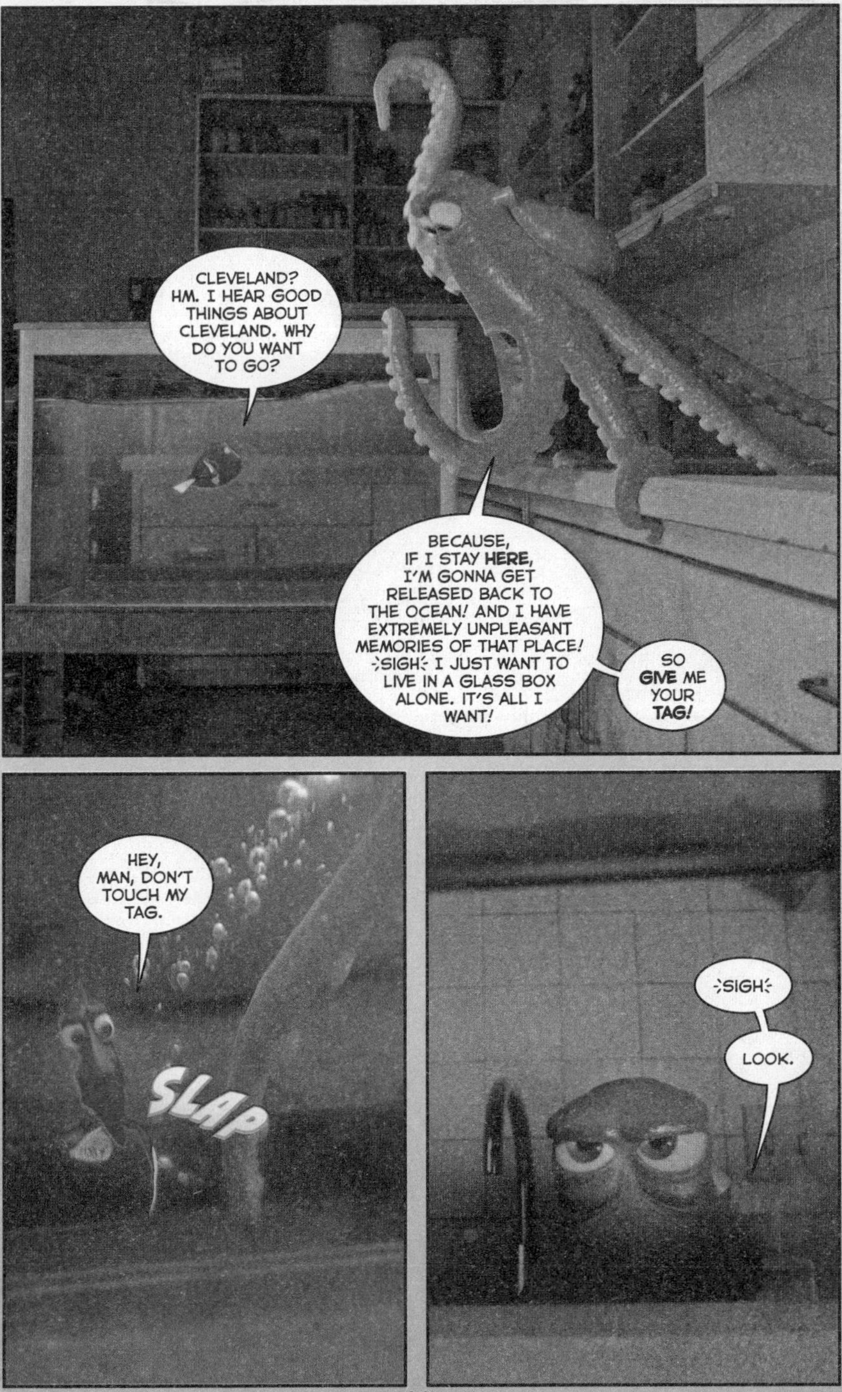
CLEVELAND? HM. I HEAR GOOD THINGS ABOUT CLEVELAND. WHY DO YOU WANT TO GO?
BECAUSE, IF I STAY **HERE**, I'M GONNA GET RELEASED BACK TO THE OCEAN! AND I HAVE EXTREMELY UNPLEASANT MEMORIES OF THAT PLACE! *SIGH* I JUST WANT TO LIVE IN A GLASS BOX ALONE. IT'S ALL I WANT!
SO **GIVE** ME YOUR **TAG!**
HEY, MAN, DON'T TOUCH MY TAG.
SLAP
SIGH
LOOK.

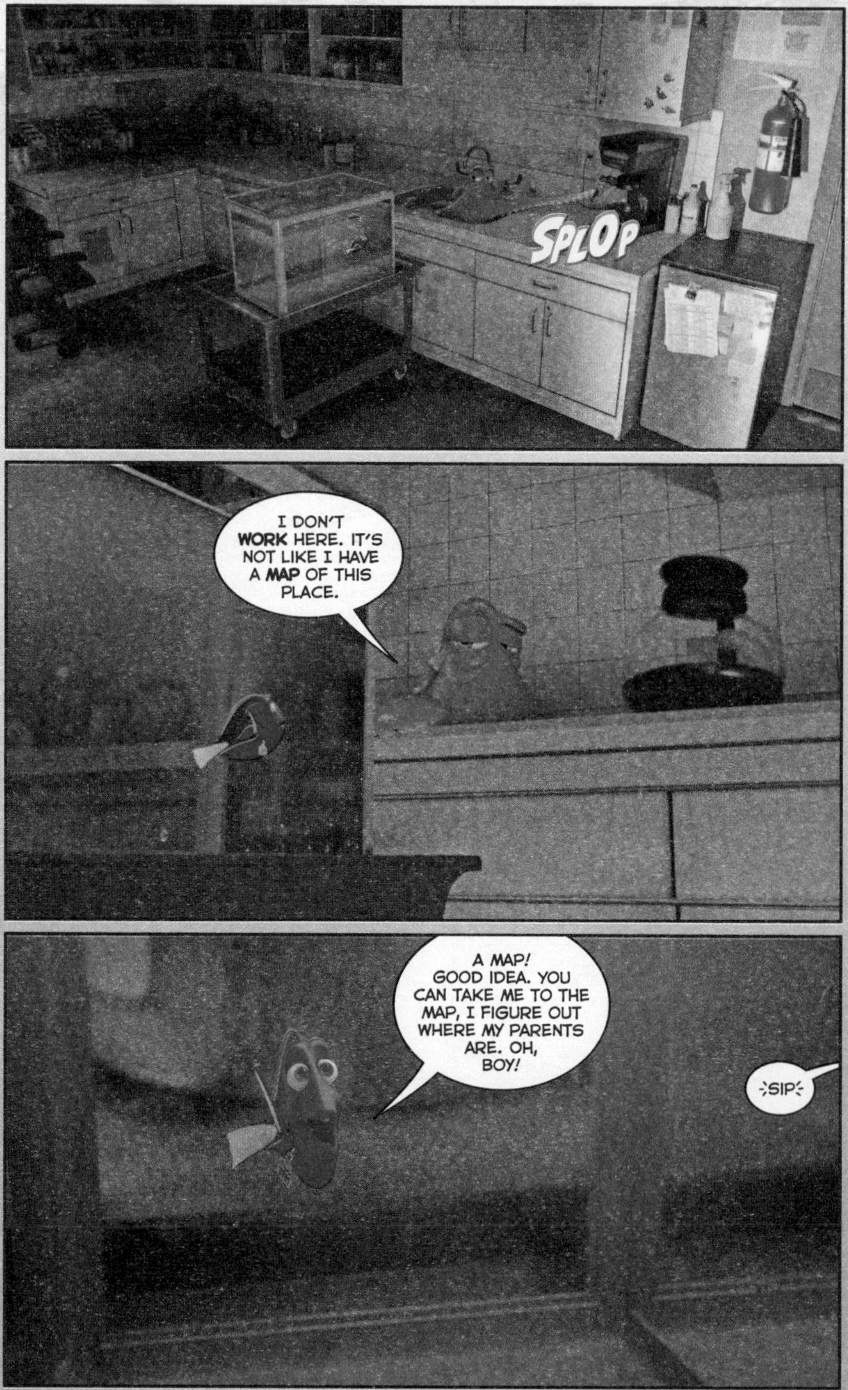
SPLOP
I DON'T **WORK** HERE. IT'S NOT LIKE I HAVE A **MAP** OF THIS PLACE.
A MAP! GOOD IDEA. YOU CAN TAKE ME TO THE MAP, I FIGURE OUT WHERE MY PARENTS ARE. OH, BOY!
SIP

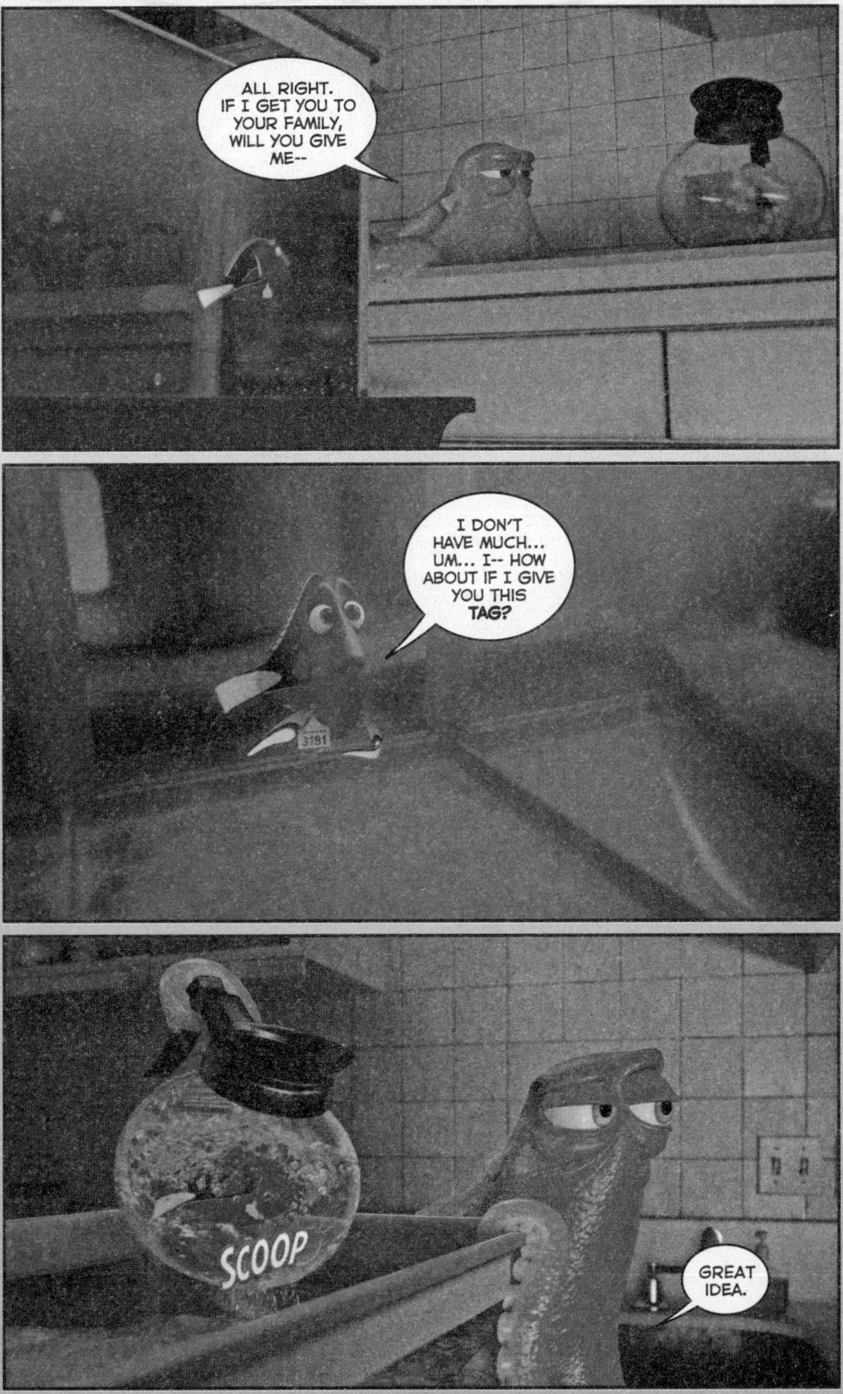
ALL RIGHT. IF I GET YOU TO YOUR FAMILY, WILL YOU GIVE ME--
I DON'T HAVE MUCH... UM... I-- HOW ABOUT IF I GIVE YOU THIS TAG?
SCOOP
GREAT IDEA.

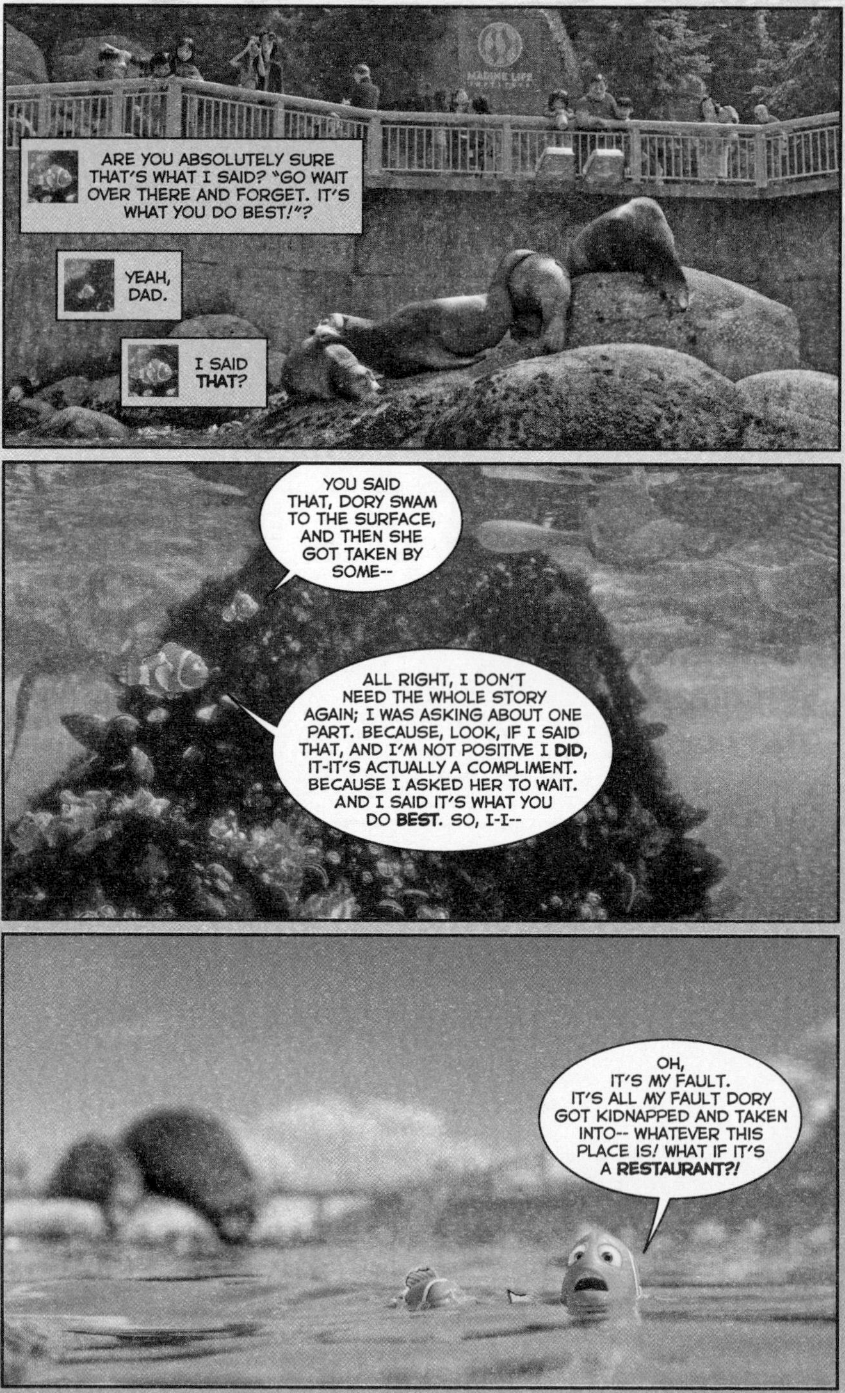
ARE YOU ABSOLUTELY SURE THAT'S WHAT I SAID? "GO WAIT OVER THERE AND FORGET. IT'S WHAT YOU DO BEST!"?
YEAH, DAD.
I SAID **THAT?**
YOU SAID THAT, DORY SWAM TO THE SURFACE, AND THEN SHE GOT TAKEN BY SOME--
ALL RIGHT, I DON'T NEED THE WHOLE STORY AGAIN; I WAS ASKING ABOUT ONE PART. BECAUSE, LOOK, IF I SAID THAT, AND I'M NOT POSITIVE I **DID**, IT-IT'S ACTUALLY A COMPLIMENT. BECAUSE I ASKED HER TO WAIT. AND I SAID IT'S WHAT YOU DO **BEST**. SO, I-I--
OH, IT'S MY FAULT. IT'S ALL MY FAULT DORY GOT KIDNAPPED AND TAKEN INTO-- WHATEVER THIS PLACE IS! WHAT IF IT'S A **RESTAURANT?!**

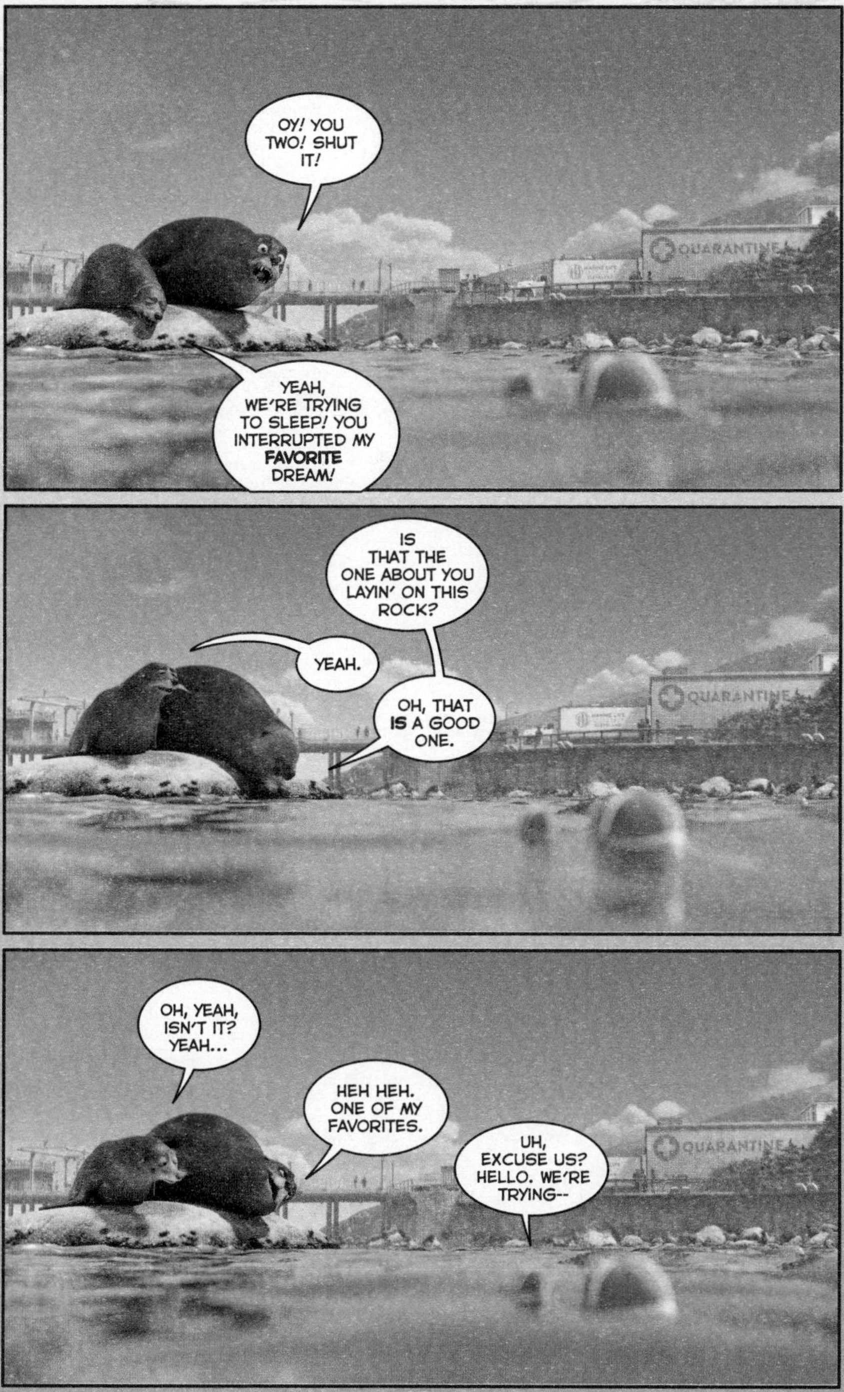
OY! YOU TWO! SHUT IT!
YEAH, WE'RE TRYING TO SLEEP! YOU INTERRUPTED MY **FAVORITE** DREAM!
IS THAT THE ONE ABOUT YOU LAYIN' ON THIS ROCK?
YEAH.
OH, THAT **IS** A GOOD ONE.
OH, YEAH, ISN'T IT? YEAH...
HEH HEH. ONE OF MY FAVORITES.
UH, EXCUSE US? HELLO. WE'RE TRYING--
QUARANTINE

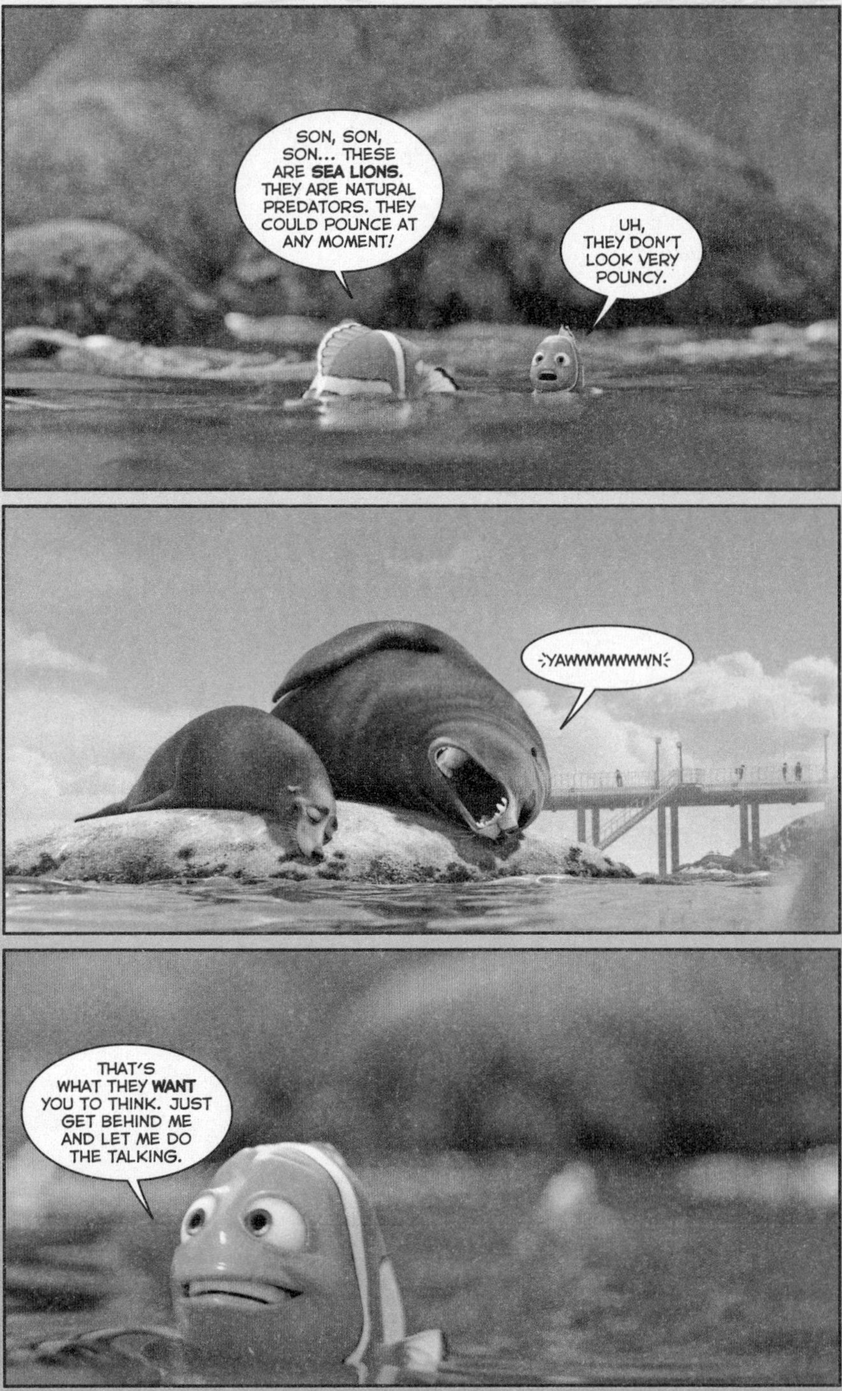
SON, SON, SON... THESE ARE **SEA LIONS.** THEY ARE NATURAL PREDATORS. THEY COULD POUNCE AT ANY MOMENT!
UH, THEY DON'T LOOK VERY POUNCY.
YAWWWWWWWWN
THAT'S WHAT THEY **WANT** YOU TO THINK. JUST GET BEHIND ME AND LET ME DO THE TALKING.

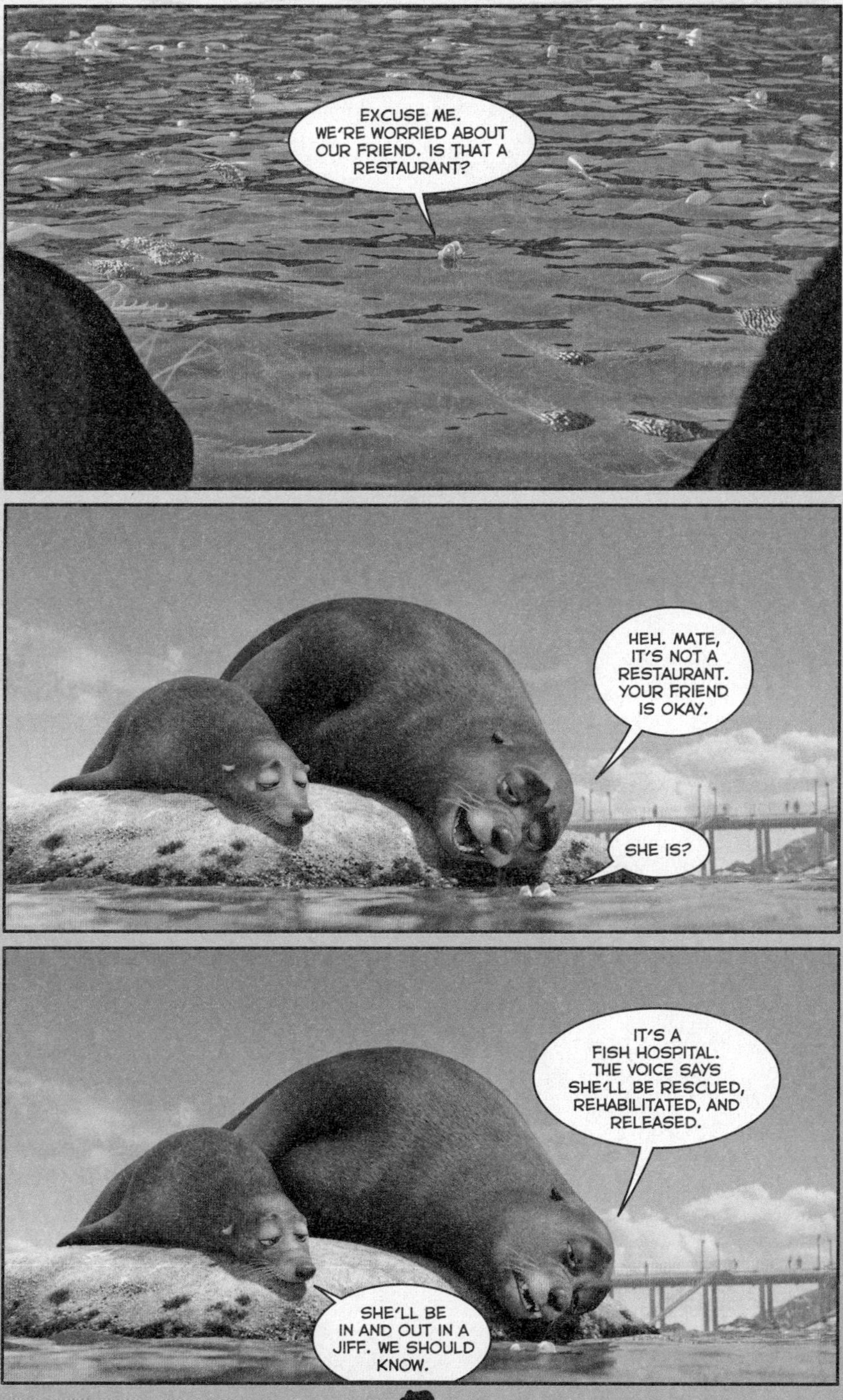
EXCUSE ME. WE'RE WORRIED ABOUT OUR FRIEND. IS THAT A RESTAURANT?
HEH. MATE, IT'S NOT A RESTAURANT. YOUR FRIEND IS OKAY.
SHE IS?
IT'S A FISH HOSPITAL. THE VOICE SAYS SHE'LL BE RESCUED, REHABILITATED, AND RELEASED.
SHE'LL BE IN AND OUT IN A JIFF. WE SHOULD KNOW.

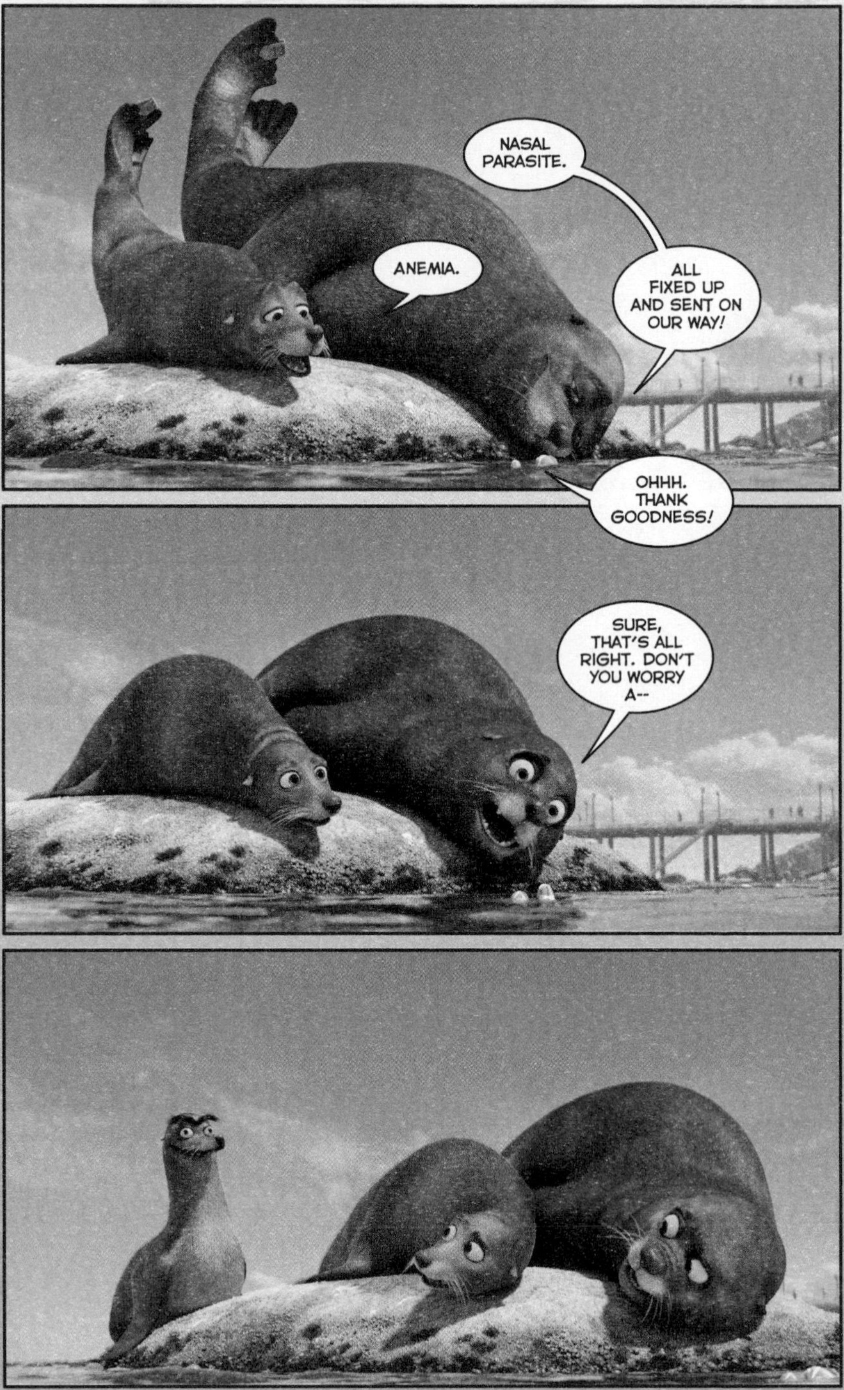
NASAL PARASITE.
ANEMIA.
ALL FIXED UP AND SENT ON OUR WAY!
OHHH. THANK GOODNESS!
SURE, THAT'S ALL RIGHT. DON'T YOU WORRY A--

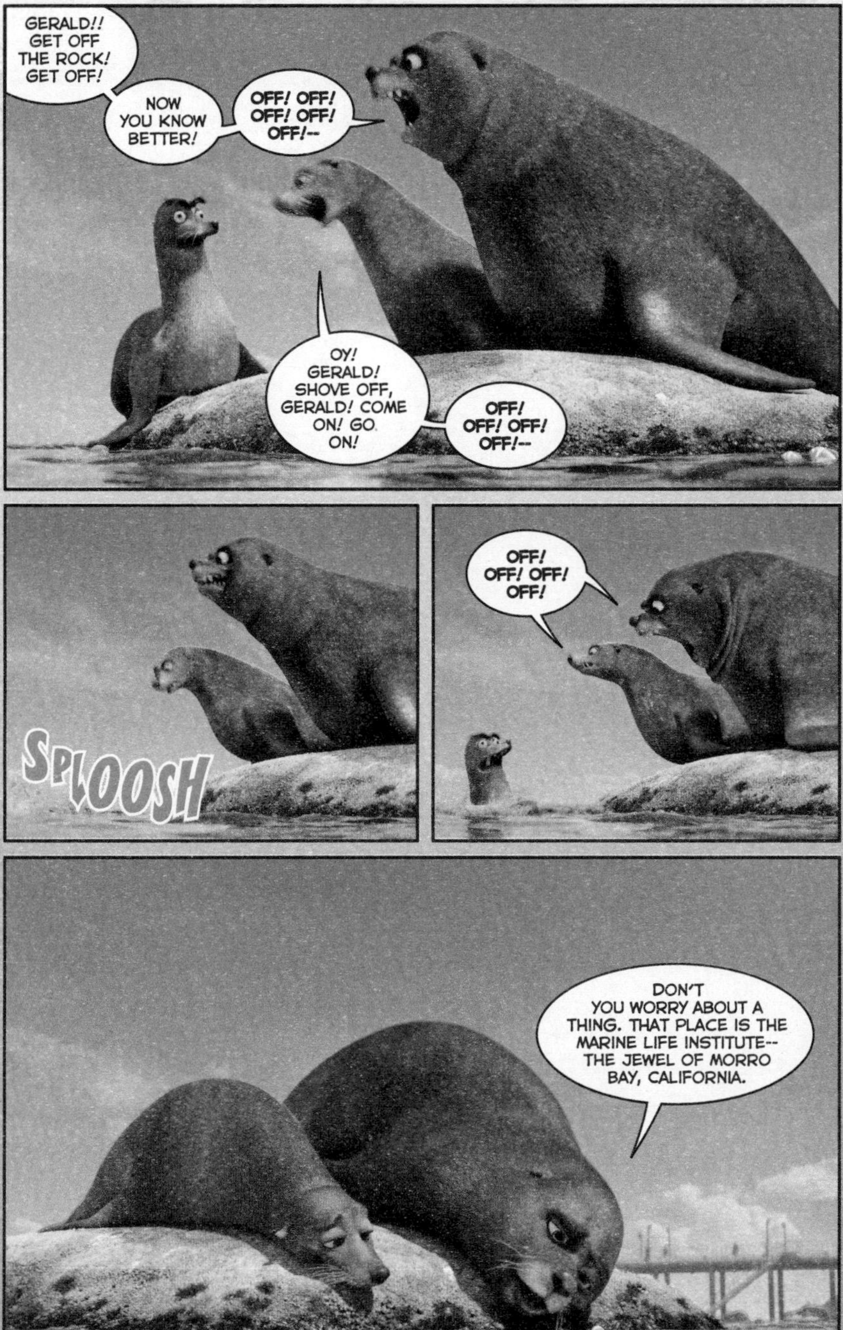
GERALD!! GET OFF THE ROCK! GET OFF!
NOW YOU KNOW BETTER!
OFF! OFF! OFF! OFF! OFF!--
OY! GERALD! SHOVE OFF, GERALD! COME ON! GO ON!
OFF! OFF! OFF! OFF!--
SPLOOSH
OFF! OFF! OFF! OFF!
DON'T YOU WORRY ABOUT A THING. THAT PLACE IS THE MARINE LIFE INSTITUTE-- THE JEWEL OF MORRO BAY, CALIFORNIA.

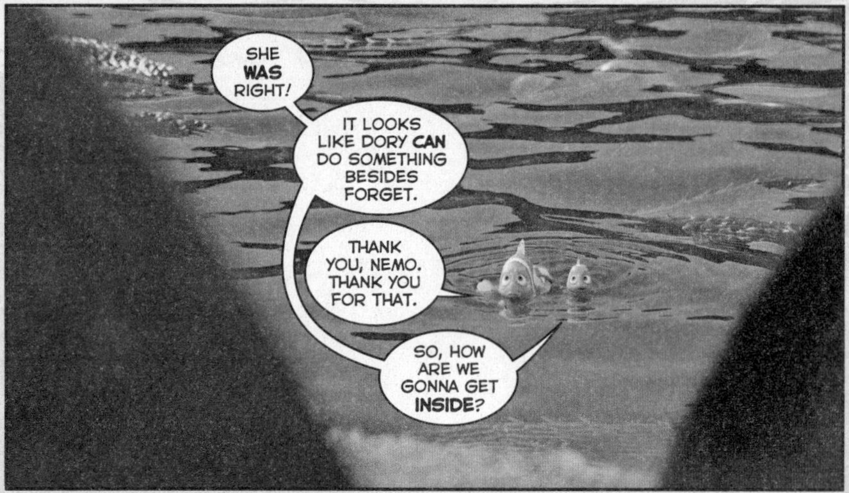
SHE **WAS** RIGHT!
IT LOOKS LIKE DORY **CAN** DO SOMETHING BESIDES FORGET.
THANK YOU, NEMO. THANK YOU FOR THAT.
SO, HOW ARE WE GONNA GET **INSIDE**?

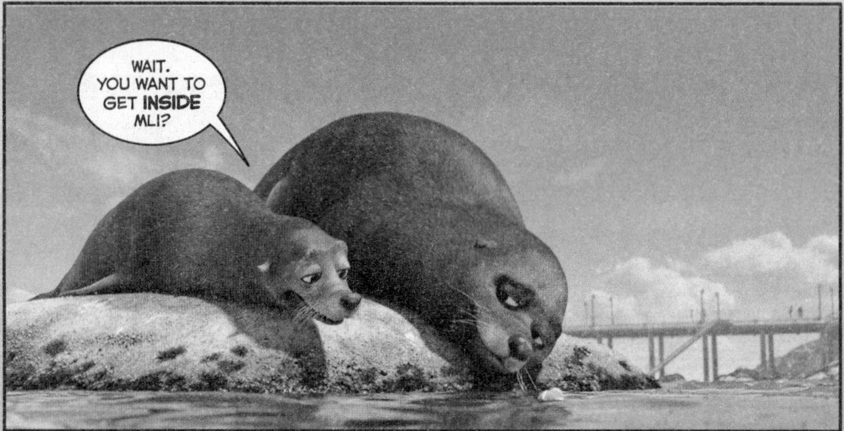
WAIT. YOU WANT TO GET **INSIDE** MLI?

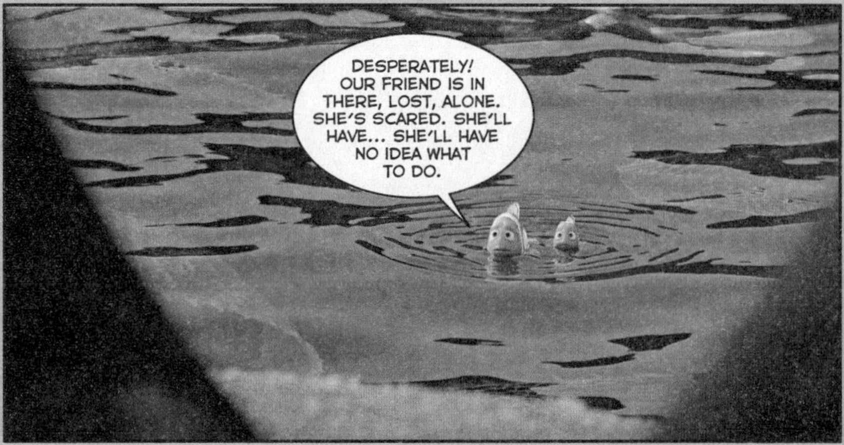
DESPERATELY! OUR FRIEND IS IN THERE, LOST, ALONE. SHE'S SCARED. SHE'LL HAVE... SHE'LL HAVE NO IDEA WHAT TO DO.

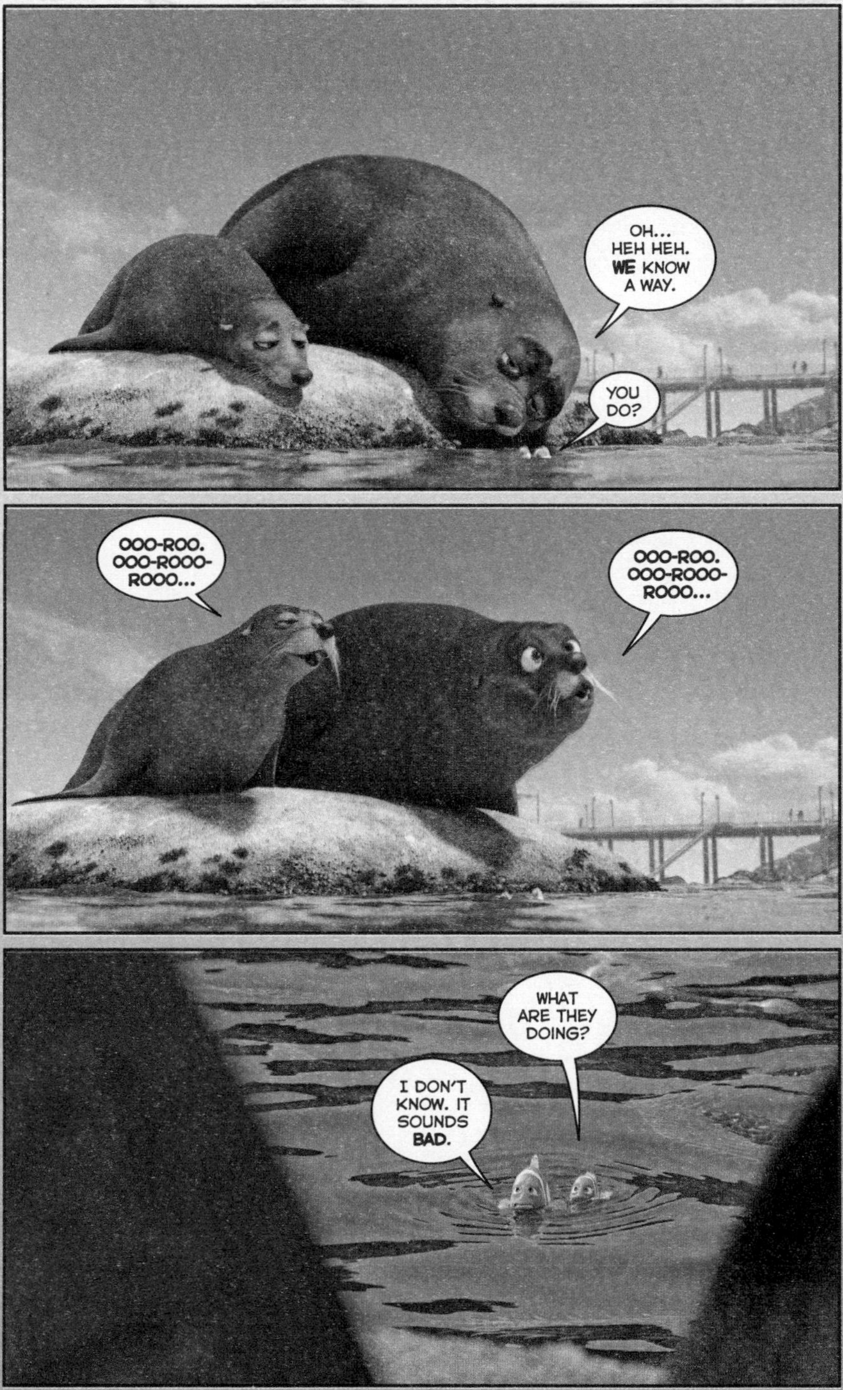
OH... HEH HEH. WE KNOW A WAY.
YOU DO?
OOO-ROO. OOO-ROOO-ROOO...
OOO-ROO. OOO-ROOO-ROOO...
WHAT ARE THEY DOING?
I DON'T KNOW. IT SOUNDS BAD.

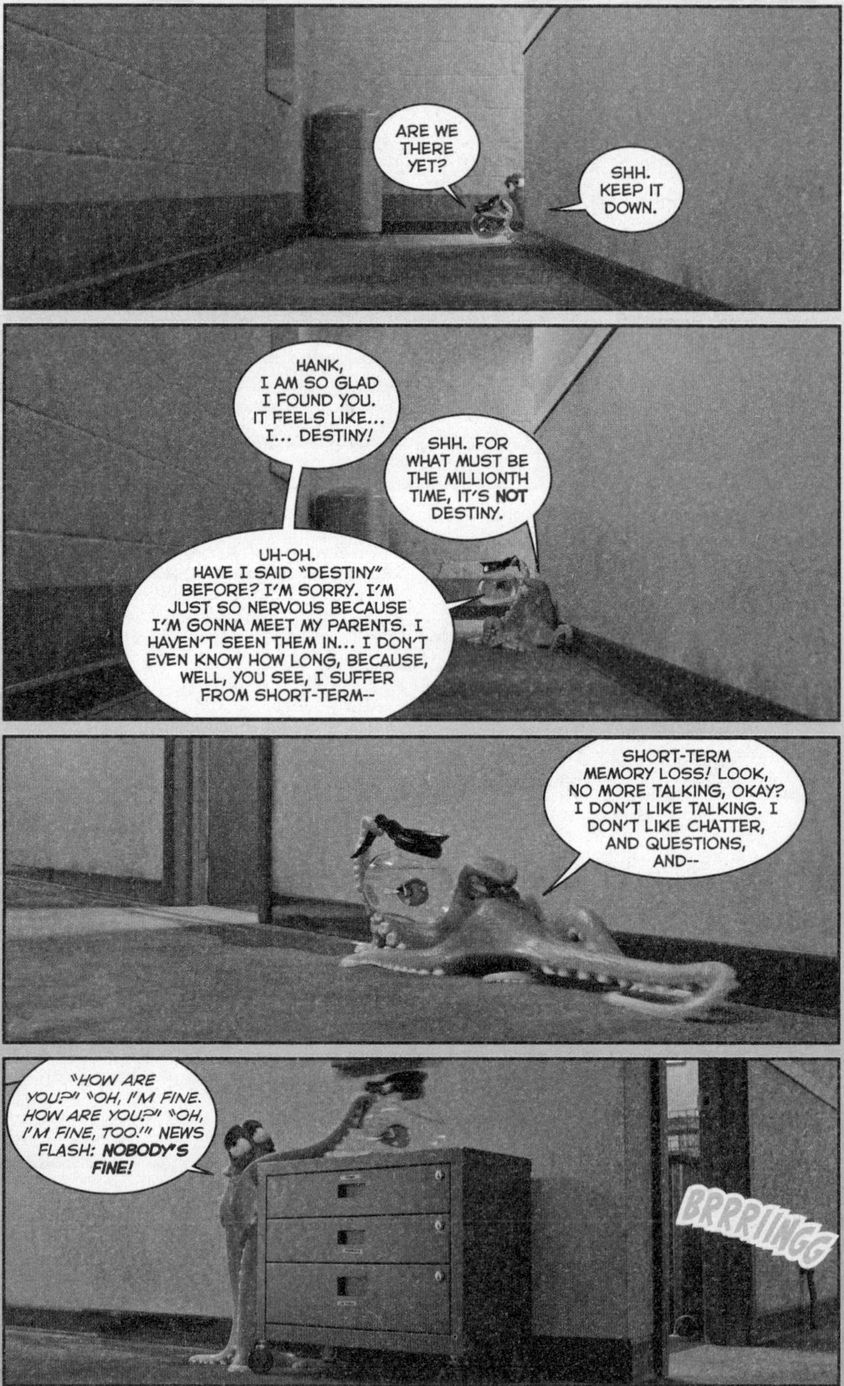
ARE WE THERE YET?
SHH. KEEP IT DOWN.
HANK, I AM SO GLAD I FOUND YOU. IT FEELS LIKE... I... DESTINY!
SHH. FOR WHAT MUST BE THE MILLIONTH TIME, IT'S NOT DESTINY.
UH-OH. HAVE I SAID "DESTINY" BEFORE? I'M SORRY. I'M JUST SO NERVOUS BECAUSE I'M GONNA MEET MY PARENTS. I HAVEN'T SEEN THEM IN... I DON'T EVEN KNOW HOW LONG, BECAUSE, WELL, YOU SEE, I SUFFER FROM SHORT-TERM--
SHORT-TERM MEMORY LOSS! LOOK, NO MORE TALKING, OKAY? I DON'T LIKE TALKING. I DON'T LIKE CHATTER, AND QUESTIONS, AND--
"HOW ARE YOU?" "OH, I'M FINE. HOW ARE YOU?" "OH, I'M FINE, TOO!" NEWS FLASH: NOBODY'S FINE!
BRRRIINGG

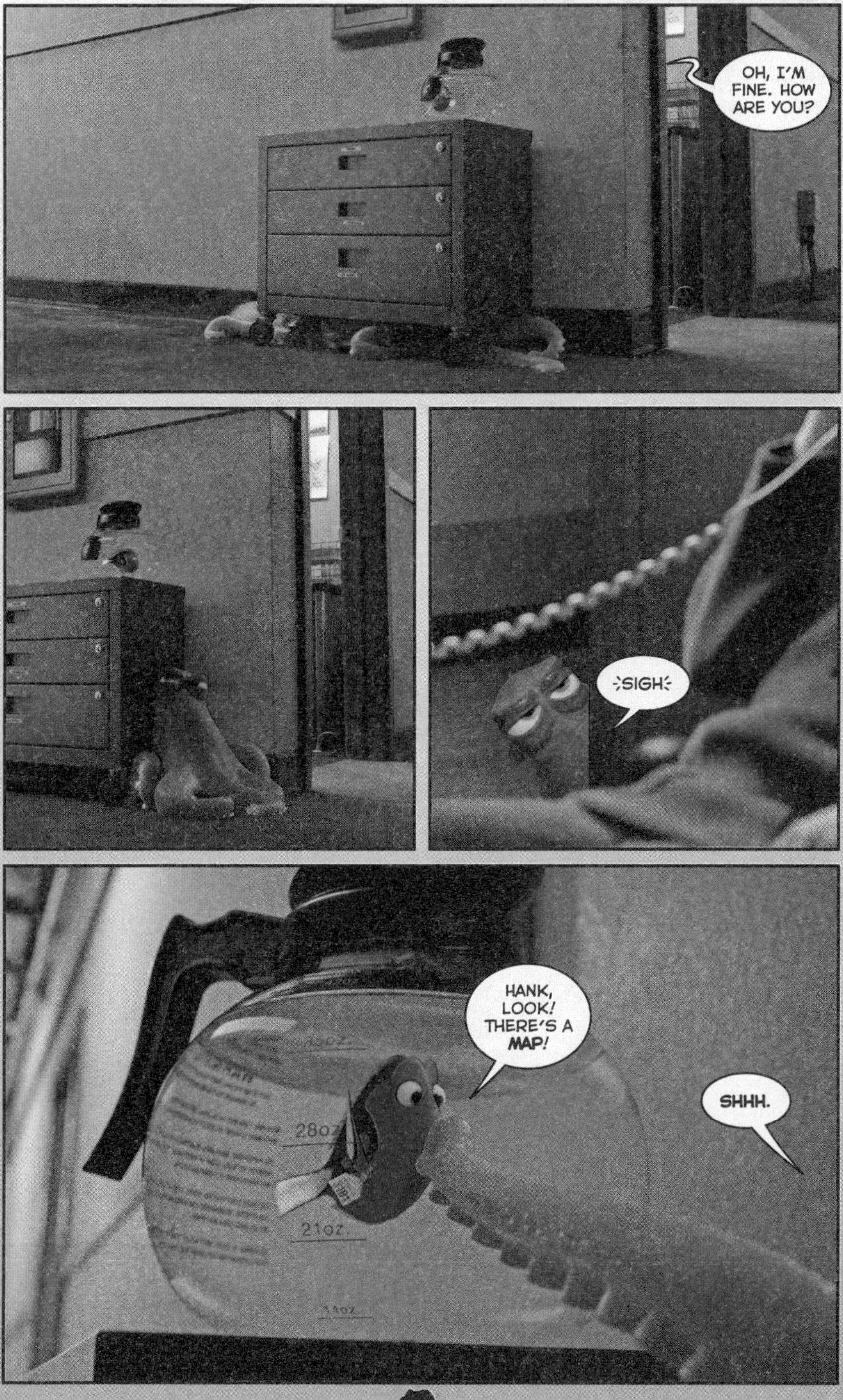
OH, I'M FINE. HOW ARE YOU?
SIGH
HANK, LOOK! THERE'S A MAP!
SHHH.

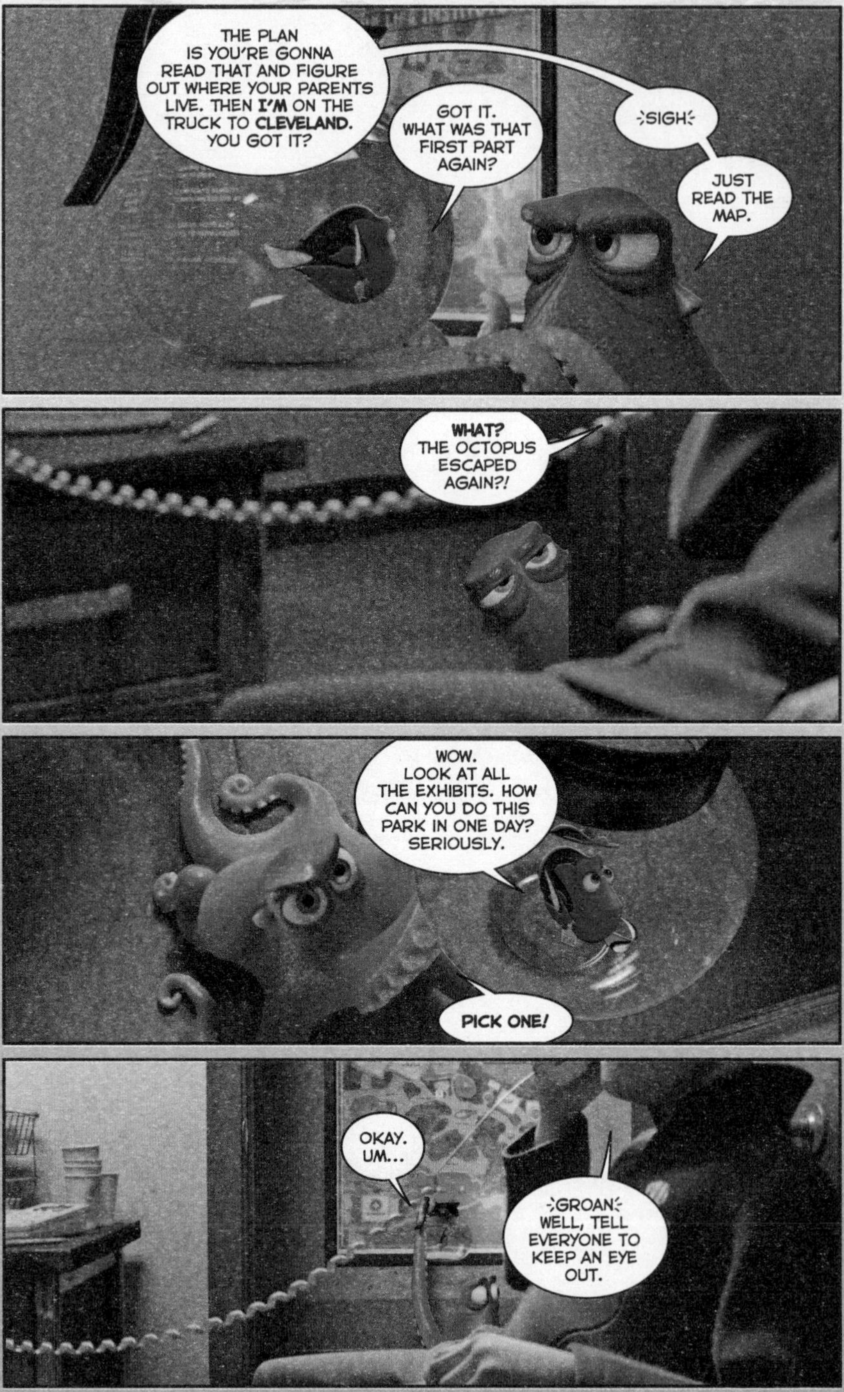
THE PLAN IS YOU'RE GONNA READ THAT AND FIGURE OUT WHERE YOUR PARENTS LIVE. THEN **I'M** ON THE TRUCK TO **CLEVELAND**. YOU GOT IT?
GOT IT. WHAT WAS THAT FIRST PART AGAIN?
SIGH
JUST READ THE MAP.
WHAT? THE OCTOPUS ESCAPED AGAIN?!
WOW. LOOK AT ALL THE EXHIBITS. HOW CAN YOU DO THIS PARK IN ONE DAY? SERIOUSLY.
PICK ONE!
OKAY. UM...
GROAN WELL, TELL EVERYONE TO KEEP AN EYE OUT.

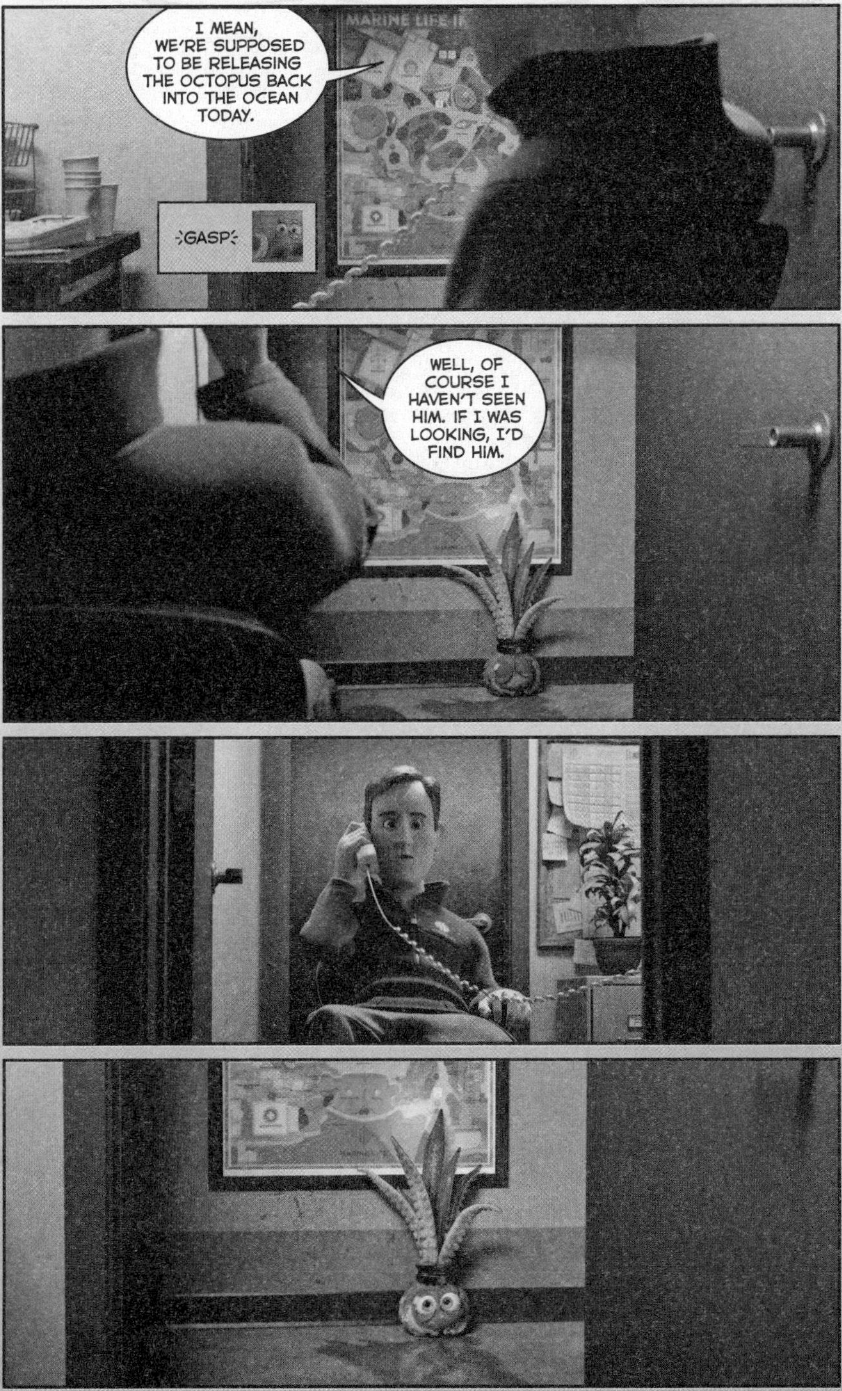
I MEAN, WE'RE SUPPOSED TO BE RELEASING THE OCTOPUS BACK INTO THE OCEAN TODAY.
GASP
WELL, OF COURSE I HAVEN'T SEEN HIM. IF I WAS LOOKING, I'D FIND HIM.

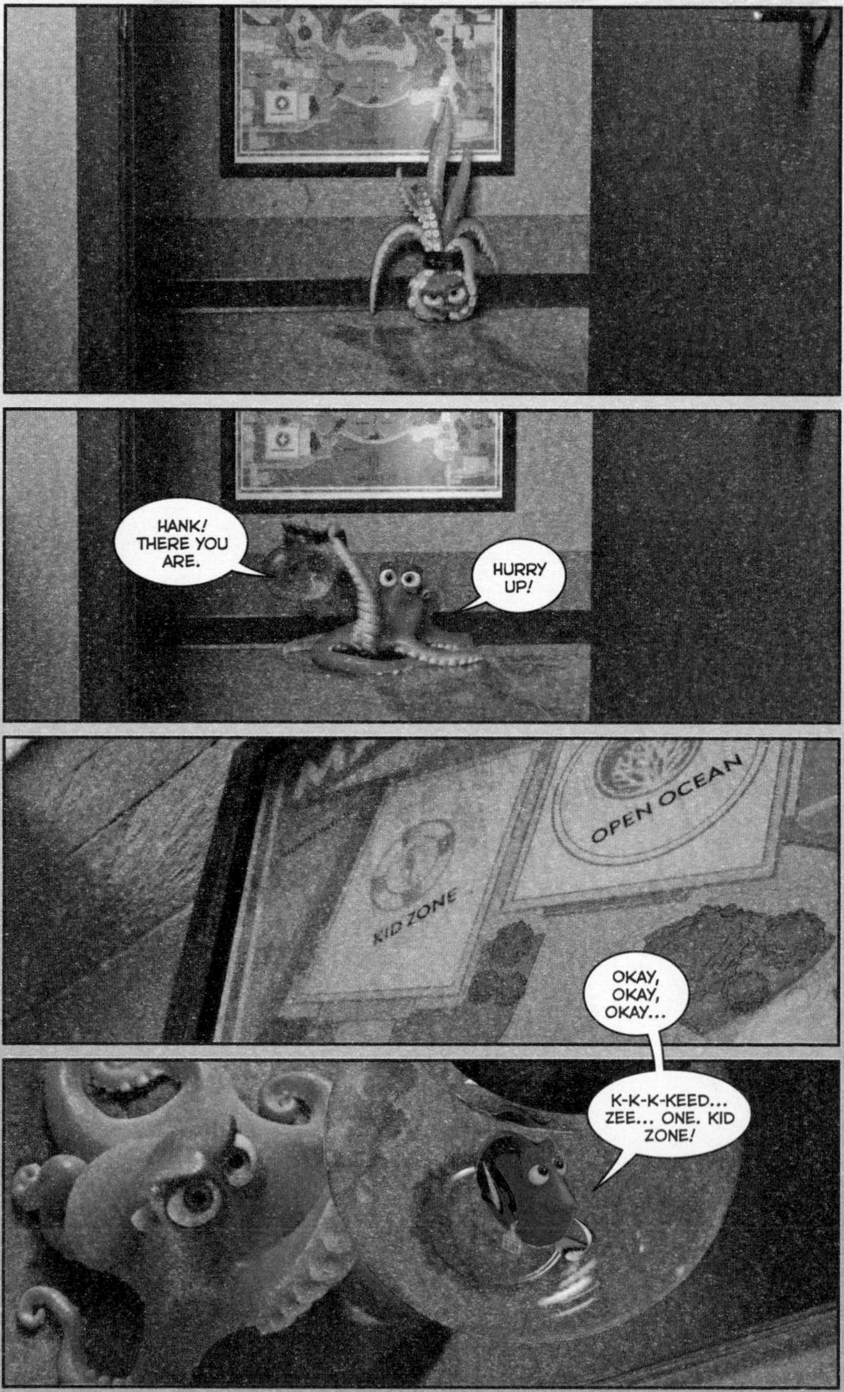
HANK! THERE YOU ARE.
HURRY UP!
OPEN OCEAN
KID ZONE
OKAY, OKAY, OKAY...
K-K-K-KEED... ZEE... ONE. KID ZONE!

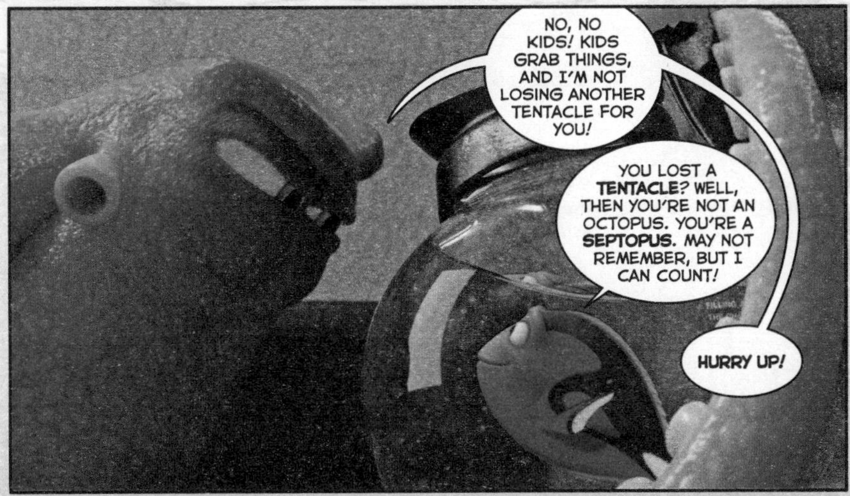
NO, NO KIDS! KIDS GRAB THINGS, AND I'M NOT LOSING ANOTHER TENTACLE FOR YOU!
YOU LOST A TENTACLE? WELL, THEN YOU'RE NOT AN OCTOPUS. YOU'RE A SEPTOPUS. MAY NOT REMEMBER, BUT I CAN COUNT!
HURRY UP!

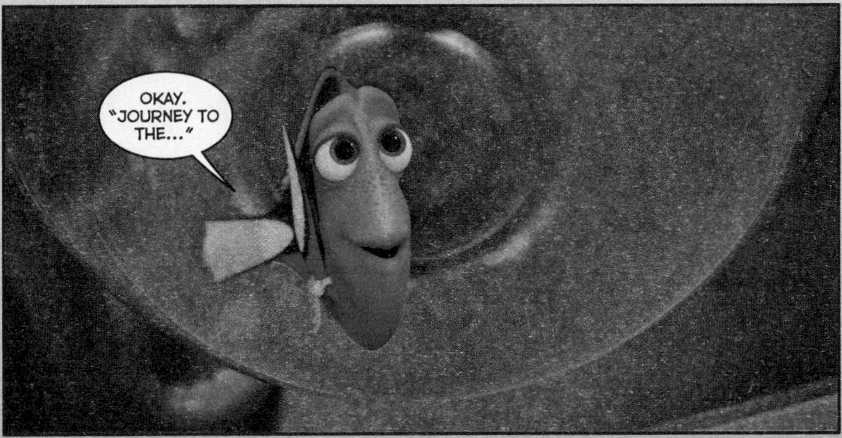
OKAY. "JOURNEY TO THE..."

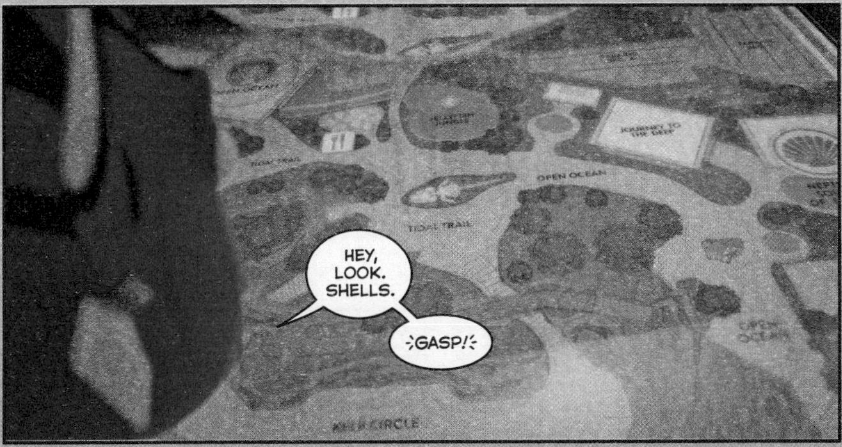
OPEN OCEAN
JOURNEY TO THE DEEP
OPEN OCEAN
TIDAL TRAIL
HEY, LOOK. SHELLS.
GASP!

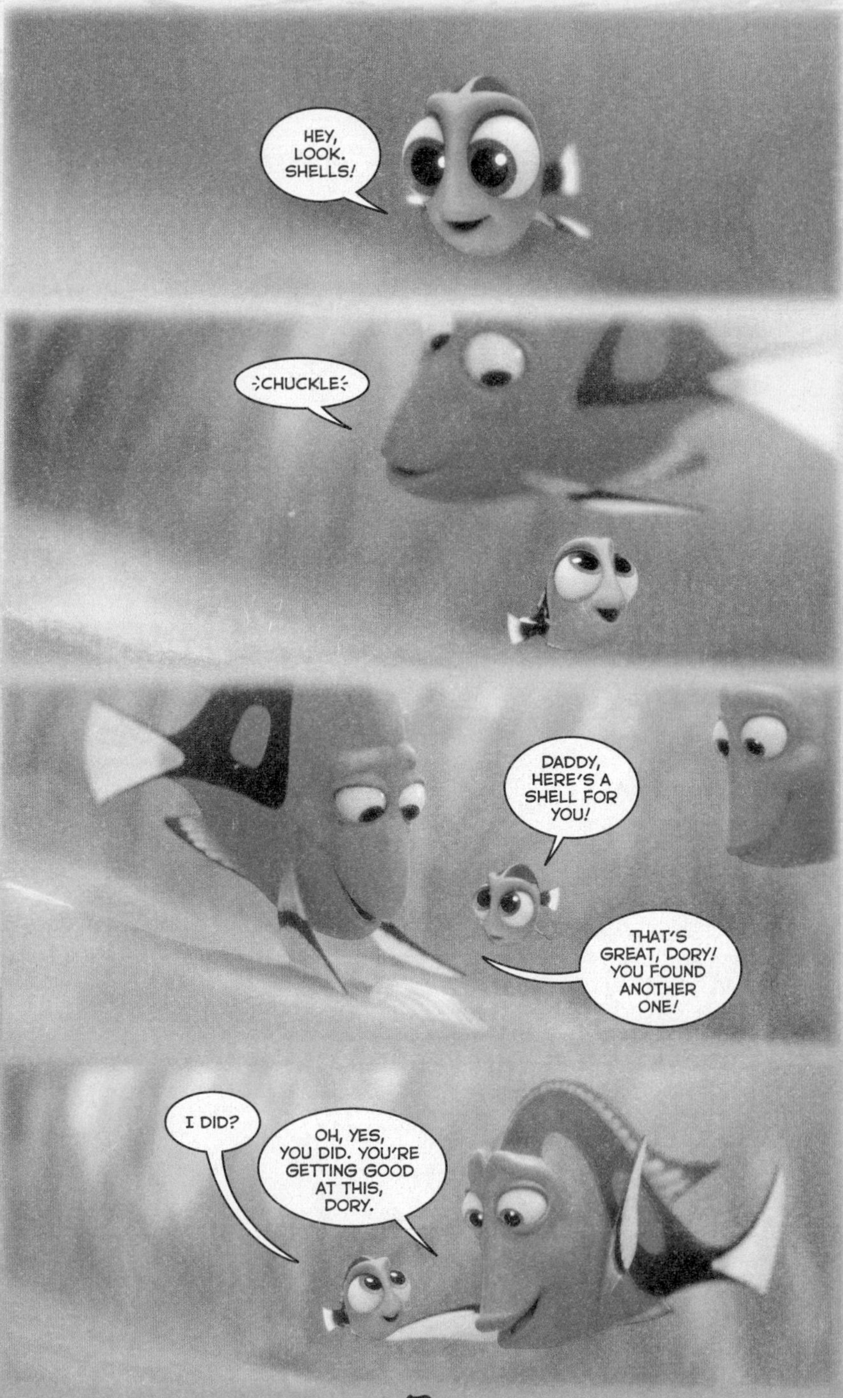
HEY, LOOK. SHELLS!
CHUCKLE
DADDY, HERE'S A SHELL FOR YOU!
THAT'S GREAT, DORY! YOU FOUND ANOTHER ONE!
I DID?
OH, YES, YOU DID. YOU'RE GETTING GOOD AT THIS, DORY.

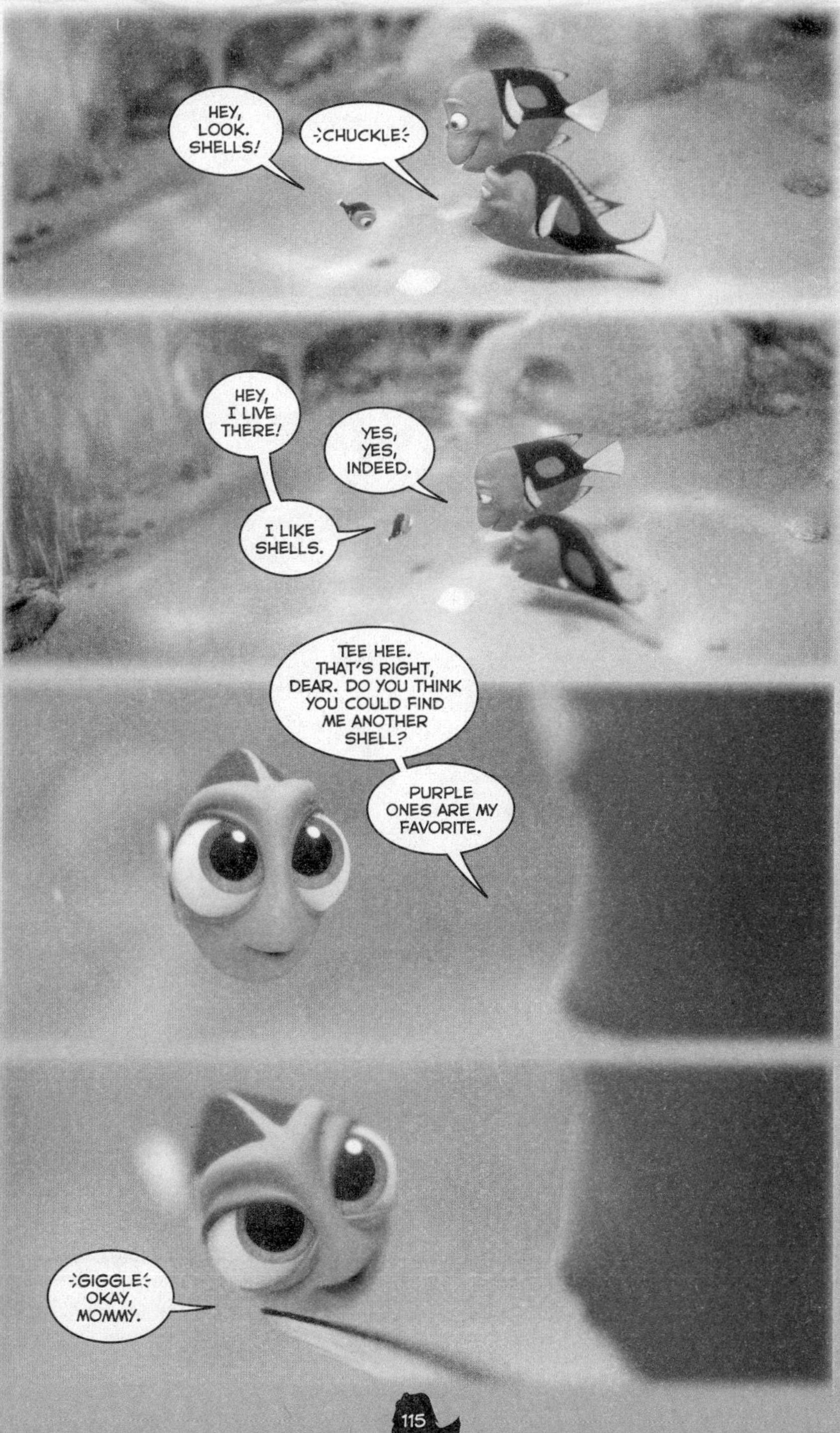
HEY, LOOK. SHELLS!
CHUCKLE
HEY, I LIVE THERE!
YES, YES, INDEED.
I LIKE SHELLS.
TEE HEE. THAT'S RIGHT, DEAR. DO YOU THINK YOU COULD FIND ME ANOTHER SHELL?
PURPLE ONES ARE MY FAVORITE.
GIGGLE OKAY, MOMMY.

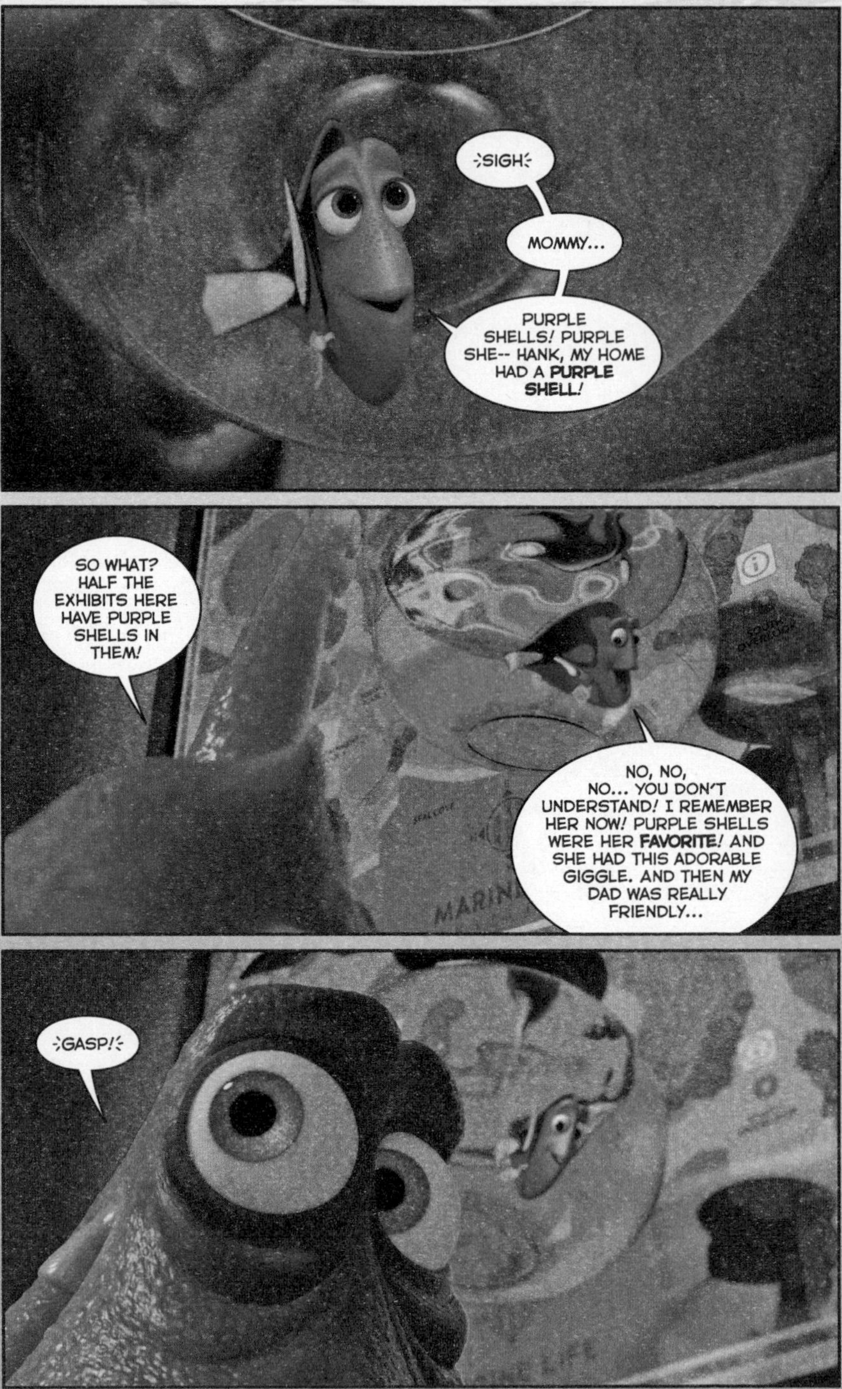
SIGH
MOMMY...
PURPLE SHELLS! PURPLE SHE-- HANK, MY HOME HAD A PURPLE SHELL!
SO WHAT? HALF THE EXHIBITS HERE HAVE PURPLE SHELLS IN THEM!
NO, NO, NO... YOU DON'T UNDERSTAND! I REMEMBER HER NOW! PURPLE SHELLS WERE HER FAVORITE! AND SHE HAD THIS ADORABLE GIGGLE. AND THEN MY DAD WAS REALLY FRIENDLY...
GASP!

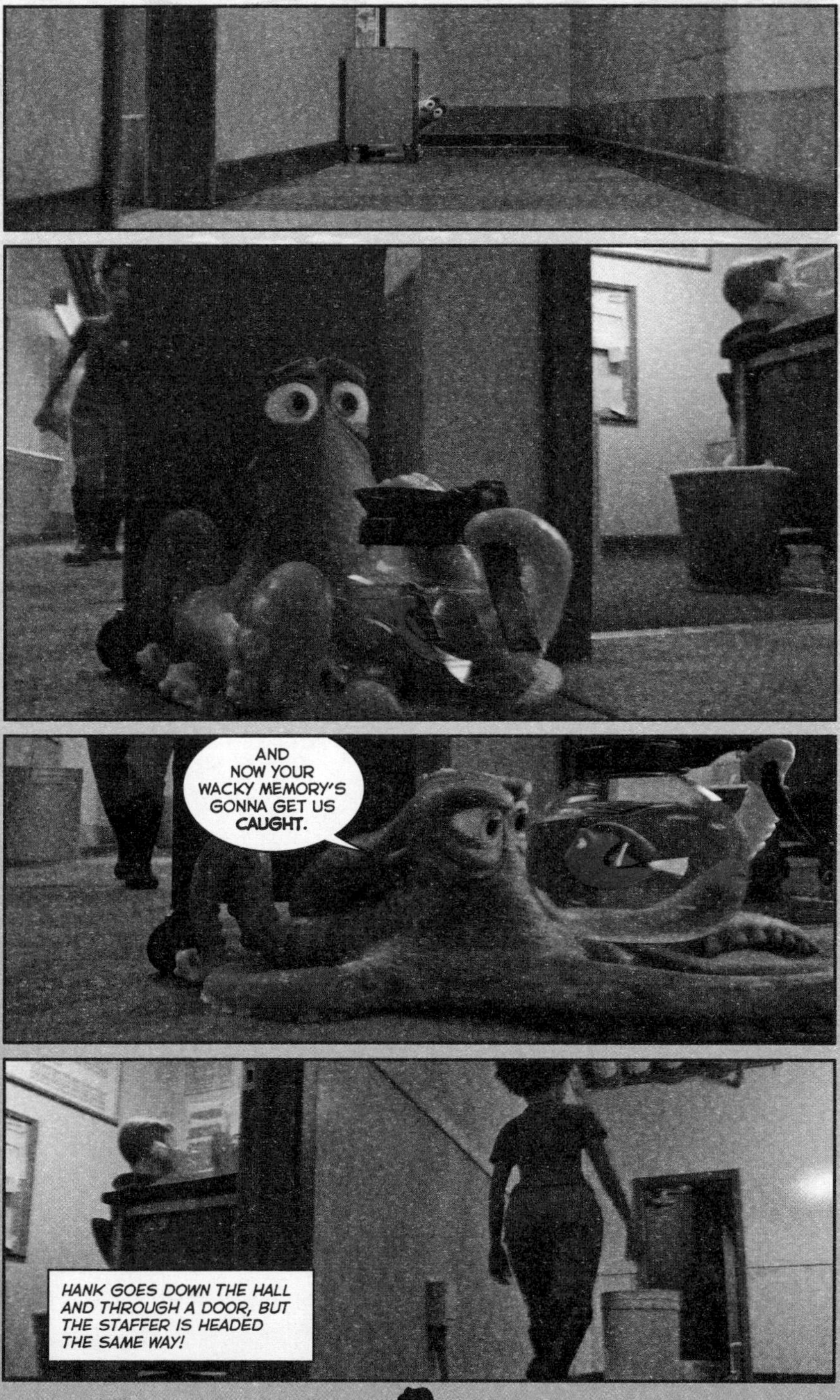
AND NOW YOUR WACKY MEMORY'S GONNA GET US CAUGHT.
HANK GOES DOWN THE HALL AND THROUGH A DOOR, BUT THE STAFFER IS HEADED THE SAME WAY!

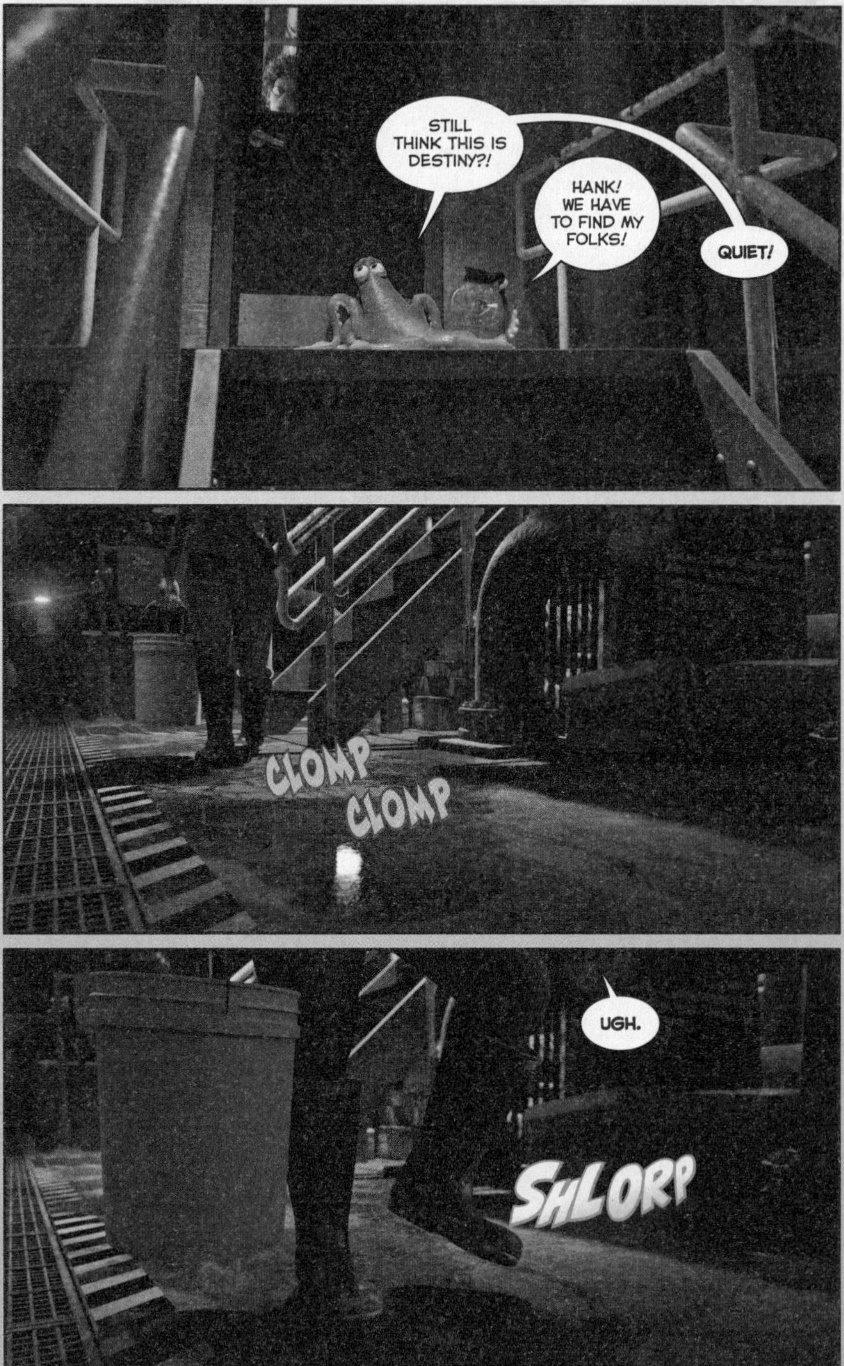
STILL THINK THIS IS DESTINY?!
HANK! WE HAVE TO FIND MY FOLKS!
QUIET!
CLOMP
CLOMP
UGH.
SHLORP

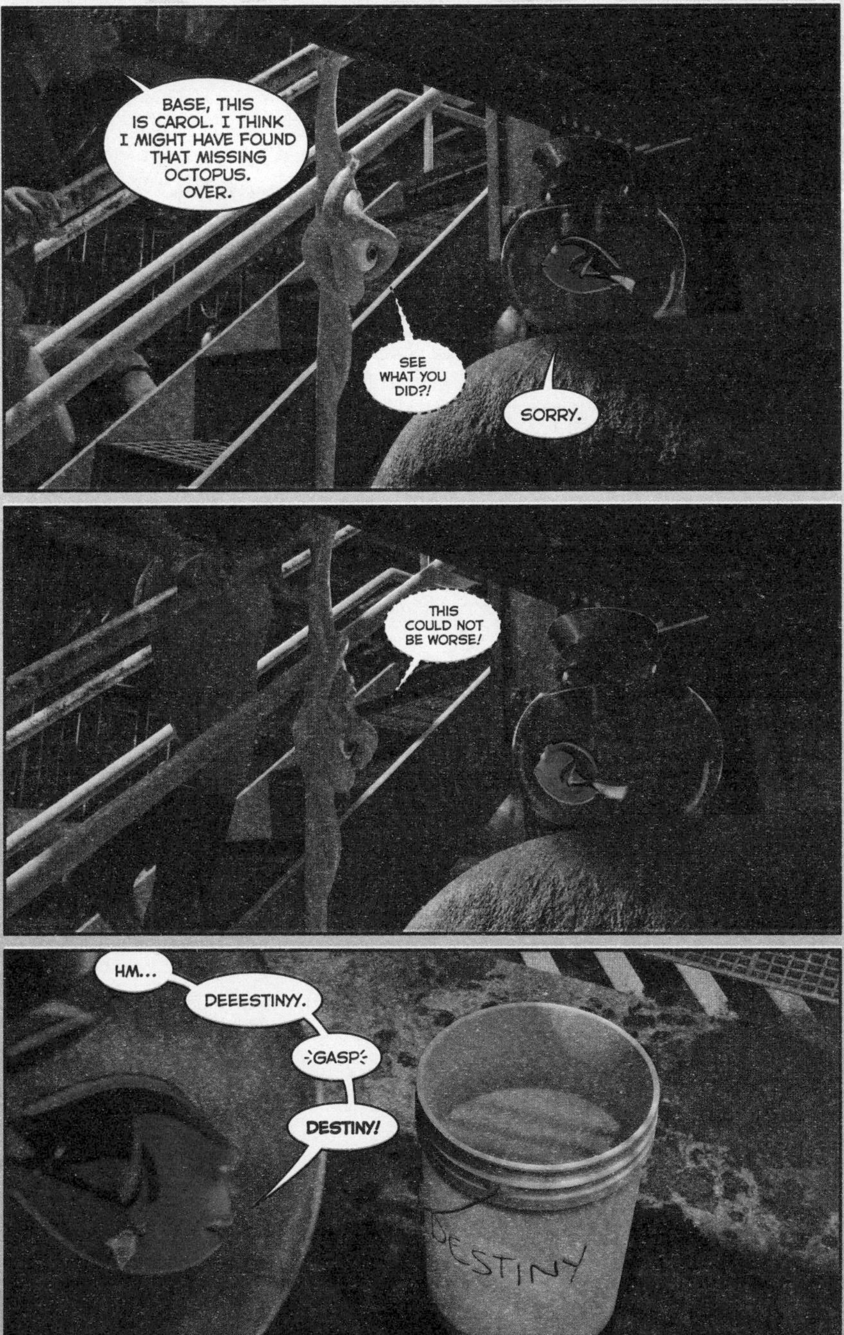
BASE, THIS IS CAROL. I THINK I MIGHT HAVE FOUND THAT MISSING OCTOPUS. OVER.
SEE WHAT YOU DID?!
SORRY.
THIS COULD NOT BE WORSE!
HM...
DEEESTINYY.
GASP
DESTINY!
DESTINY

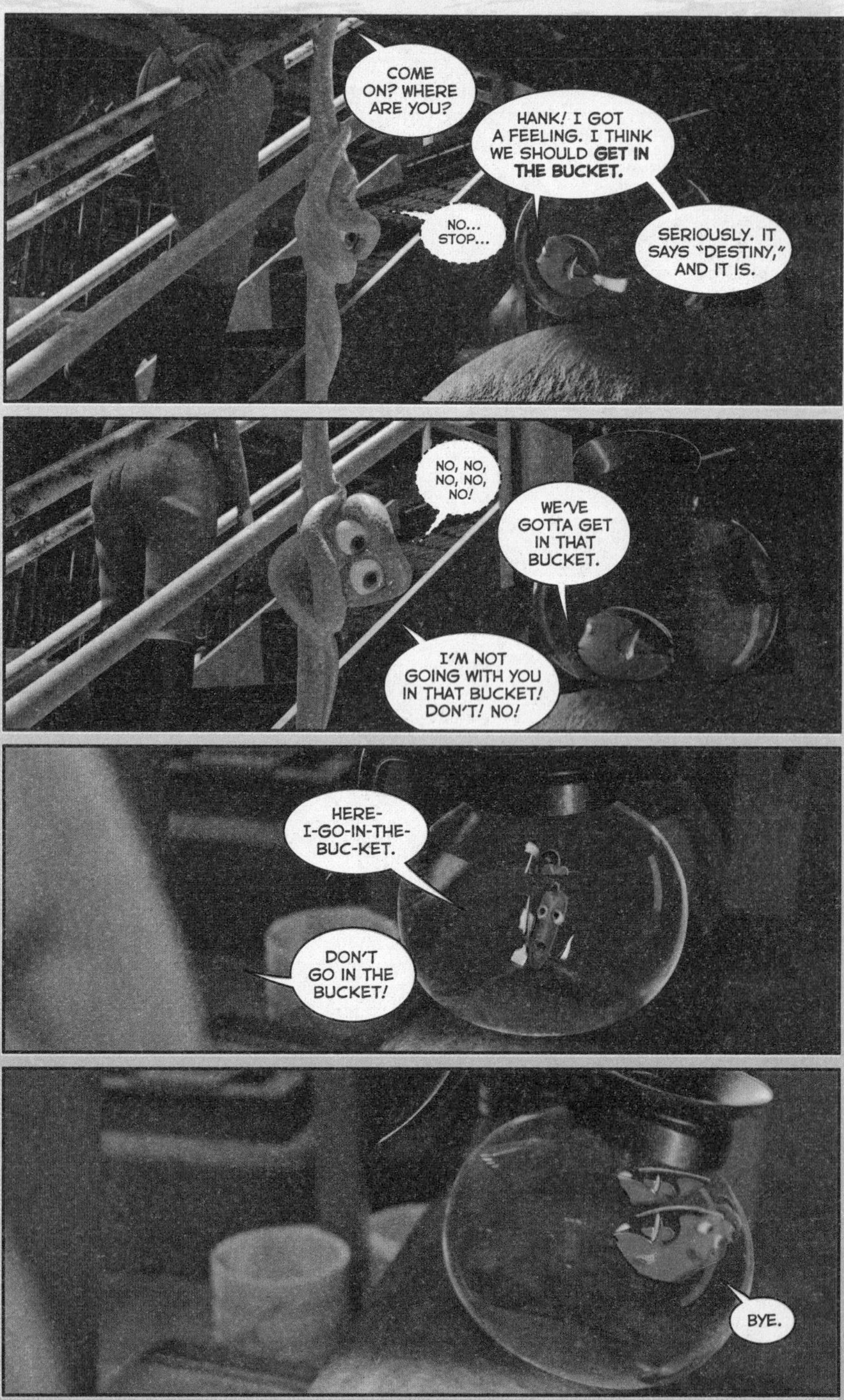
COME ON? WHERE ARE YOU?
HANK! I GOT A FEELING. I THINK WE SHOULD GET IN THE BUCKET.
NO... STOP...
SERIOUSLY. IT SAYS "DESTINY," AND IT IS.
NO, NO, NO, NO, NO!
WE'VE GOTTA GET IN THAT BUCKET.
I'M NOT GOING WITH YOU IN THAT BUCKET! DON'T! NO!
HERE-I-GO-IN-THE-BUC-KET.
DON'T GO IN THE BUCKET!
BYE.

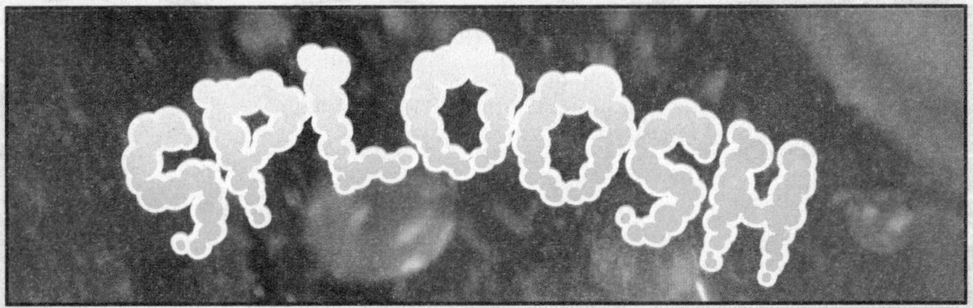
SPLOOSH

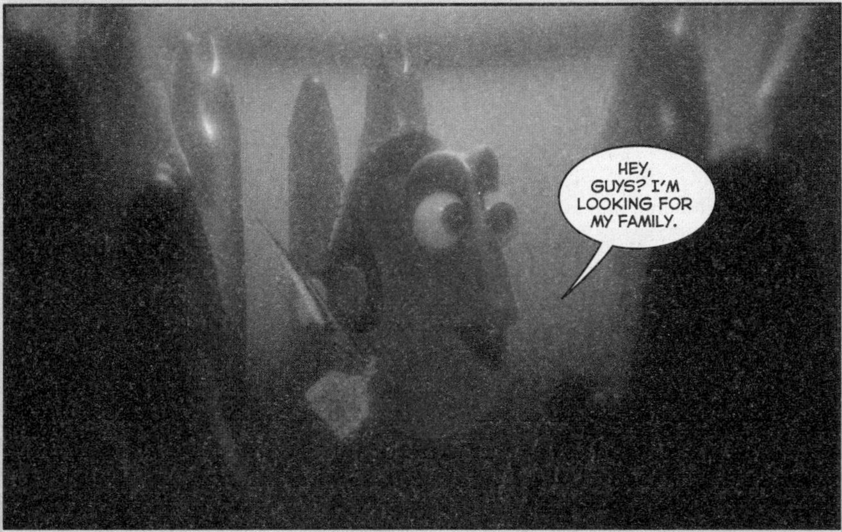
HEY, GUYS? I'M LOOKING FOR MY FAMILY.

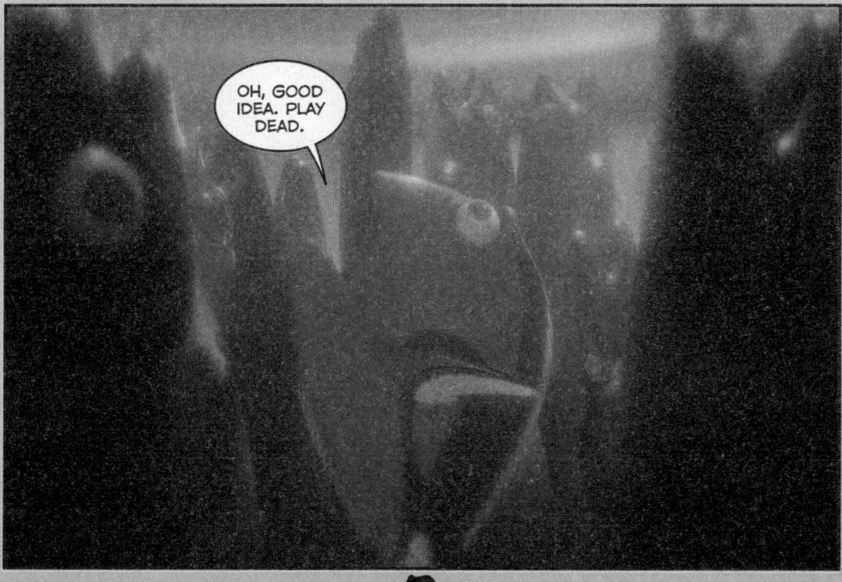
OH, GOOD IDEA. PLAY DEAD.

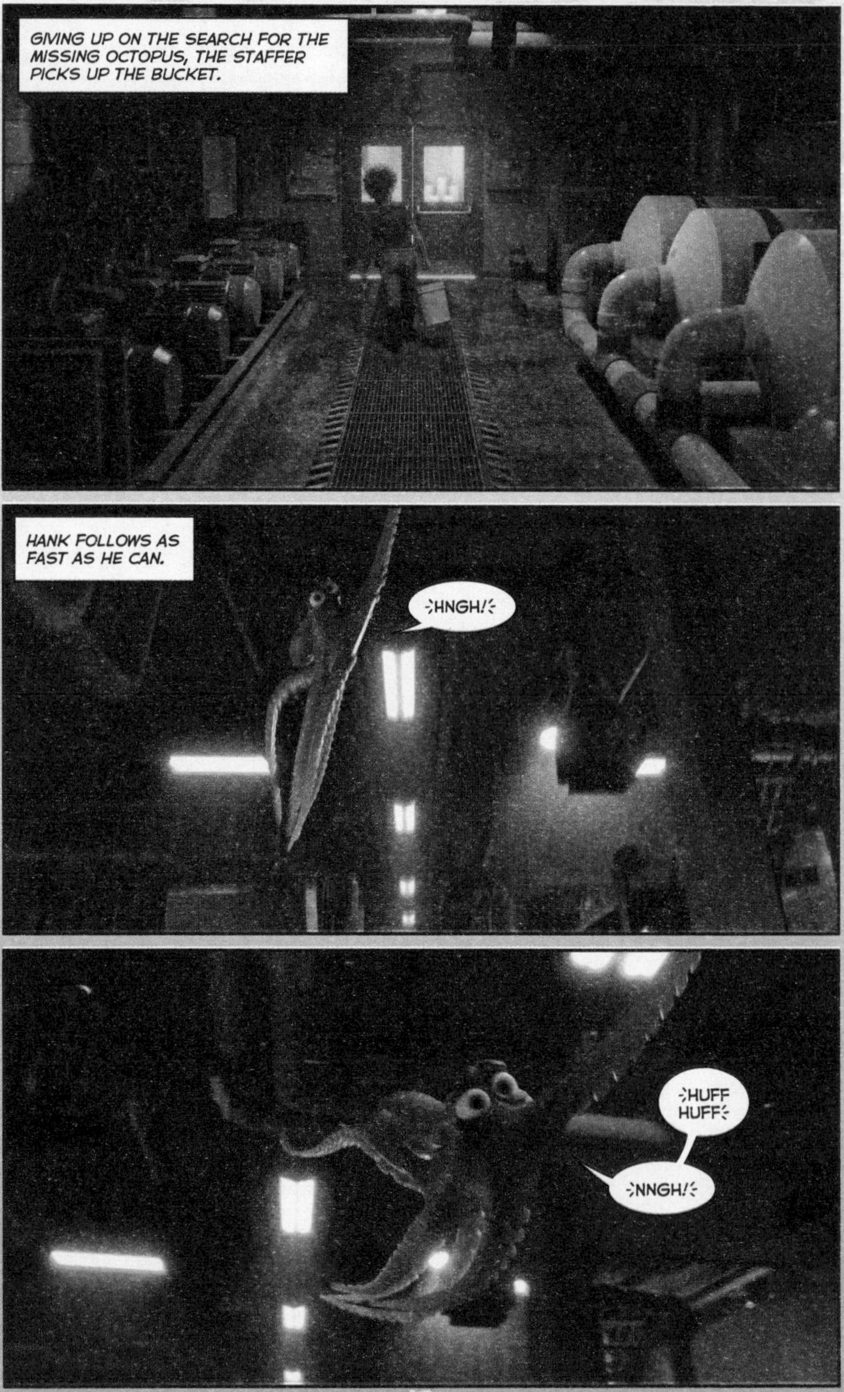
GIVING UP ON THE SEARCH FOR THE MISSING OCTOPUS, THE STAFFER PICKS UP THE BUCKET.
HANK FOLLOWS AS FAST AS HE CAN.
HNGH!
HUFF HUFF
NNGH!

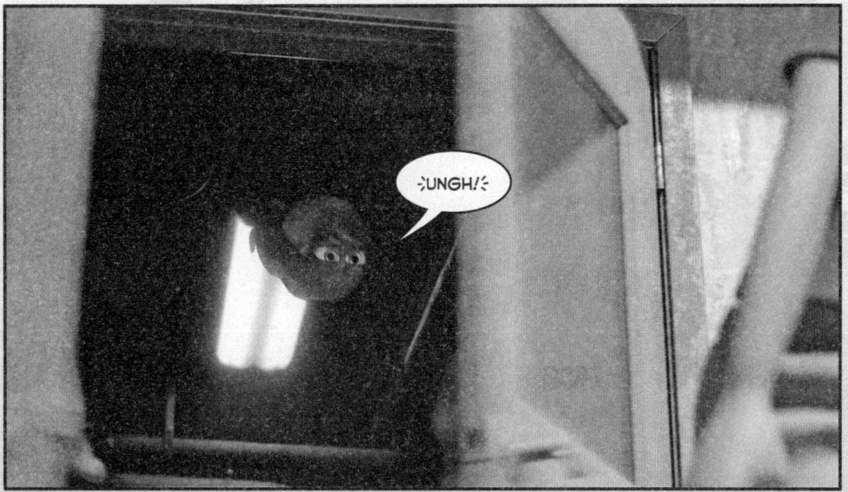
UNGH!

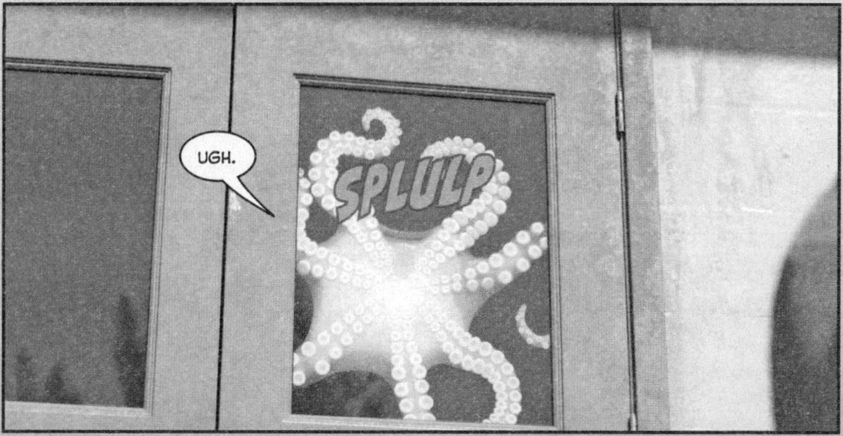
UGH.
SPLULP

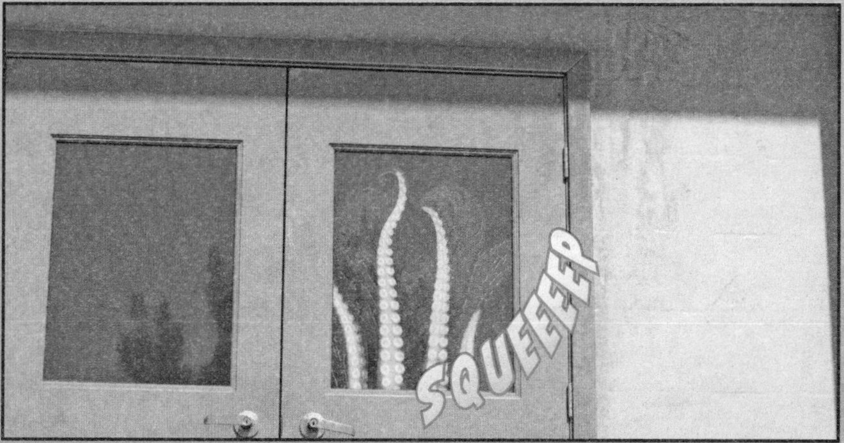
SQUEEEP

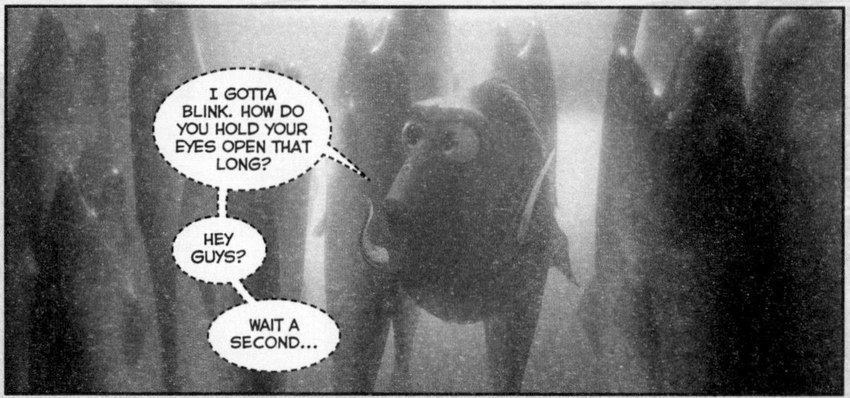
I GOTTA BLINK. HOW DO YOU HOLD YOUR EYES OPEN THAT LONG?
HEY GUYS?
WAIT A SECOND...

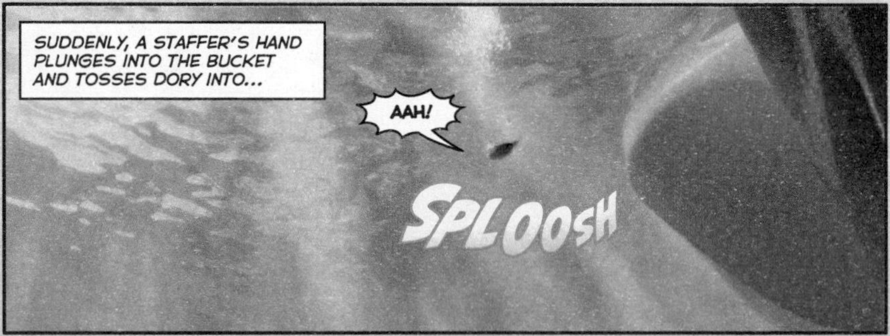
SUDDENLY, A STAFFER'S HAND PLUNGES INTO THE BUCKET AND TOSSES DORY INTO...
AAH!
SPLOOSH

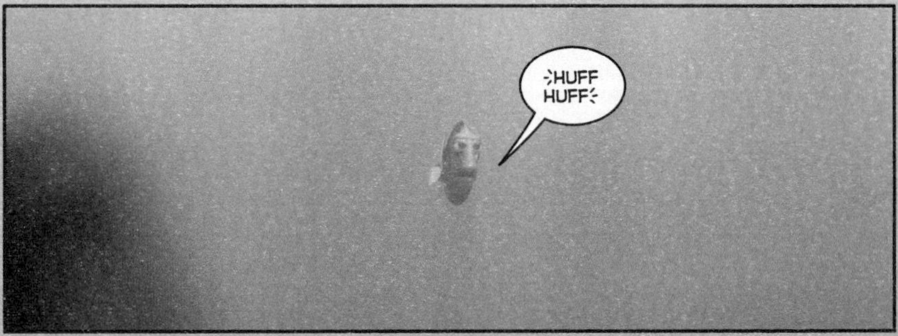
HUFF HUFF

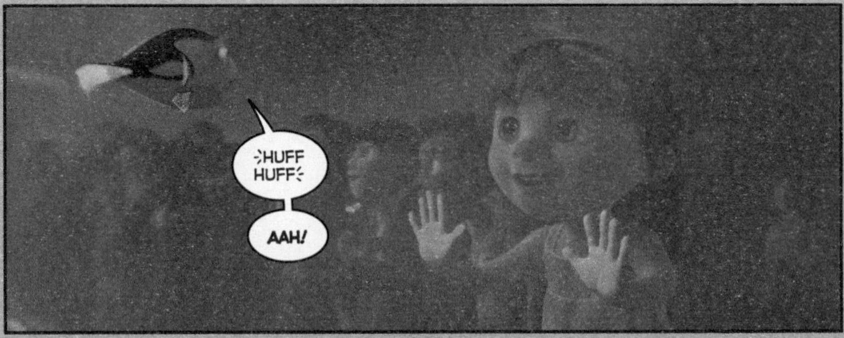
HUFF HUFF
AAH!

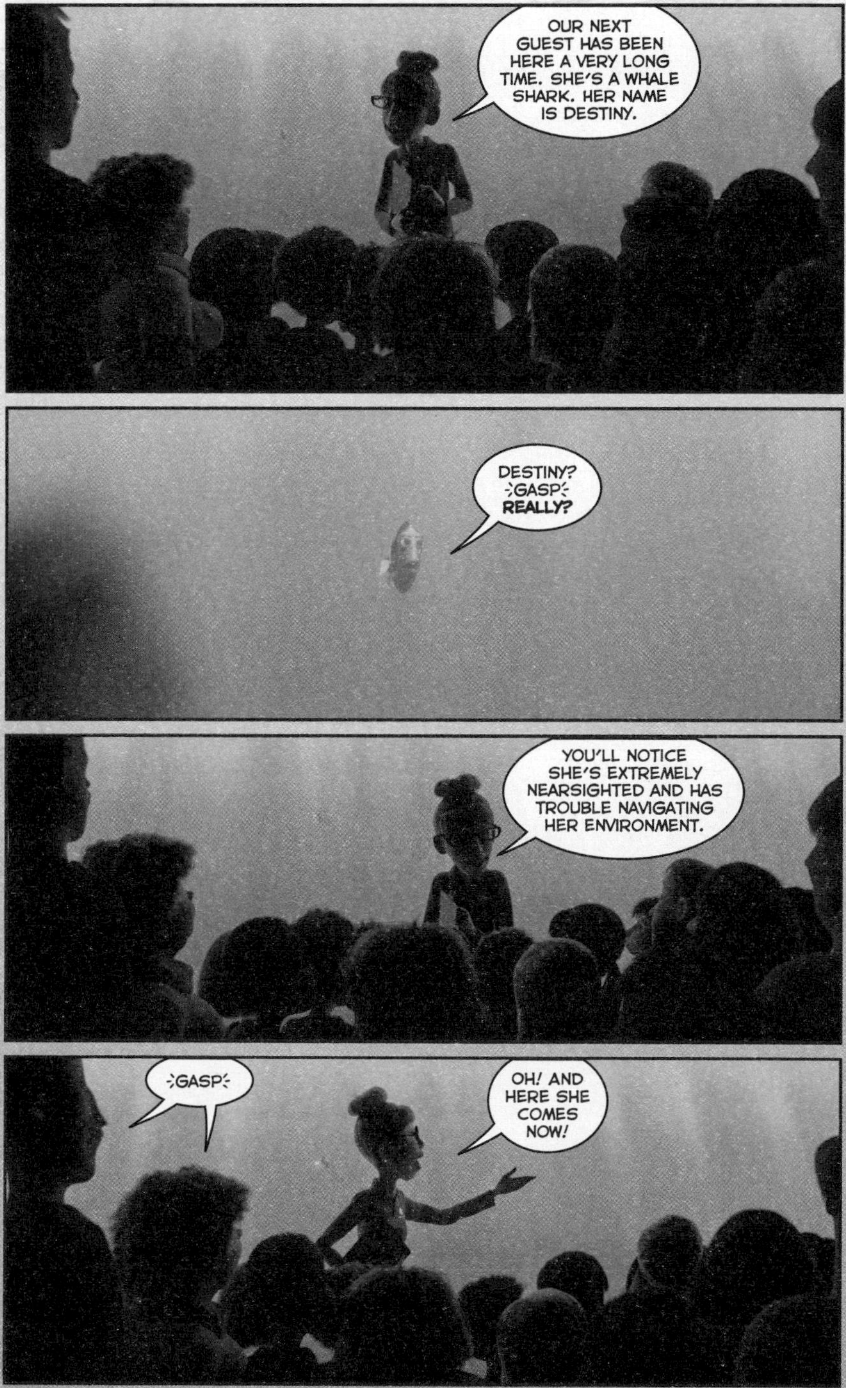

OUR NEXT GUEST HAS BEEN HERE A VERY LONG TIME. SHE'S A WHALE SHARK. HER NAME IS DESTINY.
DESTINY? *GASP* REALLY?
YOU'LL NOTICE SHE'S EXTREMELY NEARSIGHTED AND HAS TROUBLE NAVIGATING HER ENVIRONMENT.
GASP
OH! AND HERE SHE COMES NOW!

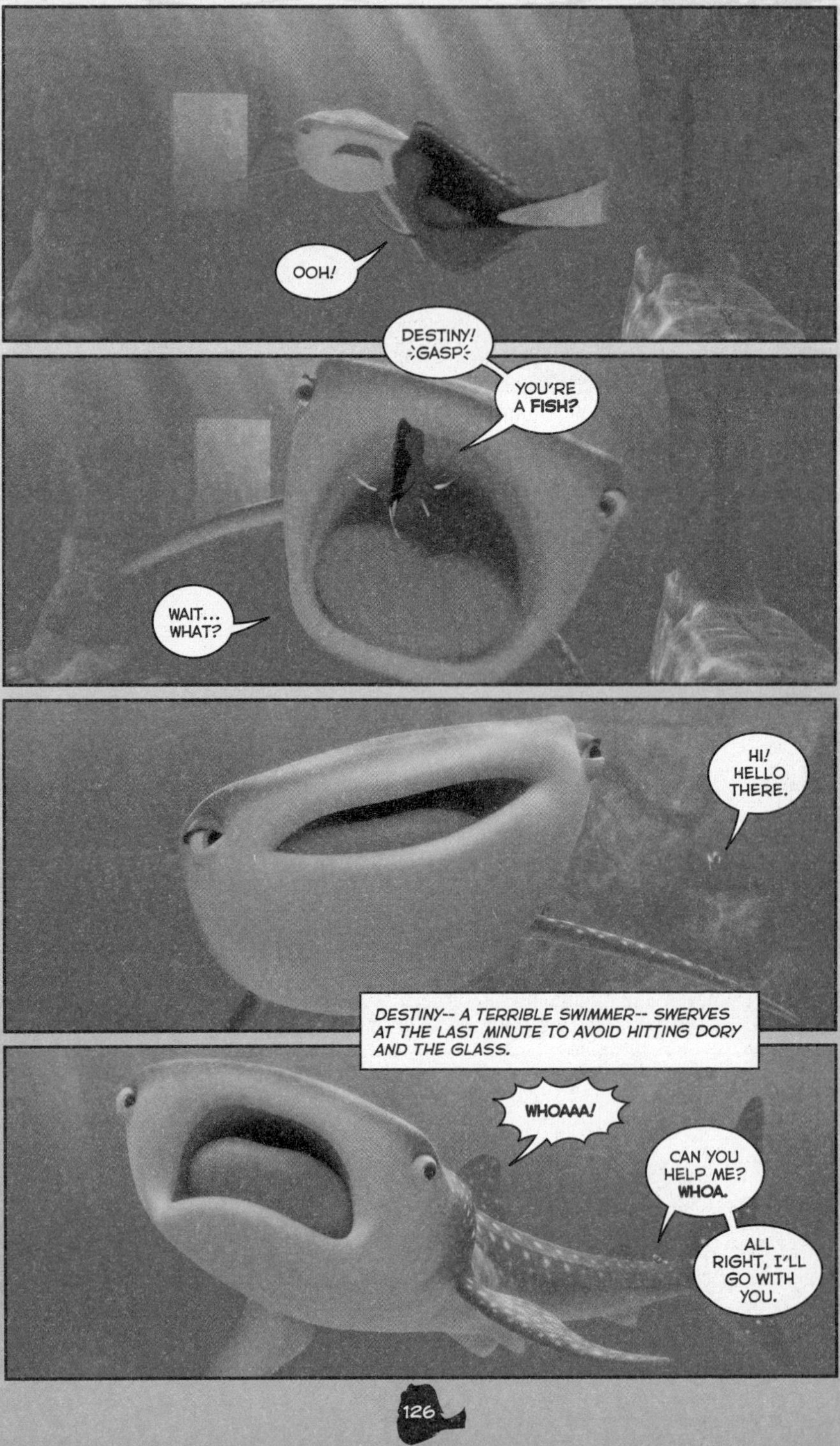
OOH!
DESTINY! -GASP-
YOU'RE A **FISH?**
WAIT... WHAT?
HI! HELLO THERE.
DESTINY-- A TERRIBLE SWIMMER-- SWERVES AT THE LAST MINUTE TO AVOID HITTING DORY AND THE GLASS.
WHOAAA!
CAN YOU HELP ME? **WHOA.**
ALL RIGHT, I'LL GO WITH YOU.

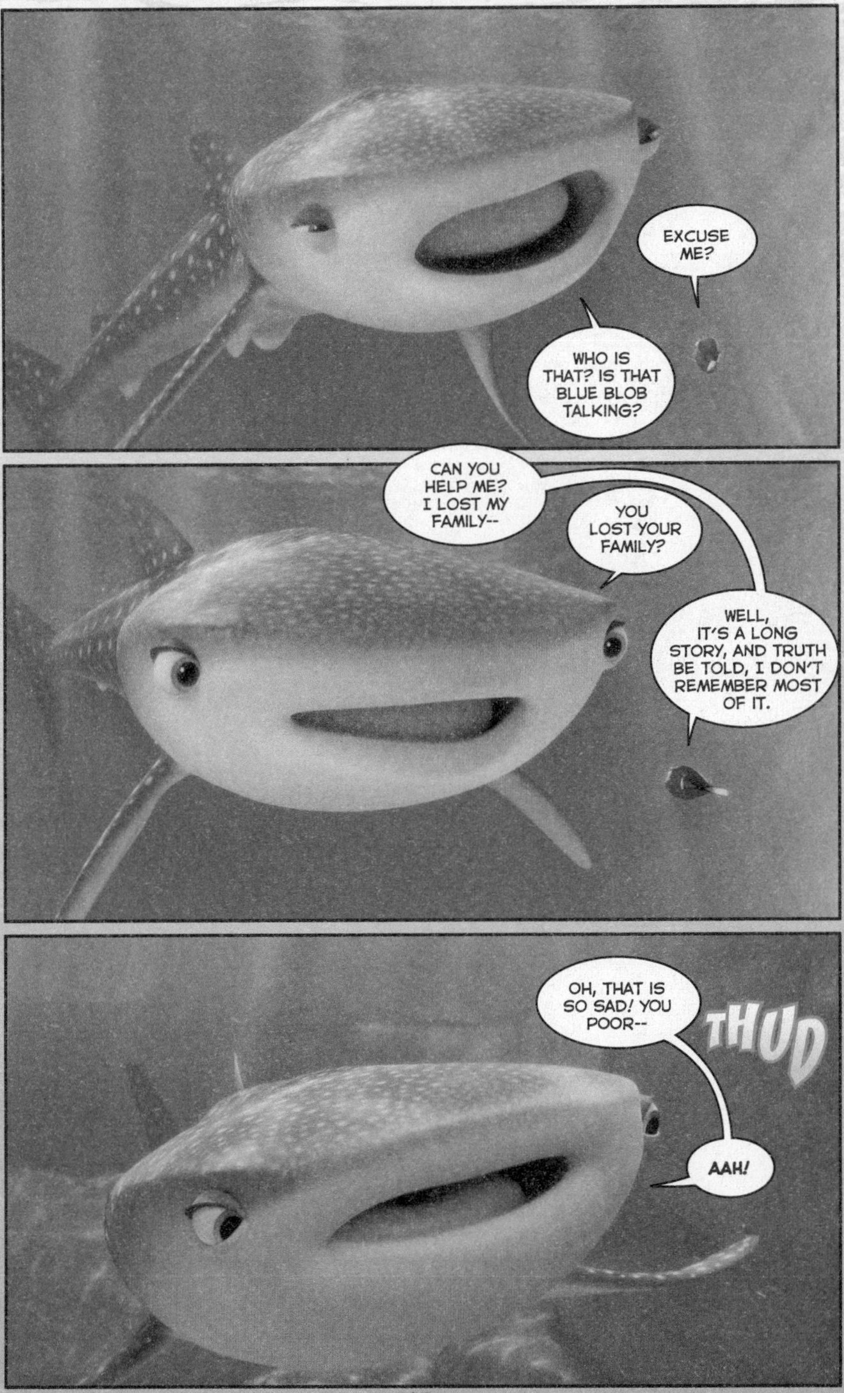
EXCUSE ME?
WHO IS THAT? IS THAT BLUE BLOB TALKING?
CAN YOU HELP ME? I LOST MY FAMILY--
YOU LOST YOUR FAMILY?
WELL, IT'S A LONG STORY, AND TRUTH BE TOLD, I DON'T REMEMBER MOST OF IT.
OH, THAT IS SO SAD! YOU POOR--
THUD
AAH!

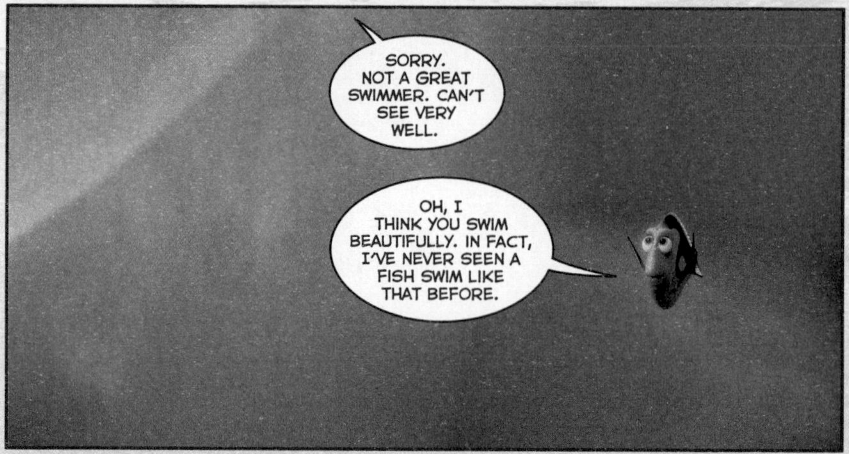
SORRY. NOT A GREAT SWIMMER. CAN'T SEE VERY WELL.
OH, I THINK YOU SWIM BEAUTIFULLY. IN FACT, I'VE NEVER SEEN A FISH SWIM LIKE THAT BEFORE.

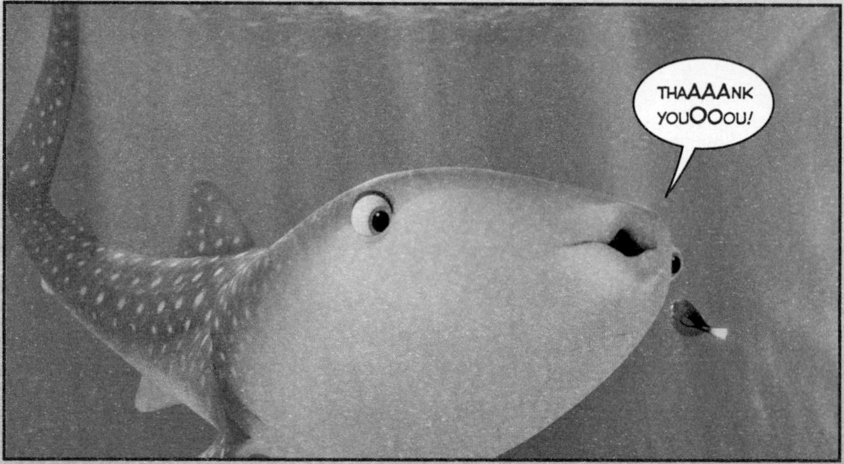
THAAAANK YOUOOou!

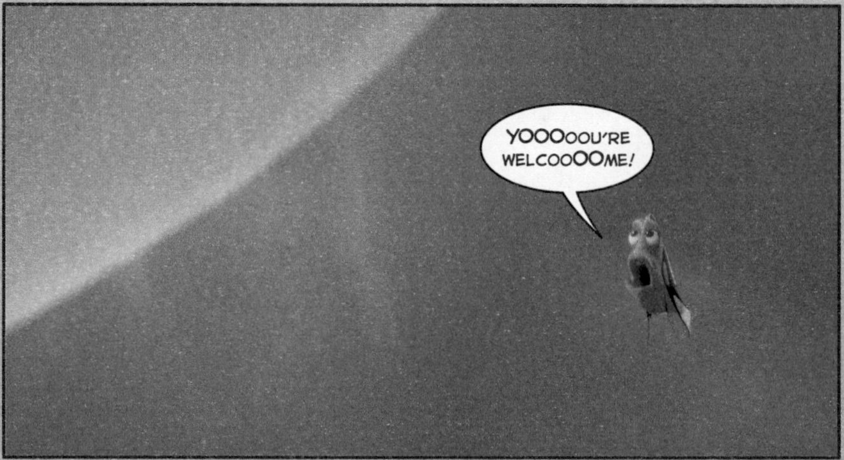
YOOOoou'RE WELCOOOOME!

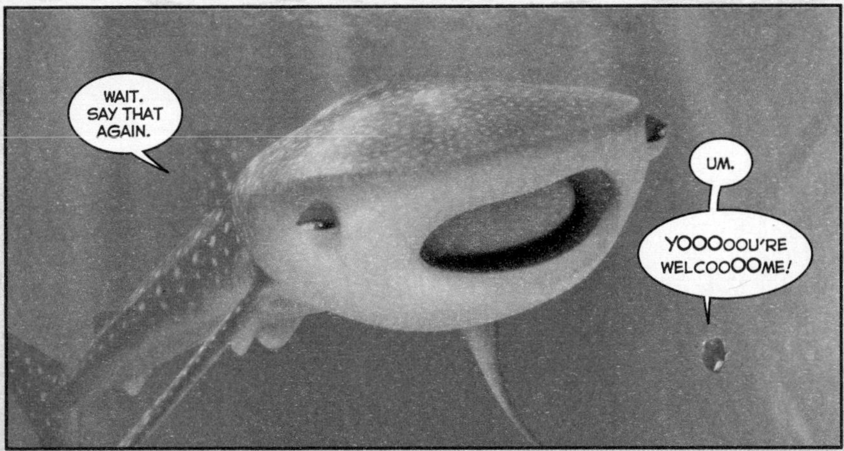
WAIT. SAY THAT AGAIN.
UM.
YOOOoou'RE WELCOoOOME!

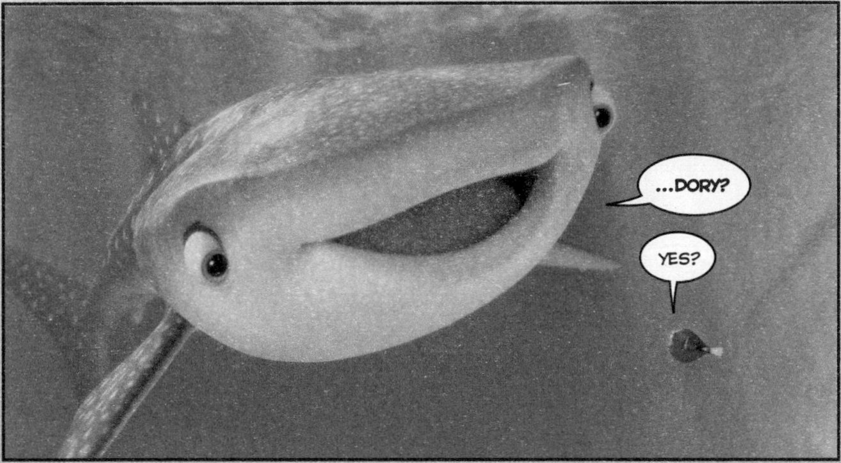
...DORY?
YES?

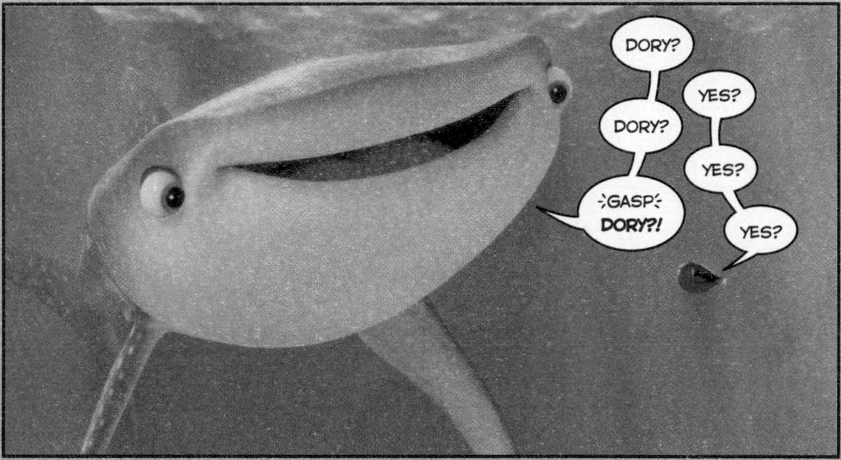
DORY?
YES?
DORY?
YES?
GASP DORY?!
YES?

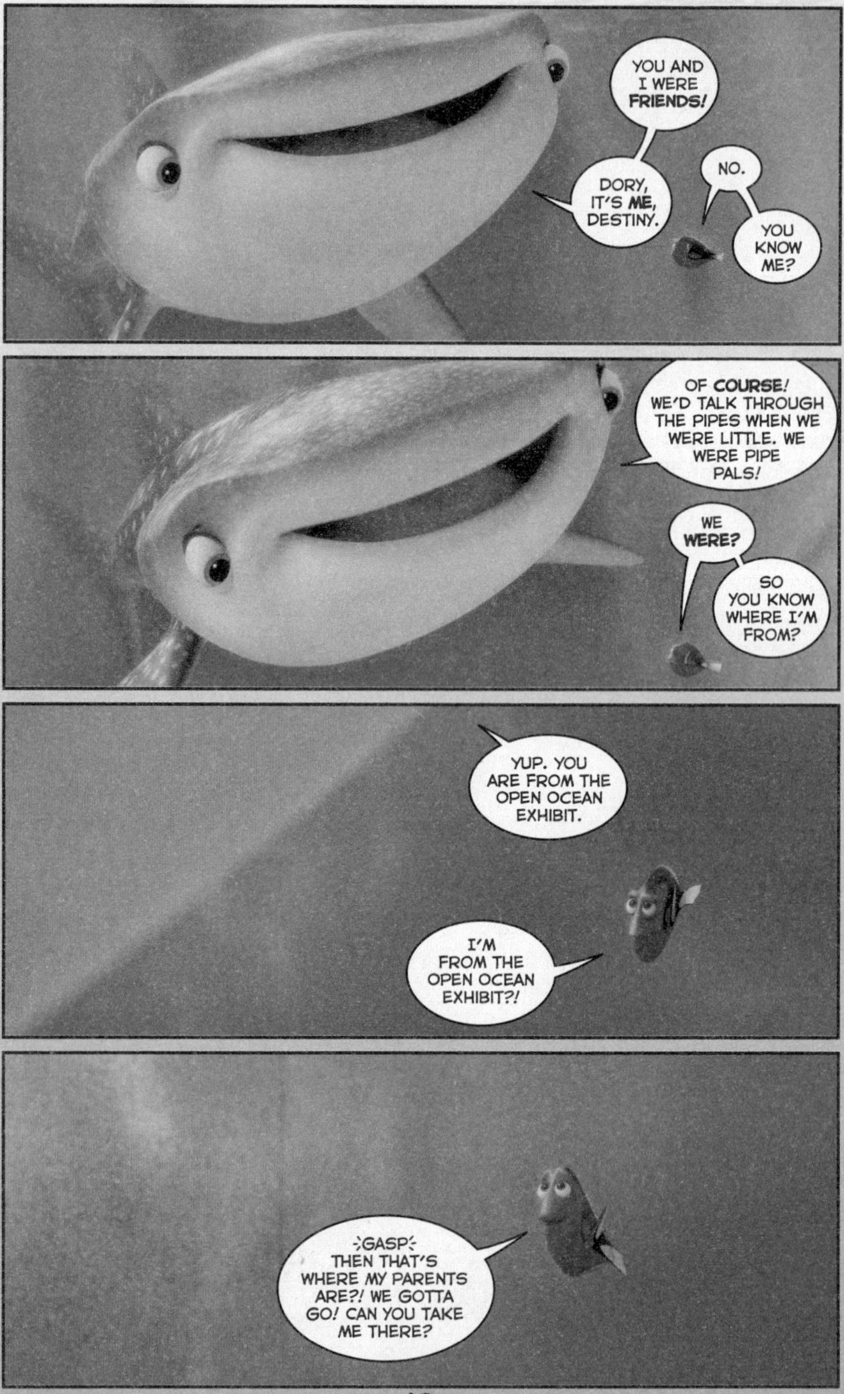
YOU AND I WERE FRIENDS!
DORY, IT'S ME, DESTINY.
NO.
YOU KNOW ME?
OF COURSE! WE'D TALK THROUGH THE PIPES WHEN WE WERE LITTLE. WE WERE PIPE PALS!
WE WERE?
SO YOU KNOW WHERE I'M FROM?
YUP. YOU ARE FROM THE OPEN OCEAN EXHIBIT.
I'M FROM THE OPEN OCEAN EXHIBIT?!
GASP
THEN THAT'S WHERE MY PARENTS ARE?! WE GOTTA GO! CAN YOU TAKE ME THERE?

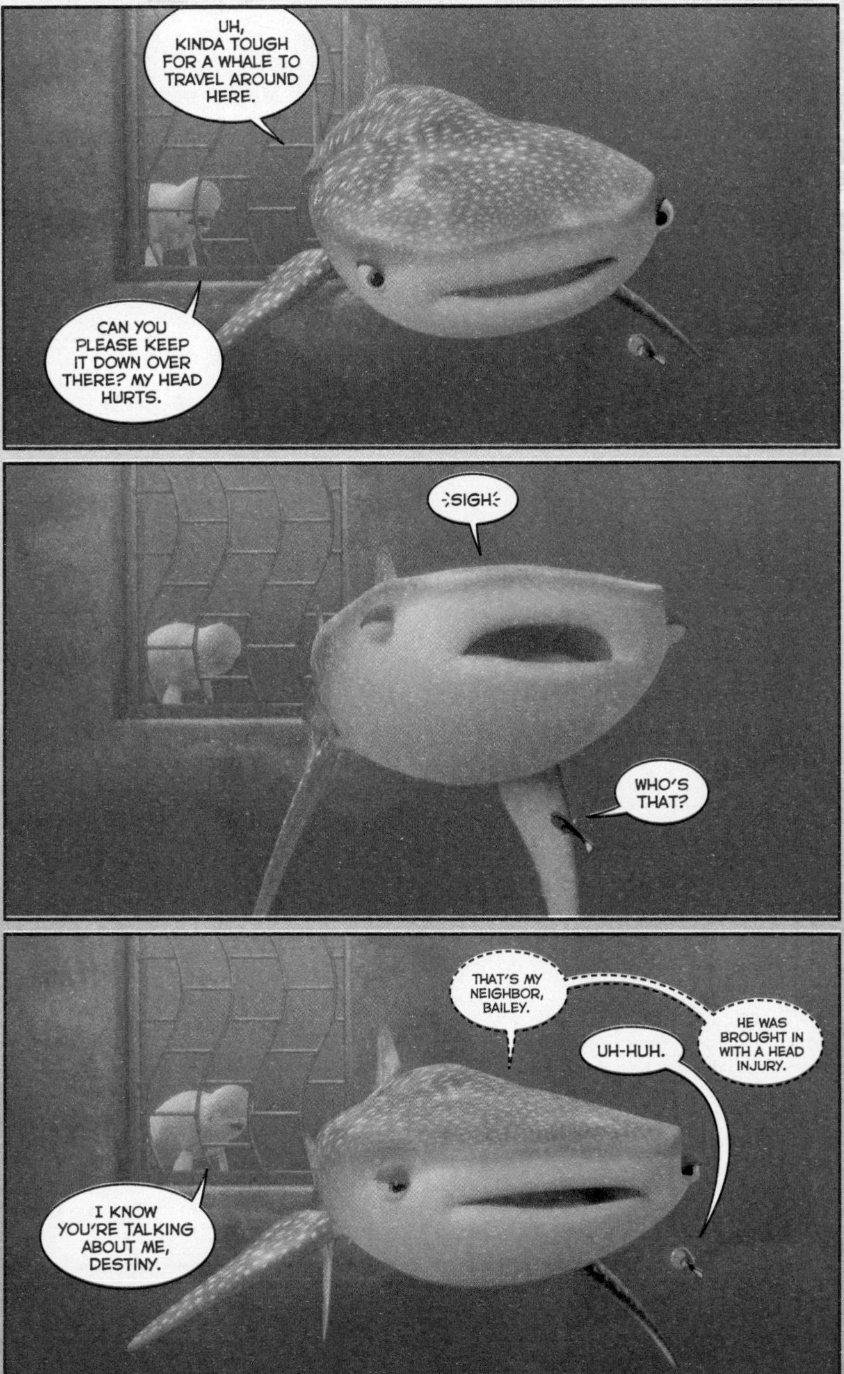
UH, KINDA TOUGH FOR A WHALE TO TRAVEL AROUND HERE.
CAN YOU PLEASE KEEP IT DOWN OVER THERE? MY HEAD HURTS.
-SIGH-
WHO'S THAT?
THAT'S MY NEIGHBOR, BAILEY.
HE WAS BROUGHT IN WITH A HEAD INJURY.
UH-HUH.
I KNOW YOU'RE TALKING ABOUT ME, DESTINY.

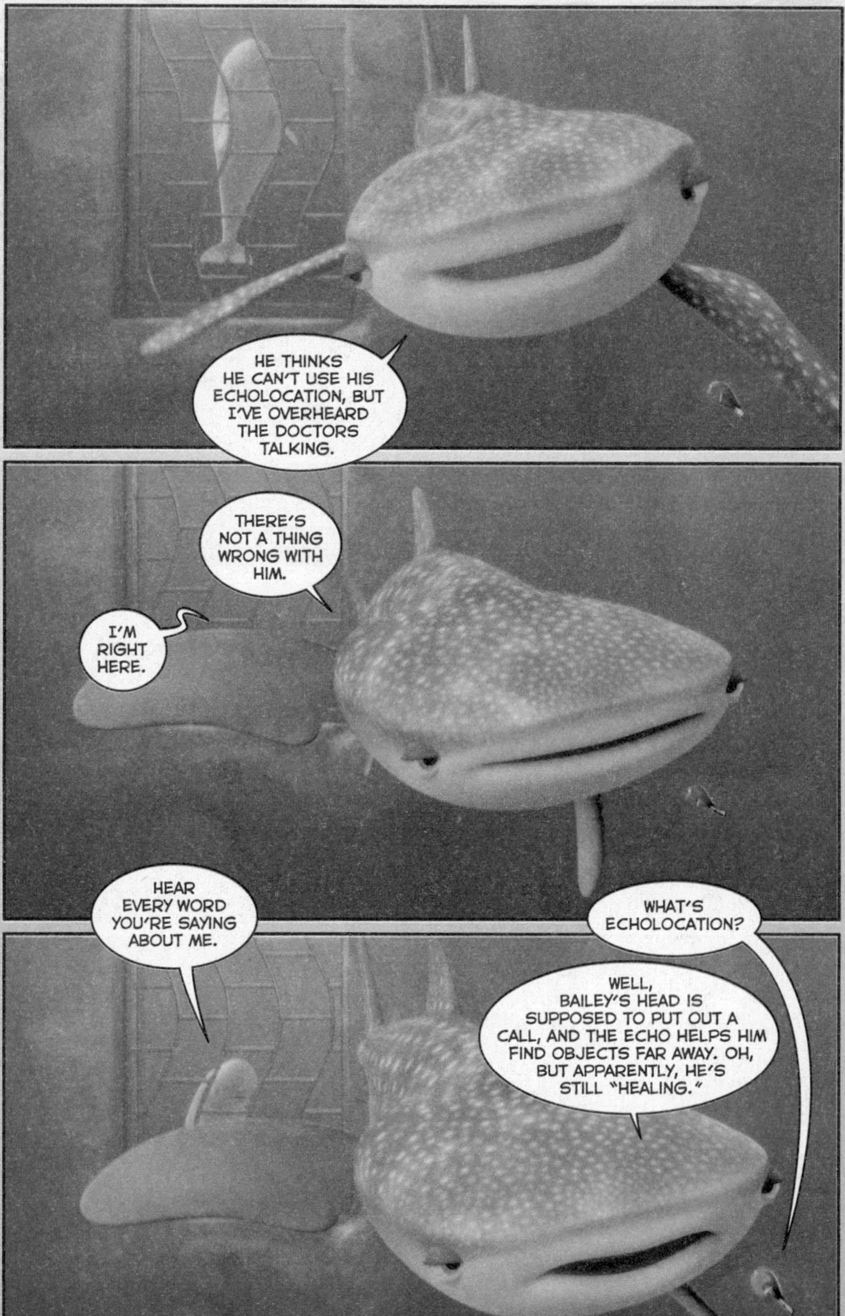
HE THINKS HE CAN'T USE HIS ECHOLOCATION, BUT I'VE OVERHEARD THE DOCTORS TALKING.
THERE'S NOT A THING WRONG WITH HIM.
I'M RIGHT HERE.
HEAR EVERY WORD YOU'RE SAYING ABOUT ME.
WHAT'S ECHOLOCATION?
WELL, BAILEY'S HEAD IS SUPPOSED TO PUT OUT A CALL, AND THE ECHO HELPS HIM FIND OBJECTS FAR AWAY. OH, BUT APPARENTLY, HE'S STILL "HEALING."

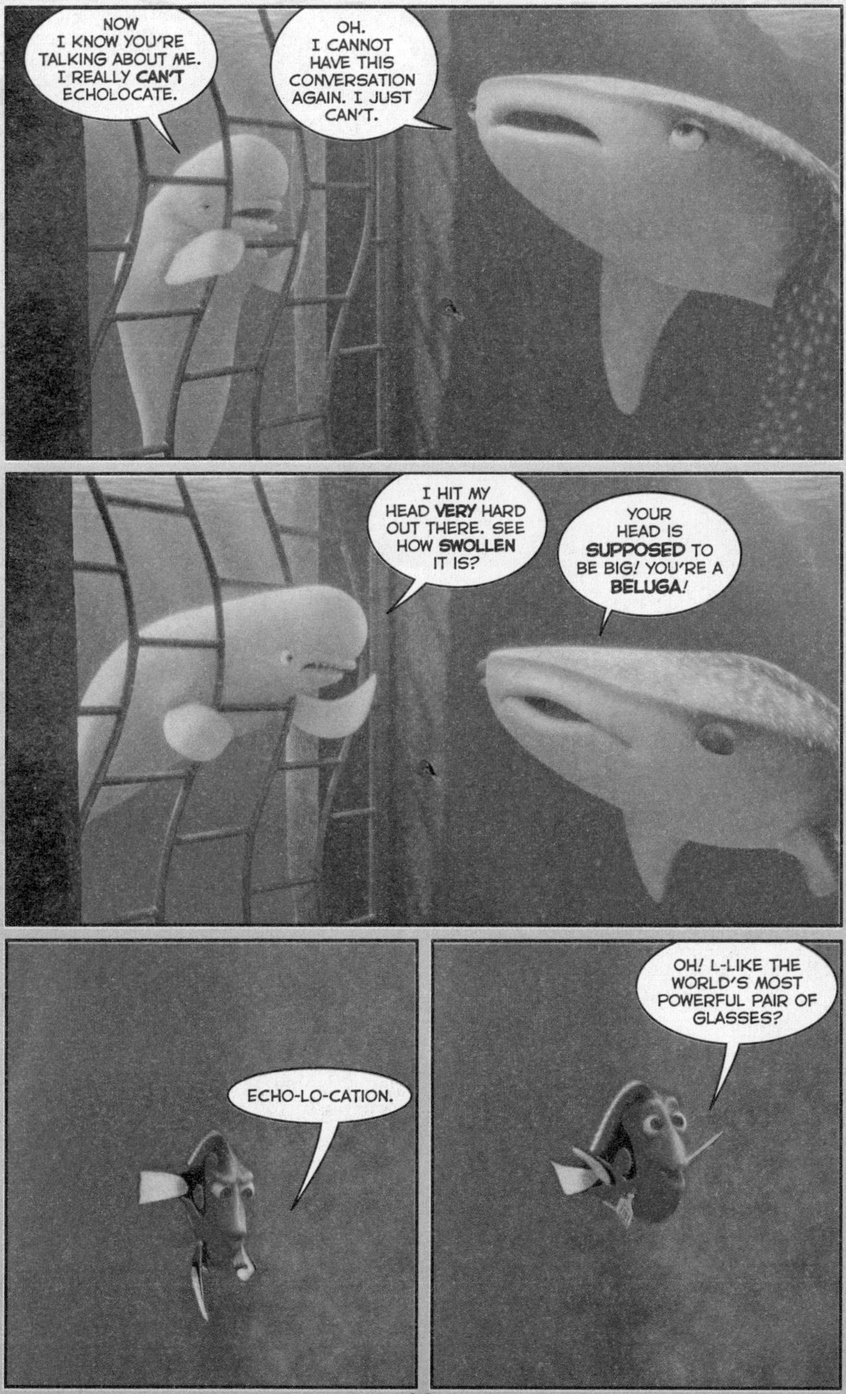
NOW I KNOW YOU'RE TALKING ABOUT ME. I REALLY **CAN'T** ECHOLOCATE.
OH. I CANNOT HAVE THIS CONVERSATION AGAIN. I JUST CAN'T.
I HIT MY HEAD **VERY** HARD OUT THERE. SEE HOW **SWOLLEN** IT IS?
YOUR HEAD IS **SUPPOSED** TO BE BIG! YOU'RE A **BELUGA**!
ECHO-LO-CATION.
OH! L-LIKE THE WORLD'S MOST POWERFUL PAIR OF GLASSES?

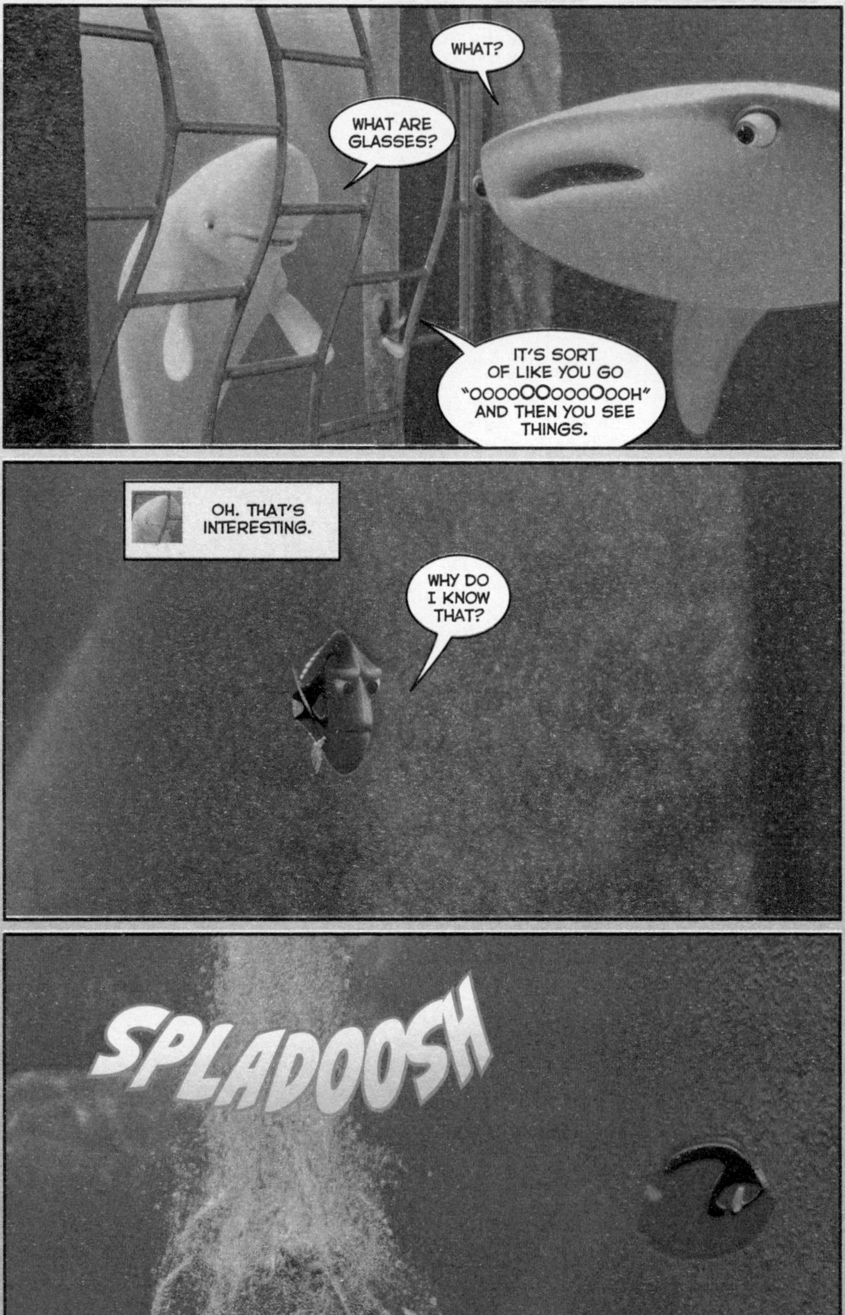

WHAT?
WHAT ARE GLASSES?
IT'S SORT OF LIKE YOU GO "OOOOOOOOOOOOH" AND THEN YOU SEE THINGS.
OH. THAT'S INTERESTING.
WHY DO I KNOW THAT?
SPLADOOSH

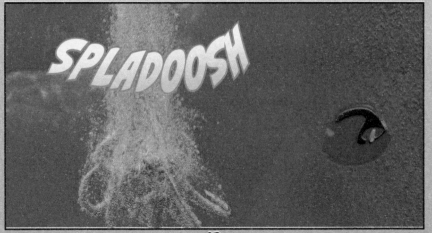

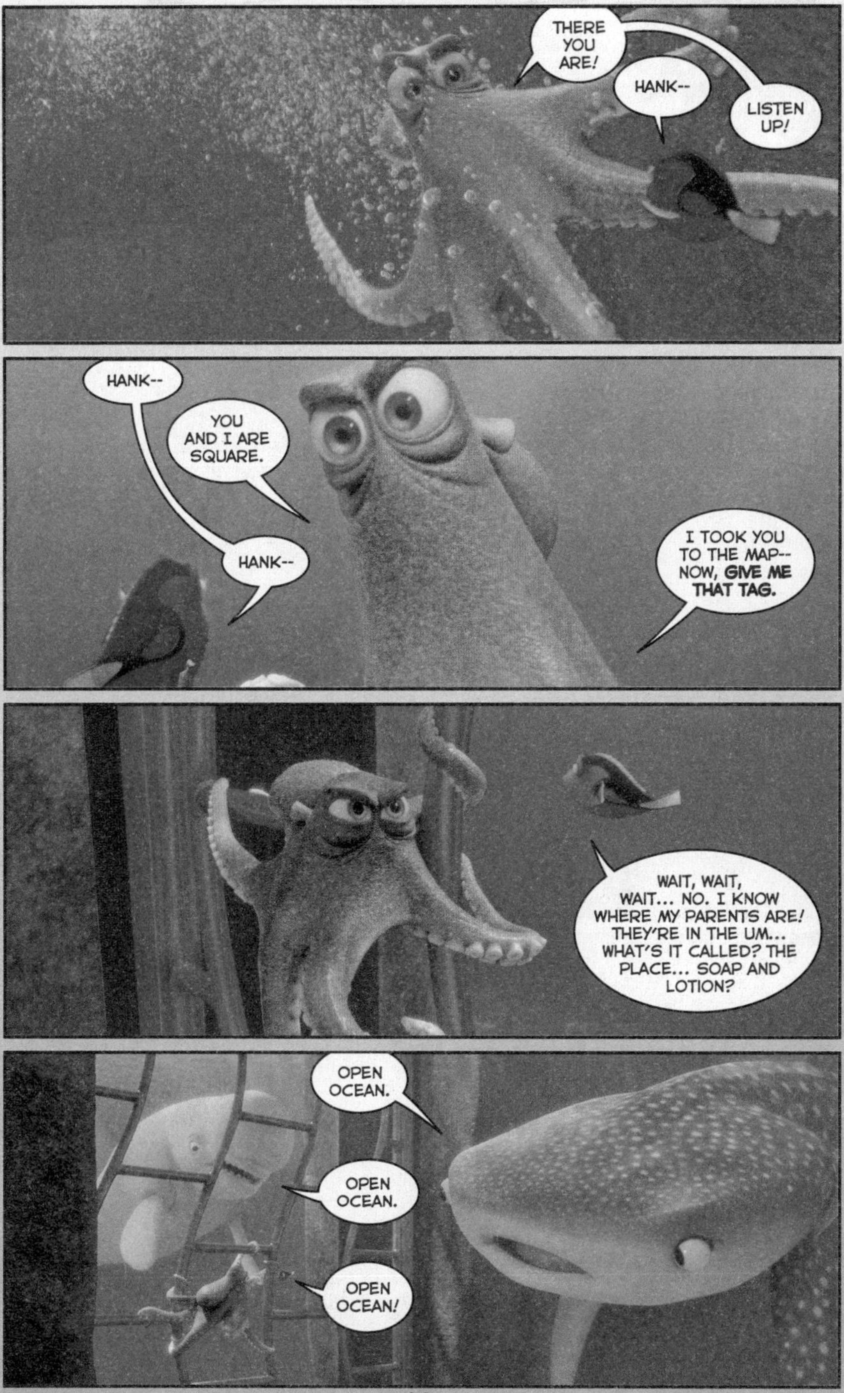
THERE YOU ARE!
HANK--
LISTEN UP!
HANK--
YOU AND I ARE SQUARE.
HANK--
I TOOK YOU TO THE MAP-- NOW, GIVE ME THAT TAG.
WAIT, WAIT, WAIT... NO. I KNOW WHERE MY PARENTS ARE! THEY'RE IN THE UM... WHAT'S IT CALLED? THE PLACE... SOAP AND LOTION?
OPEN OCEAN.
OPEN OCEAN.
OPEN OCEAN!

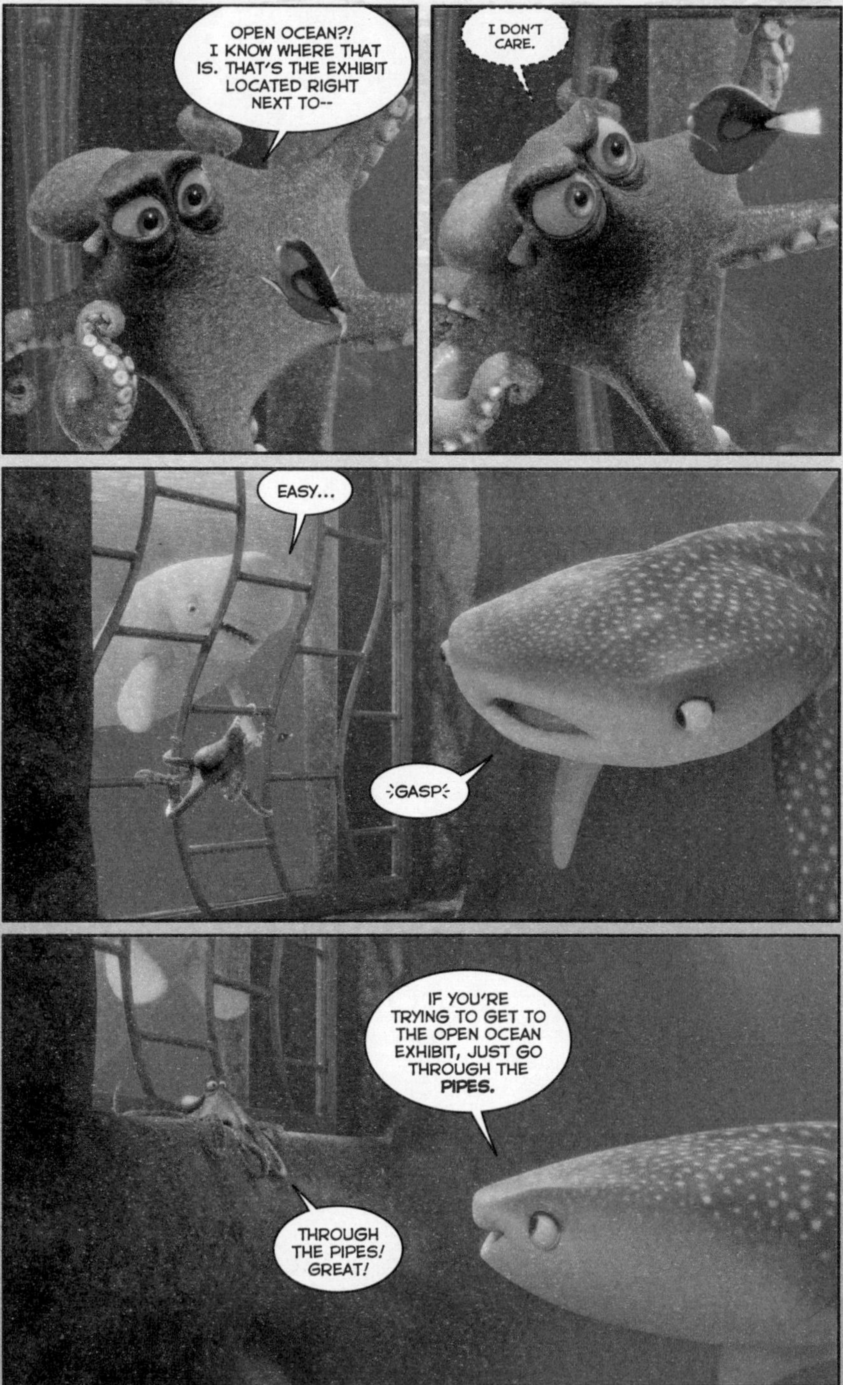
OPEN OCEAN?! I KNOW WHERE THAT IS. THAT'S THE EXHIBIT LOCATED RIGHT NEXT TO--
I DON'T CARE.
EASY...
GASP
IF YOU'RE TRYING TO GET TO THE OPEN OCEAN EXHIBIT, JUST GO THROUGH THE **PIPES.**
THROUGH THE PIPES! GREAT!

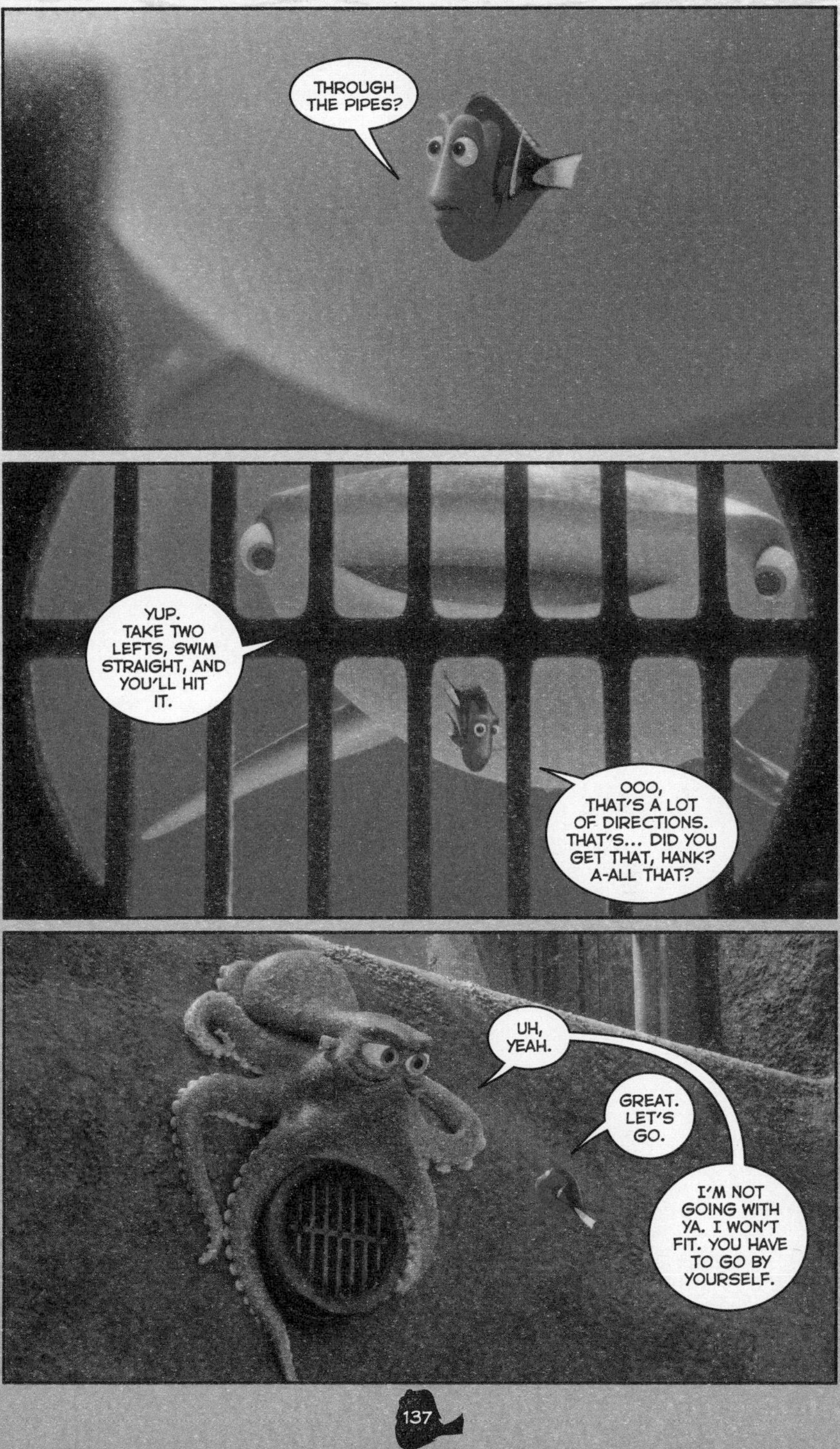
THROUGH THE PIPES?
YUP. TAKE TWO LEFTS, SWIM STRAIGHT, AND YOU'LL HIT IT.
OOO, THAT'S A LOT OF DIRECTIONS. THAT'S... DID YOU GET THAT, HANK? A-ALL THAT?
UH, YEAH.
GREAT. LET'S GO.
I'M NOT GOING WITH YA. I WON'T FIT. YOU HAVE TO GO BY YOURSELF.

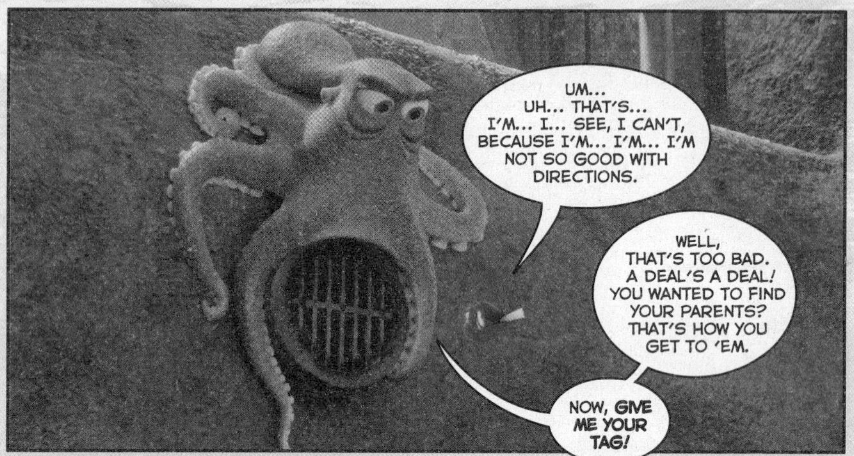
UM... UH... THAT'S... I'M... I... SEE, I CAN'T, BECAUSE I'M... I'M... I'M NOT SO GOOD WITH DIRECTIONS.
WELL, THAT'S TOO BAD. A DEAL'S A DEAL! YOU WANTED TO FIND YOUR PARENTS? THAT'S HOW YOU GET TO 'EM.
NOW, GIVE ME YOUR TAG!

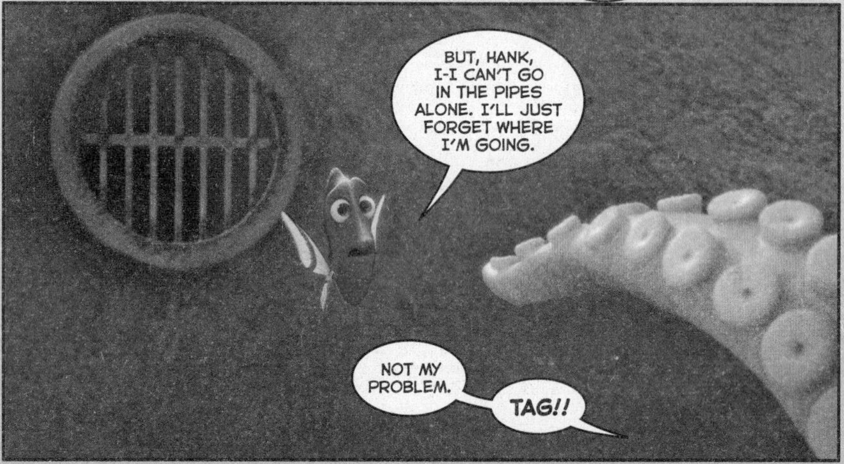
BUT, HANK, I-I CAN'T GO IN THE PIPES ALONE. I'LL JUST FORGET WHERE I'M GOING.
NOT MY PROBLEM.
TAG!!

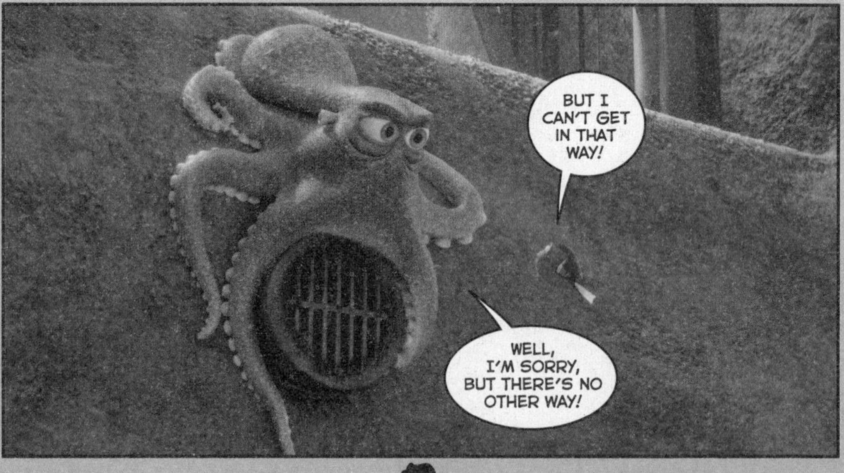
BUT I CAN'T GET IN THAT WAY!
WELL, I'M SORRY, BUT THERE'S NO OTHER WAY!

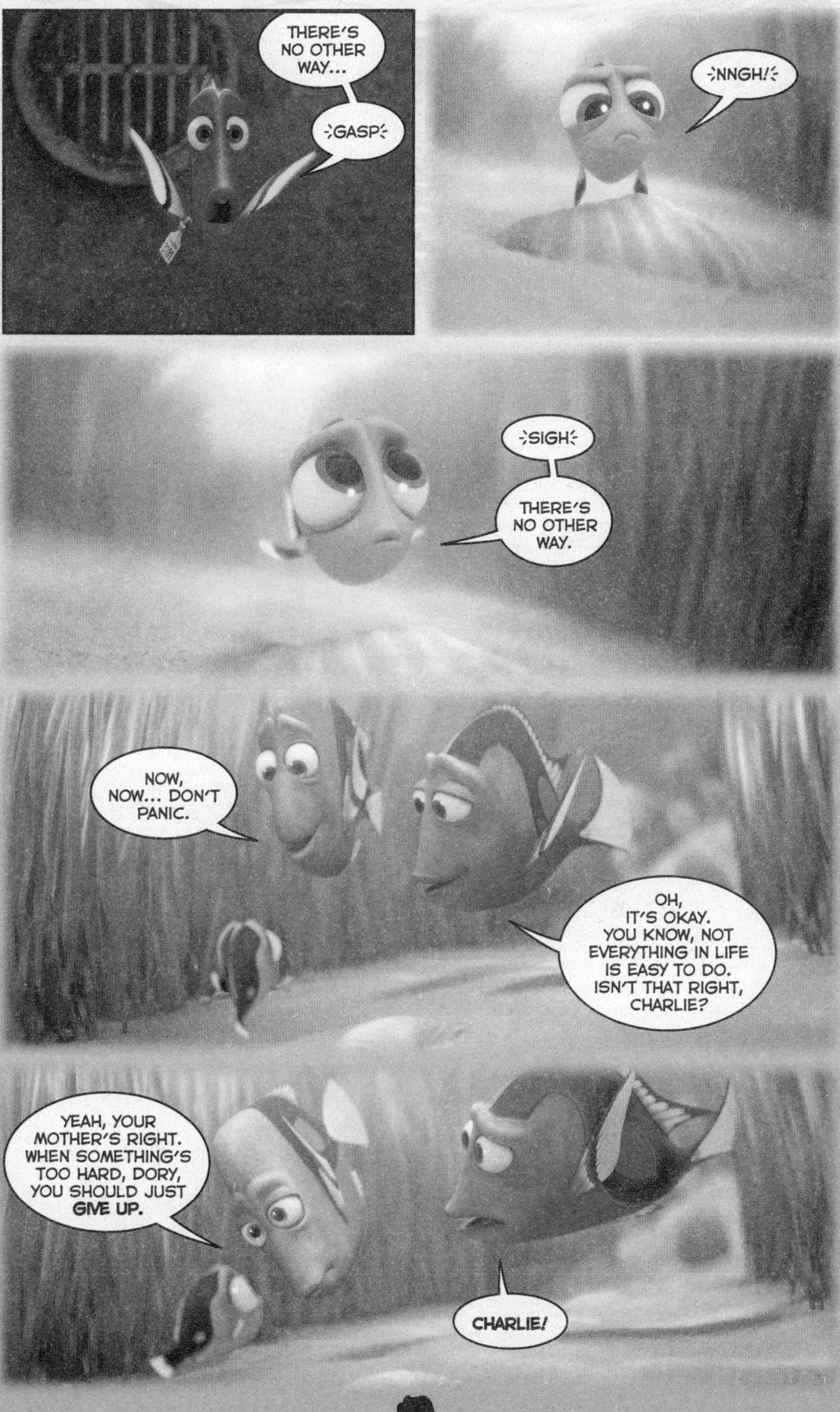
THERE'S NO OTHER WAY...
-GASP-
-NNGH!-
-SIGH-
THERE'S NO OTHER WAY.
NOW, NOW... DON'T PANIC.
OH, IT'S OKAY. YOU KNOW, NOT EVERYTHING IN LIFE IS EASY TO DO. ISN'T THAT RIGHT, CHARLIE?
YEAH, YOUR MOTHER'S RIGHT. WHEN SOMETHING'S TOO HARD, DORY, YOU SHOULD JUST **GIVE UP.**
CHARLIE!

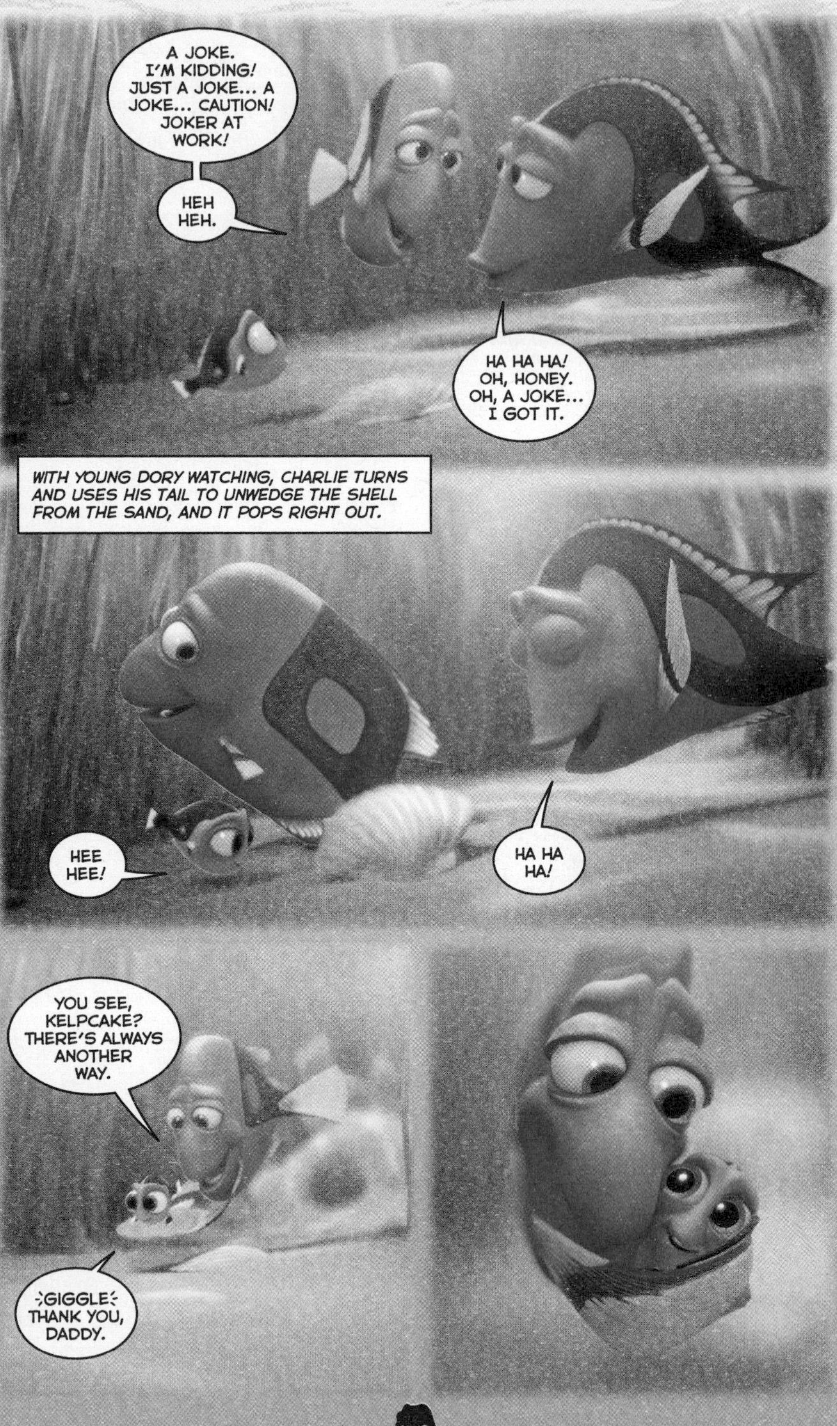
A JOKE. I'M KIDDING! JUST A JOKE... A JOKE... CAUTION! JOKER AT WORK!
HEH HEH.
HA HA HA! OH, HONEY. OH, A JOKE... I GOT IT.
WITH YOUNG DORY WATCHING, CHARLIE TURNS AND USES HIS TAIL TO UNWEDGE THE SHELL FROM THE SAND, AND IT POPS RIGHT OUT.
HEE HEE!
HA HA HA!
YOU SEE, KELPCAKE? THERE'S ALWAYS ANOTHER WAY.
GIGGLE THANK YOU, DADDY.

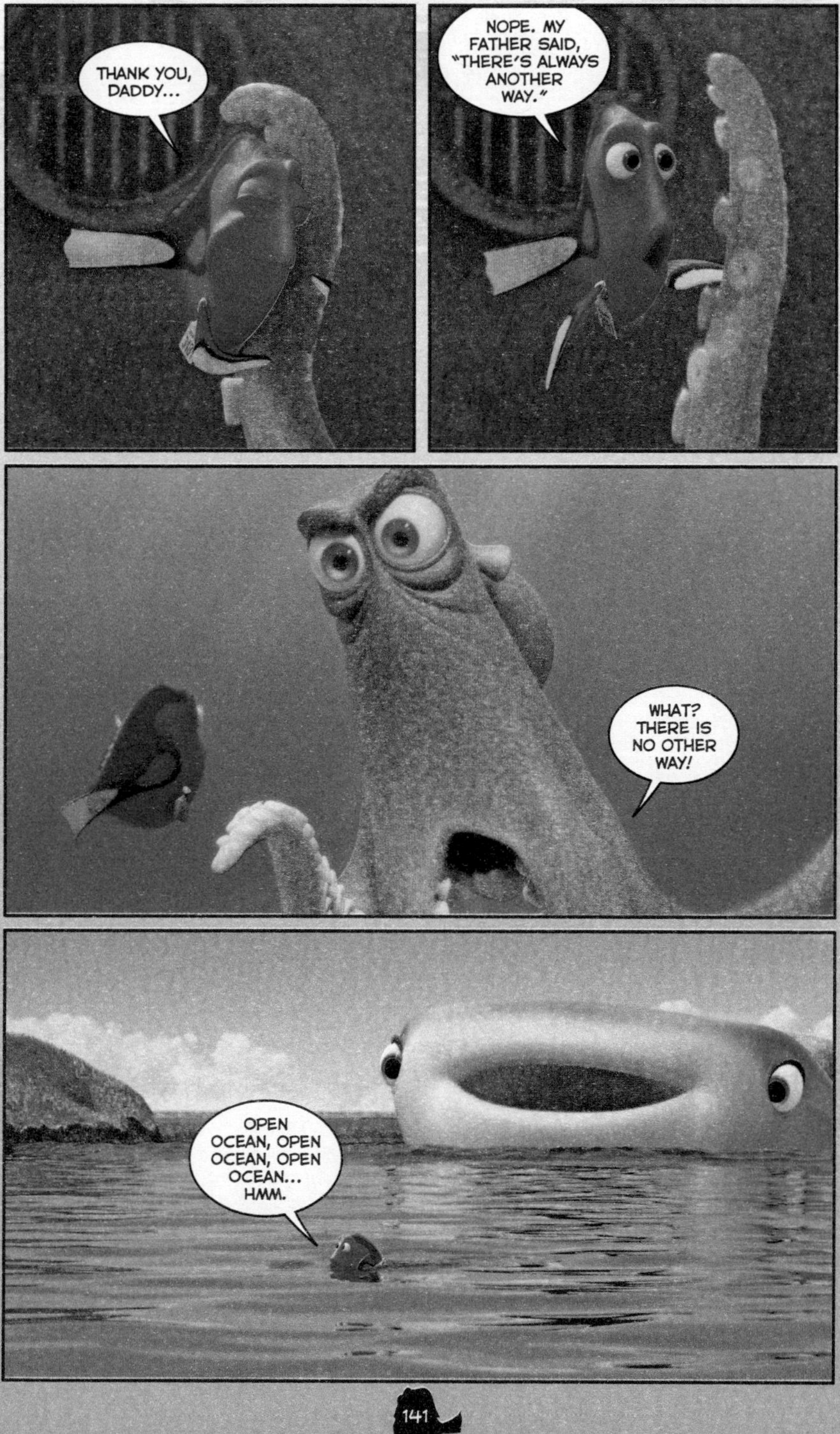
THANK YOU, DADDY...
NOPE. MY FATHER SAID, "THERE'S ALWAYS ANOTHER WAY."
WHAT? THERE IS NO OTHER WAY!
OPEN OCEAN, OPEN OCEAN, OPEN OCEAN... HMM.

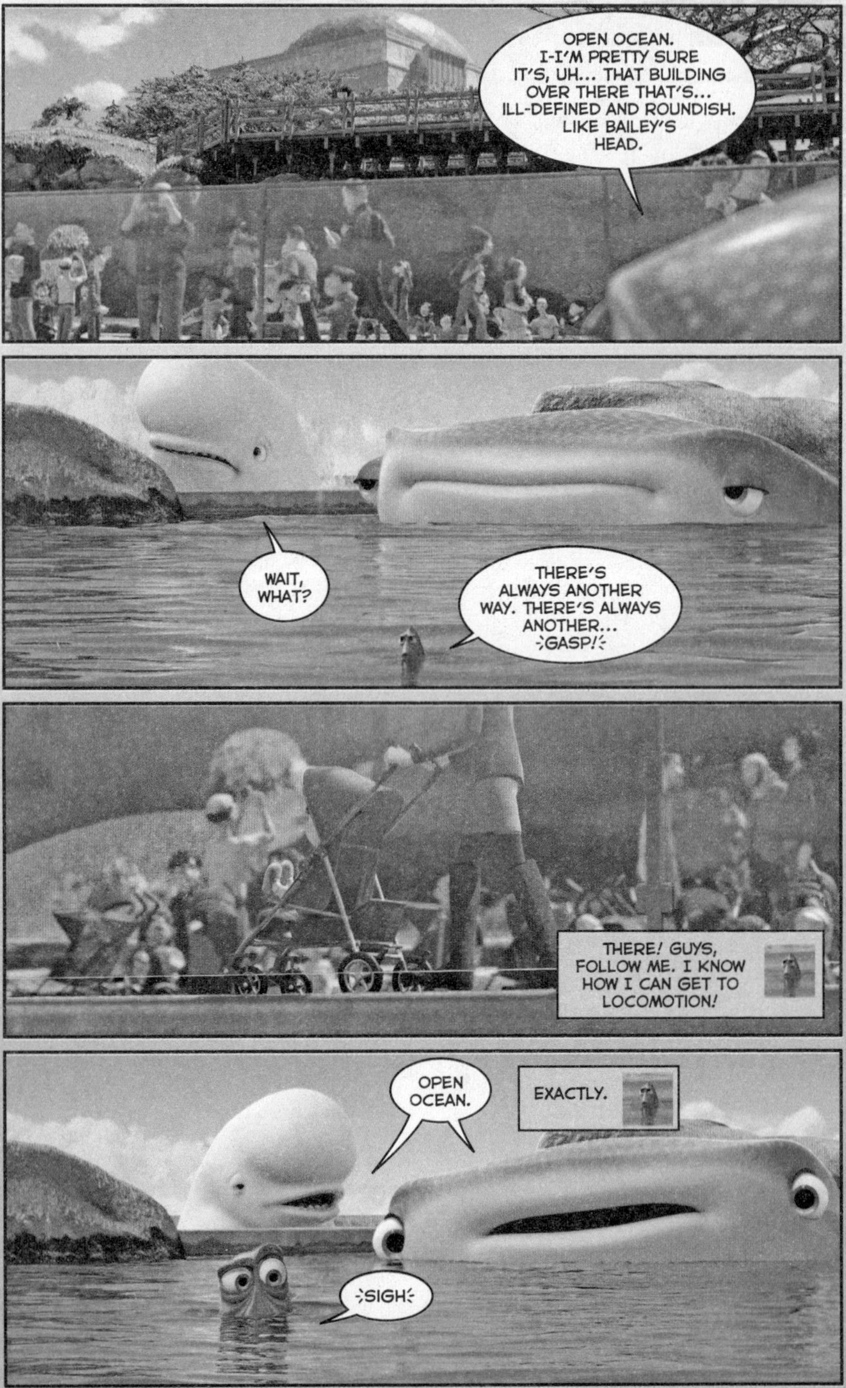

OPEN OCEAN. I-I'M PRETTY SURE IT'S, UH... THAT BUILDING OVER THERE THAT'S... ILL-DEFINED AND ROUNDISH. LIKE BAILEY'S HEAD.
WAIT, WHAT?
THERE'S ALWAYS ANOTHER WAY. THERE'S ALWAYS ANOTHER... GASP!
THERE! GUYS, FOLLOW ME. I KNOW HOW I CAN GET TO LOCOMOTION!
OPEN OCEAN.
EXACTLY.
SIGH

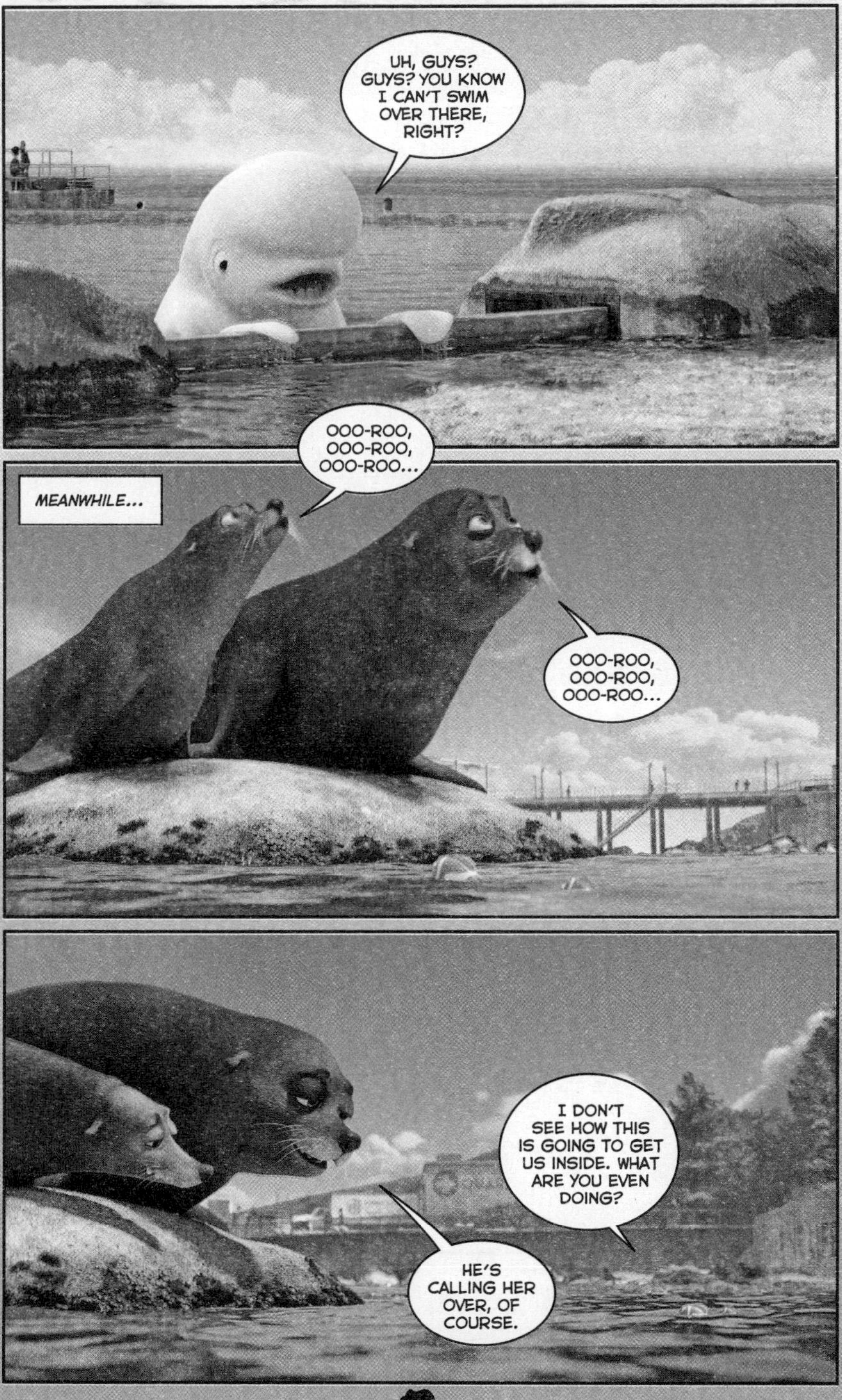
UH, GUYS? GUYS? YOU KNOW I CAN'T SWIM OVER THERE, RIGHT?
MEANWHILE...
OOO-ROO, OOO-ROO, OOO-ROO...
OOO-ROO, OOO-ROO, OOO-ROO...
I DON'T SEE HOW THIS IS GOING TO GET US INSIDE. WHAT ARE YOU EVEN DOING?
HE'S CALLING HER OVER, OF COURSE.

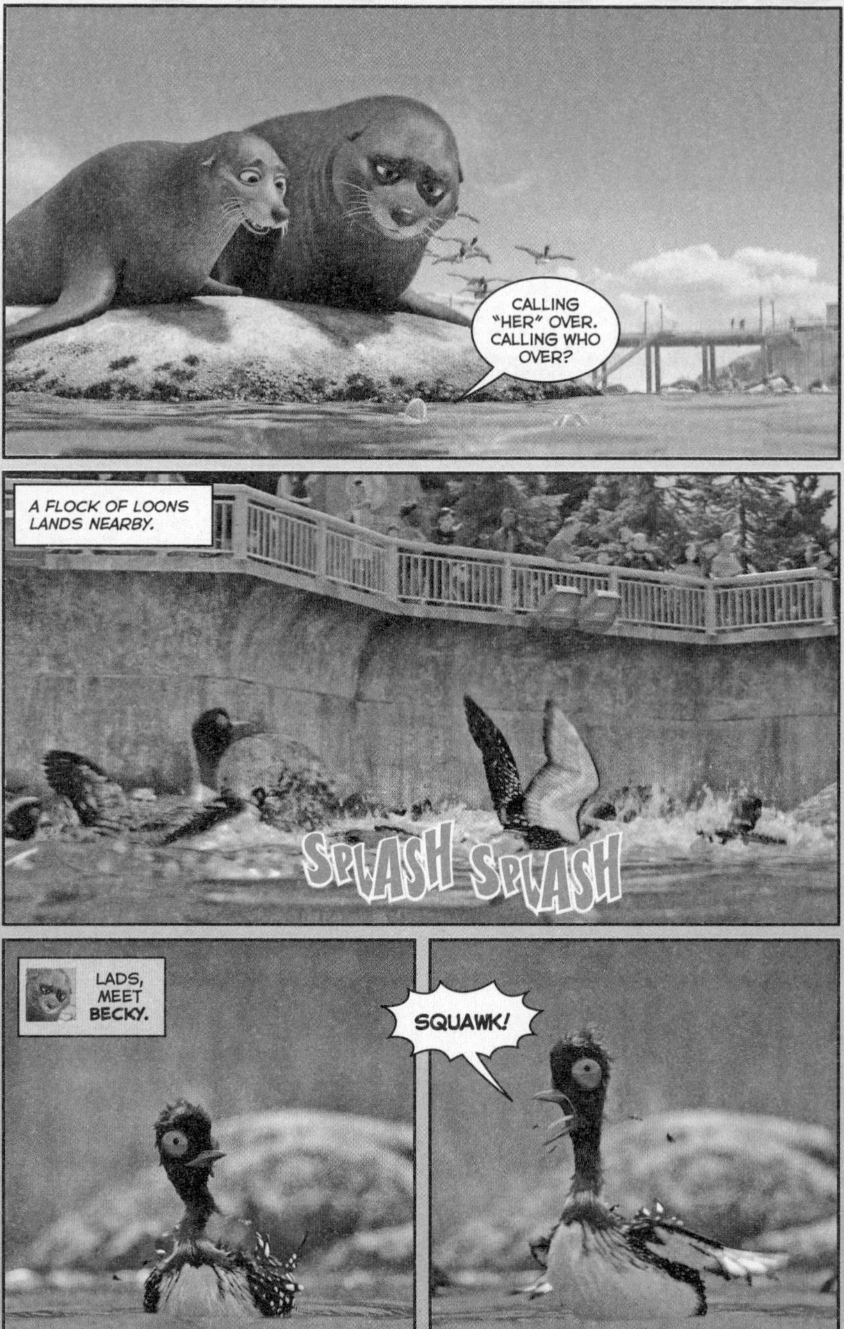
CALLING "HER" OVER. CALLING WHO OVER?
A FLOCK OF LOONS LANDS NEARBY.
SPLASH SPLASH
LADS, MEET BECKY.
SQUAWK!

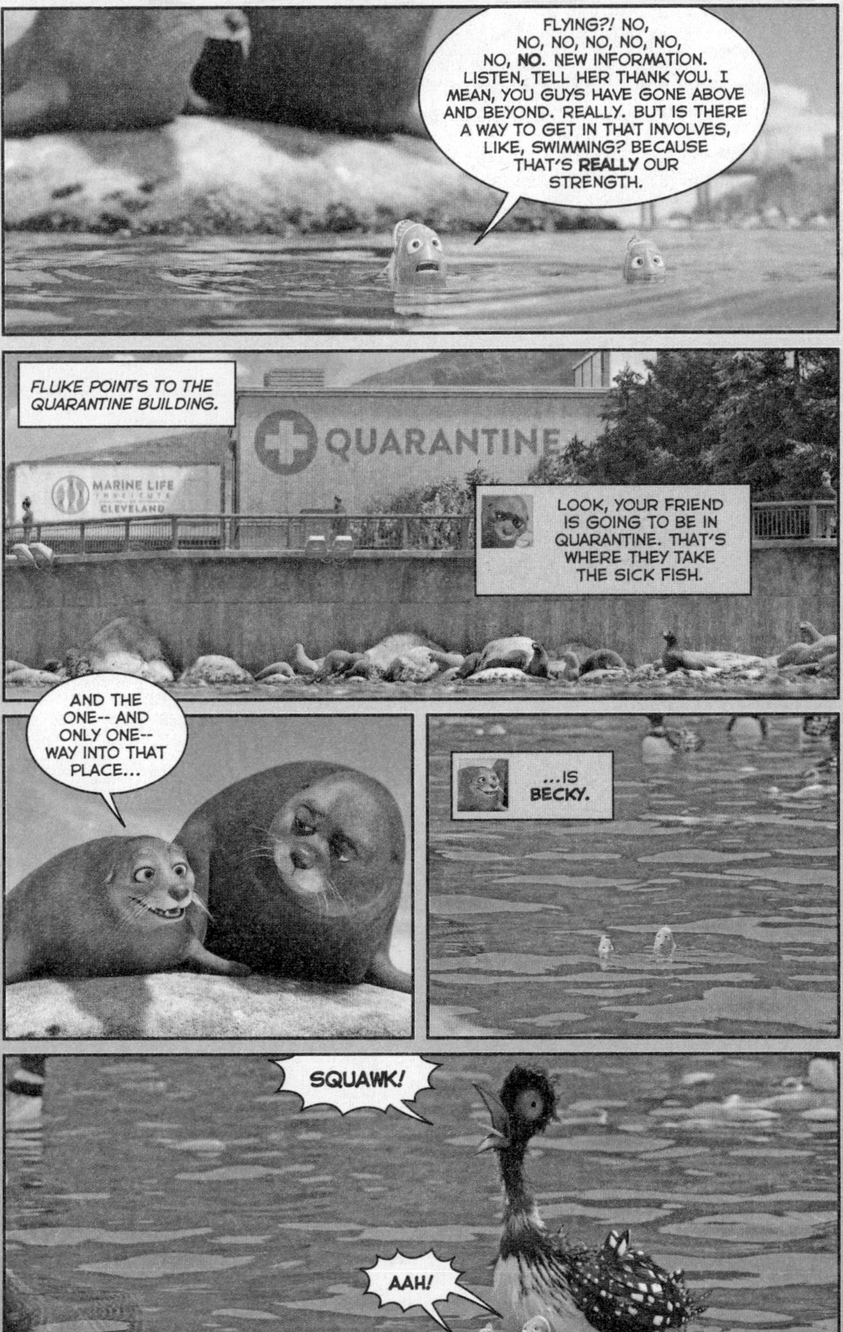
FLYING?! NO, NO, NO, NO, NO, NO, NO, **NO**. NEW INFORMATION. LISTEN, TELL HER THANK YOU. I MEAN, YOU GUYS HAVE GONE ABOVE AND BEYOND. REALLY. BUT IS THERE A WAY TO GET IN THAT INVOLVES, LIKE, SWIMMING? BECAUSE THAT'S **REALLY** OUR STRENGTH.
FLUKE POINTS TO THE QUARANTINE BUILDING.
QUARANTINE
MARINE LIFE INSTITUTE CLEVELAND
LOOK, YOUR FRIEND IS GOING TO BE IN QUARANTINE. THAT'S WHERE THEY TAKE THE SICK FISH.
AND THE ONE-- AND ONLY ONE-- WAY INTO THAT PLACE...
...IS **BECKY.**
SQUAWK!
AAH!

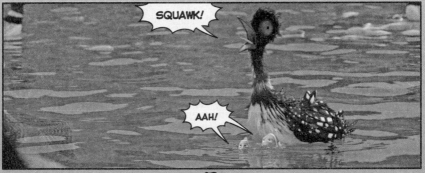

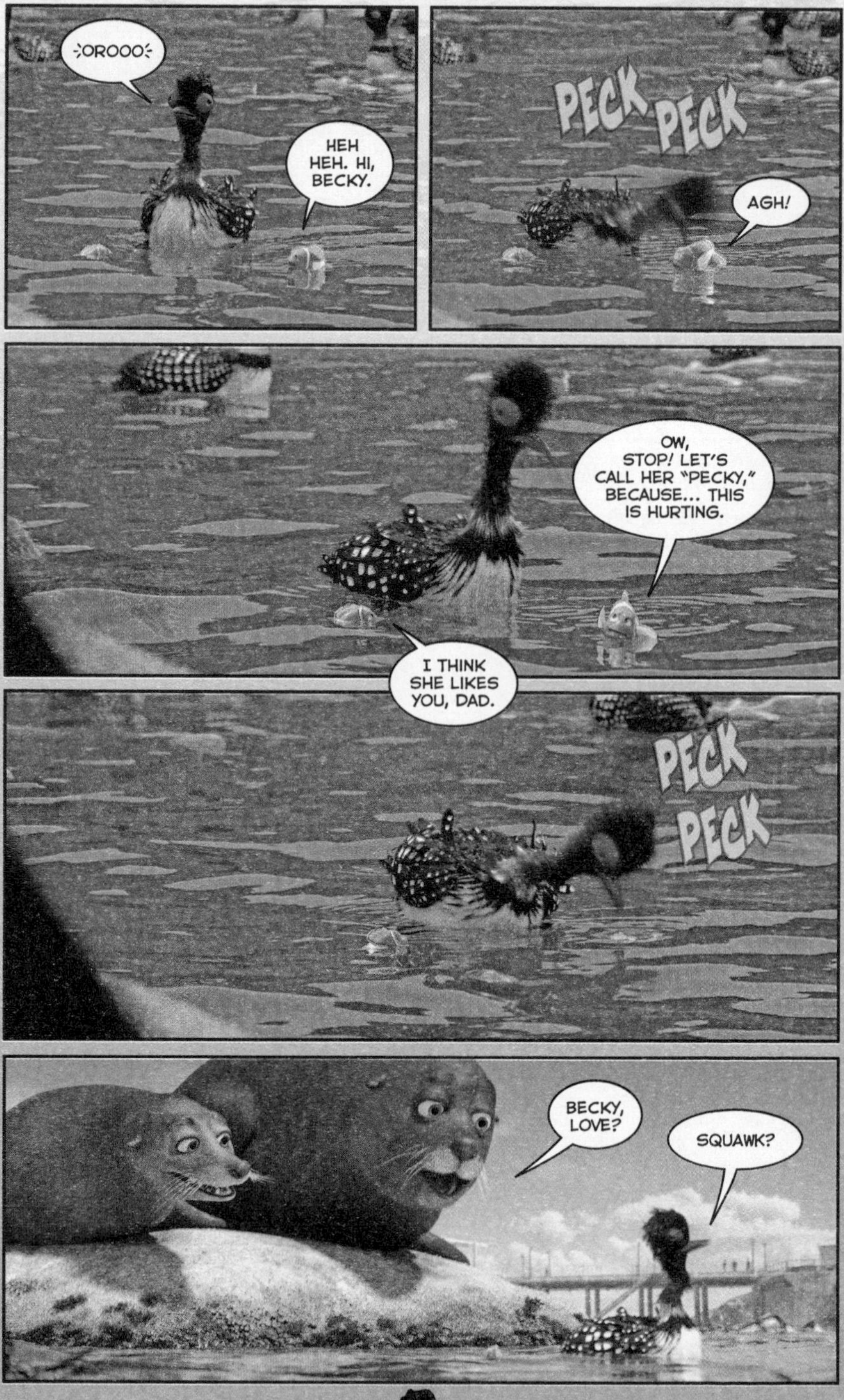
OROOO
HEH HEH. HI, BECKY.
PECK PECK
AGH!
OW, STOP! LET'S CALL HER "PECKY," BECAUSE... THIS IS HURTING.
I THINK SHE LIKES YOU, DAD.
PECK PECK
BECKY, LOVE?
SQUAWK?

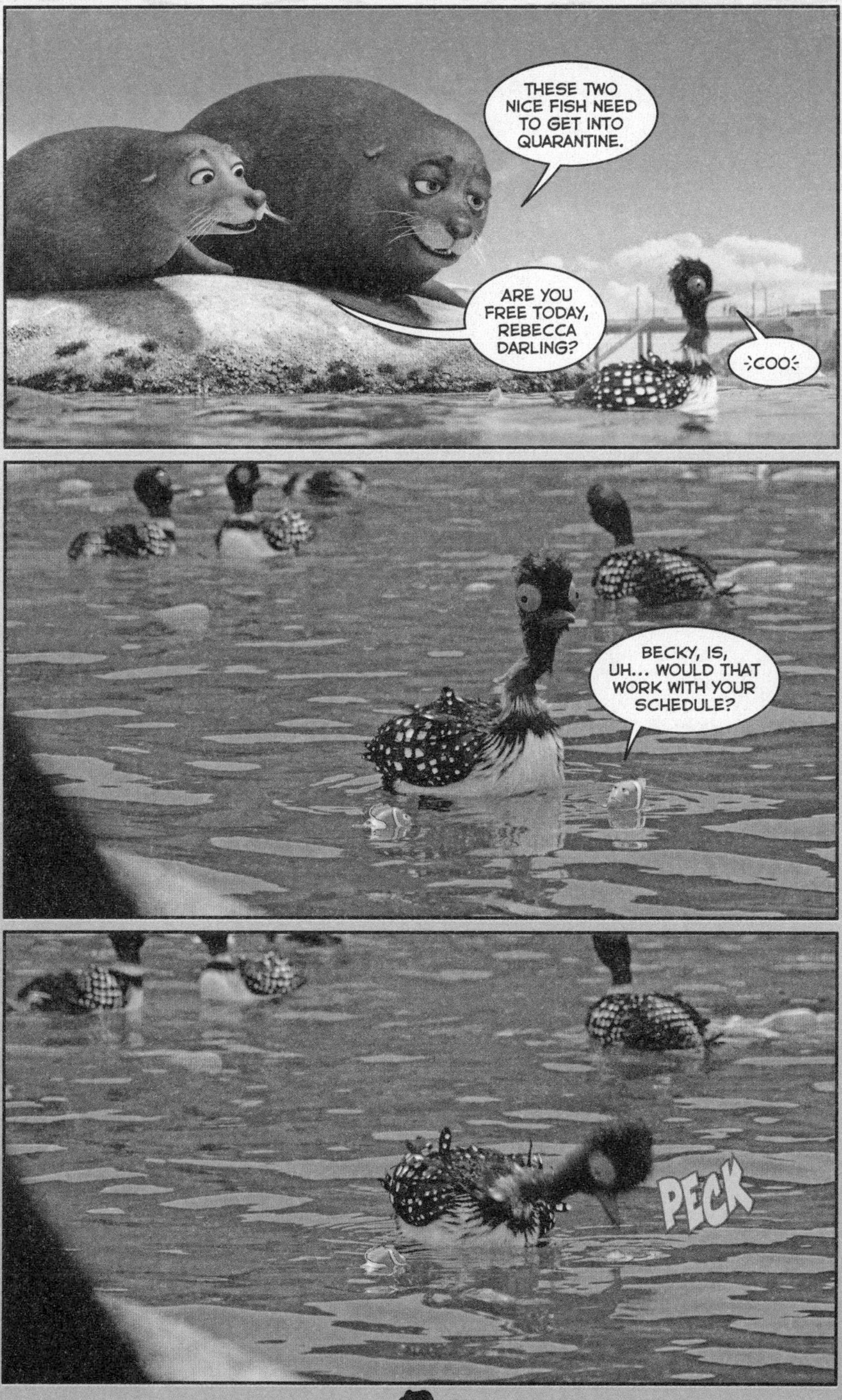
THESE TWO NICE FISH NEED TO GET INTO QUARANTINE.
ARE YOU FREE TODAY, REBECCA DARLING?
COO
BECKY, IS, UH... WOULD THAT WORK WITH YOUR SCHEDULE?
PECK

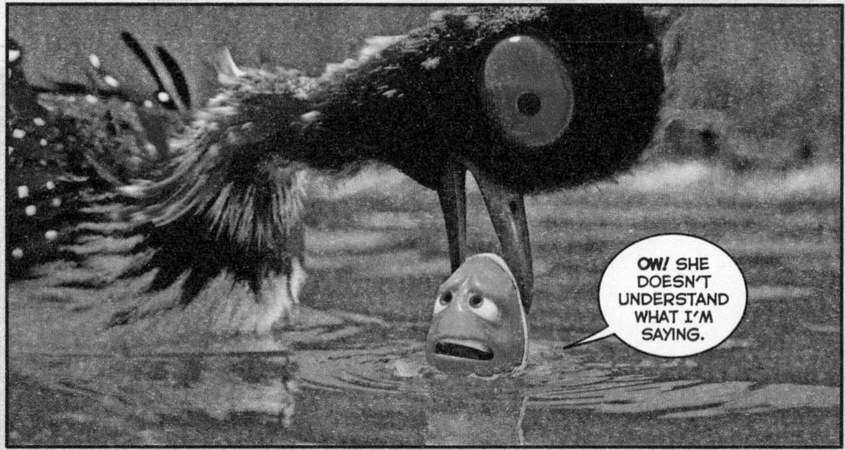
OW! SHE DOESN'T UNDERSTAND WHAT I'M SAYING.

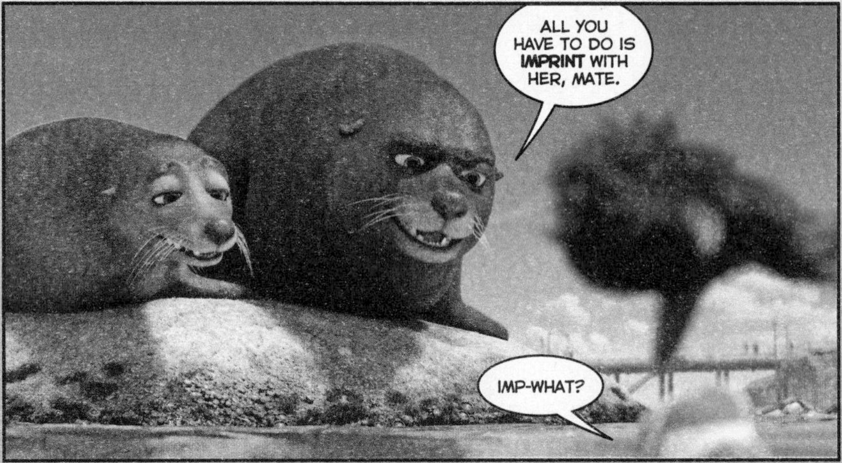
ALL YOU HAVE TO DO IS IMPRINT WITH HER, MATE.
IMP-WHAT?

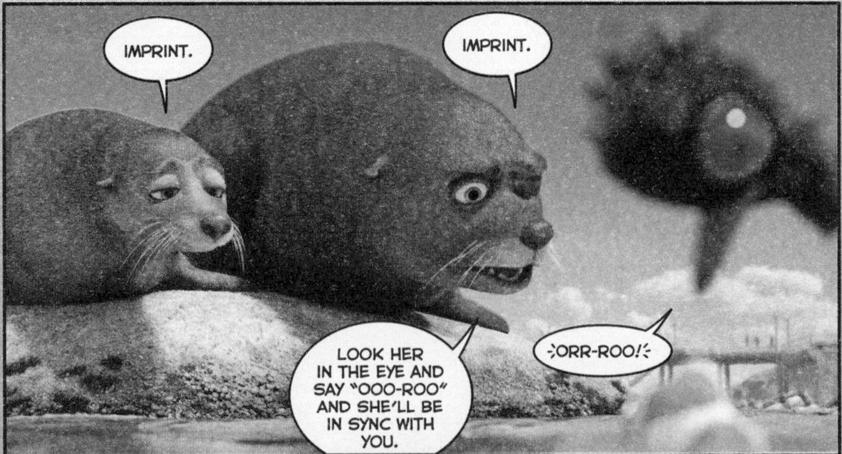
IMPRINT.
IMPRINT.
LOOK HER IN THE EYE AND SAY "OOO-ROO" AND SHE'LL BE IN SYNC WITH YOU.
ORR-ROO!

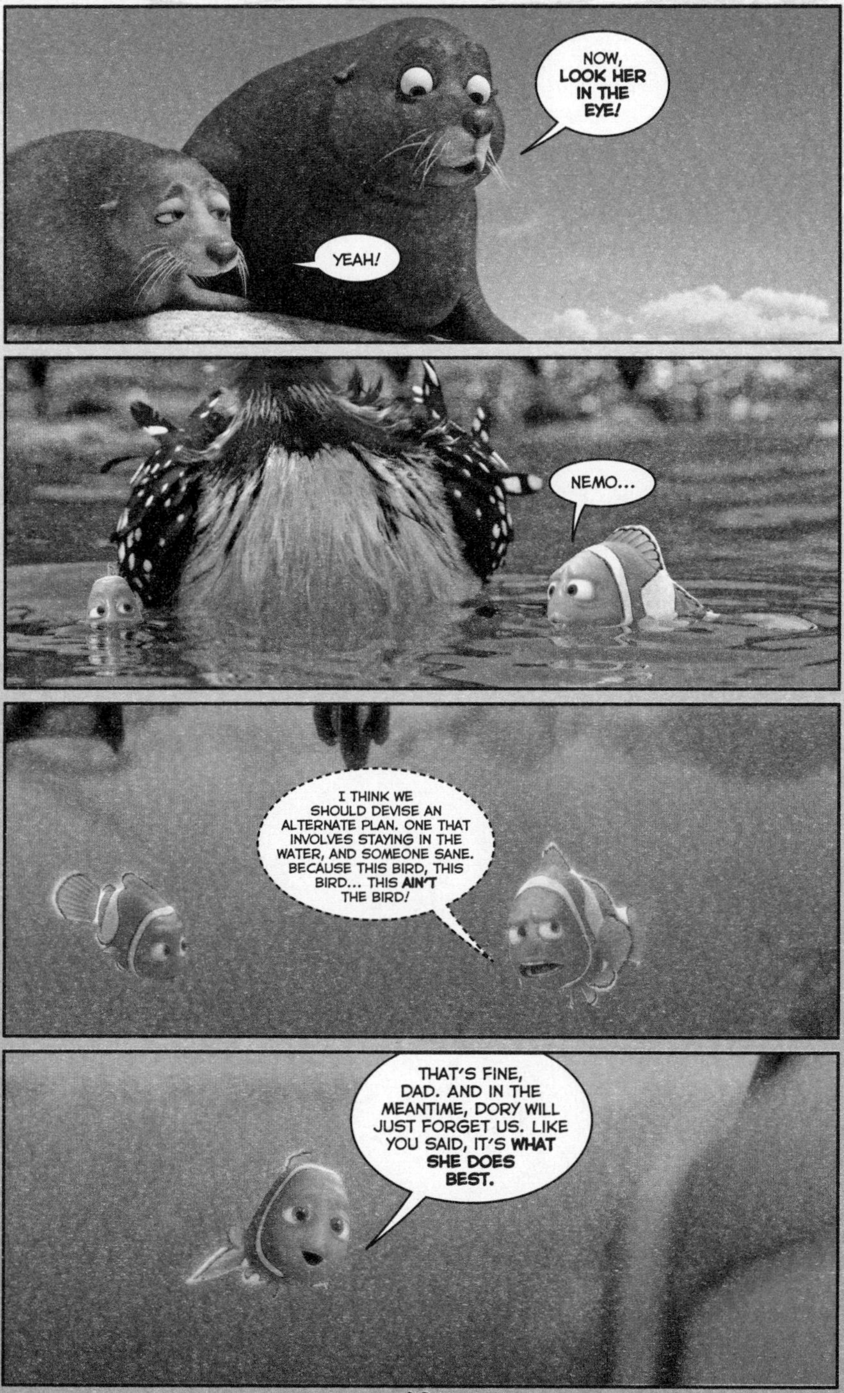
NOW, LOOK HER IN THE EYE!
YEAH!
NEMO...
I THINK WE SHOULD DEVISE AN ALTERNATE PLAN. ONE THAT INVOLVES STAYING IN THE WATER, AND SOMEONE SANE. BECAUSE THIS BIRD, THIS BIRD... THIS **AIN'T** THE BIRD!
THAT'S FINE, DAD. AND IN THE MEANTIME, DORY WILL JUST FORGET US. LIKE YOU SAID, IT'S **WHAT SHE DOES BEST.**

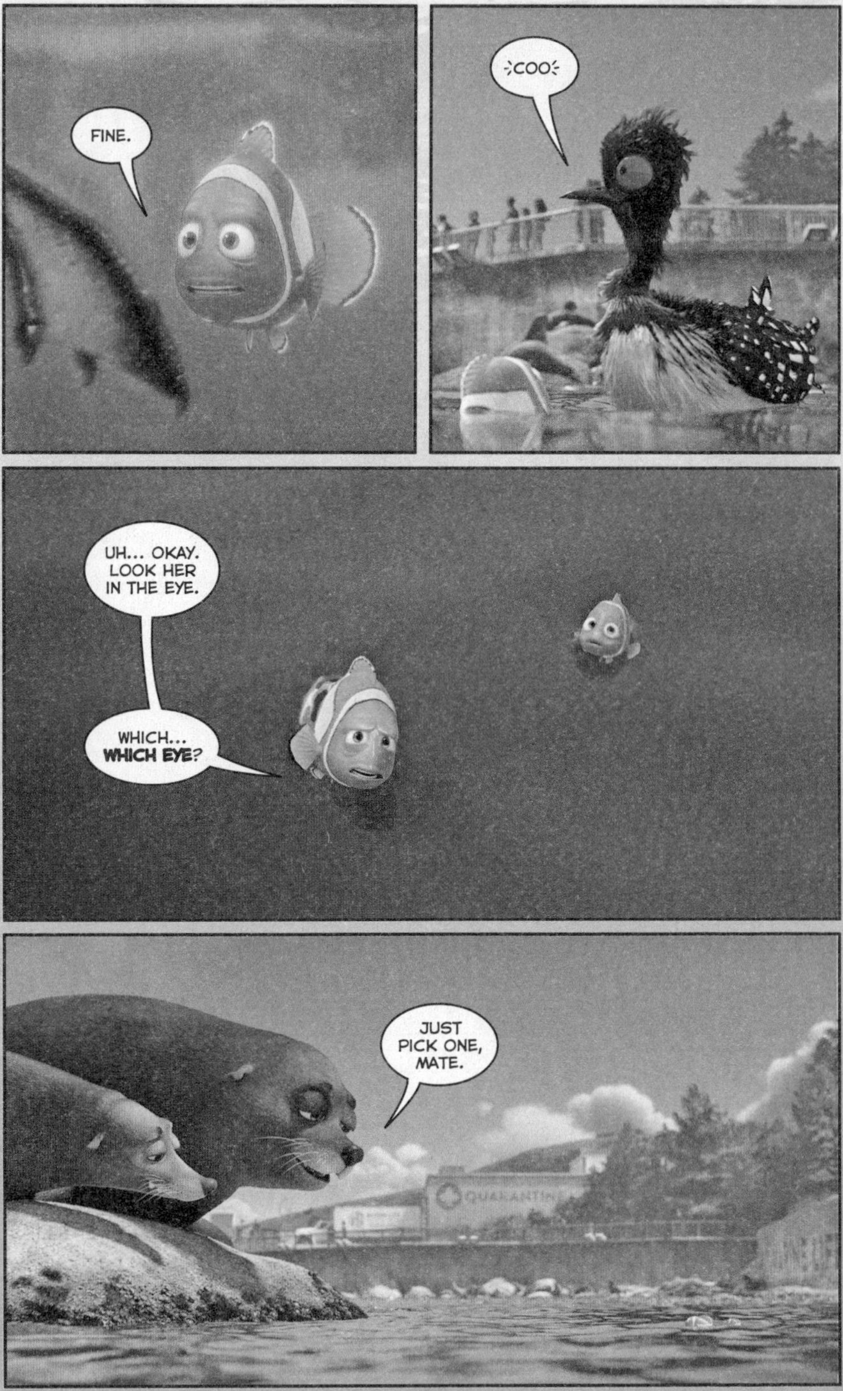
FINE.
COO
UH... OKAY. LOOK HER IN THE EYE.
WHICH... **WHICH EYE?**
JUST PICK ONE, MATE.

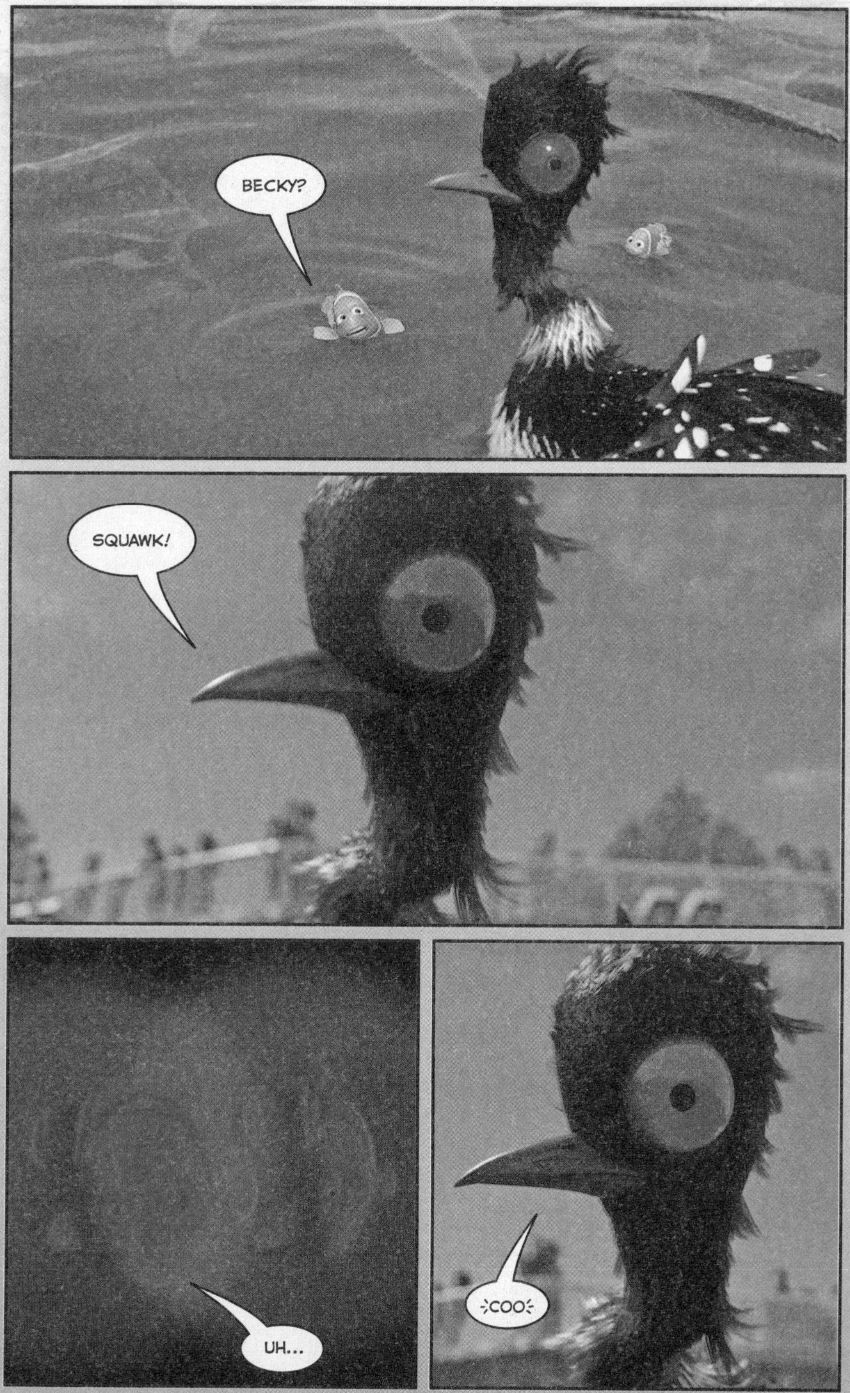
BECKY?
SQUAWK!
UH...
COO

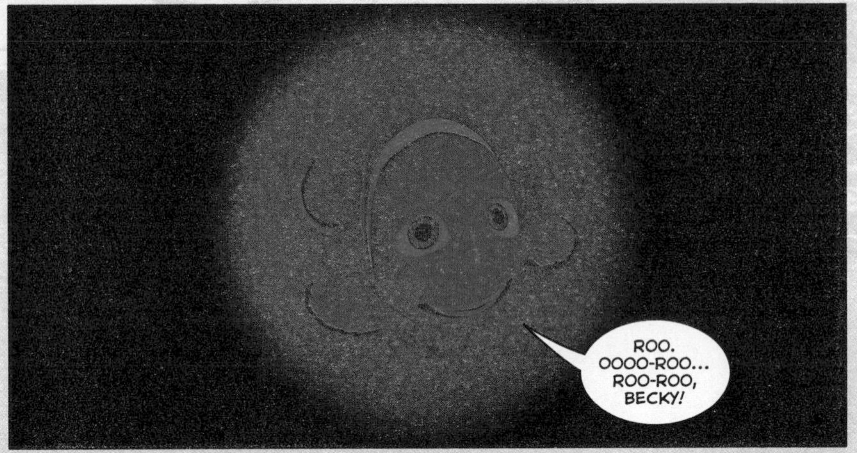
ROO. OOOO-ROO... ROO-ROO, BECKY!

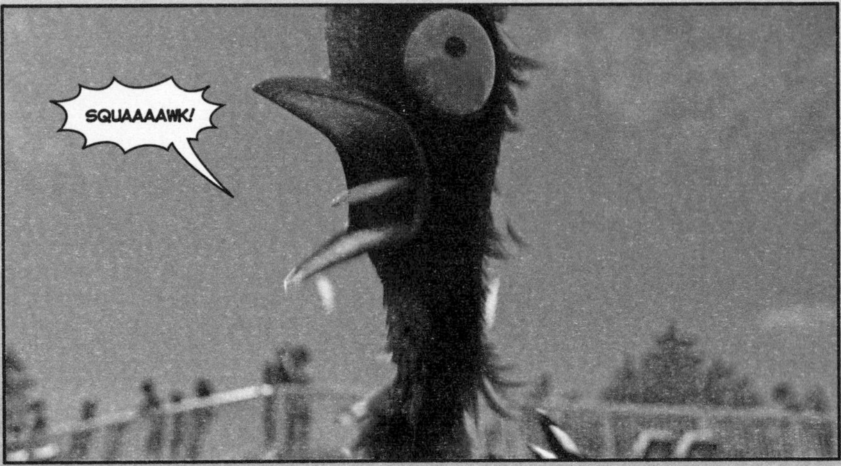
SQUAAAAWK!

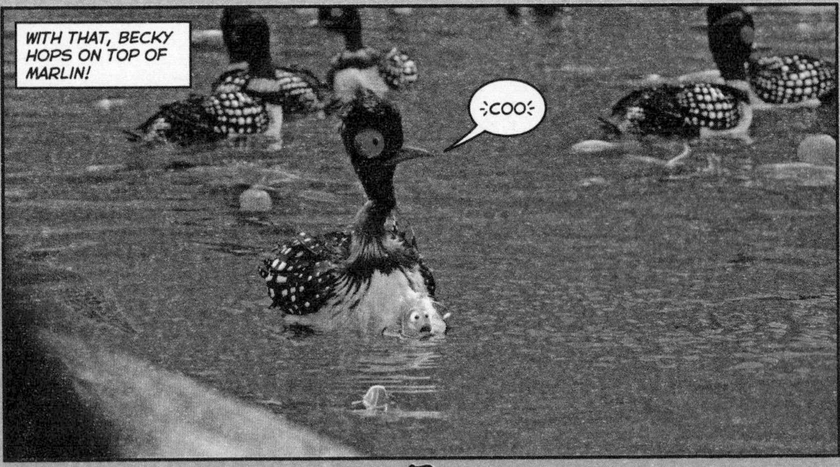
WITH THAT, BECKY HOPS ON TOP OF MARLIN!
COO

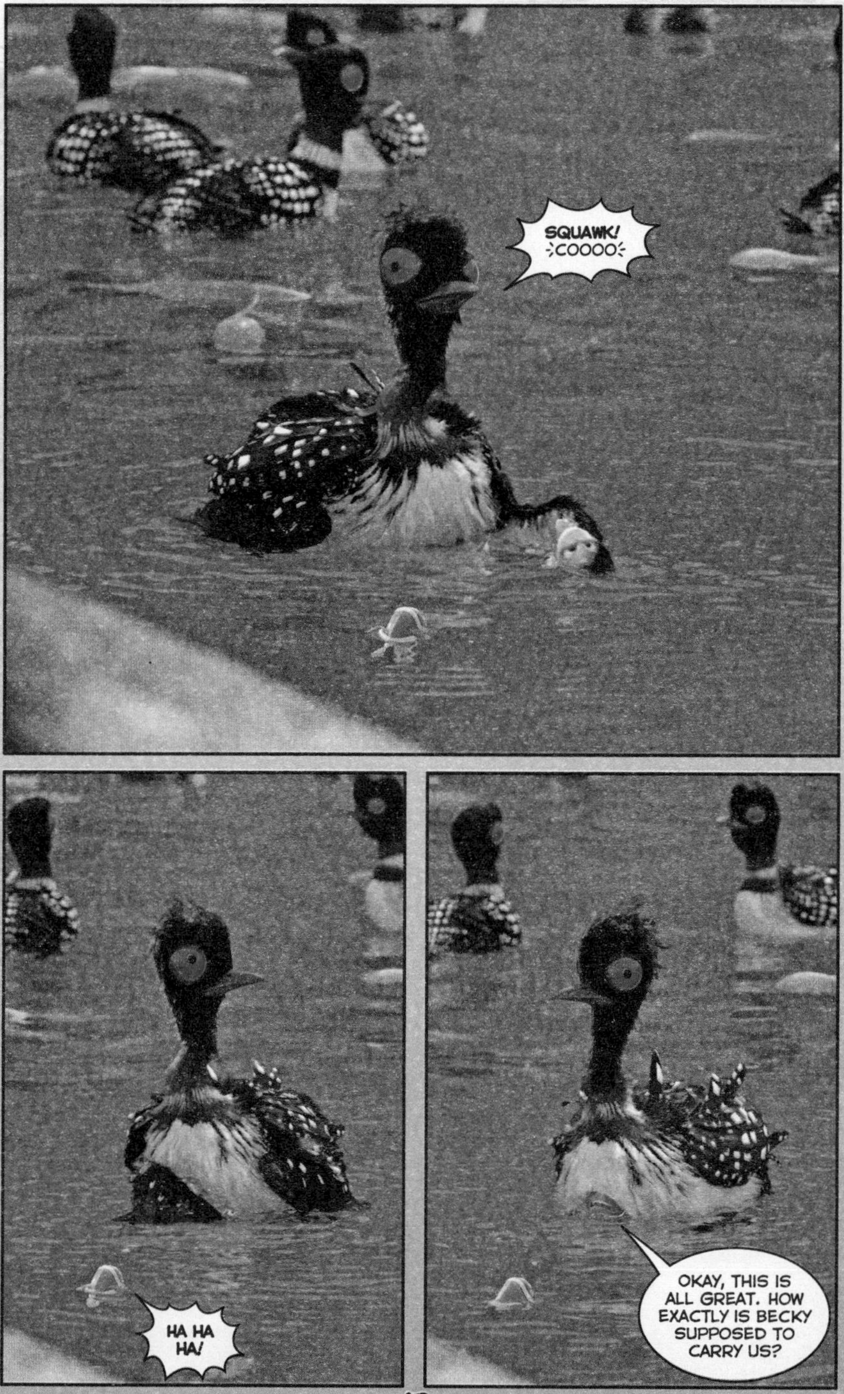
SQUAWK!
COOOO
HA HA HA!
OKAY, THIS IS ALL GREAT. HOW EXACTLY IS BECKY SUPPOSED TO CARRY US?

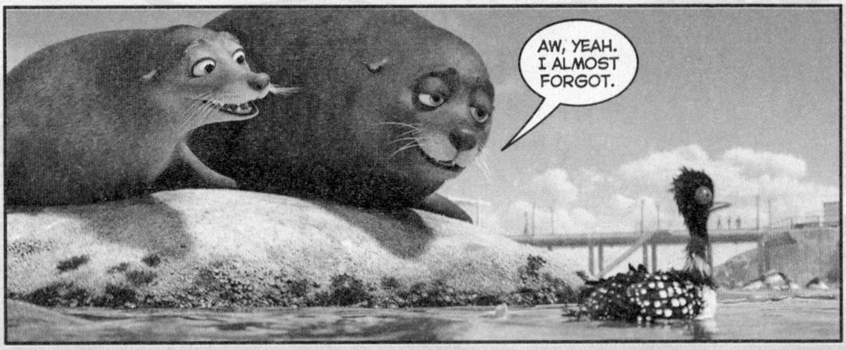
AW, YEAH.
I ALMOST
FORGOT.

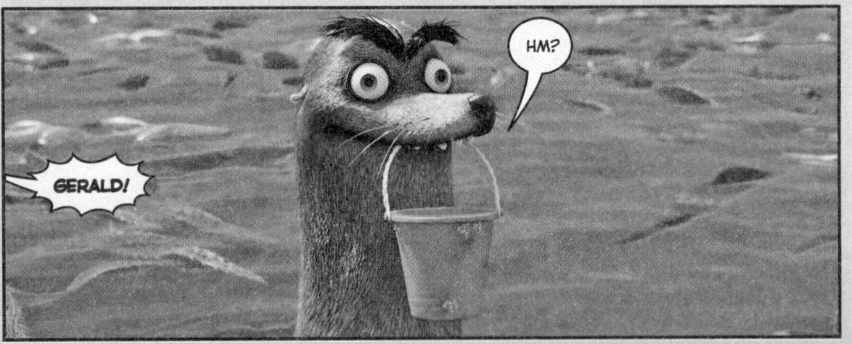
HM?
GERALD!

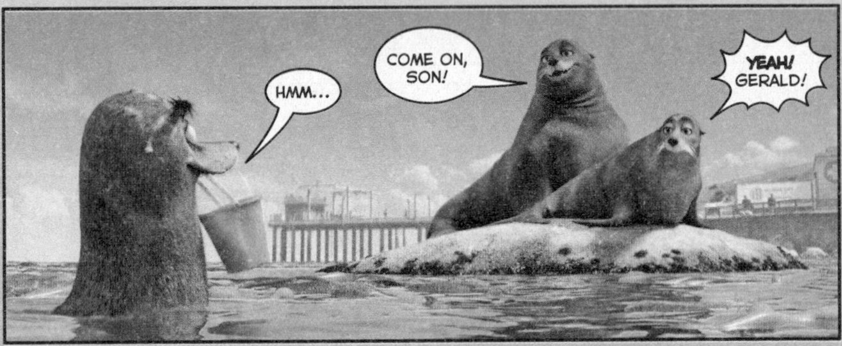
HMM...
COME ON,
SON!
YEAH!
GERALD!

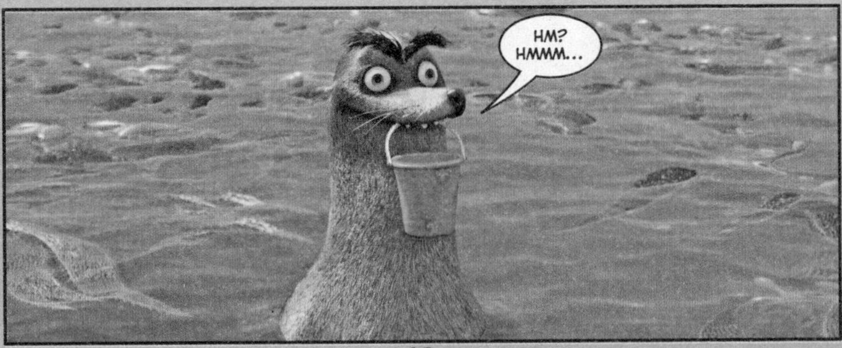
HM?
HMMM...

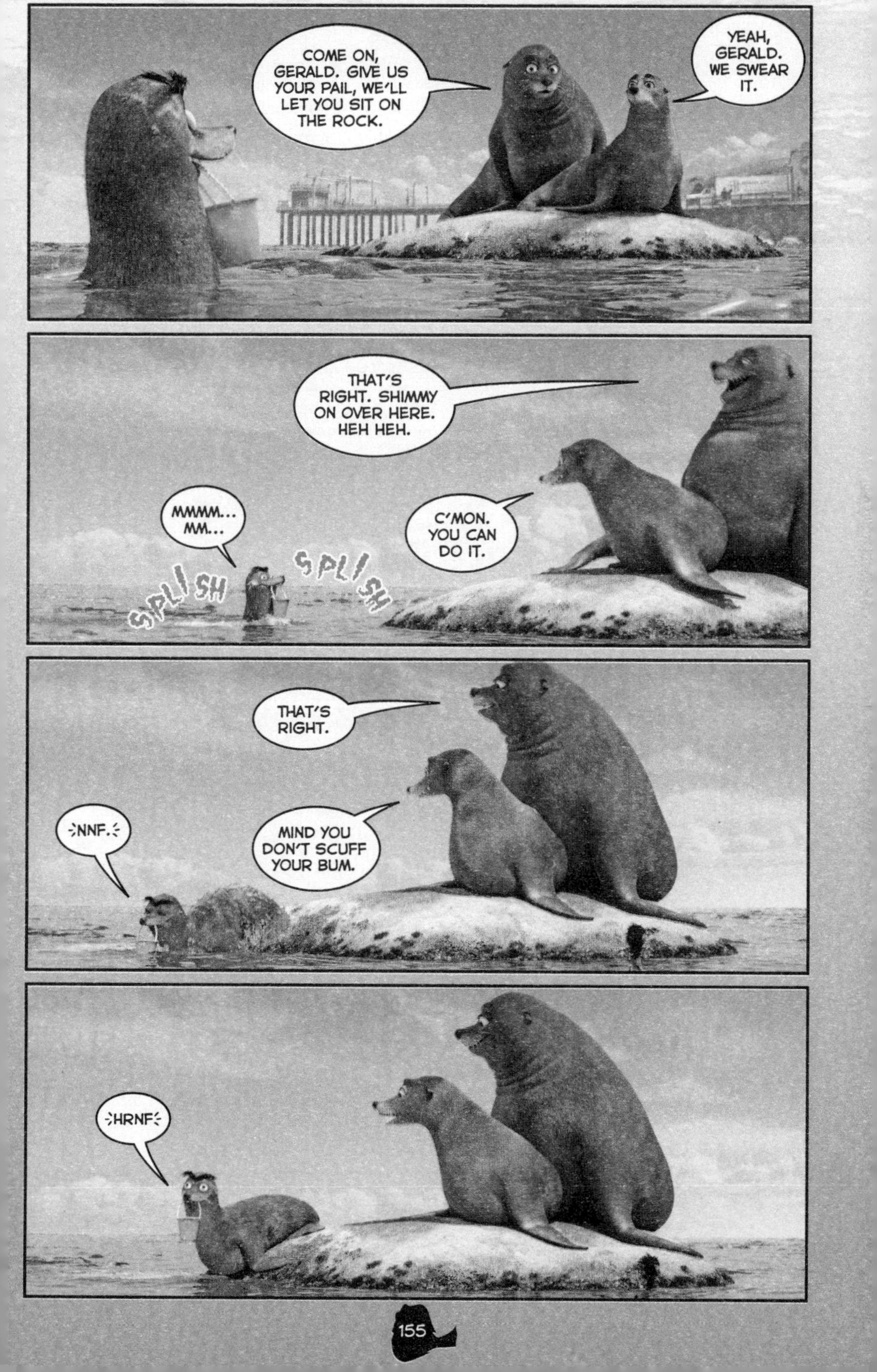
COME ON, GERALD. GIVE US YOUR PAIL, WE'LL LET YOU SIT ON THE ROCK.
YEAH, GERALD. WE SWEAR IT.
THAT'S RIGHT. SHIMMY ON OVER HERE. HEH HEH.
MMMM... MM...
SPLISH
SPLISH
C'MON. YOU CAN DO IT.
THAT'S RIGHT.
NNF.
MIND YOU DON'T SCUFF YOUR BUM.
HRNF

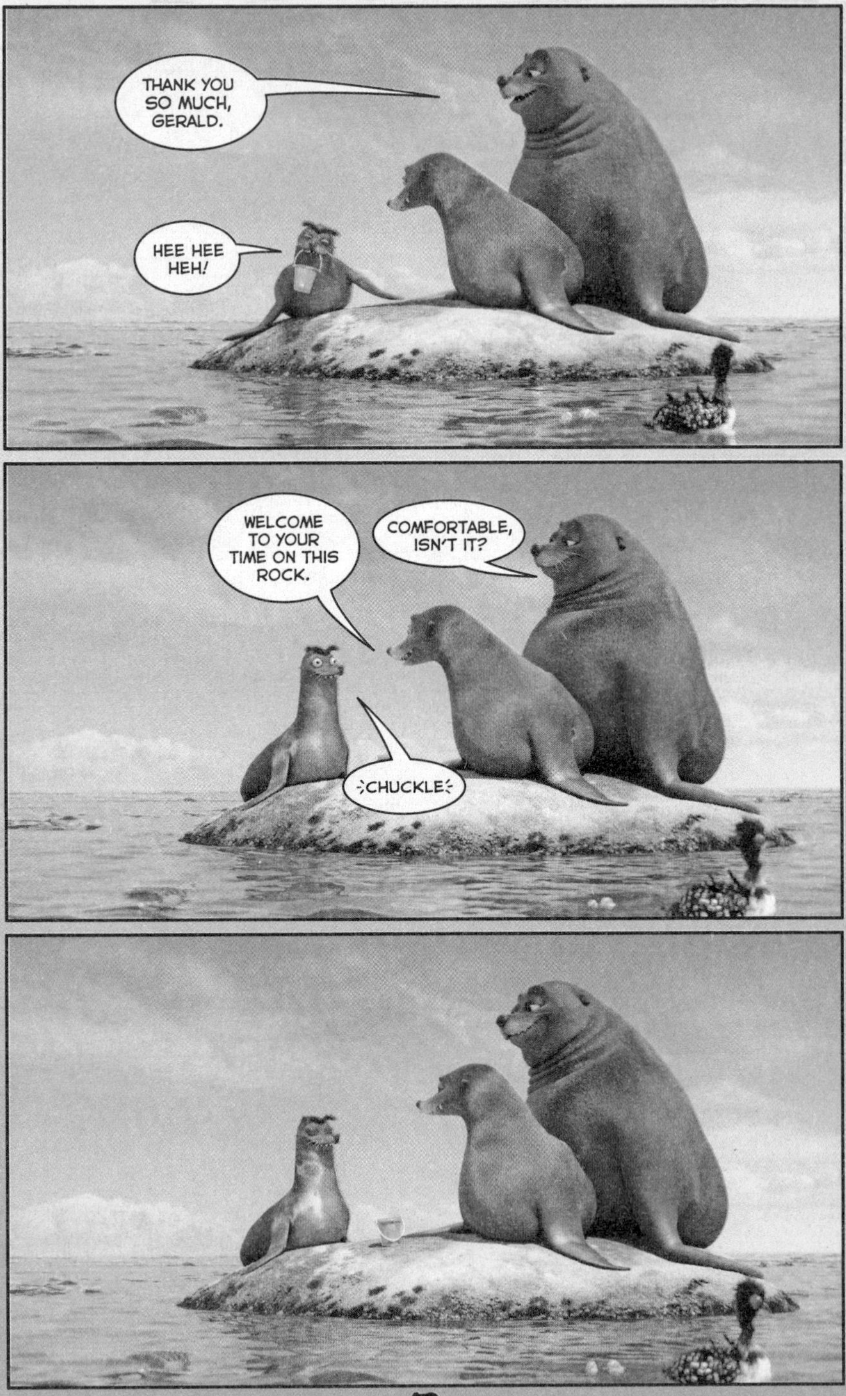
THANK YOU SO MUCH, GERALD.
HEE HEE HEH!
WELCOME TO YOUR TIME ON THIS ROCK.
COMFORTABLE, ISN'T IT?
CHUCKLE

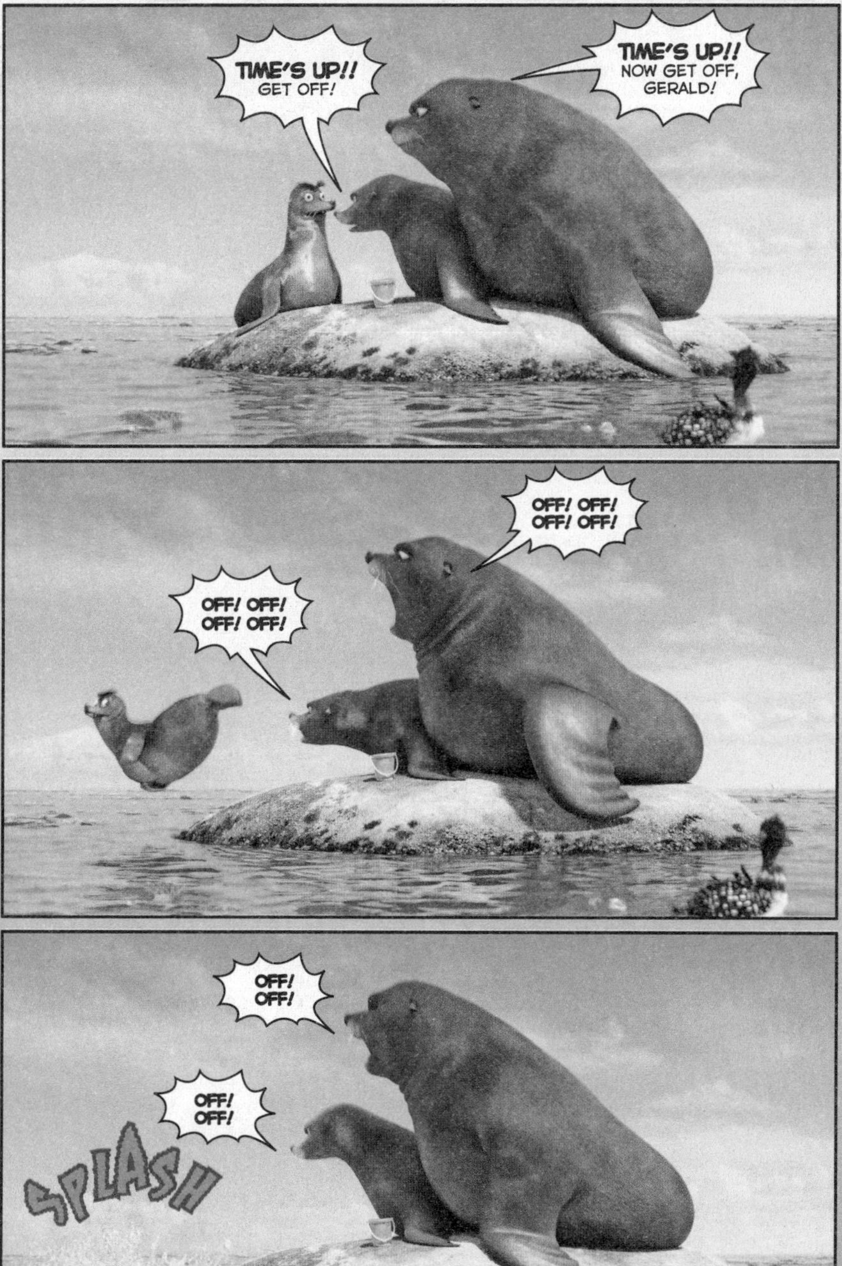
TIME'S UP!! GET OFF!
TIME'S UP!! NOW GET OFF, GERALD!
OFF! OFF! OFF! OFF!
OFF! OFF! OFF! OFF!
OFF! OFF!
OFF! OFF!
SPLASH

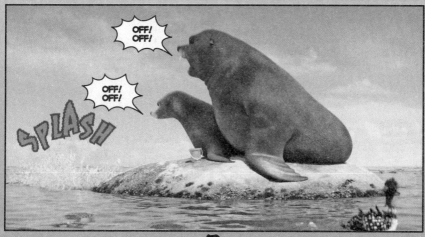

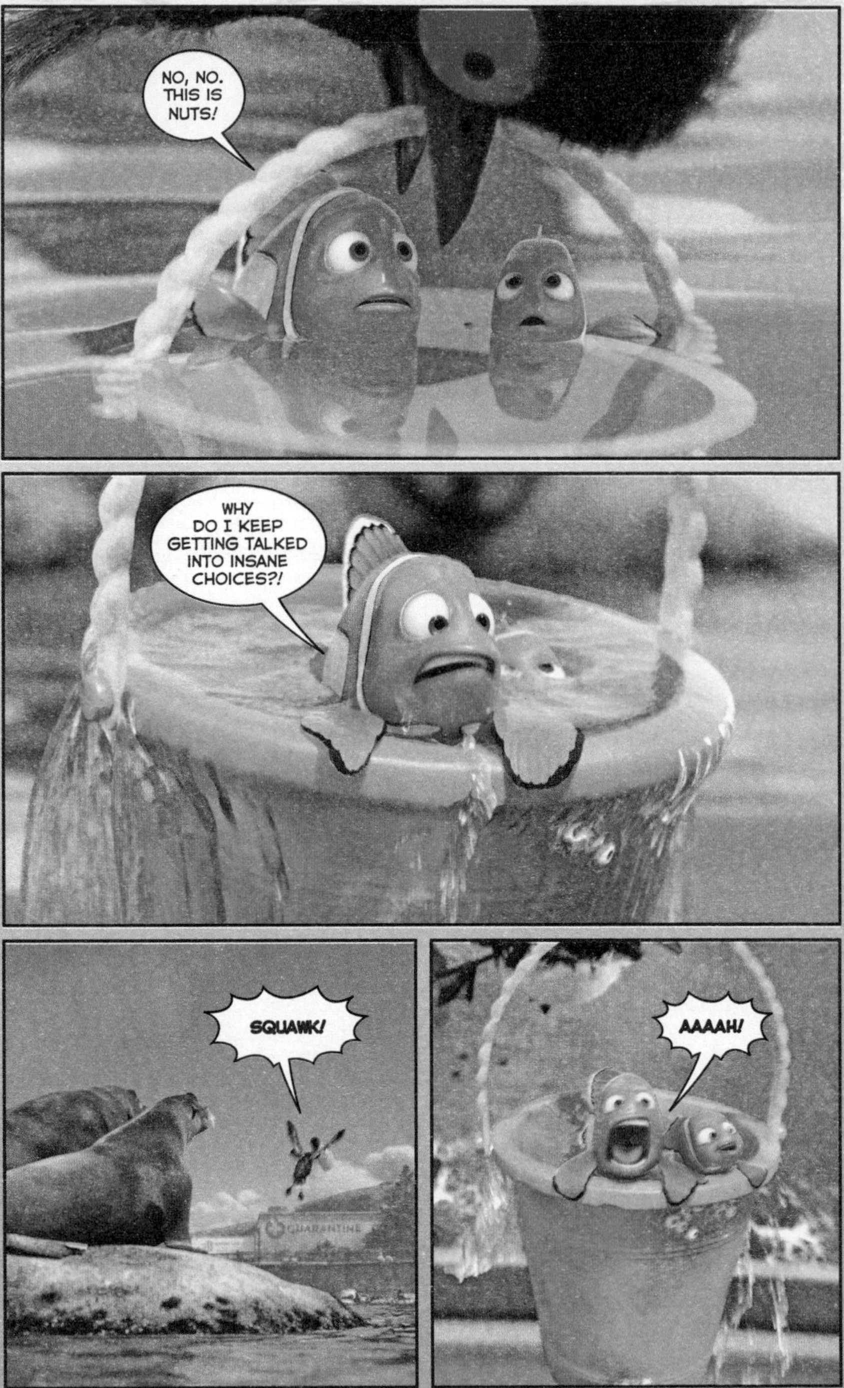
NO, NO. THIS IS NUTS!
WHY DO I KEEP GETTING TALKED INTO INSANE CHOICES?!
SQUAWK!
QUARANTINE
AAAAH!

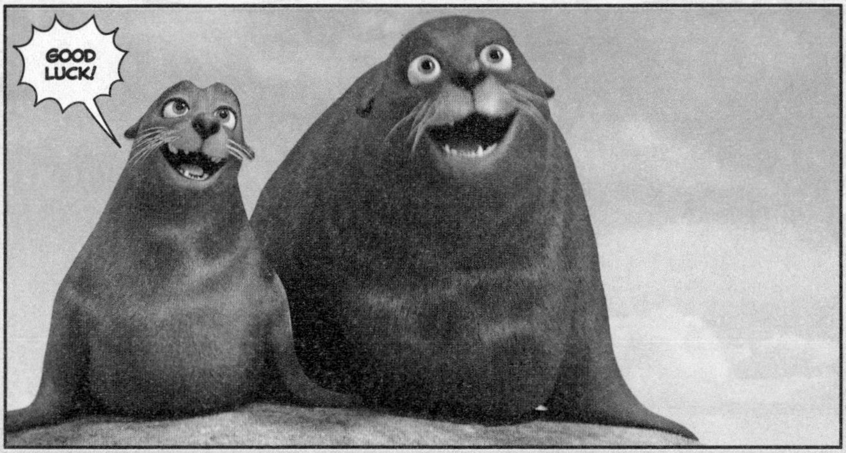
GOOD LUCK!

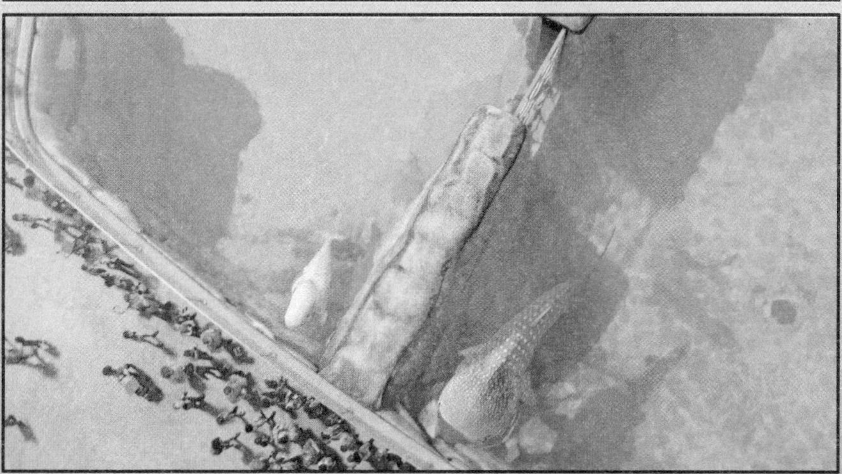

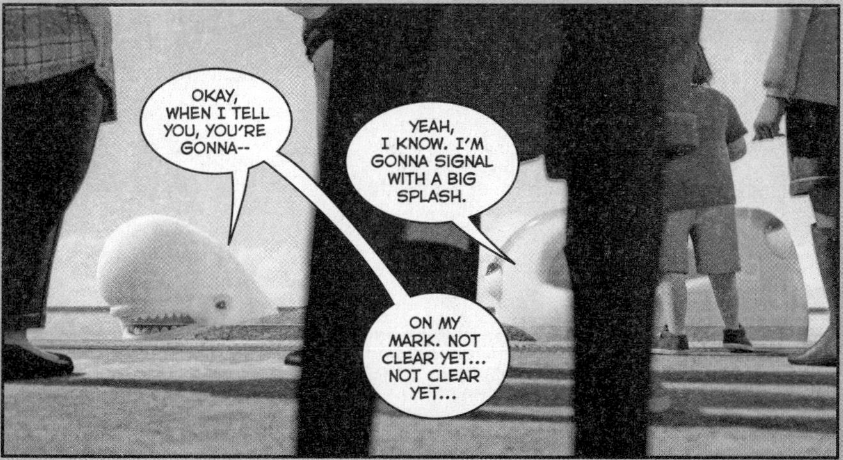
OKAY, WHEN I TELL YOU, YOU'RE GONNA--
YEAH, I KNOW. I'M GONNA SIGNAL WITH A BIG SPLASH.
ON MY MARK. NOT CLEAR YET... NOT CLEAR YET...

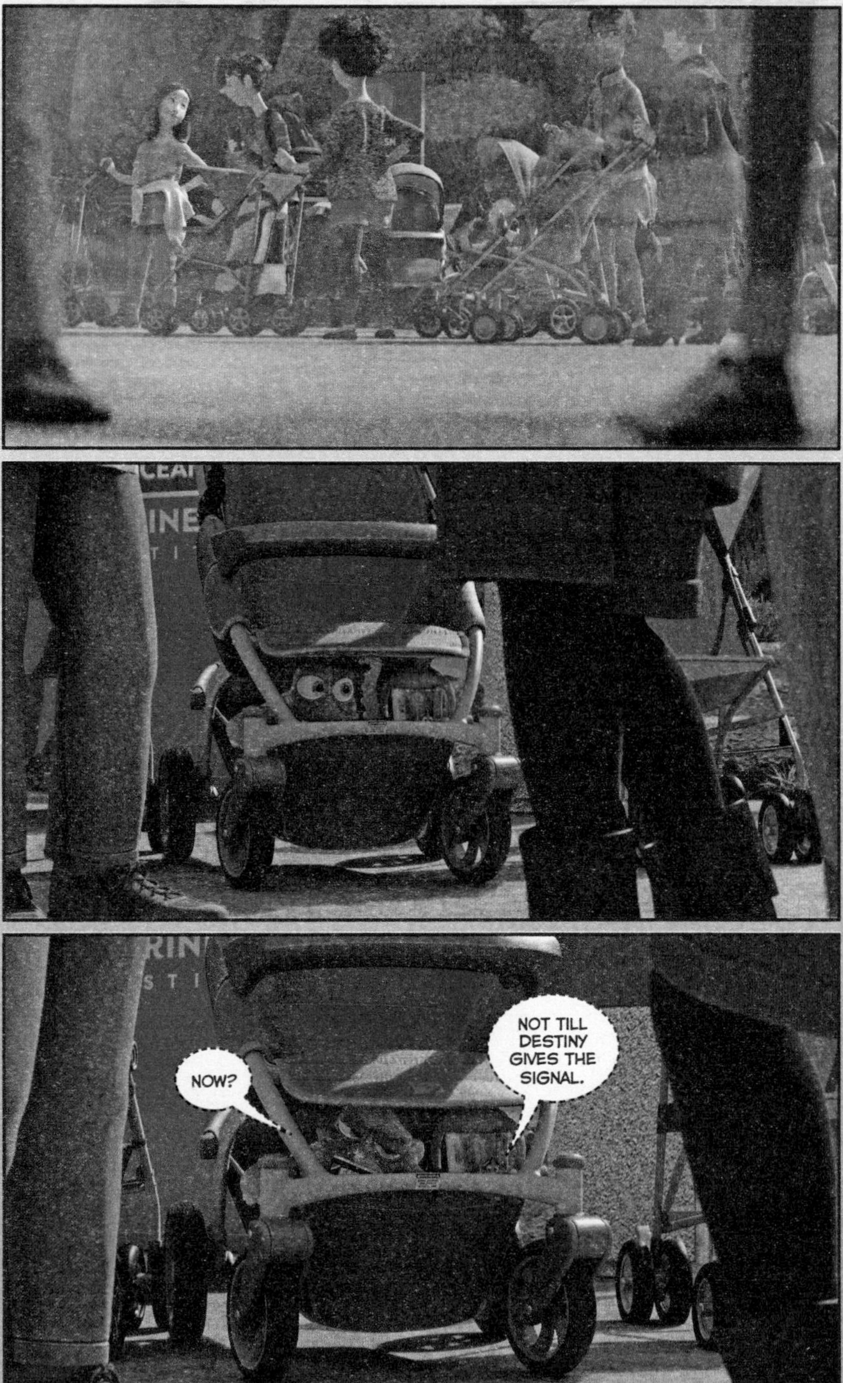
NOW?
NOT TILL DESTINY GIVES THE SIGNAL.

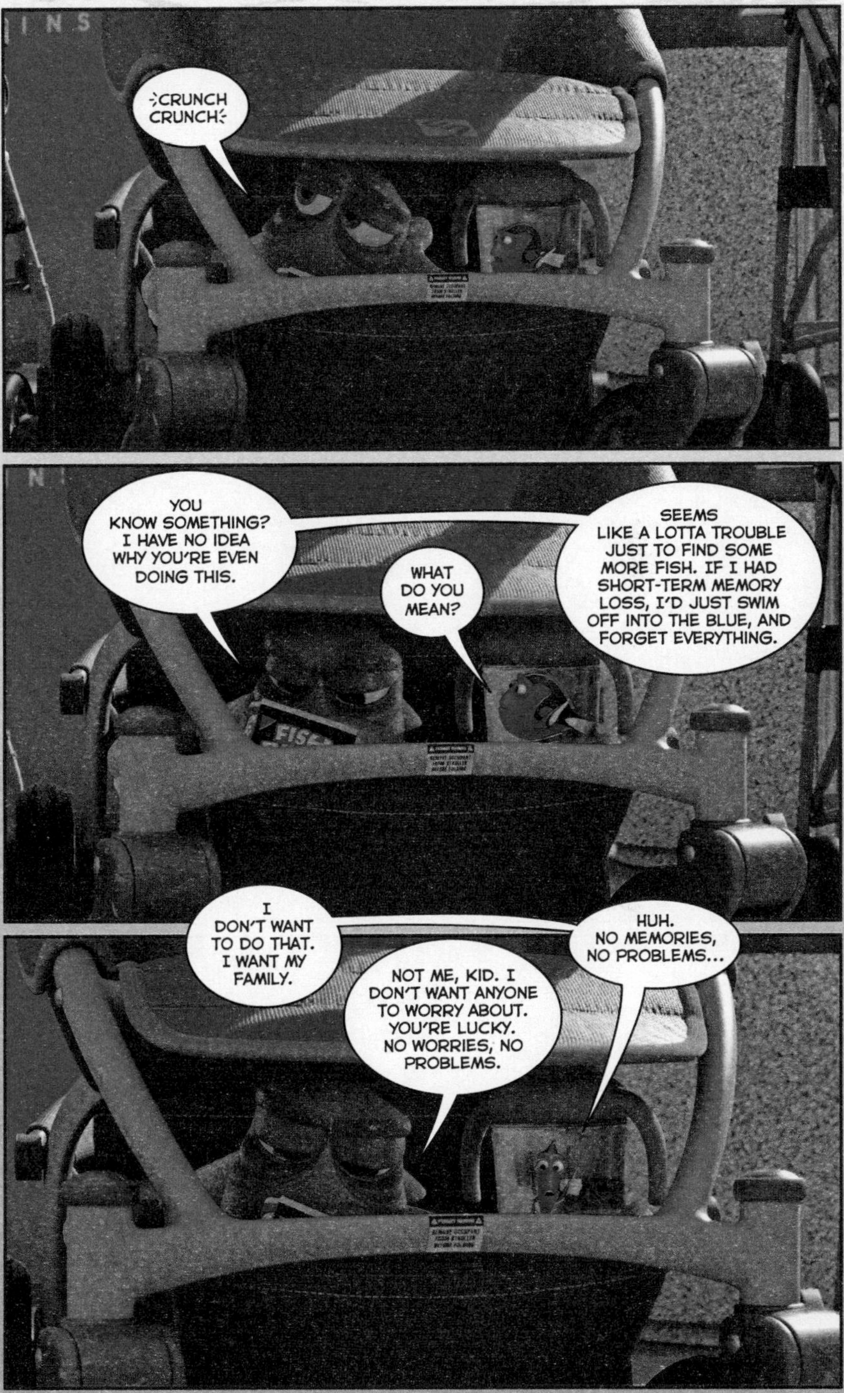

CRUNCH CRUNCH
YOU KNOW SOMETHING? I HAVE NO IDEA WHY YOU'RE EVEN DOING THIS.
WHAT DO YOU MEAN?
SEEMS LIKE A LOTTA TROUBLE JUST TO FIND SOME MORE FISH. IF I HAD SHORT-TERM MEMORY LOSS, I'D JUST SWIM OFF INTO THE BLUE, AND FORGET EVERYTHING.
I DON'T WANT TO DO THAT. I WANT MY FAMILY.
HUH. NO MEMORIES, NO PROBLEMS...
NOT ME, KID. I DON'T WANT ANYONE TO WORRY ABOUT. YOU'RE LUCKY. NO WORRIES, NO PROBLEMS.

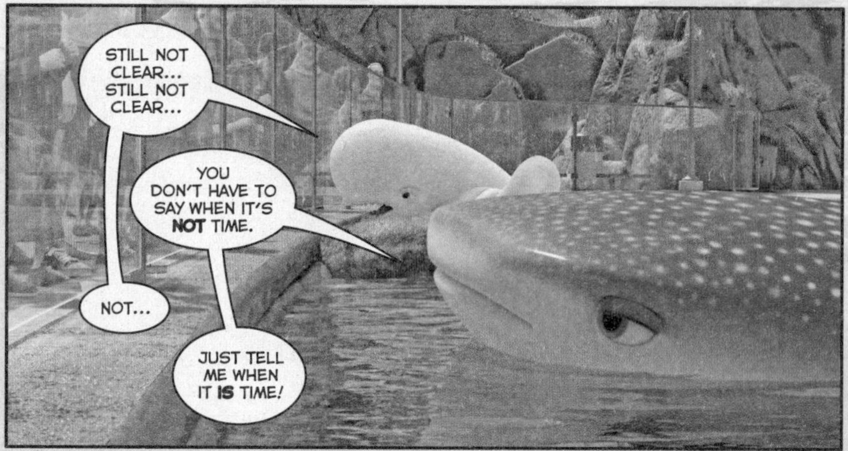
STILL NOT CLEAR... STILL NOT CLEAR...
YOU DON'T HAVE TO SAY WHEN IT'S **NOT** TIME.
NOT...
JUST TELL ME WHEN IT **IS** TIME!

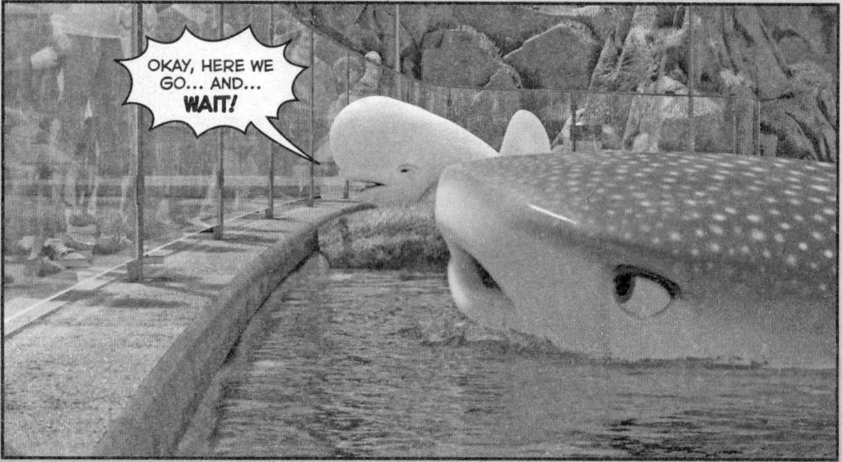
OKAY, HERE WE GO... AND... **WAIT!**

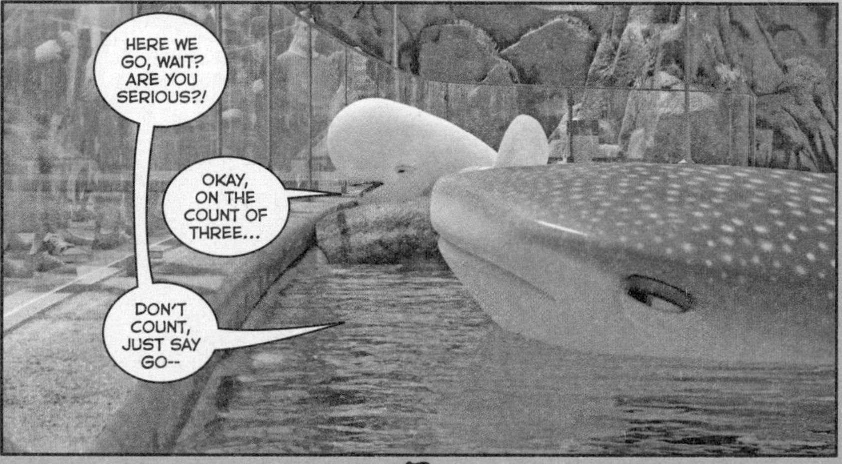
HERE WE GO, WAIT? ARE YOU SERIOUS?!
OKAY, ON THE COUNT OF THREE...
DON'T COUNT, JUST SAY GO--

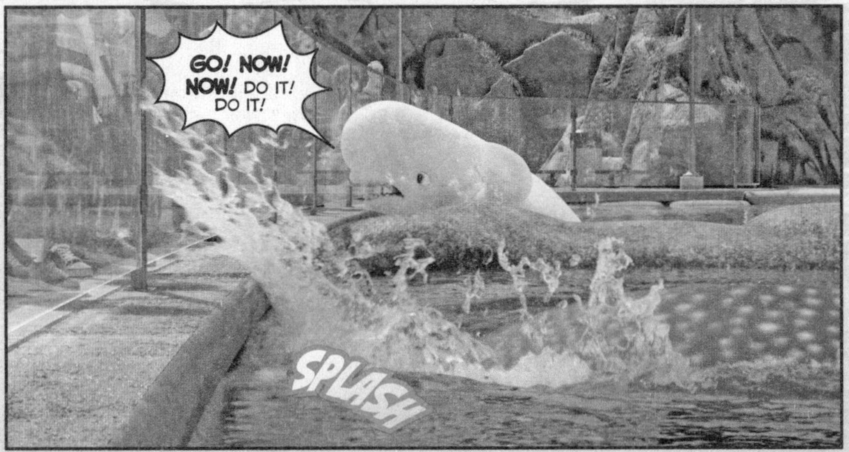
GO! NOW! NOW! DO IT! DO IT!
SPLASH

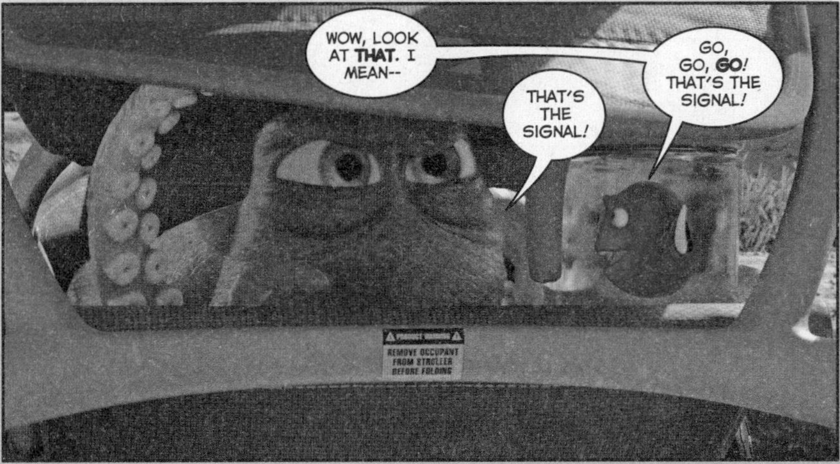
WOW, LOOK AT THAT. I MEAN--
GO, GO, GO! THAT'S THE SIGNAL!
THAT'S THE SIGNAL!
REMOVE OCCUPANT FROM STROLLER BEFORE FOLDING

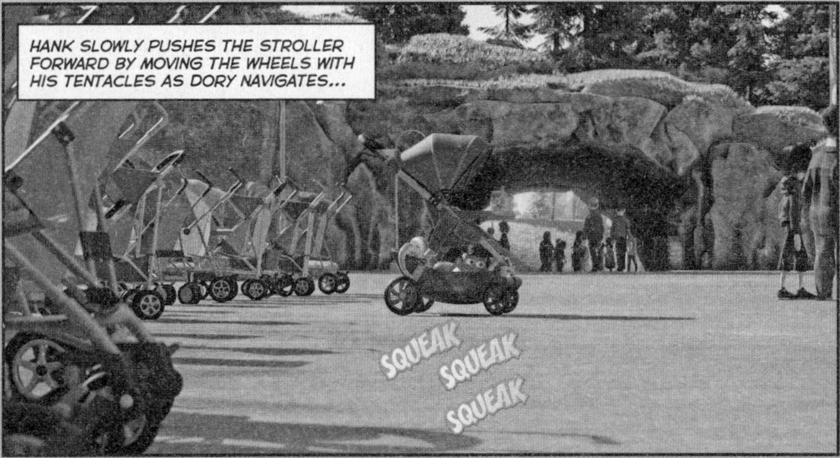
HANK SLOWLY PUSHES THE STROLLER FORWARD BY MOVING THE WHEELS WITH HIS TENTACLES AS DORY NAVIGATES...
SQUEAK
SQUEAK
SQUEAK

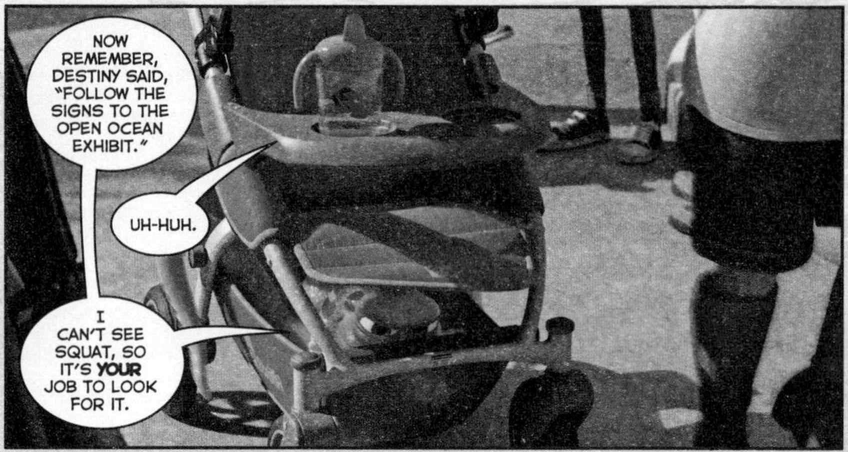
NOW REMEMBER, DESTINY SAID, "FOLLOW THE SIGNS TO THE OPEN OCEAN EXHIBIT."
UH-HUH.
I CAN'T SEE SQUAT, SO IT'S **YOUR** JOB TO LOOK FOR IT.

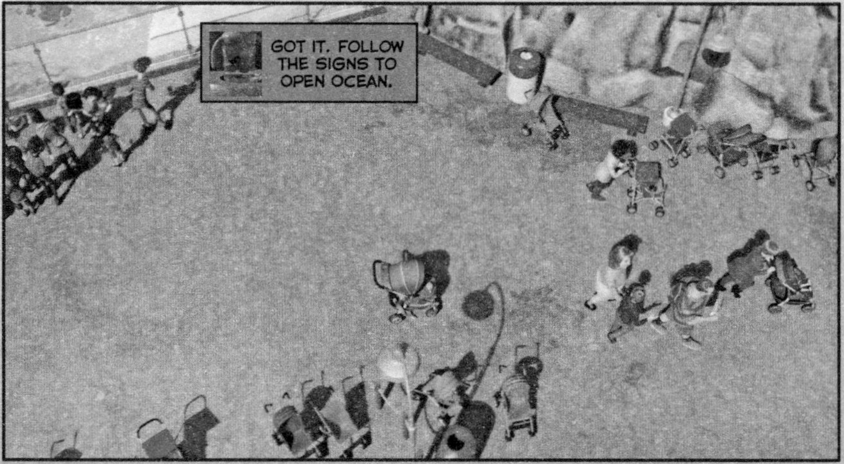
GOT IT. FOLLOW THE SIGNS TO OPEN OCEAN.

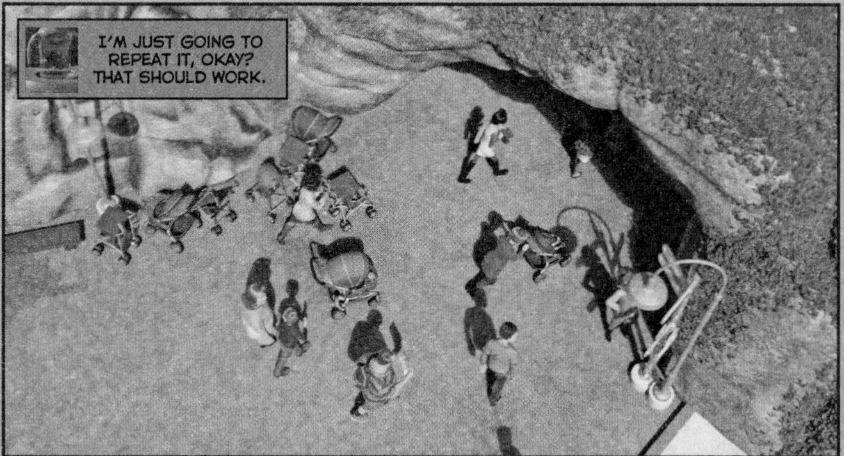
I'M JUST GOING TO REPEAT IT, OKAY? THAT SHOULD WORK.

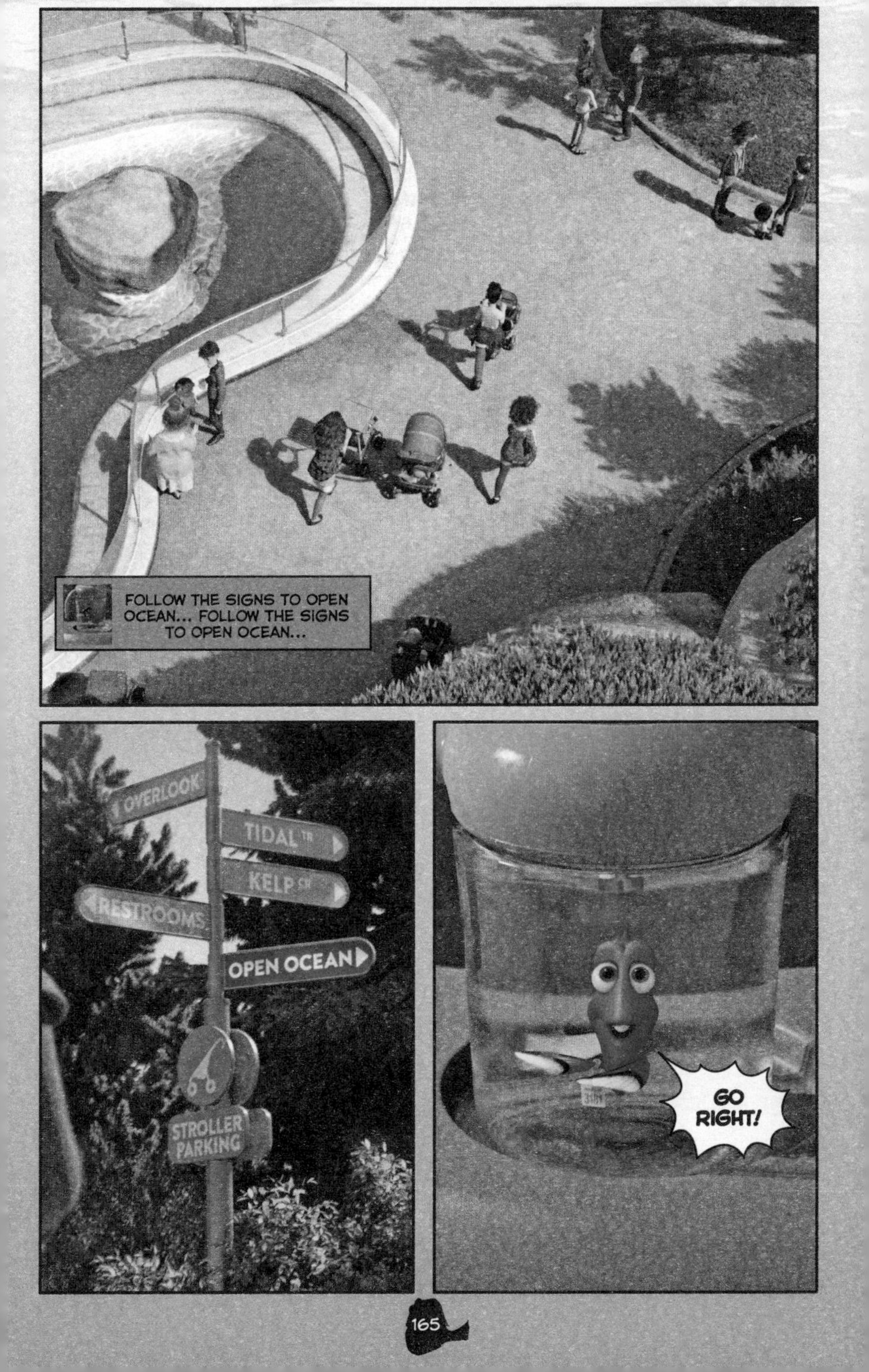
FOLLOW THE SIGNS TO OPEN OCEAN... FOLLOW THE SIGNS TO OPEN OCEAN...
OVERLOOK
TIDAL TR
KELP ST
RESTROOMS
OPEN OCEAN
STROLLER PARKING
GO RIGHT!

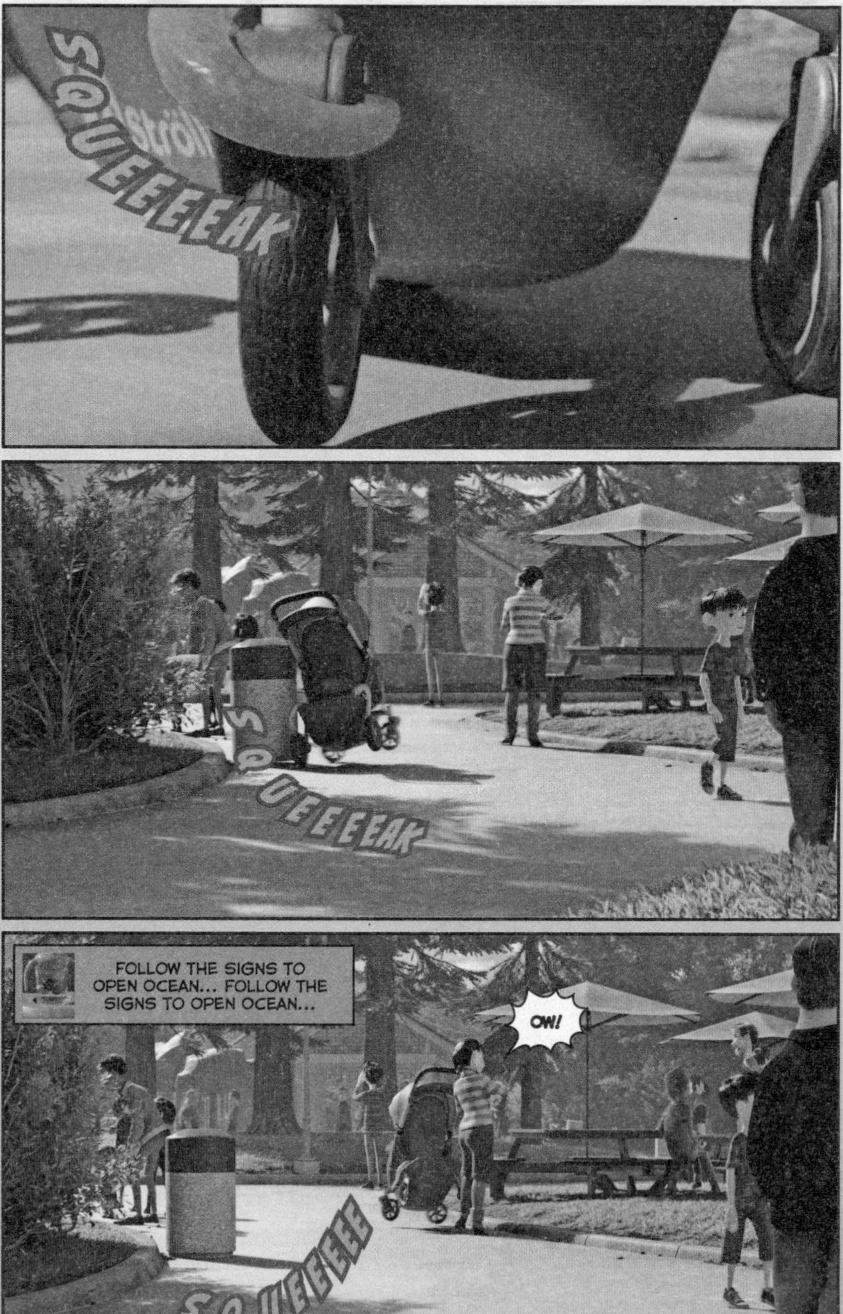
SQUEEEEAK
SQUEEEEAK
FOLLOW THE SIGNS TO OPEN OCEAN... FOLLOW THE SIGNS TO OPEN OCEAN...
OW!
SQUEEEEE

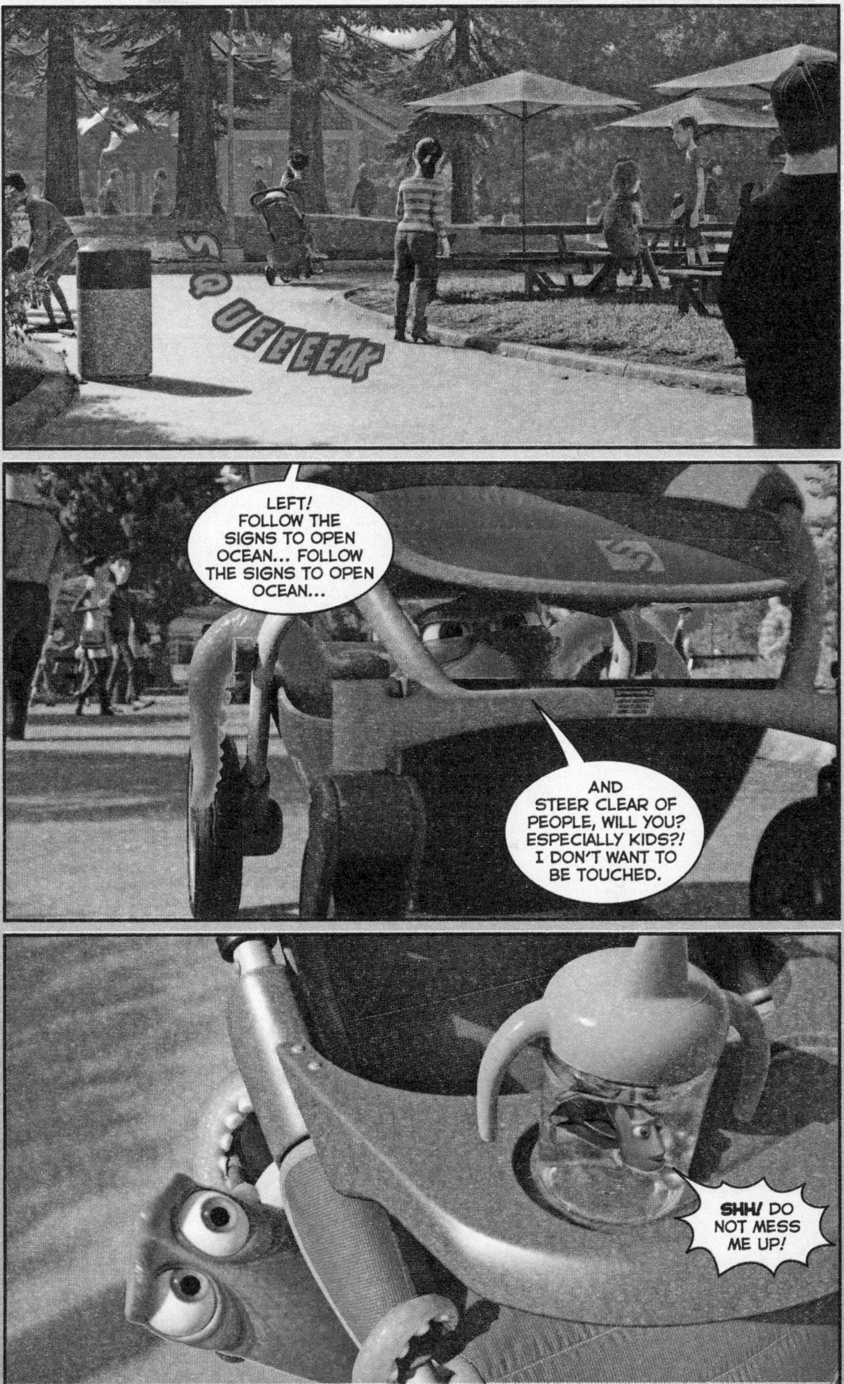
SQUEEEEAK
LEFT! FOLLOW THE SIGNS TO OPEN OCEAN... FOLLOW THE SIGNS TO OPEN OCEAN...
AND STEER CLEAR OF PEOPLE, WILL YOU? ESPECIALLY KIDS?! I DON'T WANT TO BE TOUCHED.
SHH! DO NOT MESS ME UP!

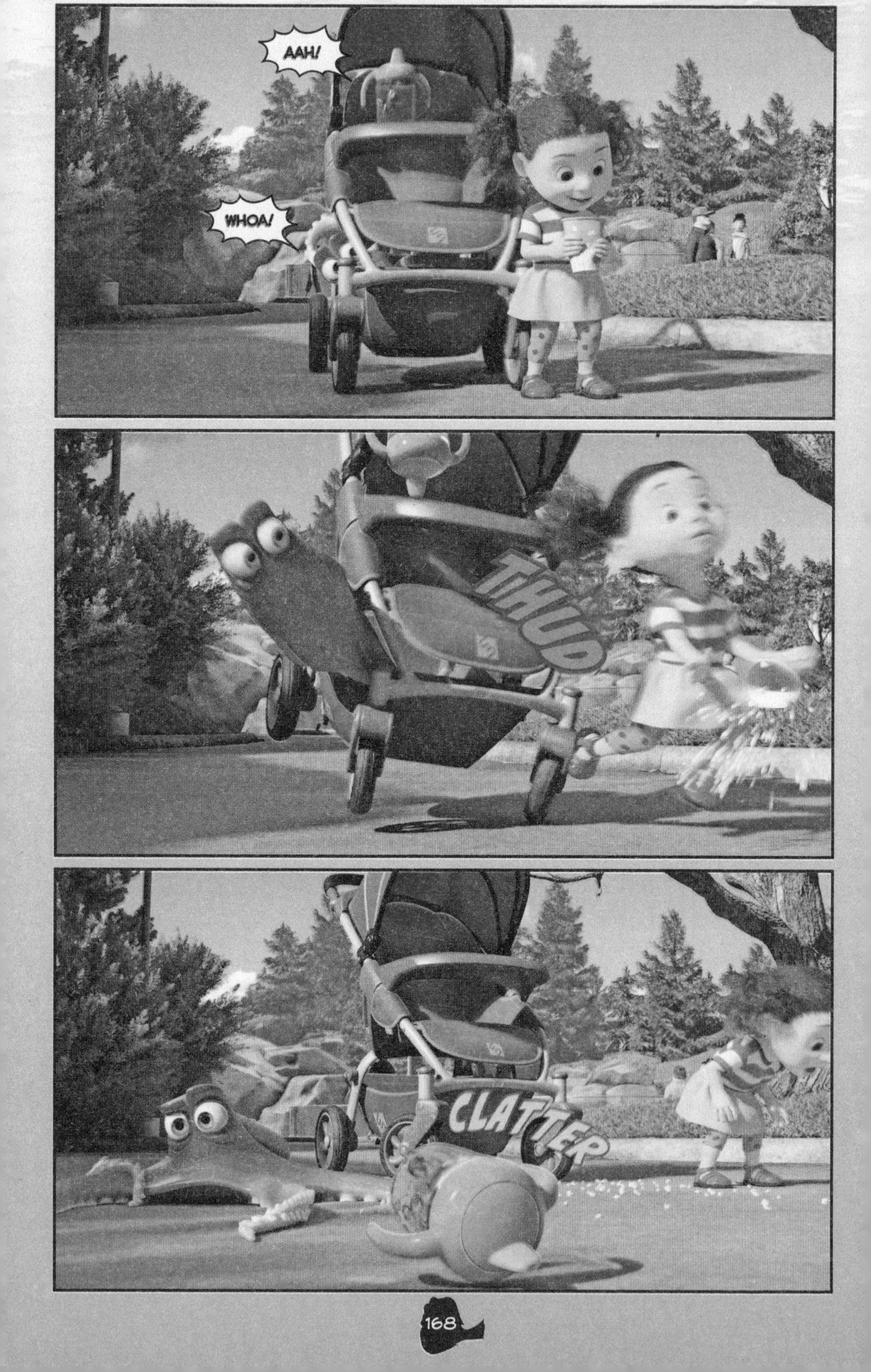
AAH!
WHOA!
THUD
CLATTER

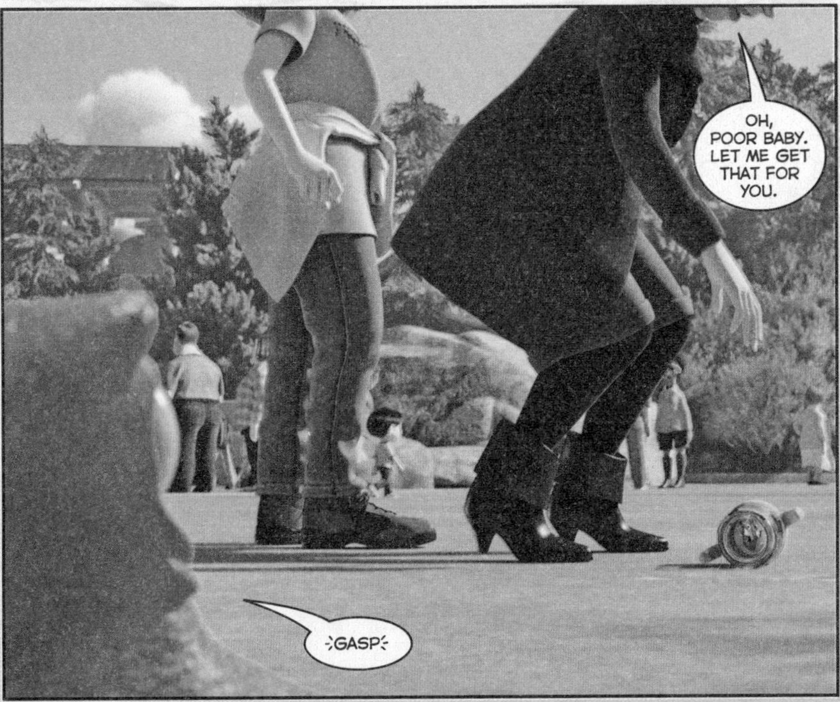
OH, POOR BABY. LET ME GET THAT FOR YOU.
GASP

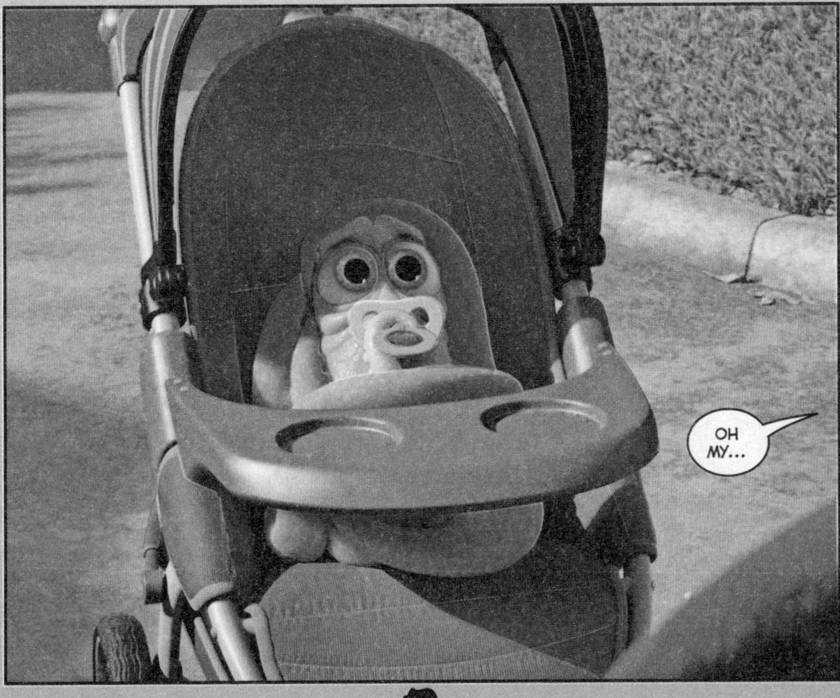
OH MY...

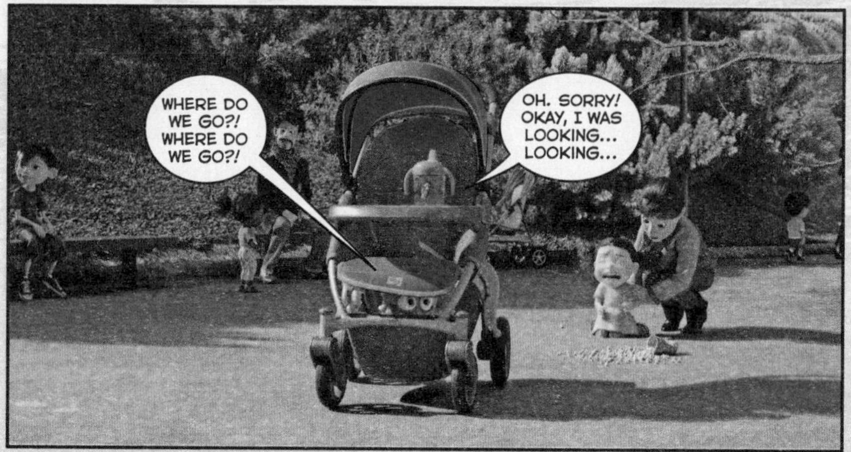
WHERE DO WE GO?! WHERE DO WE GO?!
OH. SORRY! OKAY, I WAS LOOKING... LOOKING...

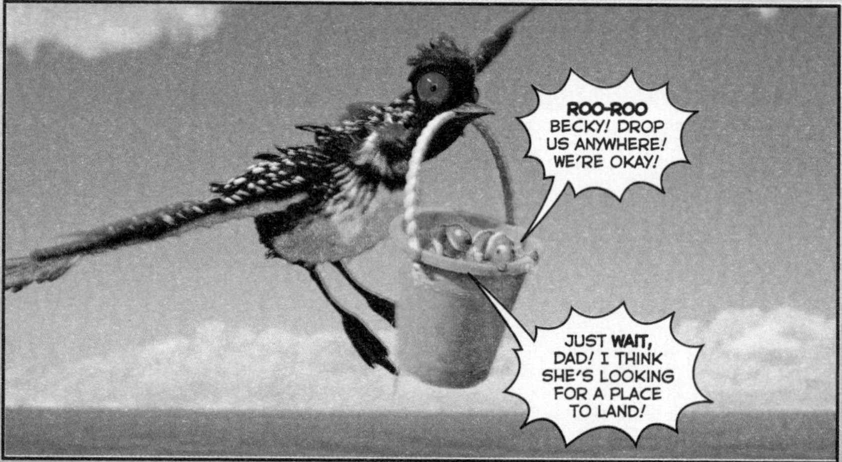
ROO-ROO BECKY! DROP US ANYWHERE! WE'RE OKAY!
JUST WAIT, DAD! I THINK SHE'S LOOKING FOR A PLACE TO LAND!

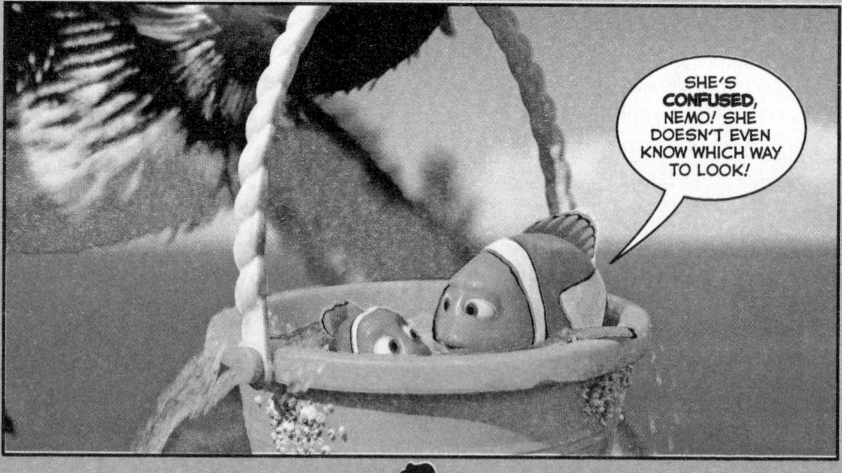
SHE'S CONFUSED, NEMO! SHE DOESN'T EVEN KNOW WHICH WAY TO LOOK!

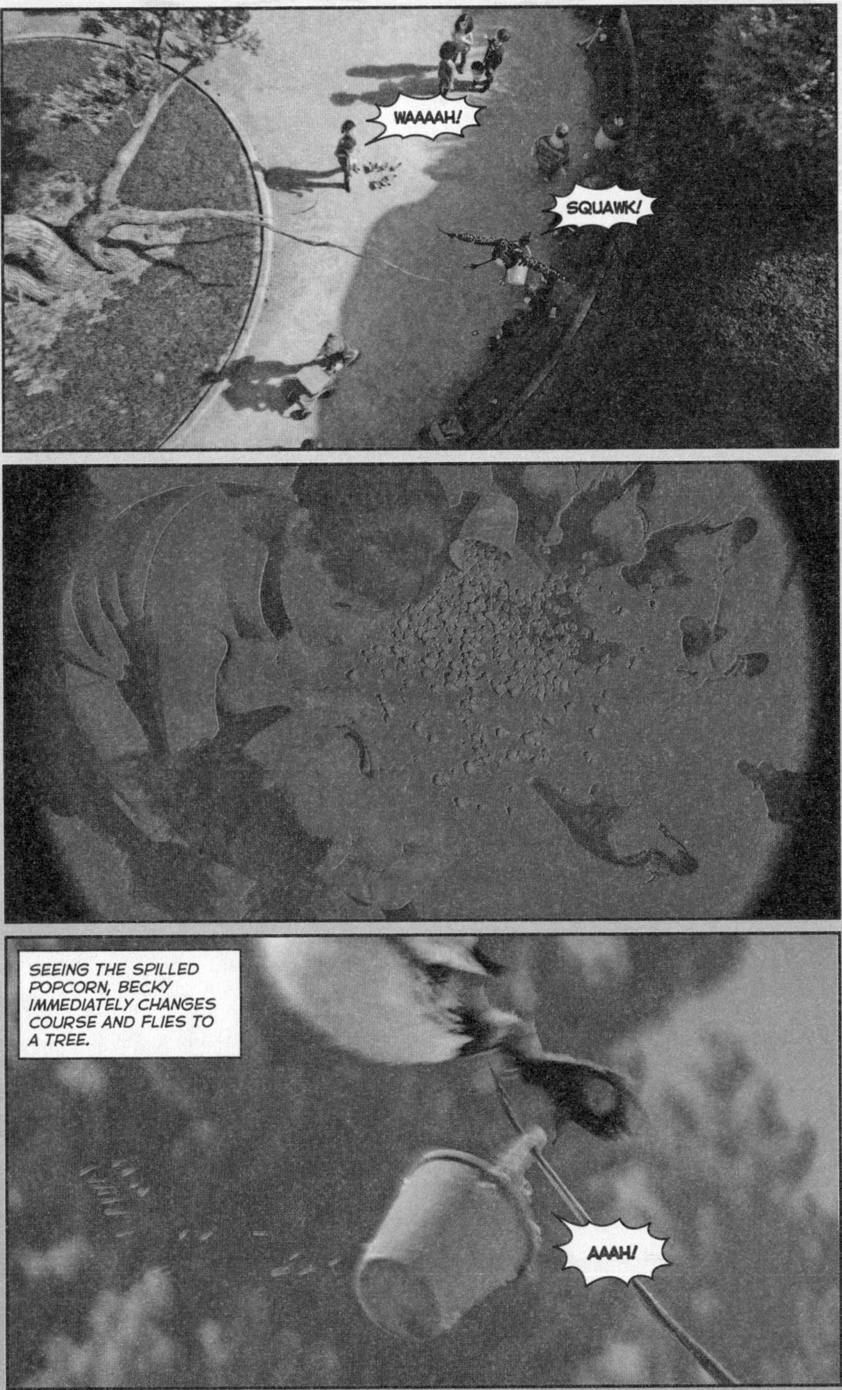
WAAAAH!
SQUAWK!
SEEING THE SPILLED POPCORN, BECKY IMMEDIATELY CHANGES COURSE AND FLIES TO A TREE.
AAAH!

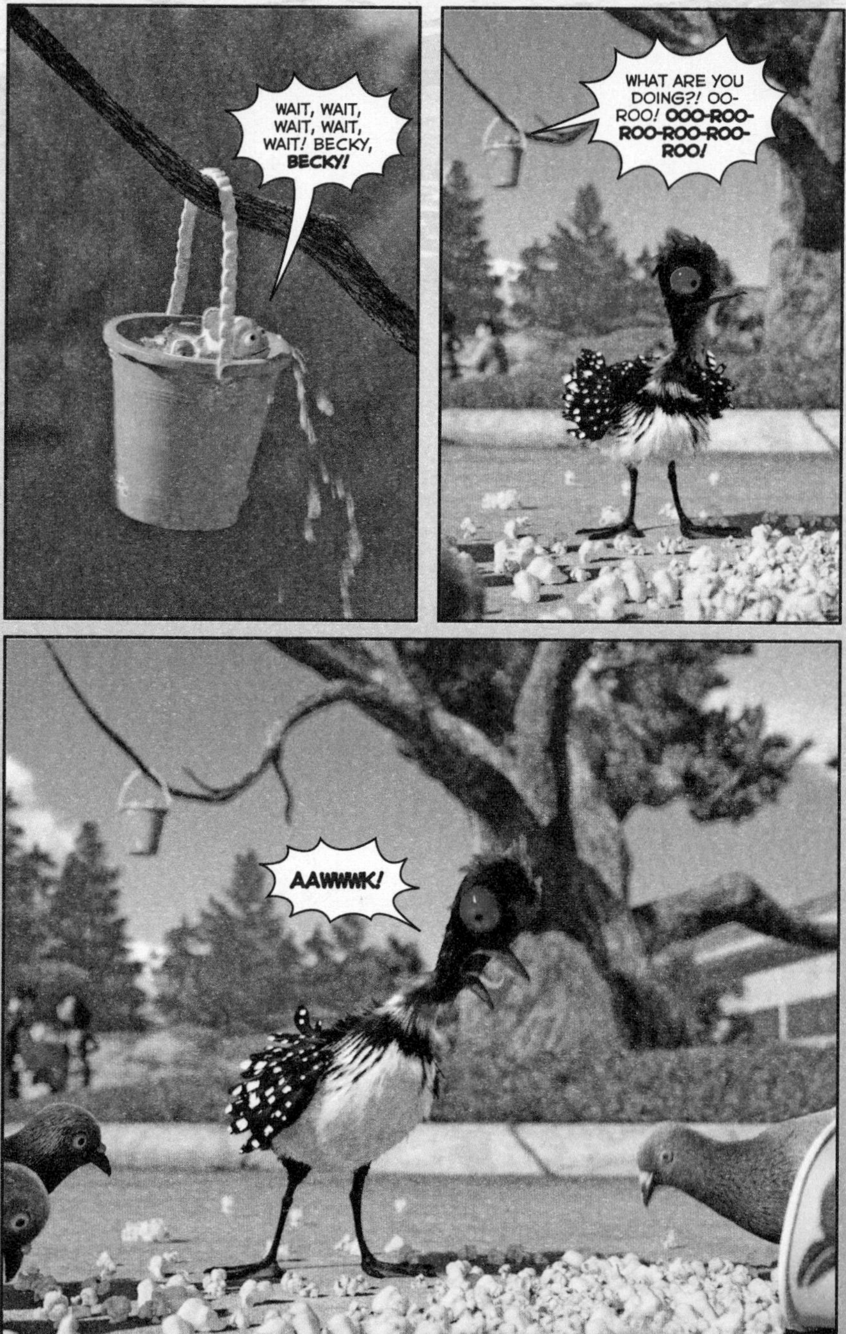
WAIT, WAIT, WAIT, WAIT, WAIT! BECKY, **BECKY!**
WHAT ARE YOU DOING?! OO-ROO! **OOO-ROO-ROO-ROO-ROO-ROO!**
AAWWWK!

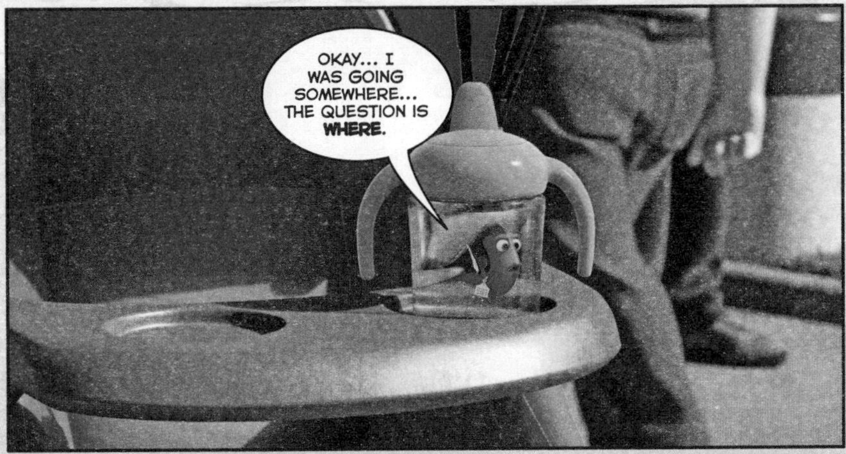
OKAY... I WAS GOING SOMEWHERE... THE QUESTION IS **WHERE**.

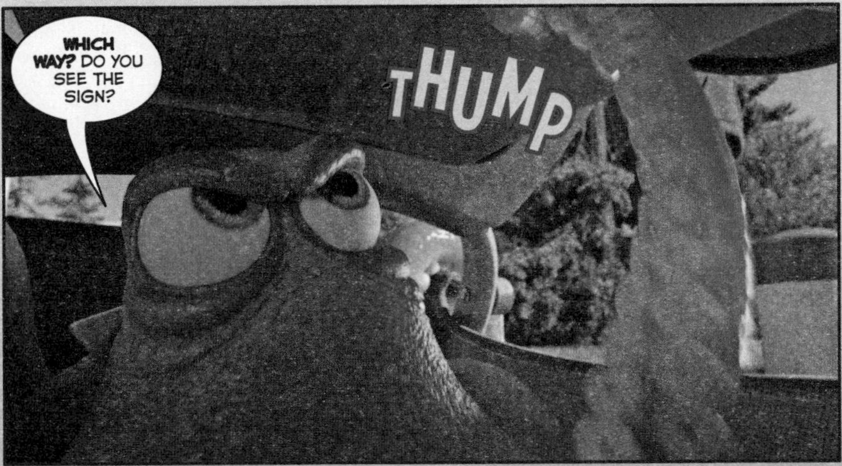
WHICH WAY? DO YOU SEE THE SIGN?
THUMP

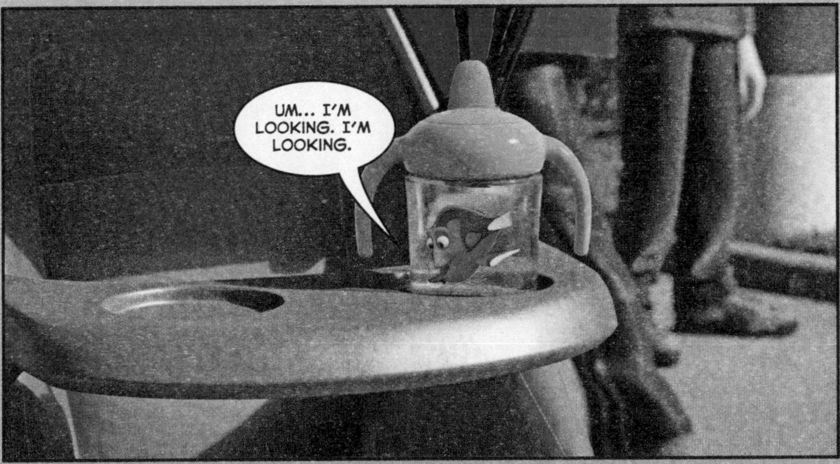
UM... I'M LOOKING. I'M LOOKING.

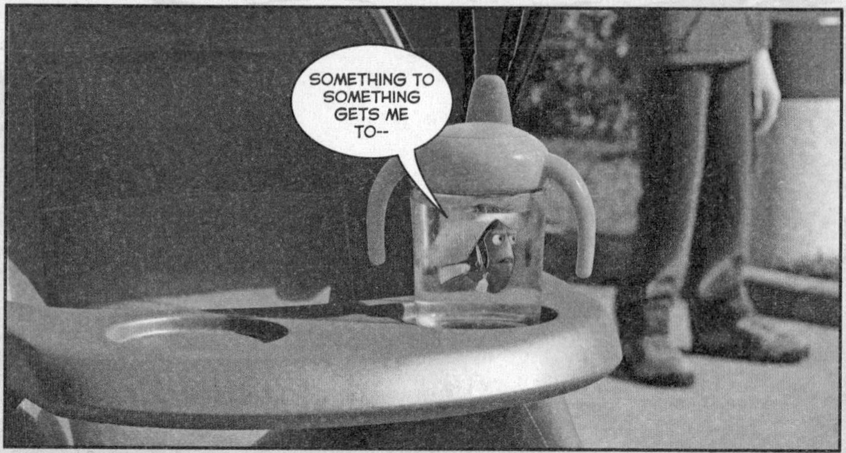
SOMETHING TO SOMETHING GETS ME TO--

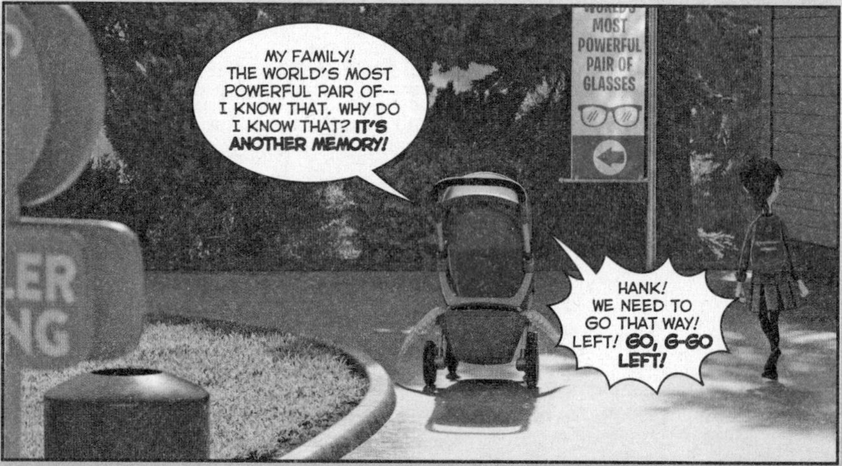
MOST POWERFUL PAIR OF GLASSES
MY FAMILY! THE WORLD'S MOST POWERFUL PAIR OF-- I KNOW THAT. WHY DO I KNOW THAT? **IT'S ANOTHER MEMORY!**
HANK! WE NEED TO GO THAT WAY! LEFT! **GO, G-GO LEFT!**

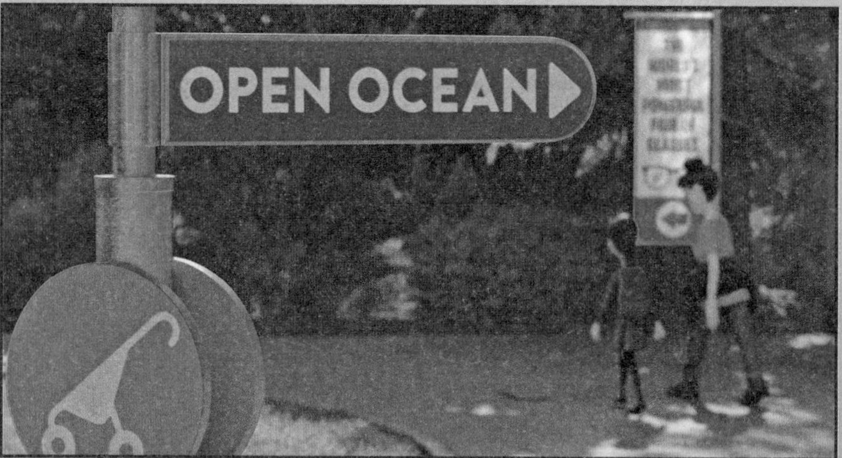
OPEN OCEAN

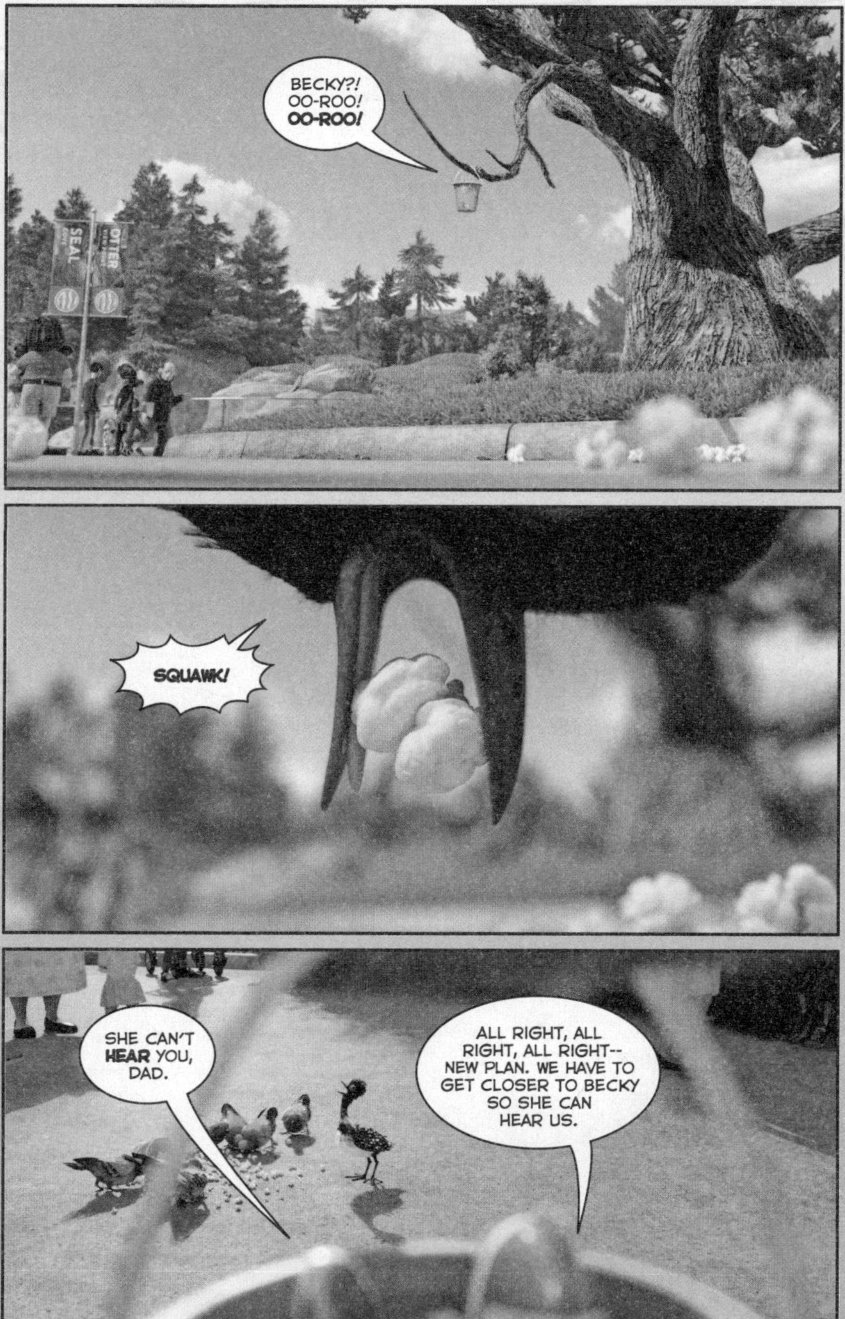
BECKY?! OO-ROO! **OO-ROO!**
SEAL
OTTER
SQUAWK!
SHE CAN'T **HEAR** YOU, DAD.
ALL RIGHT, ALL RIGHT, ALL RIGHT-- NEW PLAN. WE HAVE TO GET CLOSER TO BECKY SO SHE CAN HEAR US.

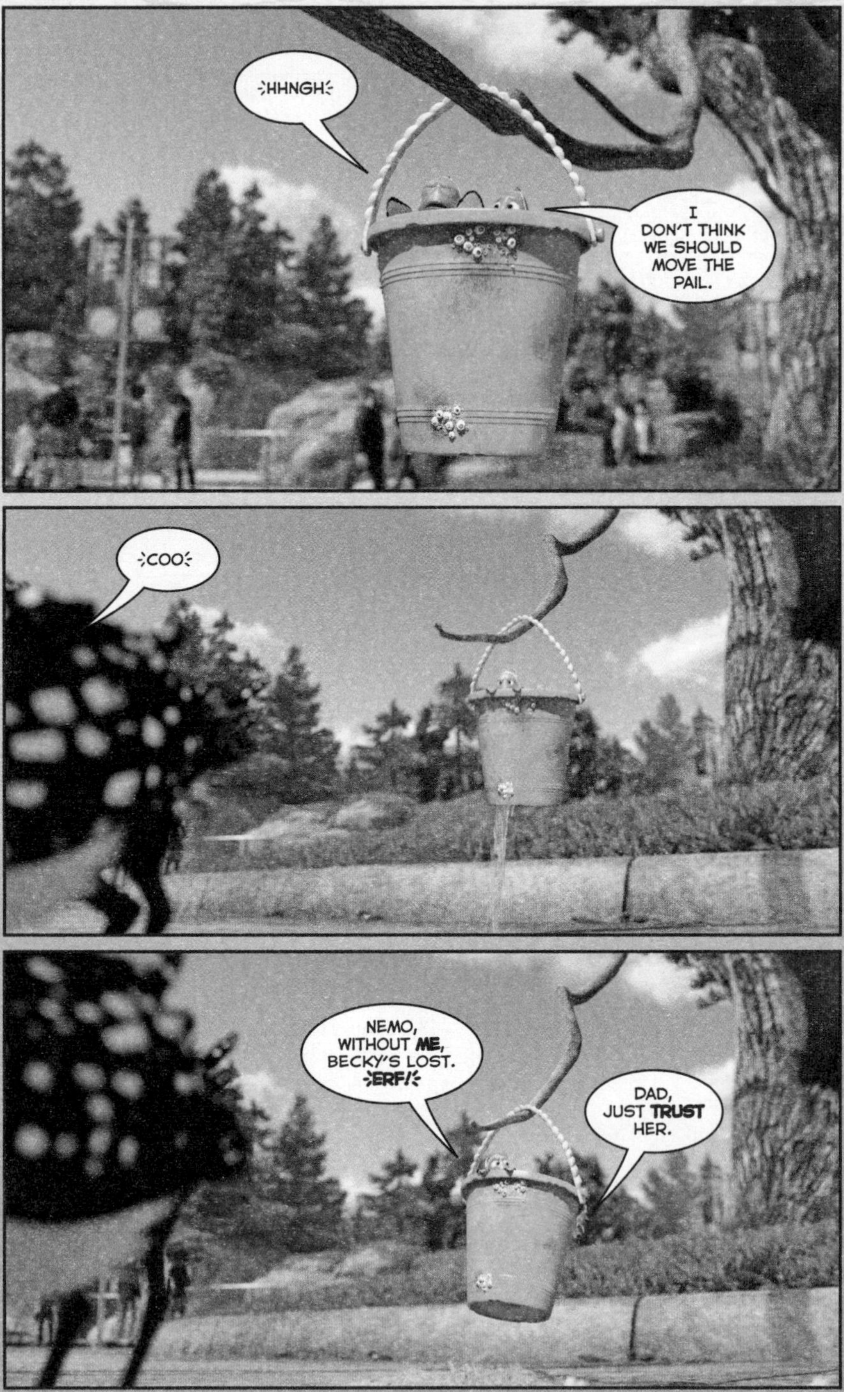
HHNGH
I DON'T THINK WE SHOULD MOVE THE PAIL.
COO
NEMO, WITHOUT **ME**, BECKY'S LOST. **ERF!**
DAD, JUST **TRUST** HER.

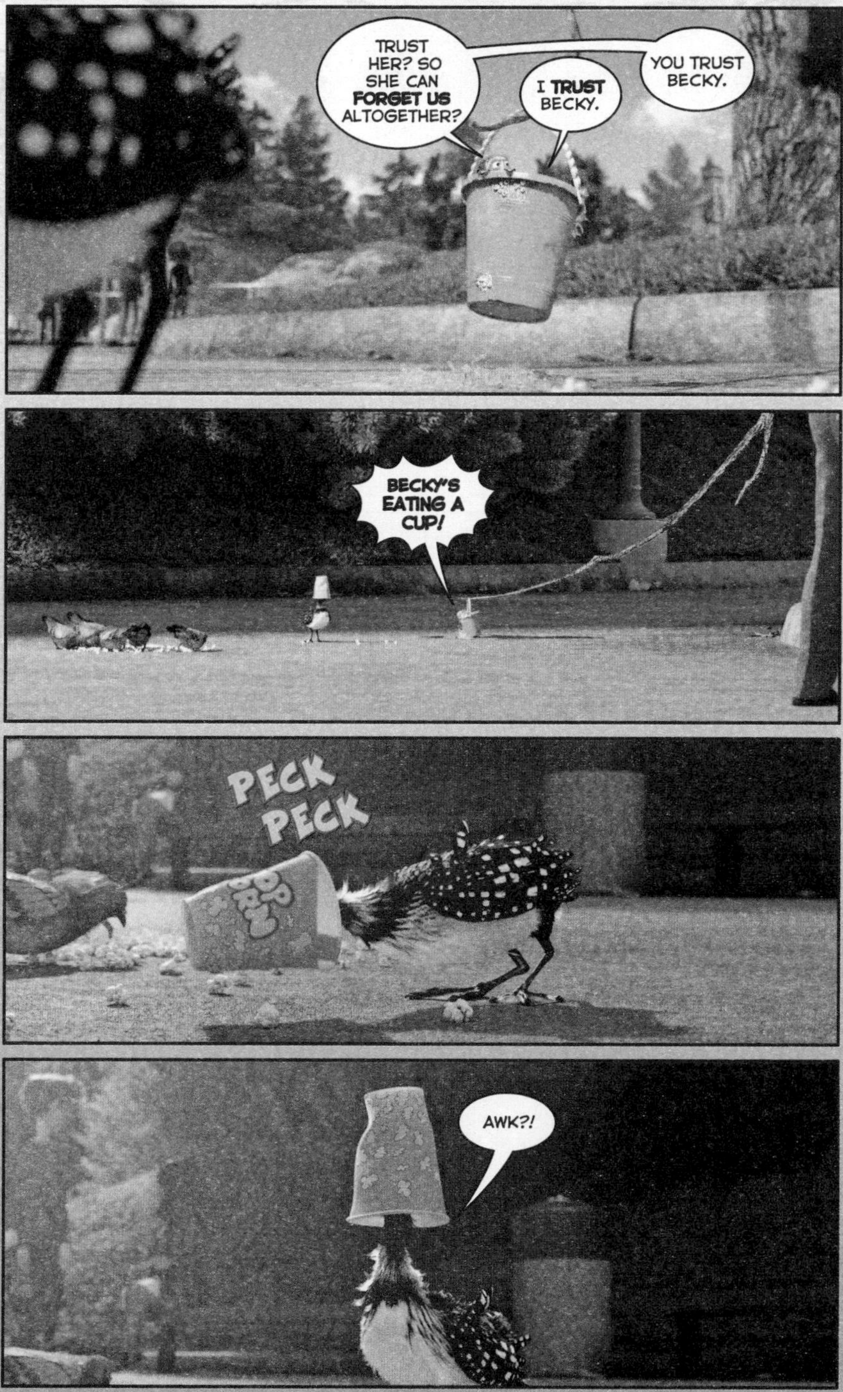
TRUST HER? SO SHE CAN FORGET US ALTOGETHER?
I TRUST BECKY.
YOU TRUST BECKY.
BECKY'S EATING A CUP!
PECK PECK
AWK?!

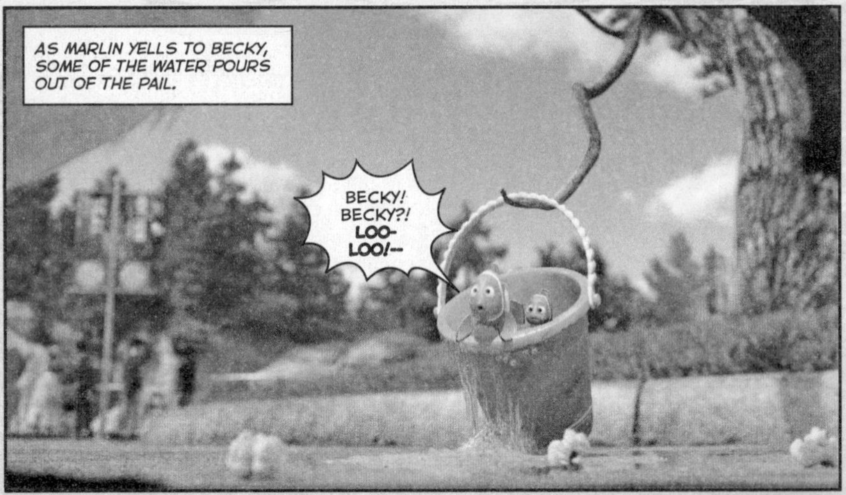
AS MARLIN YELLS TO BECKY, SOME OF THE WATER POURS OUT OF THE PAIL.
BECKY! BECKY?! LOO-LOO!--

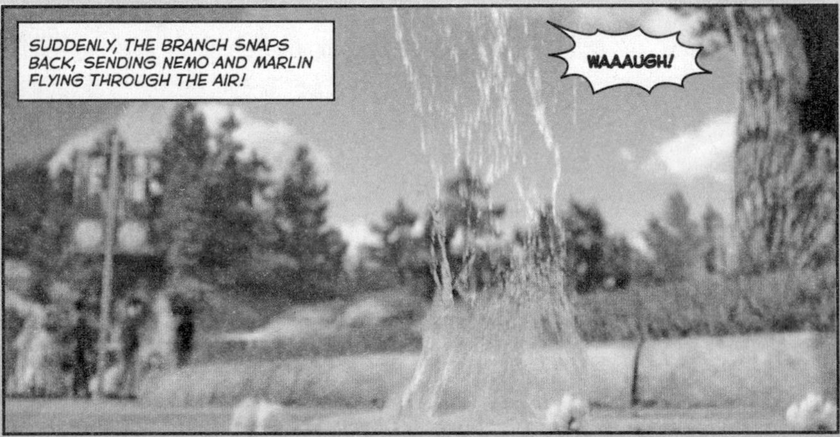
SUDDENLY, THE BRANCH SNAPS BACK, SENDING NEMO AND MARLIN FLYING THROUGH THE AIR!
WAAAUGH!

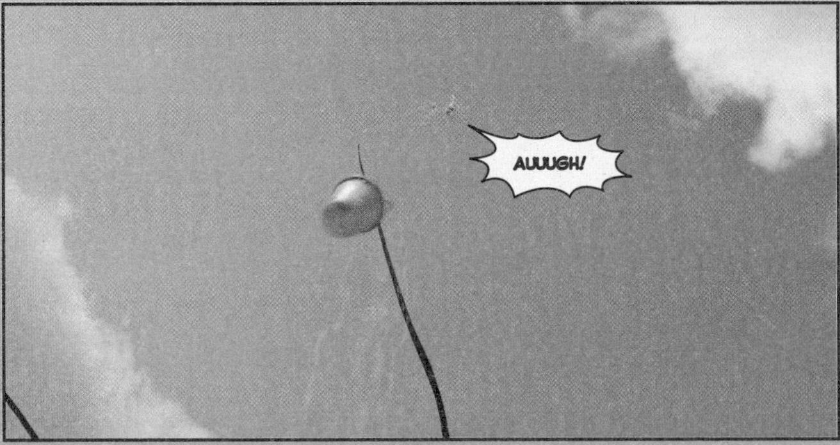
AUUUGH!

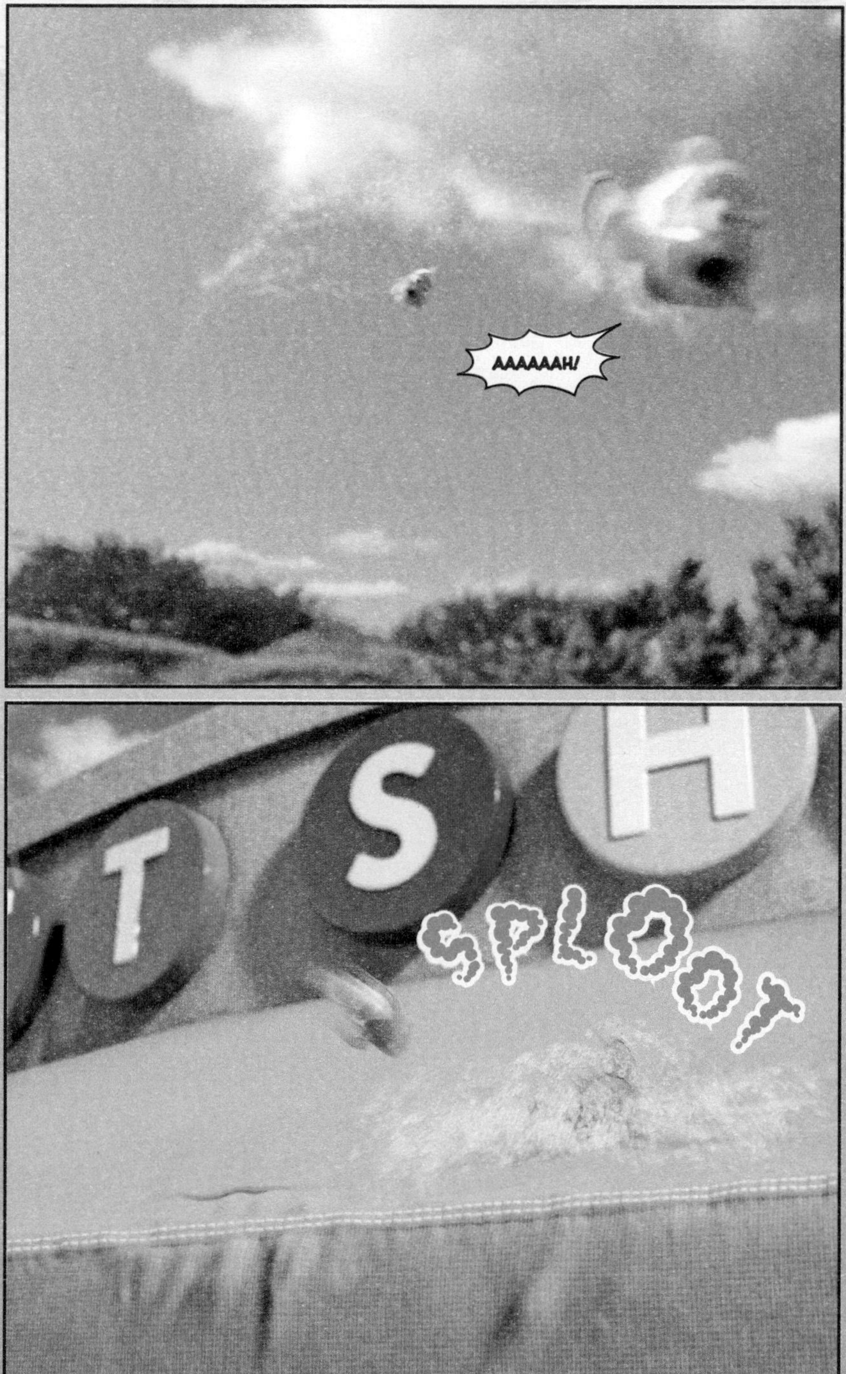
AAAAAAH!
SPLOOT

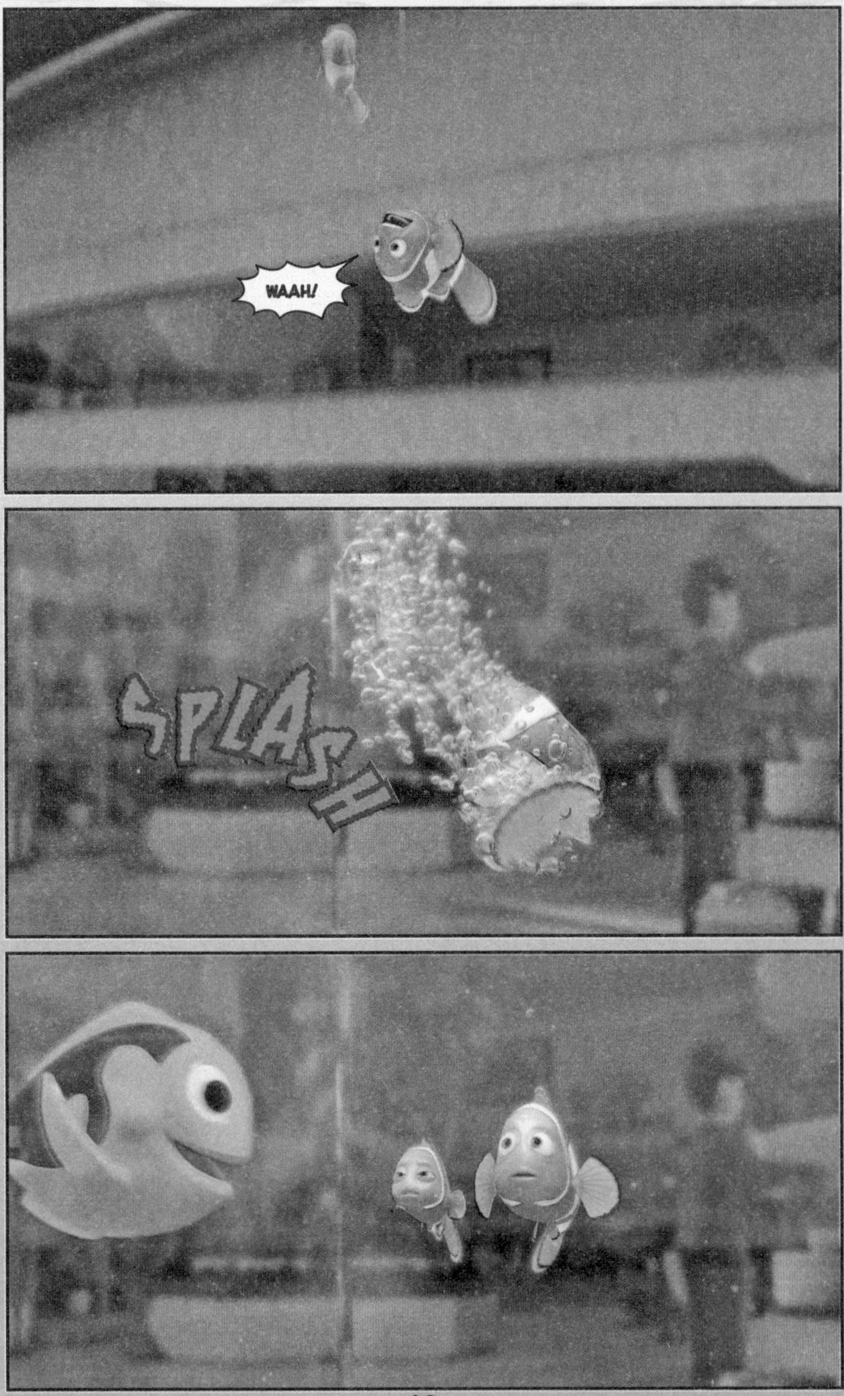
WAAH!
SPLASH

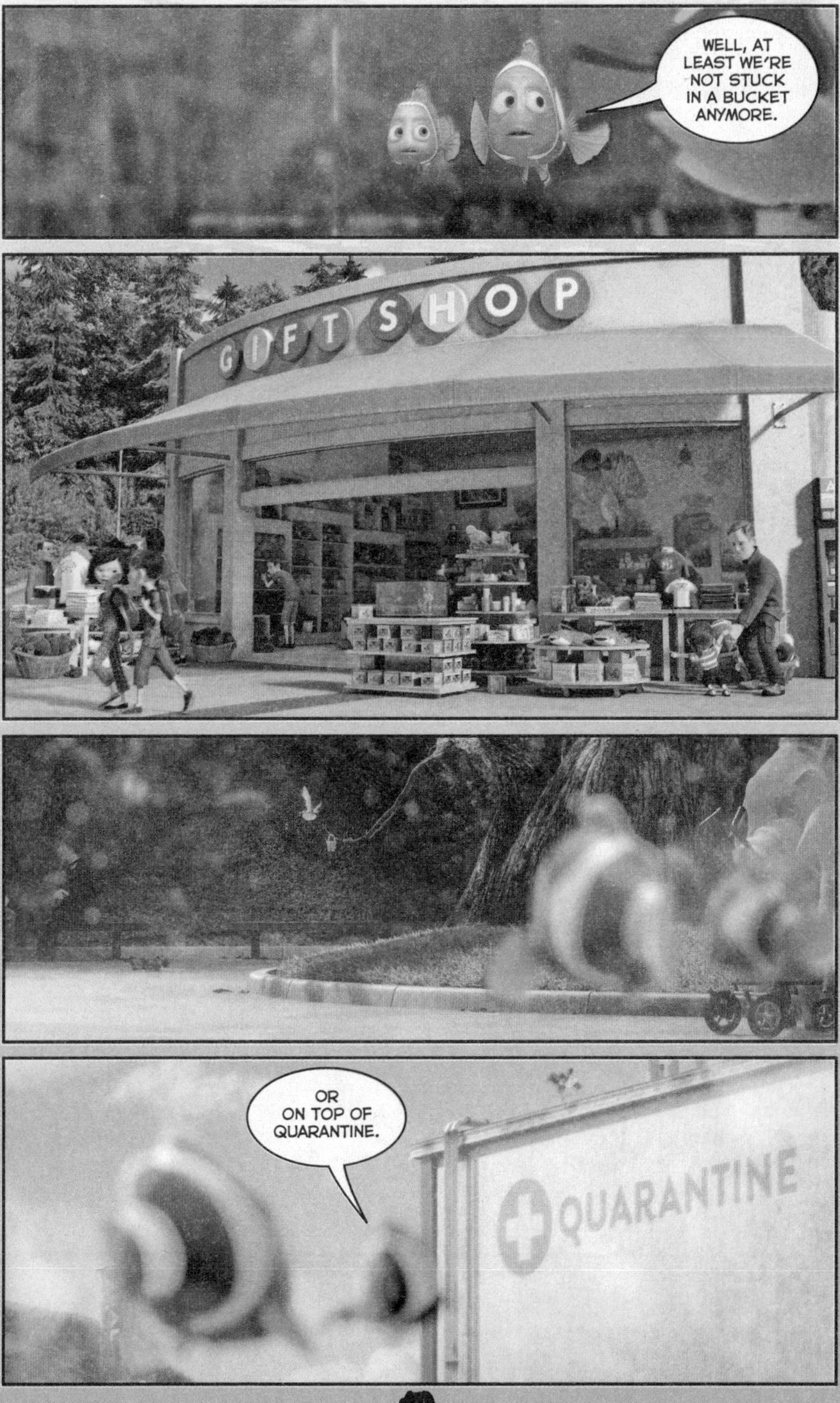
WELL, AT LEAST WE'RE NOT STUCK IN A BUCKET ANYMORE.
GIFT SHOP
OR ON TOP OF QUARANTINE.
QUARANTINE

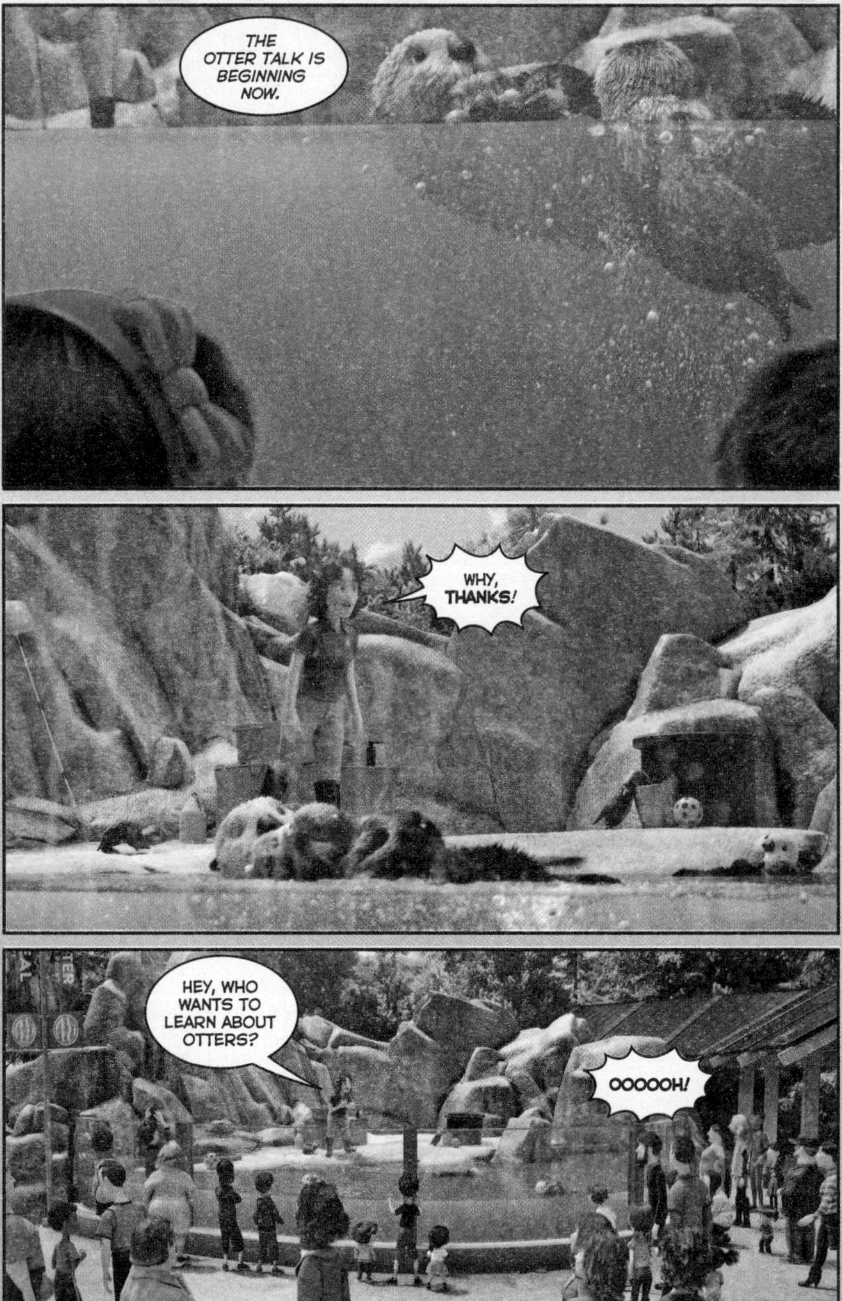
THE OTTER TALK IS BEGINNING NOW.
WHY, THANKS!
HEY, WHO WANTS TO LEARN ABOUT OTTERS?
OOOOOH!

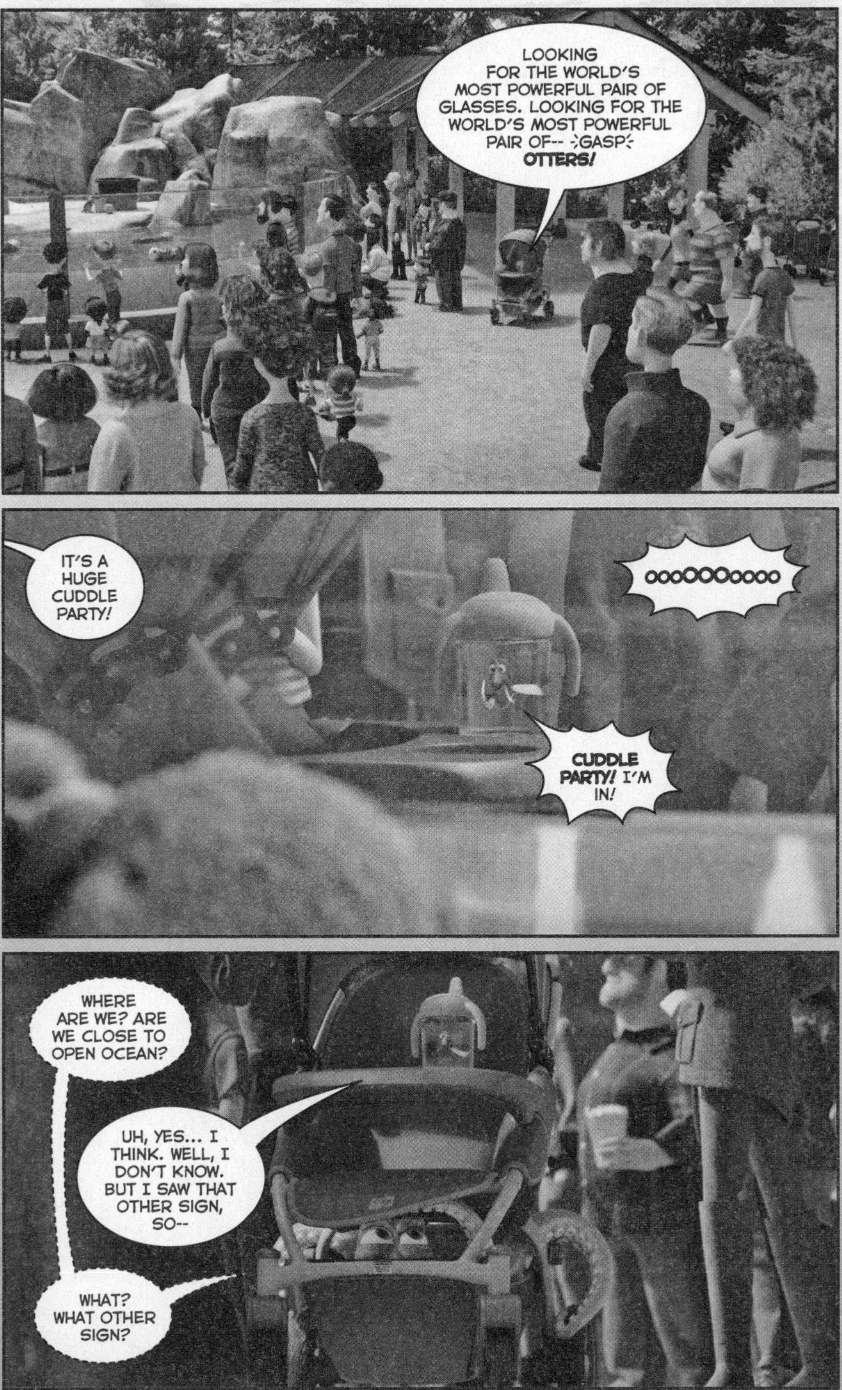
LOOKING FOR THE WORLD'S MOST POWERFUL PAIR OF GLASSES. LOOKING FOR THE WORLD'S MOST POWERFUL PAIR OF-- GASP OTTERS!
IT'S A HUGE CUDDLE PARTY!
oooOOOoooo
CUDDLE PARTY! I'M IN!
WHERE ARE WE? ARE WE CLOSE TO OPEN OCEAN?
UH, YES... I THINK. WELL, I DON'T KNOW. BUT I SAW THAT OTHER SIGN, SO--
WHAT? WHAT OTHER SIGN?

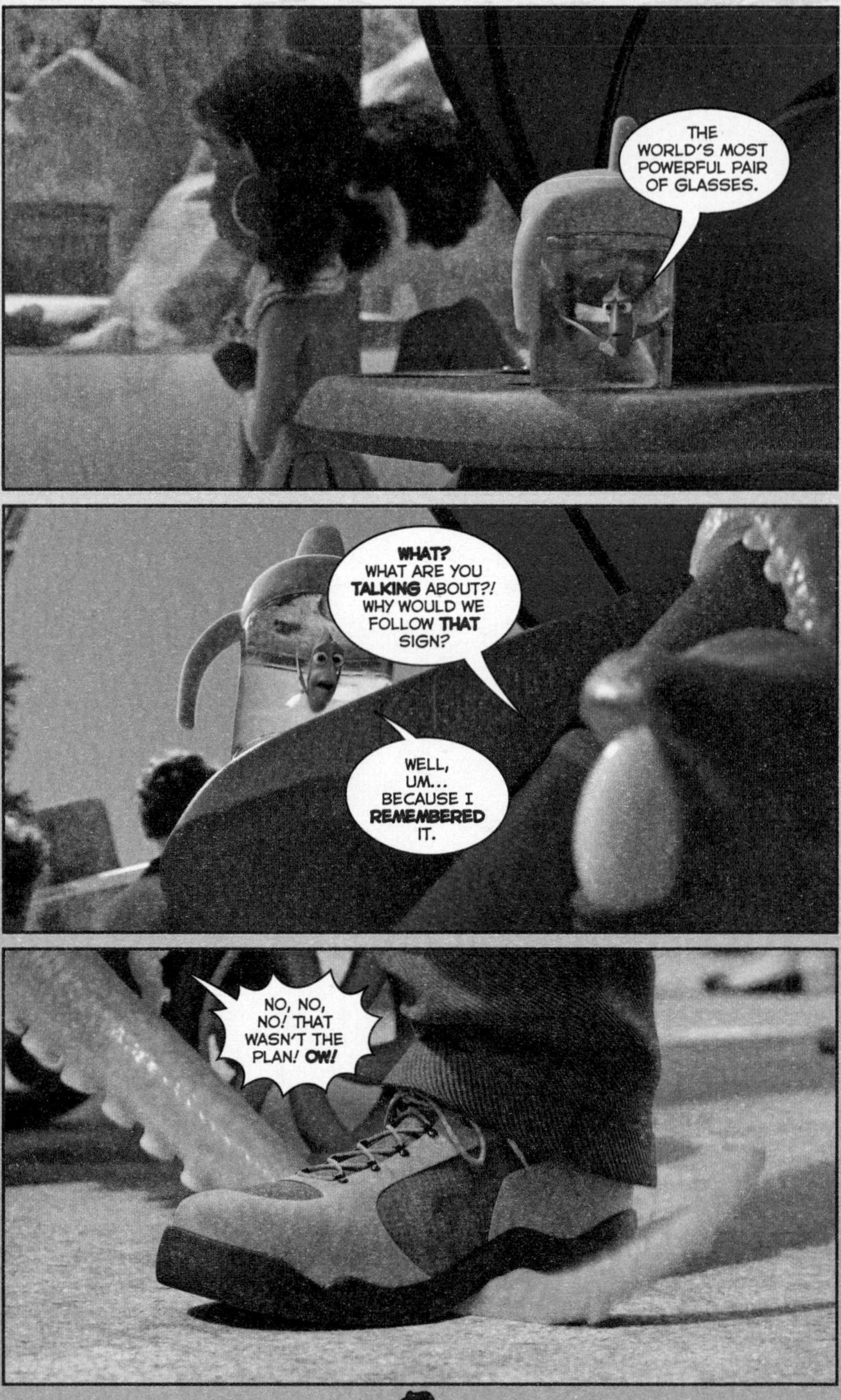
THE WORLD'S MOST POWERFUL PAIR OF GLASSES.
WHAT? WHAT ARE YOU TALKING ABOUT?! WHY WOULD WE FOLLOW THAT SIGN?
WELL, UM... BECAUSE I REMEMBERED IT.
NO, NO, NO! THAT WASN'T THE PLAN! OW!

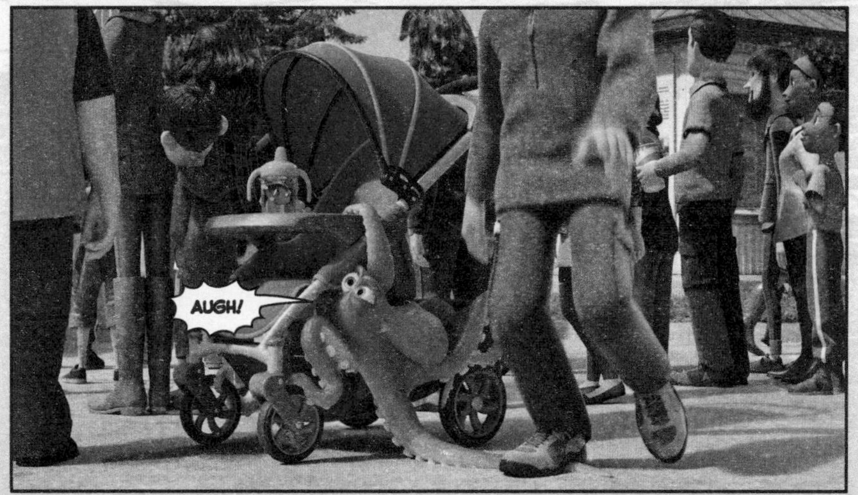
AUGH!

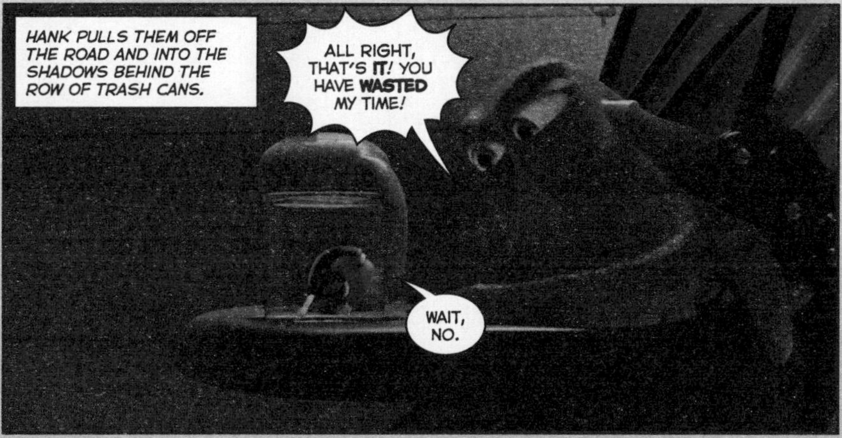
HANK PULLS THEM OFF THE ROAD AND INTO THE SHADOWS BEHIND THE ROW OF TRASH CANS.
ALL RIGHT, THAT'S IT! YOU HAVE WASTED MY TIME!
WAIT, NO.

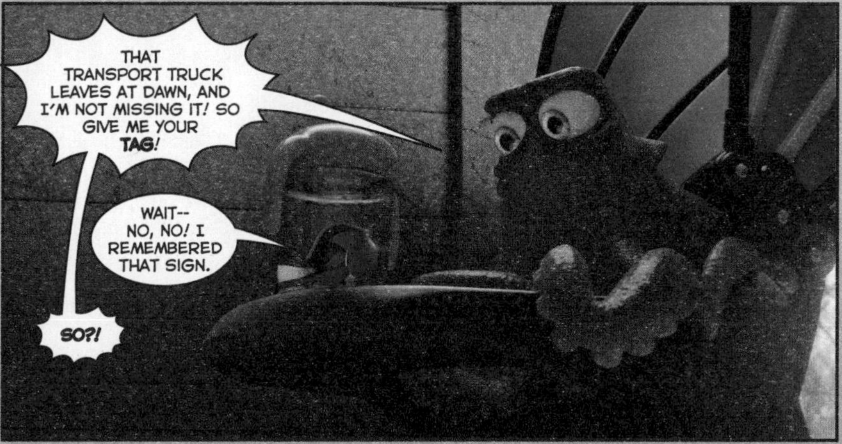
THAT TRANSPORT TRUCK LEAVES AT DAWN, AND I'M NOT MISSING IT! SO GIVE ME YOUR TAG!
WAIT-- NO, NO! I REMEMBERED THAT SIGN.
SO?!

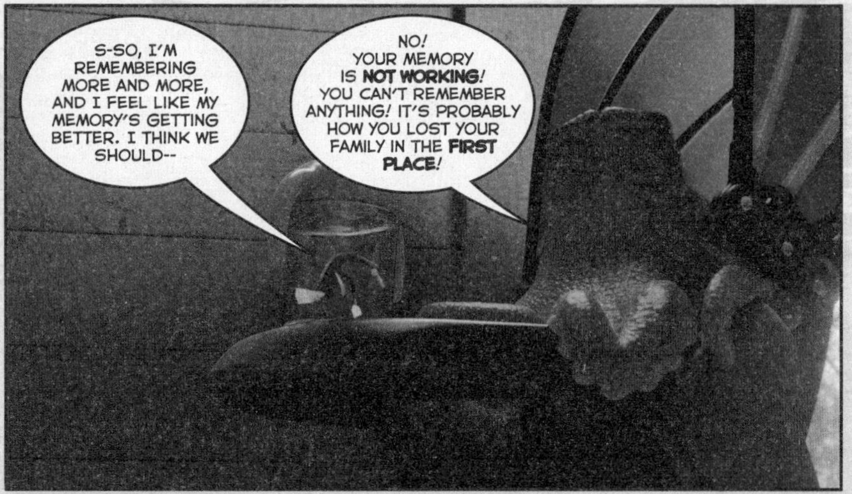
S-SO, I'M REMEMBERING MORE AND MORE, AND I FEEL LIKE MY MEMORY'S GETTING BETTER. I THINK WE SHOULD--
NO! YOUR MEMORY IS **NOT WORKING**! YOU CAN'T REMEMBER ANYTHING! IT'S PROBABLY HOW YOU LOST YOUR FAMILY IN THE **FIRST PLACE**!

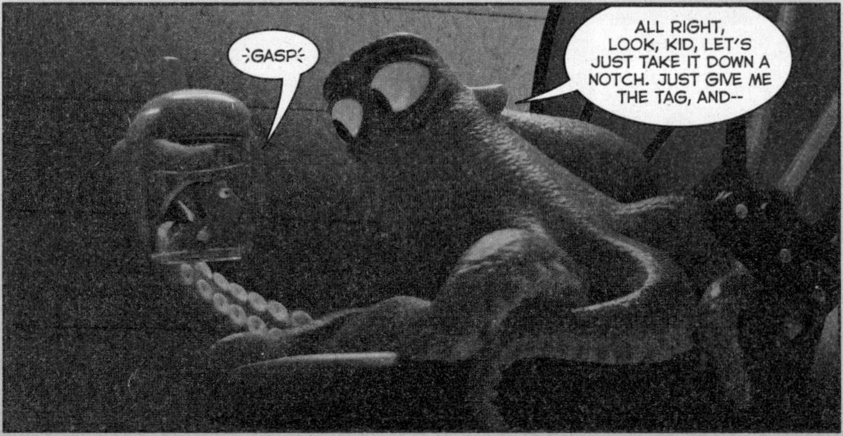
GASP
ALL RIGHT, LOOK, KID, LET'S JUST TAKE IT DOWN A NOTCH. JUST GIVE ME THE TAG, AND--

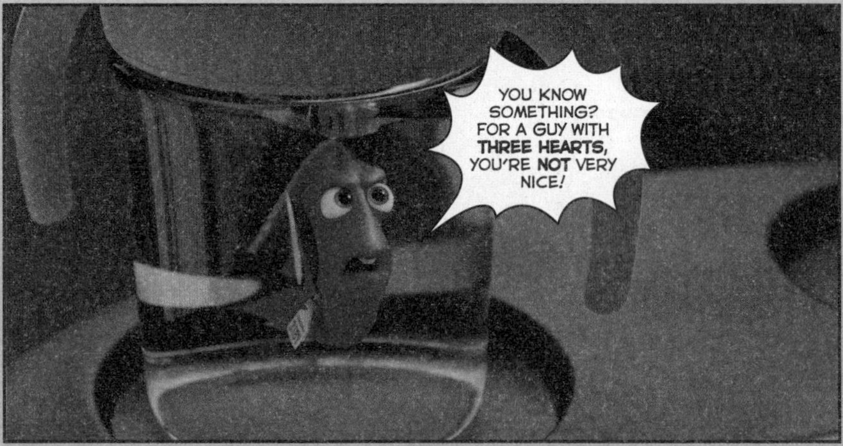
YOU KNOW SOMETHING? FOR A GUY WITH **THREE HEARTS**, YOU'RE **NOT** VERY NICE!

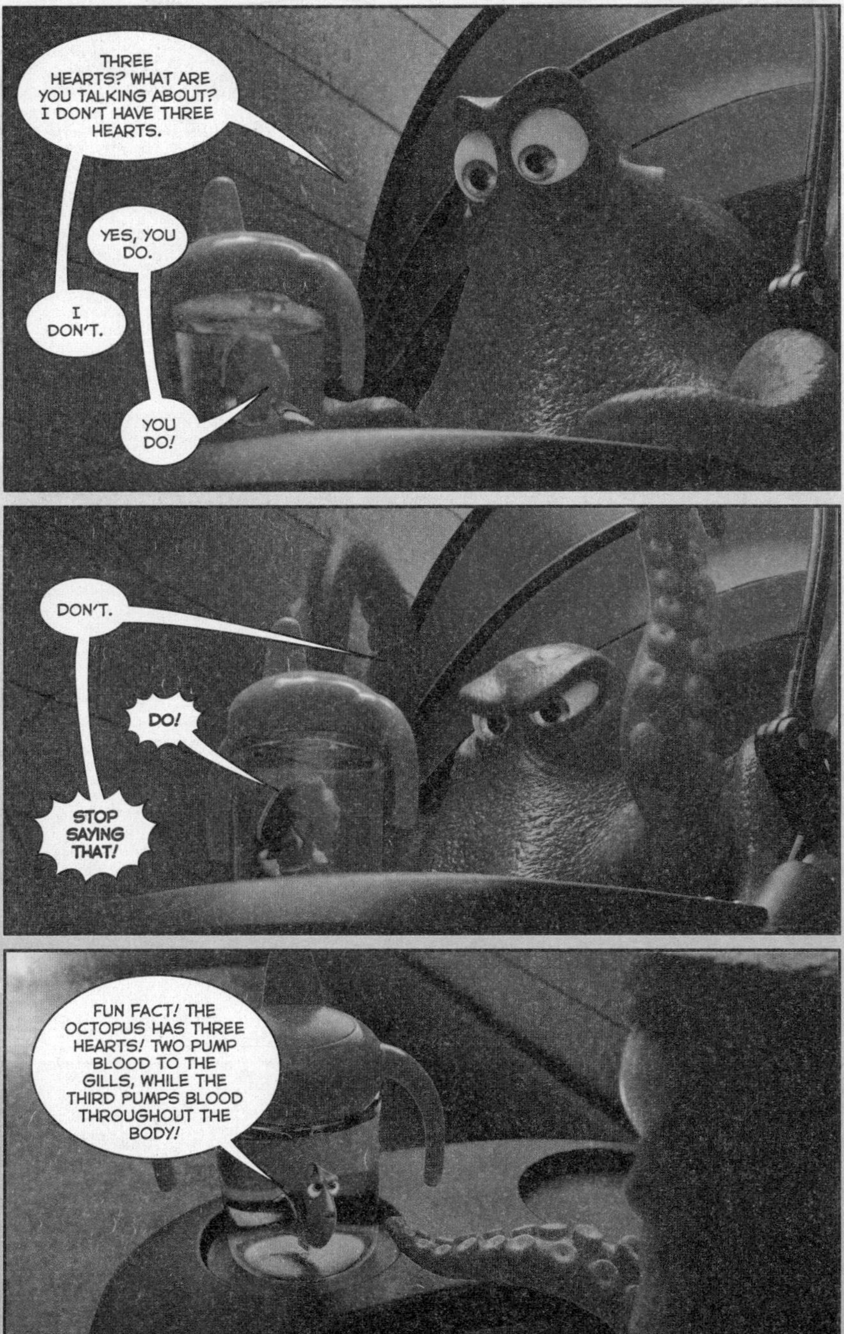
THREE HEARTS? WHAT ARE YOU TALKING ABOUT? I DON'T HAVE THREE HEARTS.
YES, YOU DO.
I DON'T.
YOU DO!
DON'T.
DO!
STOP SAYING THAT!
FUN FACT! THE OCTOPUS HAS THREE HEARTS! TWO PUMP BLOOD TO THE GILLS, WHILE THE THIRD PUMPS BLOOD THROUGHOUT THE BODY!

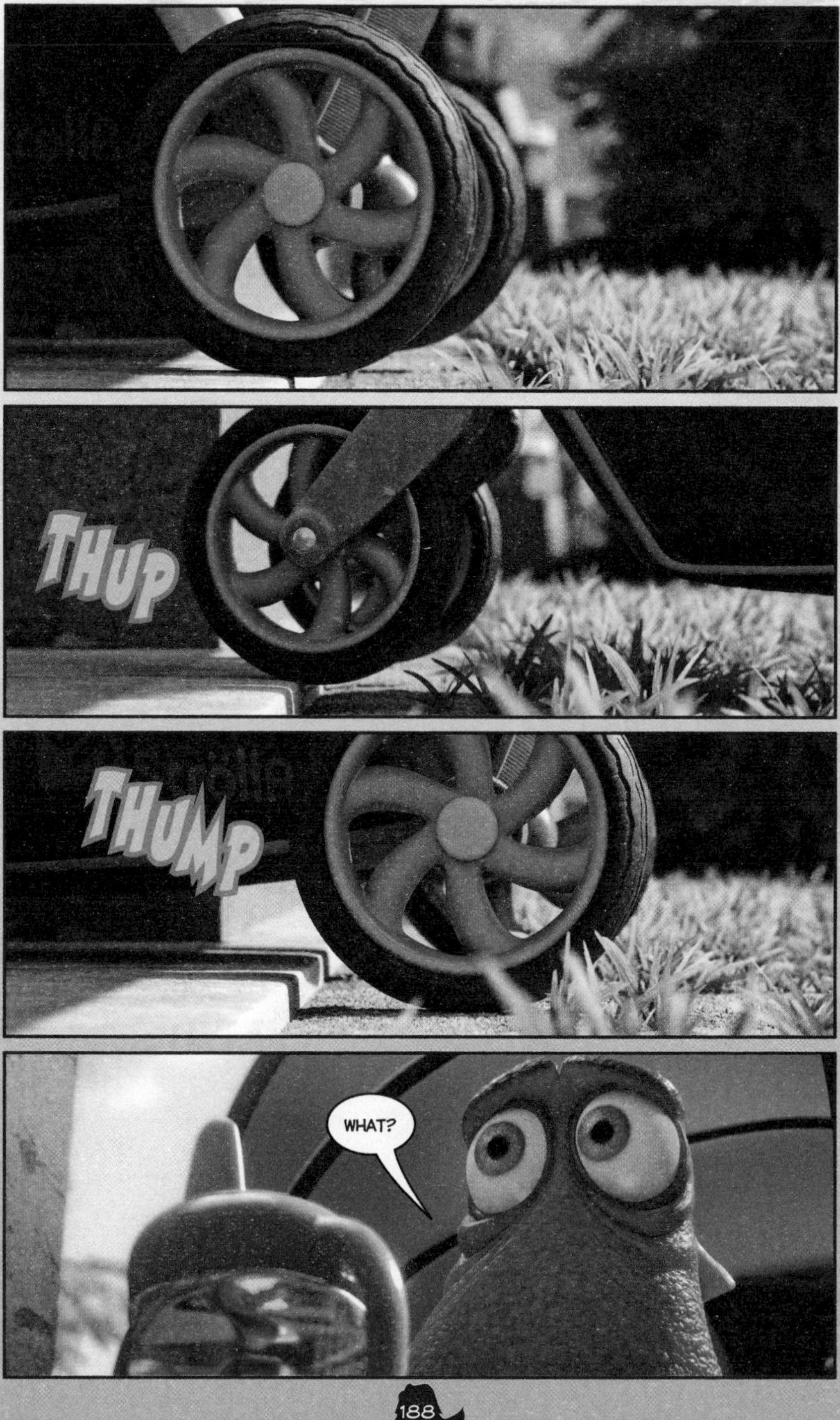
THUP
THUMP
WHAT?

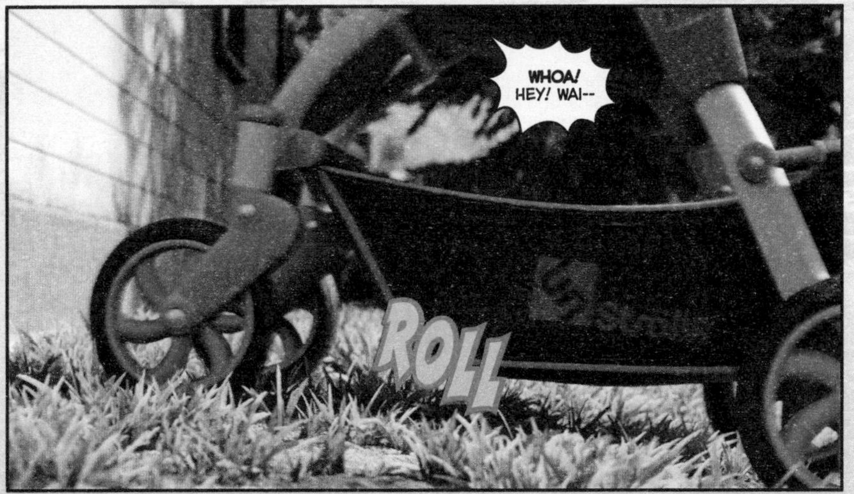
WHOA! HEY! WAI--
ROLL

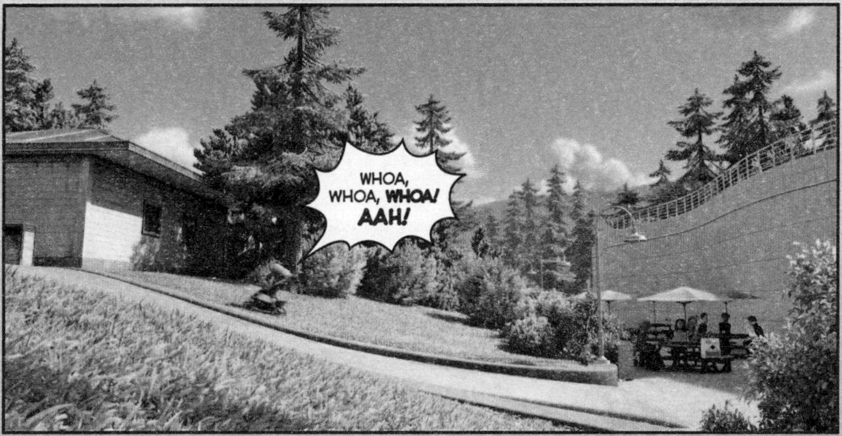
WHOA, WHOA, WHOA! AAH!

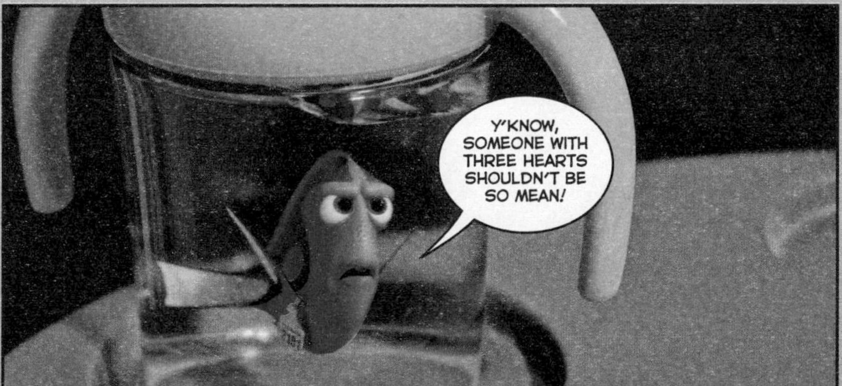
Y'KNOW, SOMEONE WITH THREE HEARTS SHOULDN'T BE SO MEAN!

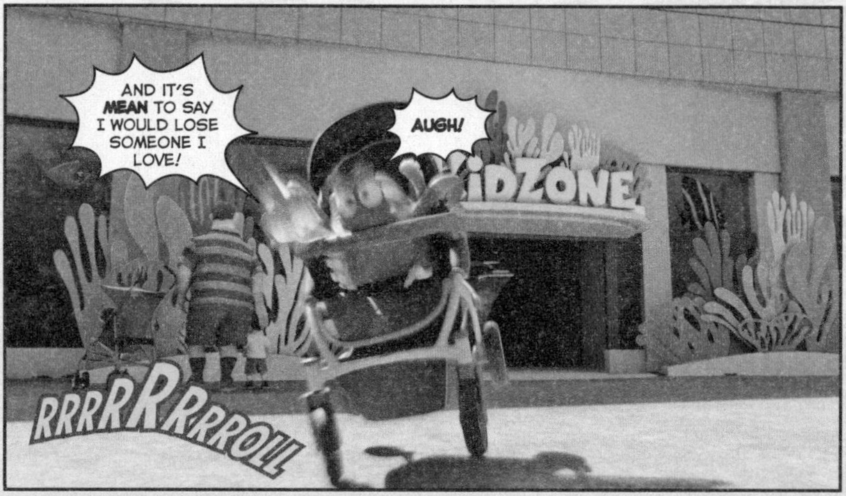
AND IT'S **MEAN** TO SAY I WOULD LOSE SOMEONE I LOVE!
AUGH!
KIDZONE
RRRRRRRROLL

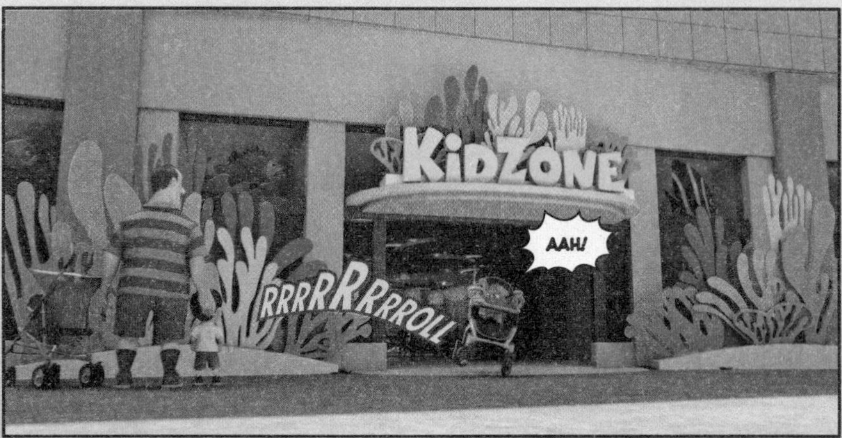
KIDZONE
AAH!
RRRRRRRROLL

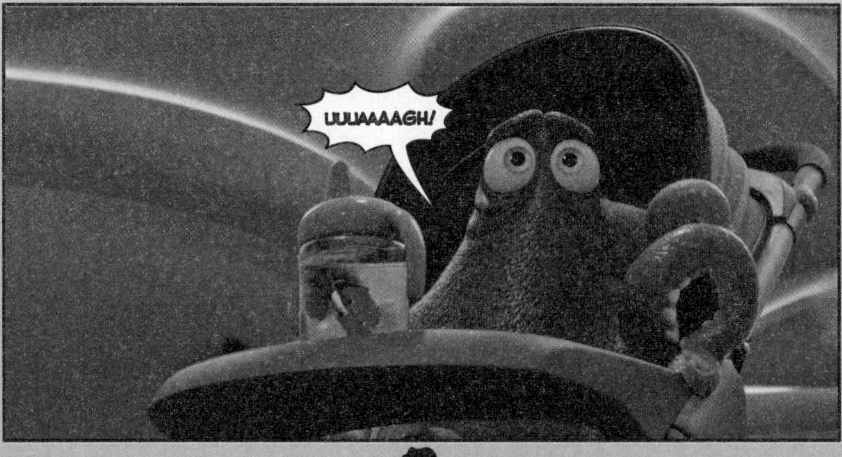
UUUAAAAGH!

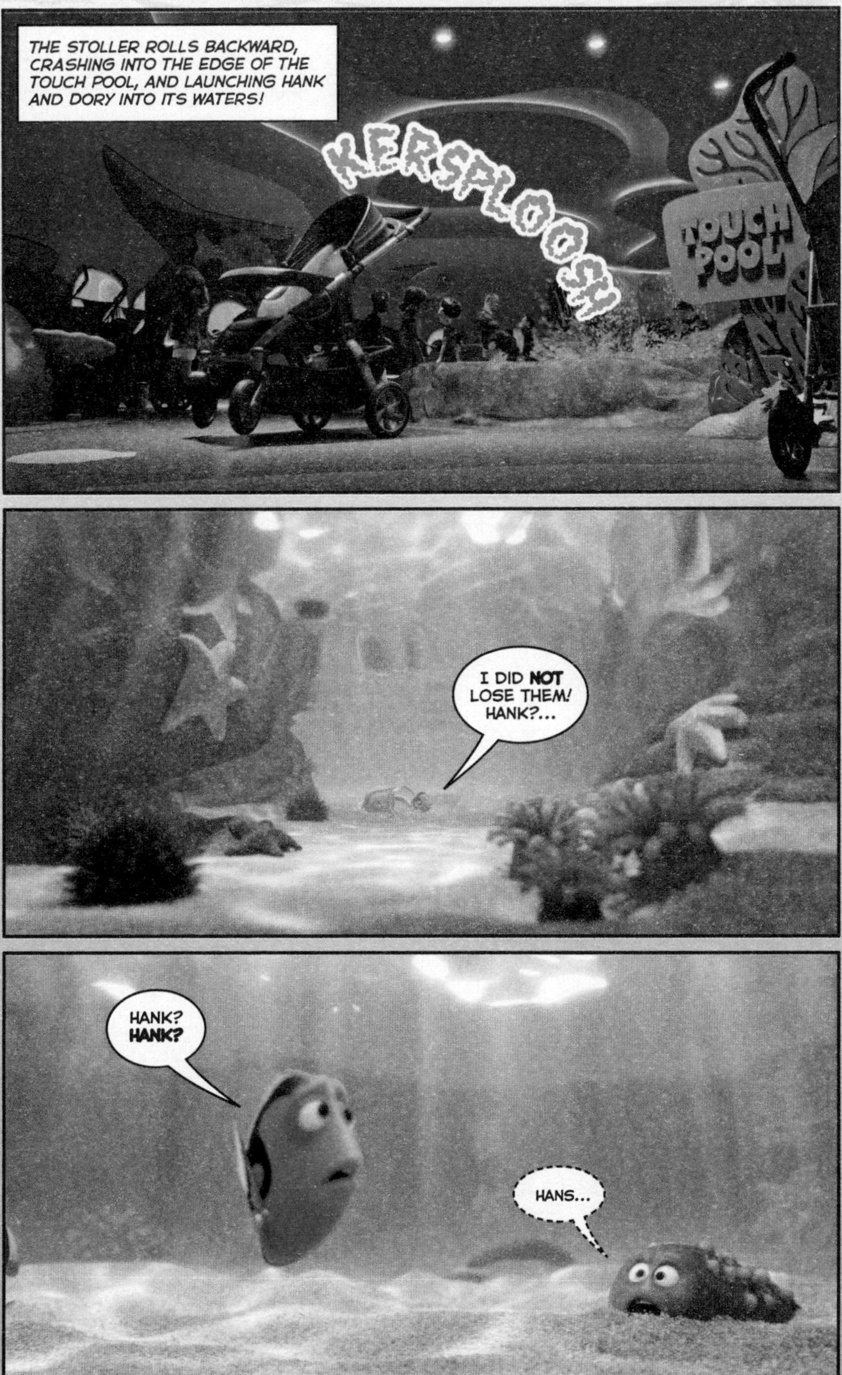
THE STOLLER ROLLS BACKWARD, CRASHING INTO THE EDGE OF THE TOUCH POOL, AND LAUNCHING HANK AND DORY INTO ITS WATERS!
KERSPLOOSH
TOUCH POOL
I DID **NOT** LOSE THEM! HANK?...
HANK? **HANK?**
HANS...

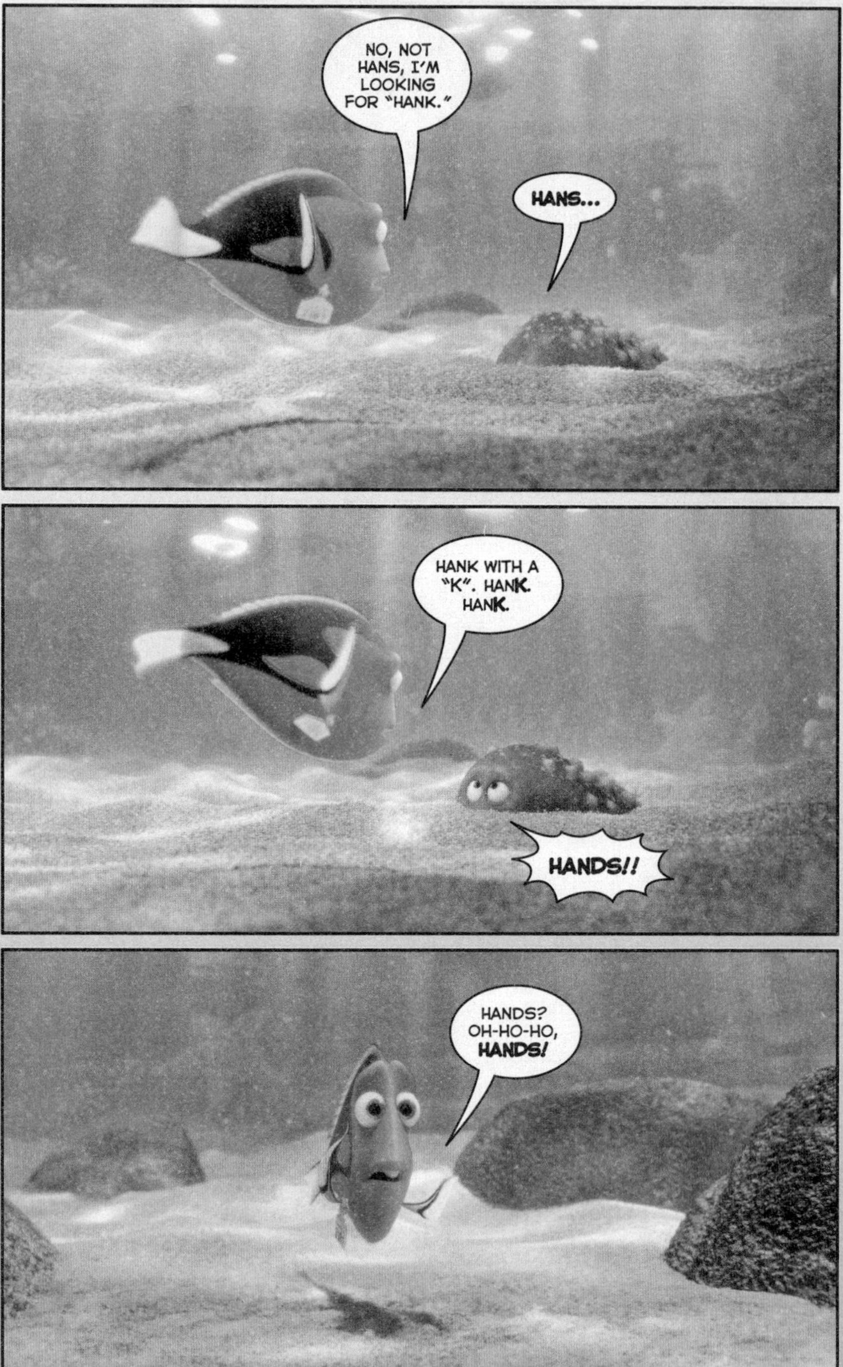
NO, NOT HANS, I'M LOOKING FOR "HANK."
HANS...
HANK WITH A "K". HANK. HANK.
HANDS!!
HANDS? OH-HO-HO, HANDS!

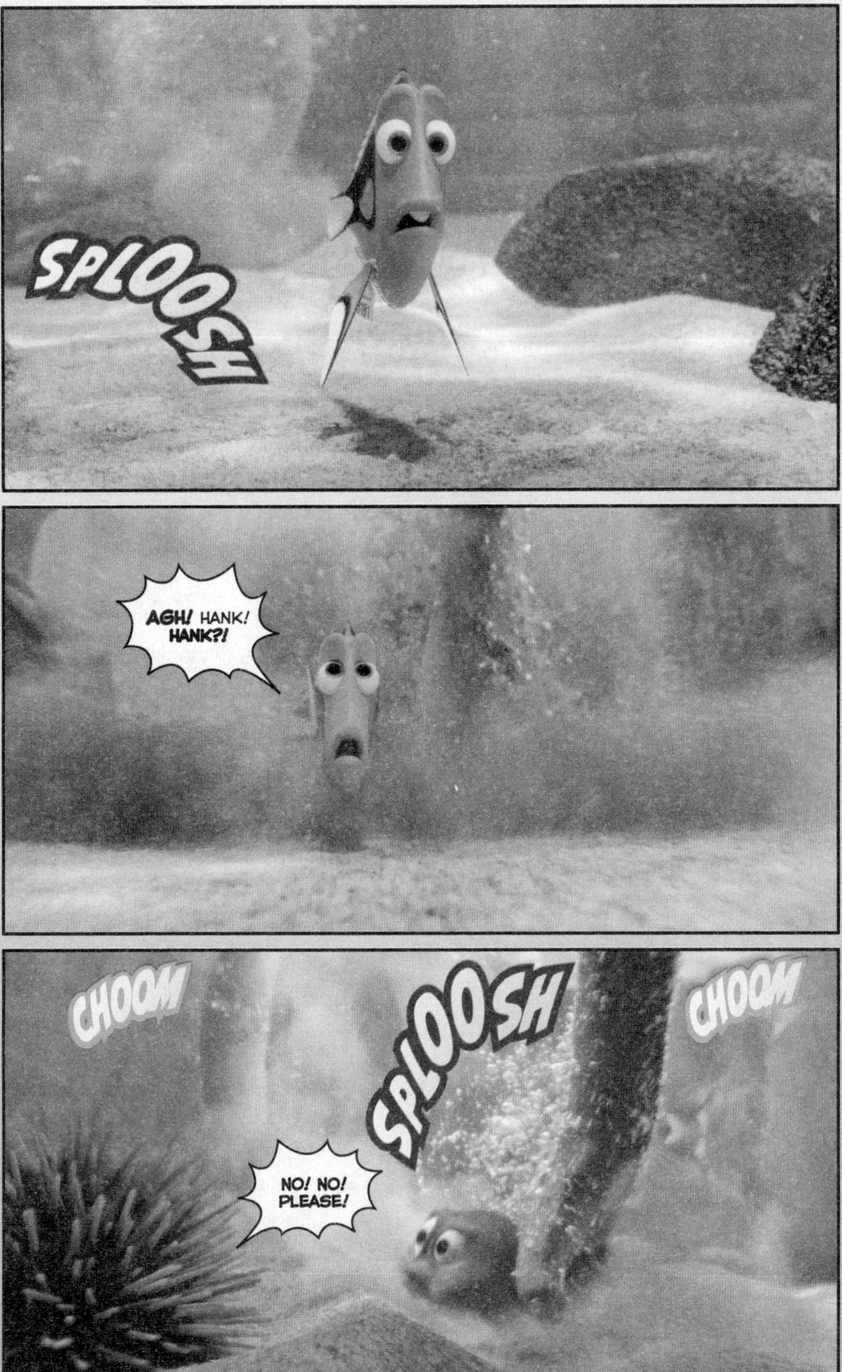
SPLOOSH
AGH! HANK! HANK?!
CHOOM
SPLOOSH
CHOOM
NO! NO! PLEASE!

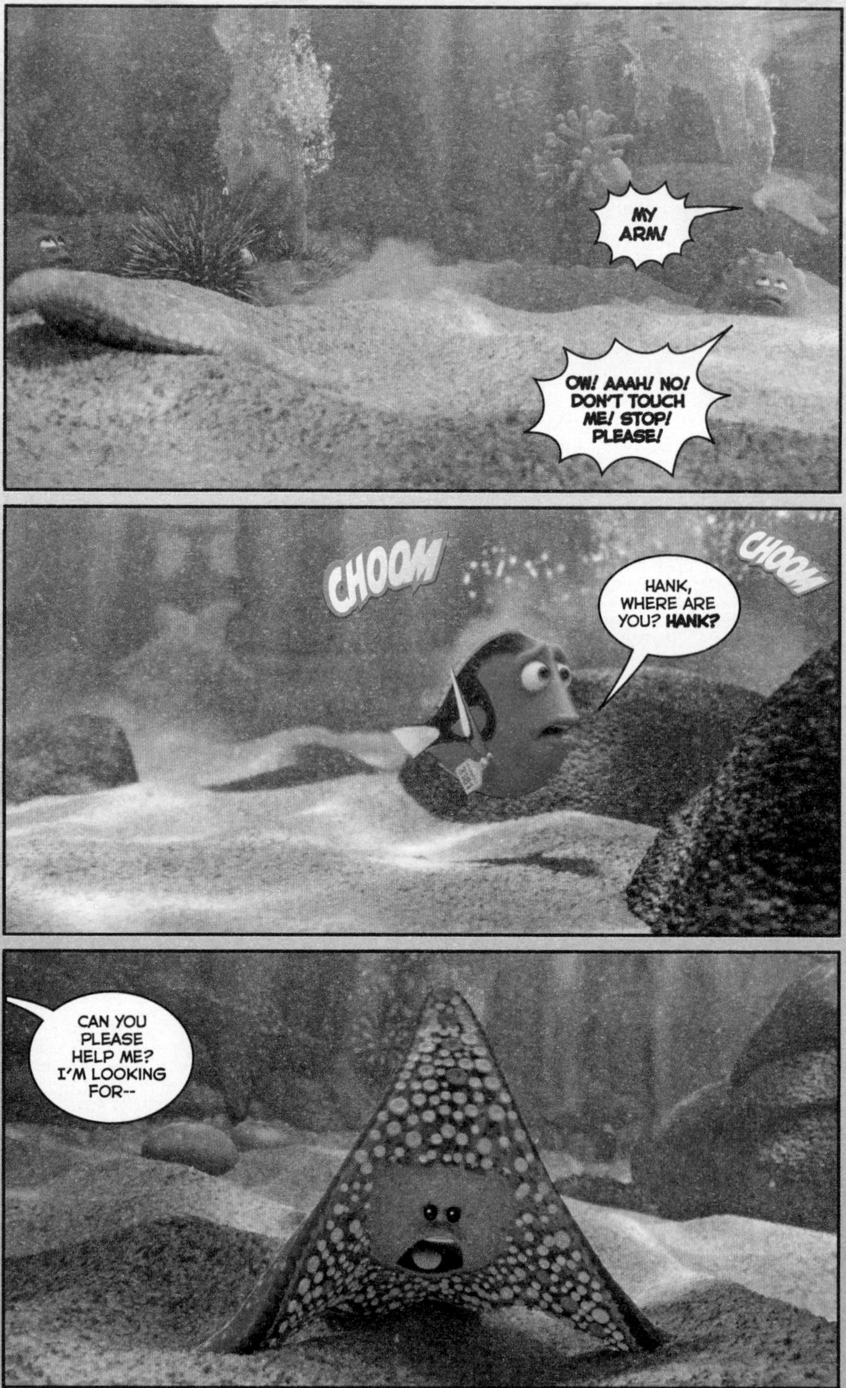
MY ARM!
OW! AAAH! NO! DON'T TOUCH ME! STOP! PLEASE!
CHOOM
HANK, WHERE ARE YOU? HANK?
CHOOM
CAN YOU PLEASE HELP ME? I'M LOOKING FOR--

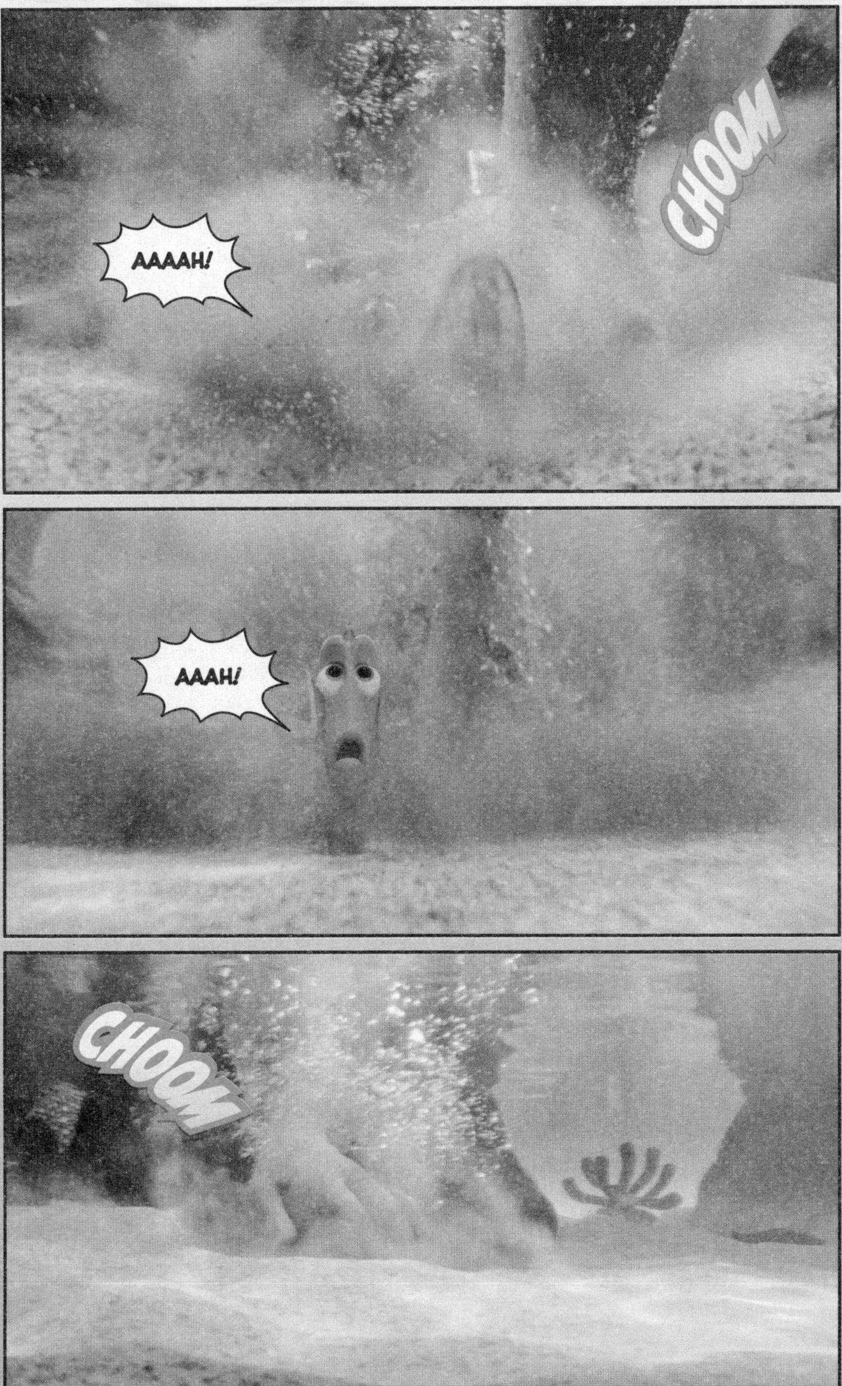
AAAAH!
CHOOM
AAAH!
CHOOM

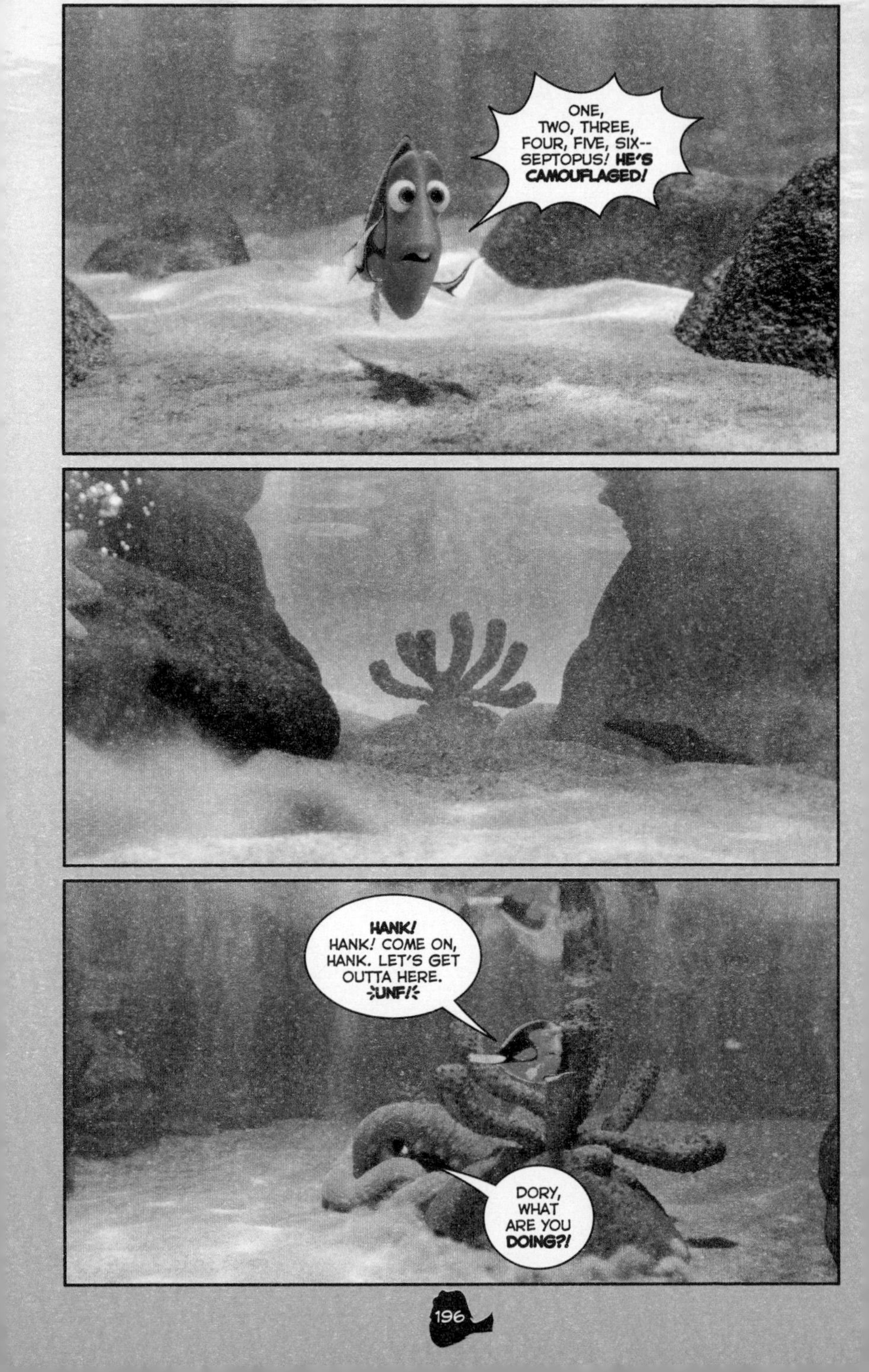
ONE, TWO, THREE, FOUR, FIVE, SIX-- SEPTOPUS! **HE'S CAMOUFLAGED!**
HANK! HANK! COME ON, HANK. LET'S GET OUTTA HERE. **UNF!**
DORY, WHAT ARE YOU **DOING?!**

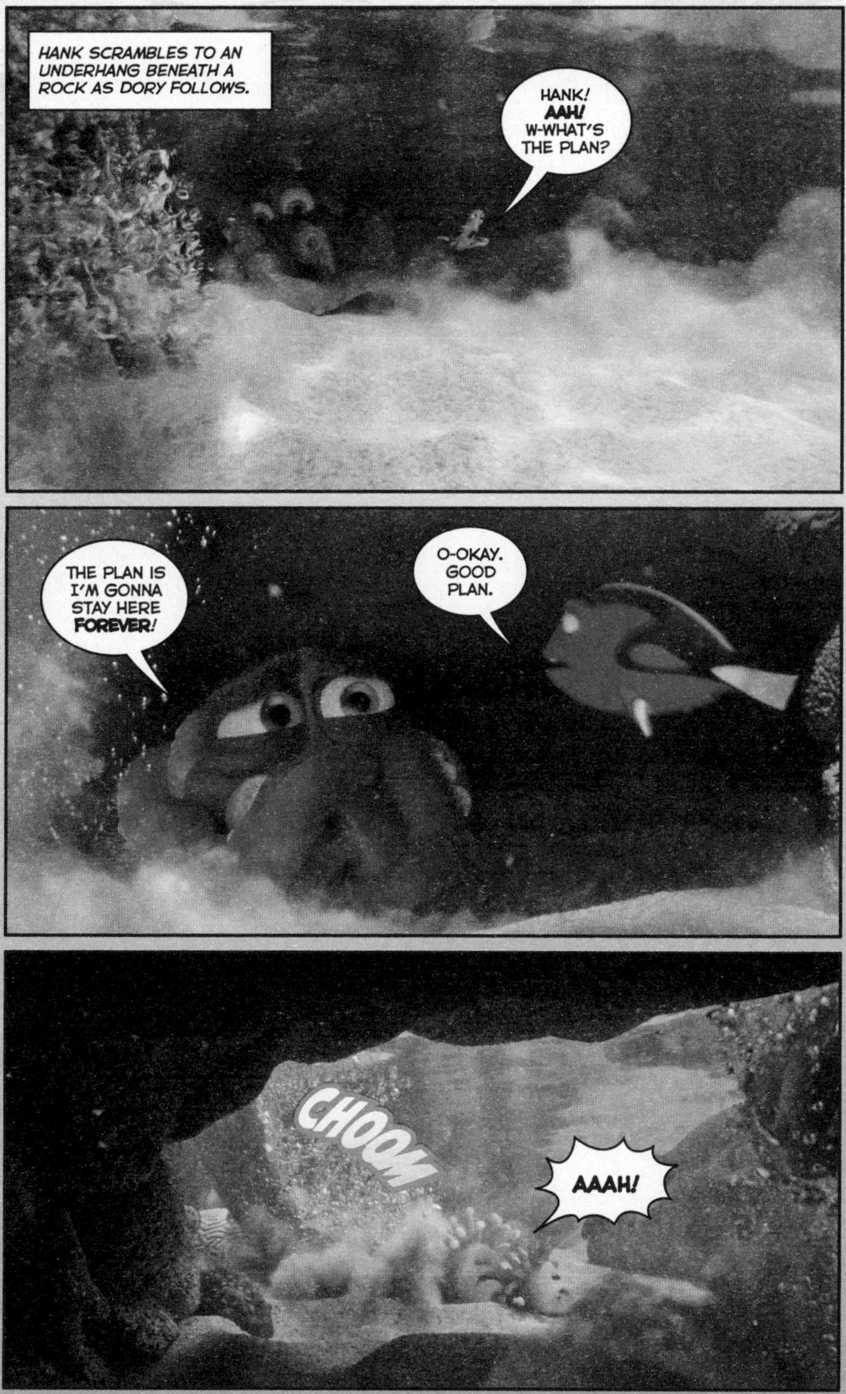
HANK SCRAMBLES TO AN UNDERHANG BENEATH A ROCK AS DORY FOLLOWS.
HANK! AAH! W-WHAT'S THE PLAN?
THE PLAN IS I'M GONNA STAY HERE FOREVER!
O-OKAY. GOOD PLAN.
CHOOM
AAAH!

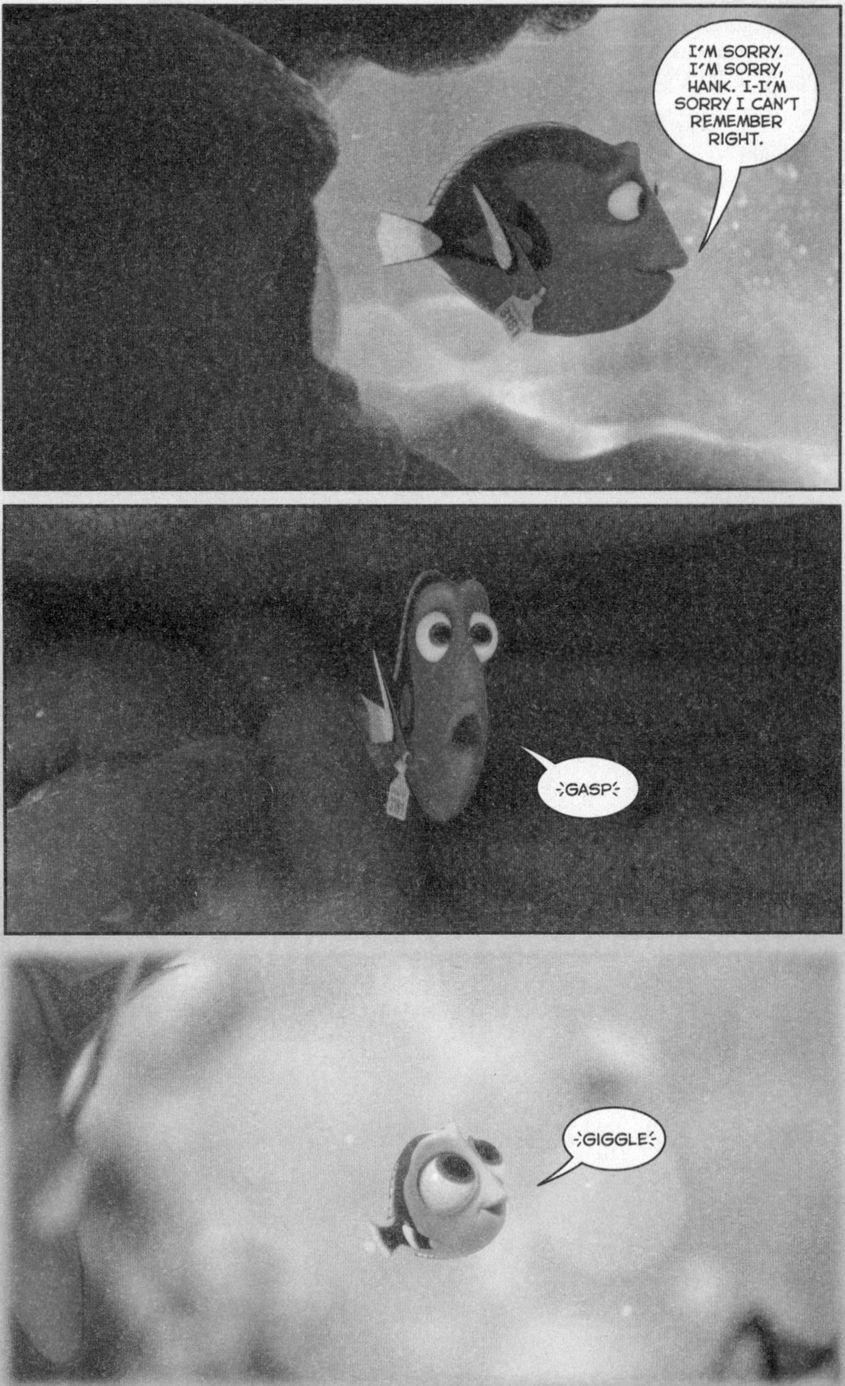
I'M SORRY. I'M SORRY, HANK. I-I'M SORRY I CAN'T REMEMBER RIGHT.
GASP
GIGGLE

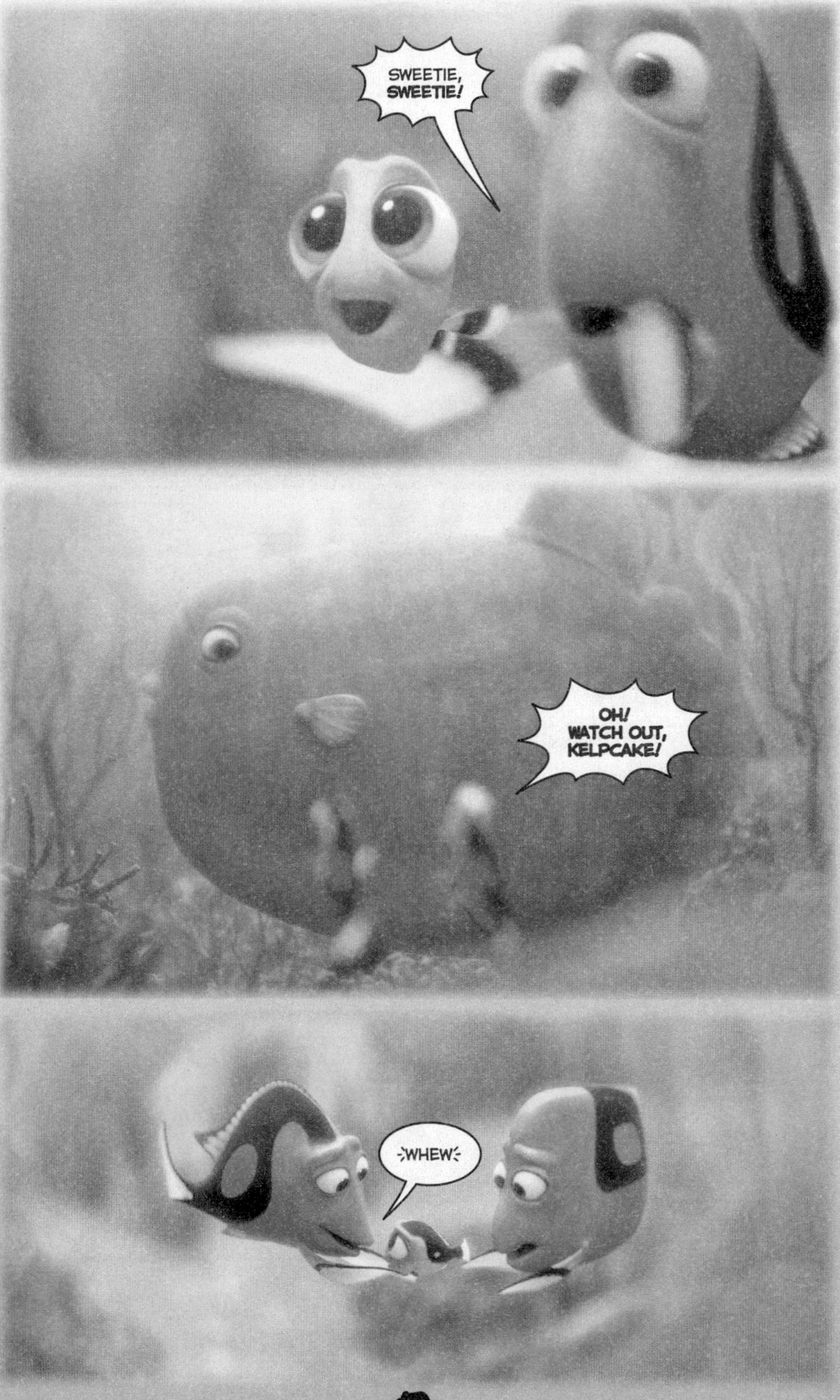
SWEETIE, SWEETIE!
OH! WATCH OUT, KELPCAKE!
WHEW

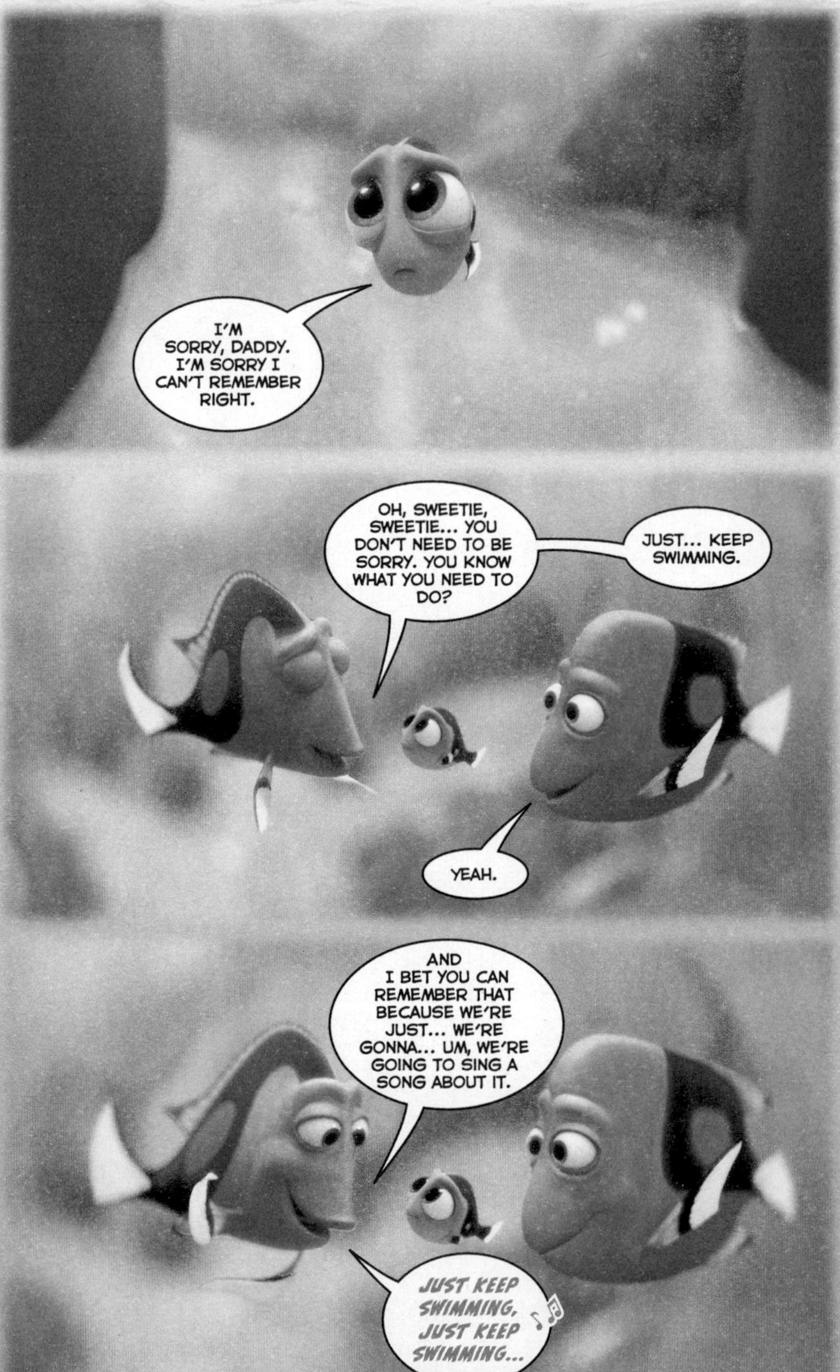
I'M SORRY, DADDY. I'M SORRY I CAN'T REMEMBER RIGHT.
OH, SWEETIE, SWEETIE... YOU DON'T NEED TO BE SORRY. YOU KNOW WHAT YOU NEED TO DO?
JUST... KEEP SWIMMING.
YEAH.
AND I BET YOU CAN REMEMBER THAT BECAUSE WE'RE JUST... WE'RE GONNA... UM, WE'RE GOING TO SING A SONG ABOUT IT.
JUST KEEP SWIMMING, JUST KEEP SWIMMING...

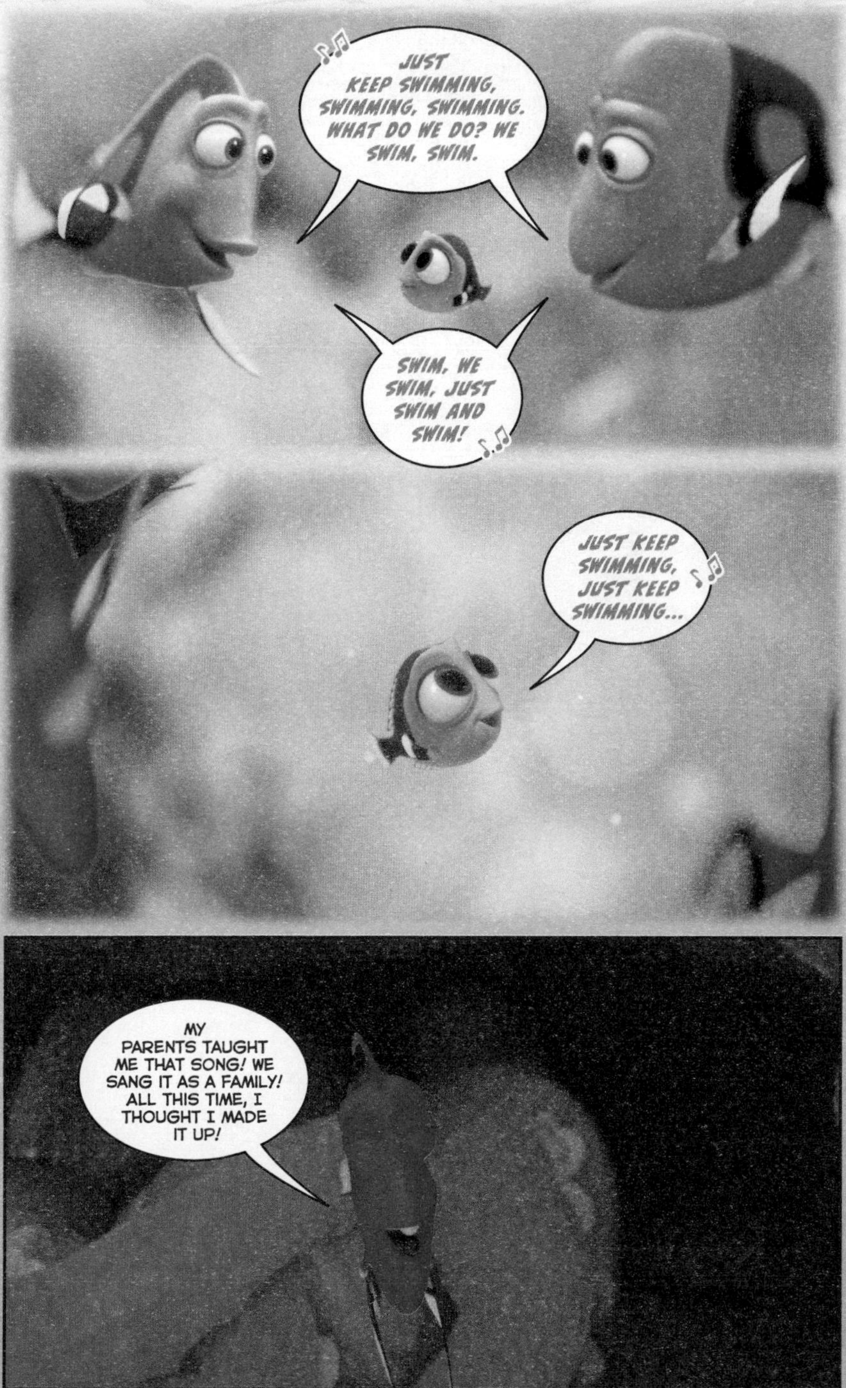

JUST KEEP SWIMMING, SWIMMING, SWIMMING. WHAT DO WE DO? WE SWIM, SWIM.
SWIM, WE SWIM, JUST SWIM AND SWIM!
JUST KEEP SWIMMING, JUST KEEP SWIMMING...
MY PARENTS TAUGHT ME THAT SONG! WE SANG IT AS A FAMILY! ALL THIS TIME, I THOUGHT I MADE IT UP!

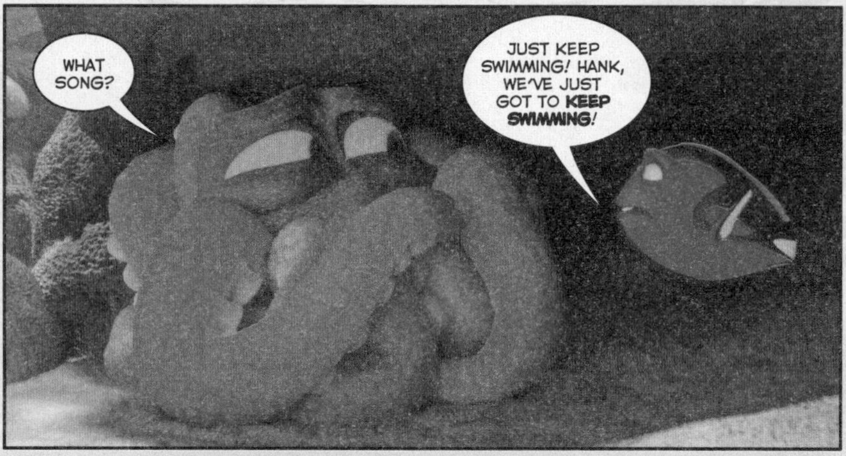
WHAT SONG?
JUST KEEP SWIMMING! HANK, WE'VE JUST GOT TO KEEP SWIMMING!

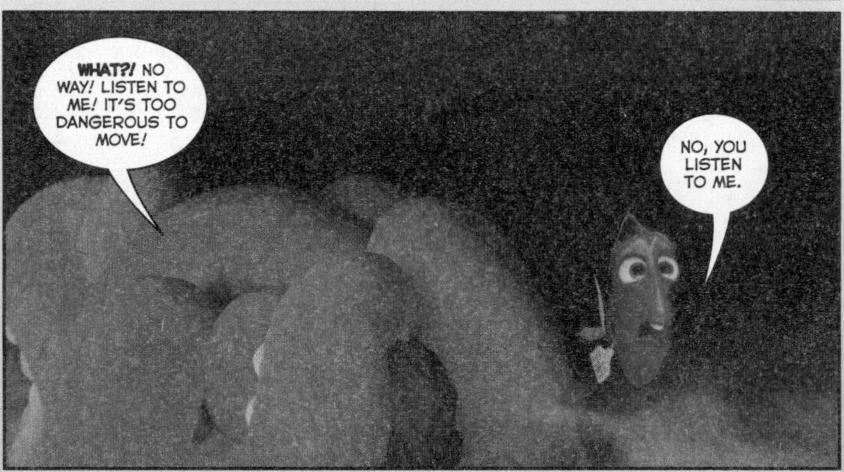
WHAT?! NO WAY! LISTEN TO ME! IT'S TOO DANGEROUS TO MOVE!
NO, YOU LISTEN TO ME.

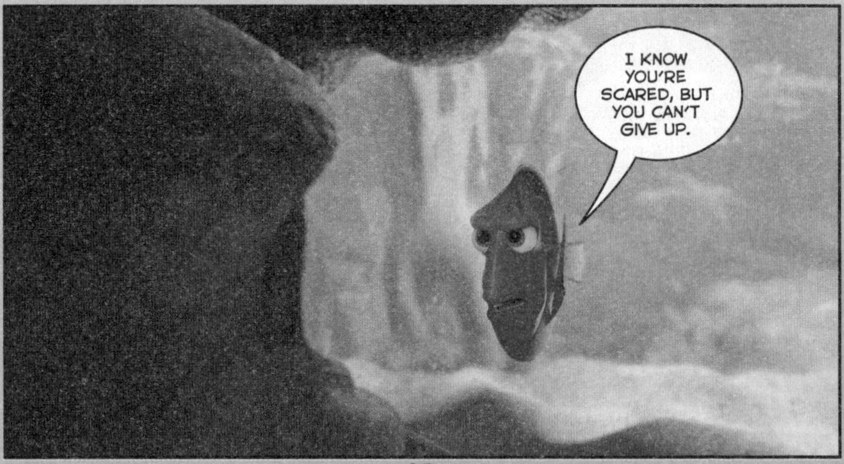
I KNOW YOU'RE SCARED, BUT YOU CAN'T GIVE UP.

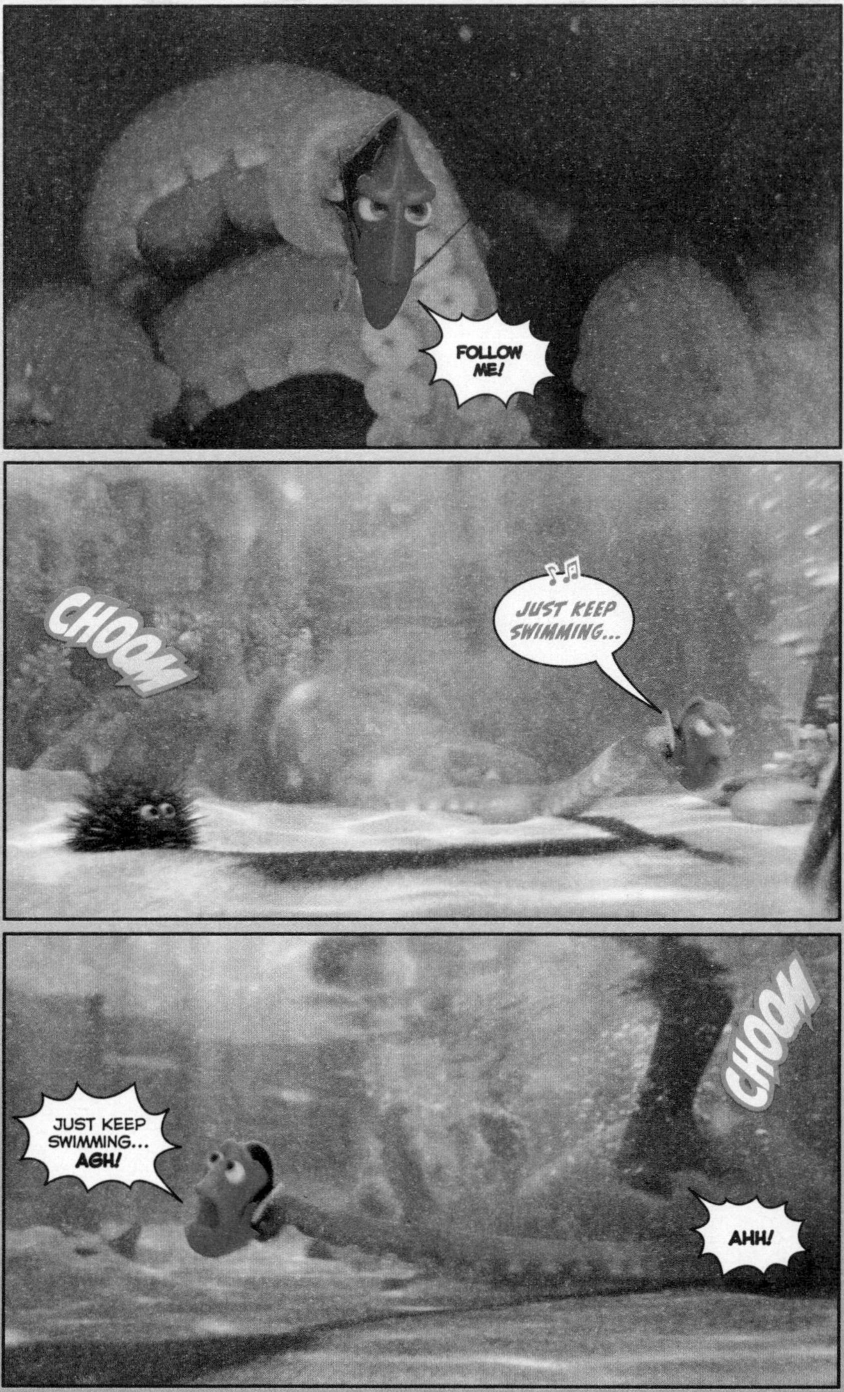
FOLLOW ME!
CHOOM
JUST KEEP SWIMMING...
JUST KEEP SWIMMING... AGH!
CHOOM
AHH!

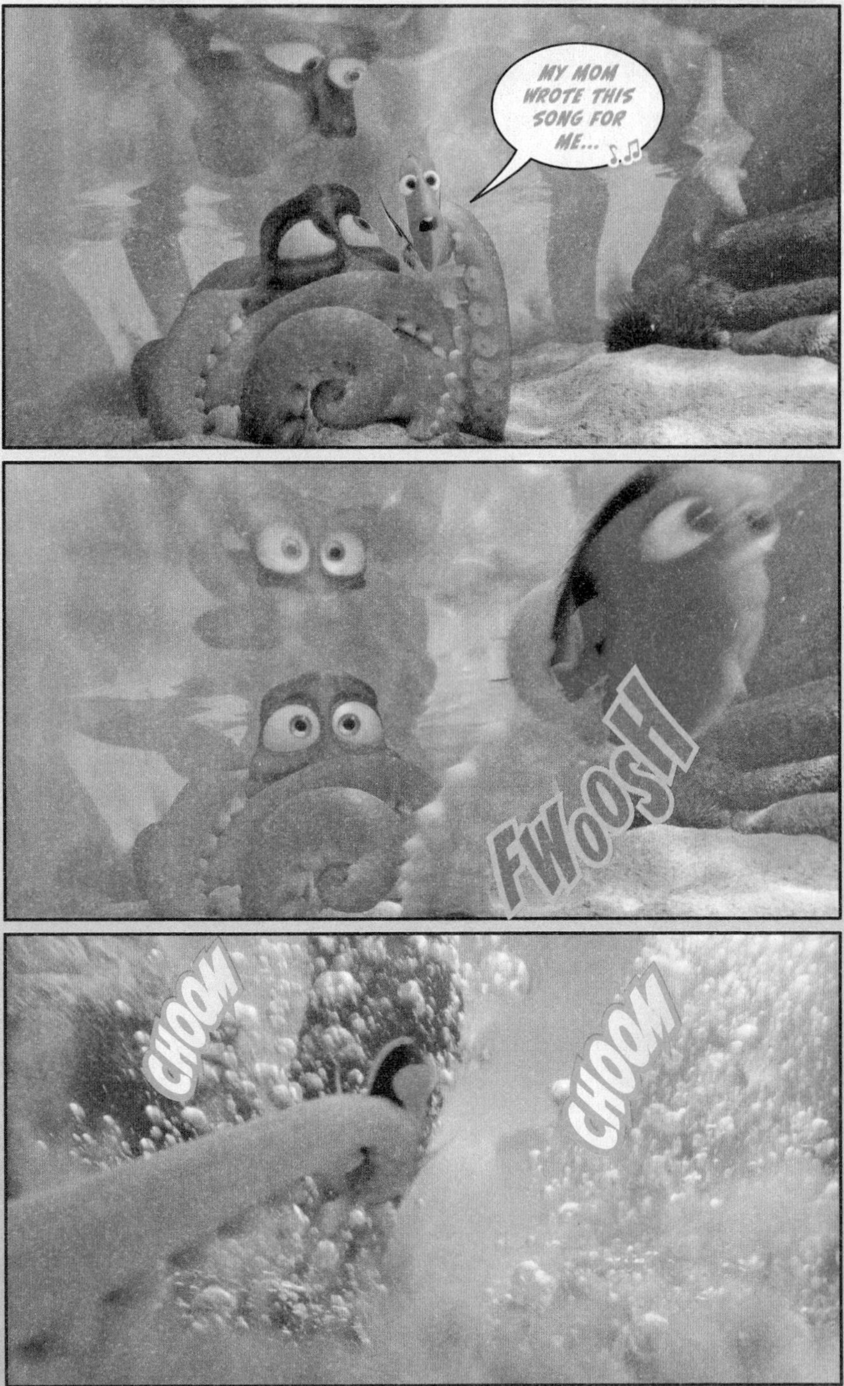

MY MOM WROTE THIS SONG FOR ME...
FWOOSH
CHOOM
CHOOM

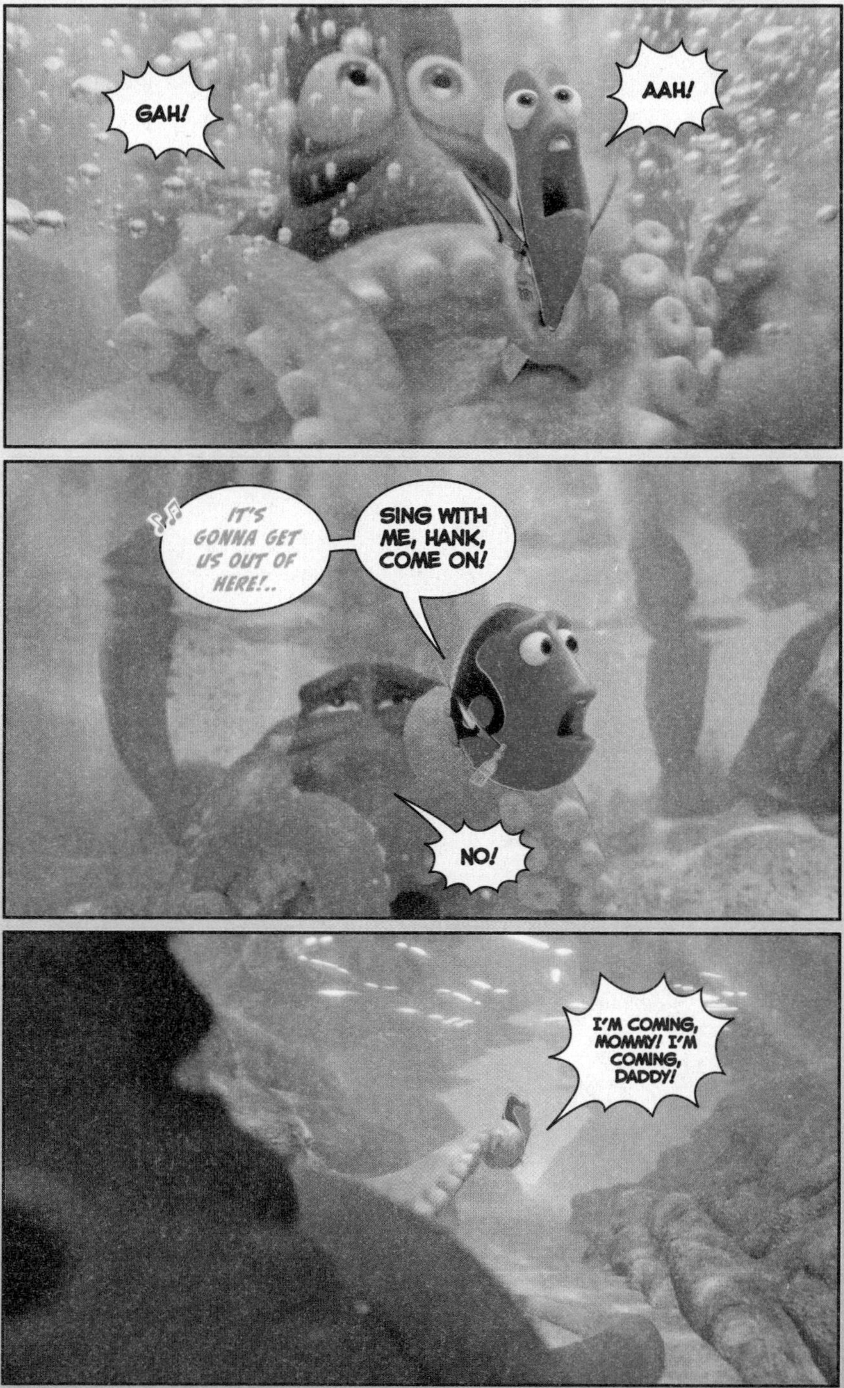
GAH!
AAH!
IT'S GONNA GET US OUT OF HERE!..
SING WITH ME, HANK, COME ON!
NO!
I'M COMING, MOMMY! I'M COMING, DADDY!

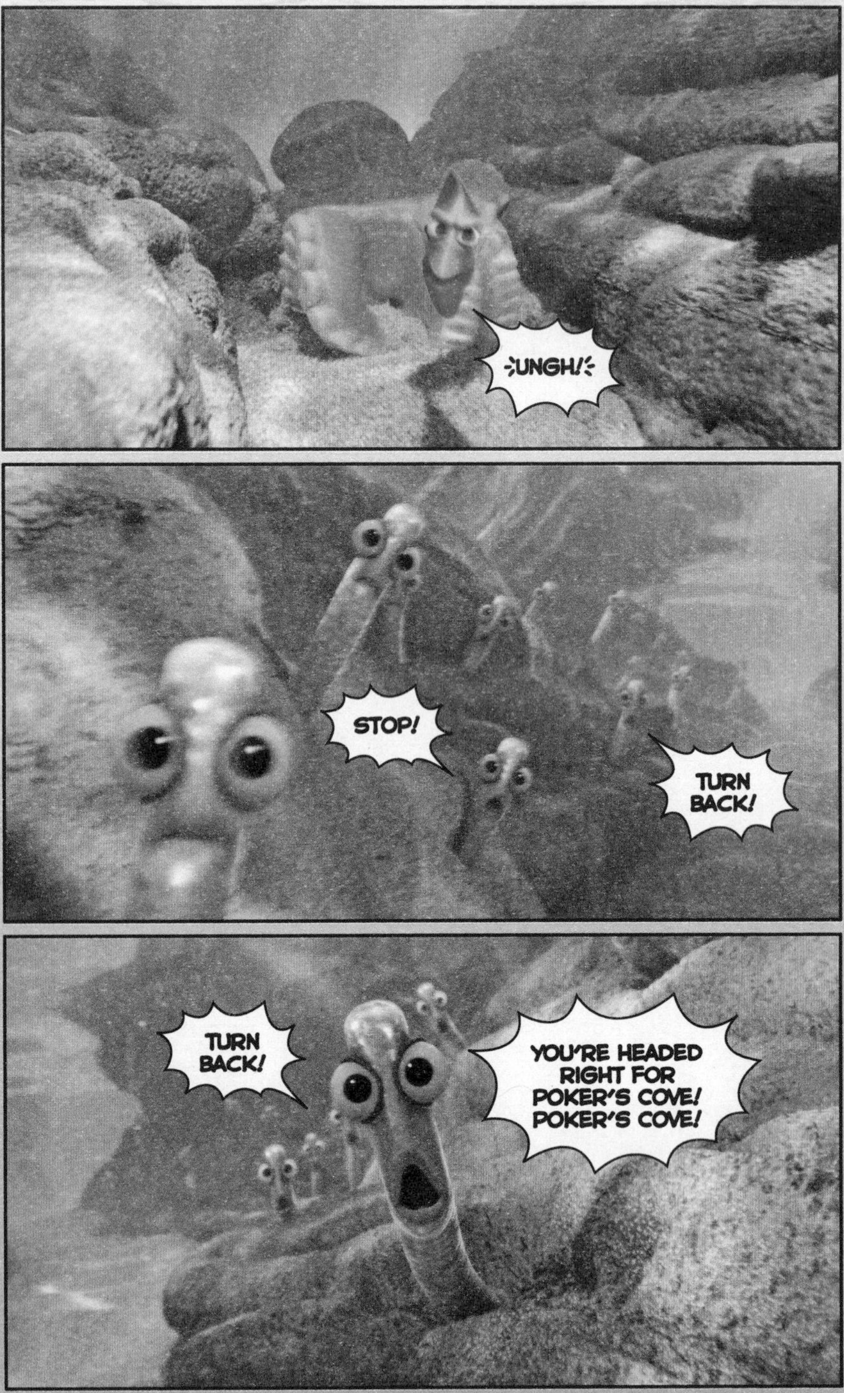
UNGH!
STOP!
TURN BACK!
TURN BACK!
YOU'RE HEADED RIGHT FOR POKER'S COVE! POKER'S COVE!

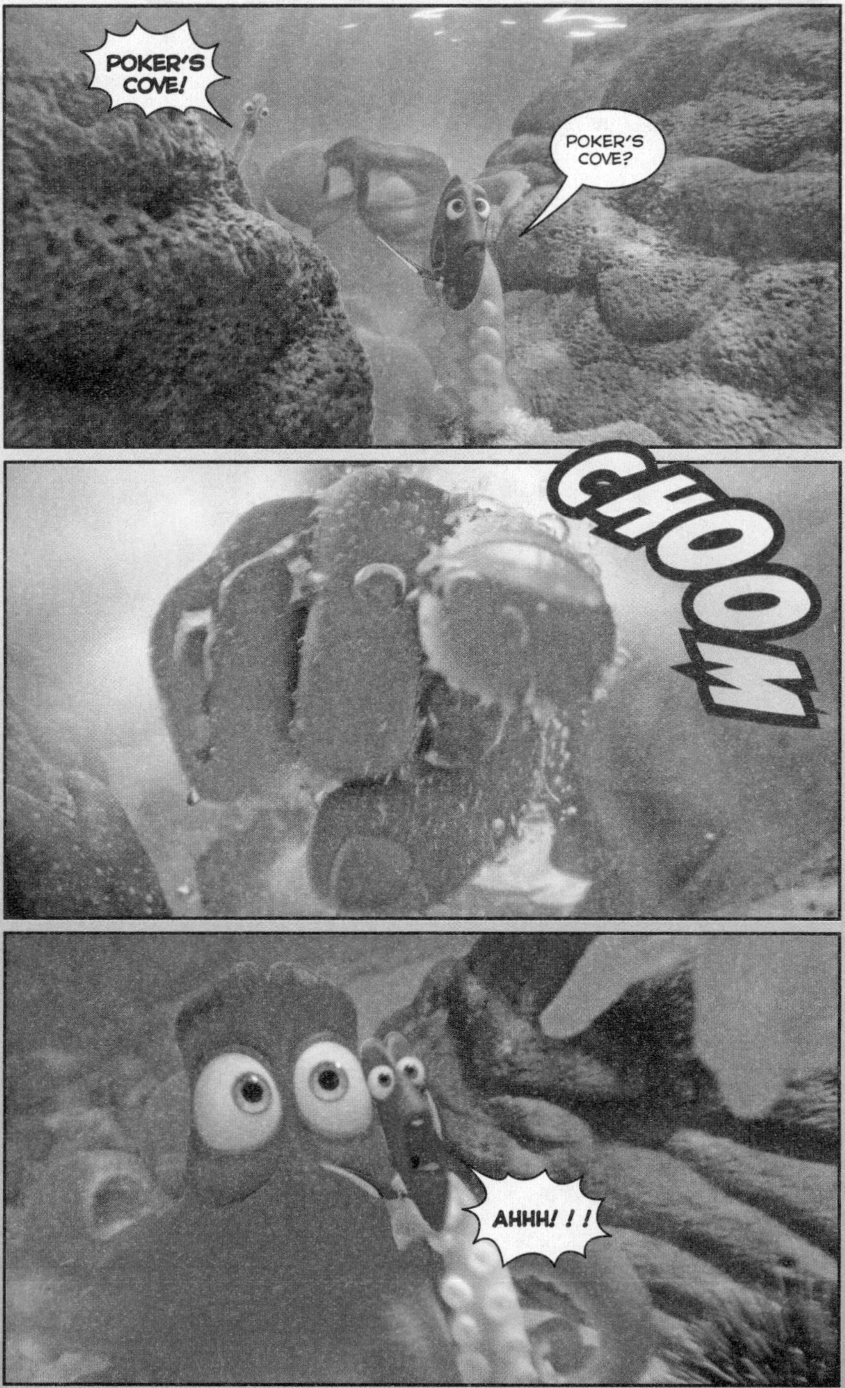
POKER'S COVE!
POKER'S COVE?
CHOOOM
AHHH! ! !

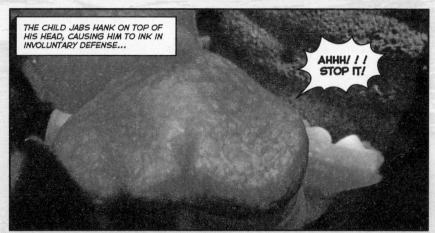

THE CHILD JABS HANK ON TOP OF HIS HEAD, CAUSING HIM TO INK IN INVOLUNTARY DEFENSE...

AHHH! ! ! STOP IT!

EW! WHAT IS IT?!

AHH!

EEEEK!

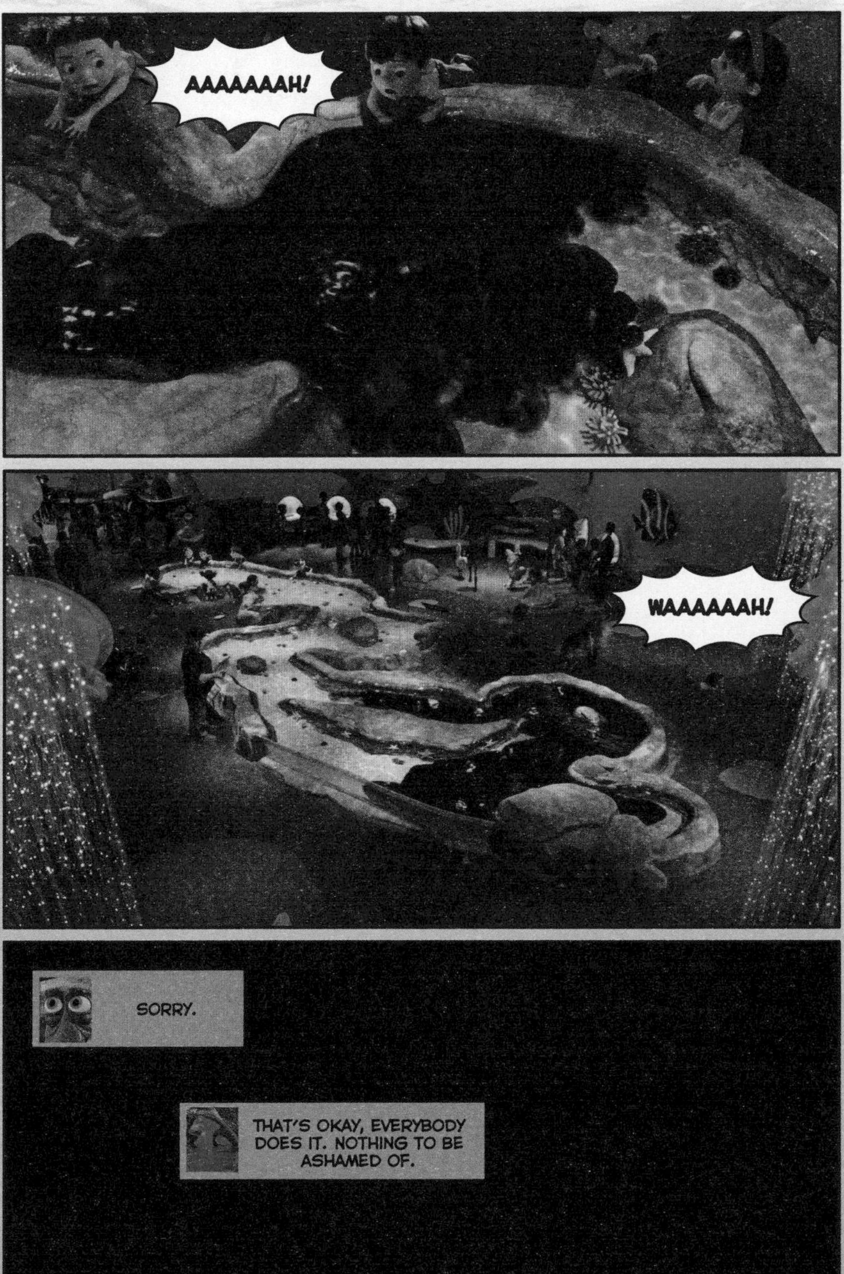
AAAAAAAH!
WAAAAAAH!
SORRY.
THAT'S OKAY, EVERYBODY DOES IT. NOTHING TO BE ASHAMED OF.

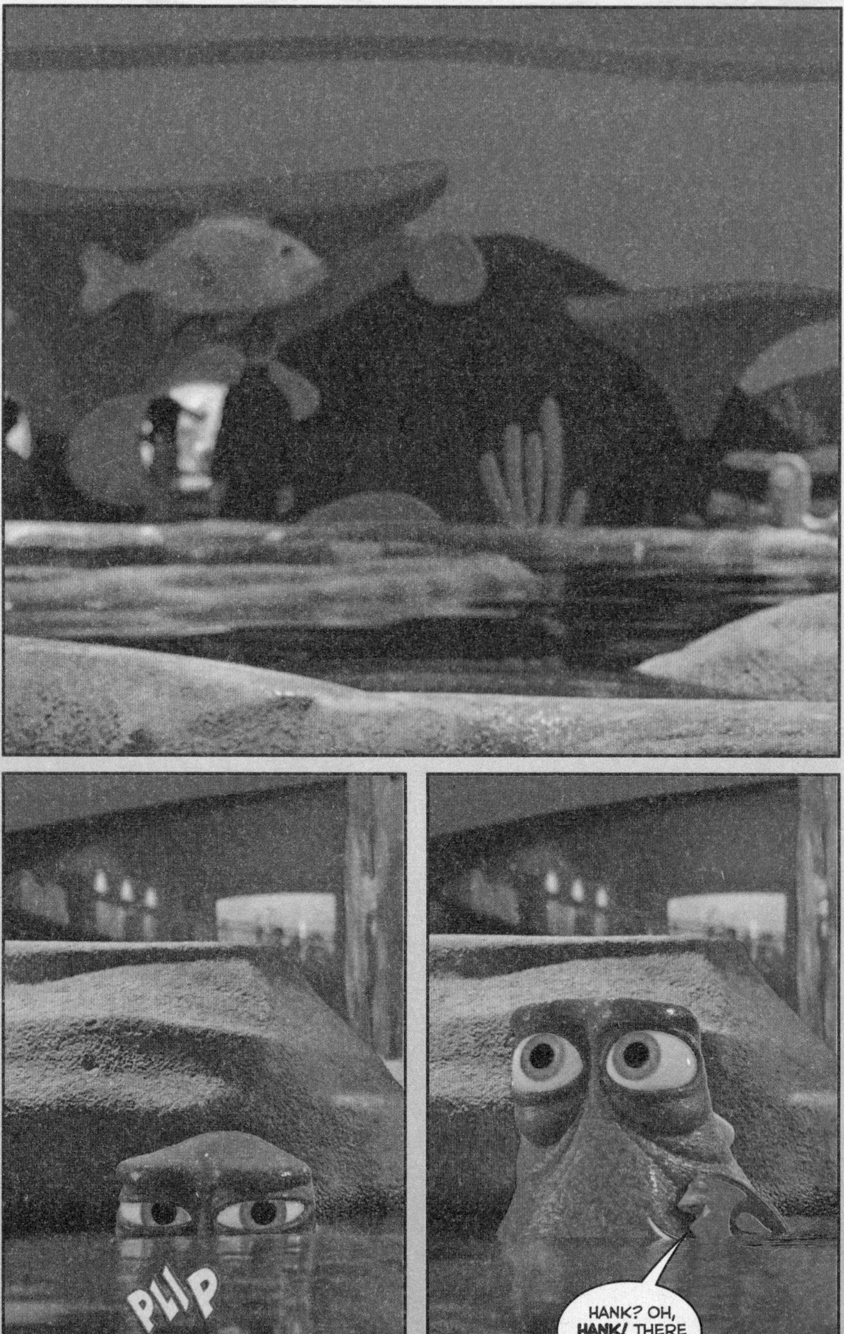
PLIP
HANK? OH, HANK! THERE YOU ARE!

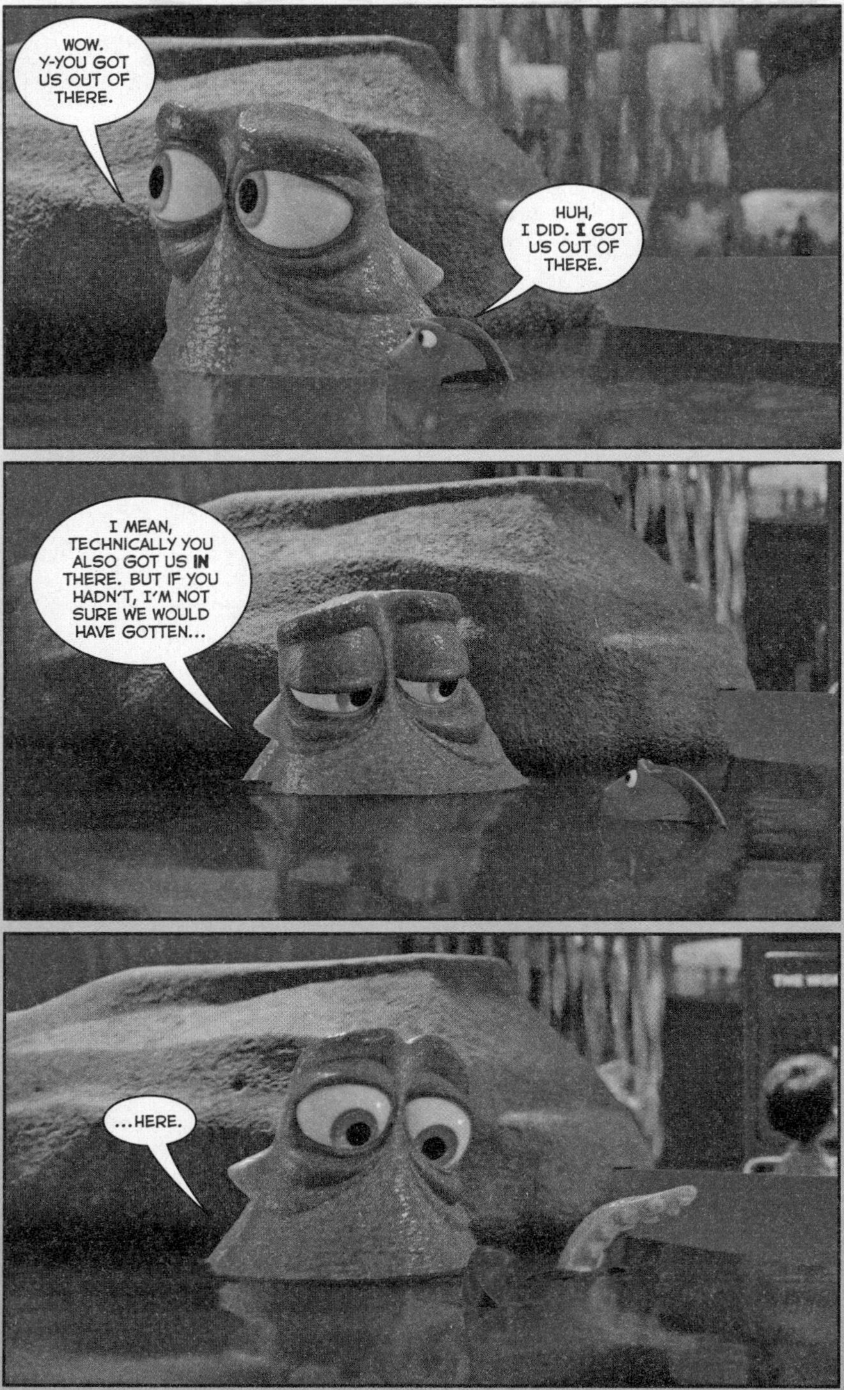
WOW. Y-YOU GOT US OUT OF THERE.
HUH, I DID. I GOT US OUT OF THERE.
I MEAN, TECHNICALLY YOU ALSO GOT US IN THERE. BUT IF YOU HADN'T, I'M NOT SURE WE WOULD HAVE GOTTEN...
...HERE.

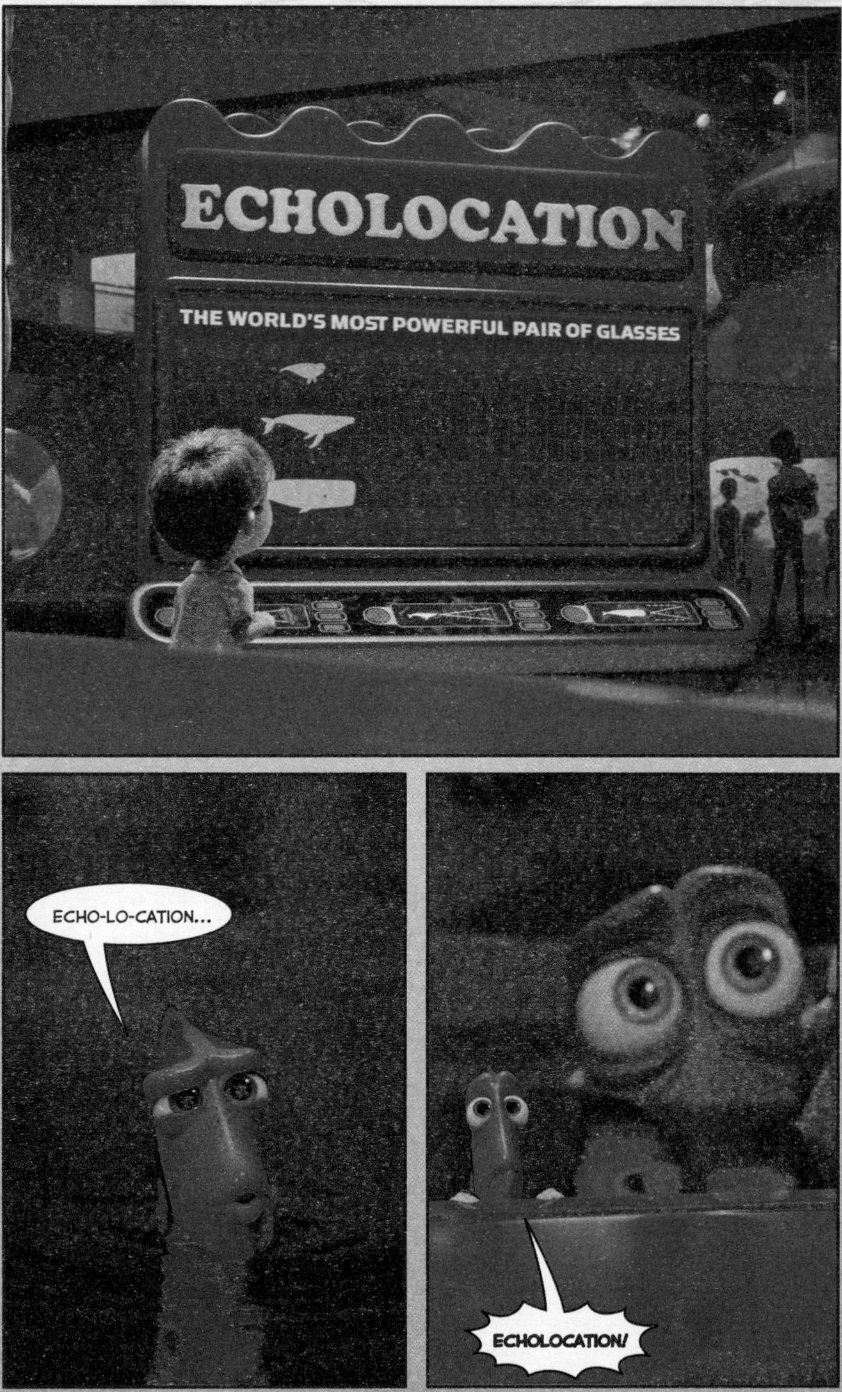
ECHOLOCATION
THE WORLD'S MOST POWERFUL PAIR OF GLASSES
ECHO-LO-CATION...
ECHOLOCATION!

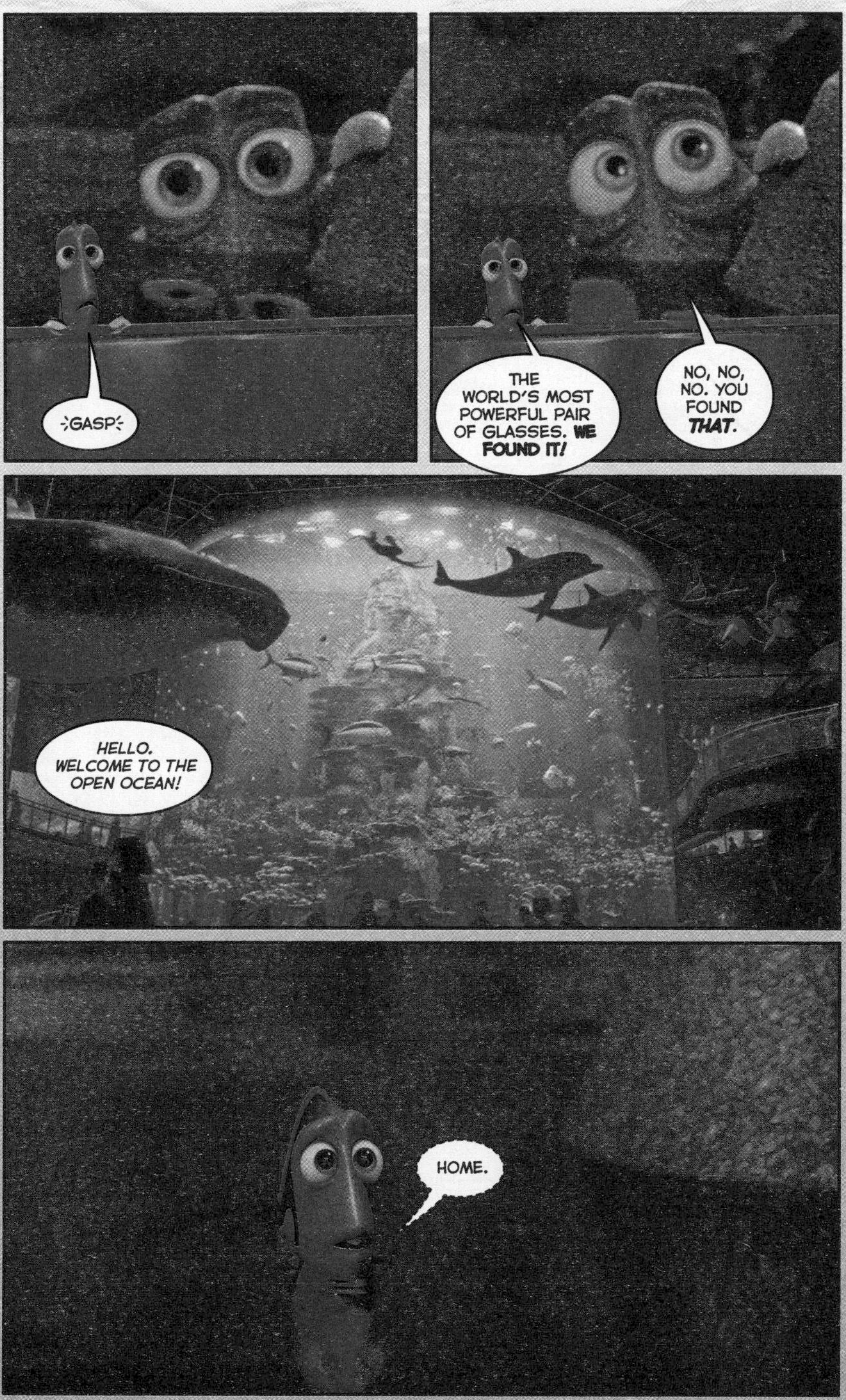
GASP
THE WORLD'S MOST POWERFUL PAIR OF GLASSES. WE FOUND IT!
NO, NO, NO. YOU FOUND THAT.
HELLO. WELCOME TO THE OPEN OCEAN!
HOME.

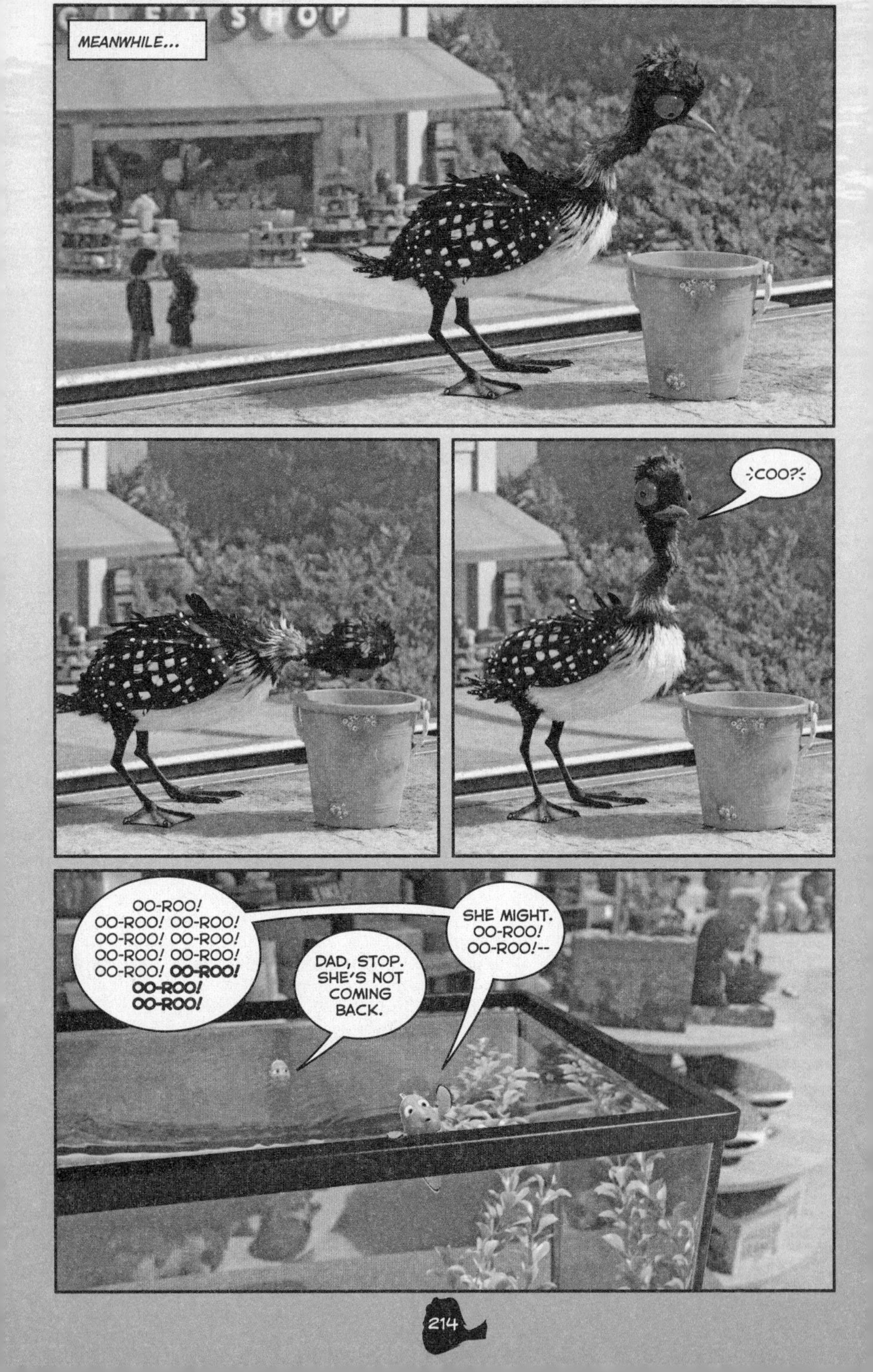
MEANWHILE...
SHOP
COO?
OO-ROO! OO-ROO! OO-ROO! OO-ROO! OO-ROO! OO-ROO! OO-ROO! OO-ROO! **OO-ROO! OO-ROO! OO-ROO!**
DAD, STOP. SHE'S NOT COMING BACK.
SHE MIGHT. OO-ROO! OO-ROO!--

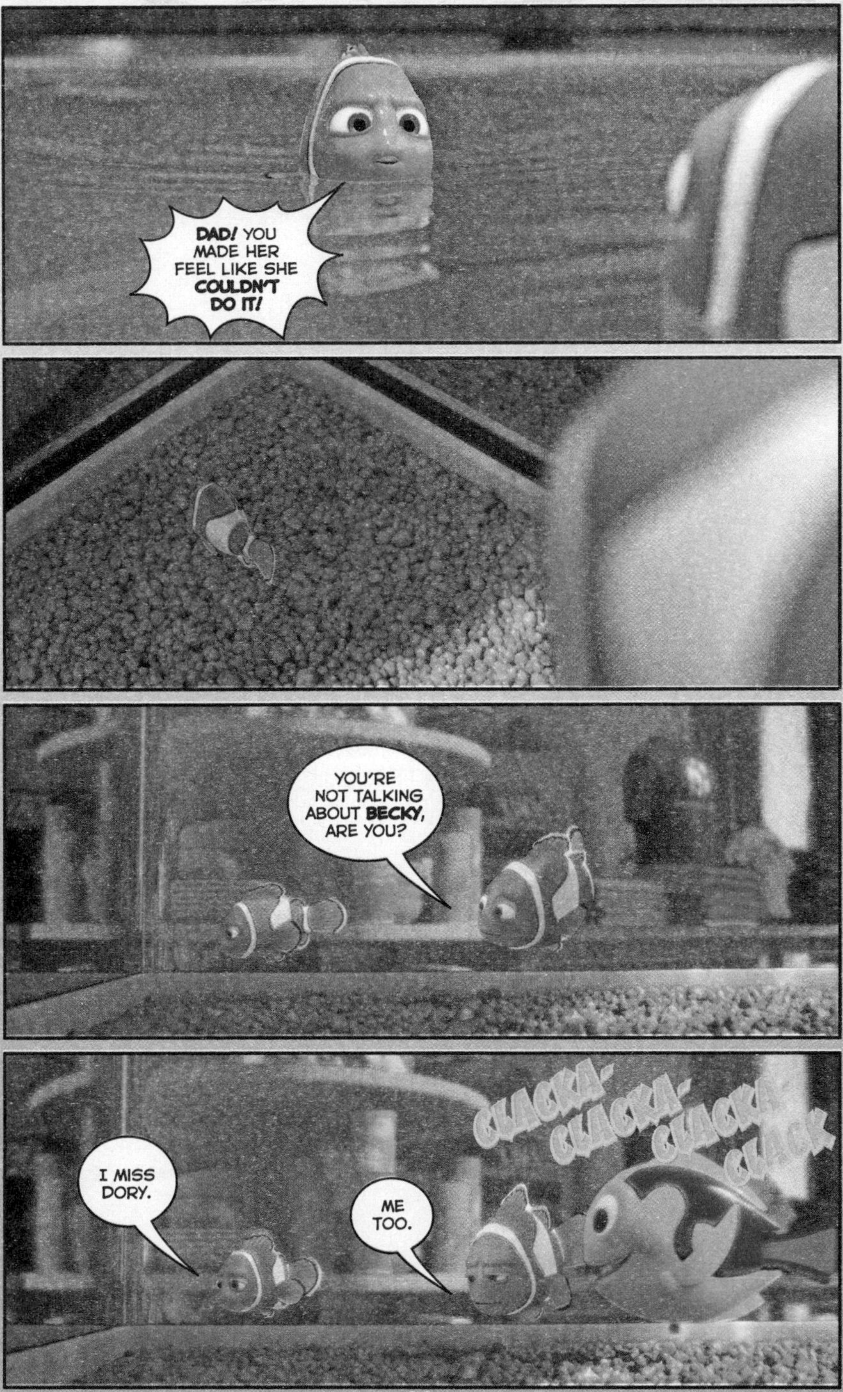
DAD! YOU MADE HER FEEL LIKE SHE COULDN'T DO IT!
YOU'RE NOT TALKING ABOUT BECKY, ARE YOU?
I MISS DORY.
ME TOO.
CLACKA-CLACKA-CLACKA-CLACK

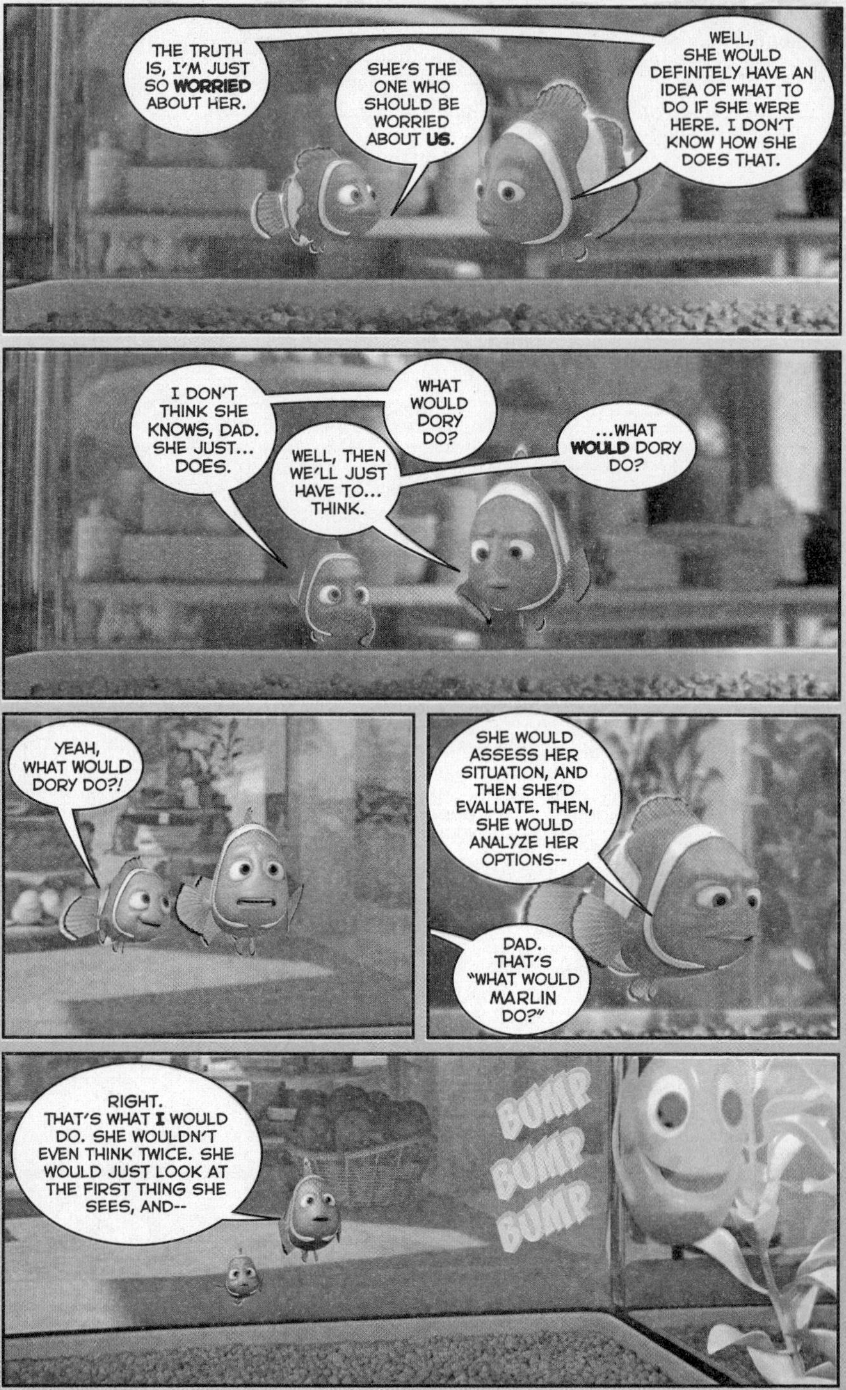
THE TRUTH IS, I'M JUST SO **WORRIED** ABOUT HER.
SHE'S THE ONE WHO SHOULD BE WORRIED ABOUT **US**.
WELL, SHE WOULD DEFINITELY HAVE AN IDEA OF WHAT TO DO IF SHE WERE HERE. I DON'T KNOW HOW SHE DOES THAT.
I DON'T THINK SHE KNOWS, DAD. SHE JUST... DOES.
WHAT WOULD DORY DO?
WELL, THEN WE'LL JUST HAVE TO... THINK.
...WHAT **WOULD** DORY DO?
YEAH, WHAT WOULD DORY DO?!
SHE WOULD ASSESS HER SITUATION, AND THEN SHE'D EVALUATE. THEN, SHE WOULD ANALYZE HER OPTIONS--
DAD. THAT'S "WHAT WOULD MARLIN DO?"
RIGHT. THAT'S WHAT **I** WOULD DO. SHE WOULDN'T EVEN THINK TWICE. SHE WOULD JUST LOOK AT THE FIRST THING SHE SEES, AND--
BUMP BUMP BUMP

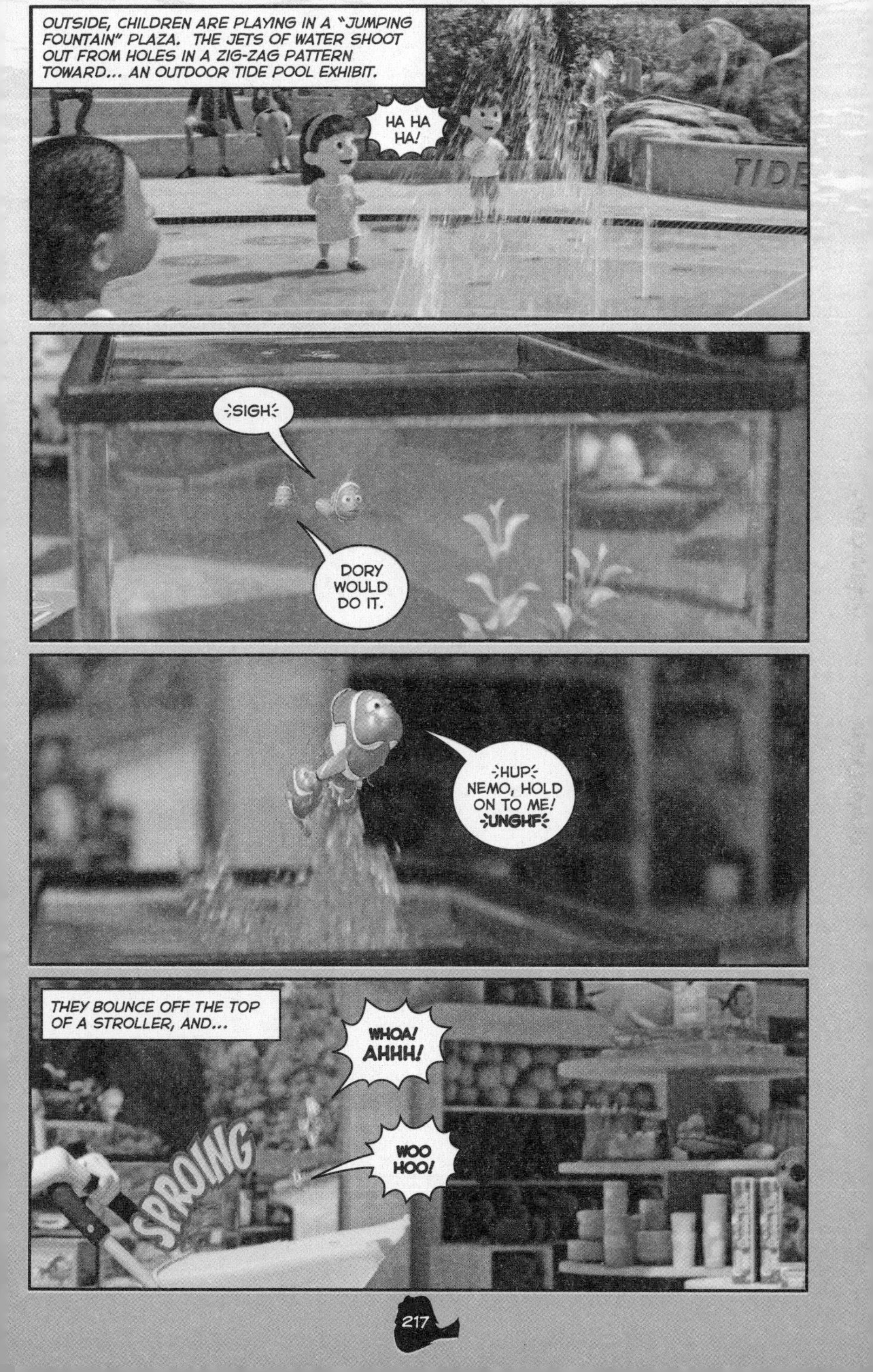
OUTSIDE, CHILDREN ARE PLAYING IN A "JUMPING FOUNTAIN" PLAZA. THE JETS OF WATER SHOOT OUT FROM HOLES IN A ZIG-ZAG PATTERN TOWARD... AN OUTDOOR TIDE POOL EXHIBIT.
HA HA HA!
TIDE
-SIGH-
DORY WOULD DO IT.
-HUP- NEMO, HOLD ON TO ME! -UNGHF-
THEY BOUNCE OFF THE TOP OF A STROLLER, AND...
WHOA! AHHH!
WOO HOO!
SPROING

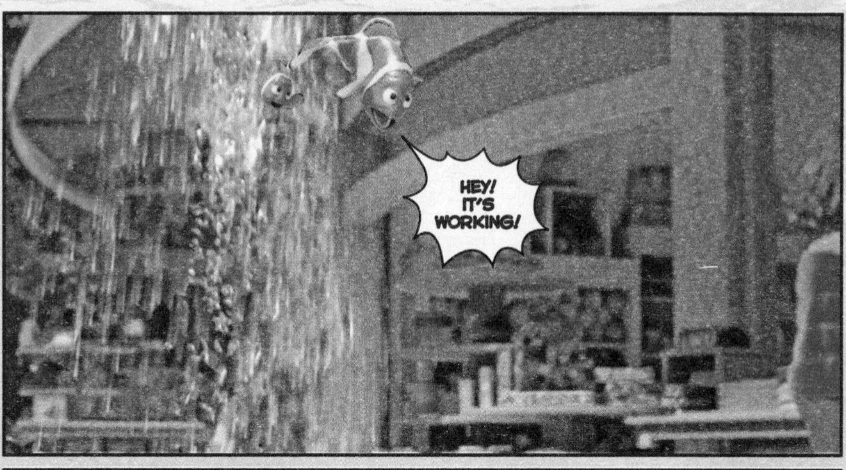
HEY! IT'S WORKING!

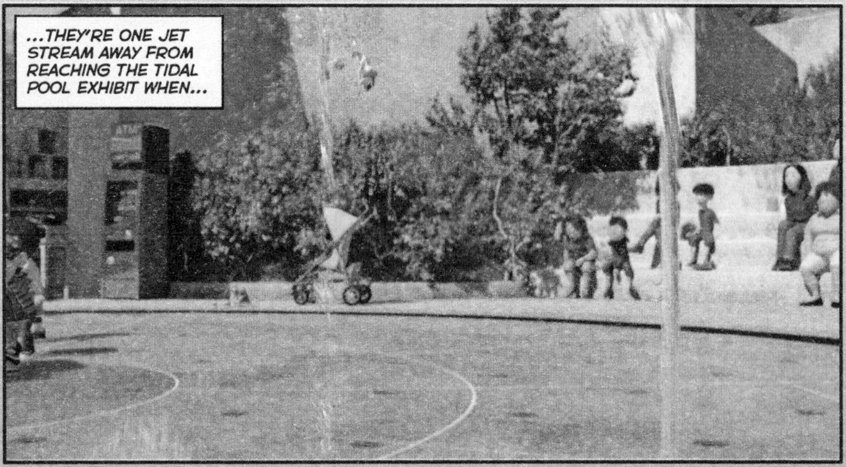
...THEY'RE ONE JET STREAM AWAY FROM REACHING THE TIDAL POOL EXHIBIT WHEN...

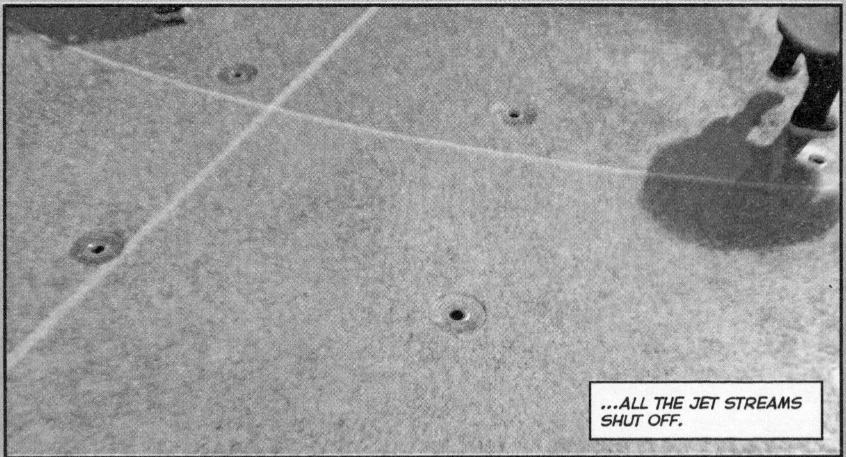
...ALL THE JET STREAMS SHUT OFF.

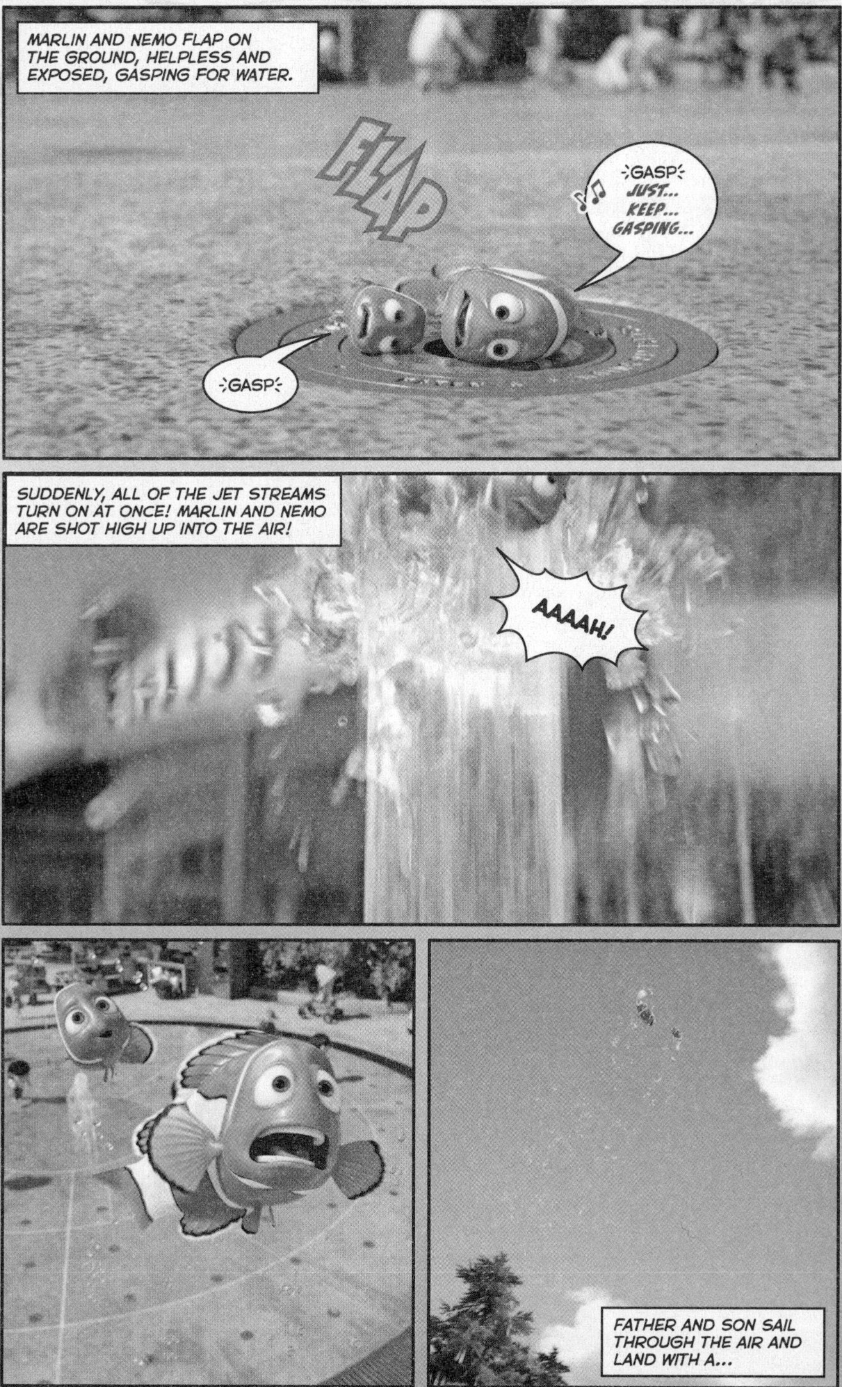
MARLIN AND NEMO FLAP ON THE GROUND, HELPLESS AND EXPOSED, GASPING FOR WATER.
FLAP
GASP JUST... KEEP... GASPING...
GASP
SUDDENLY, ALL OF THE JET STREAMS TURN ON AT ONCE! MARLIN AND NEMO ARE SHOT HIGH UP INTO THE AIR!
AAAAH!
FATHER AND SON SAIL THROUGH THE AIR AND LAND WITH A...

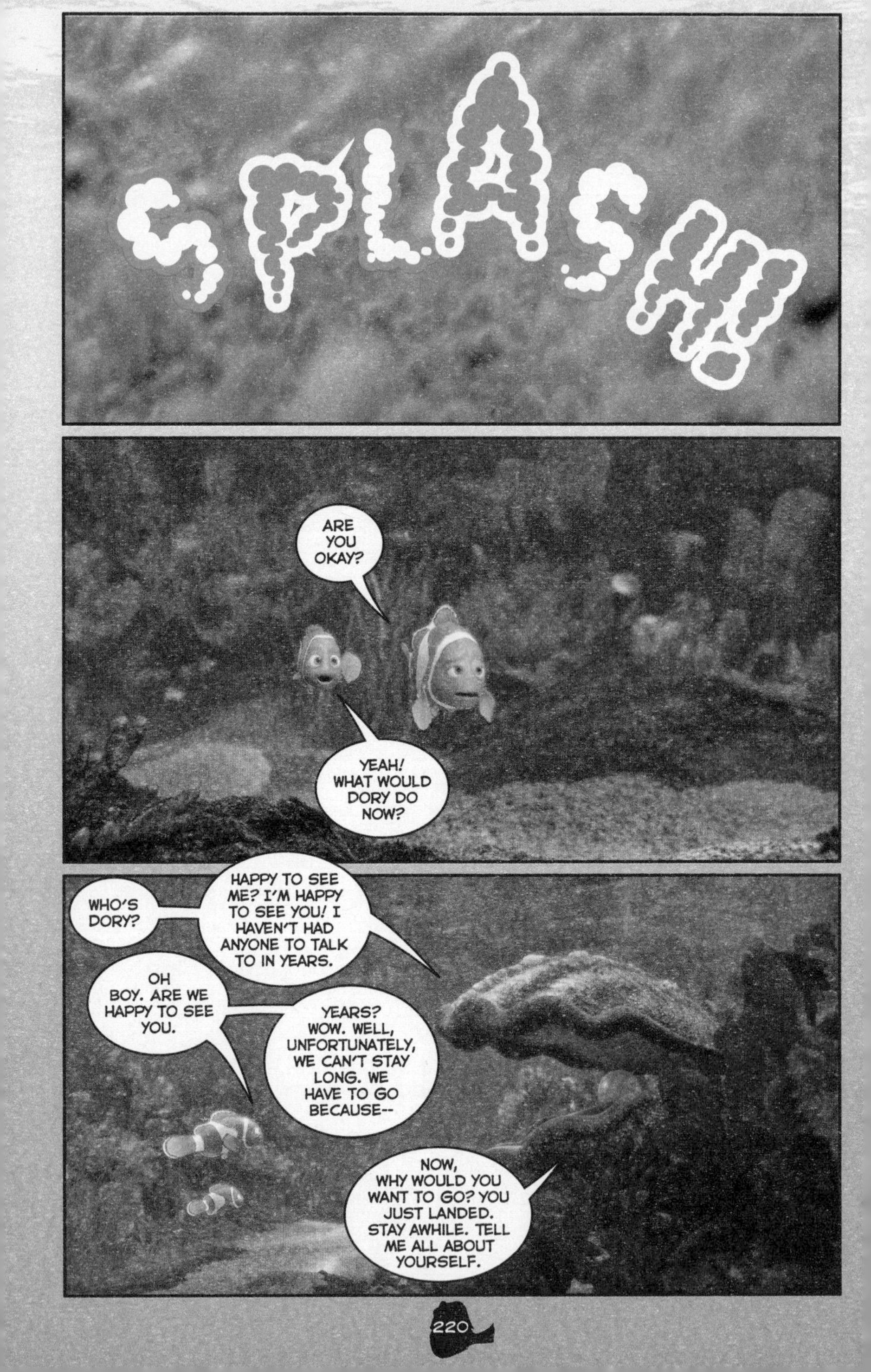
SPLASH!
ARE YOU OKAY?
YEAH! WHAT WOULD DORY DO NOW?
WHO'S DORY?
HAPPY TO SEE ME? I'M HAPPY TO SEE YOU! I HAVEN'T HAD ANYONE TO TALK TO IN YEARS.
OH BOY. ARE WE HAPPY TO SEE YOU.
YEARS? WOW. WELL, UNFORTUNATELY, WE CAN'T STAY LONG. WE HAVE TO GO BECAUSE--
NOW, WHY WOULD YOU WANT TO GO? YOU JUST LANDED. STAY AWHILE. TELL ME ALL ABOUT YOURSELF.

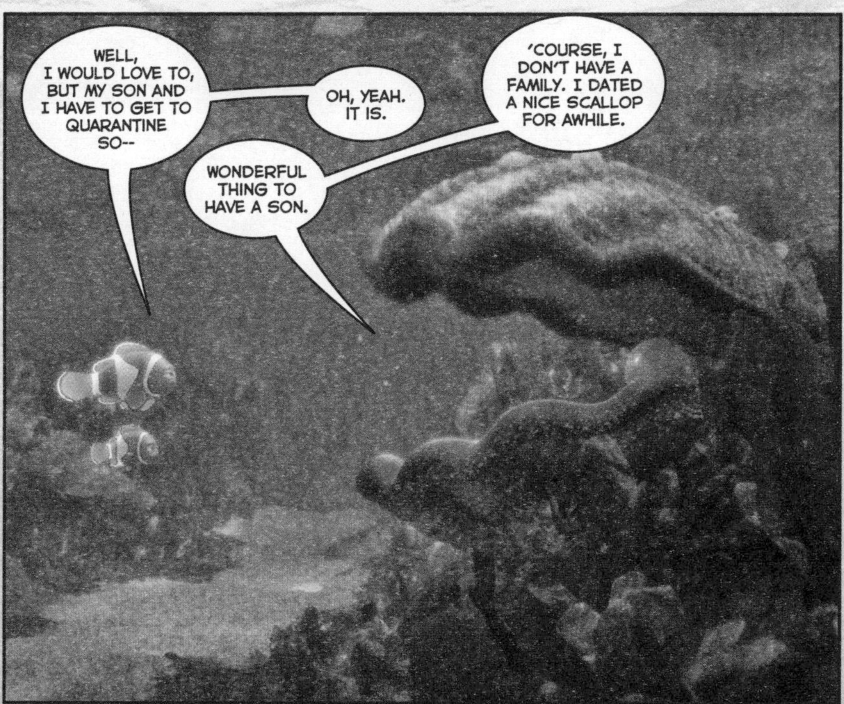
WELL, I WOULD LOVE TO, BUT MY SON AND I HAVE TO GET TO QUARANTINE SO--
OH, YEAH. IT IS.
'COURSE, I DON'T HAVE A FAMILY. I DATED A NICE SCALLOP FOR AWHILE.
WONDERFUL THING TO HAVE A SON.

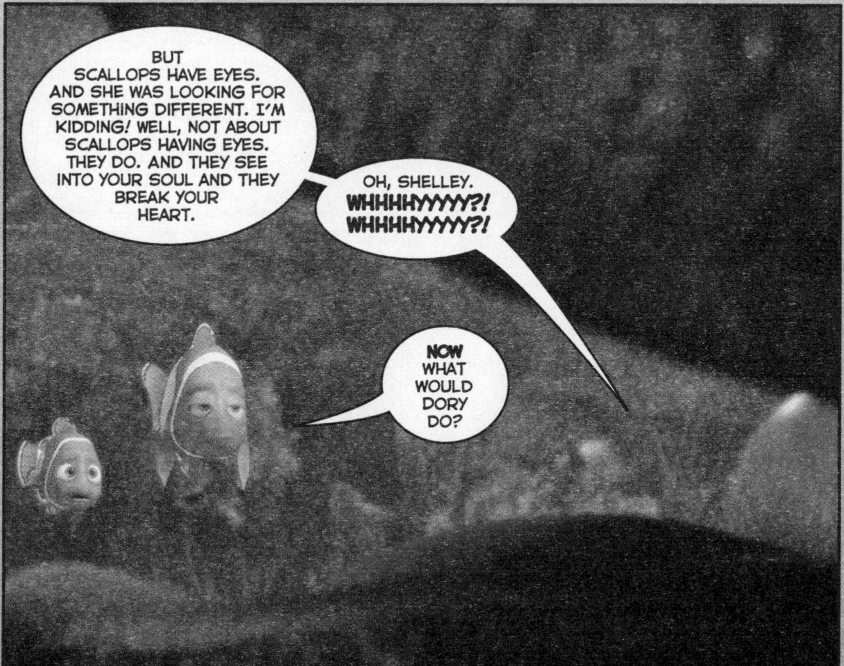
BUT SCALLOPS HAVE EYES. AND SHE WAS LOOKING FOR SOMETHING DIFFERENT. I'M KIDDING! WELL, NOT ABOUT SCALLOPS HAVING EYES. THEY DO. AND THEY SEE INTO YOUR SOUL AND THEY BREAK YOUR HEART.
OH, SHELLEY. WHHHHYYYYY?! WHHHHYYYYY?!
NOW WHAT WOULD DORY DO?

COME WITH US, AS WE EXPLORE THE MYSTERIOUS WORLD OF THE OPEN OCEAN.

OKAY, HANK, FOLLOW ME.

YOU'RE IN A CUP.

RIGHT. I'LL FOLLOW YOU, THEN.

PANGEA

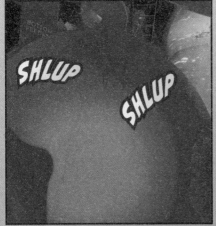

SHLUP

SHLUP

HANK MAKES HIS WAY ACROSS THE ROOM BY CLIMBING A CEILING BANNER...

222

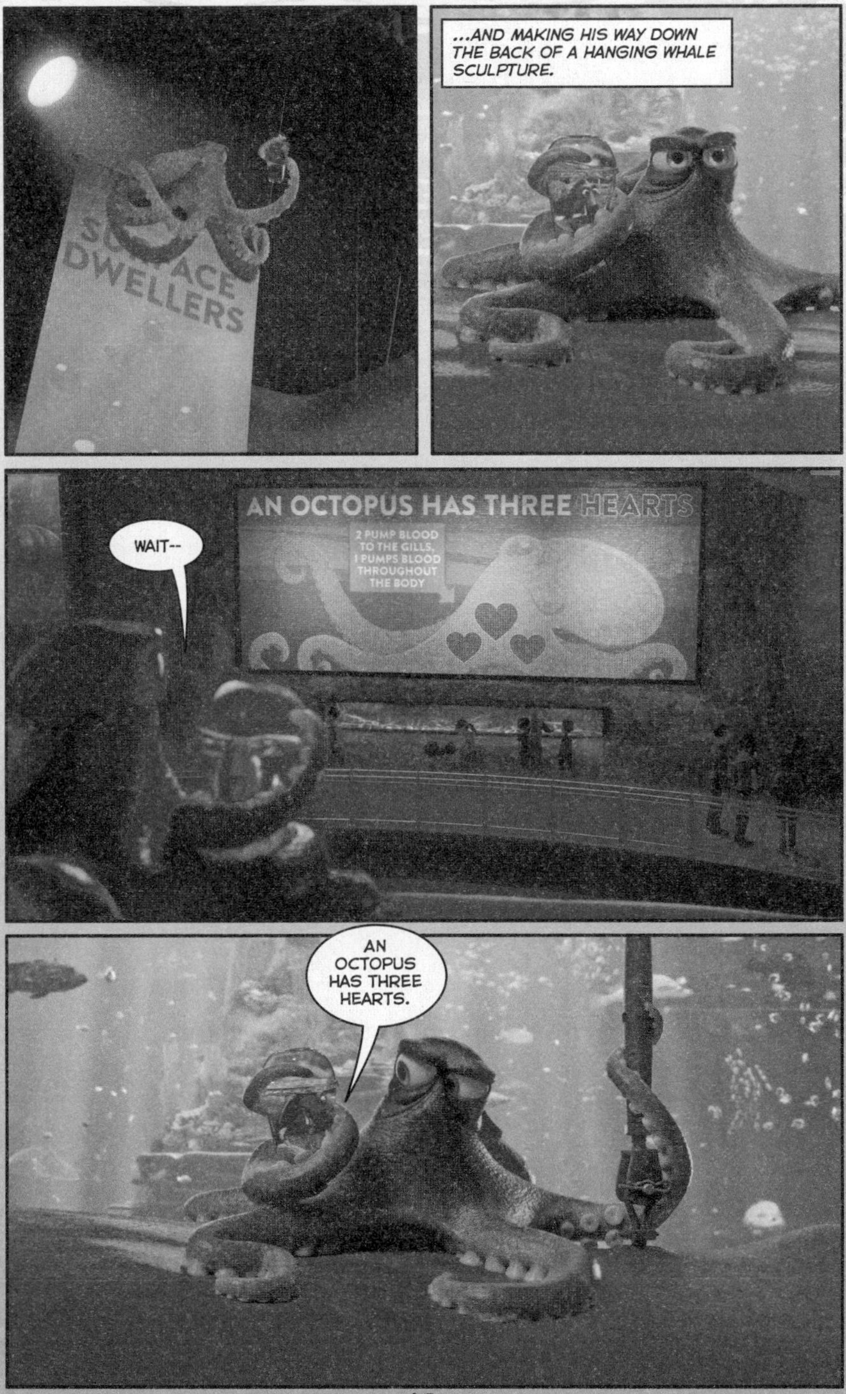
DWELLERS
...AND MAKING HIS WAY DOWN THE BACK OF A HANGING WHALE SCULPTURE.
AN OCTOPUS HAS THREE HEARTS
2 PUMP BLOOD TO THE GILLS, 1 PUMPS BLOOD THROUGHOUT THE BODY
WAIT--
AN OCTOPUS HAS THREE HEARTS.

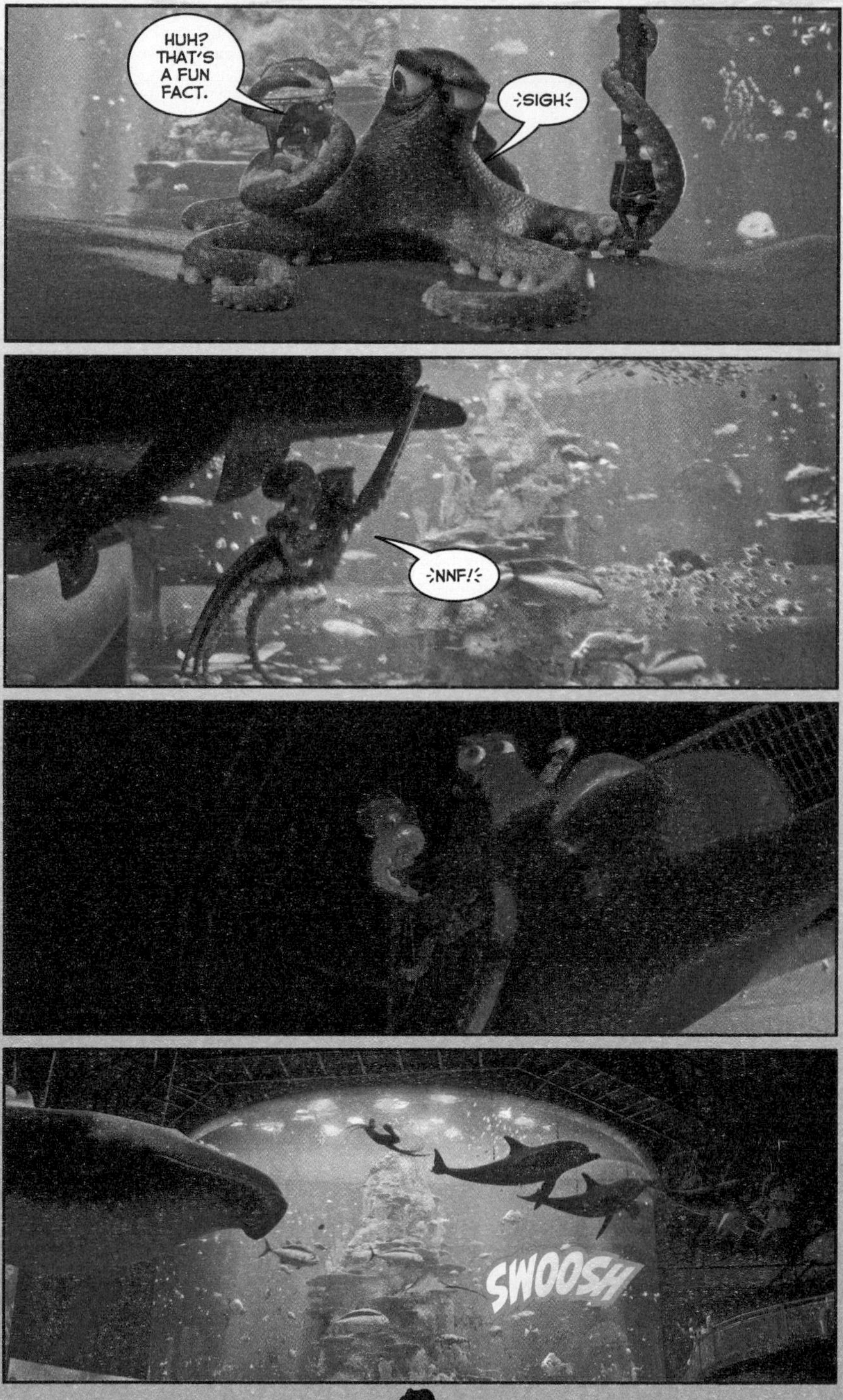
HUH? THAT'S A FUN FACT.
SIGH
NNF!
SWOOSH

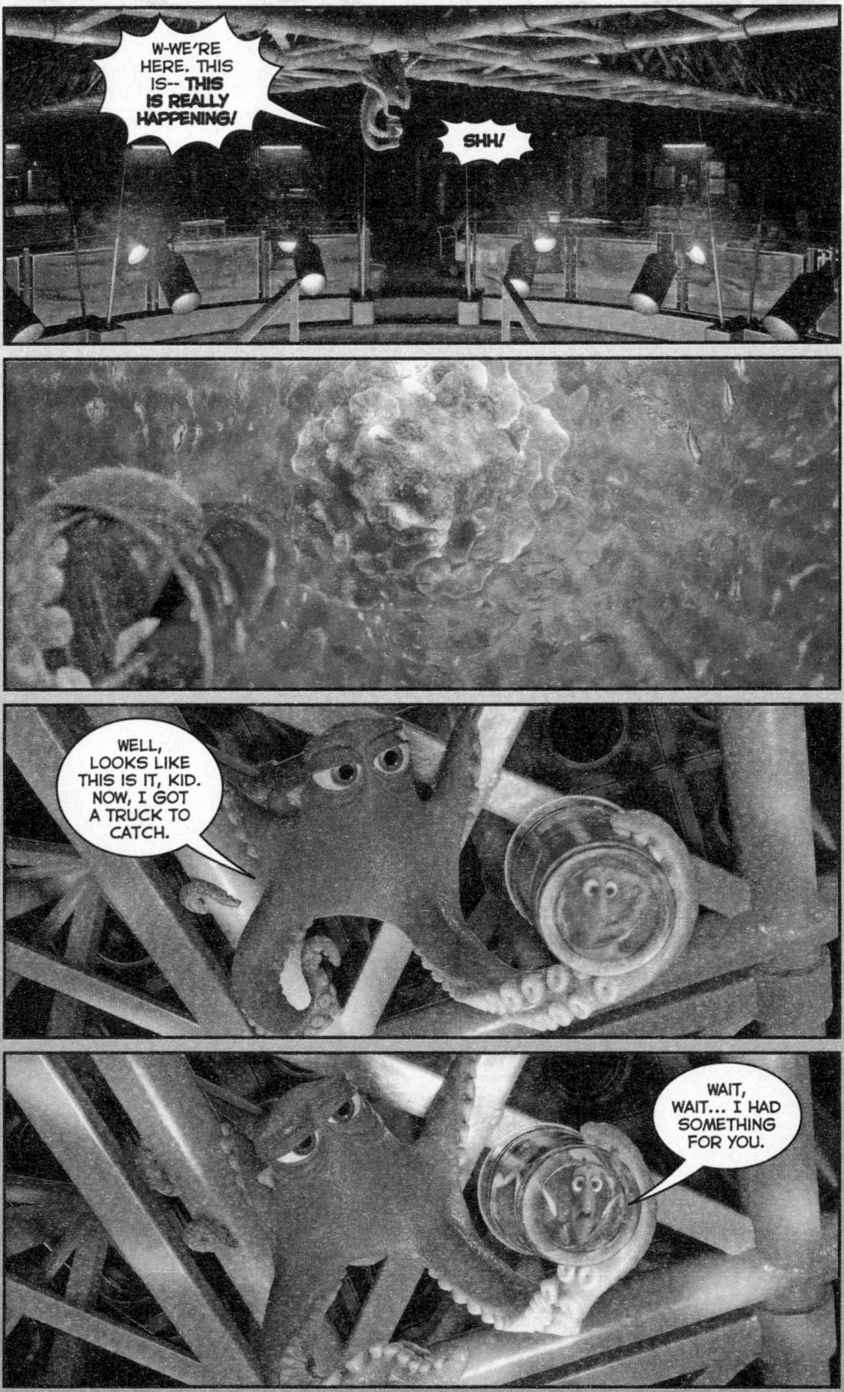
W-WE'RE HERE. THIS IS-- THIS IS REALLY HAPPENING!
SHH!
WELL, LOOKS LIKE THIS IS IT, KID. NOW, I GOT A TRUCK TO CATCH.
WAIT, WAIT... I HAD SOMETHING FOR YOU.

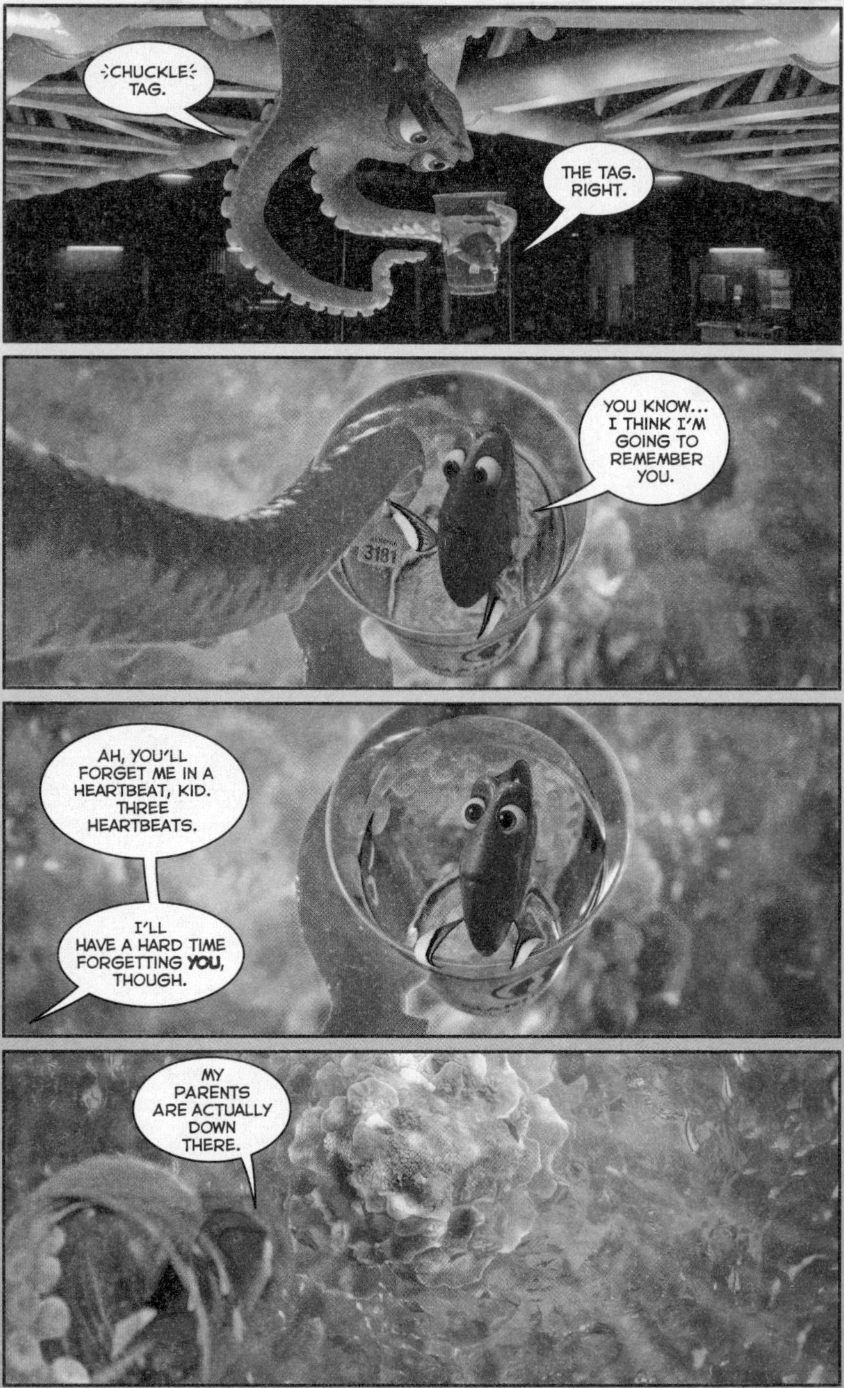

-:CHUCKLE:-
TAG.
THE TAG. RIGHT.
YOU KNOW... I THINK I'M GOING TO REMEMBER YOU.
3181
AH, YOU'LL FORGET ME IN A HEARTBEAT, KID. THREE HEARTBEATS.
I'LL HAVE A HARD TIME FORGETTING **YOU**, THOUGH.
MY PARENTS ARE ACTUALLY DOWN THERE.

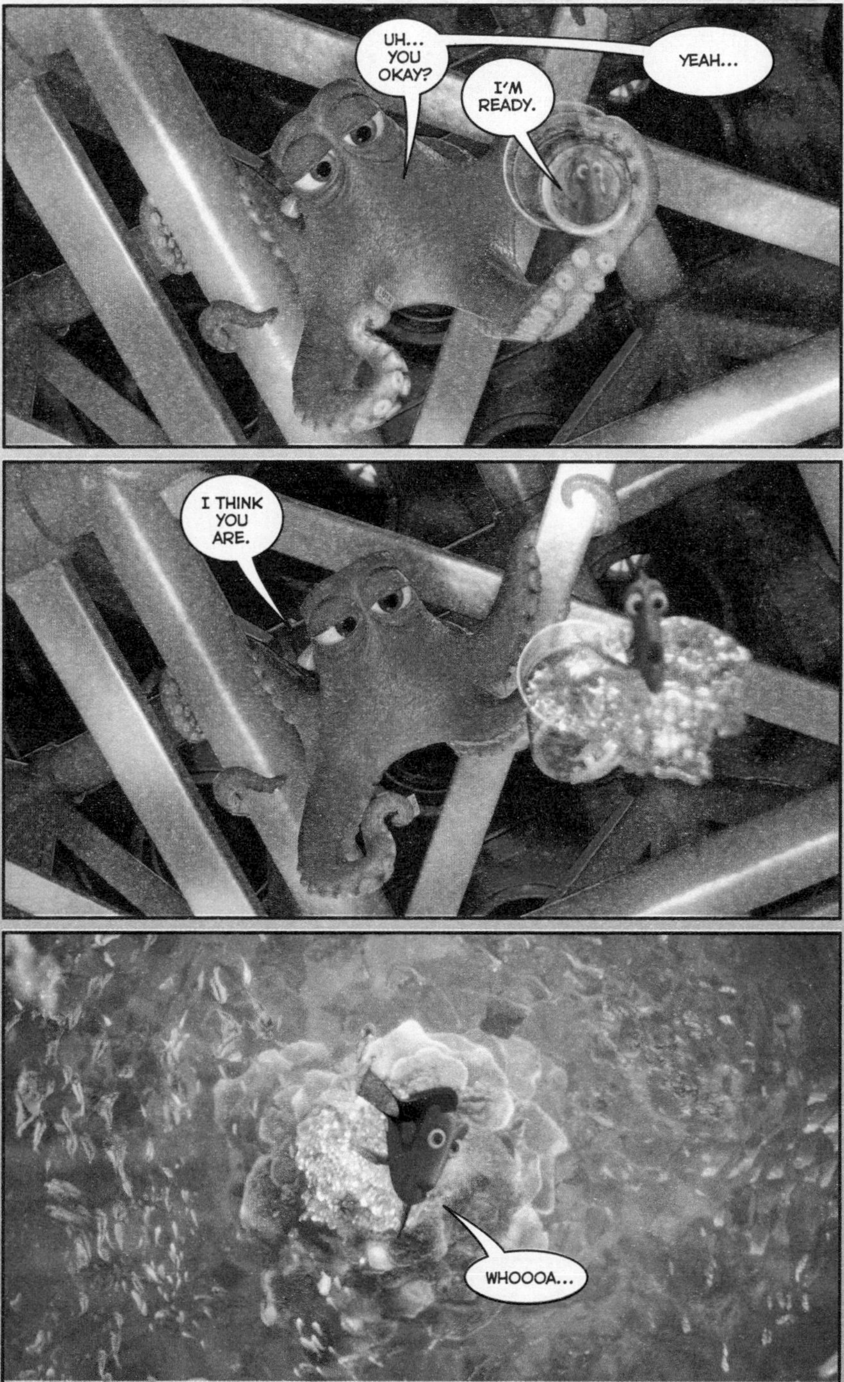
UH... YOU OKAY?
YEAH...
I'M READY.
I THINK YOU ARE.
WHOOOA...

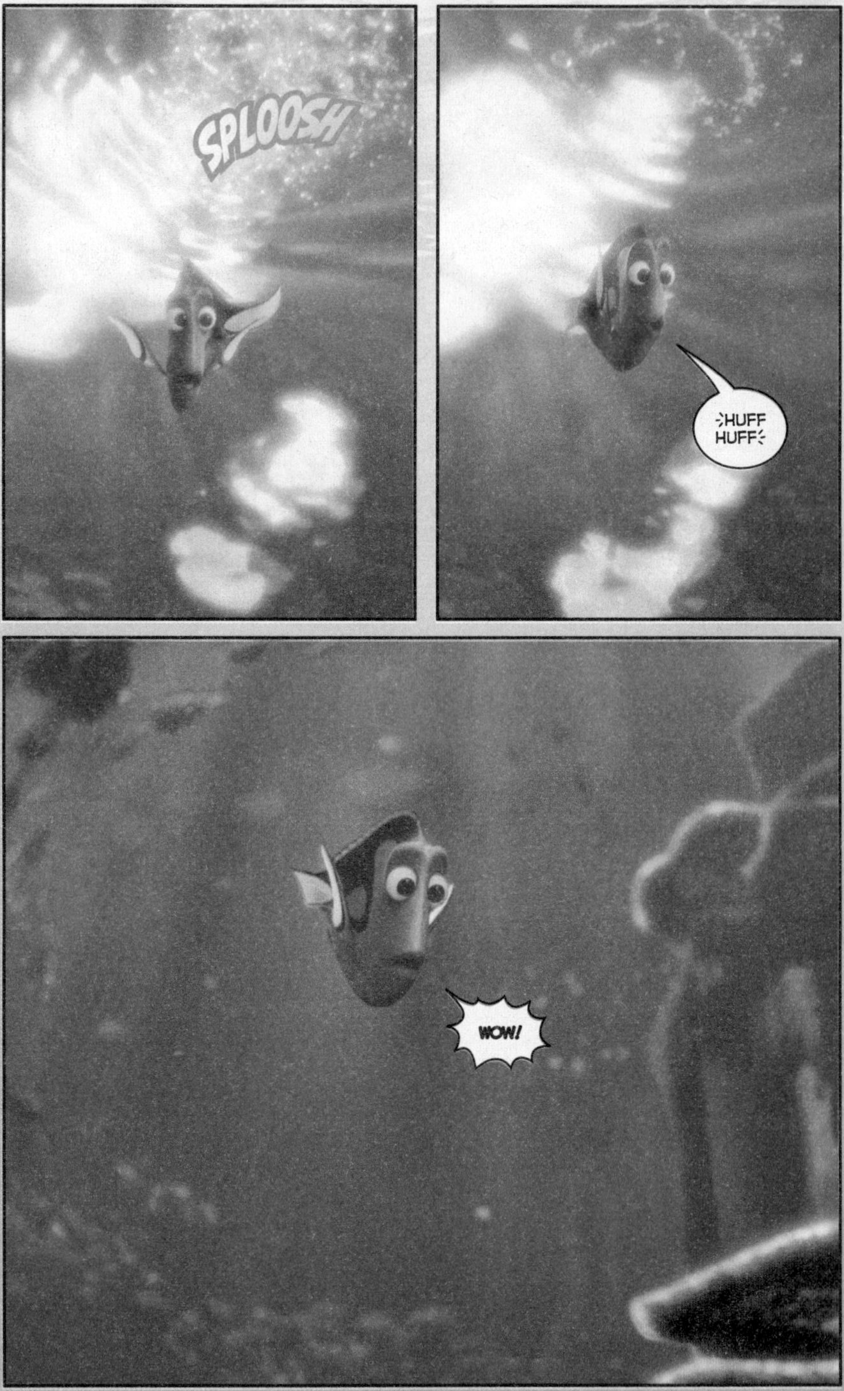
SPLOOSH
HUFF HUFF
WOW!

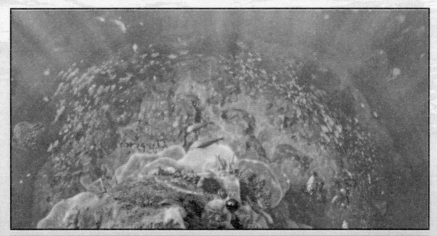

WHERE ARE THEY? WHERE ARE THEY? WHERE ARE THEY? OKAY, OKAY...

PARDON ME, AH, OH...

EXCUSE ME, HAVE YOU SEEN A COUPLE-- THEY'RE OLD, LIKE YOU-- NOT OLD LIKE YOU-- BUT OLDER THAN YOU, EVEN.

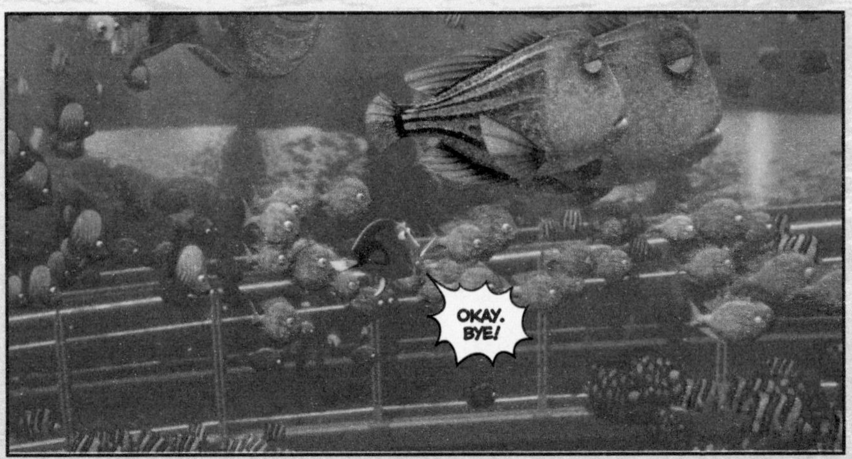
OKAY. BYE!

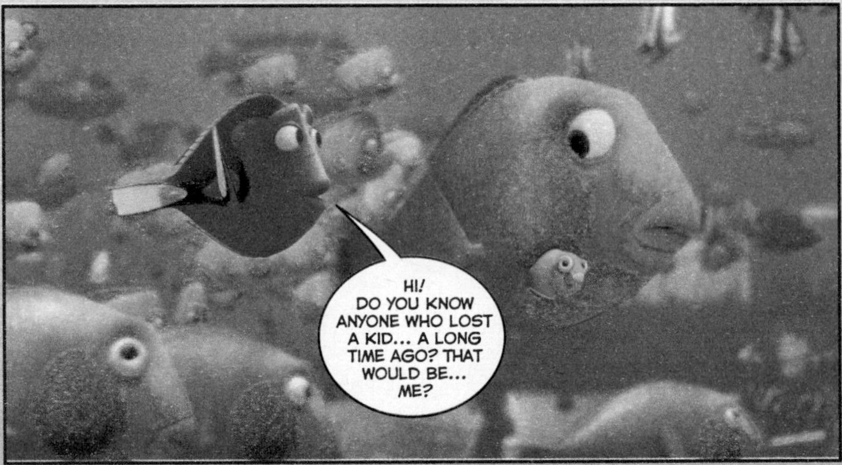
HI! DO YOU KNOW ANYONE WHO LOST A KID... A LONG TIME AGO? THAT WOULD BE... ME?

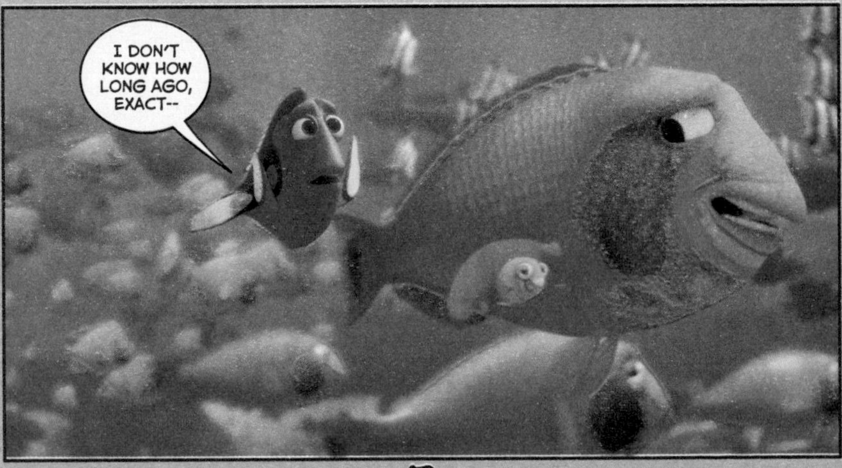
I DON'T KNOW HOW LONG AGO, EXACT--

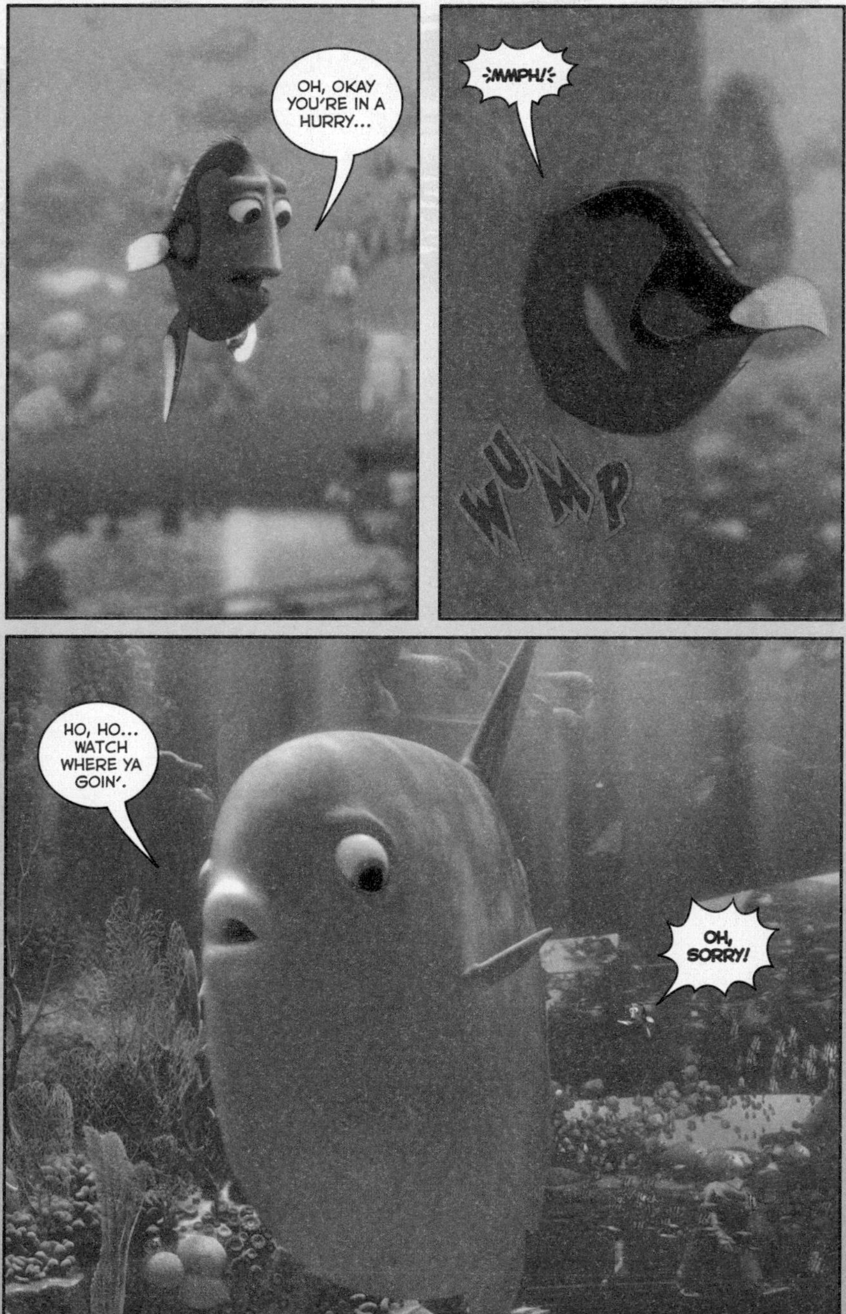
OH, OKAY YOU'RE IN A HURRY...
MMPH!
WUMP
HO, HO... WATCH WHERE YA GOIN'.
OH, SORRY!

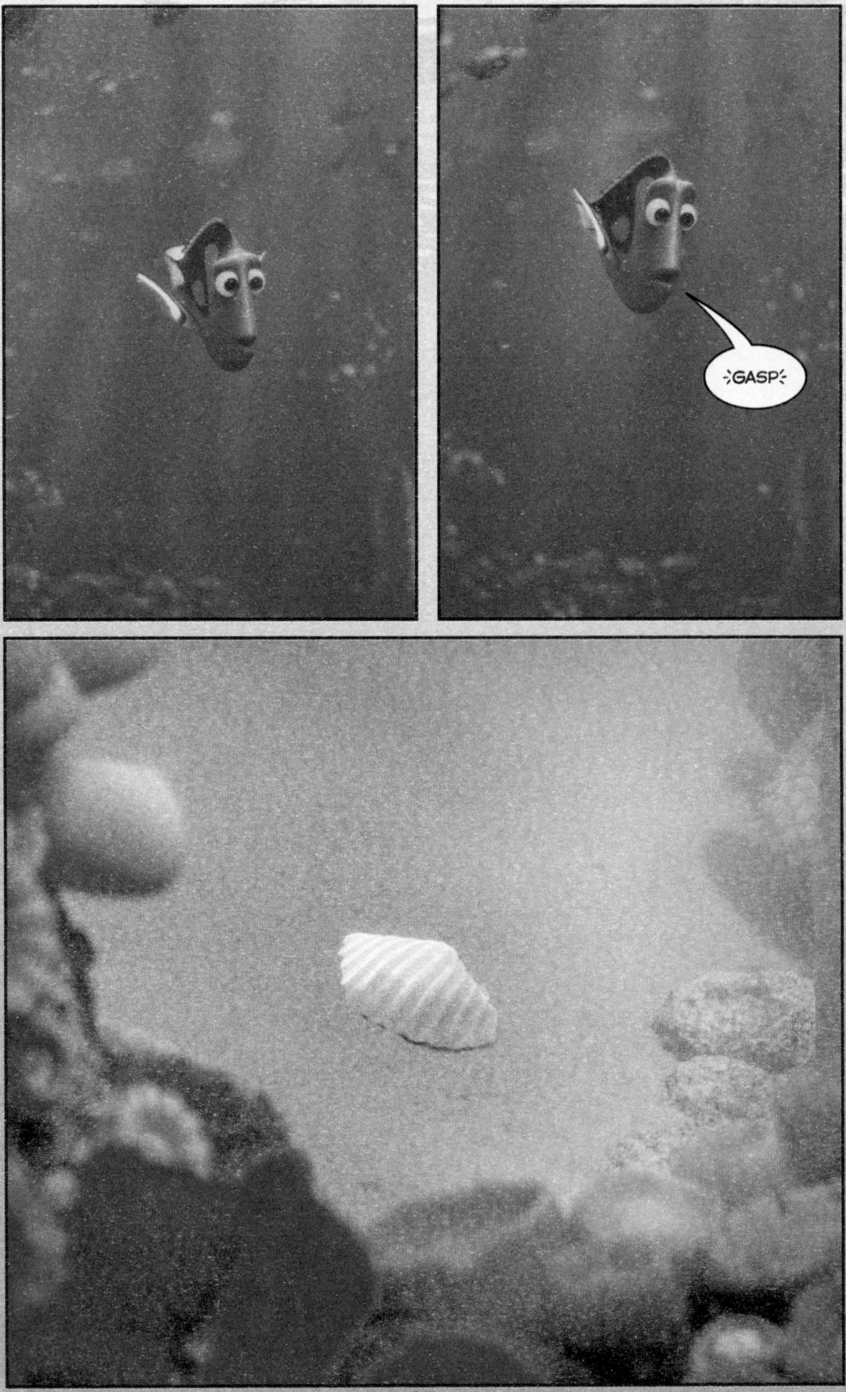
GASP

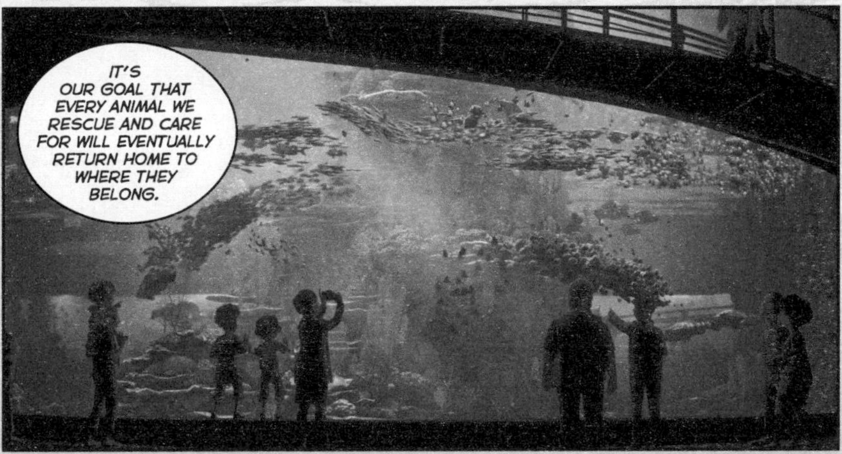
IT'S OUR GOAL THAT EVERY ANIMAL WE RESCUE AND CARE FOR WILL EVENTUALLY RETURN HOME TO WHERE THEY BELONG.

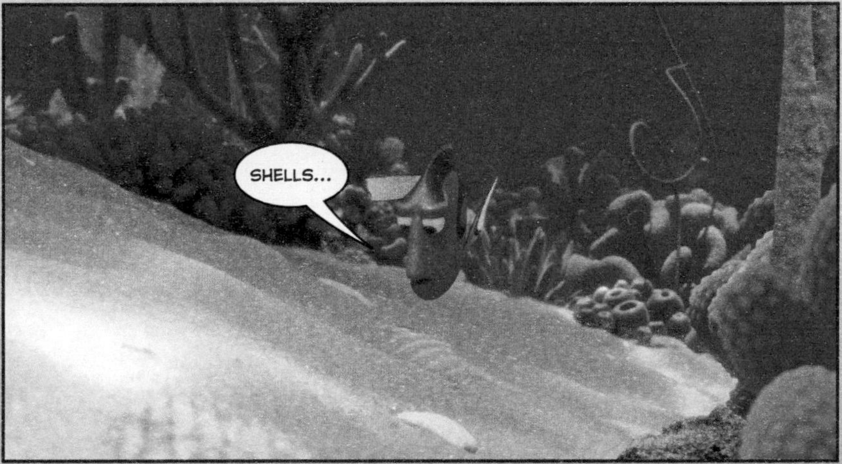
SHELLS...

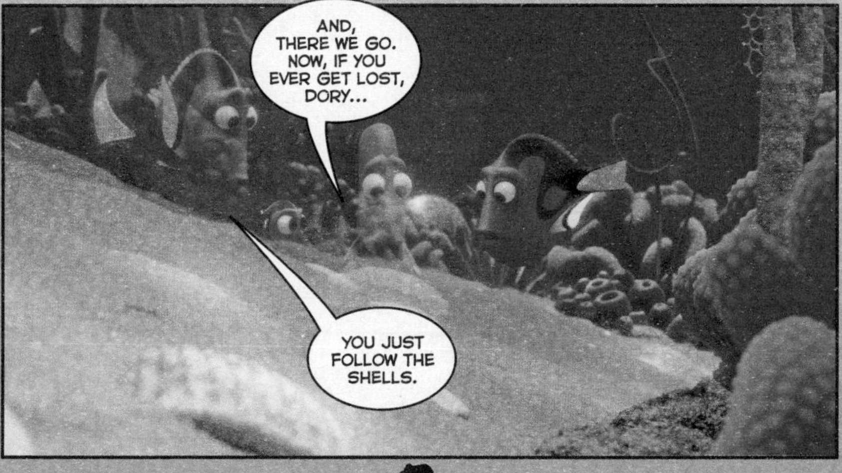
AND, THERE WE GO. NOW, IF YOU EVER GET LOST, DORY...
YOU JUST FOLLOW THE SHELLS.

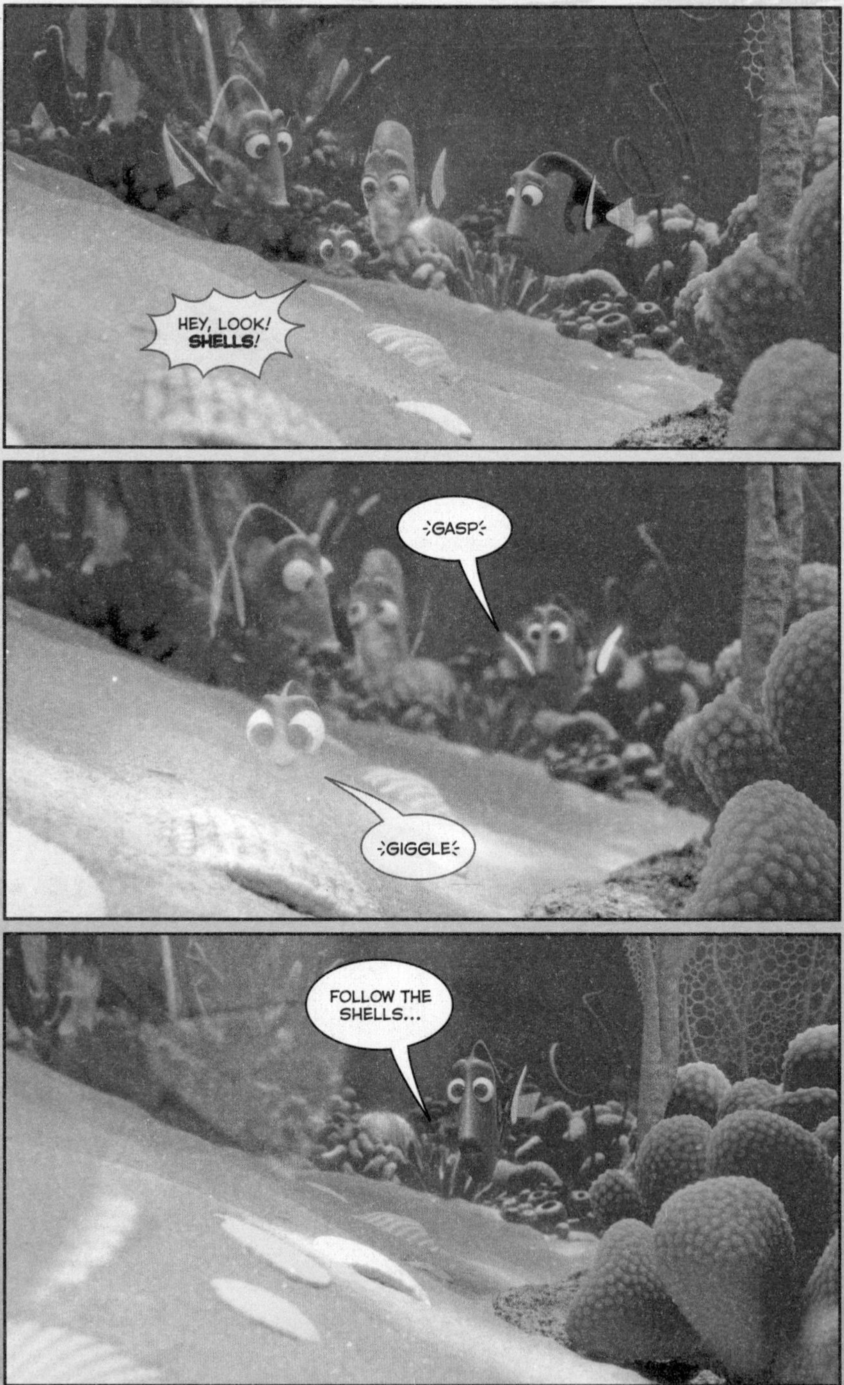
HEY, LOOK! **SHELLS!**
GASP
GIGGLE
FOLLOW THE SHELLS...

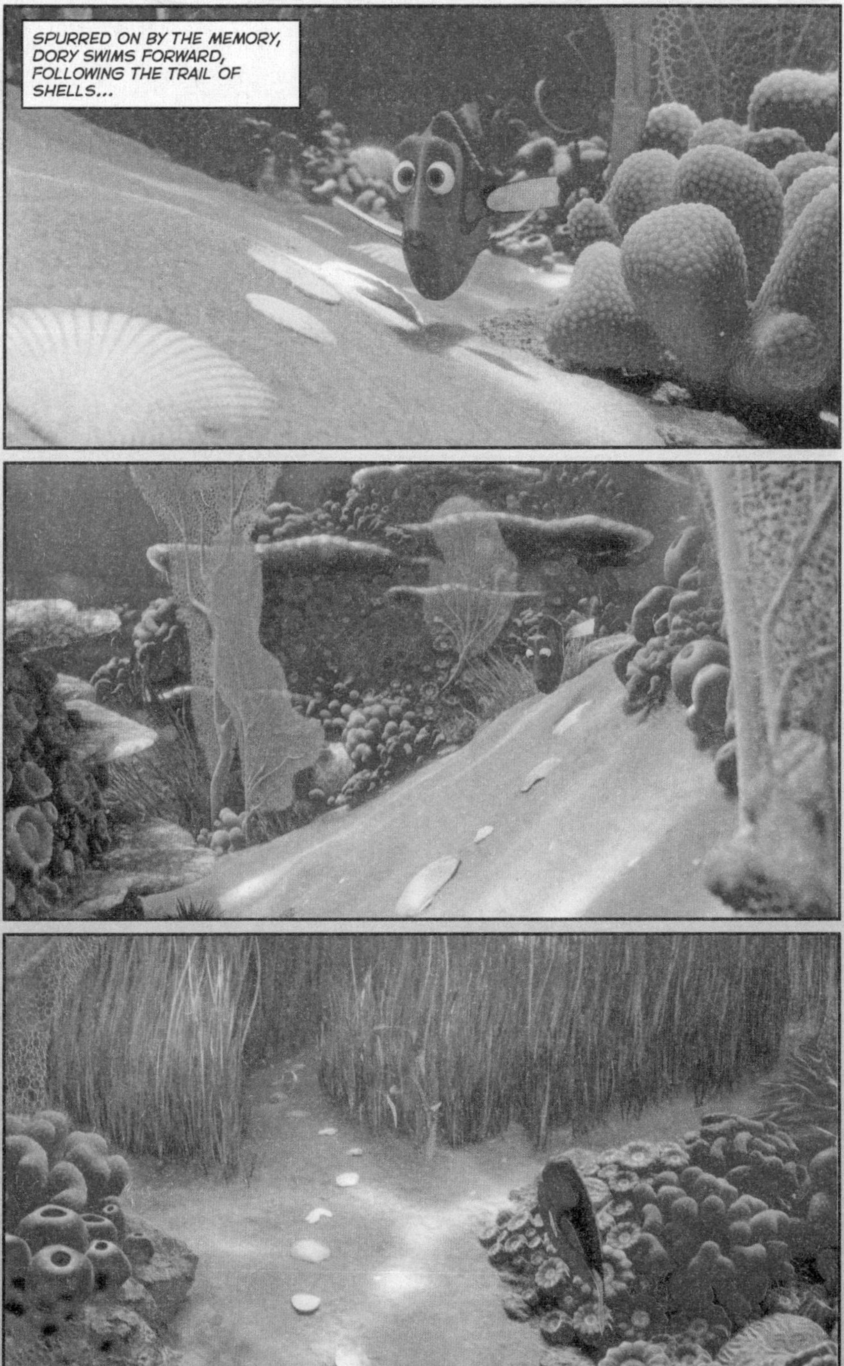
SPURRED ON BY THE MEMORY, DORY SWIMS FORWARD, FOLLOWING THE TRAIL OF SHELLS...

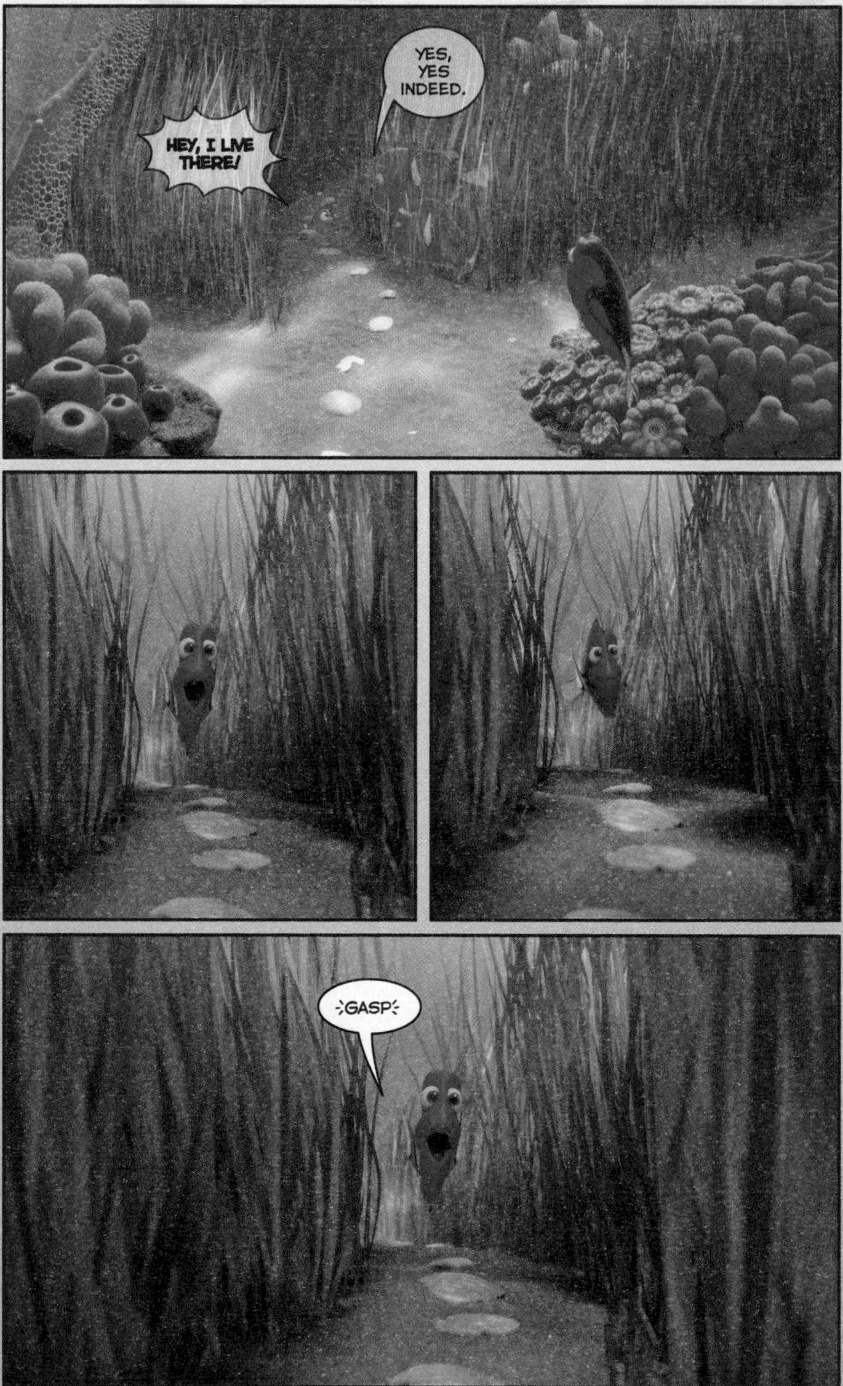
HEY, I LIVE THERE!
YES, YES INDEED.
GASP

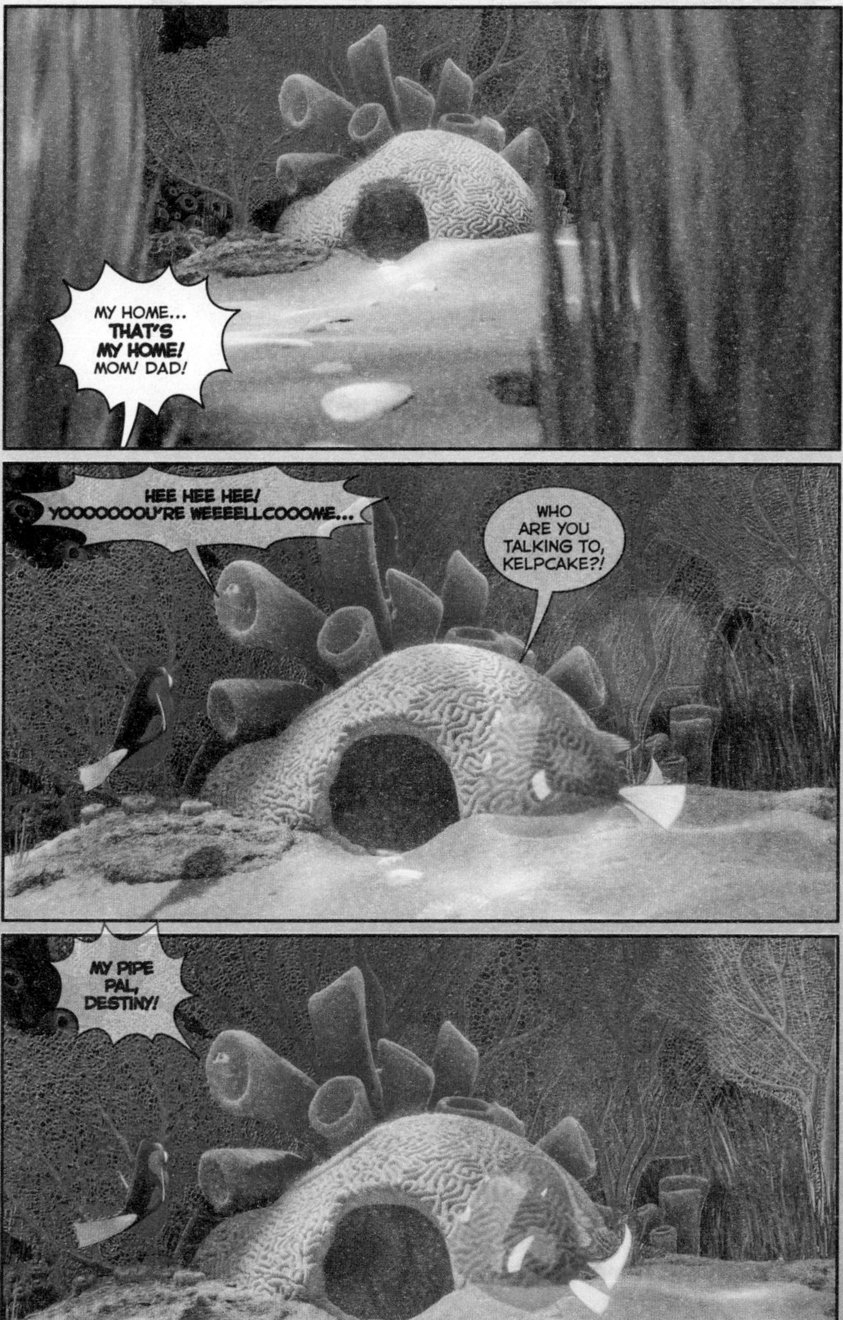
MY HOME... THAT'S MY HOME! MOM! DAD!
HEE HEE HEE! YOOOOOOOU'RE WEEEELLCOOOME...
WHO ARE YOU TALKING TO, KELPCAKE?!
MY PIPE PAL, DESTINY!

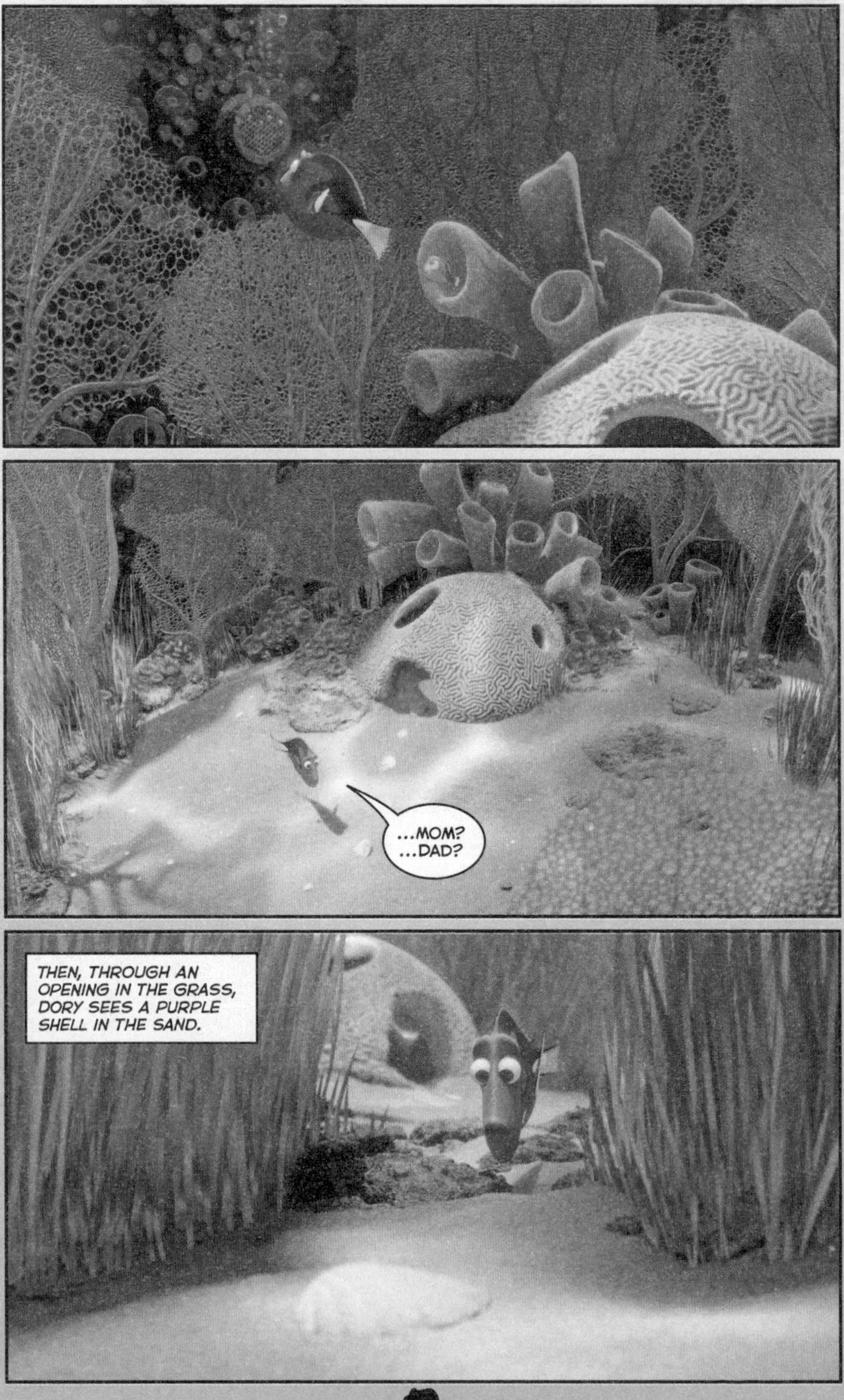
...MOM?
...DAD?
THEN, THROUGH AN OPENING IN THE GRASS, DORY SEES A PURPLE SHELL IN THE SAND.

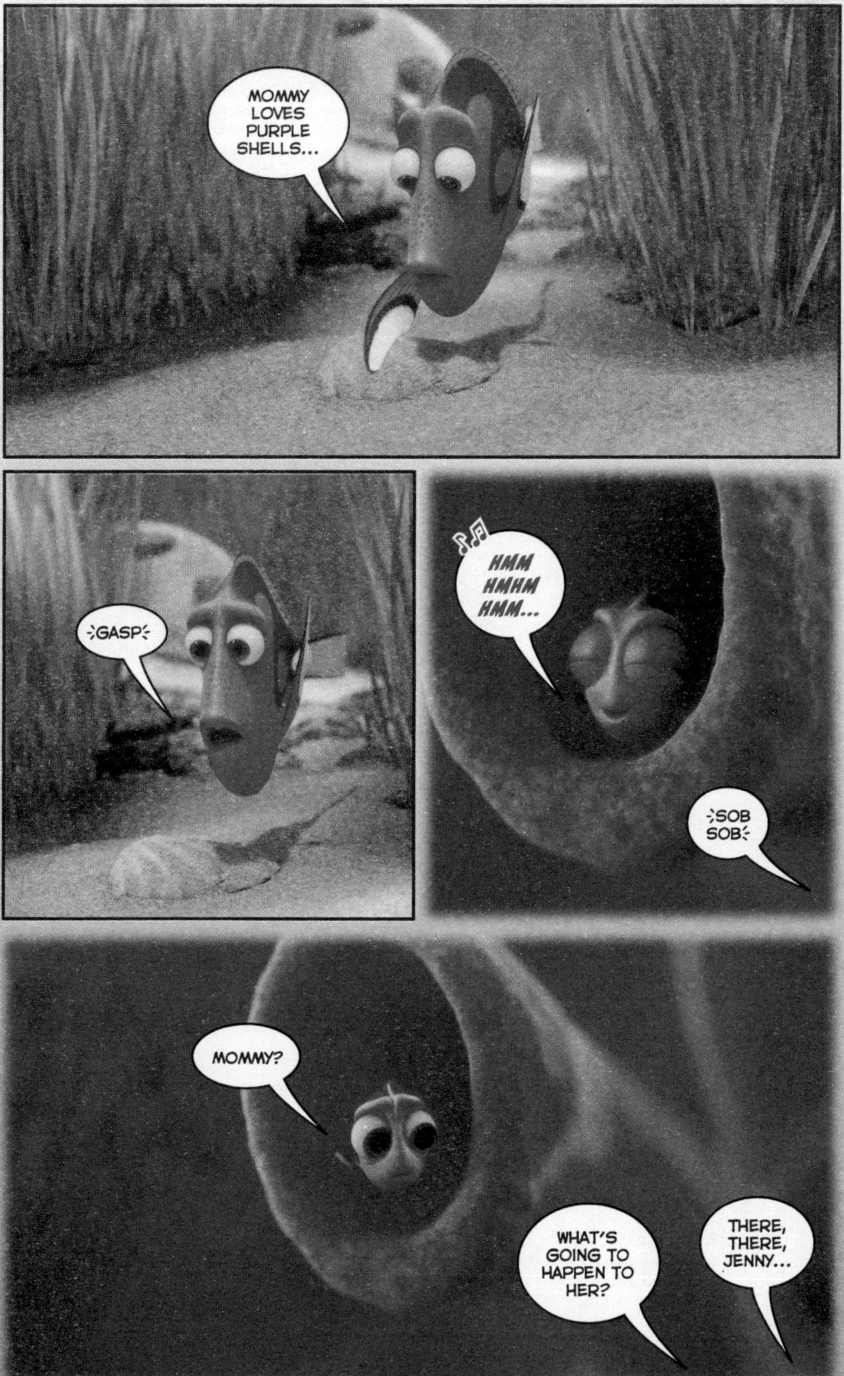
MOMMY LOVES PURPLE SHELLS...
GASP
HMM HMHM HMM...
SOB SOB
MOMMY?
WHAT'S GOING TO HAPPEN TO HER?
THERE, THERE, JENNY...

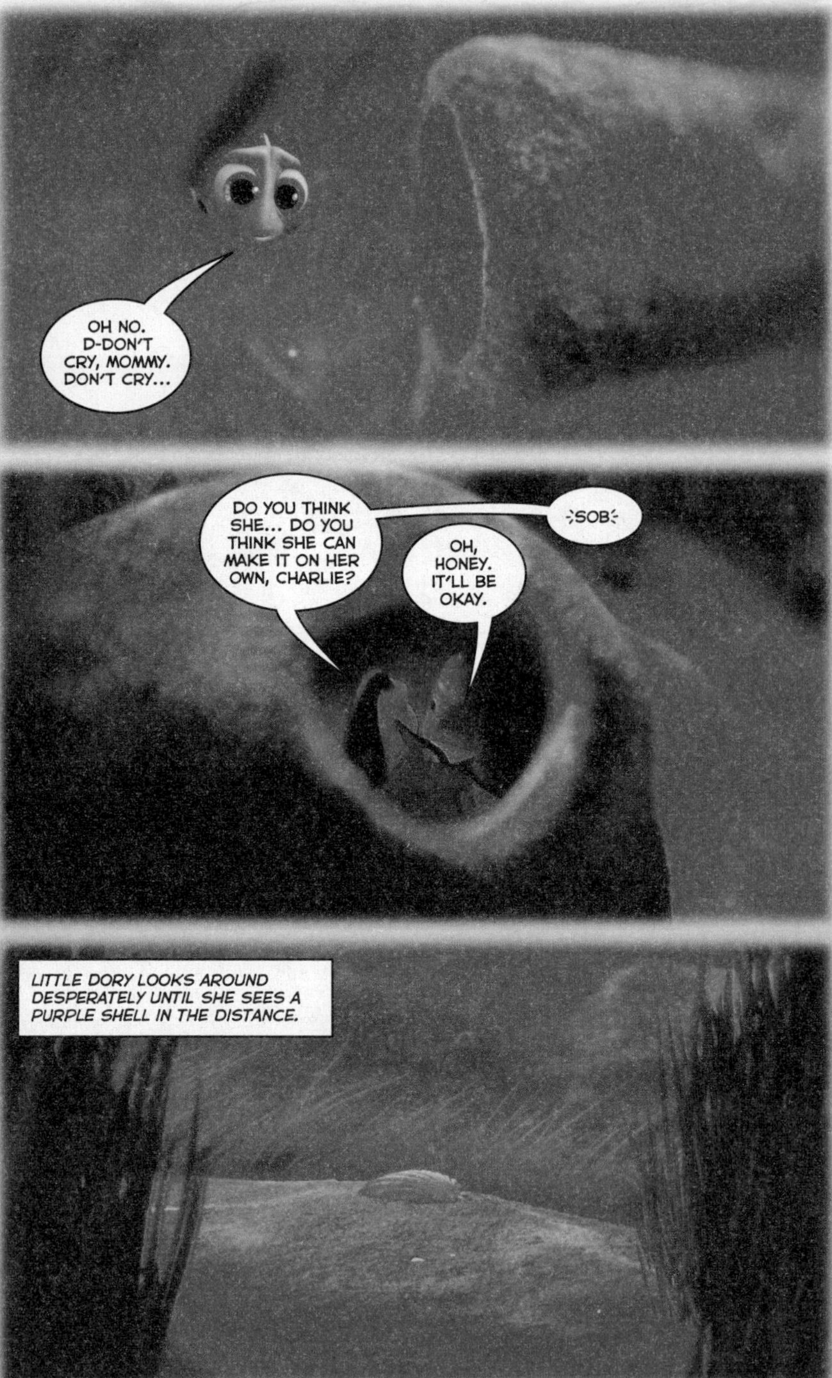
OH NO. D-DON'T CRY, MOMMY. DON'T CRY...
DO YOU THINK SHE... DO YOU THINK SHE CAN MAKE IT ON HER OWN, CHARLIE?
SOB
OH, HONEY. IT'LL BE OKAY.
LITTLE DORY LOOKS AROUND DESPERATELY UNTIL SHE SEES A PURPLE SHELL IN THE DISTANCE.

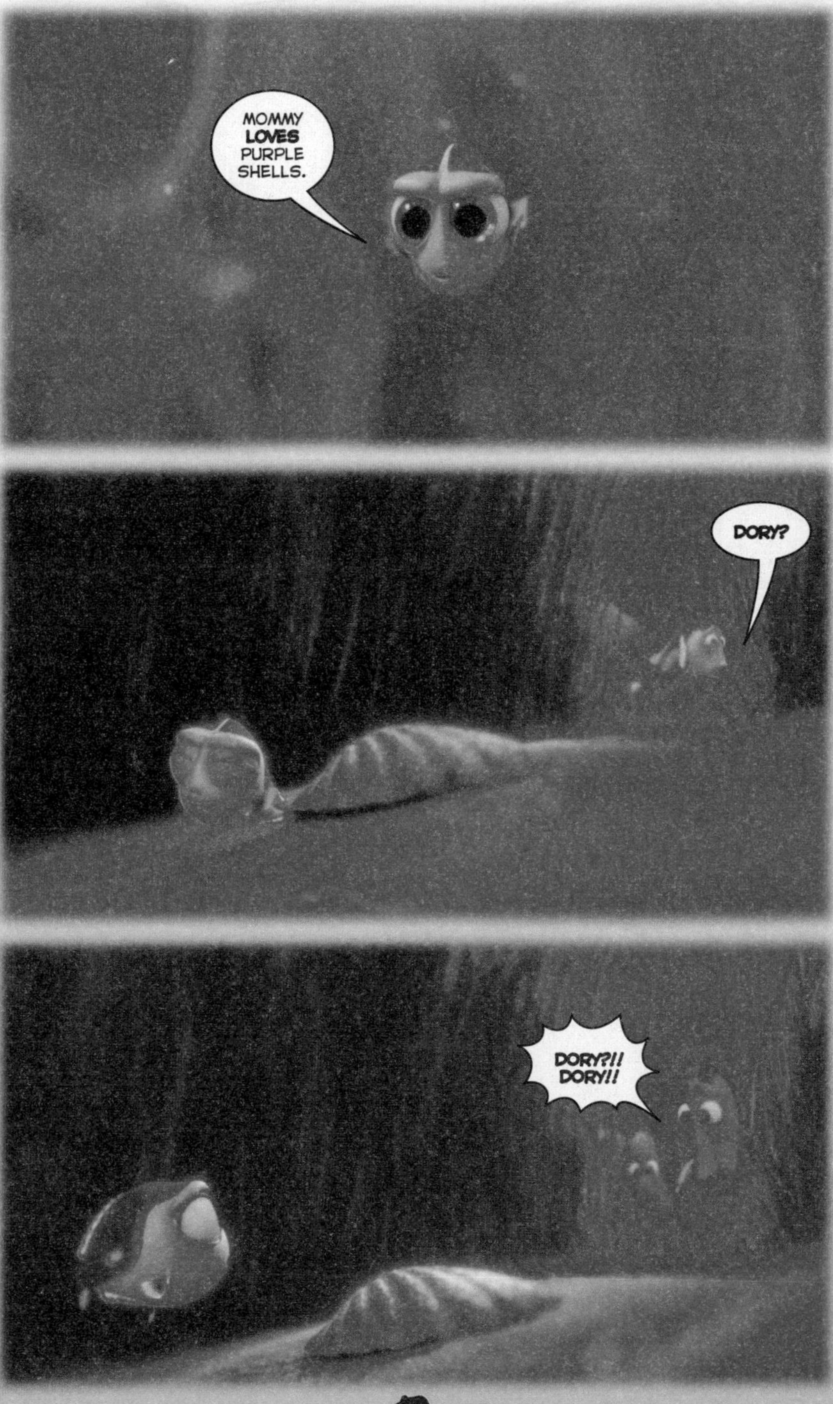
MOMMY LOVES PURPLE SHELLS.
DORY?
DORY?!! DORY!!

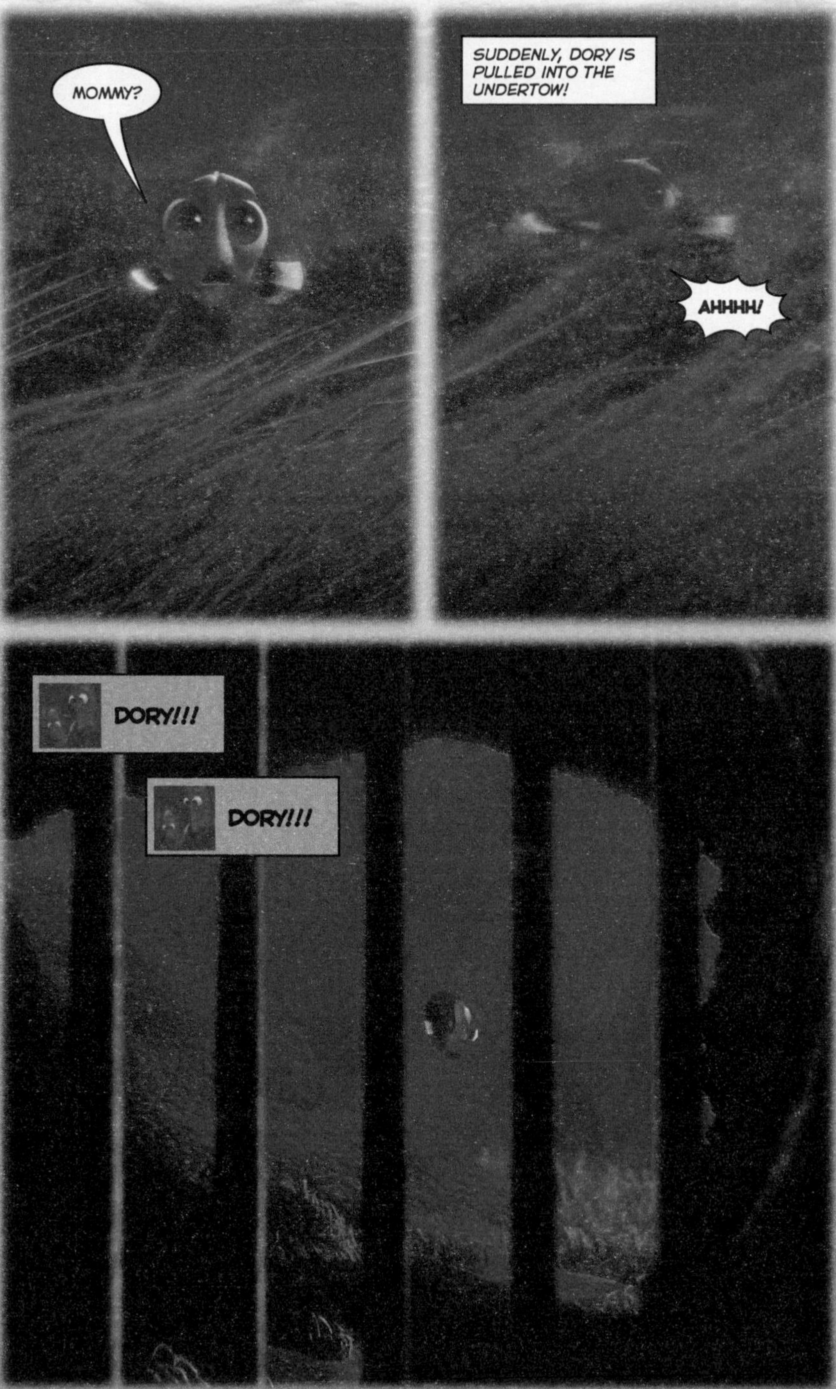
MOMMY?
SUDDENLY, DORY IS PULLED INTO THE UNDERTOW!
AHHHH!
DORY!!!
DORY!!!

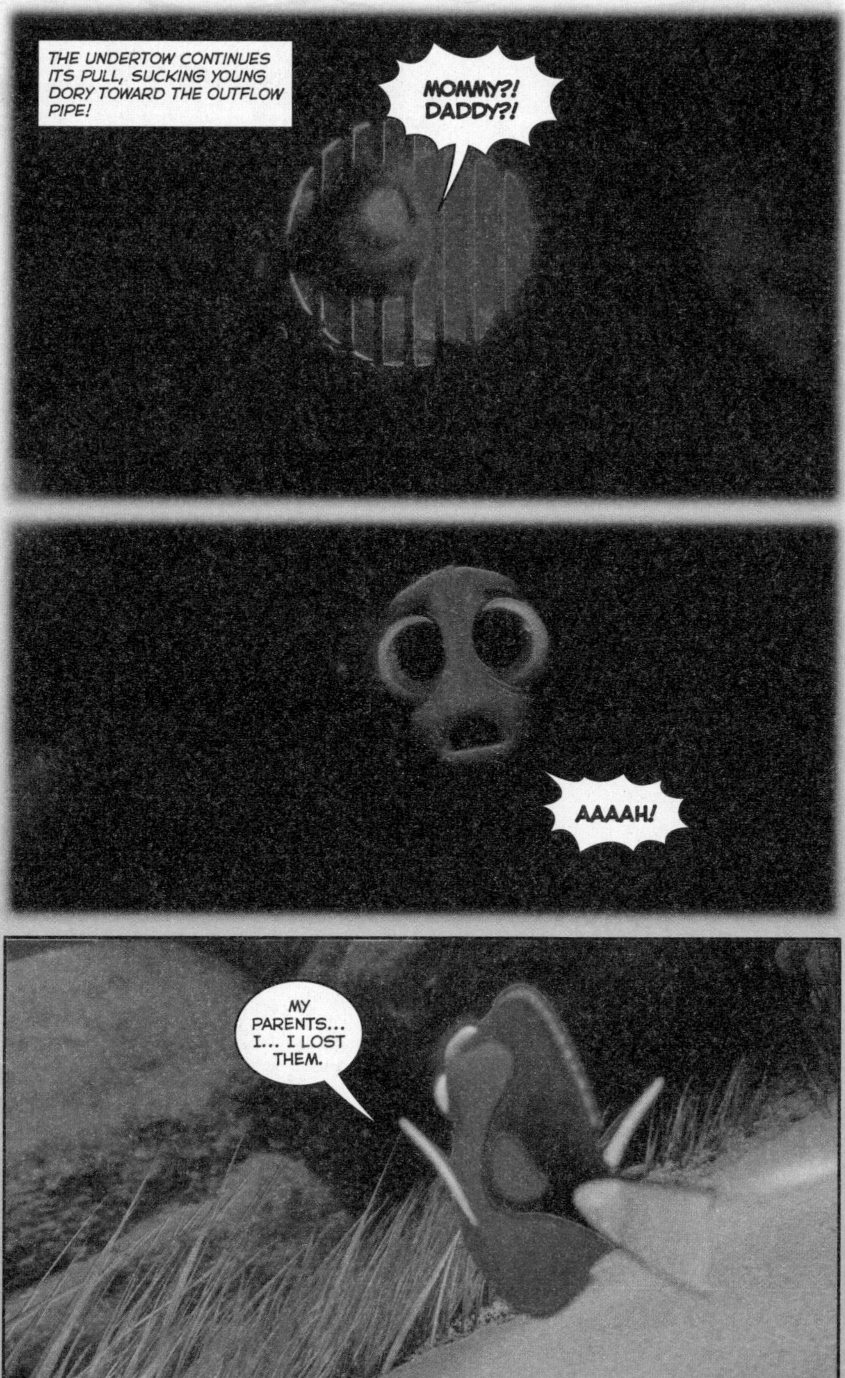
THE UNDERTOW CONTINUES ITS PULL, SUCKING YOUNG DORY TOWARD THE OUTFLOW PIPE!
MOMMY?! DADDY?!
AAAAH!
MY PARENTS... I... I LOST THEM.

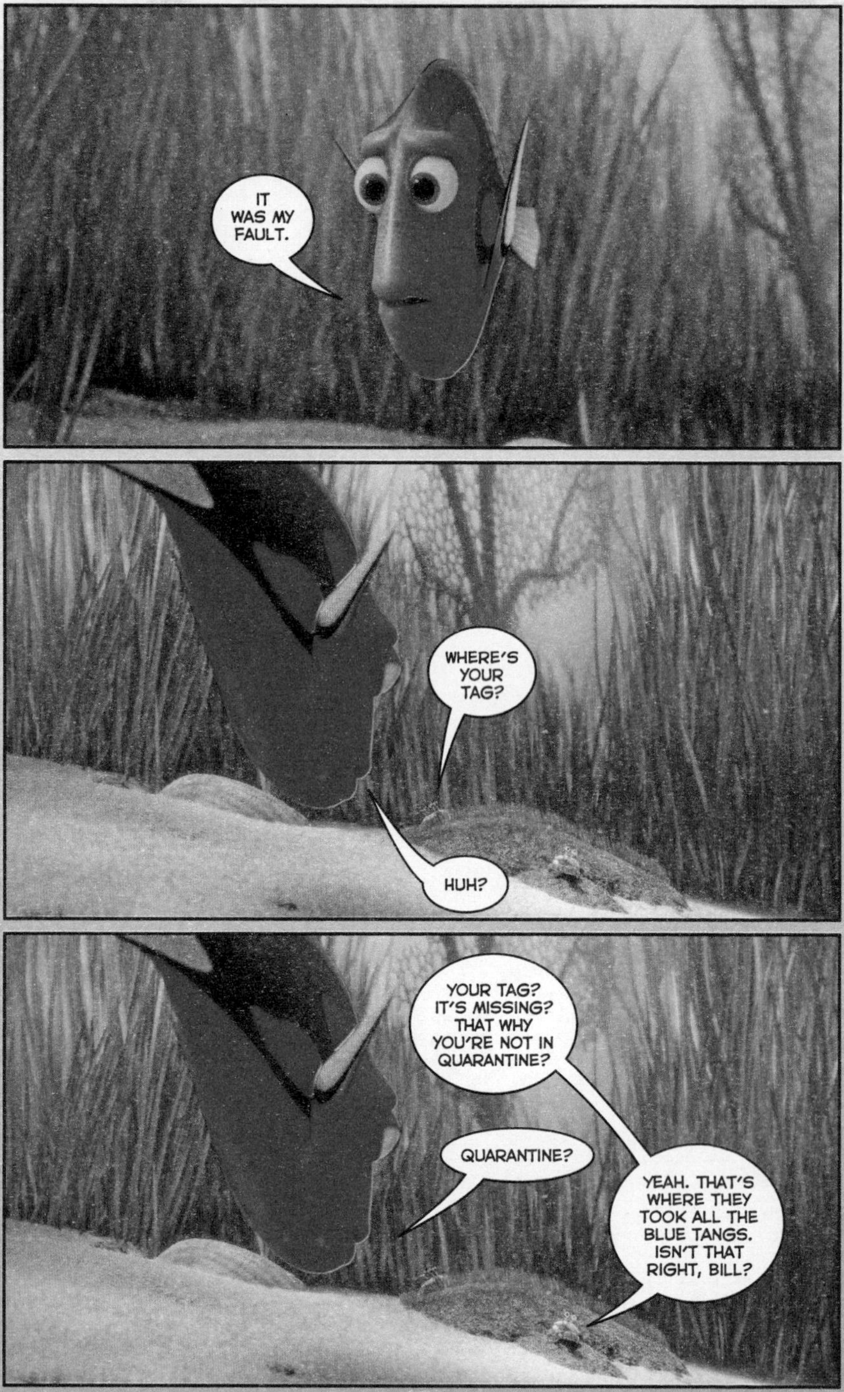
IT WAS MY FAULT.
WHERE'S YOUR TAG?
HUH?
YOUR TAG? IT'S MISSING? THAT WHY YOU'RE NOT IN QUARANTINE?
QUARANTINE?
YEAH. THAT'S WHERE THEY TOOK ALL THE BLUE TANGS. ISN'T THAT RIGHT, BILL?

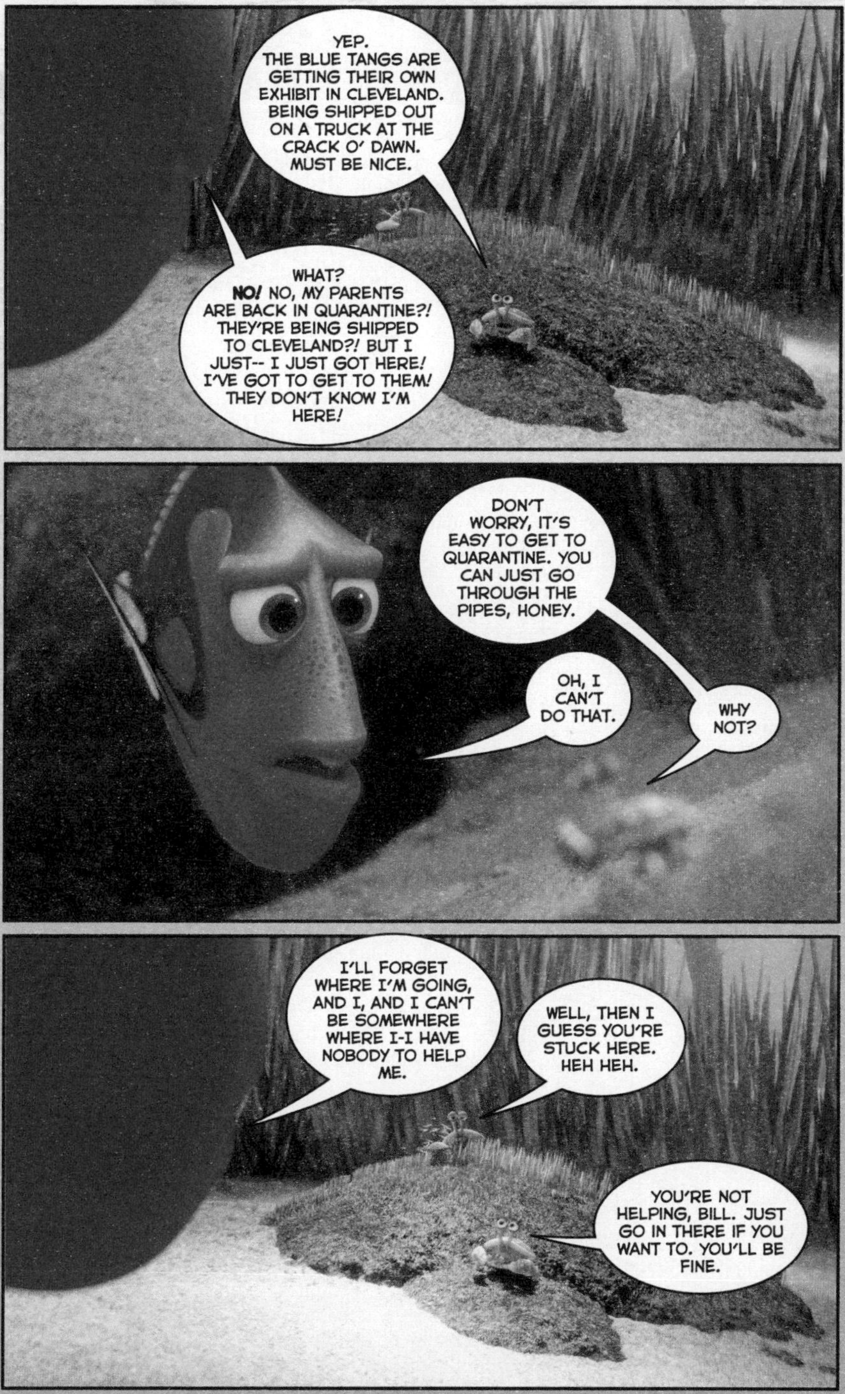
YEP. THE BLUE TANGS ARE GETTING THEIR OWN EXHIBIT IN CLEVELAND. BEING SHIPPED OUT ON A TRUCK AT THE CRACK O' DAWN. MUST BE NICE.
WHAT? **NO!** NO, MY PARENTS ARE BACK IN QUARANTINE?! THEY'RE BEING SHIPPED TO CLEVELAND?! BUT I JUST-- I JUST GOT HERE! I'VE GOT TO GET TO THEM! THEY DON'T KNOW I'M HERE!
DON'T WORRY, IT'S EASY TO GET TO QUARANTINE. YOU CAN JUST GO THROUGH THE PIPES, HONEY.
OH, I CAN'T DO THAT.
WHY NOT?
I'LL FORGET WHERE I'M GOING, AND I, AND I CAN'T BE SOMEWHERE WHERE I-I HAVE NOBODY TO HELP ME.
WELL, THEN I GUESS YOU'RE STUCK HERE. HEH HEH.
YOU'RE NOT HELPING, BILL. JUST GO IN THERE IF YOU WANT TO. YOU'LL BE FINE.

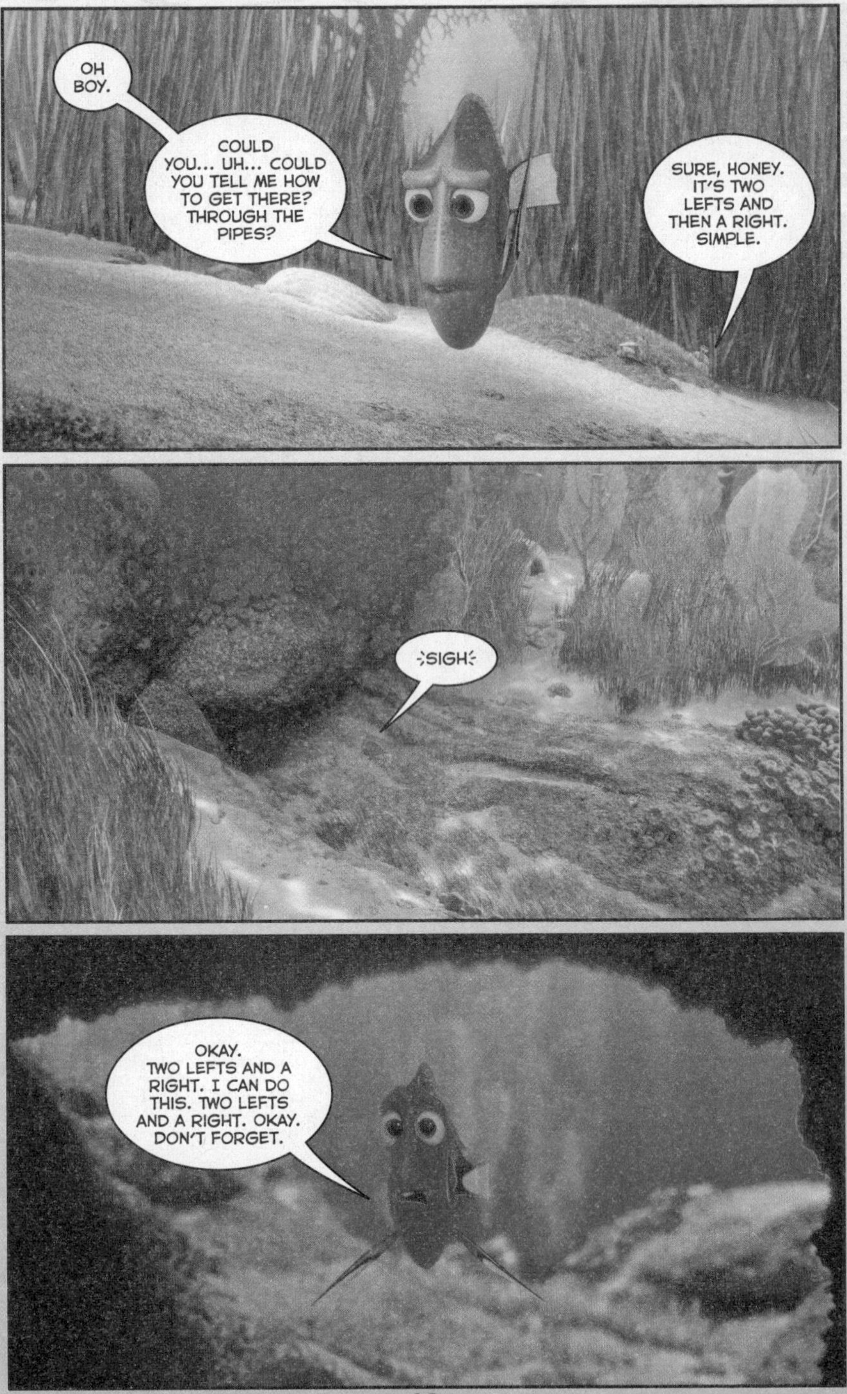
OH BOY.
COULD YOU... UH... COULD YOU TELL ME HOW TO GET THERE? THROUGH THE PIPES?
SURE, HONEY. IT'S TWO LEFTS AND THEN A RIGHT. SIMPLE.
SIGH
OKAY. TWO LEFTS AND A RIGHT. I CAN DO THIS. TWO LEFTS AND A RIGHT. OKAY. DON'T FORGET.

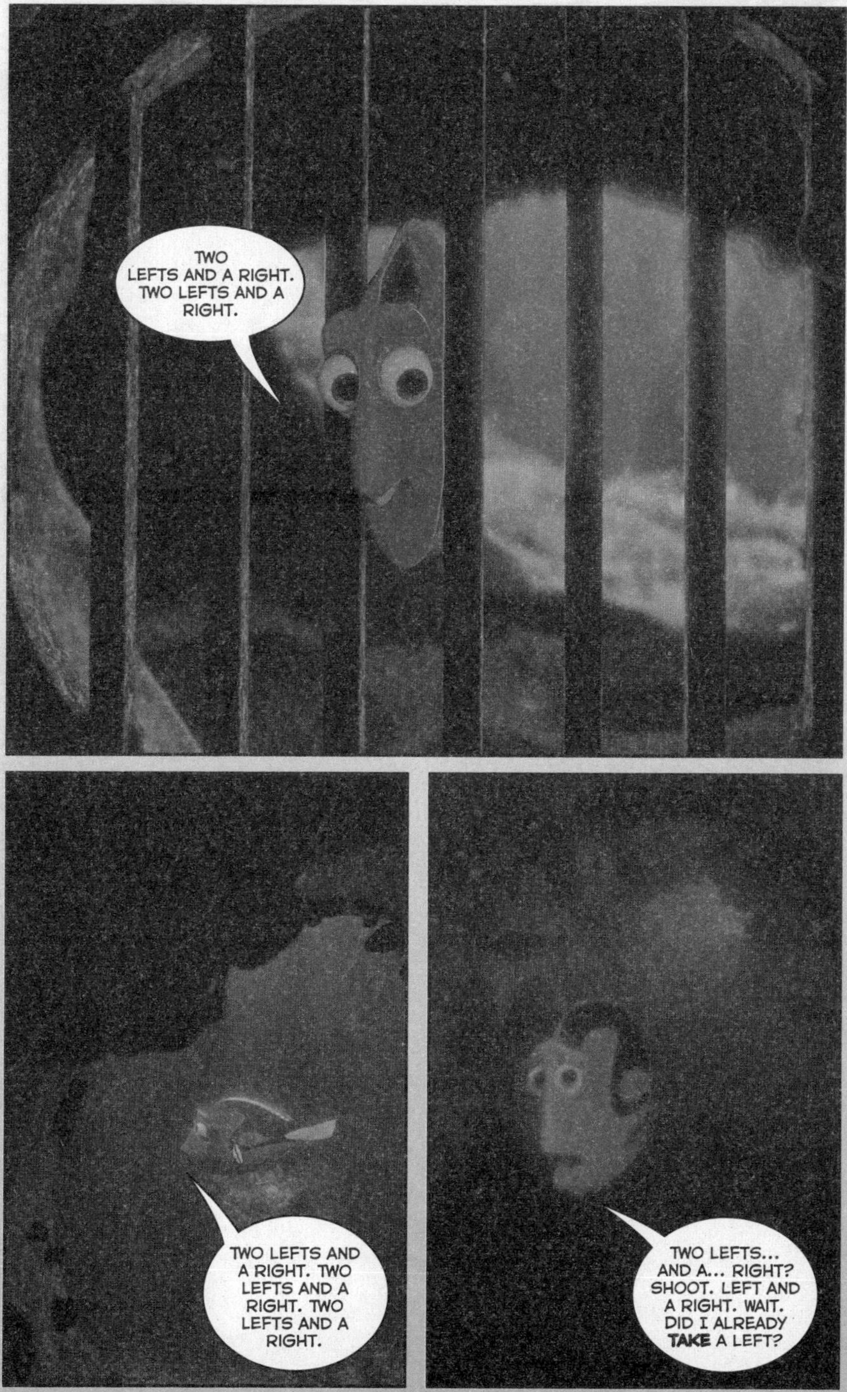
TWO LEFTS AND A RIGHT. TWO LEFTS AND A RIGHT.
TWO LEFTS AND A RIGHT. TWO LEFTS AND A RIGHT. TWO LEFTS AND A RIGHT.
TWO LEFTS... AND A... RIGHT? SHOOT. LEFT AND A RIGHT. WAIT. DID I ALREADY **TAKE** A LEFT?

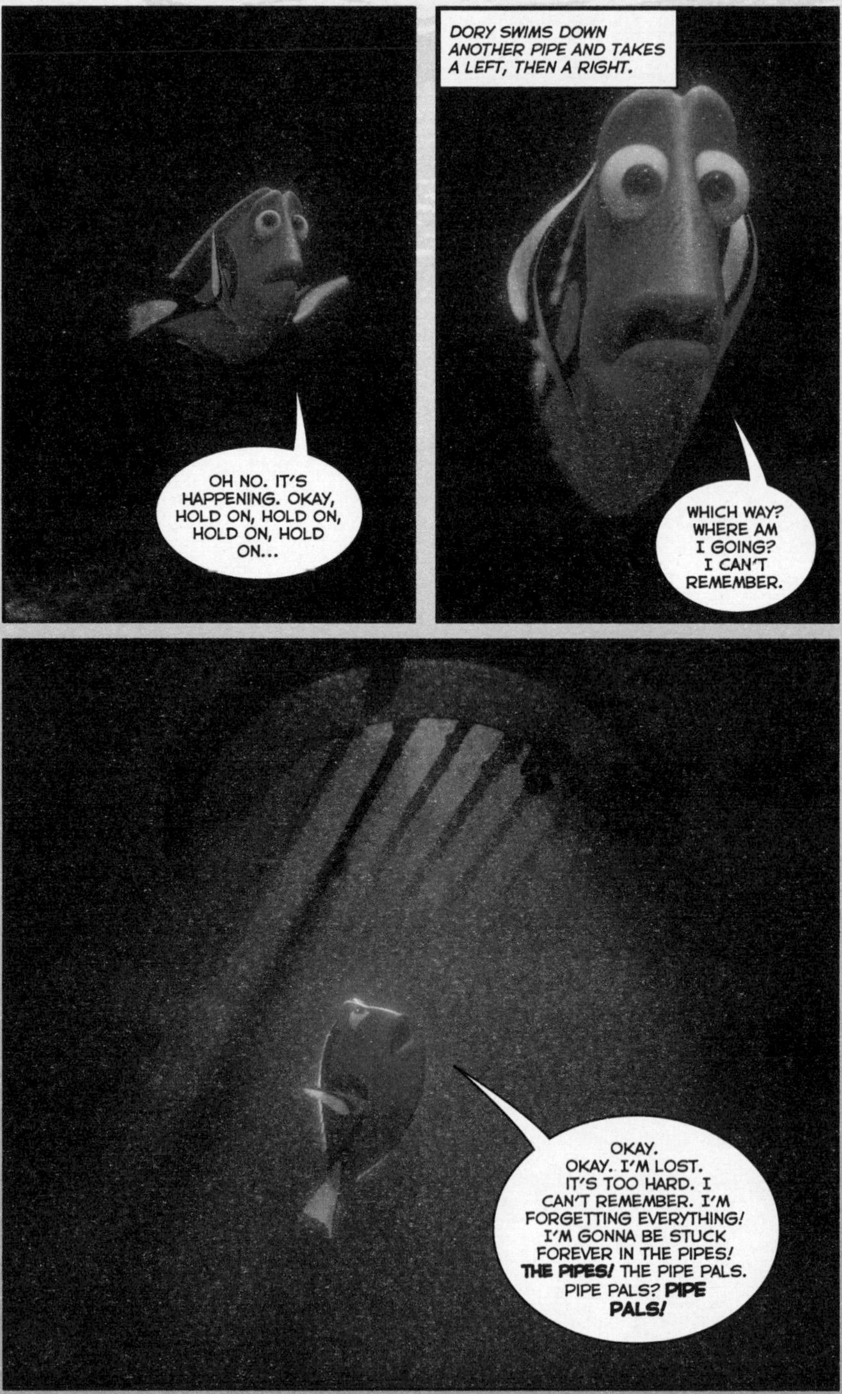
OH NO. IT'S HAPPENING. OKAY, HOLD ON, HOLD ON, HOLD ON, HOLD ON...
DORY SWIMS DOWN ANOTHER PIPE AND TAKES A LEFT, THEN A RIGHT.
WHICH WAY? WHERE AM I GOING? I CAN'T REMEMBER.
OKAY. OKAY. I'M LOST. IT'S TOO HARD. I CAN'T REMEMBER. I'M FORGETTING EVERYTHING! I'M GONNA BE STUCK FOREVER IN THE PIPES! **THE PIPES!** THE PIPE PALS. PIPE PALS? **PIPE PALS!**

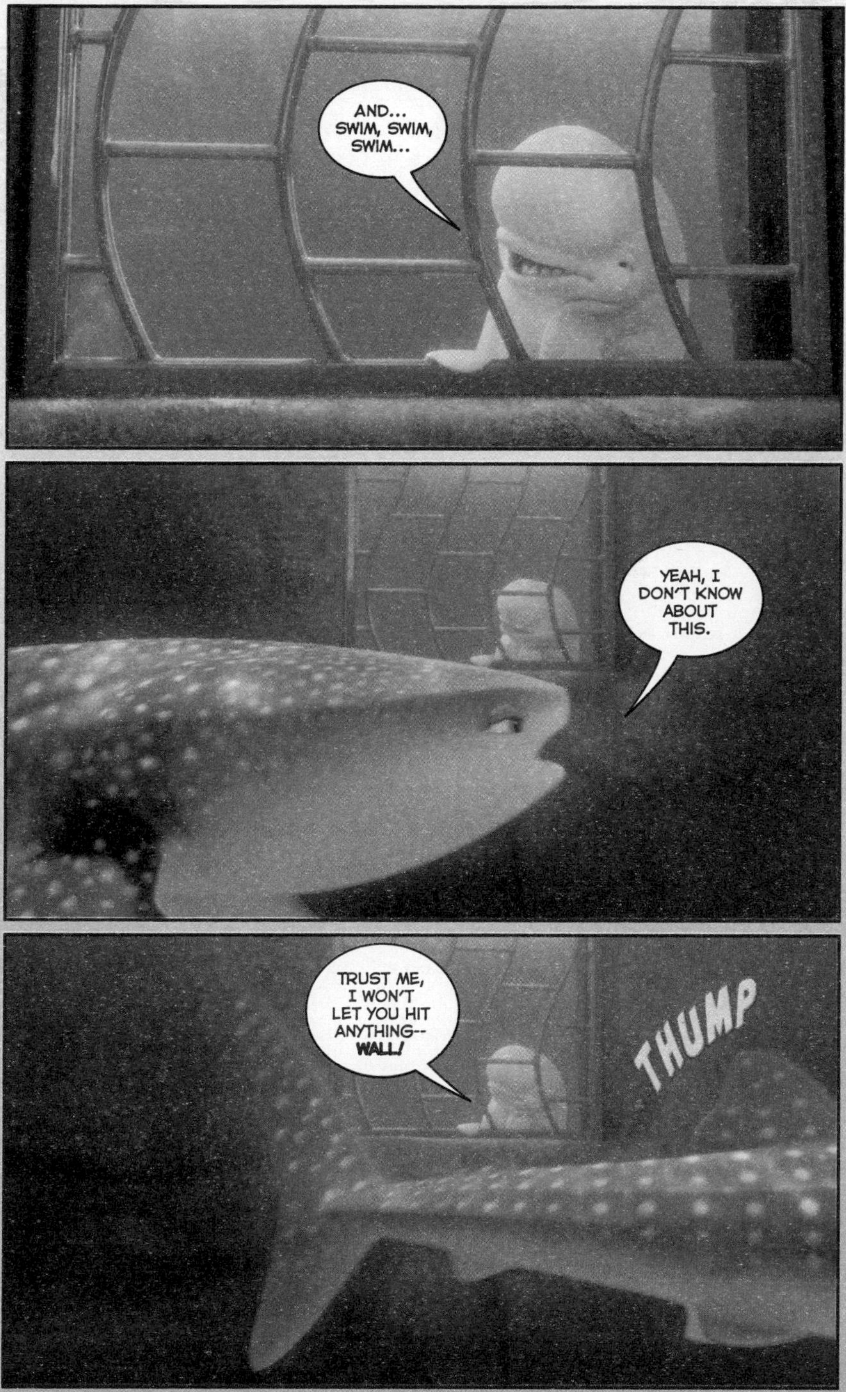
AND... SWIM, SWIM, SWIM...
YEAH, I DON'T KNOW ABOUT THIS.
TRUST ME, I WON'T LET YOU HIT ANYTHING-- WALL!
THUMP

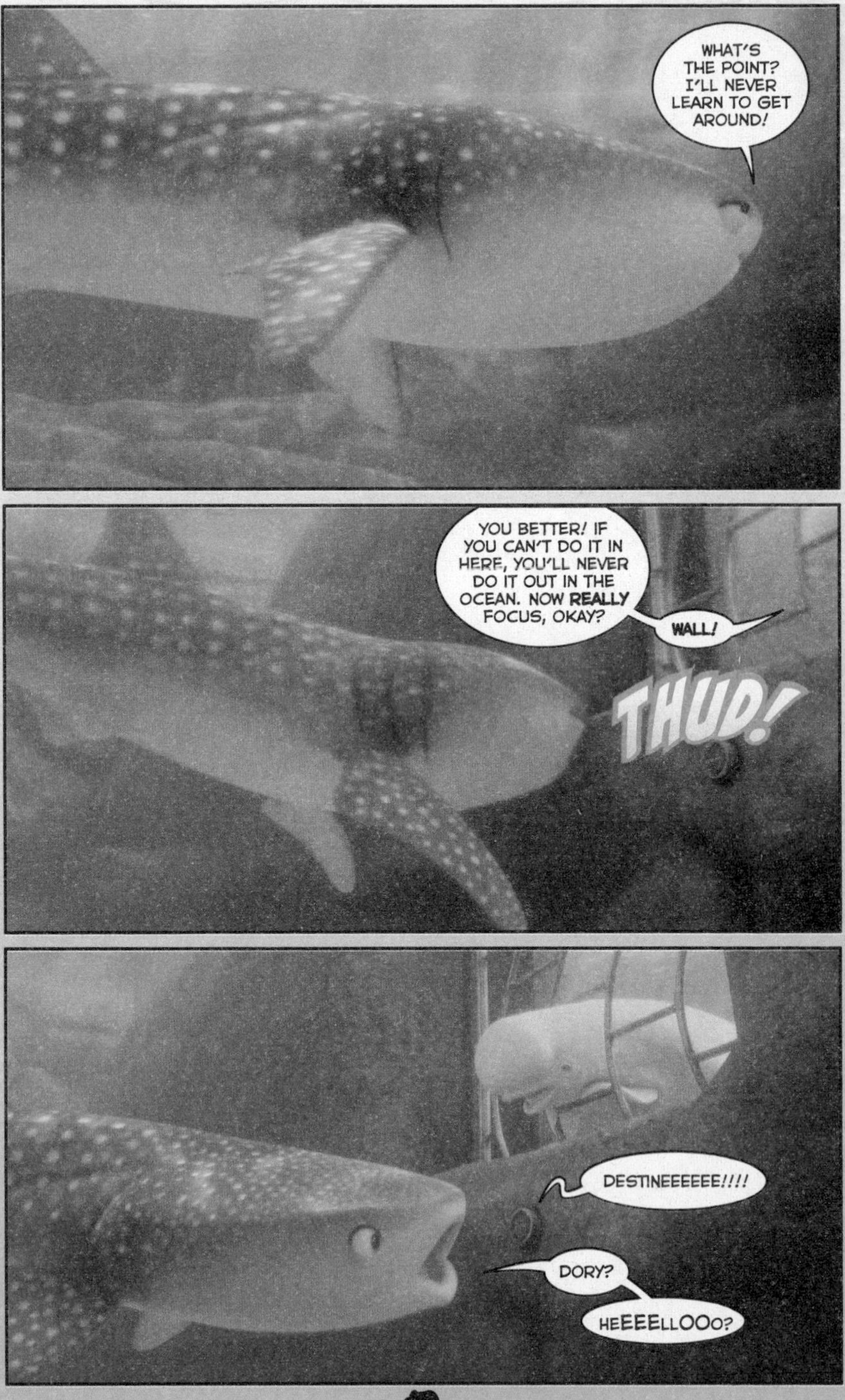
WHAT'S THE POINT? I'LL NEVER LEARN TO GET AROUND!
YOU BETTER! IF YOU CAN'T DO IT IN HERE, YOU'LL NEVER DO IT OUT IN THE OCEAN. NOW REALLY FOCUS, OKAY?
WALL!
THUD!
DESTINEEEEEE!!!!
DORY?
HEEEELLOOo?

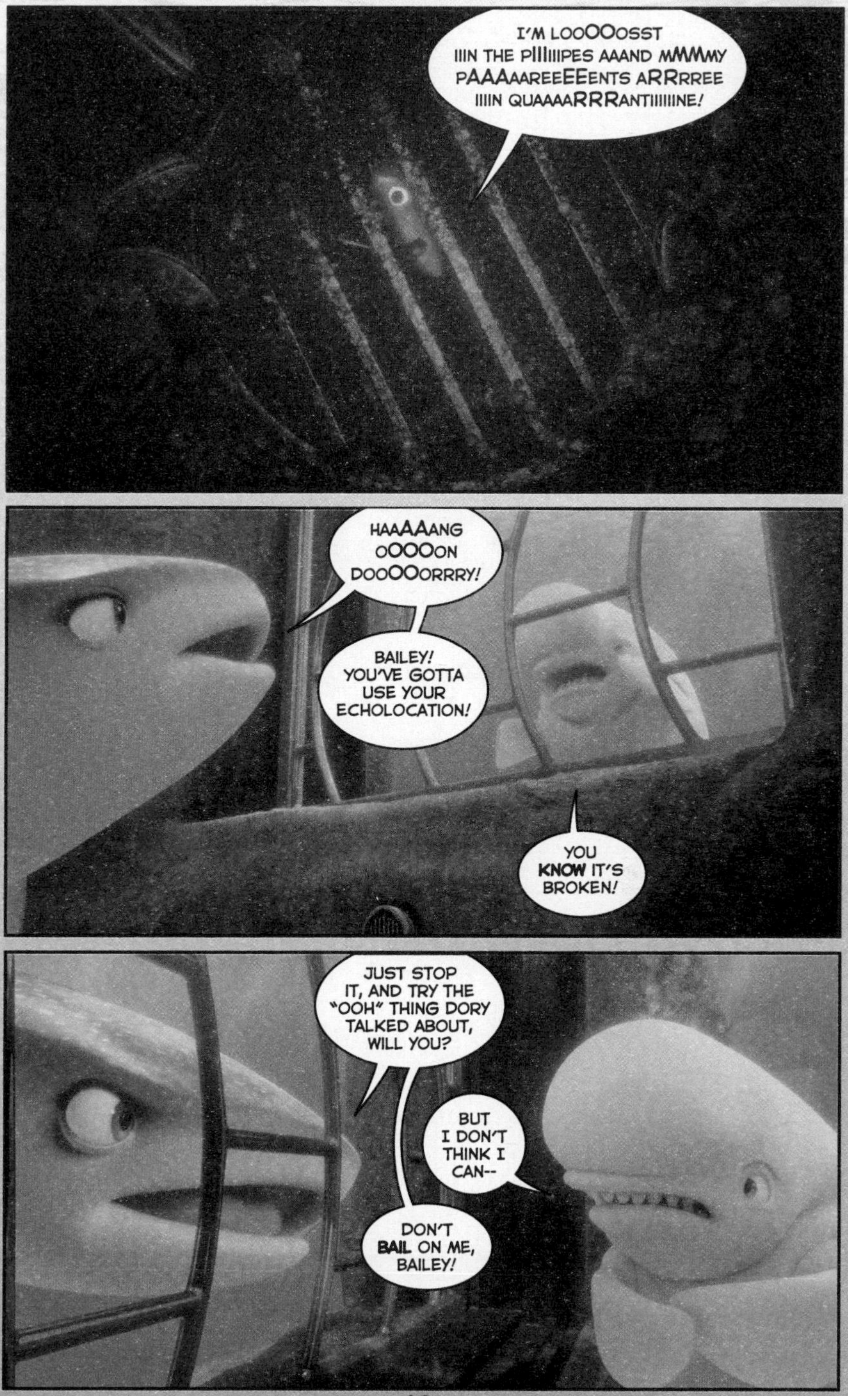
I'M LOOOOOSST IIIN THE PIIIIIPES AAAND MMMMY PAAAAAREEEEENTS ARRRREE IIIN QUAAAARRRANTIIIIINE!
HAAAAANG OOOOON DOOOOORRRY!
BAILEY! YOU'VE GOTTA USE YOUR ECHOLOCATION!
YOU KNOW IT'S BROKEN!
JUST STOP IT, AND TRY THE "OOH" THING DORY TALKED ABOUT, WILL YOU?
BUT I DON'T THINK I CAN--
DON'T BAIL ON ME, BAILEY!

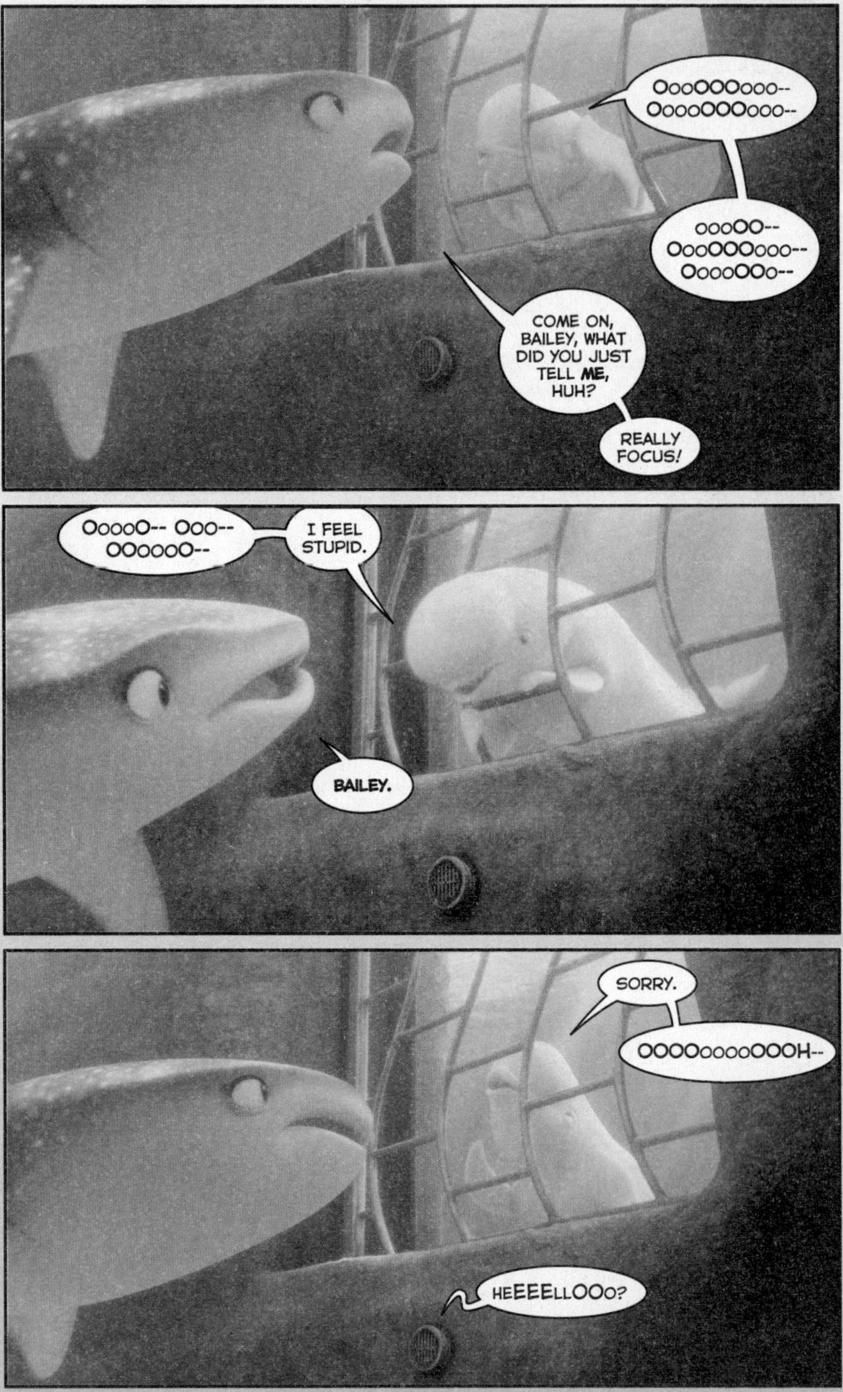
OooOOOooo--
OoooOOOooo--
oooOO--
OooOOOooo--
OoooOOo--
COME ON, BAILEY, WHAT DID YOU JUST TELL **ME**, HUH?
REALLY FOCUS!
OoooO-- Ooo-- OOoooO--
I FEEL STUPID.
BAILEY.
SORRY.
OOOOooooOOOH--
HEEEELLOOo?

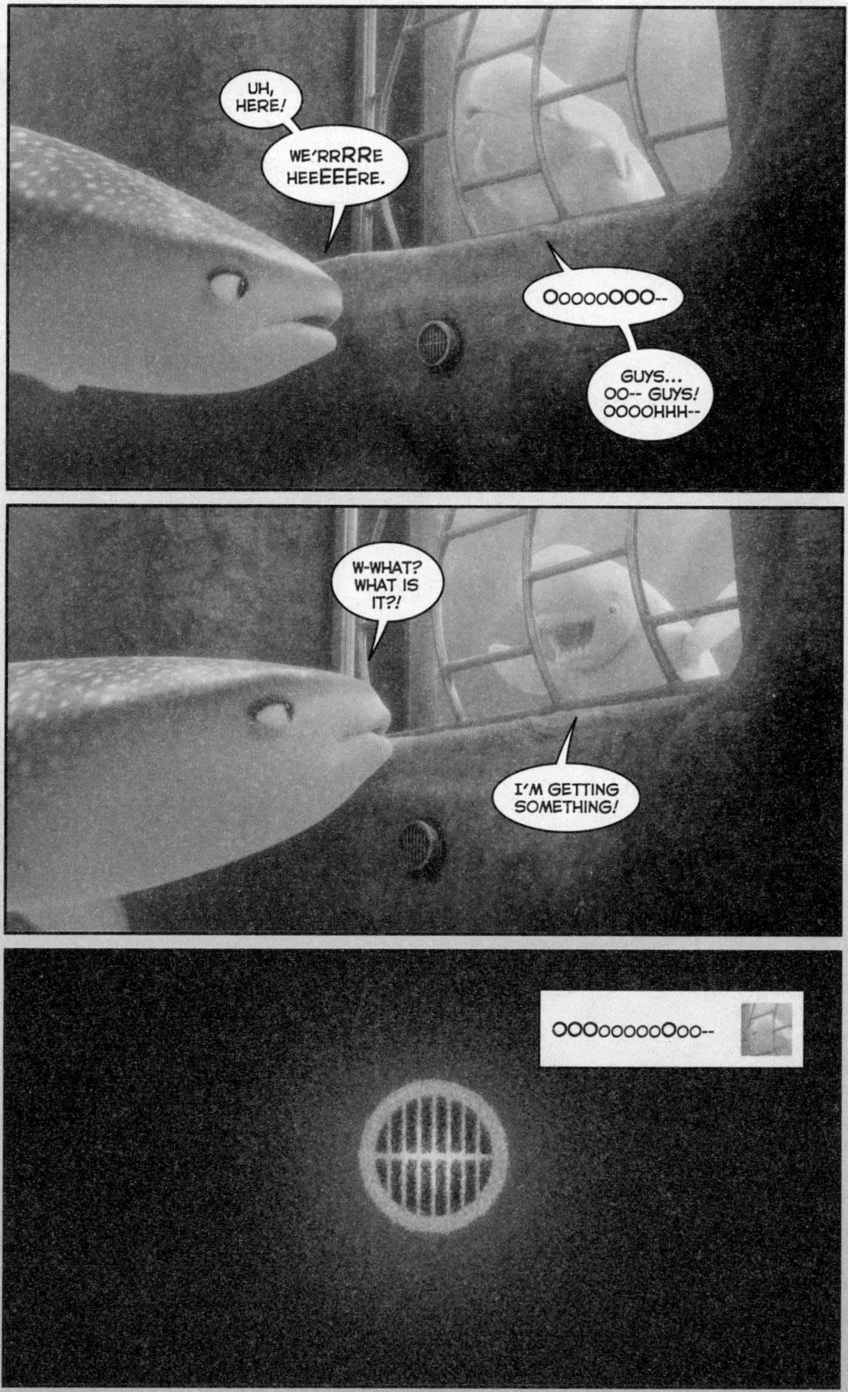
UH, HERE!
WE'RRRRE HEEEEEre.
OooooOOO--
GUYS... OO-- GUYS! OOOOHHH--
W-WHAT? WHAT IS IT?!
I'M GETTING SOMETHING!
OOOooooooOoo--

OOOoooooOoo--
OOOoooooOoo--
OOOoooooOoo--
HERE WE GO!
OooooOoo-- **OH YES!**
OOooo-- I CAN SEE
THE QUARANTINE!

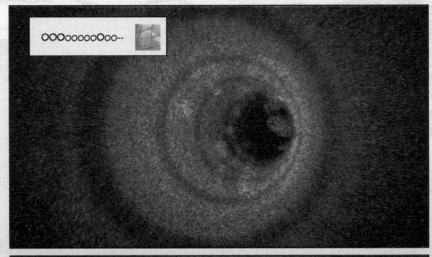

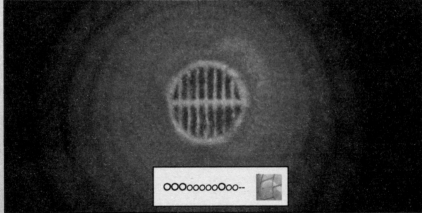

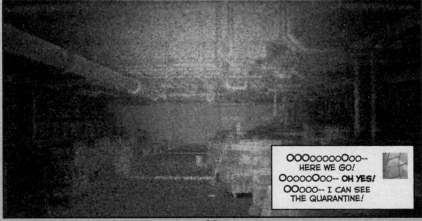

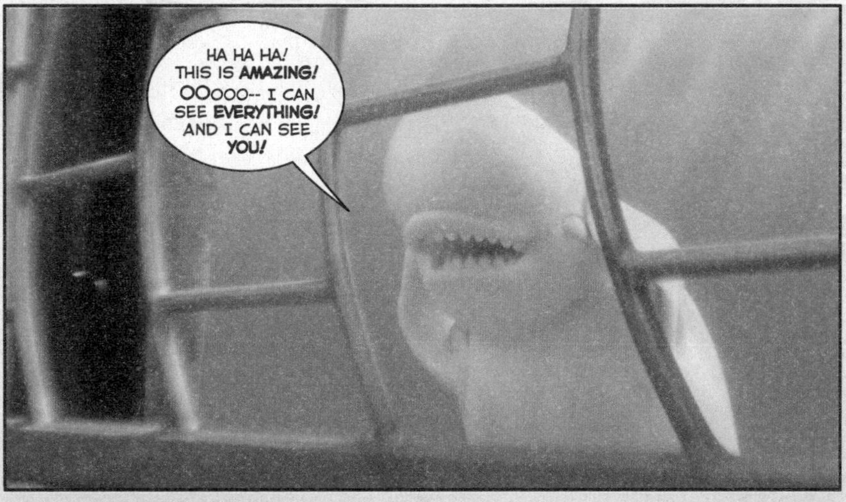
HA HA HA! THIS IS AMAZING! OOooo-- I CAN SEE EVERYTHING! AND I CAN SEE YOU!

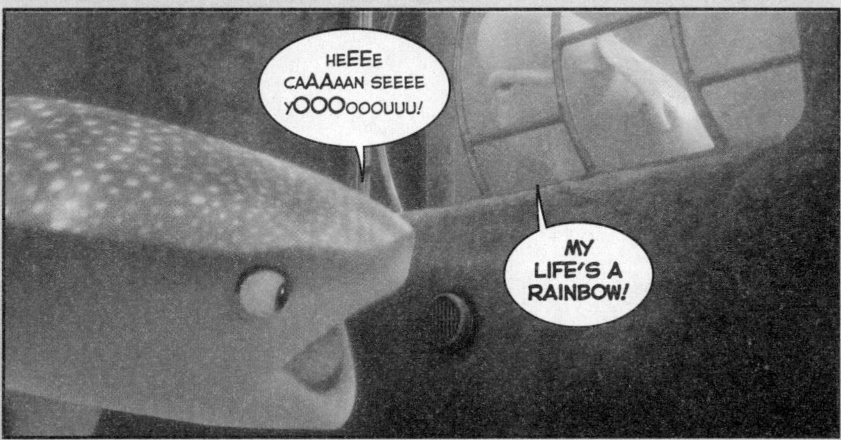
HeEEe CaAAaan SEEEE yOOOooouuu!
MY LIFE'S A RAINBOW!

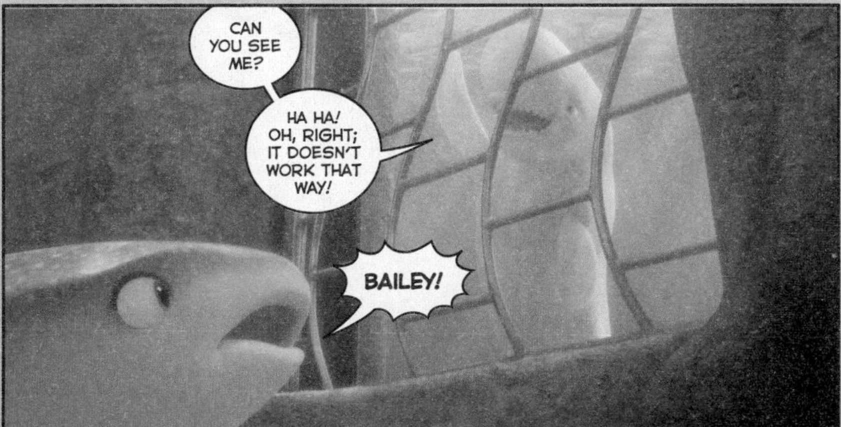
CAN YOU SEE ME?
HA HA! OH, RIGHT; IT DOESN'T WORK THAT WAY!
BAILEY!

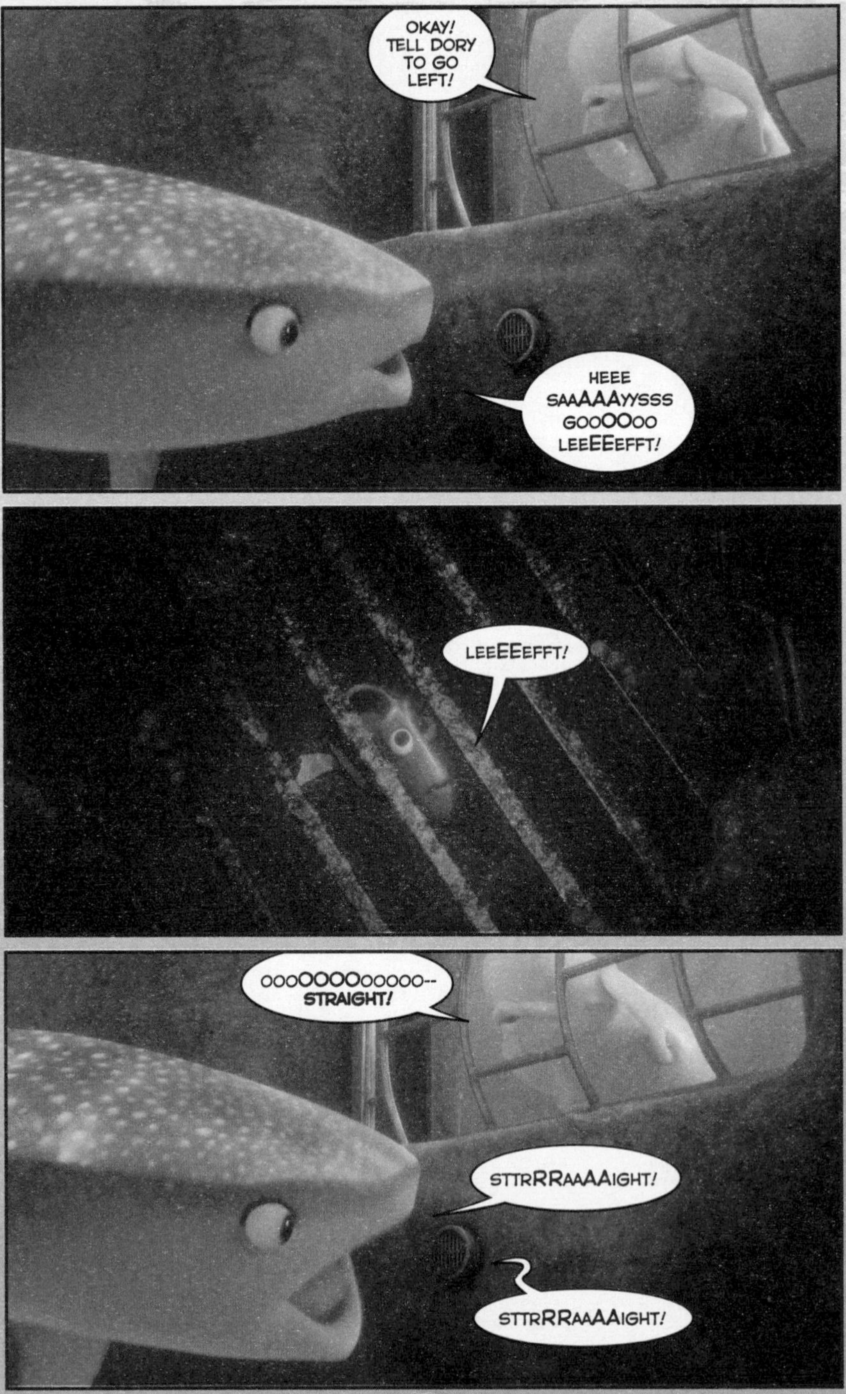
OKAY! TELL DORY TO GO LEFT!
HEEE SAAAAAYYSSS GOOOOOO LEEEEEFFT!
LEEEEEFFT!
OOOOOOOOOOOO--
STRAIGHT!
STTRRRAAAAIGHT!
STTRRRAAAAIGHT!

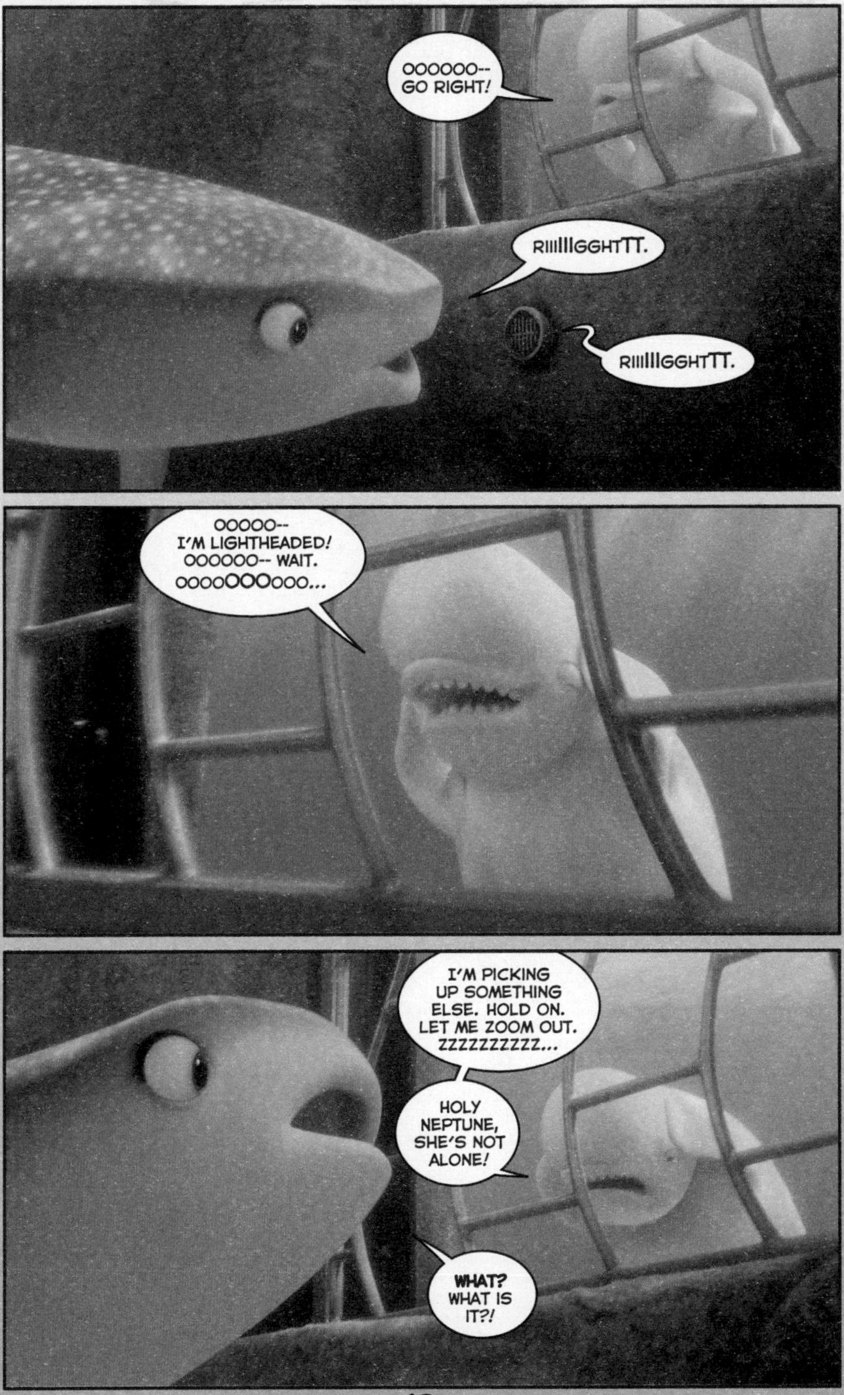
OOOOOO--
GO RIGHT!
RIIIIIGGHTTT.
RIIIIIGGHTTT.
OOOOO--
I'M LIGHTHEADED!
OOOOOO-- WAIT.
ooooOOOooo...
I'M PICKING
UP SOMETHING
ELSE. HOLD ON.
LET ME ZOOM OUT.
ZZZZZZZZZZ...
HOLY
NEPTUNE,
SHE'S NOT
ALONE!
WHAT?
WHAT IS
IT?!

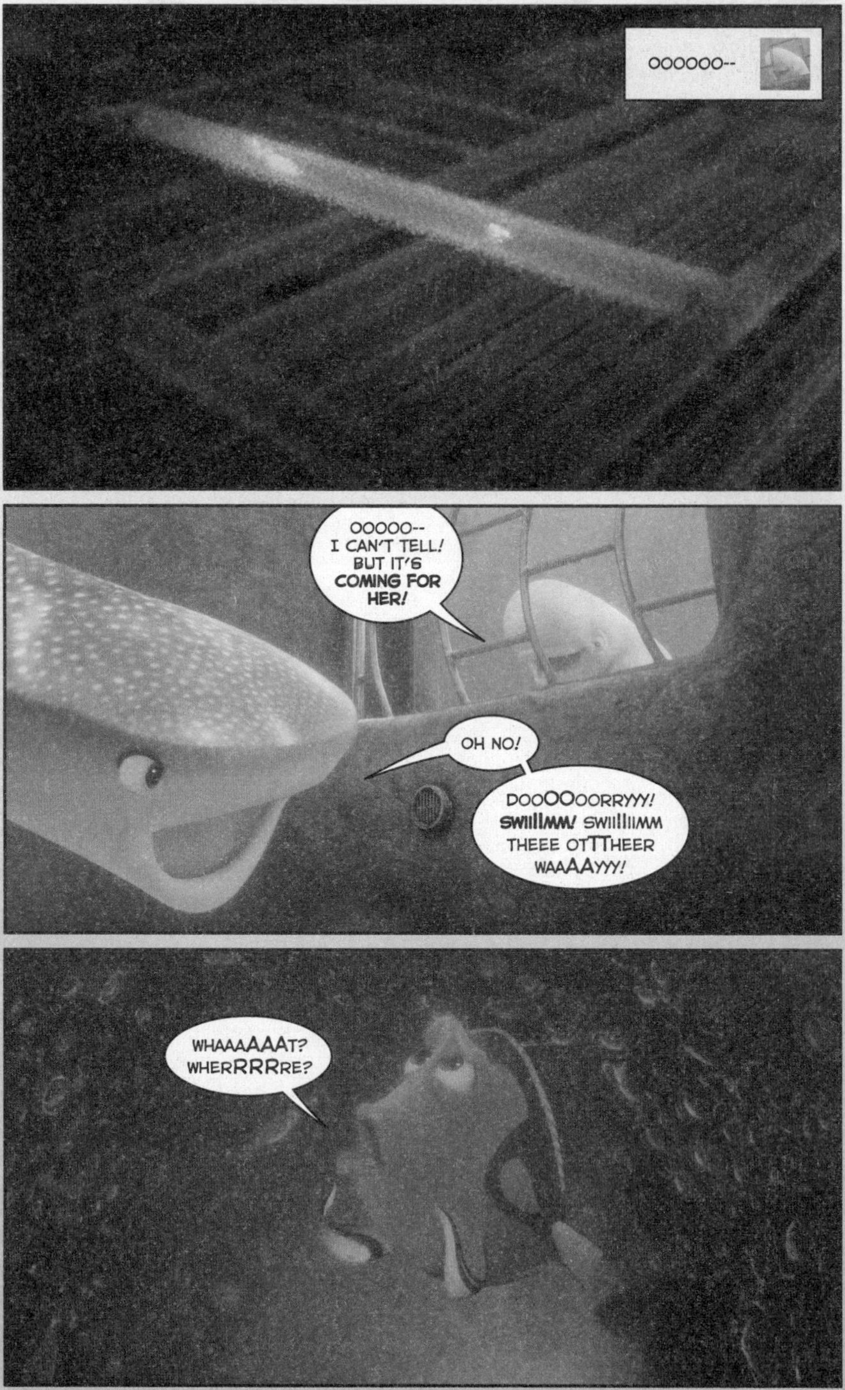
OOOOOO--
OOOOO-- I CAN'T TELL! BUT IT'S COMING FOR HER!
OH NO!
DOOOOOORRYYY! SWIIIIIMM! SWIIIIIIIMM THEEE OTTTHEER WAAAAYYY!
WHAAAAAAT? WHERRRRRE?

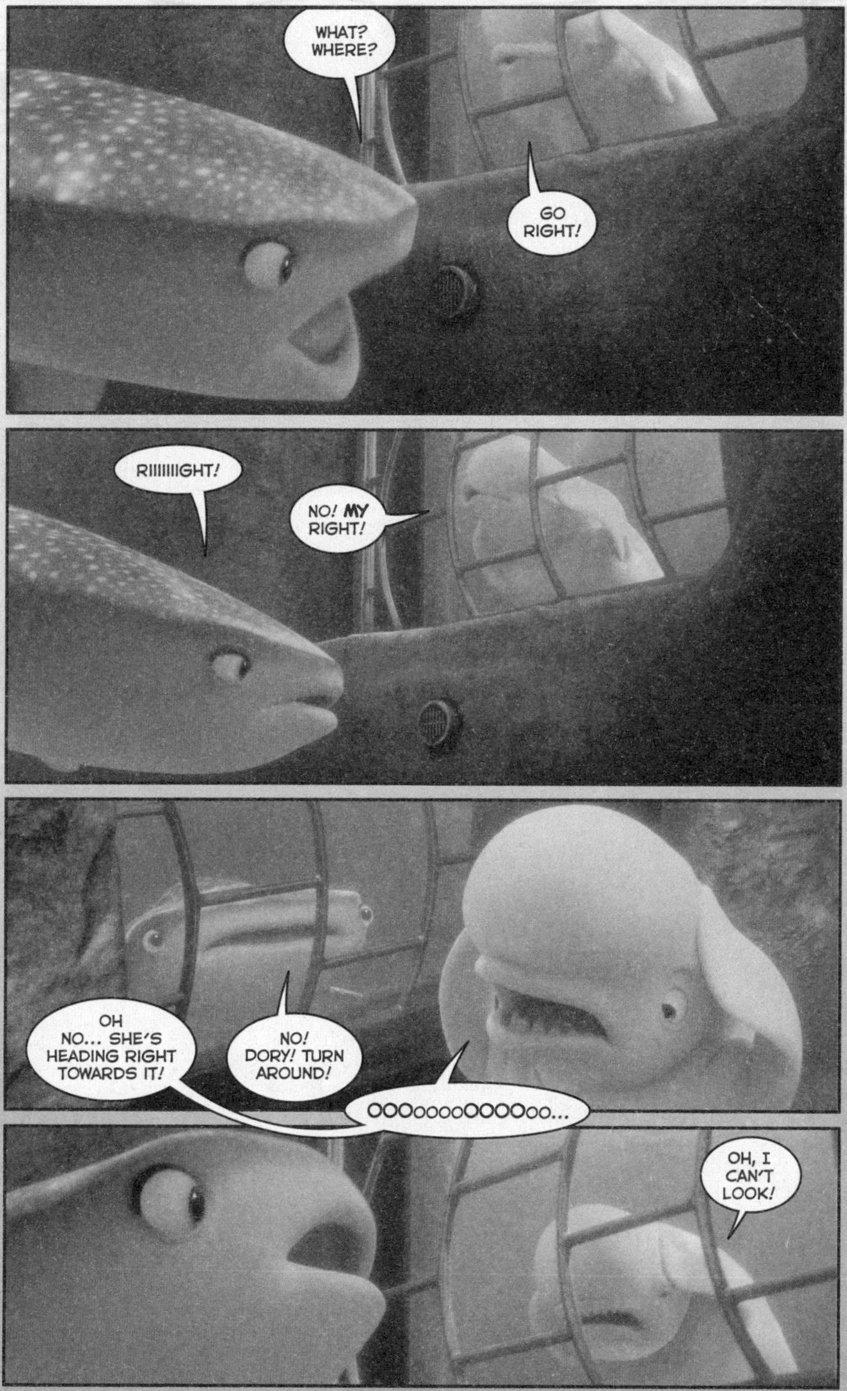
WHAT? WHERE?
GO RIGHT!
RIIIIIIIGHT!
NO! MY RIGHT!
OH NO... SHE'S HEADING RIGHT TOWARDS IT!
NO! DORY! TURN AROUND!
OOOoooo0000oo...
OH, I CAN'T LOOK!

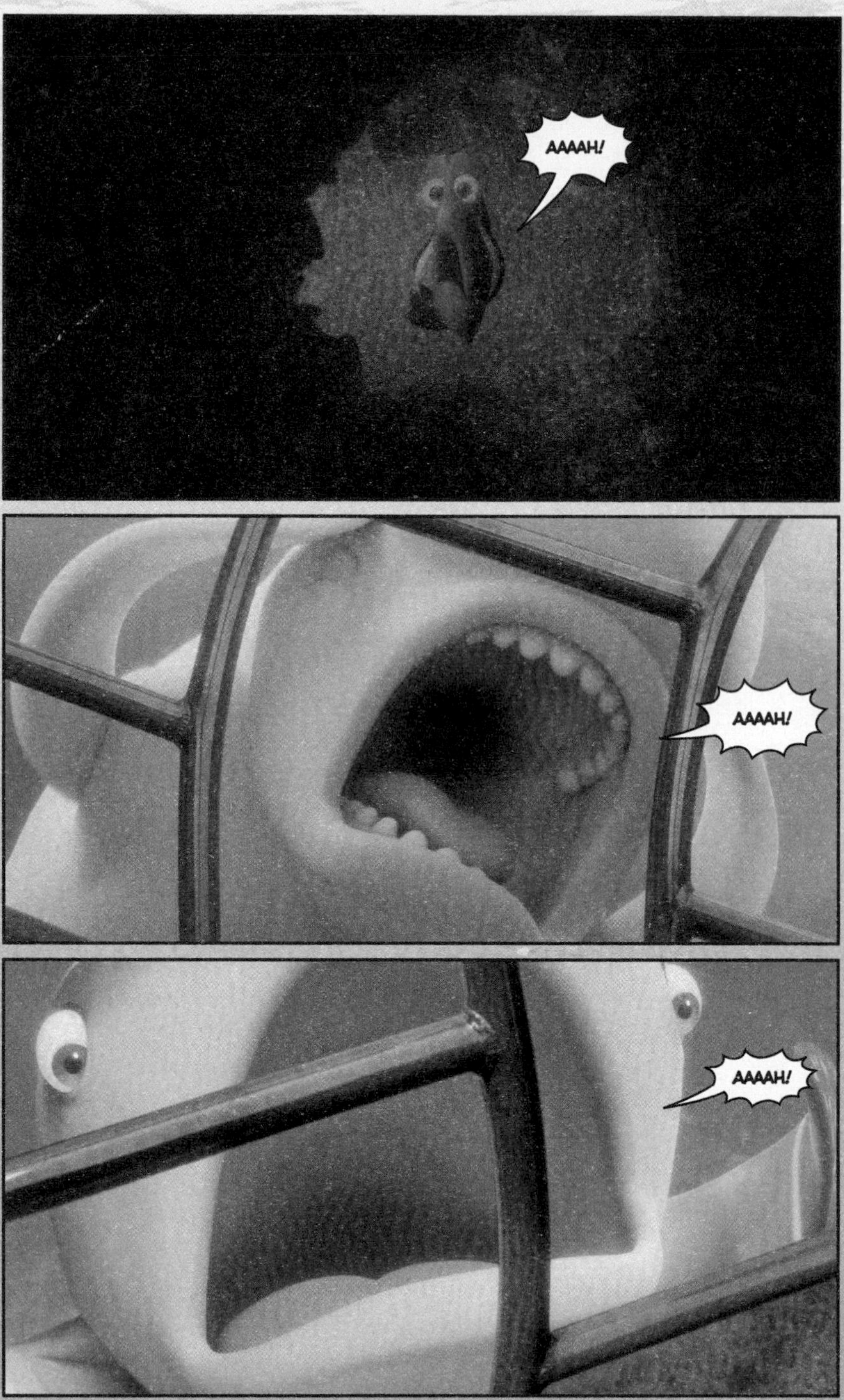
AAAAH!
AAAAH!
AAAAH!

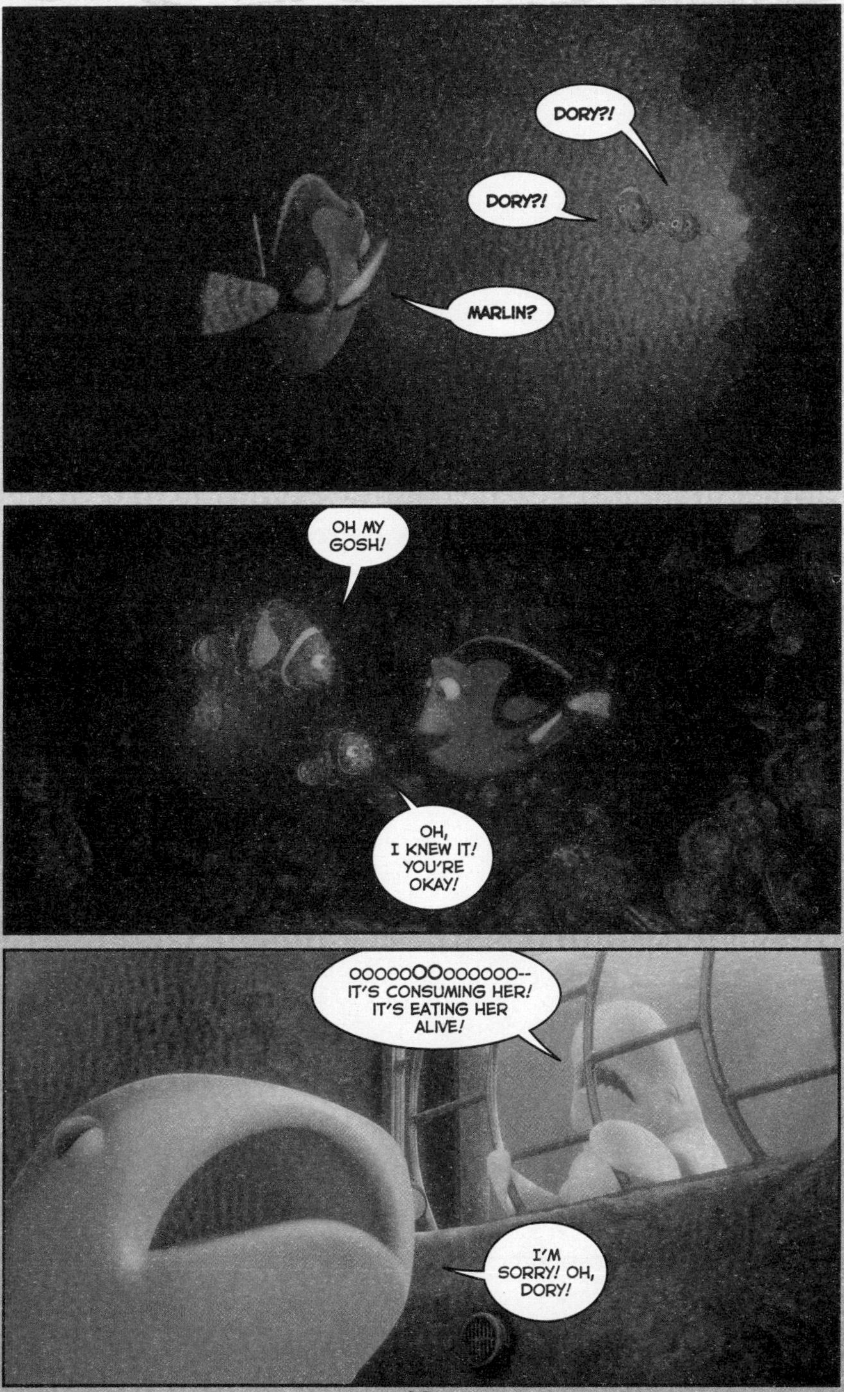
DORY?!
DORY?!
MARLIN?
OH MY GOSH!
OH, I KNEW IT! YOU'RE OKAY!
OOOOOOOOOOOOO-- IT'S CONSUMING HER! IT'S EATING HER ALIVE!
I'M SORRY! OH, DORY!

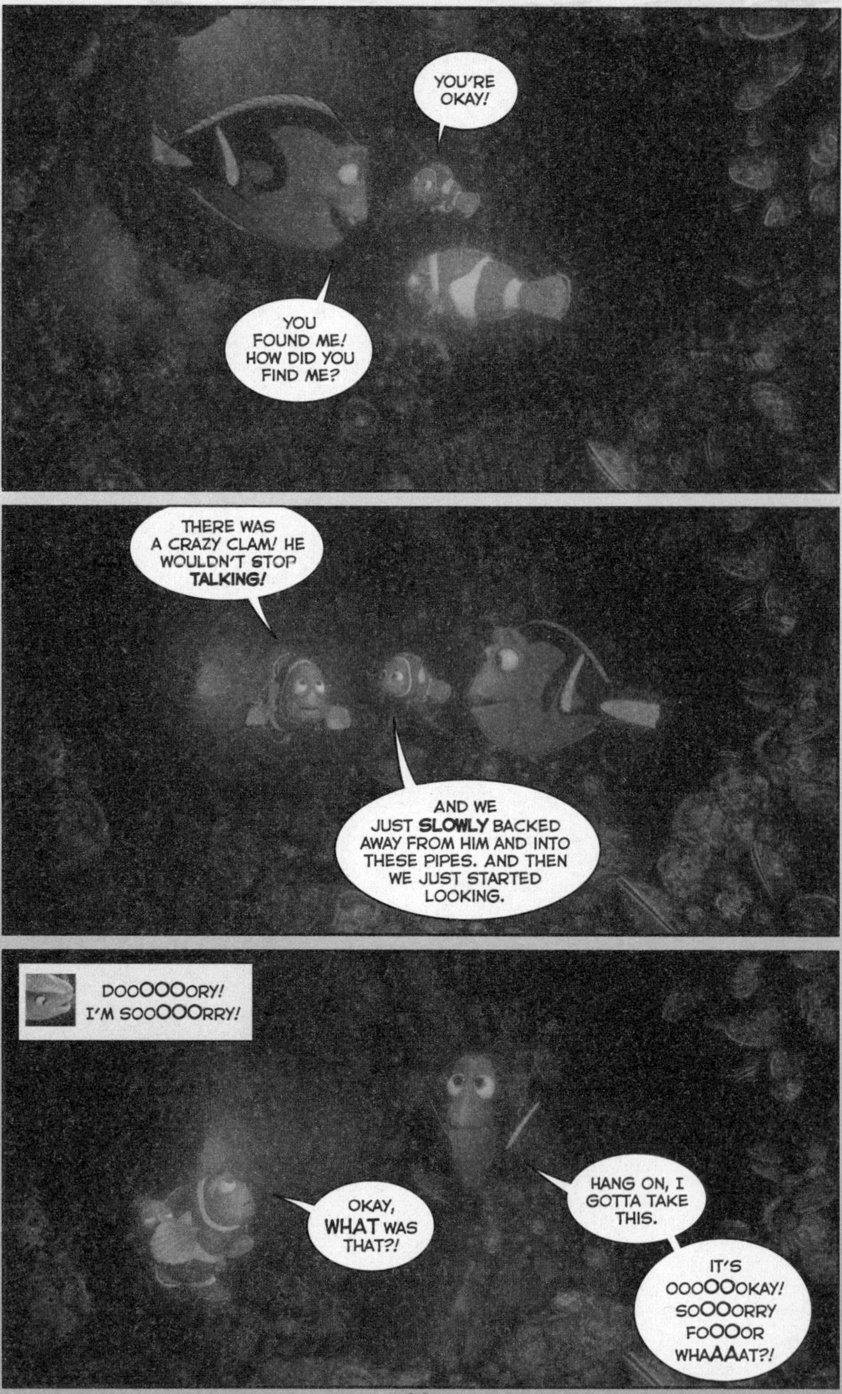
YOU'RE OKAY!
YOU FOUND ME! HOW DID YOU FIND ME?
THERE WAS A CRAZY CLAM! HE WOULDN'T STOP TALKING!
AND WE JUST SLOWLY BACKED AWAY FROM HIM AND INTO THESE PIPES. AND THEN WE JUST STARTED LOOKING.
DOOOOOORY! I'M SOOOOORRY!
OKAY, WHAT WAS THAT?!
HANG ON, I GOTTA TAKE THIS.
IT'S OOOOOOKAY! SOOOORRY FOOOOR WHAAAAT?!

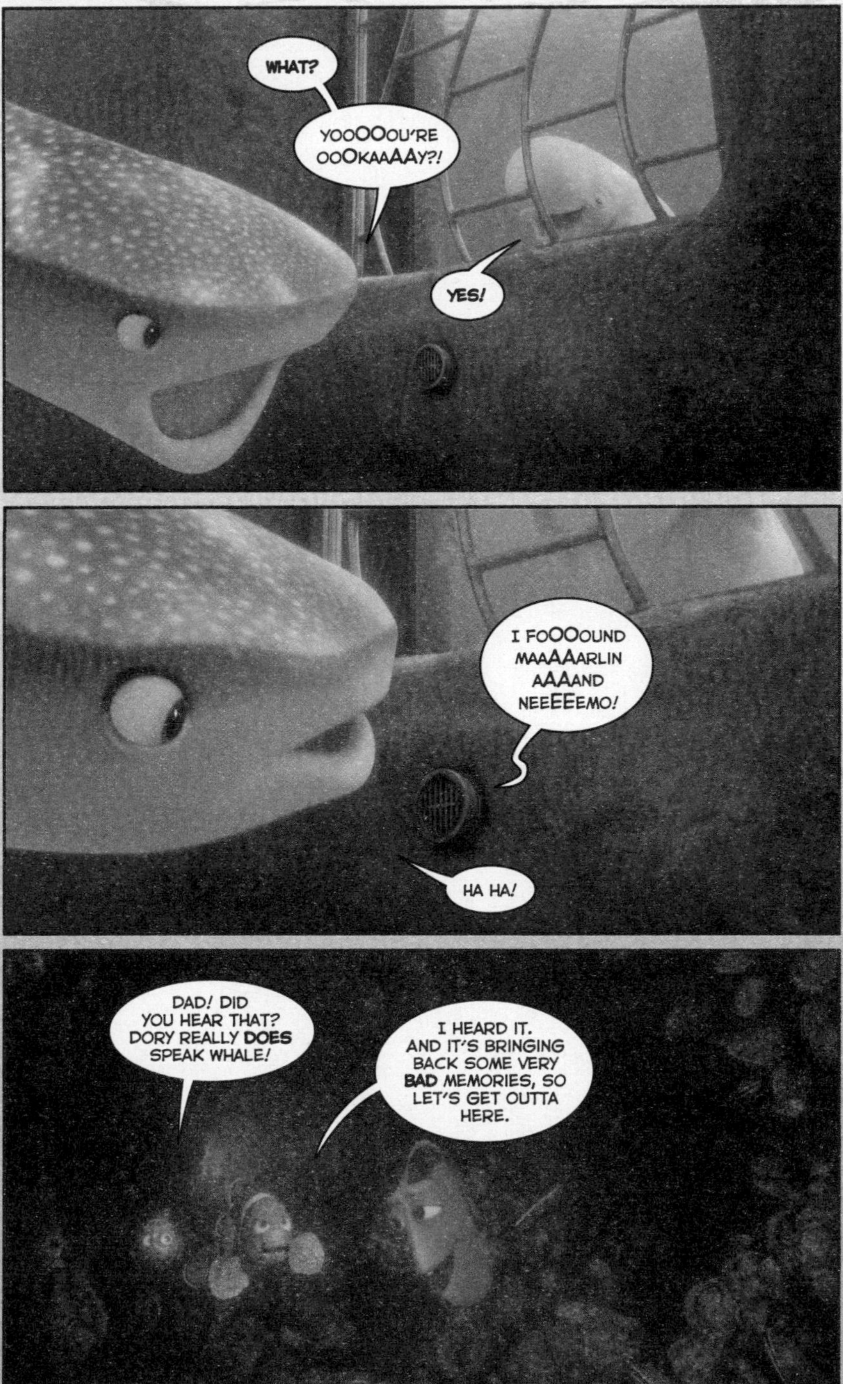
WHAT?
YOOOOOU'RE OOOKAAAAY?!
YES!
I FOOOOUND MAAAAARLIN AAAAND NEEEEEMO!
HA HA!
DAD! DID YOU HEAR THAT? DORY REALLY **DOES** SPEAK WHALE!
I HEARD IT. AND IT'S BRINGING BACK SOME VERY **BAD** MEMORIES, SO LET'S GET OUTTA HERE.

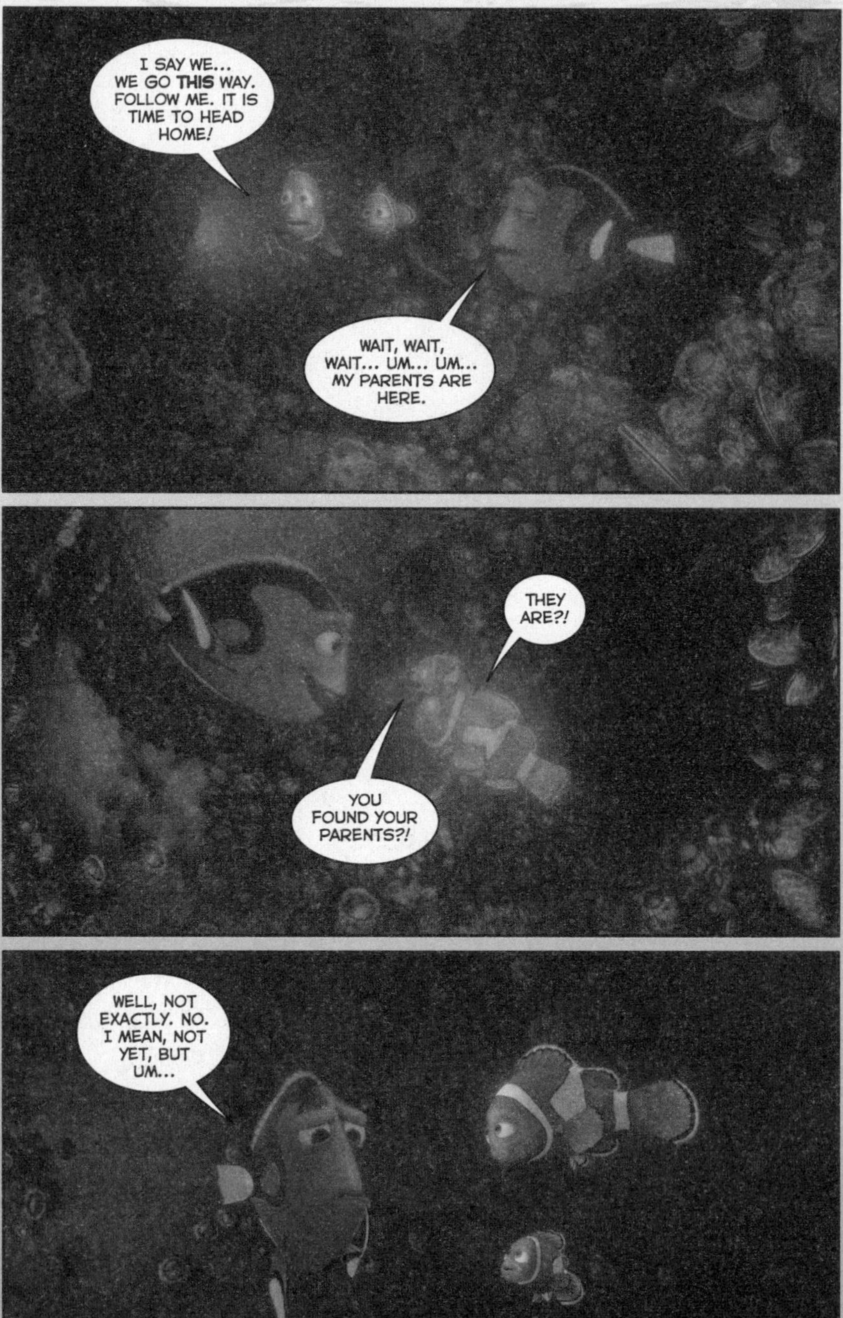
I SAY WE... WE GO THIS WAY. FOLLOW ME. IT IS TIME TO HEAD HOME!
WAIT, WAIT, WAIT... UM... UM... MY PARENTS ARE HERE.
THEY ARE?!
YOU FOUND YOUR PARENTS?!
WELL, NOT EXACTLY. NO. I MEAN, NOT YET, BUT UM...

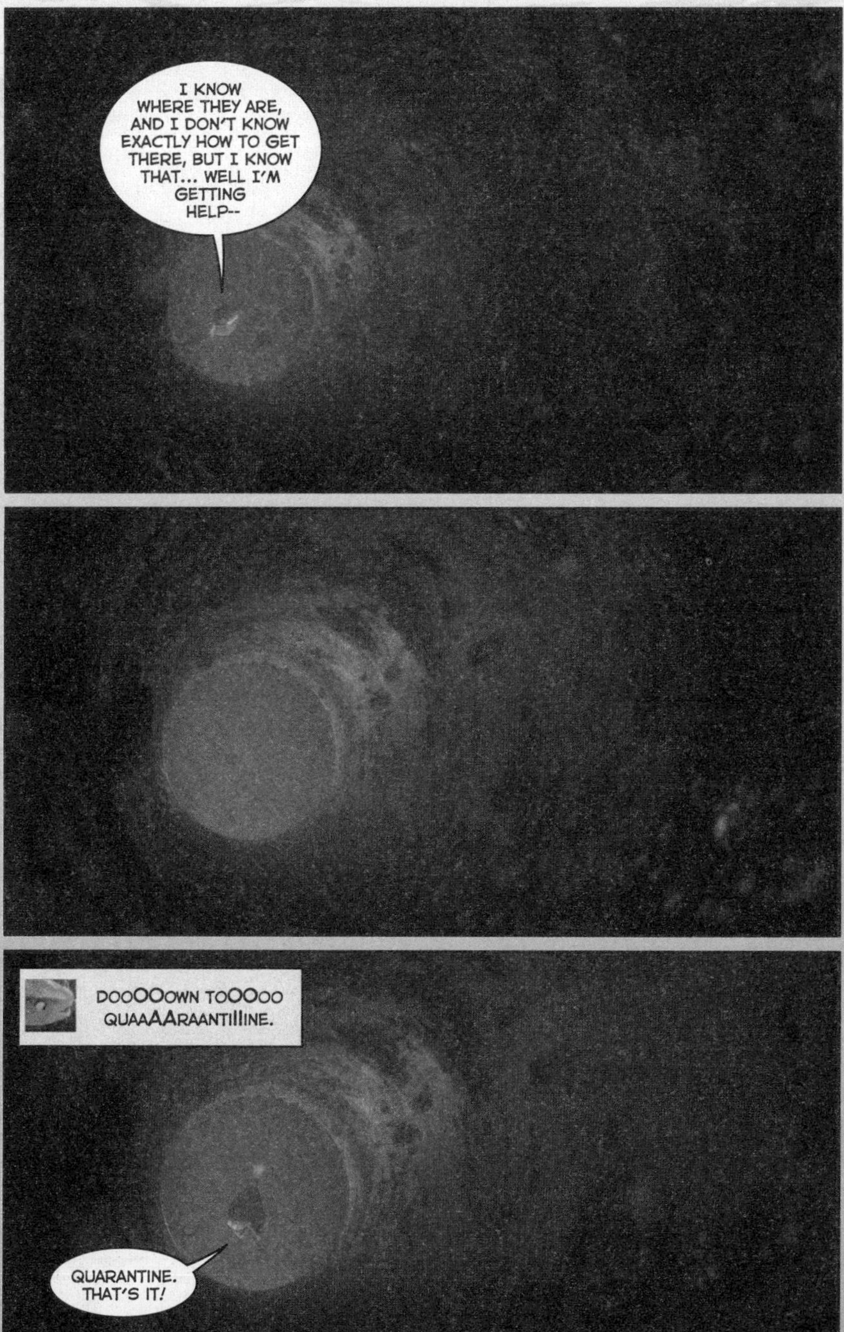
I KNOW WHERE THEY ARE, AND I DON'T KNOW EXACTLY HOW TO GET THERE, BUT I KNOW THAT... WELL I'M GETTING HELP--
DOOOOOWN TOOOOO QUAAAARAANTIIIINE.
QUARANTINE. THAT'S IT!

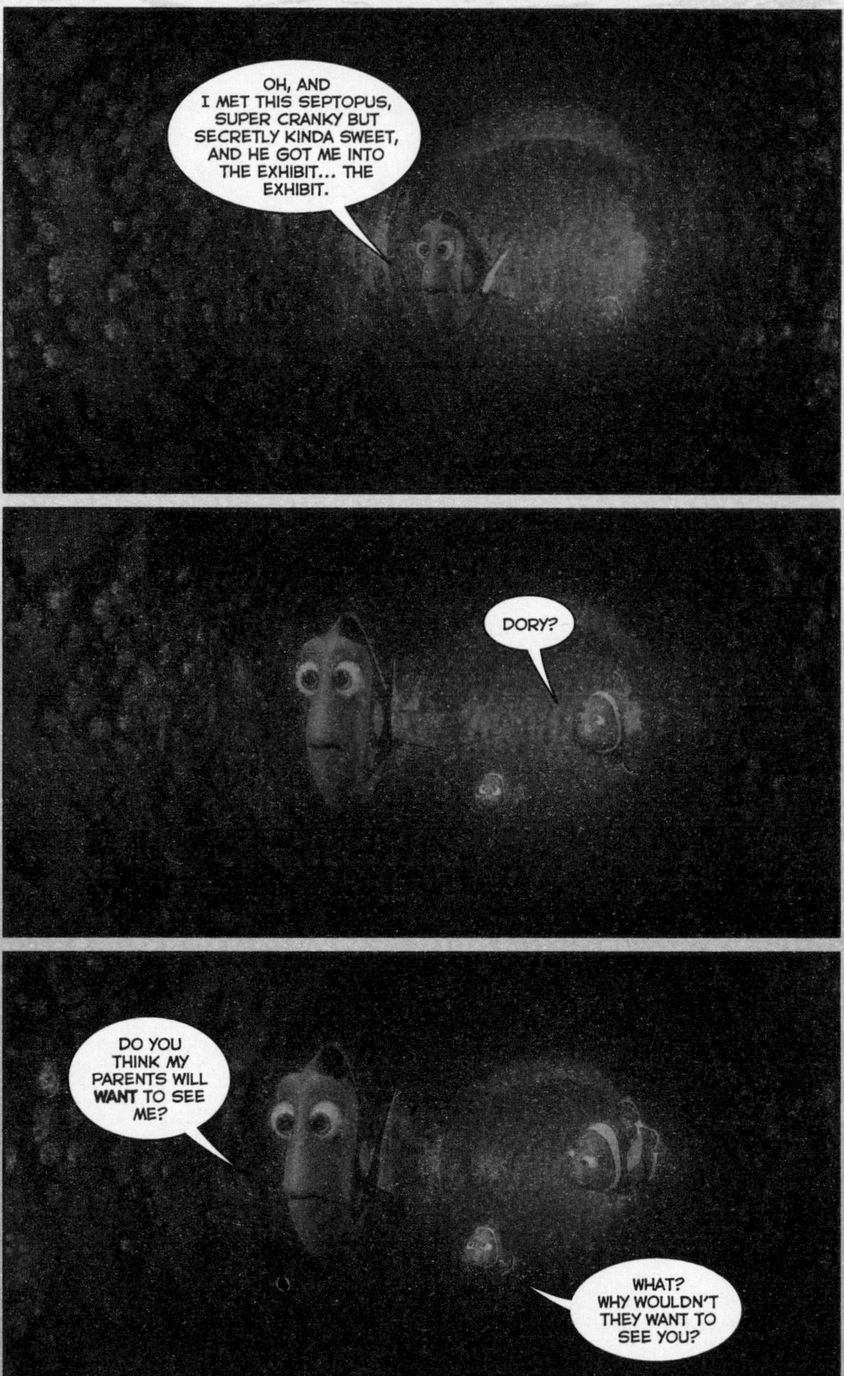
OH, AND I MET THIS SEPTOPUS, SUPER CRANKY BUT SECRETLY KINDA SWEET, AND HE GOT ME INTO THE EXHIBIT... THE EXHIBIT.
DORY?
DO YOU THINK MY PARENTS WILL **WANT** TO SEE ME?
WHAT? WHY WOULDN'T THEY WANT TO SEE YOU?

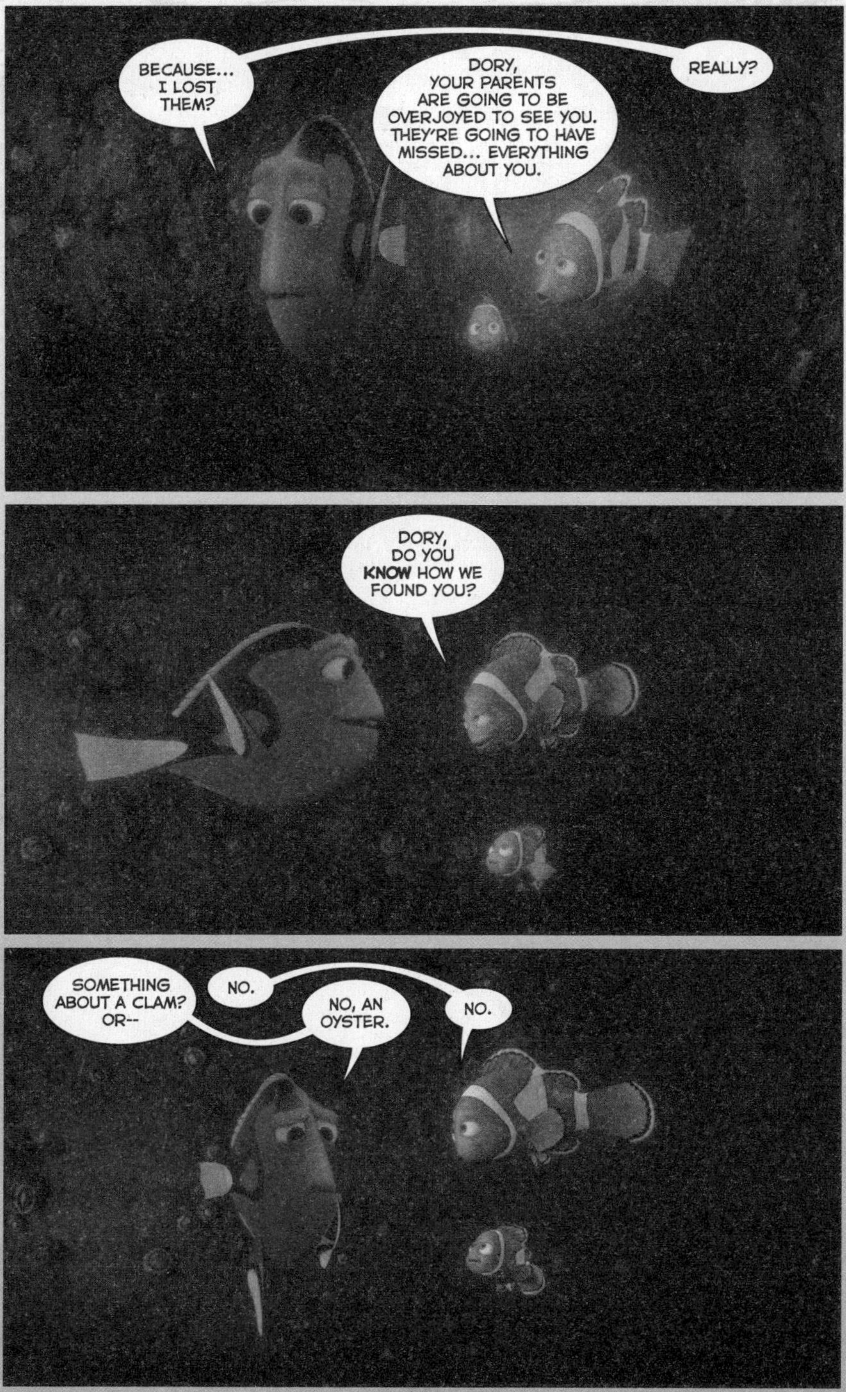
BECAUSE... I LOST THEM?
DORY, YOUR PARENTS ARE GOING TO BE OVERJOYED TO SEE YOU. THEY'RE GOING TO HAVE MISSED... EVERYTHING ABOUT YOU.
REALLY?
DORY, DO YOU **KNOW** HOW WE FOUND YOU?
SOMETHING ABOUT A CLAM? OR--
NO.
NO, AN OYSTER.
NO.

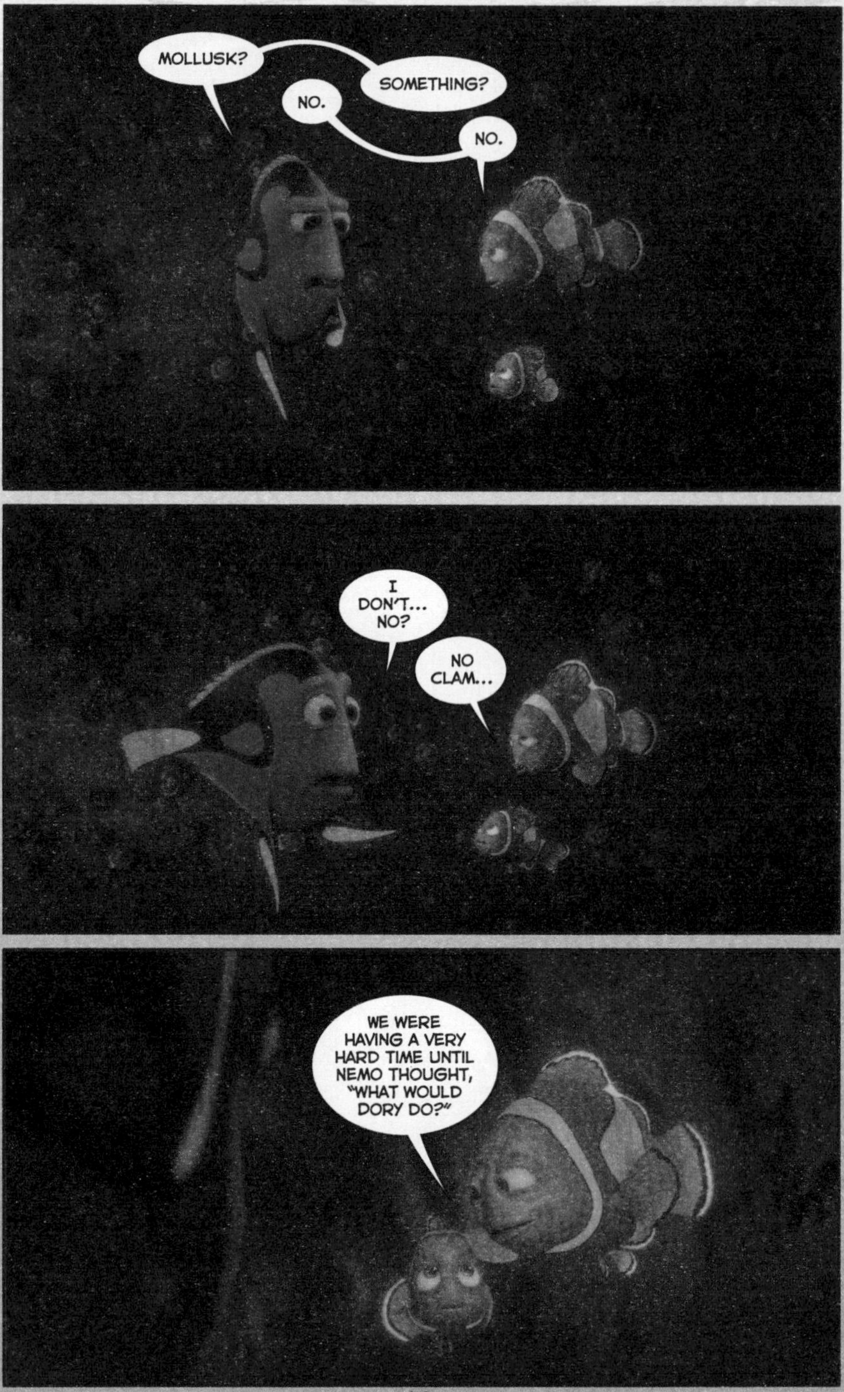
MOLLUSK?
SOMETHING?
NO.
NO.
I DON'T... NO?
NO CLAM...
WE WERE HAVING A VERY HARD TIME UNTIL NEMO THOUGHT, "WHAT WOULD DORY DO?"

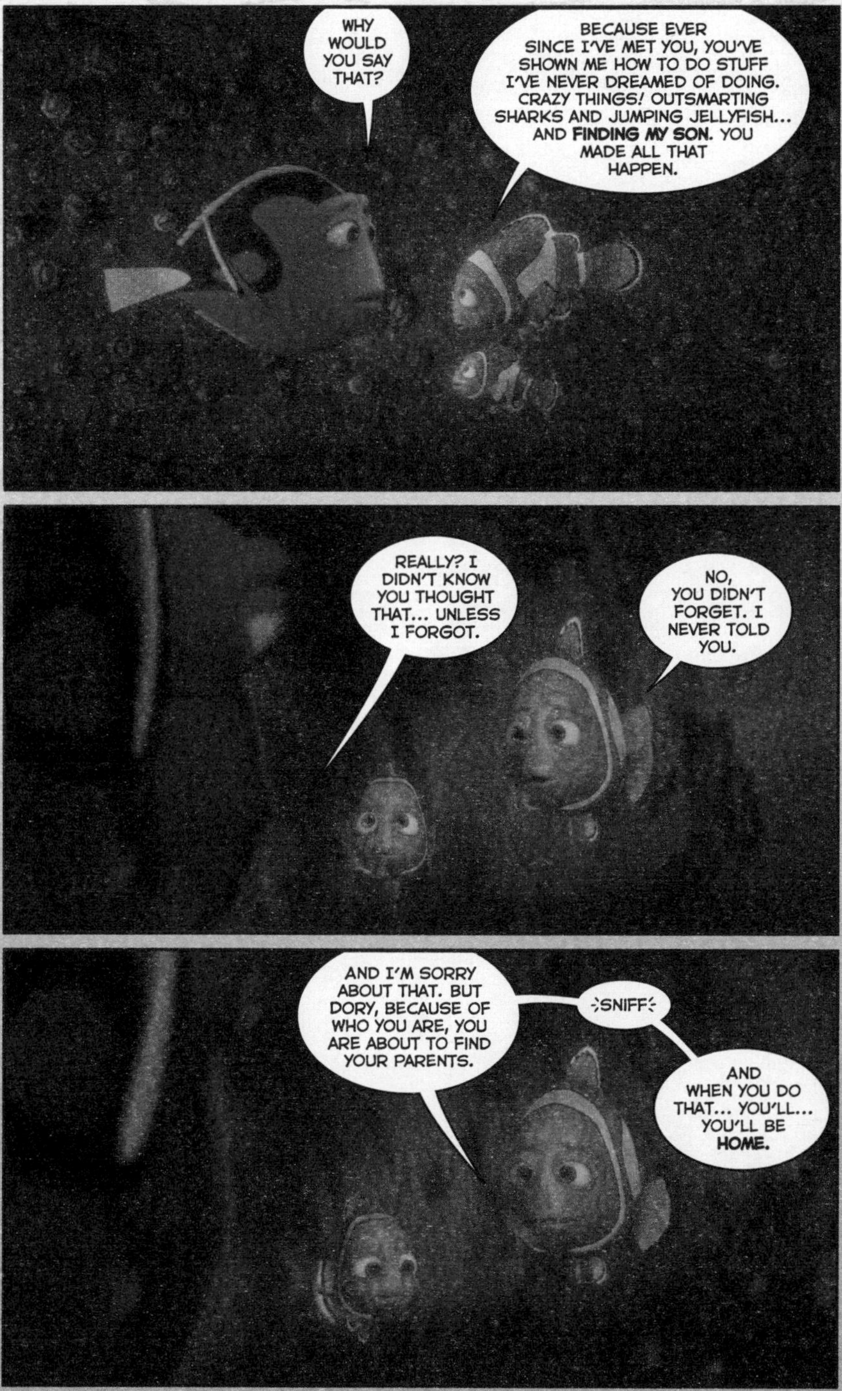
WHY WOULD YOU SAY THAT?
BECAUSE EVER SINCE I'VE MET YOU, YOU'VE SHOWN ME HOW TO DO STUFF I'VE NEVER DREAMED OF DOING. CRAZY THINGS! OUTSMARTING SHARKS AND JUMPING JELLYFISH... AND **FINDING MY SON**. YOU MADE ALL THAT HAPPEN.
REALLY? I DIDN'T KNOW YOU THOUGHT THAT... UNLESS I FORGOT.
NO, YOU DIDN'T FORGET. I NEVER TOLD YOU.
AND I'M SORRY ABOUT THAT. BUT DORY, BECAUSE OF WHO YOU ARE, YOU ARE ABOUT TO FIND YOUR PARENTS.
SNIFF
AND WHEN YOU DO THAT... YOU'LL... YOU'LL BE **HOME.**

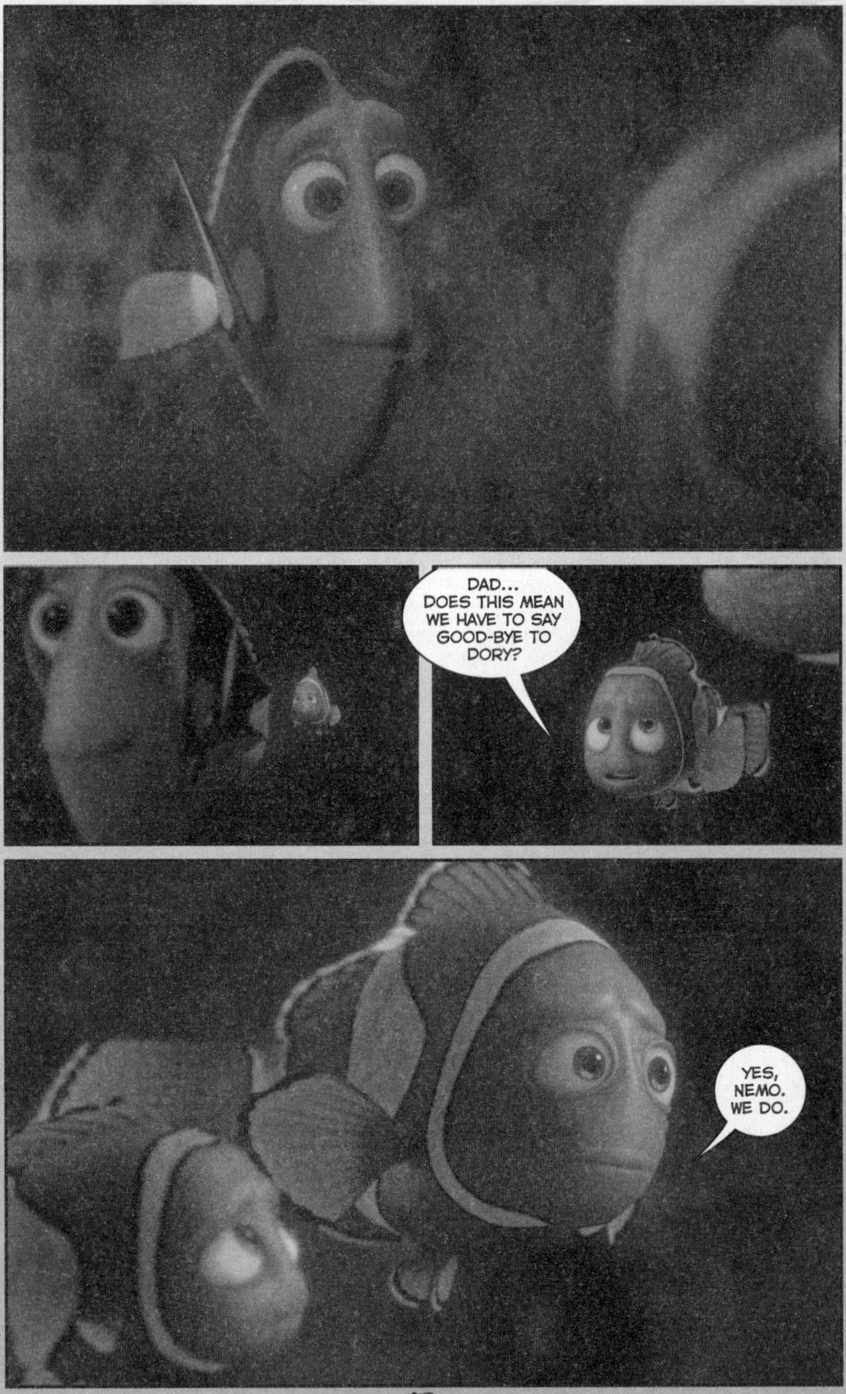
DAD... DOES THIS MEAN WE HAVE TO SAY GOOD-BYE TO DORY?
YES, NEMO. WE DO.

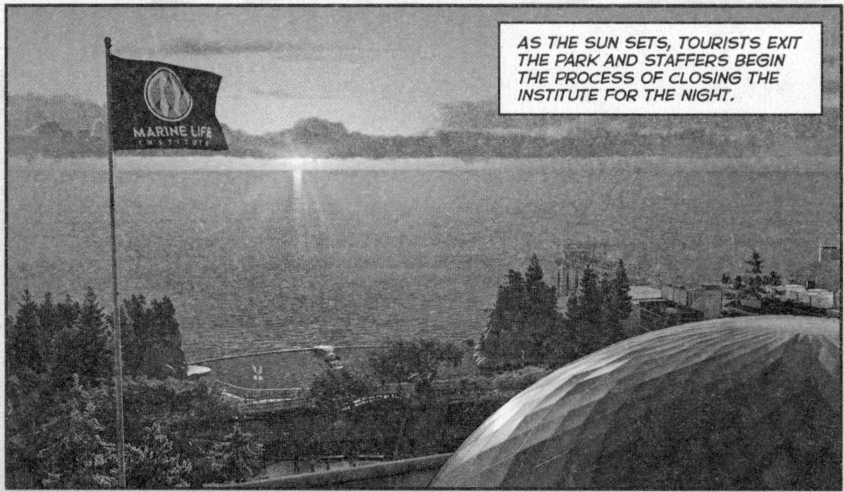
AS THE SUN SETS, TOURISTS EXIT THE PARK AND STAFFERS BEGIN THE PROCESS OF CLOSING THE INSTITUTE FOR THE NIGHT.
MARINE LIFE INSTITUTE

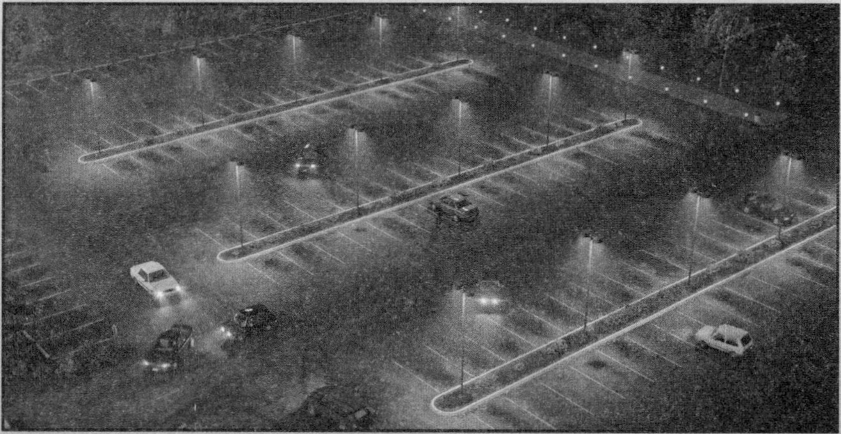

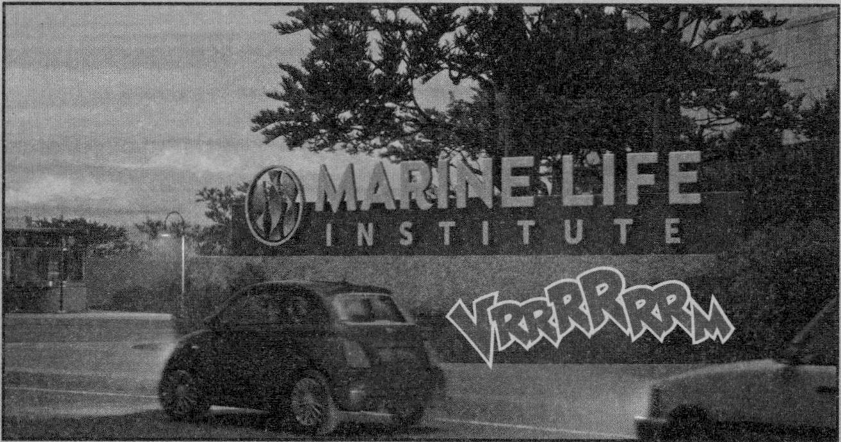
MARINE LIFE INSTITUTE
VRRRRRRM

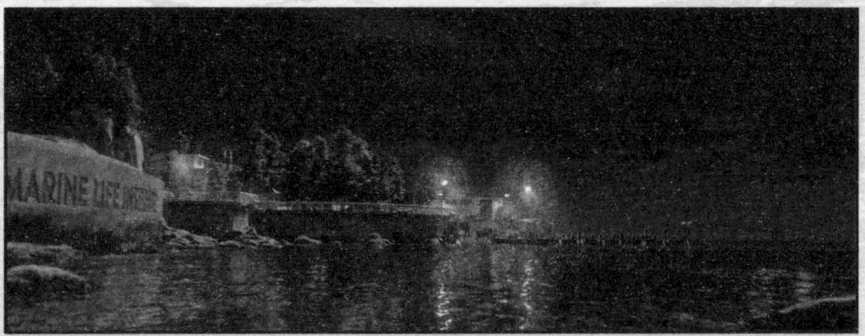
MARINE LIFE INSTITUTE

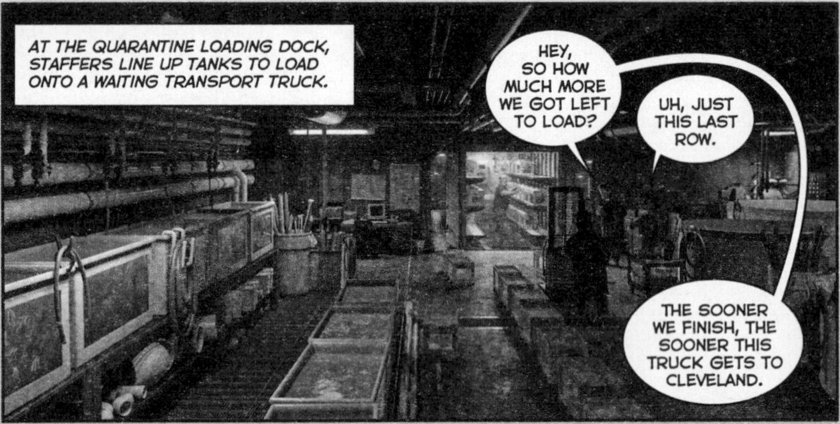
AT THE QUARANTINE LOADING DOCK, STAFFERS LINE UP TANKS TO LOAD ONTO A WAITING TRANSPORT TRUCK.
HEY, SO HOW MUCH MORE WE GOT LEFT TO LOAD?
UH, JUST THIS LAST ROW.
THE SOONER WE FINISH, THE SOONER THIS TRUCK GETS TO CLEVELAND.

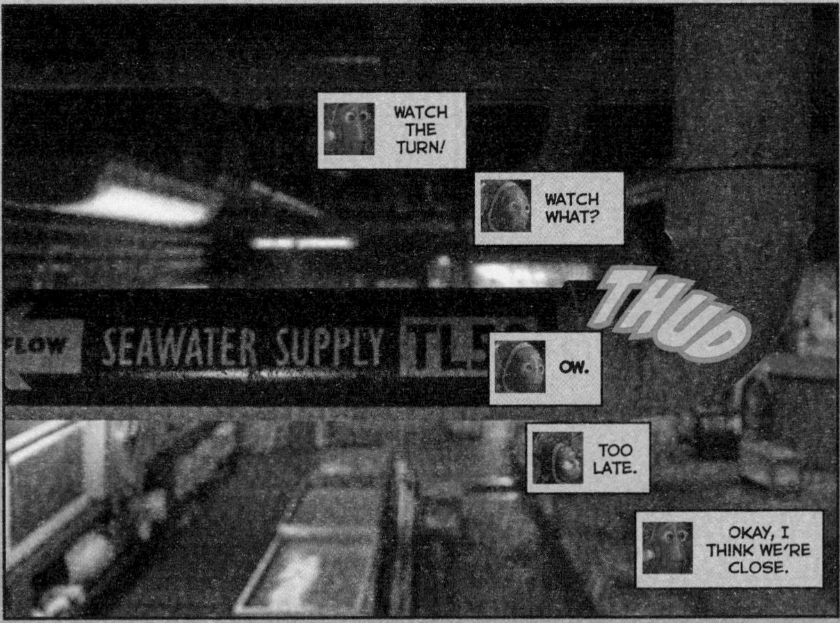
WATCH THE TURN!
WATCH WHAT?
THUD
FLOW
SEAWATER SUPPLY
OW.
TOO LATE.
OKAY, I THINK WE'RE CLOSE.

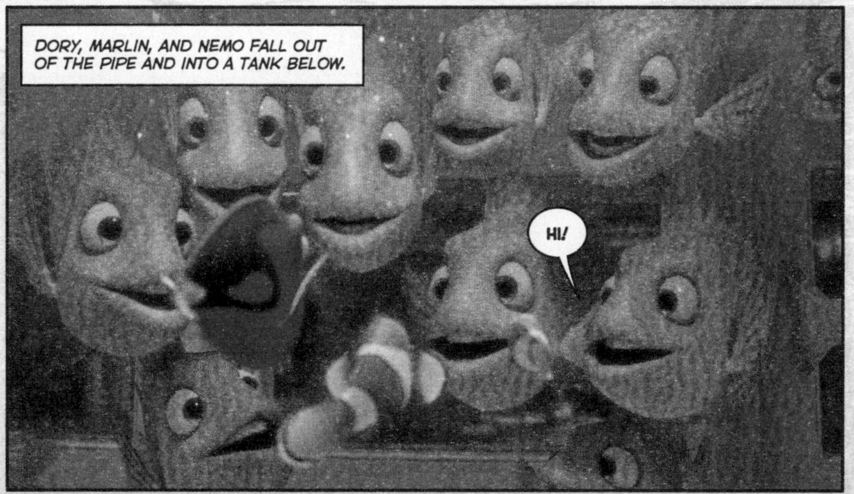
DORY, MARLIN, AND NEMO FALL OUT OF THE PIPE AND INTO A TANK BELOW.
HI!

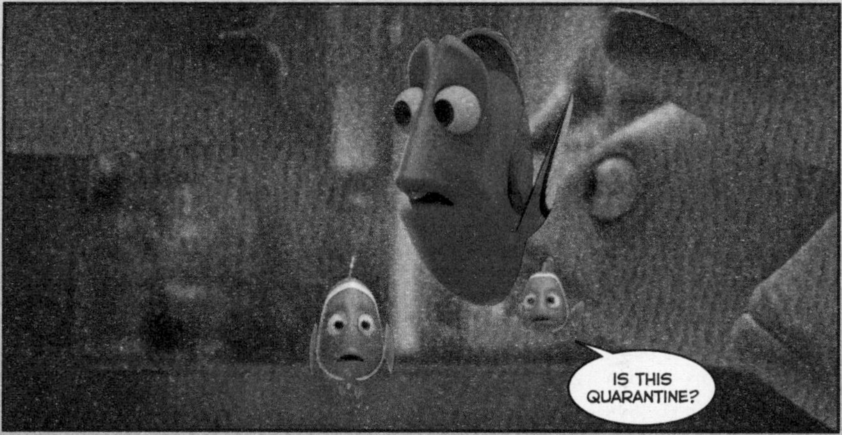
IS THIS QUARANTINE?

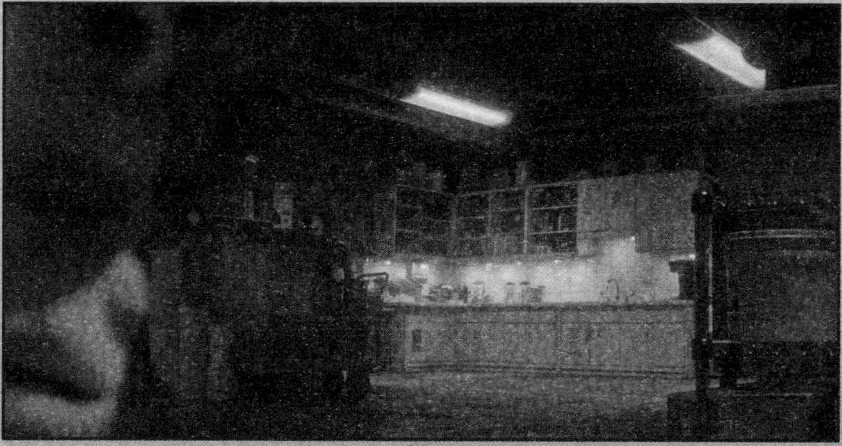

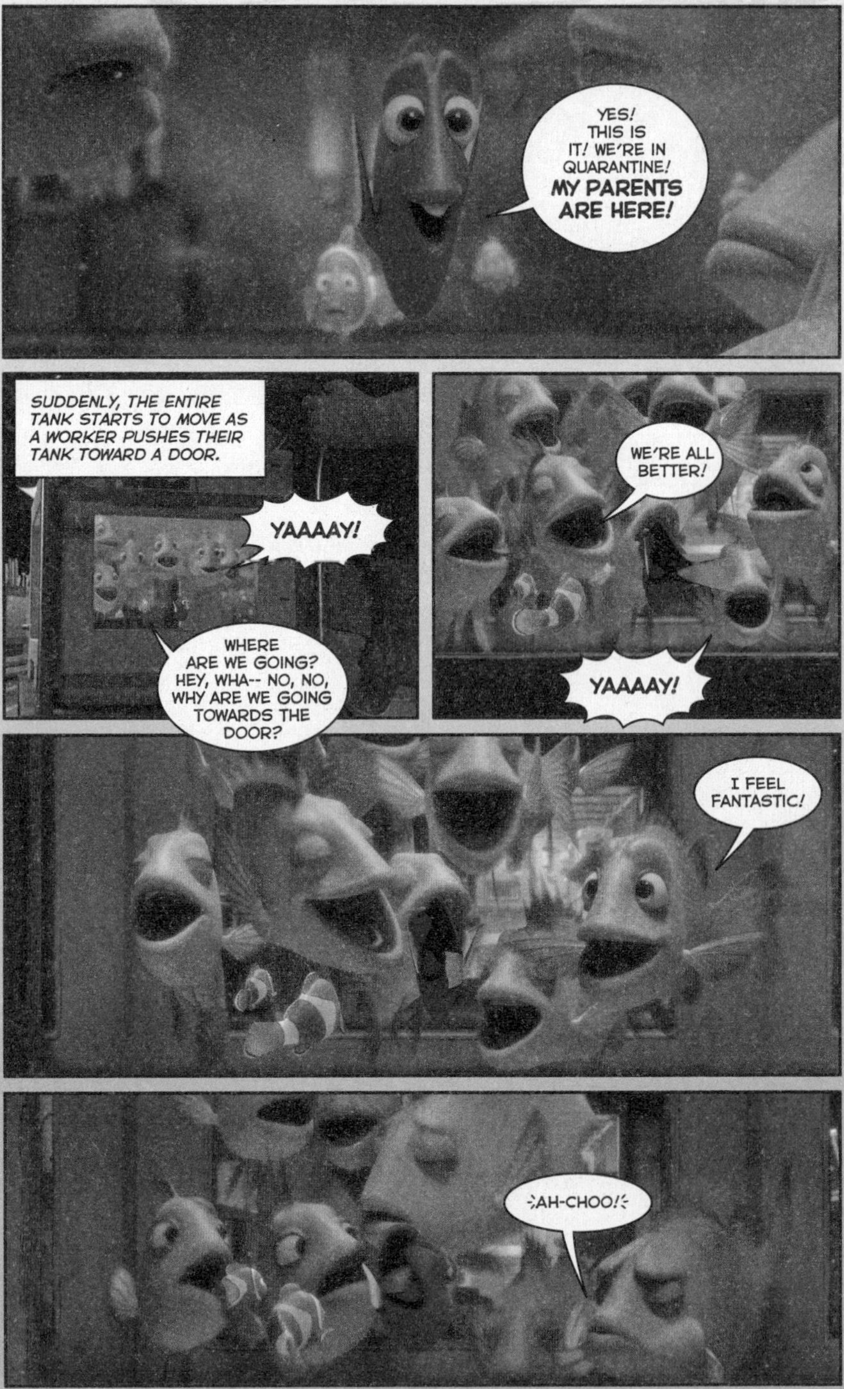
YES! THIS IS IT! WE'RE IN QUARANTINE! MY PARENTS ARE HERE!
SUDDENLY, THE ENTIRE TANK STARTS TO MOVE AS A WORKER PUSHES THEIR TANK TOWARD A DOOR.
YAAAAY!
WHERE ARE WE GOING? HEY, WHA-- NO, NO, WHY ARE WE GOING TOWARDS THE DOOR?
WE'RE ALL BETTER!
YAAAAY!
I FEEL FANTASTIC!
AH-CHOO!

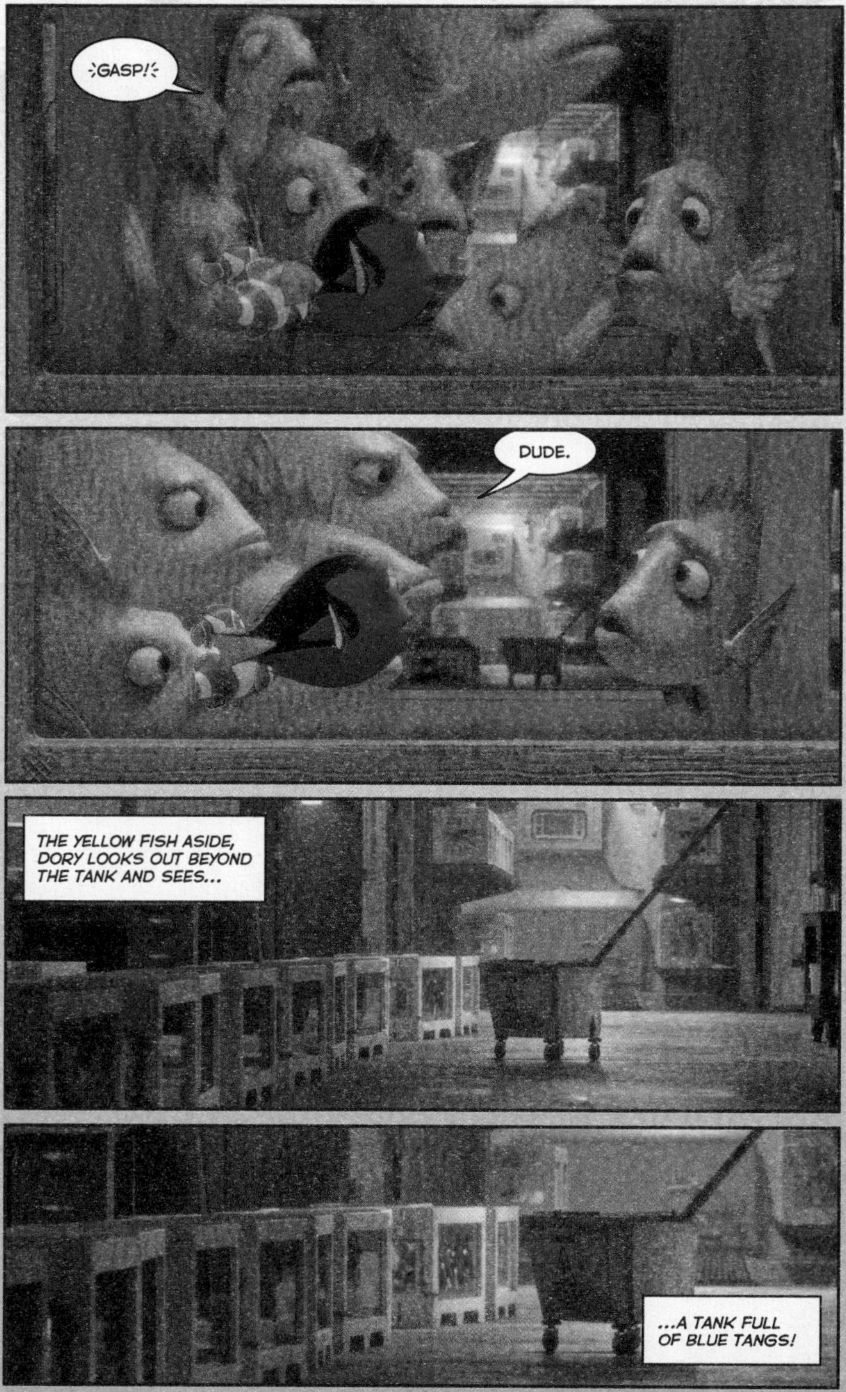
GASP!
DUDE.
THE YELLOW FISH ASIDE, DORY LOOKS OUT BEYOND THE TANK AND SEES...
...A TANK FULL OF BLUE TANGS!

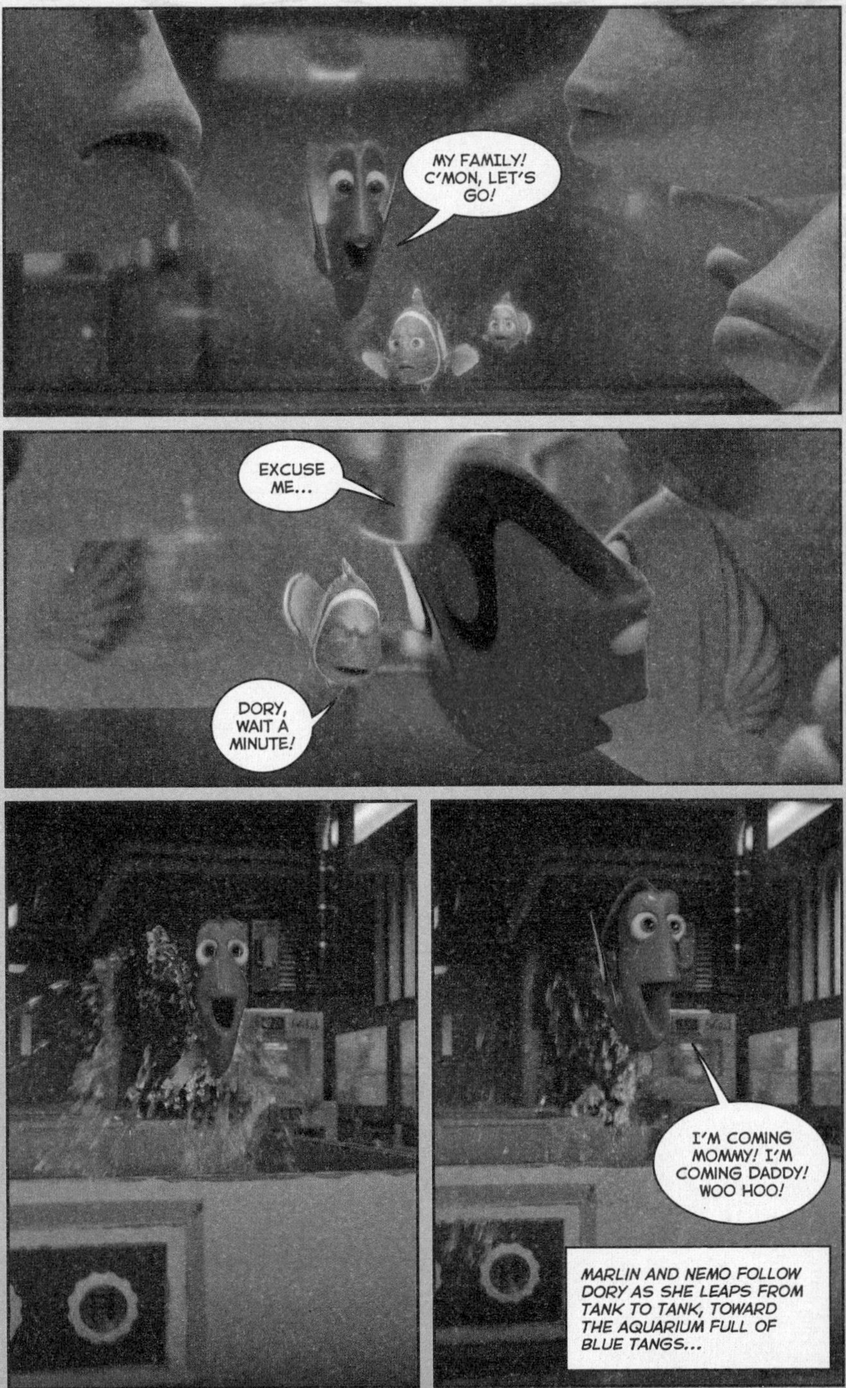
MY FAMILY! C'MON, LET'S GO!
EXCUSE ME...
DORY, WAIT A MINUTE!
I'M COMING MOMMY! I'M COMING DADDY! WOO HOO!
MARLIN AND NEMO FOLLOW DORY AS SHE LEAPS FROM TANK TO TANK, TOWARD THE AQUARIUM FULL OF BLUE TANGS...

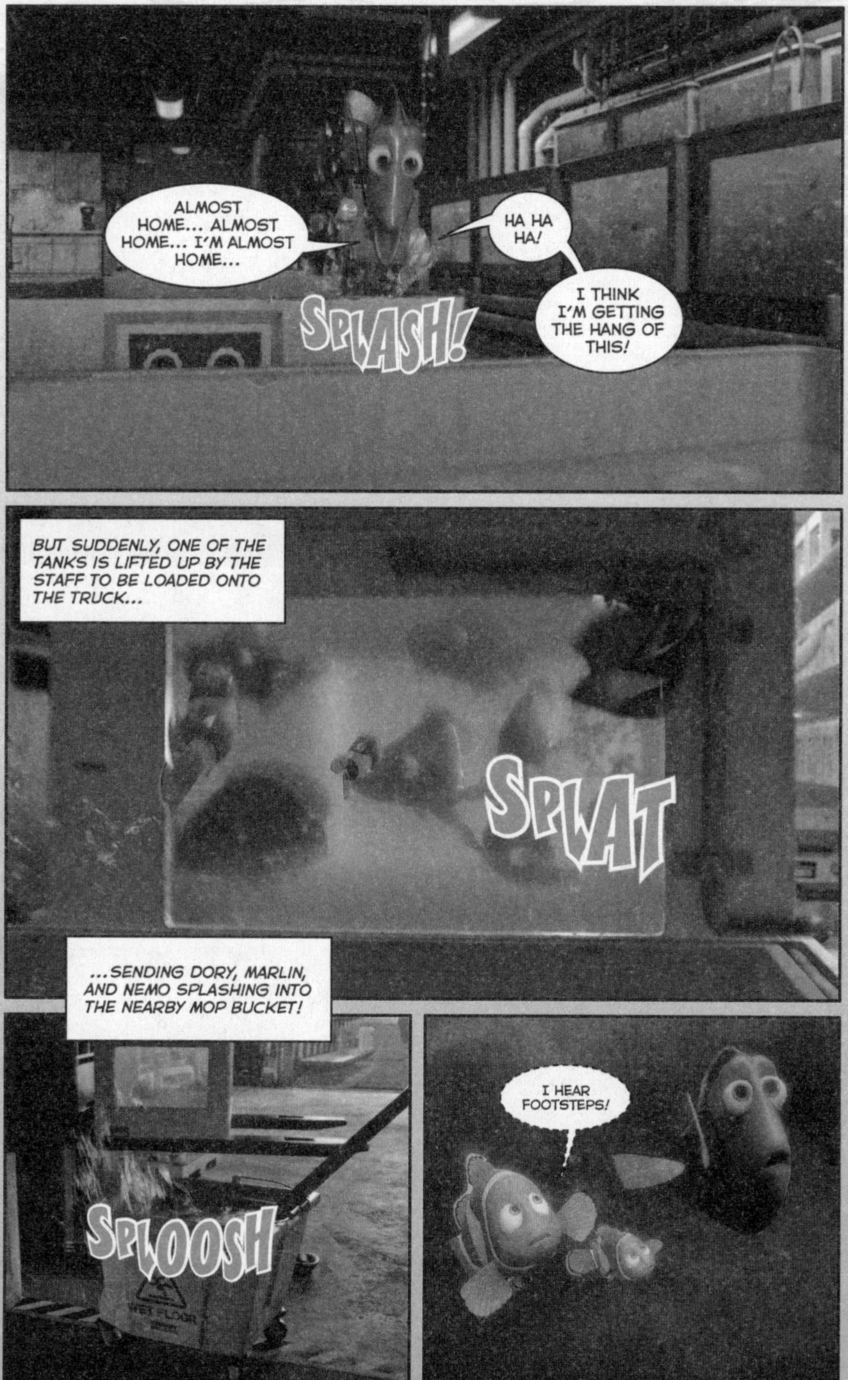
ALMOST HOME... ALMOST HOME... I'M ALMOST HOME...
HA HA HA!
I THINK I'M GETTING THE HANG OF THIS!
SPLASH!
BUT SUDDENLY, ONE OF THE TANKS IS LIFTED UP BY THE STAFF TO BE LOADED ONTO THE TRUCK...
SPLAT
...SENDING DORY, MARLIN, AND NEMO SPLASHING INTO THE NEARBY MOP BUCKET!
SPLOOSH
I HEAR FOOTSTEPS!

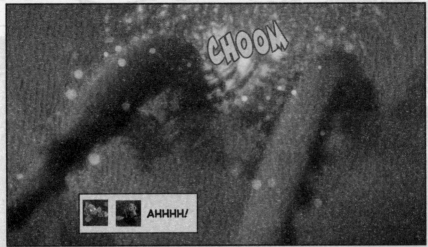

CHOOM

AHHHH!

-:GASP:- -:GASP:-

-:GASP:-

HANK DROPS THE THREE FISH INTO A CONTAINER OF WATER.

HANK!

QUIET.

HANK, WE NEED TO GET IN THAT TANK.

THAT RHYMED!

278

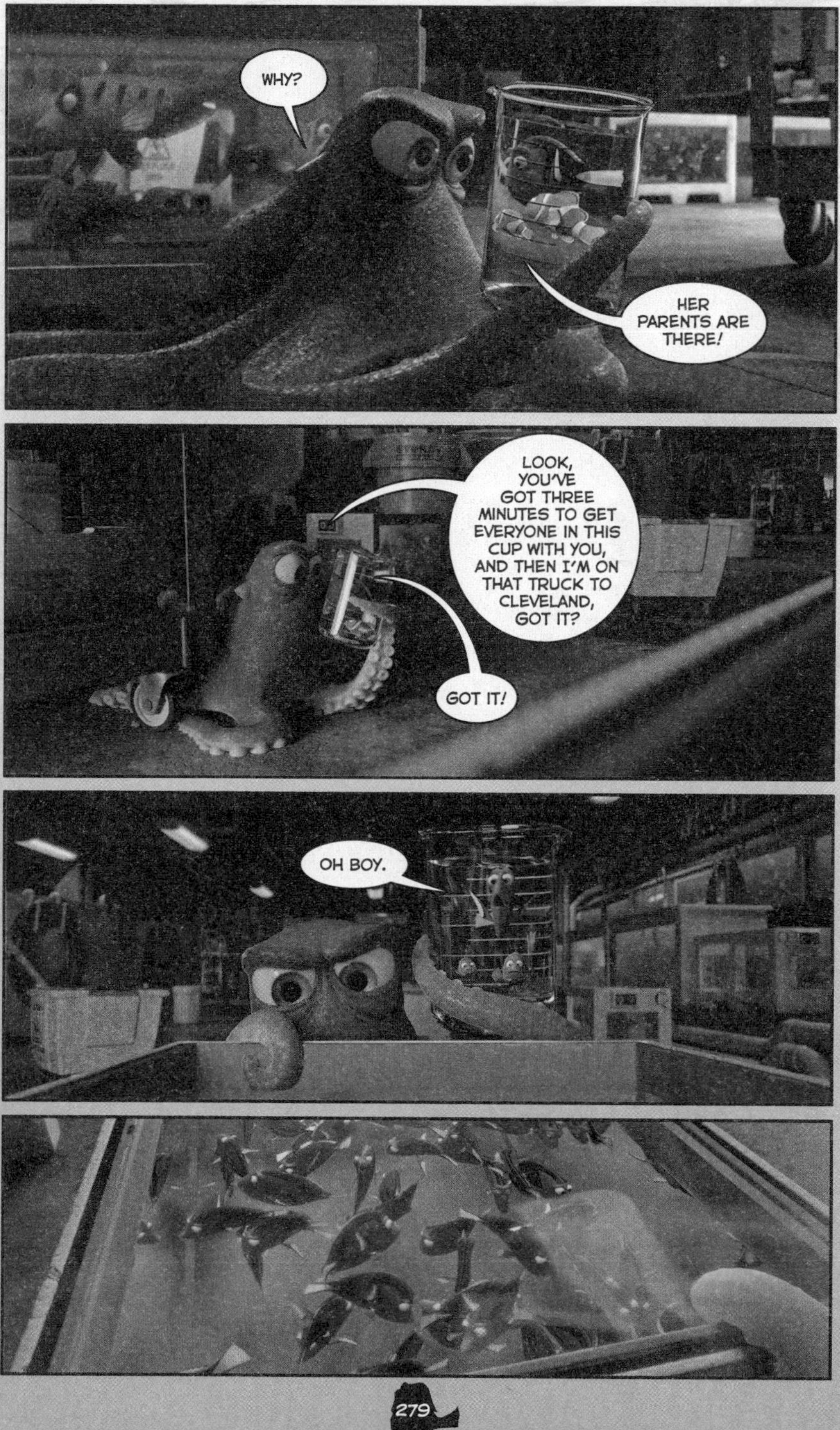
WHY?
HER PARENTS ARE THERE!
LOOK, YOU'VE GOT THREE MINUTES TO GET EVERYONE IN THIS CUP WITH YOU, AND THEN I'M ON THAT TRUCK TO CLEVELAND, GOT IT?
GOT IT!
OH BOY.

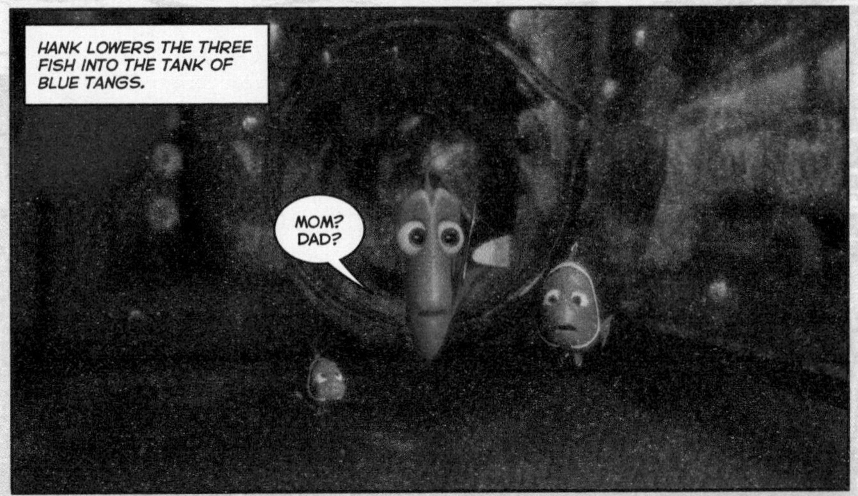
HANK LOWERS THE THREE FISH INTO THE TANK OF BLUE TANGS.
MOM? DAD?

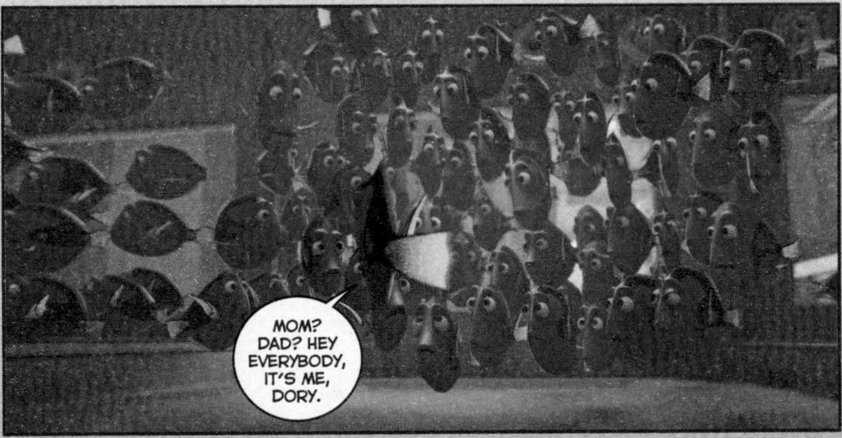
MOM? DAD? HEY EVERYBODY, IT'S ME, DORY.

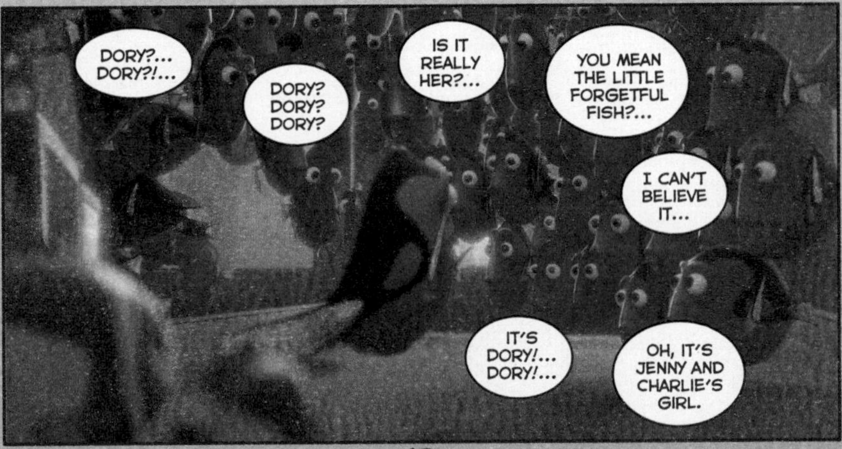
DORY?... DORY?!...
DORY? DORY? DORY?
IS IT REALLY HER?...
YOU MEAN THE LITTLE FORGETFUL FISH?...
I CAN'T BELIEVE IT...
IT'S DORY!... DORY!...
OH, IT'S JENNY AND CHARLIE'S GIRL.

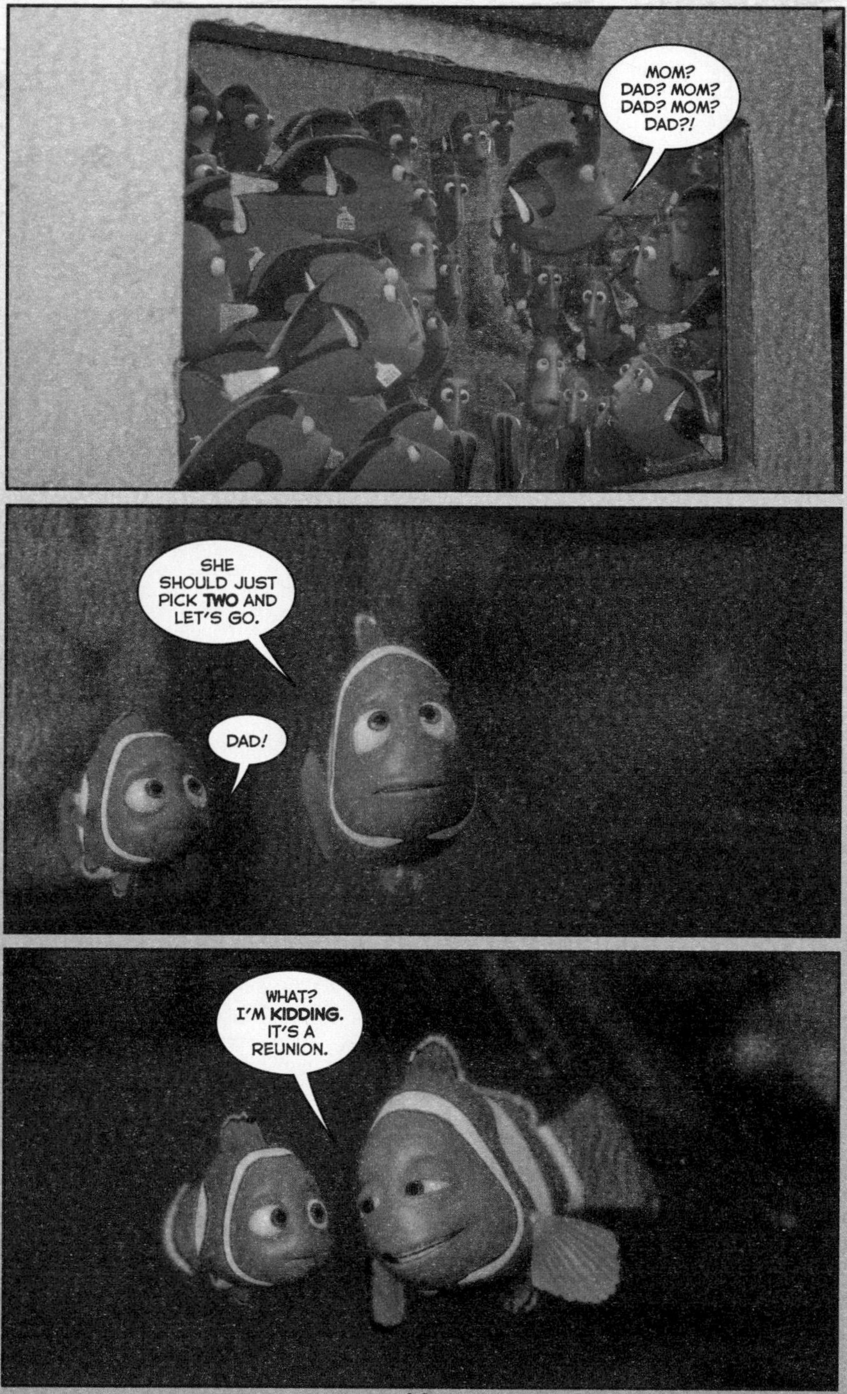
MOM? DAD? MOM? DAD? MOM? DAD?!
SHE SHOULD JUST PICK **TWO** AND LET'S GO.
DAD!
WHAT? I'M **KIDDING.** IT'S A REUNION.

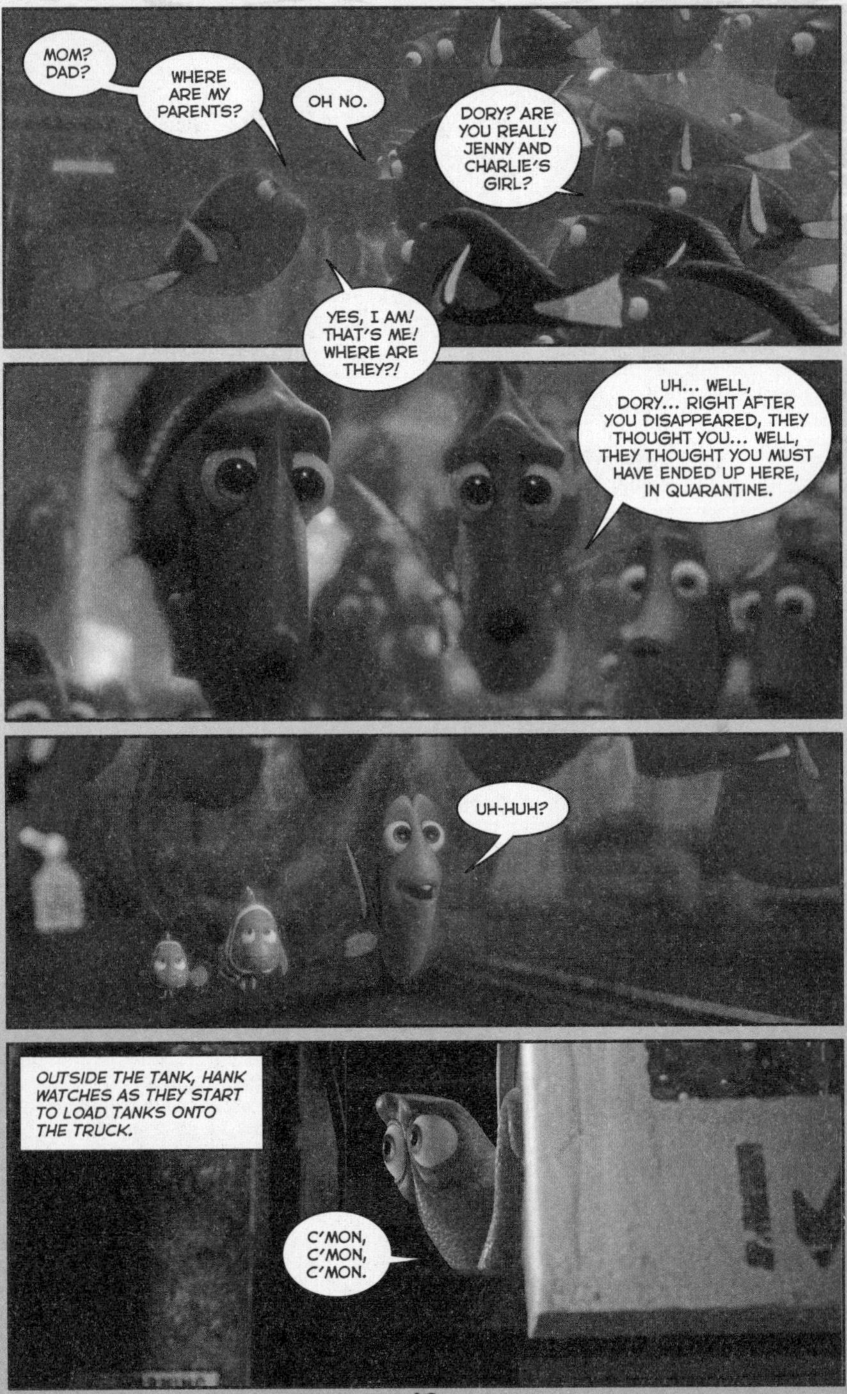
MOM? DAD?
WHERE ARE MY PARENTS?
OH NO.
DORY? ARE YOU REALLY JENNY AND CHARLIE'S GIRL?
YES, I AM! THAT'S ME! WHERE ARE THEY?!
UH... WELL, DORY... RIGHT AFTER YOU DISAPPEARED, THEY THOUGHT YOU... WELL, THEY THOUGHT YOU MUST HAVE ENDED UP HERE, IN QUARANTINE.
UH-HUH?
OUTSIDE THE TANK, HANK WATCHES AS THEY START TO LOAD TANKS ONTO THE TRUCK.
C'MON, C'MON, C'MON.

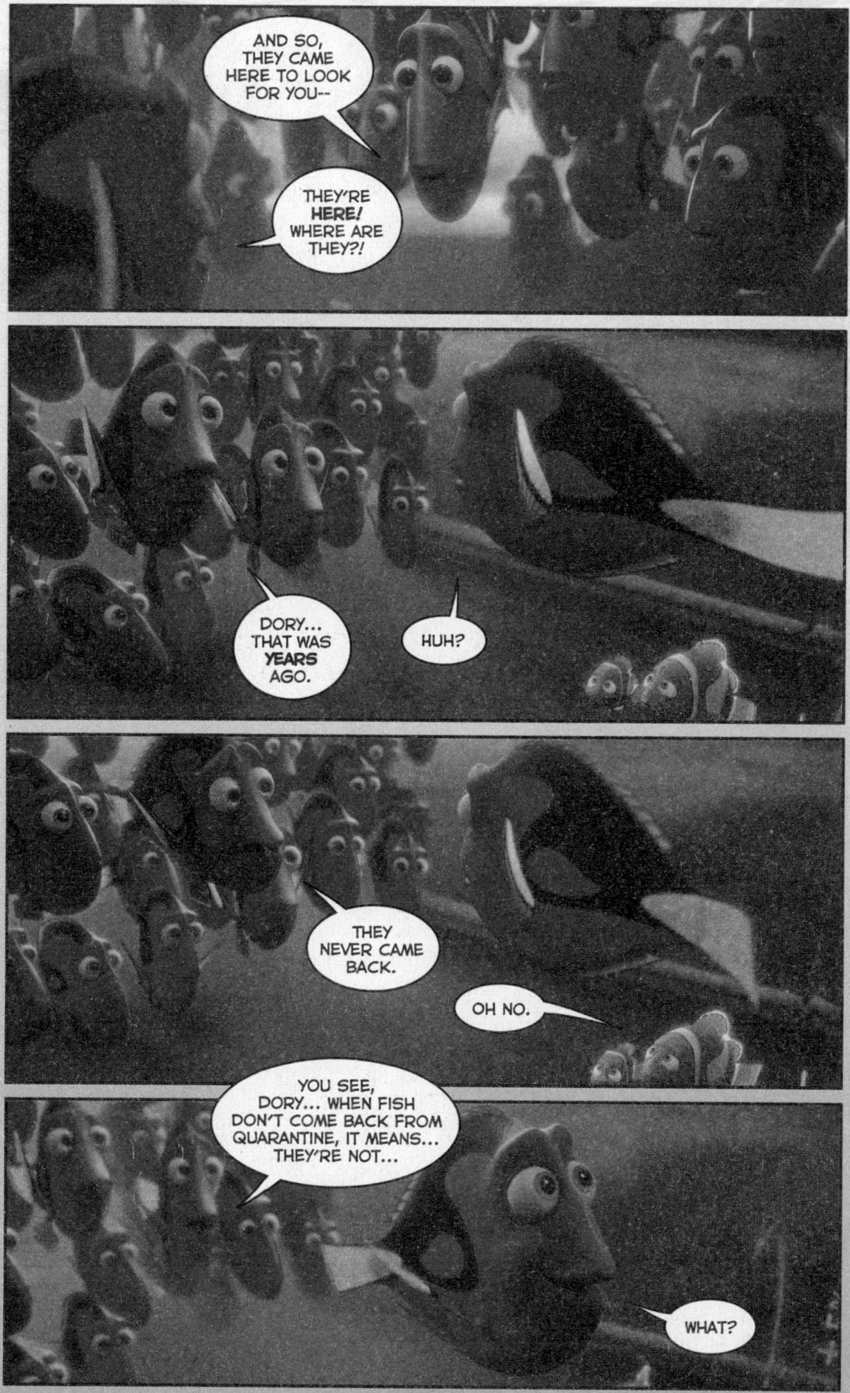
AND SO, THEY CAME HERE TO LOOK FOR YOU--
THEY'RE **HERE!** WHERE ARE THEY?!
DORY... THAT WAS **YEARS** AGO.
HUH?
THEY NEVER CAME BACK.
OH NO.
YOU SEE, DORY... WHEN FISH DON'T COME BACK FROM QUARANTINE, IT MEANS... THEY'RE NOT...
WHAT?

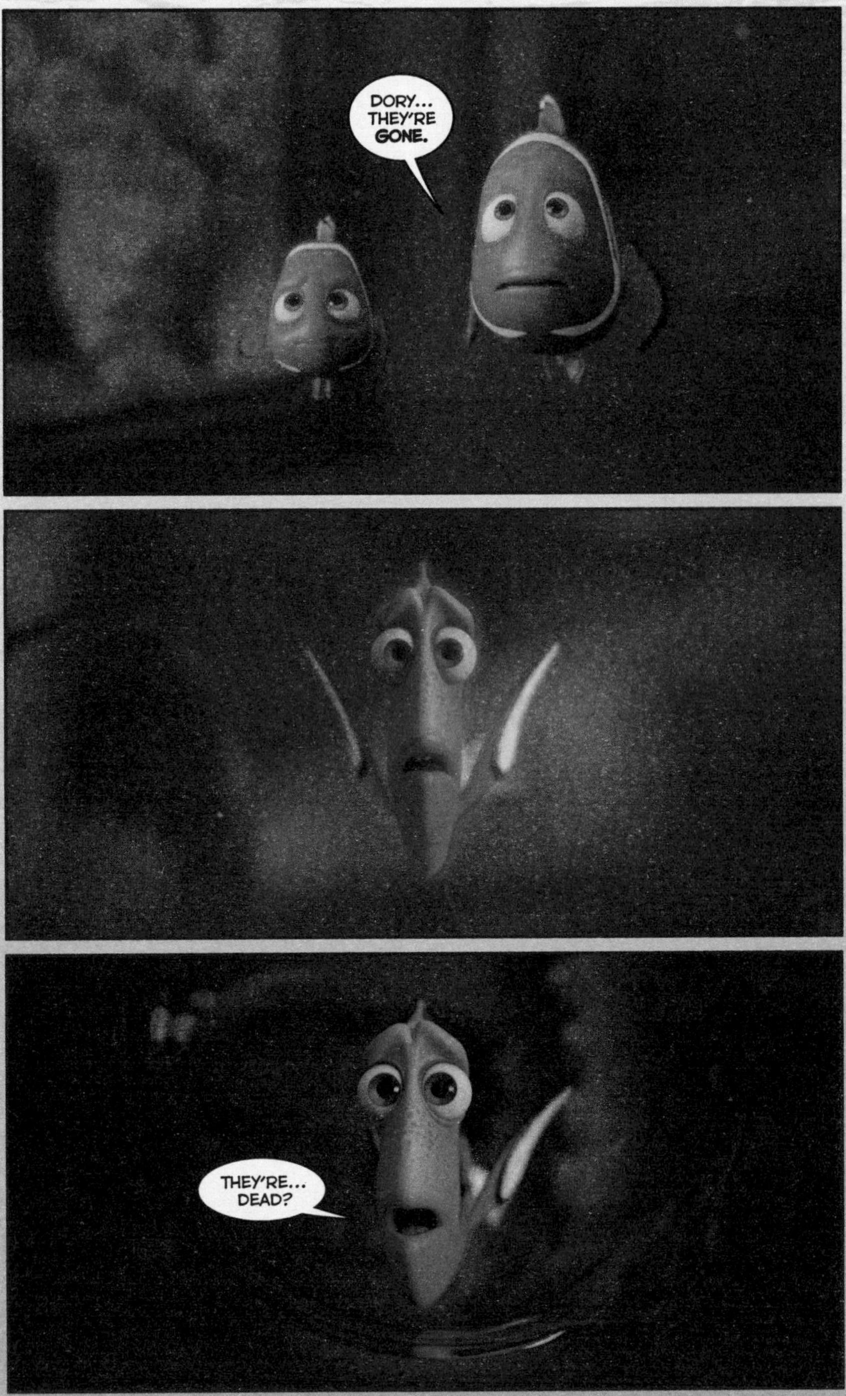
DORY... THEY'RE GONE.
THEY'RE... DEAD?

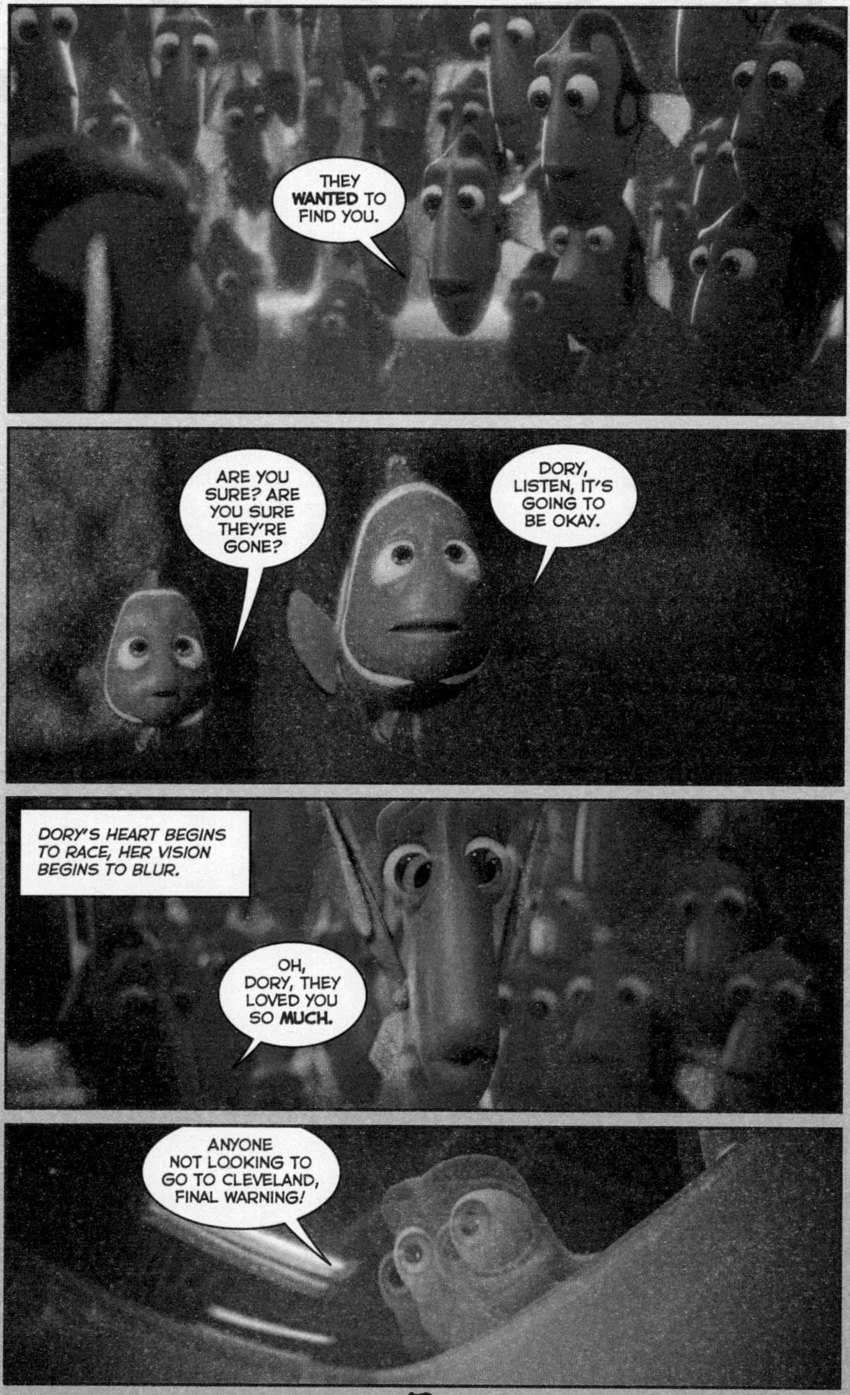
THEY WANTED TO FIND YOU.
ARE YOU SURE? ARE YOU SURE THEY'RE GONE?
DORY, LISTEN, IT'S GOING TO BE OKAY.
DORY'S HEART BEGINS TO RACE, HER VISION BEGINS TO BLUR.
OH, DORY, THEY LOVED YOU SO MUCH.
ANYONE NOT LOOKING TO GO TO CLEVELAND, FINAL WARNING!

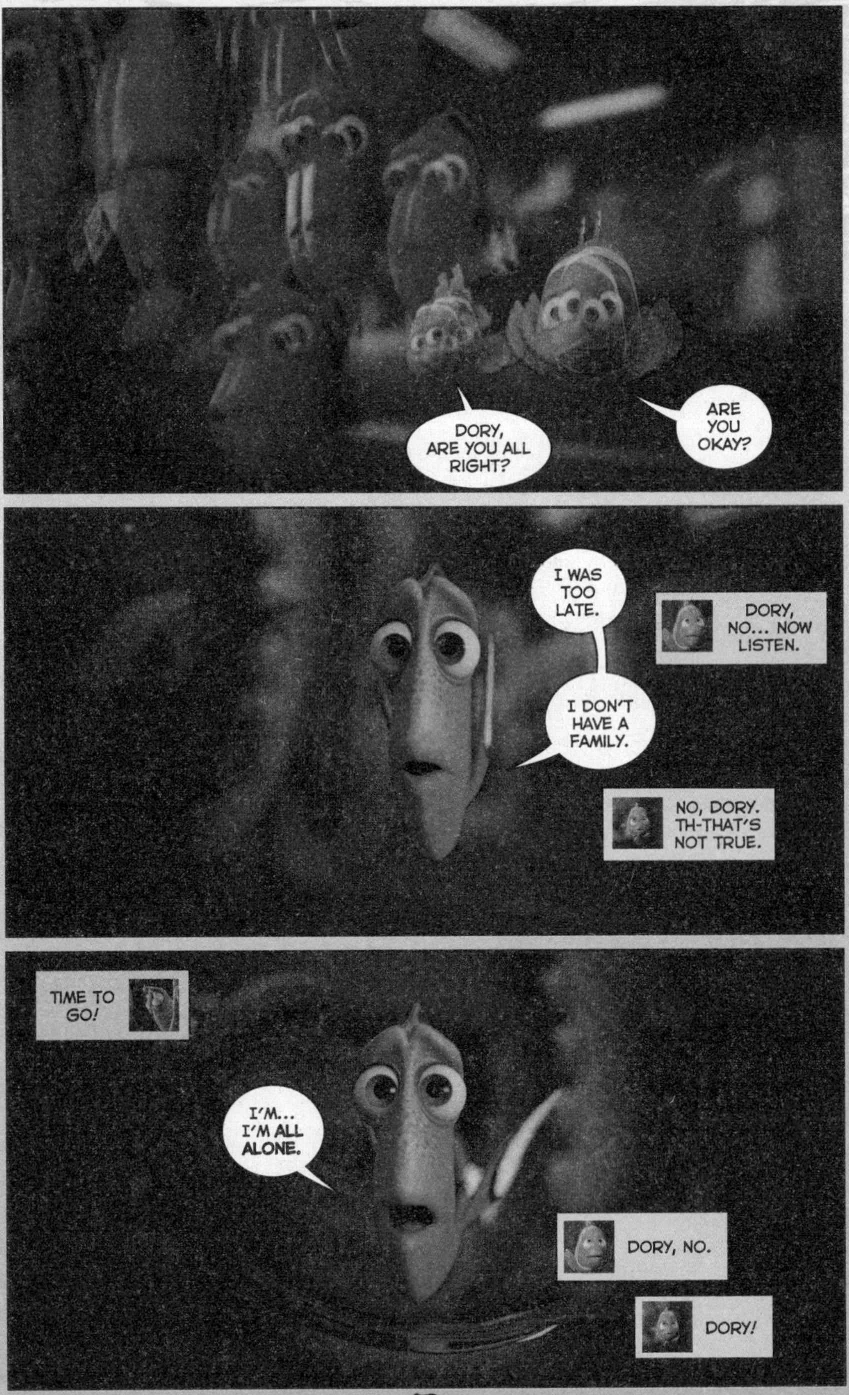
DORY, ARE YOU ALL RIGHT?
ARE YOU OKAY?
I WAS TOO LATE.
DORY, NO... NOW LISTEN.
I DON'T HAVE A FAMILY.
NO, DORY. TH-THAT'S NOT TRUE.
TIME TO GO!
I'M... I'M ALL ALONE.
DORY, NO.
DORY!

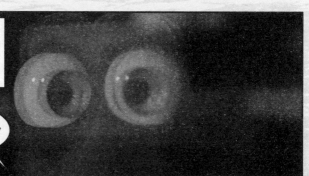

HANK WATCHES THE FORKLIFT GO UNDER THE TANK AND QUICKLY SCOOPS UP DORY, MISSING MARLIN AND NEMO.

WHERE'S EVERYBODY ELSE?

:GASP:

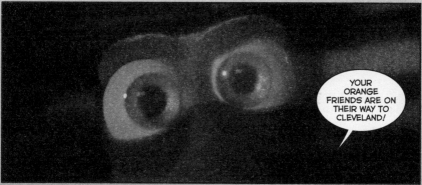

YOUR ORANGE FRIENDS ARE ON THEIR WAY TO CLEVELAND!

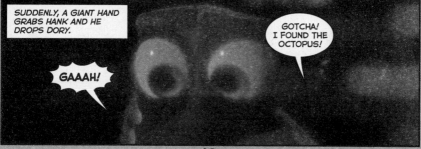

SUDDENLY, A GIANT HAND GRABS HANK AND HE DROPS DORY.

GOTCHA! I FOUND THE OCTOPUS!

GAAAH!

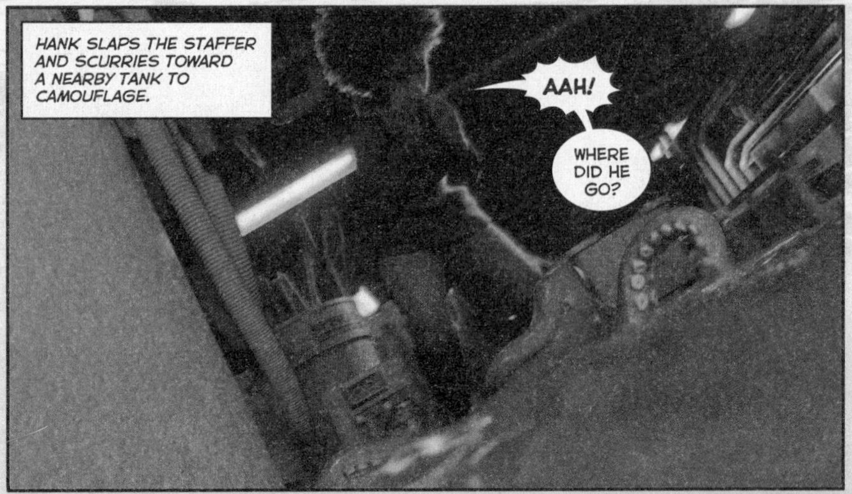
HANK SLAPS THE STAFFER AND SCURRIES TOWARD A NEARBY TANK TO CAMOUFLAGE.
AAH!
WHERE DID HE GO?

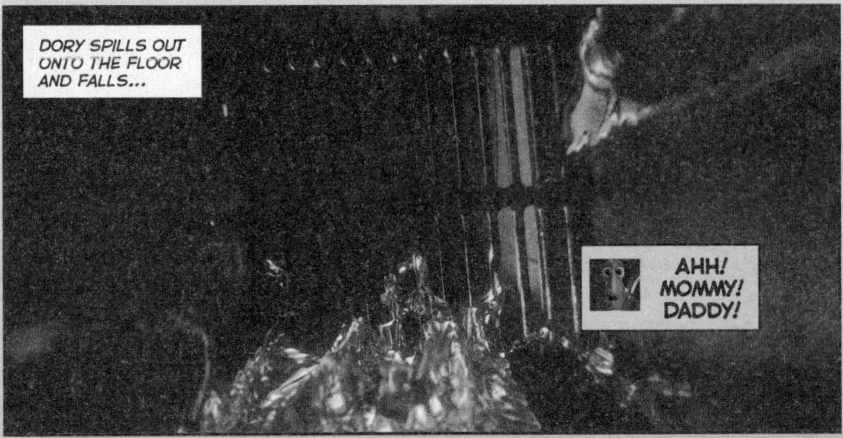
DORY SPILLS OUT ONTO THE FLOOR AND FALLS...
AHH! MOMMY! DADDY!

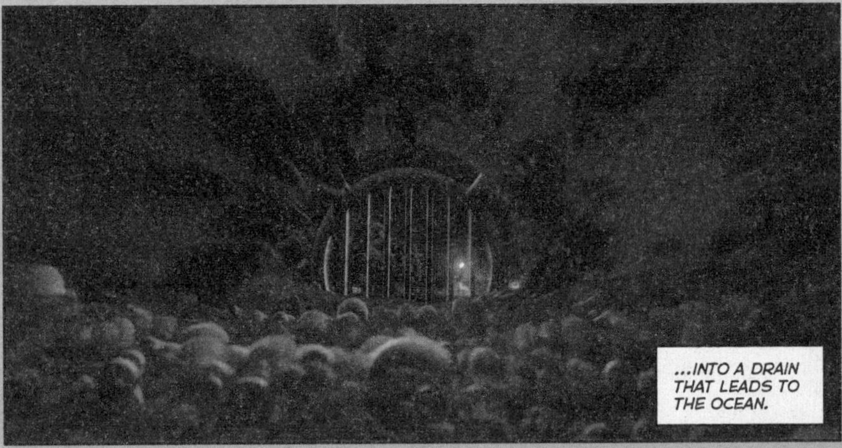
...INTO A DRAIN THAT LEADS TO THE OCEAN.

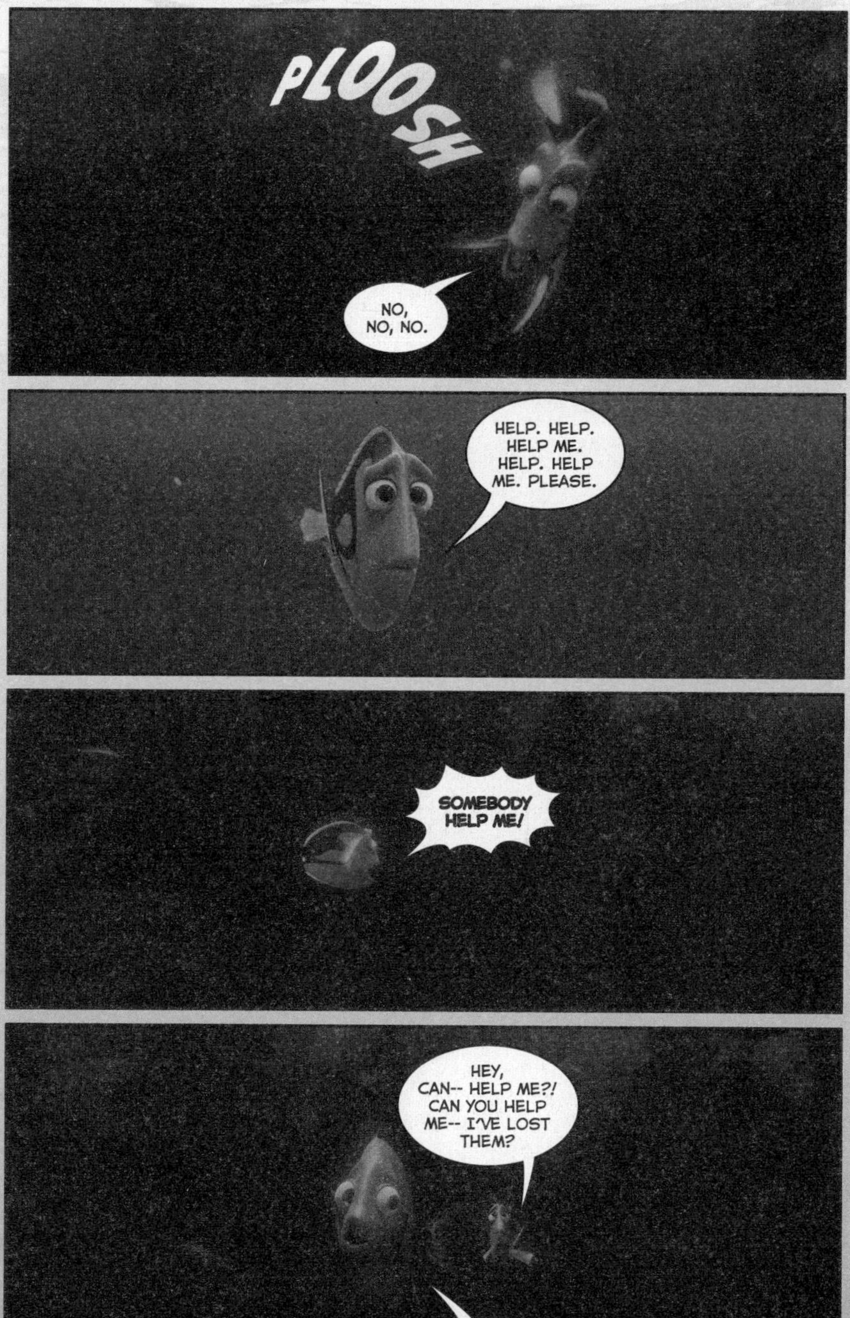
PLOOSH
NO, NO, NO.
HELP. HELP. HELP ME. HELP. HELP ME. PLEASE.
SOMEBODY HELP ME!
HEY, CAN-- HELP ME?! CAN YOU HELP ME-- I'VE LOST THEM?
OH. LOST WHO?

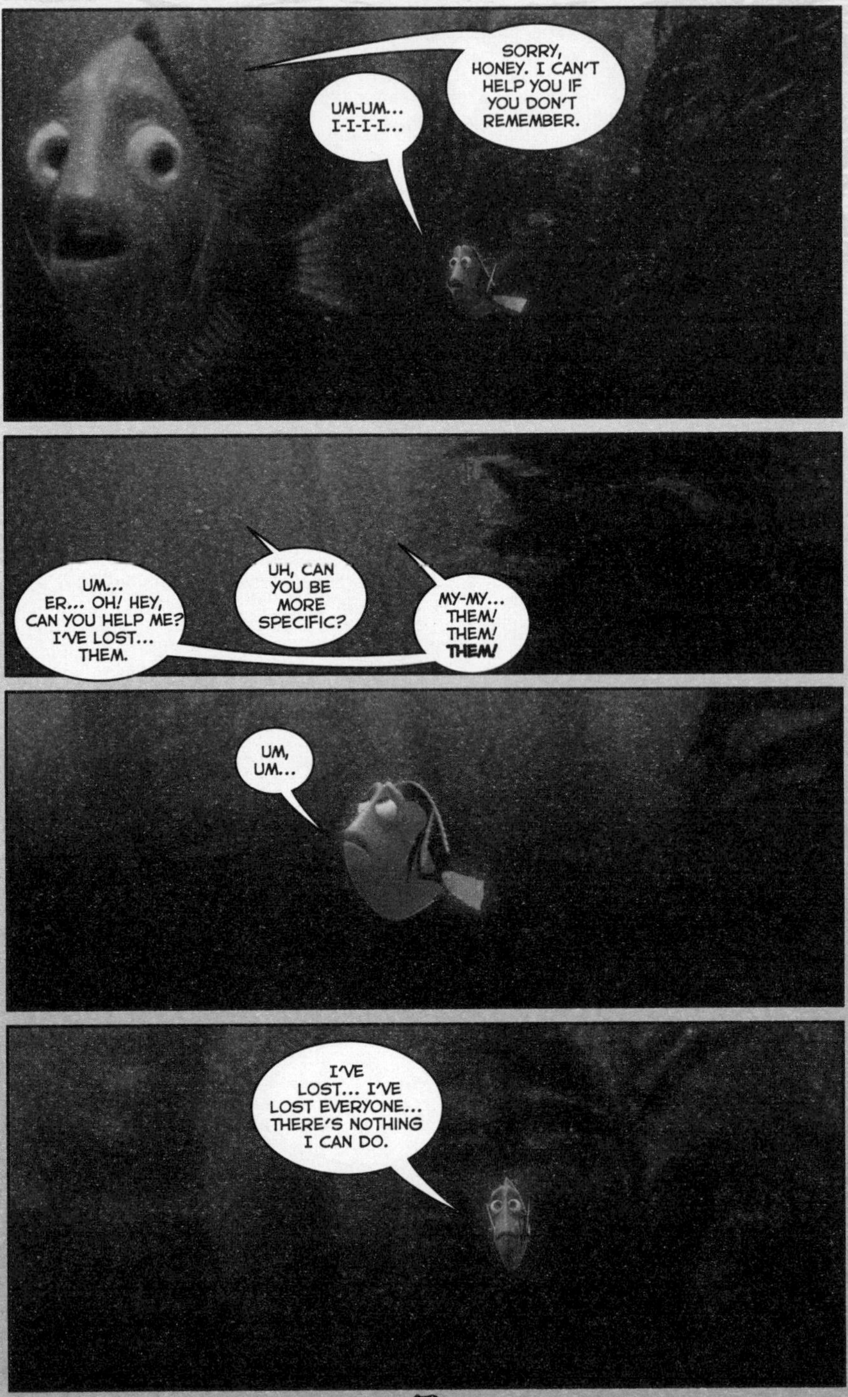
SORRY, HONEY. I CAN'T HELP YOU IF YOU DON'T REMEMBER.
UM-UM... I-I-I-I...
UM... ER... OH! HEY, CAN YOU HELP ME? I'VE LOST... THEM.
UH, CAN YOU BE MORE SPECIFIC?
MY-MY... THEM! THEM! THEM!
UM, UM...
I'VE LOST... I'VE LOST EVERYONE... THERE'S NOTHING I CAN DO.

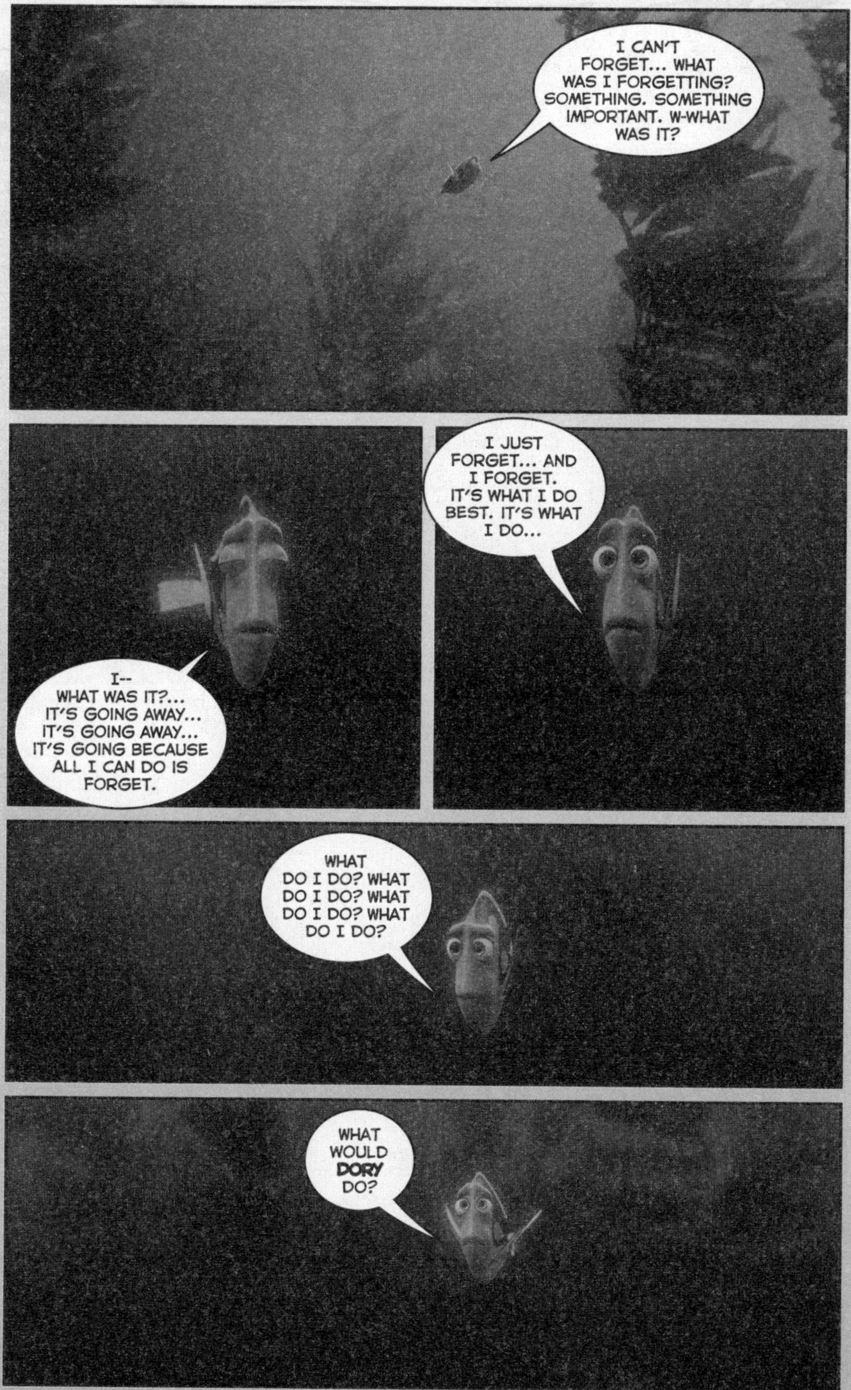
I CAN'T FORGET... WHAT WAS I FORGETTING? SOMETHING. SOMETHING IMPORTANT. W-WHAT WAS IT?
I-- WHAT WAS IT?... IT'S GOING AWAY... IT'S GOING AWAY... IT'S GOING BECAUSE ALL I CAN DO IS FORGET.
I JUST FORGET... AND I FORGET. IT'S WHAT I DO BEST. IT'S WHAT I DO...
WHAT DO I DO? WHAT DO I DO? WHAT DO I DO? WHAT DO I DO?
WHAT WOULD **DORY** DO?

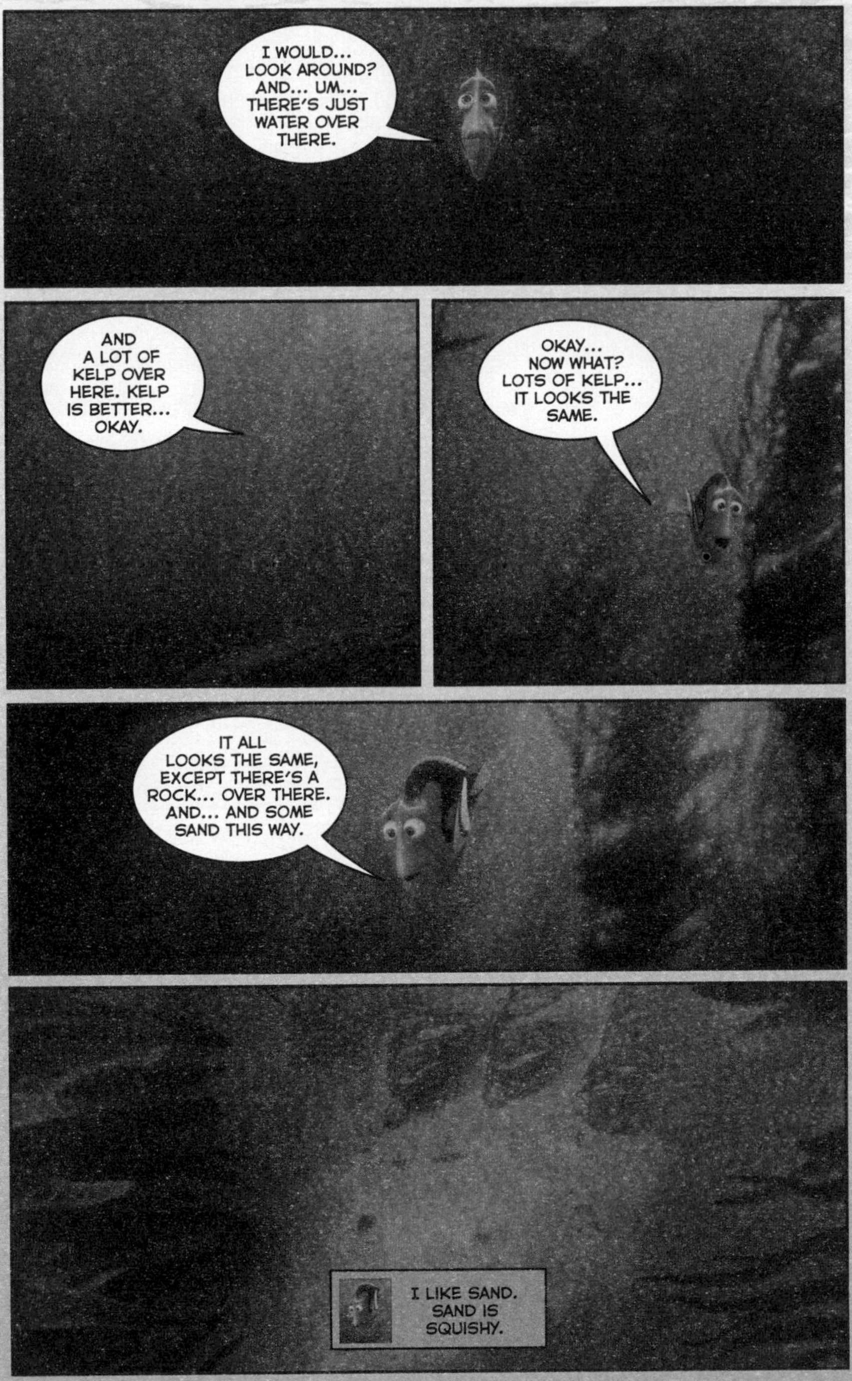
I WOULD... LOOK AROUND? AND... UM... THERE'S JUST WATER OVER THERE.
AND A LOT OF KELP OVER HERE. KELP IS BETTER... OKAY.
OKAY... NOW WHAT? LOTS OF KELP... IT LOOKS THE SAME.
IT ALL LOOKS THE SAME, EXCEPT THERE'S A ROCK... OVER THERE. AND... AND SOME SAND THIS WAY.
I LIKE SAND. SAND IS SQUISHY.

THIS ISN'T GOING ANYWHERE. THERE'S NOTHING HERE. NOTHING BUT KELP.
LOTS OF KELP, AND SOME SHELLS... THIS... WAY.

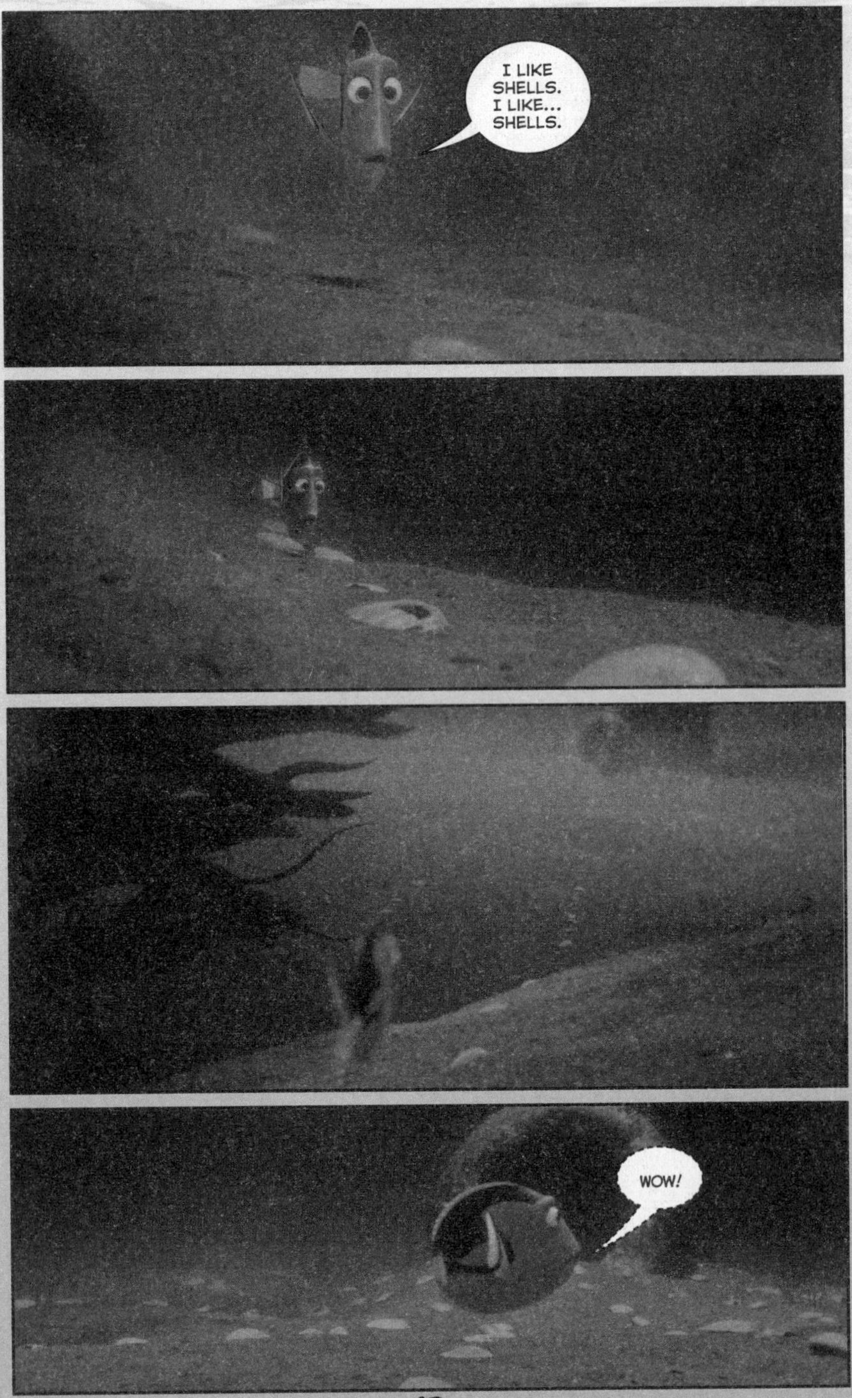
I LIKE SHELLS. I LIKE... SHELLS.
WOW!

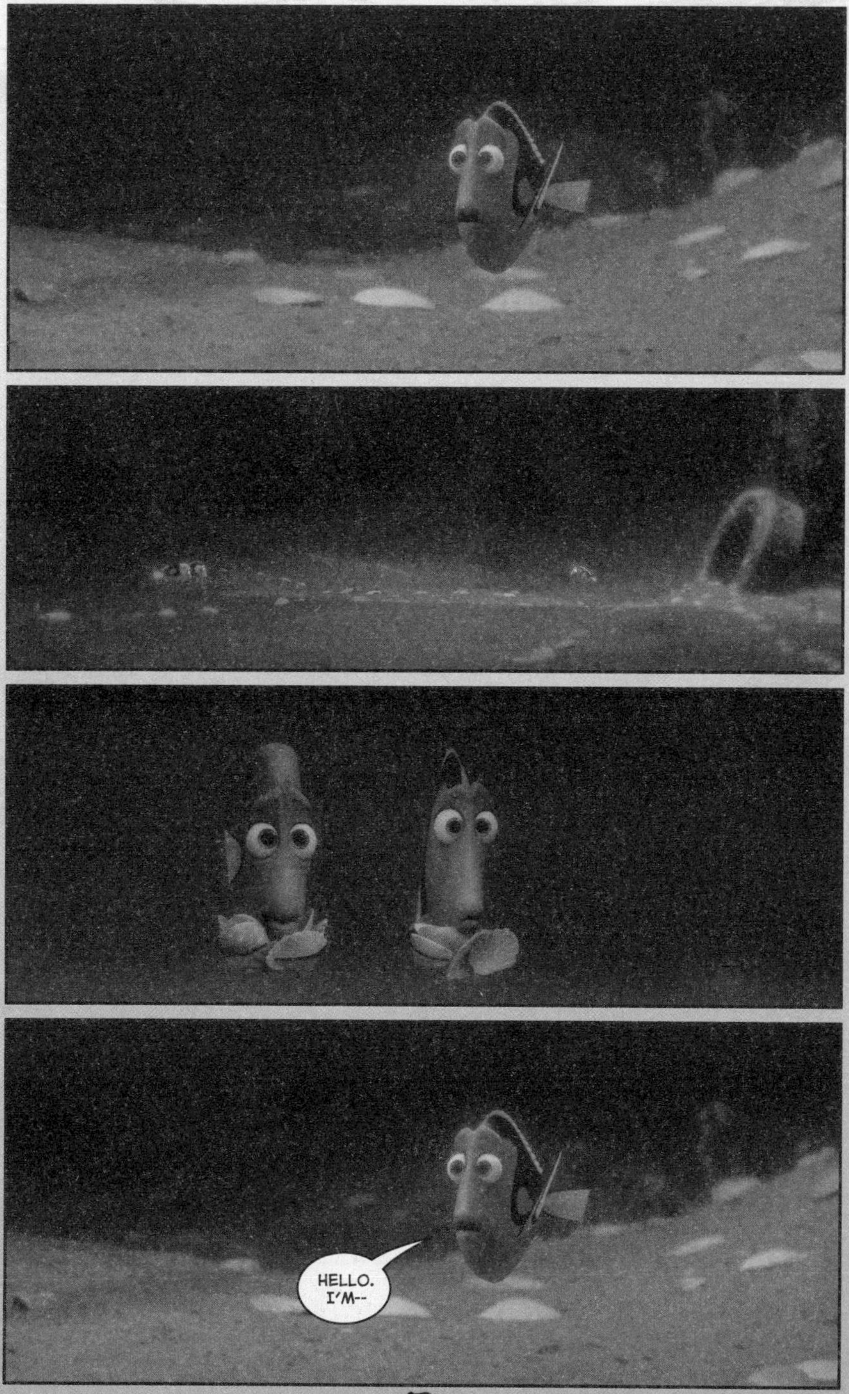
HELLO. I'M--

DORY!

DORY!

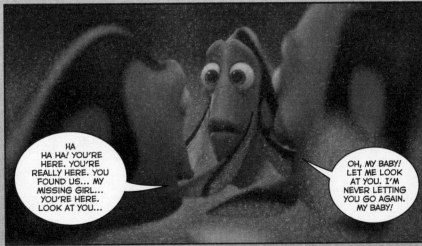

HA HA HA! YOU'RE HERE. YOU'RE REALLY HERE. YOU FOUND US... MY MISSING GIRL... YOU'RE HERE. LOOK AT YOU...

OH, MY BABY! LET ME LOOK AT YOU. I'M NEVER LETTING YOU GO AGAIN. MY BABY!

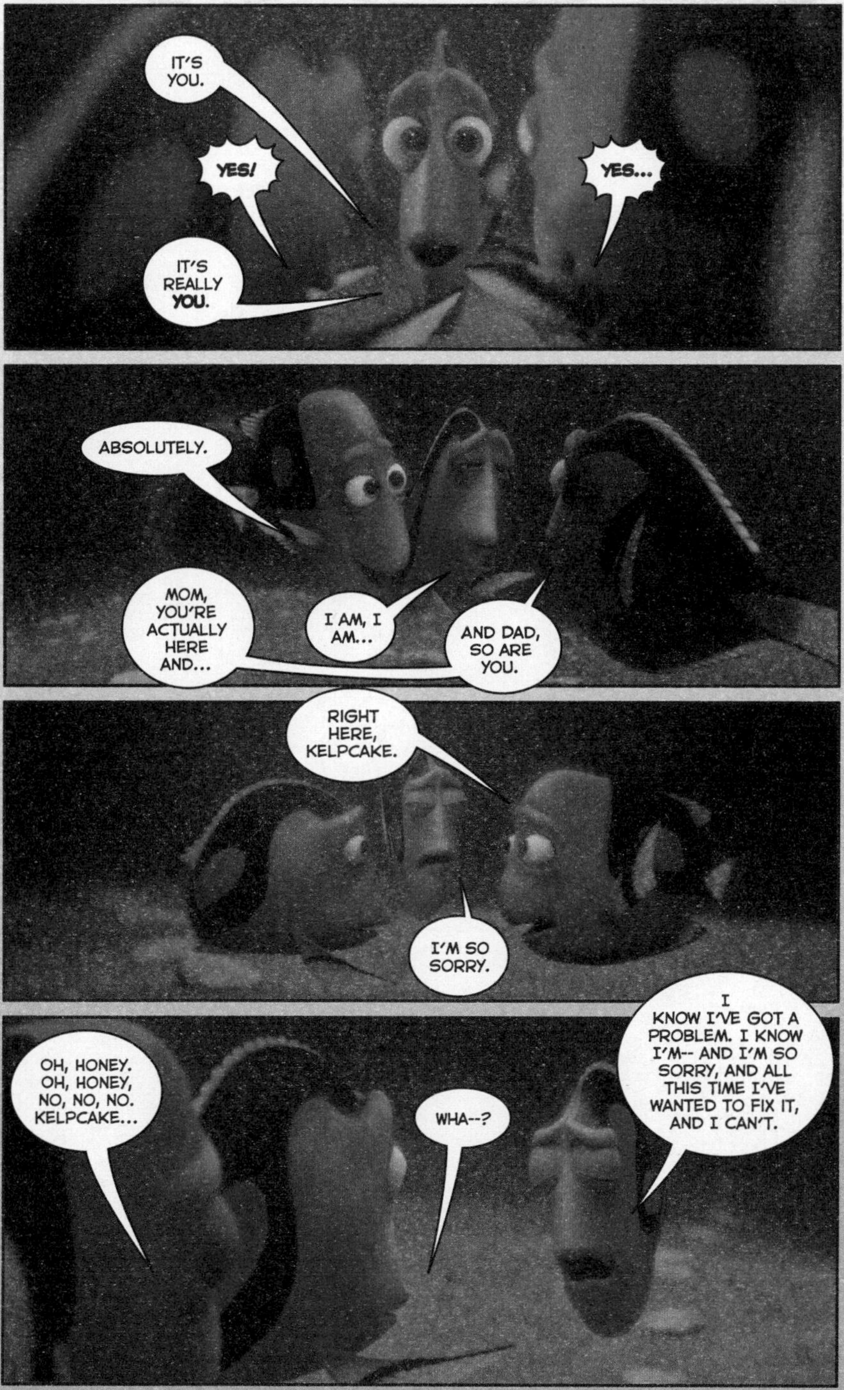
IT'S YOU.
YES!
IT'S REALLY YOU.
YES...
ABSOLUTELY.
MOM, YOU'RE ACTUALLY HERE AND...
I AM, I AM...
AND DAD, SO ARE YOU.
RIGHT HERE, KELPCAKE.
I'M SO SORRY.
I KNOW I'VE GOT A PROBLEM. I KNOW I'M-- AND I'M SO SORRY, AND ALL THIS TIME I'VE WANTED TO FIX IT, AND I CAN'T.
OH, HONEY. OH, HONEY, NO, NO, NO. KELPCAKE...
WHA--?

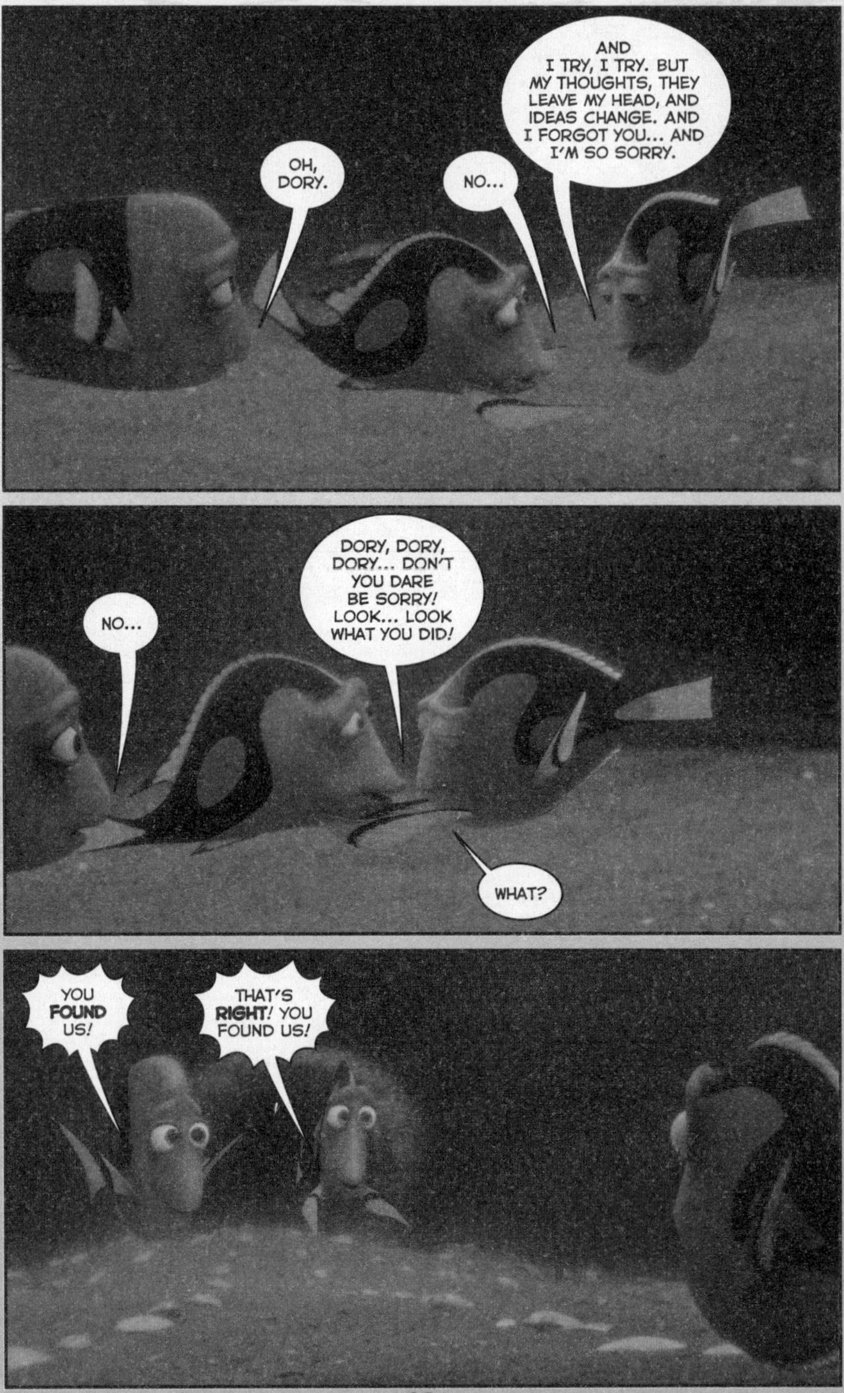
AND I TRY, I TRY. BUT MY THOUGHTS, THEY LEAVE MY HEAD, AND IDEAS CHANGE. AND I FORGOT YOU... AND I'M SO SORRY.
OH, DORY.
NO...
NO...
DORY, DORY, DORY... DON'T YOU DARE BE SORRY! LOOK... LOOK WHAT YOU DID!
WHAT?
YOU **FOUND** US!
THAT'S **RIGHT**! YOU FOUND US!

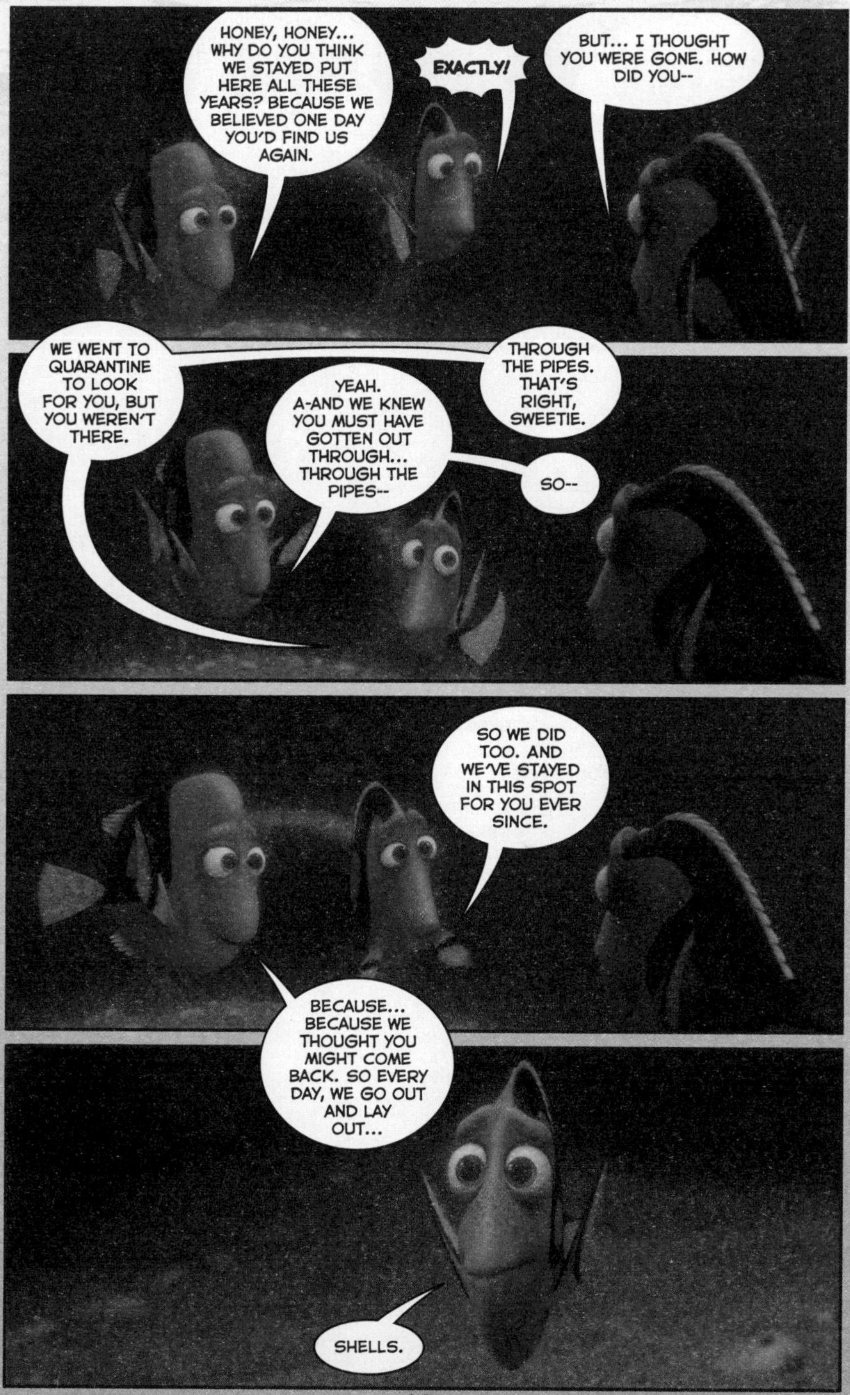
HONEY, HONEY... WHY DO YOU THINK WE STAYED PUT HERE ALL THESE YEARS? BECAUSE WE BELIEVED ONE DAY YOU'D FIND US AGAIN.
EXACTLY!
BUT... I THOUGHT YOU WERE GONE. HOW DID YOU--
WE WENT TO QUARANTINE TO LOOK FOR YOU, BUT YOU WEREN'T THERE.
YEAH. A-AND WE KNEW YOU MUST HAVE GOTTEN OUT THROUGH... THROUGH THE PIPES--
THROUGH THE PIPES. THAT'S RIGHT, SWEETIE.
SO--
SO WE DID TOO. AND WE'VE STAYED IN THIS SPOT FOR YOU EVER SINCE.
BECAUSE... BECAUSE WE THOUGHT YOU MIGHT COME BACK. SO EVERY DAY, WE GO OUT AND LAY OUT...
SHELLS.

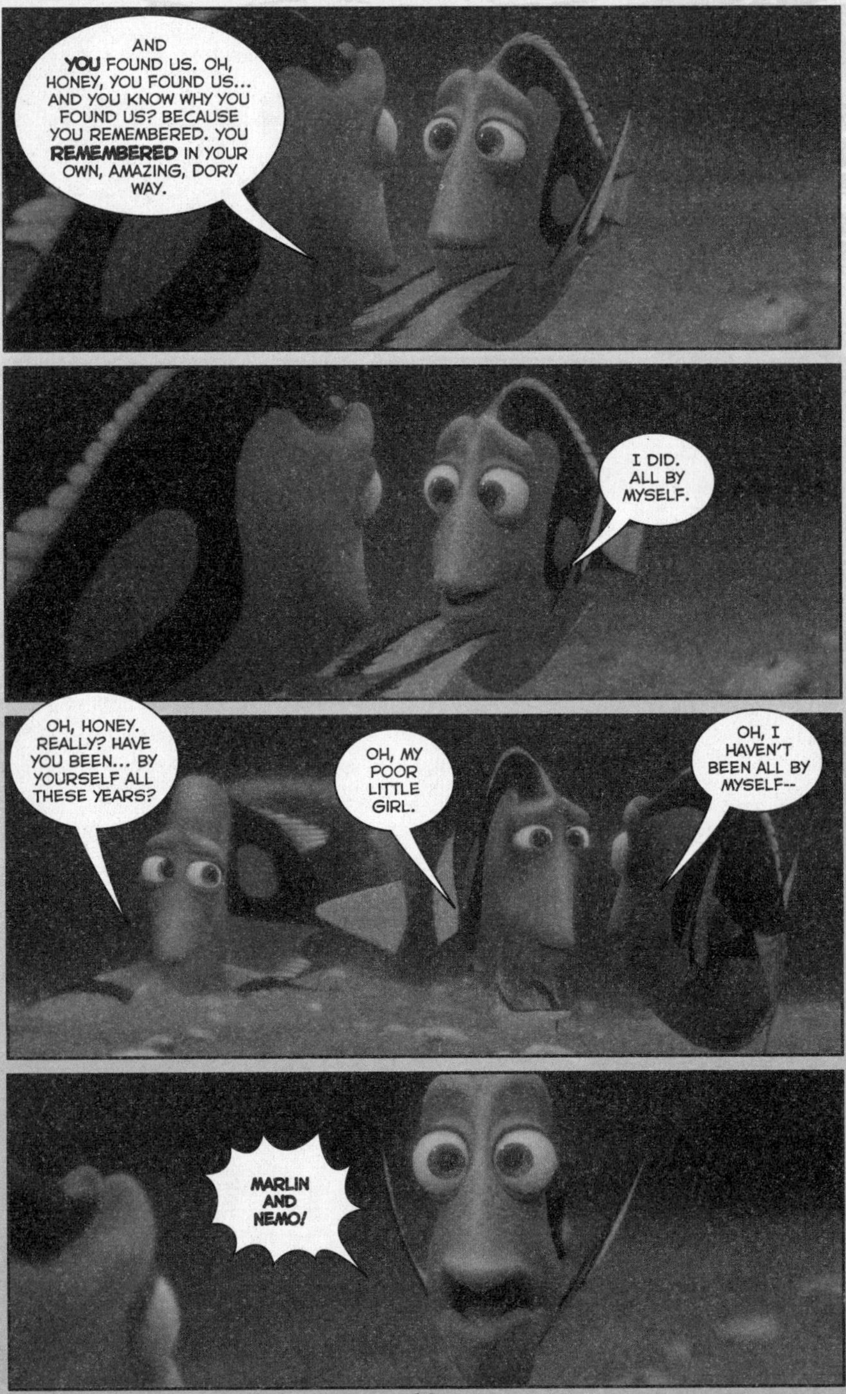
AND **YOU** FOUND US. OH, HONEY, YOU FOUND US... AND YOU KNOW WHY YOU FOUND US? BECAUSE YOU REMEMBERED. YOU **REMEMBERED** IN YOUR OWN, AMAZING, DORY WAY.
I DID. ALL BY MYSELF.
OH, HONEY. REALLY? HAVE YOU BEEN... BY YOURSELF ALL THESE YEARS?
OH, MY POOR LITTLE GIRL.
OH, I HAVEN'T BEEN ALL BY MYSELF--
MARLIN AND NEMO!

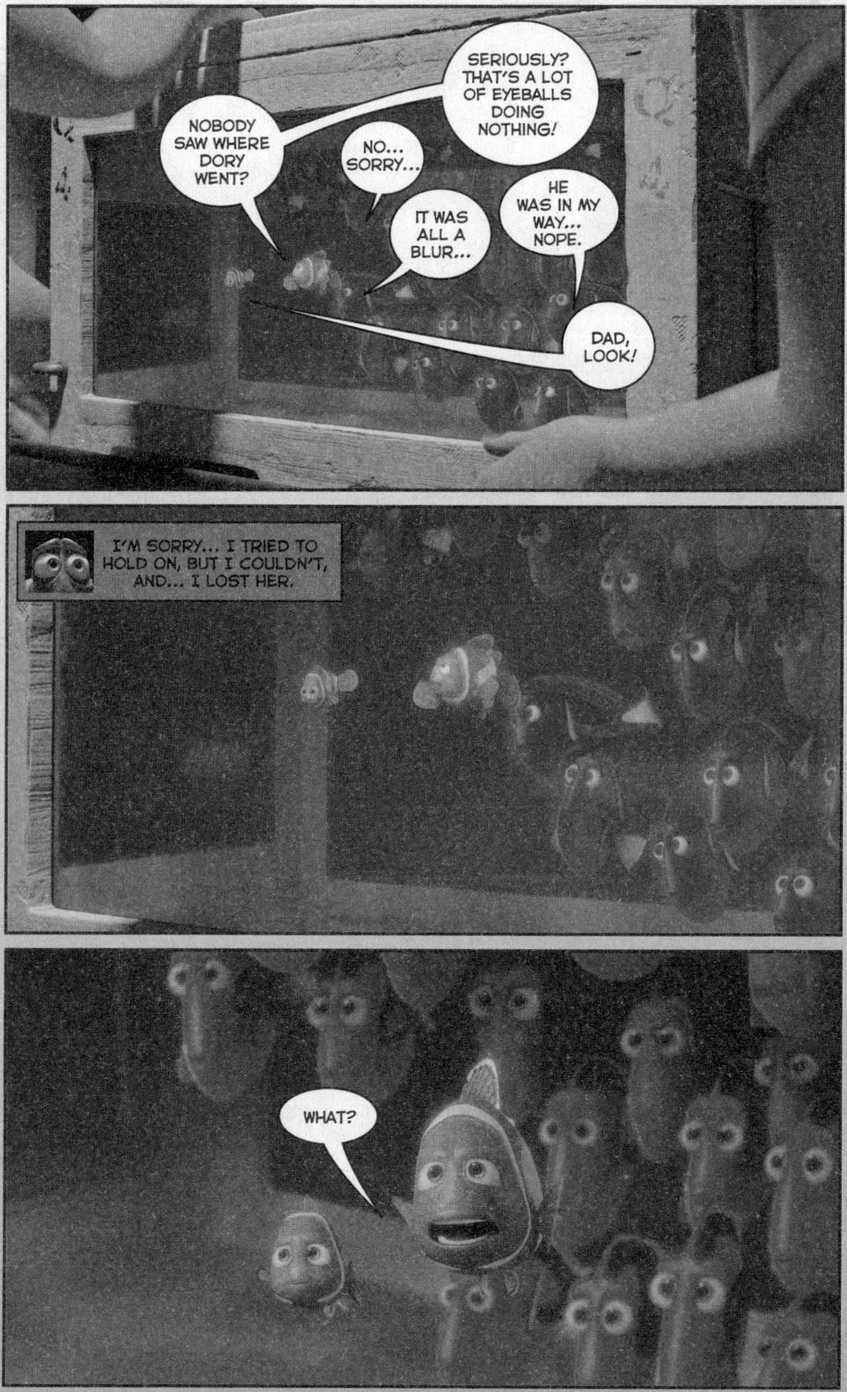
NOBODY SAW WHERE DORY WENT?
SERIOUSLY? THAT'S A LOT OF EYEBALLS DOING NOTHING!
NO... SORRY...
IT WAS ALL A BLUR...
HE WAS IN MY WAY... NOPE.
DAD, LOOK!
I'M SORRY... I TRIED TO HOLD ON, BUT I COULDN'T, AND... I LOST HER.
WHAT?

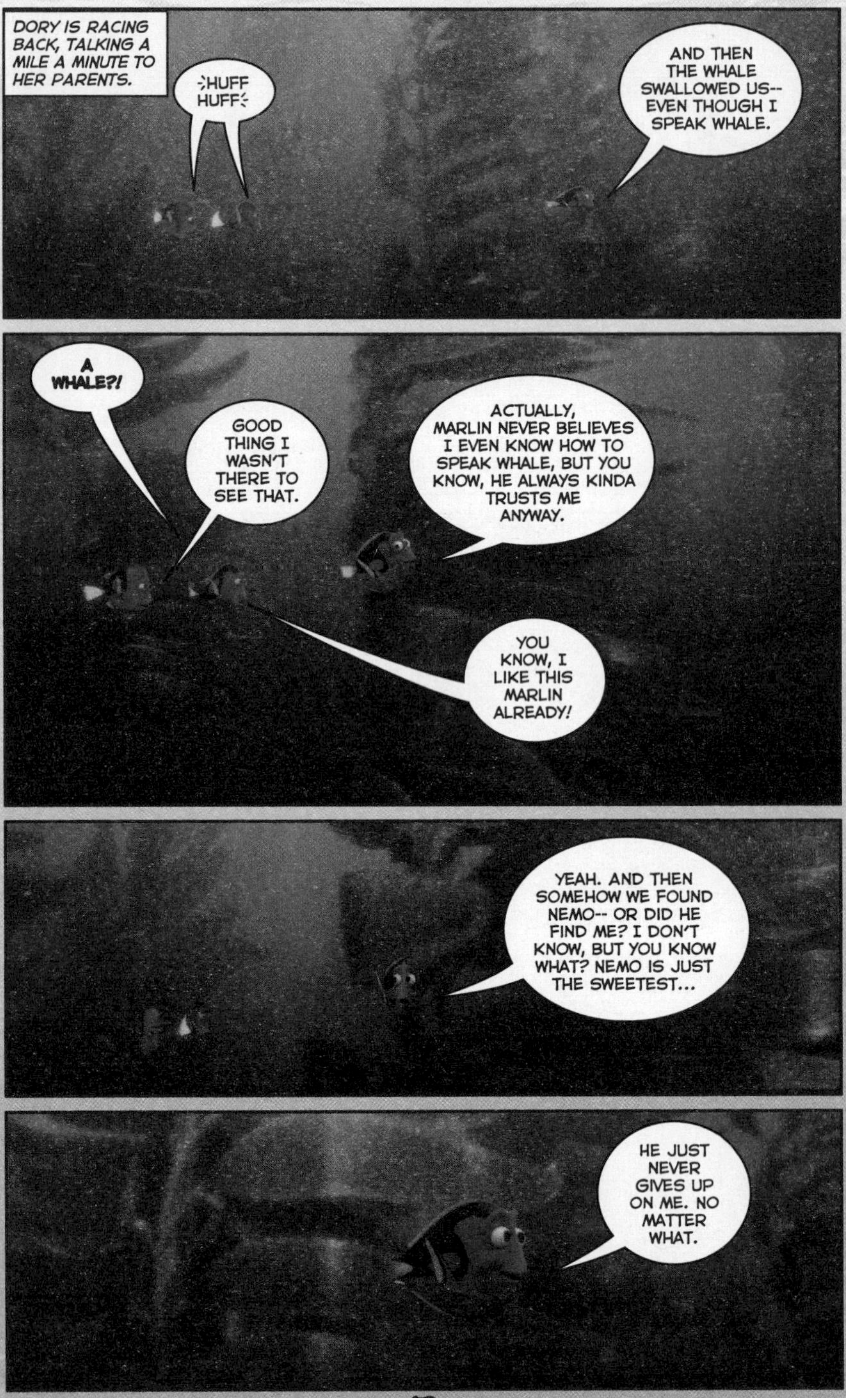
DORY IS RACING BACK, TALKING A MILE A MINUTE TO HER PARENTS.
HUFF HUFF
AND THEN THE WHALE SWALLOWED US-- EVEN THOUGH I SPEAK WHALE.
A WHALE?!
GOOD THING I WASN'T THERE TO SEE THAT.
ACTUALLY, MARLIN NEVER BELIEVES I EVEN KNOW HOW TO SPEAK WHALE, BUT YOU KNOW, HE ALWAYS KINDA TRUSTS ME ANYWAY.
YOU KNOW, I LIKE THIS MARLIN ALREADY!
YEAH. AND THEN SOMEHOW WE FOUND NEMO-- OR DID HE FIND ME? I DON'T KNOW, BUT YOU KNOW WHAT? NEMO IS JUST THE SWEETEST...
HE JUST NEVER GIVES UP ON ME. NO MATTER WHAT.

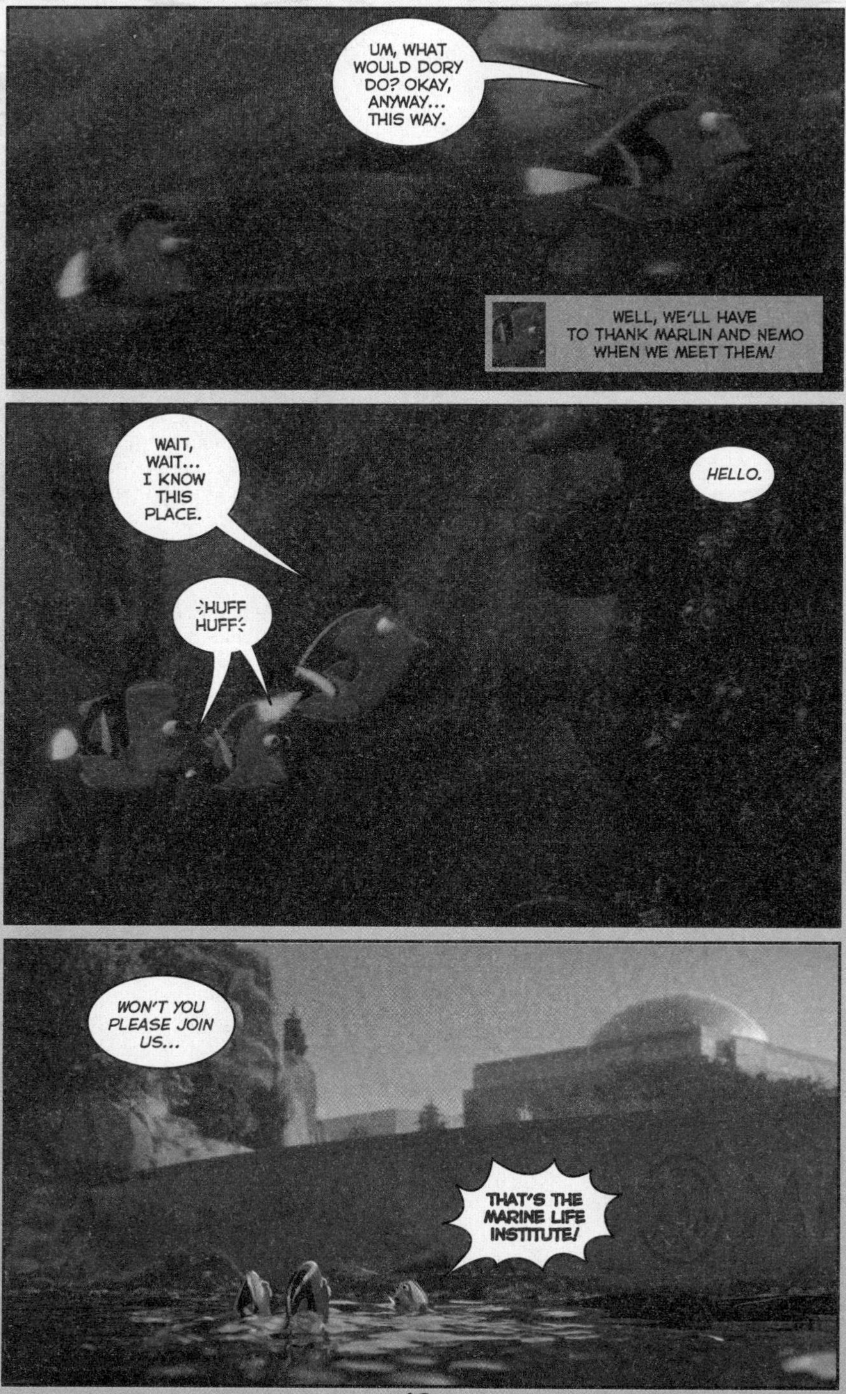
UM, WHAT WOULD DORY DO? OKAY, ANYWAY... THIS WAY.
WELL, WE'LL HAVE TO THANK MARLIN AND NEMO WHEN WE MEET THEM!
WAIT, WAIT... I KNOW THIS PLACE.
HELLO.
HUFF HUFF
WON'T YOU PLEASE JOIN US...
THAT'S THE MARINE LIFE INSTITUTE!

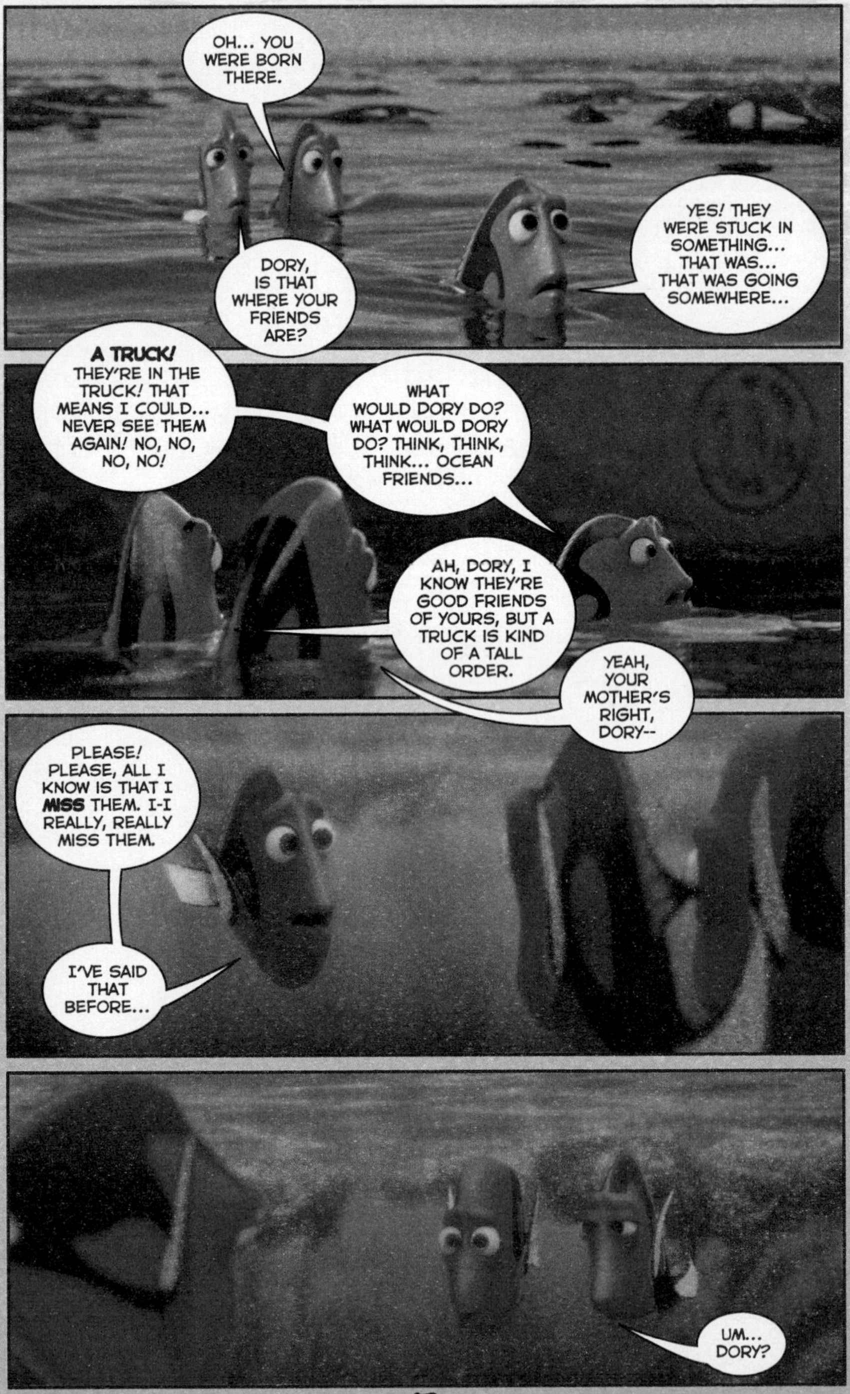
OH... YOU WERE BORN THERE.
DORY, IS THAT WHERE YOUR FRIENDS ARE?
YES! THEY WERE STUCK IN SOMETHING... THAT WAS... THAT WAS GOING SOMEWHERE...
A TRUCK! THEY'RE IN THE TRUCK! THAT MEANS I COULD... NEVER SEE THEM AGAIN! NO, NO, NO, NO!
WHAT WOULD DORY DO? WHAT WOULD DORY DO? THINK, THINK, THINK... OCEAN FRIENDS...
AH, DORY, I KNOW THEY'RE GOOD FRIENDS OF YOURS, BUT A TRUCK IS KIND OF A TALL ORDER.
YEAH, YOUR MOTHER'S RIGHT, DORY--
PLEASE! PLEASE, ALL I KNOW IS THAT I MISS THEM. I-I REALLY, REALLY MISS THEM.
I'VE SAID THAT BEFORE...
UM... DORY?

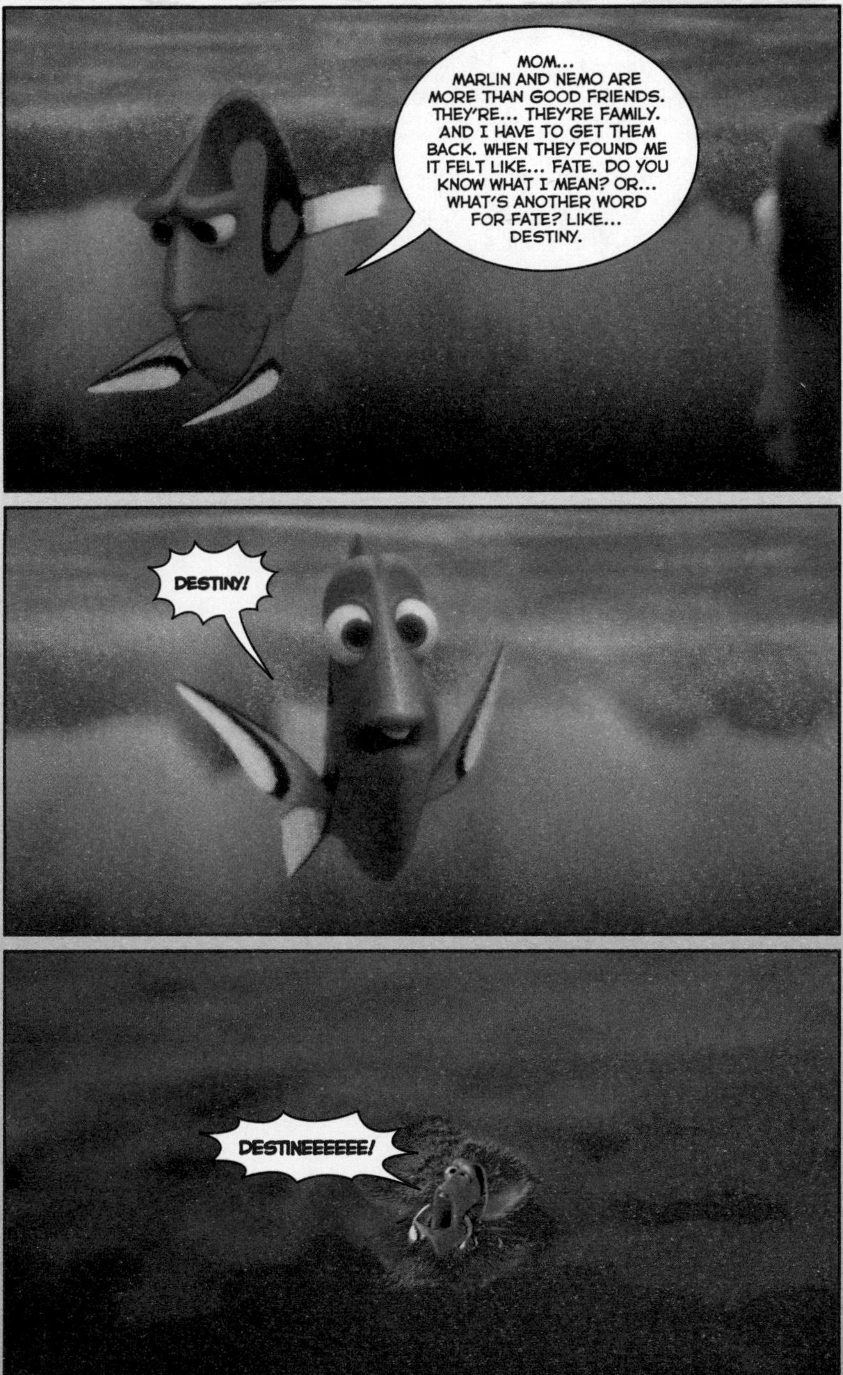
MOM... MARLIN AND NEMO ARE MORE THAN GOOD FRIENDS. THEY'RE... THEY'RE FAMILY. AND I HAVE TO GET THEM BACK. WHEN THEY FOUND ME IT FELT LIKE... FATE. DO YOU KNOW WHAT I MEAN? OR... WHAT'S ANOTHER WORD FOR FATE? LIKE... DESTINY.
DESTINY!
DESTINEEEEEE!

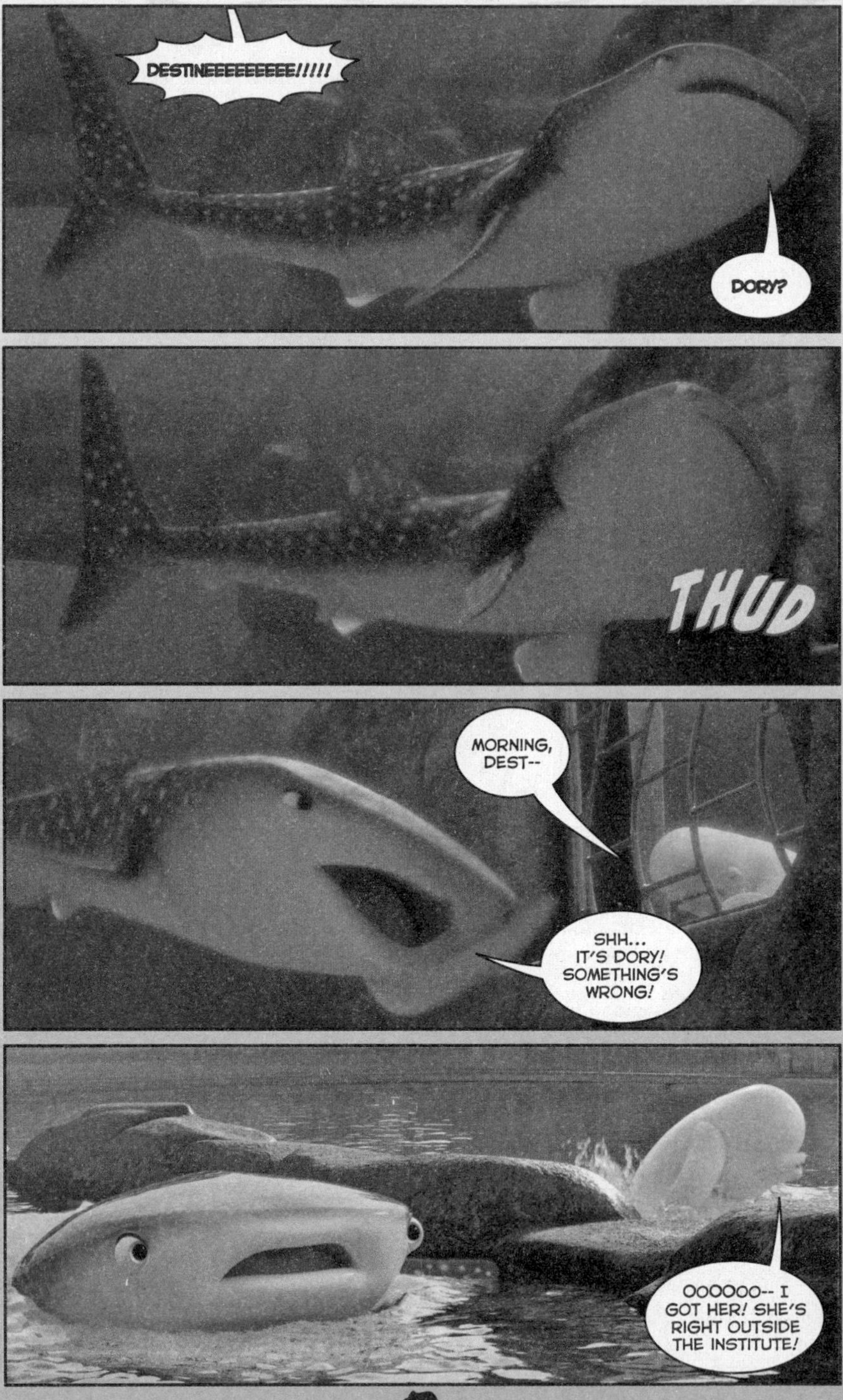
DESTINEEEEEEEEEE!!!!!
DORY?
THUD
MORNING, DEST--
SHH... IT'S DORY! SOMETHING'S WRONG!
OOOOOO-- I GOT HER! SHE'S RIGHT OUTSIDE THE INSTITUTE!

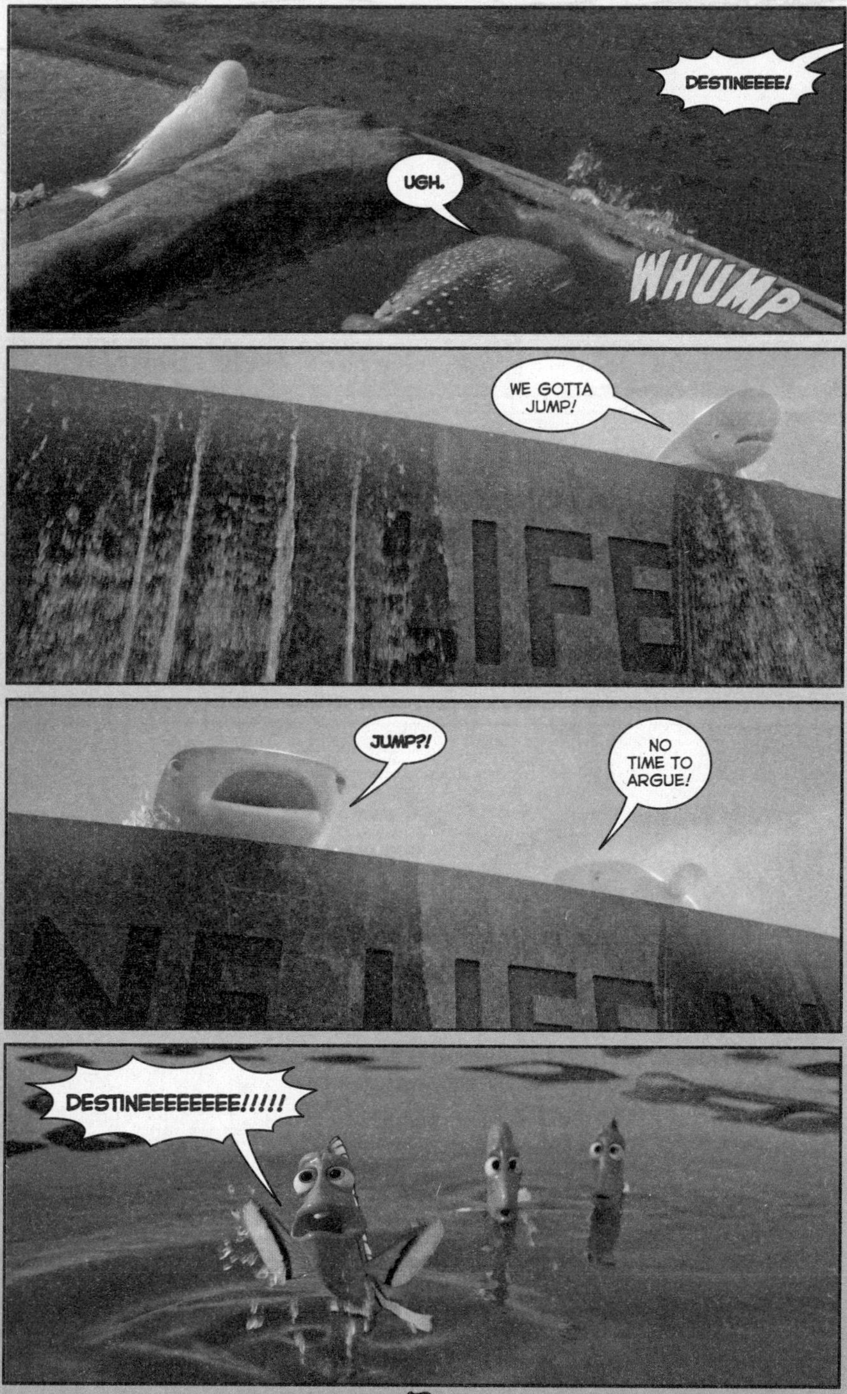
DESTINEEEEE!
UGH.
WHUMP
WE GOTTA JUMP!
JUMP?!
NO TIME TO ARGUE!
DESTINEEEEEEEE!!!!!!

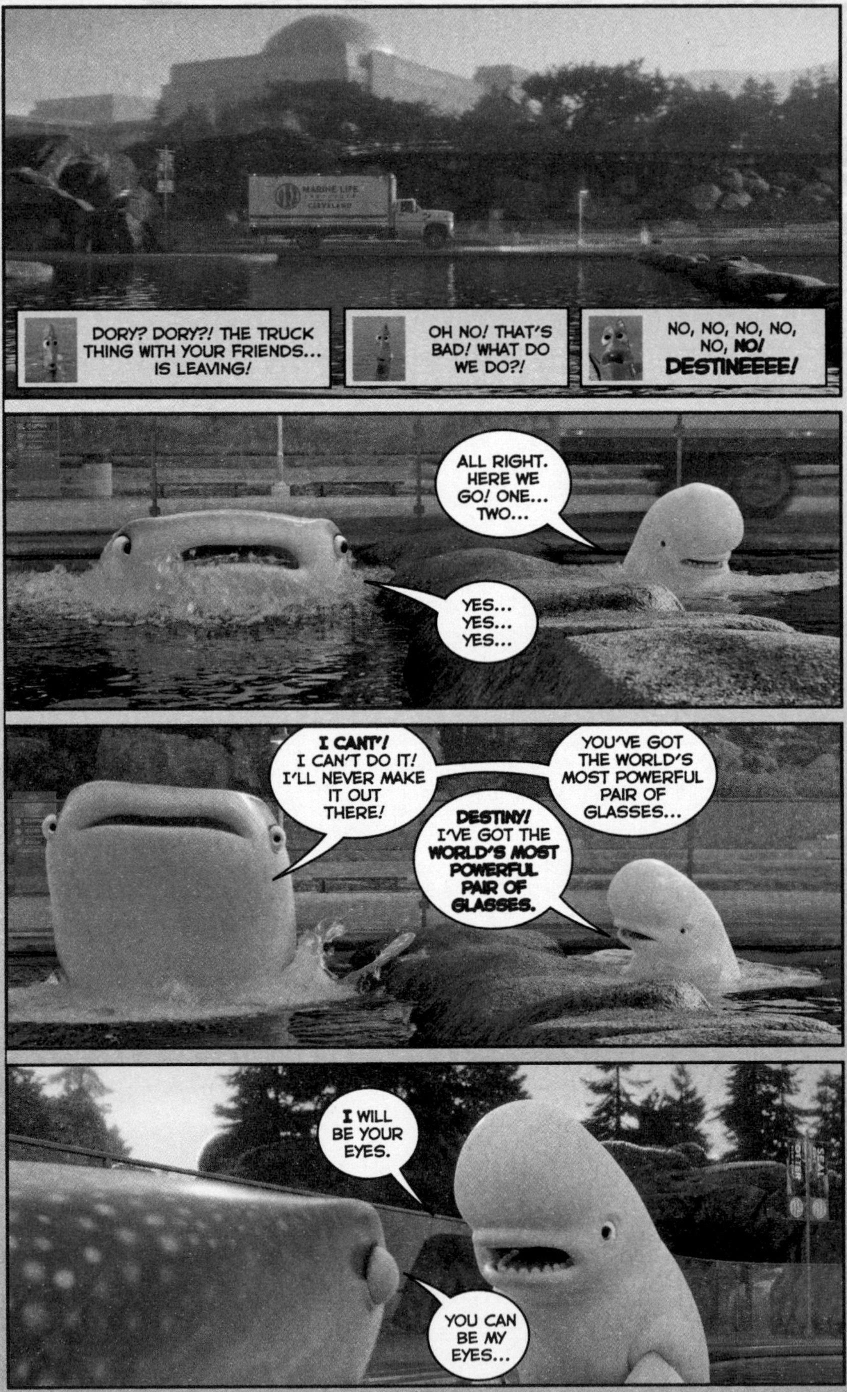
DORY? DORY?! THE TRUCK THING WITH YOUR FRIENDS... IS LEAVING!
OH NO! THAT'S BAD! WHAT DO WE DO?!
NO, NO, NO, NO, NO, NO! DESTINEEEE!
ALL RIGHT. HERE WE GO! ONE... TWO...
YES... YES... YES...
I CAN'T! I CAN'T DO IT! I'LL NEVER MAKE IT OUT THERE!
YOU'VE GOT THE WORLD'S MOST POWERFUL PAIR OF GLASSES...
DESTINY! I'VE GOT THE WORLD'S MOST POWERFUL PAIR OF GLASSES.
I WILL BE YOUR EYES.
YOU CAN BE MY EYES...

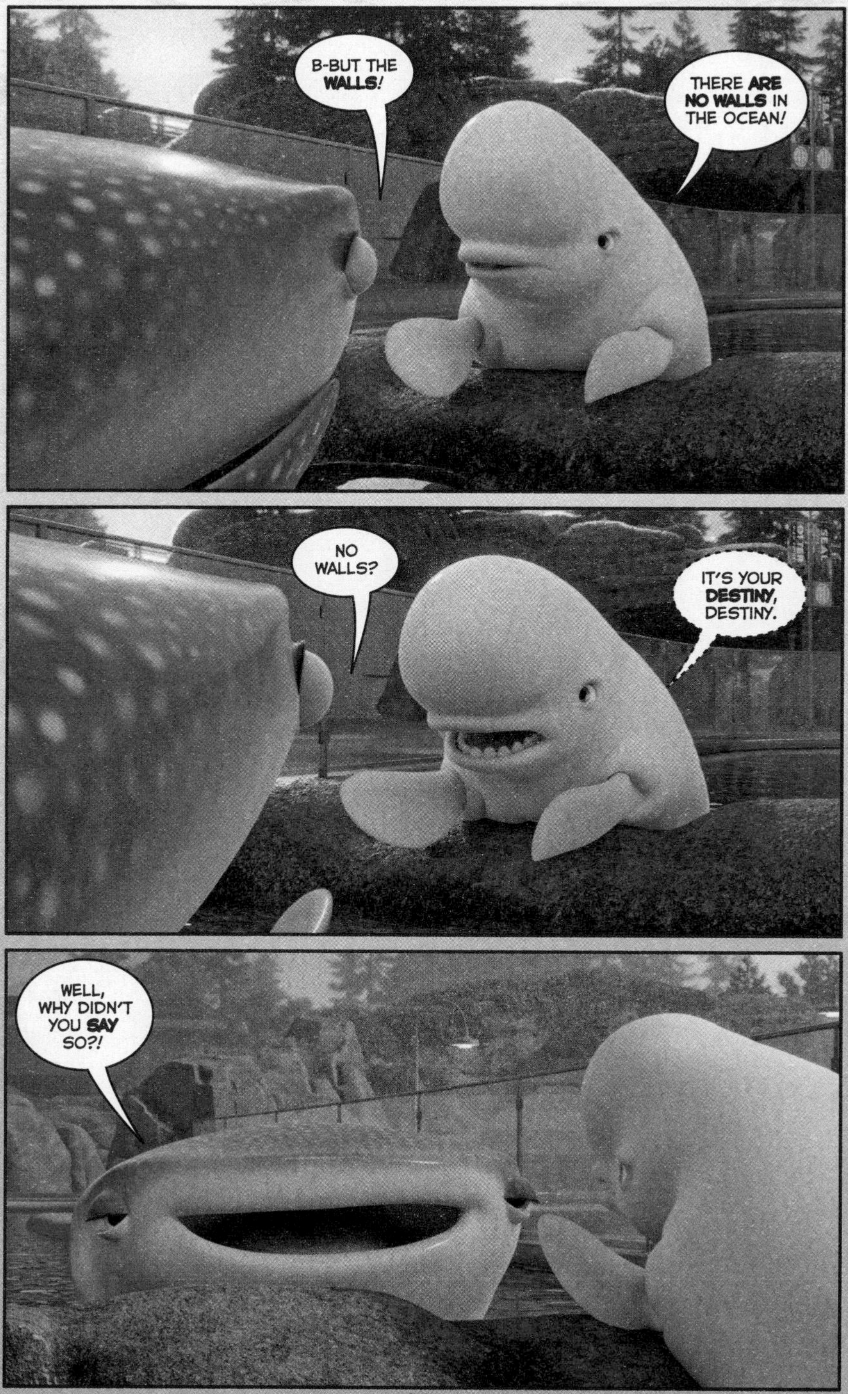
B-BUT THE WALLS!
THERE ARE NO WALLS IN THE OCEAN!
NO WALLS?
IT'S YOUR DESTINY, DESTINY.
WELL, WHY DIDN'T YOU SAY SO?!

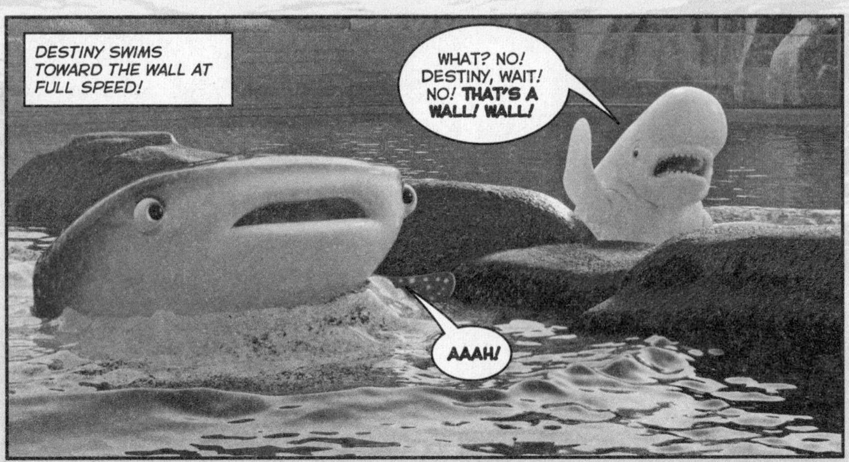
DESTINY SWIMS TOWARD THE WALL AT FULL SPEED!
WHAT? NO! DESTINY, WAIT! NO! THAT'S A WALL! WALL!
AAAH!

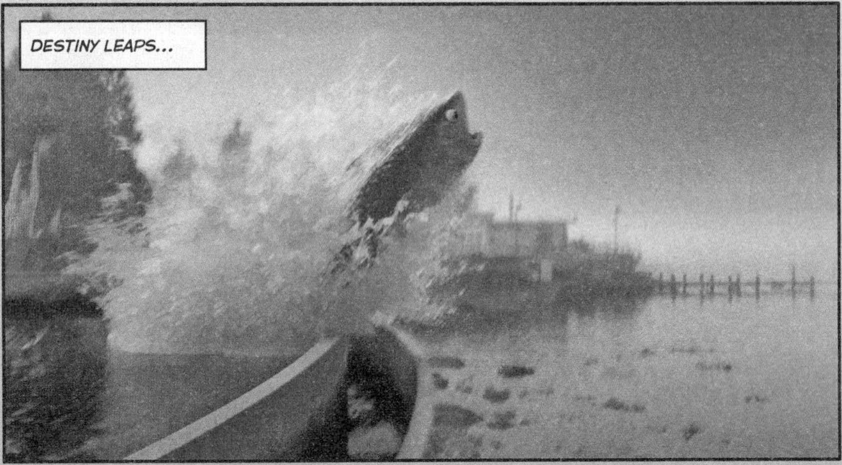
DESTINY LEAPS...

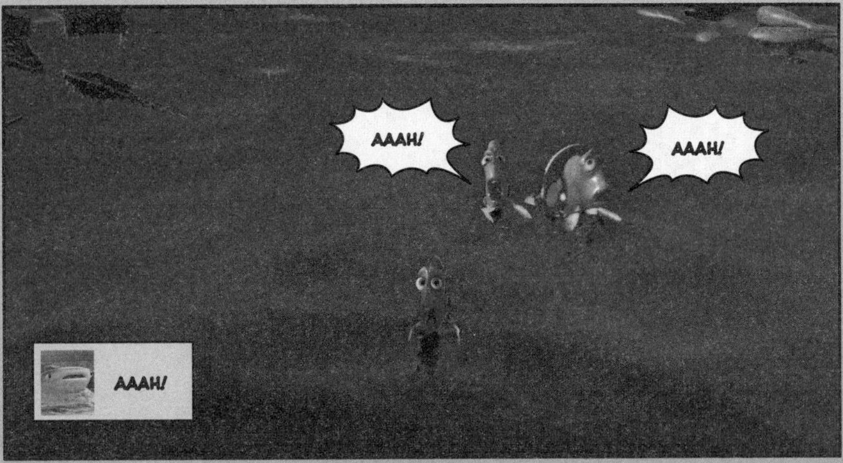
AAAH!
AAAH!
AAAH!

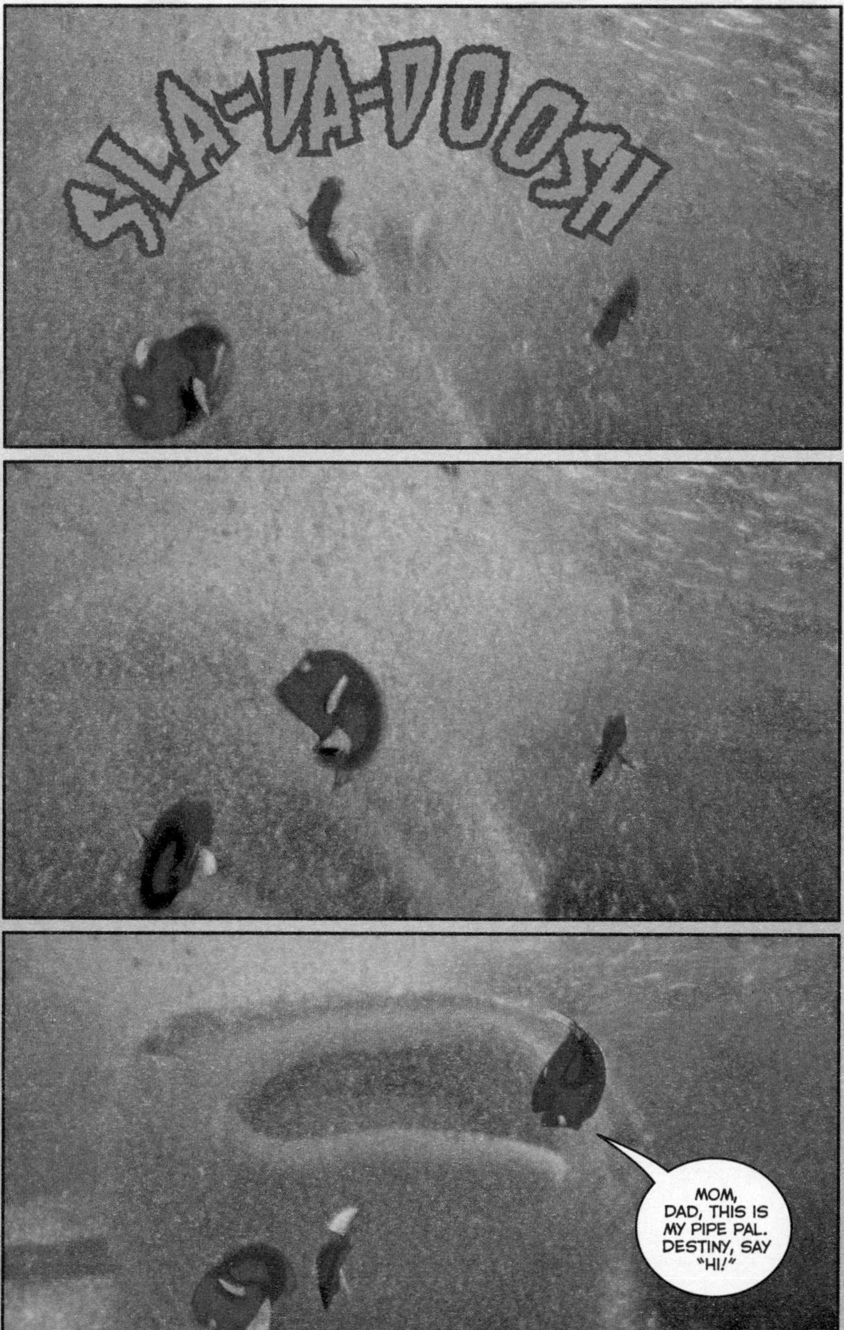
SLA-DA-DOOSH
MOM, DAD, THIS IS MY PIPE PAL. DESTINY, SAY "HI!"

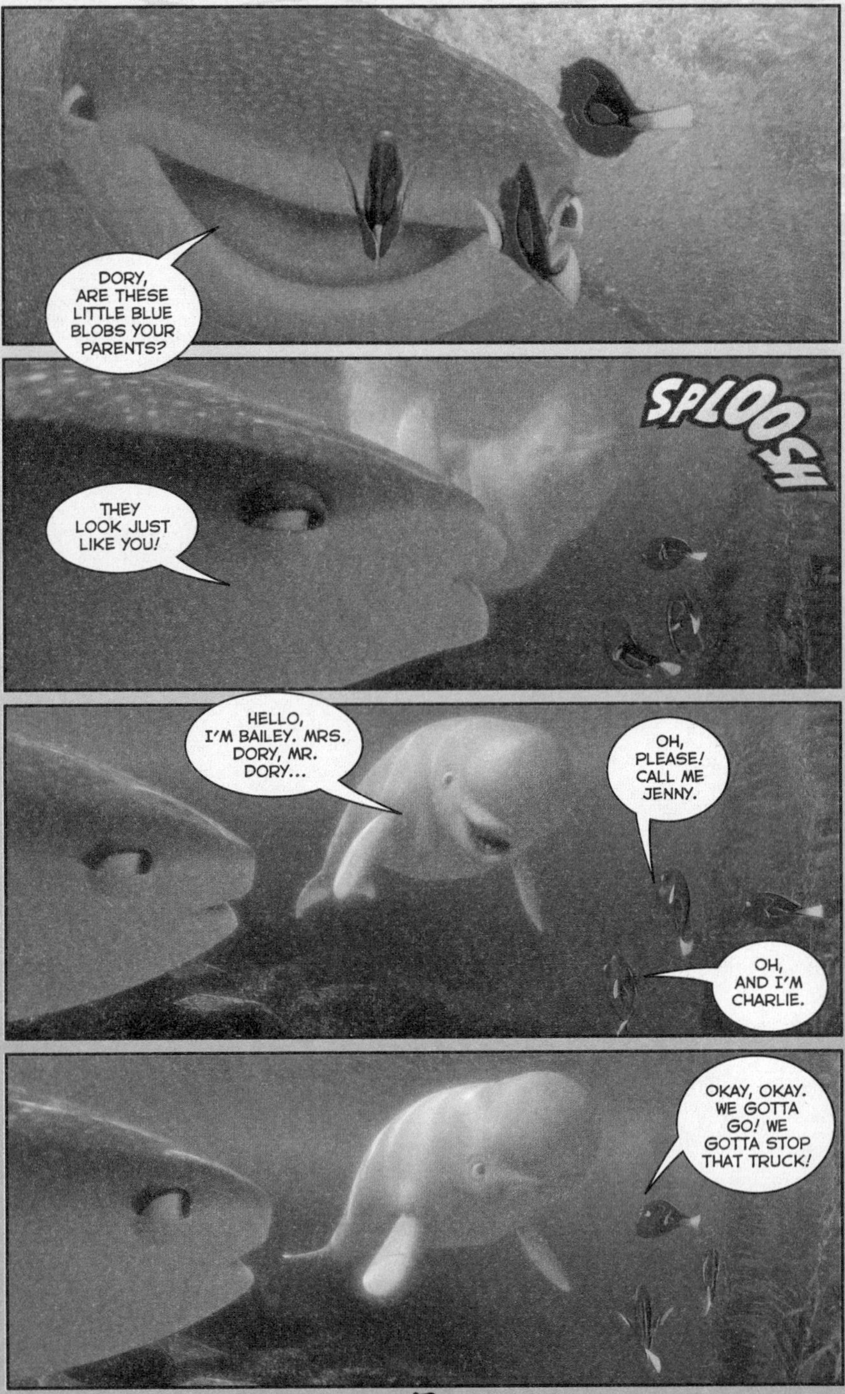
DORY, ARE THESE LITTLE BLUE BLOBS YOUR PARENTS?
SPLOOSH
THEY LOOK JUST LIKE YOU!
HELLO, I'M BAILEY. MRS. DORY, MR. DORY...
OH, PLEASE! CALL ME JENNY.
OH, AND I'M CHARLIE.
OKAY, OKAY. WE GOTTA GO! WE GOTTA STOP THAT TRUCK!

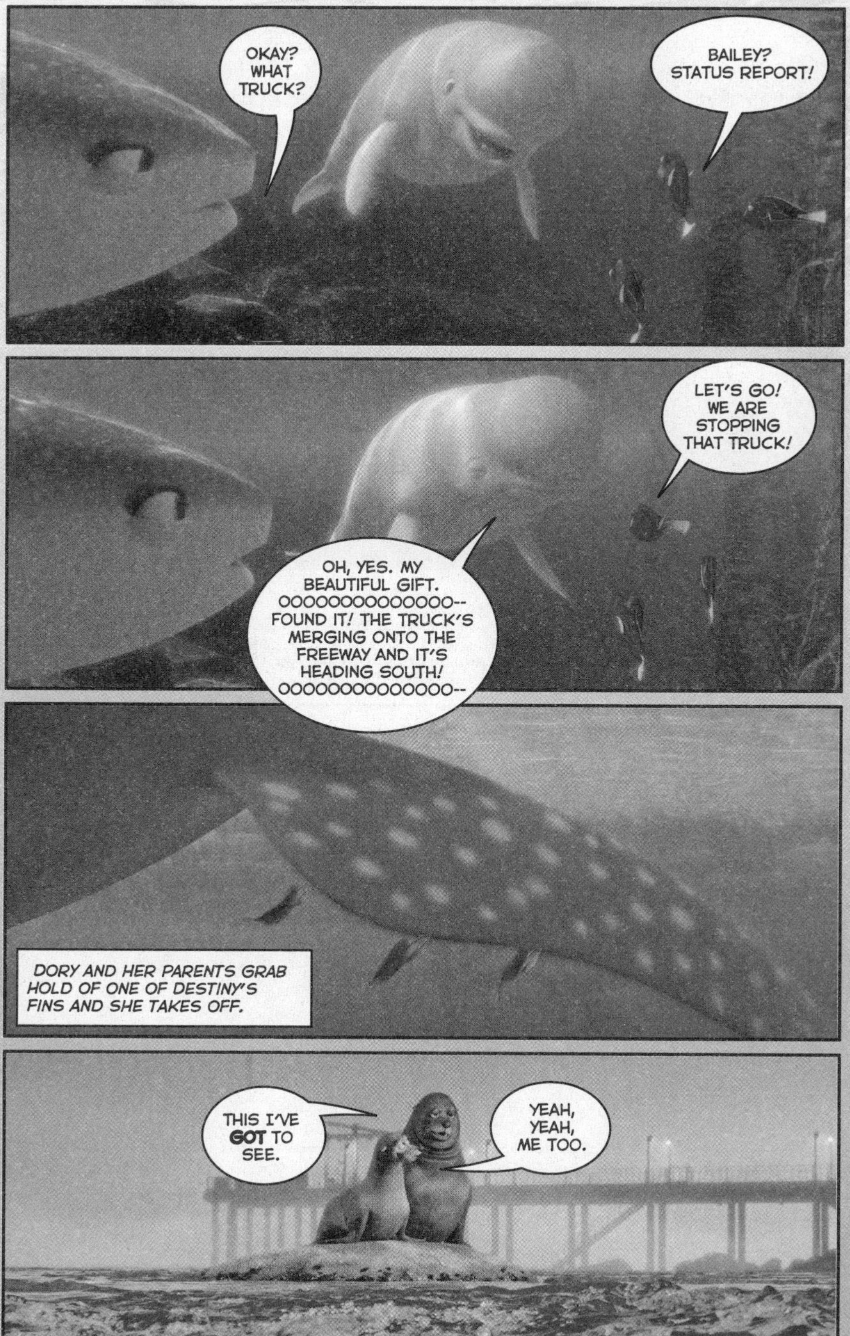
OKAY? WHAT TRUCK?
BAILEY? STATUS REPORT!
LET'S GO! WE ARE STOPPING THAT TRUCK!
OH, YES. MY BEAUTIFUL GIFT. OOOOOOOOOOOOOO-- FOUND IT! THE TRUCK'S MERGING ONTO THE FREEWAY AND IT'S HEADING SOUTH! OOOOOOOOOOOOOOO--
DORY AND HER PARENTS GRAB HOLD OF ONE OF DESTINY'S FINS AND SHE TAKES OFF.
THIS I'VE **GOT** TO SEE.
YEAH, YEAH, ME TOO.

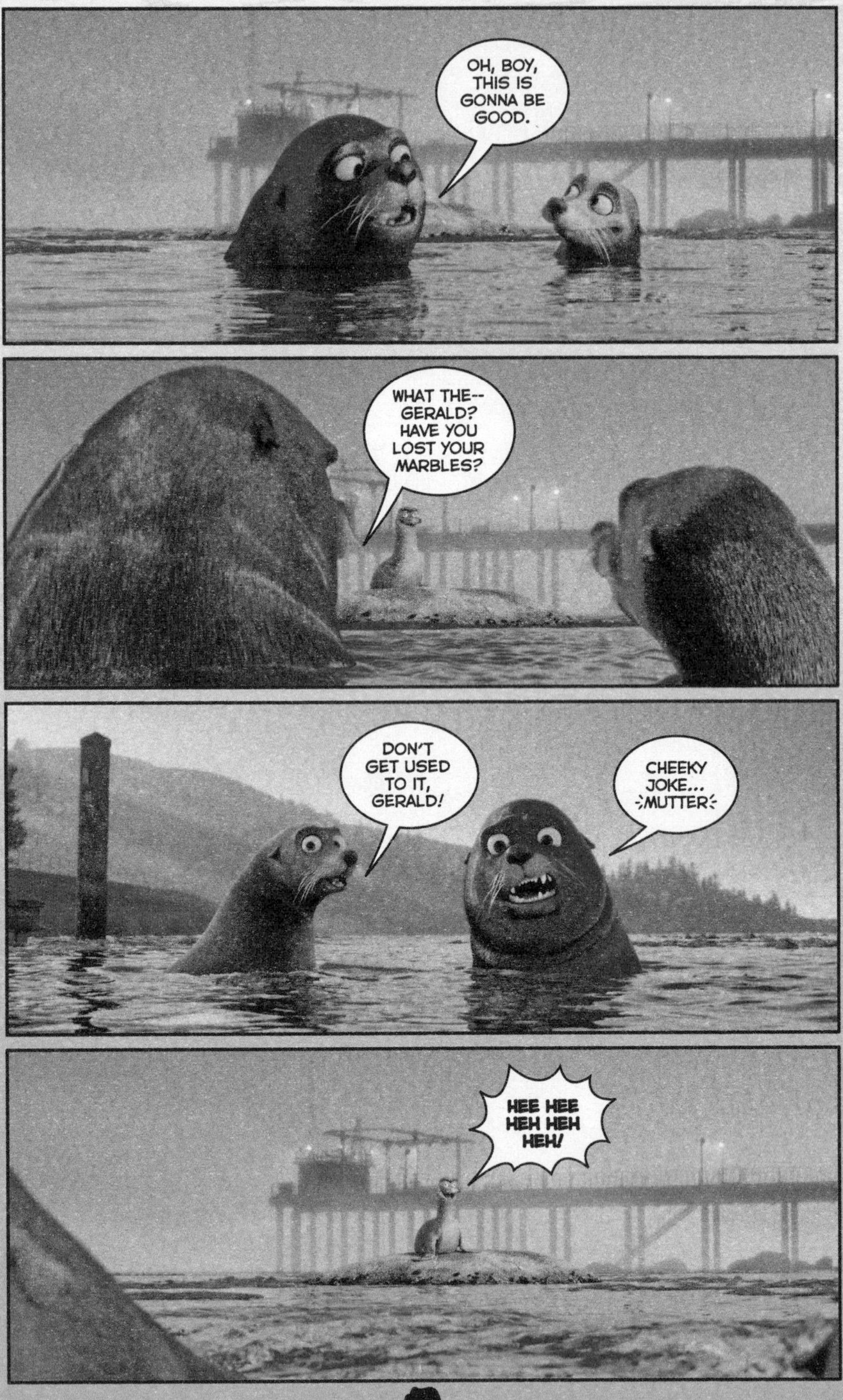
OH, BOY, THIS IS GONNA BE GOOD.
WHAT THE-- GERALD? HAVE YOU LOST YOUR MARBLES?
DON'T GET USED TO IT, GERALD!
CHEEKY JOKE... MUTTER
HEE HEE HEH HEH HEH!

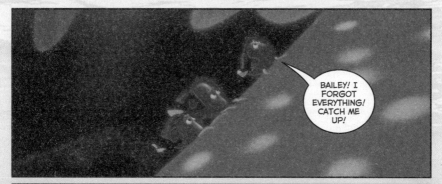

BAILEY! I FORGOT EVERYTHING! CATCH ME UP!

YES, MA'AM! OOOOOOOOOOOOooooooo....

YOUR FRIENDS ARE STILL ON THE TRUCK! OOOOoo-- THEY'RE HEADED NORTH TOWARDS THE BRIDGE! OOOOoo--

OH, LOOK! THERE'S A BUNCH OF CUTE OTTERS OVER THERE! I WANT ONE!

OW!

AGH!

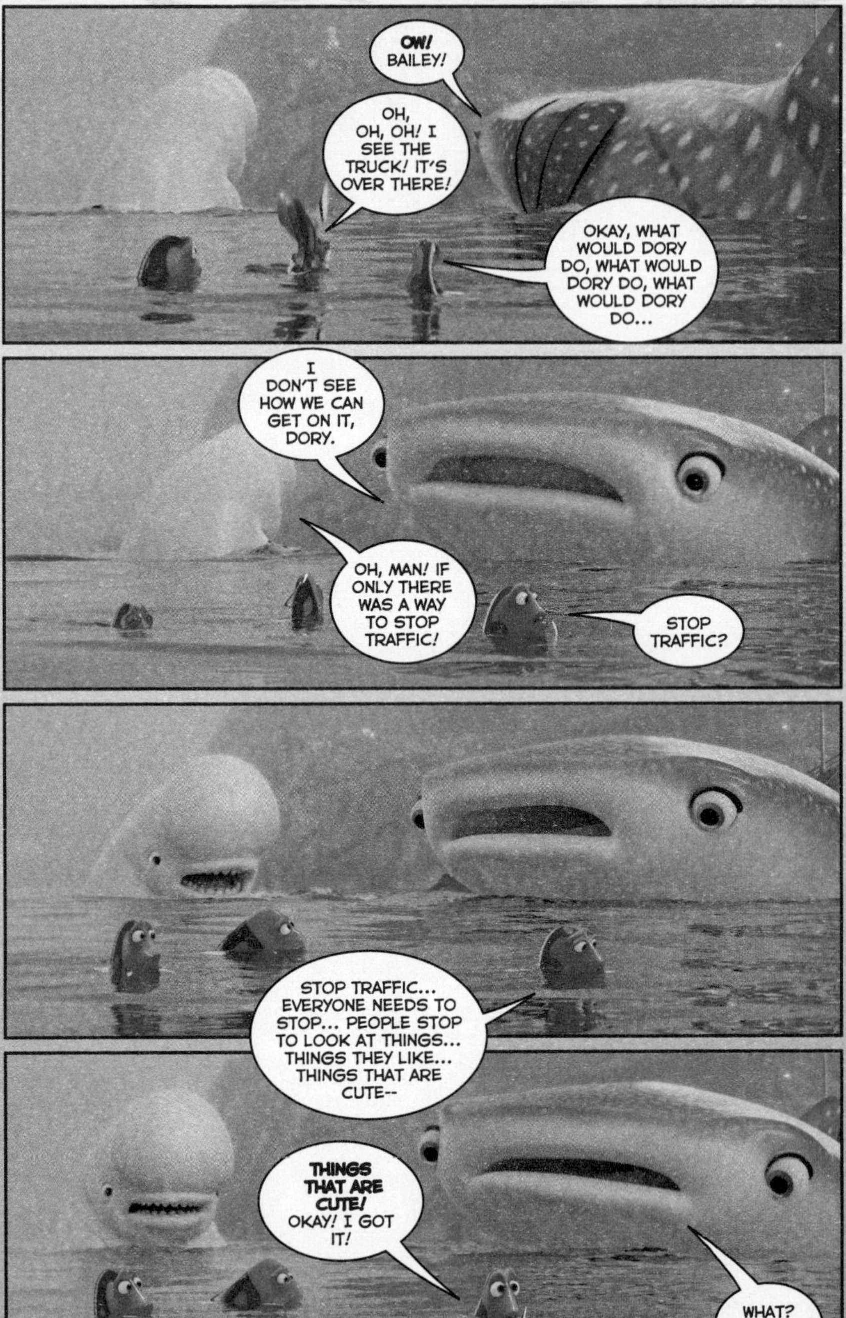
OW! BAILEY!
OH, OH, OH! I SEE THE TRUCK! IT'S OVER THERE!
OKAY, WHAT WOULD DORY DO, WHAT WOULD DORY DO, WHAT WOULD DORY DO...
I DON'T SEE HOW WE CAN GET ON IT, DORY.
OH, MAN! IF ONLY THERE WAS A WAY TO STOP TRAFFIC!
STOP TRAFFIC?
STOP TRAFFIC... EVERYONE NEEDS TO STOP... PEOPLE STOP TO LOOK AT THINGS... THINGS THEY LIKE... THINGS THAT ARE CUTE--
THINGS THAT ARE CUTE! OKAY! I GOT IT!
WHAT? WHAT IS IT?

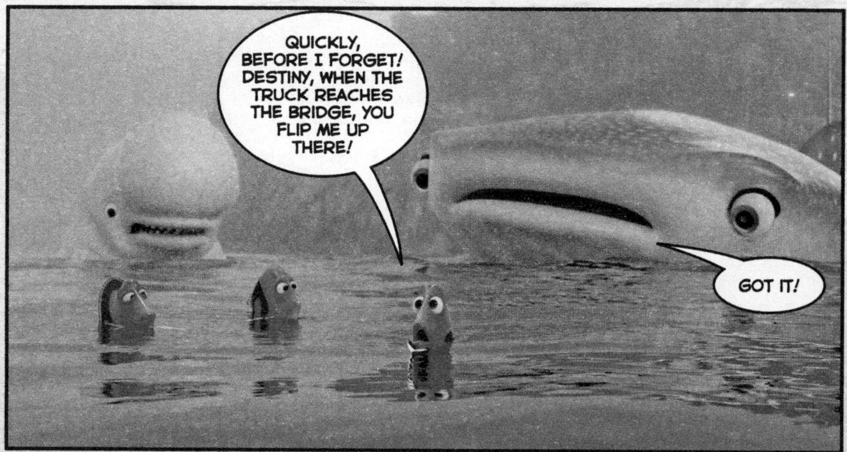
QUICKLY, BEFORE I FORGET! DESTINY, WHEN THE TRUCK REACHES THE BRIDGE, YOU FLIP ME UP THERE!
GOT IT!

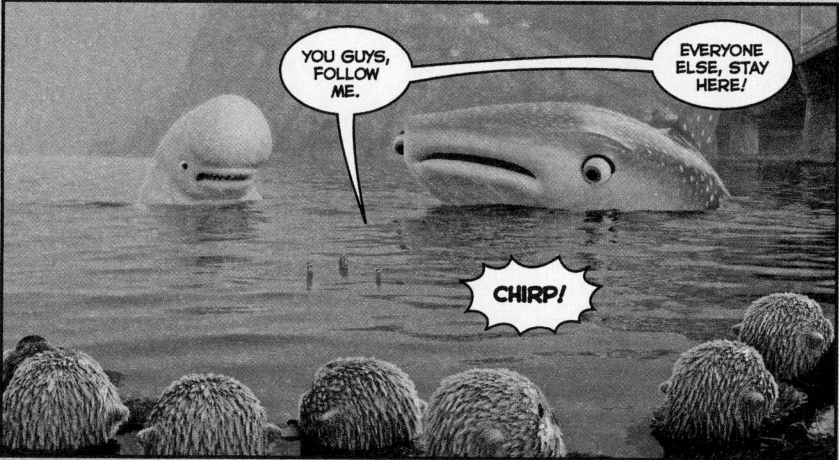
YOU GUYS, FOLLOW ME.
EVERYONE ELSE, STAY HERE!
CHIRP!

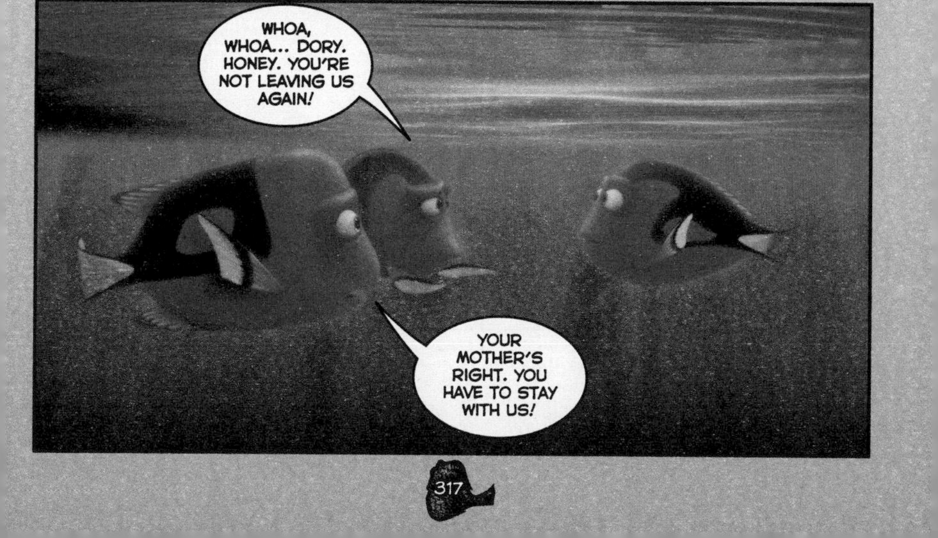
WHOA, WHOA... DORY. HONEY. YOU'RE NOT LEAVING US AGAIN!
YOUR MOTHER'S RIGHT. YOU HAVE TO STAY WITH US!

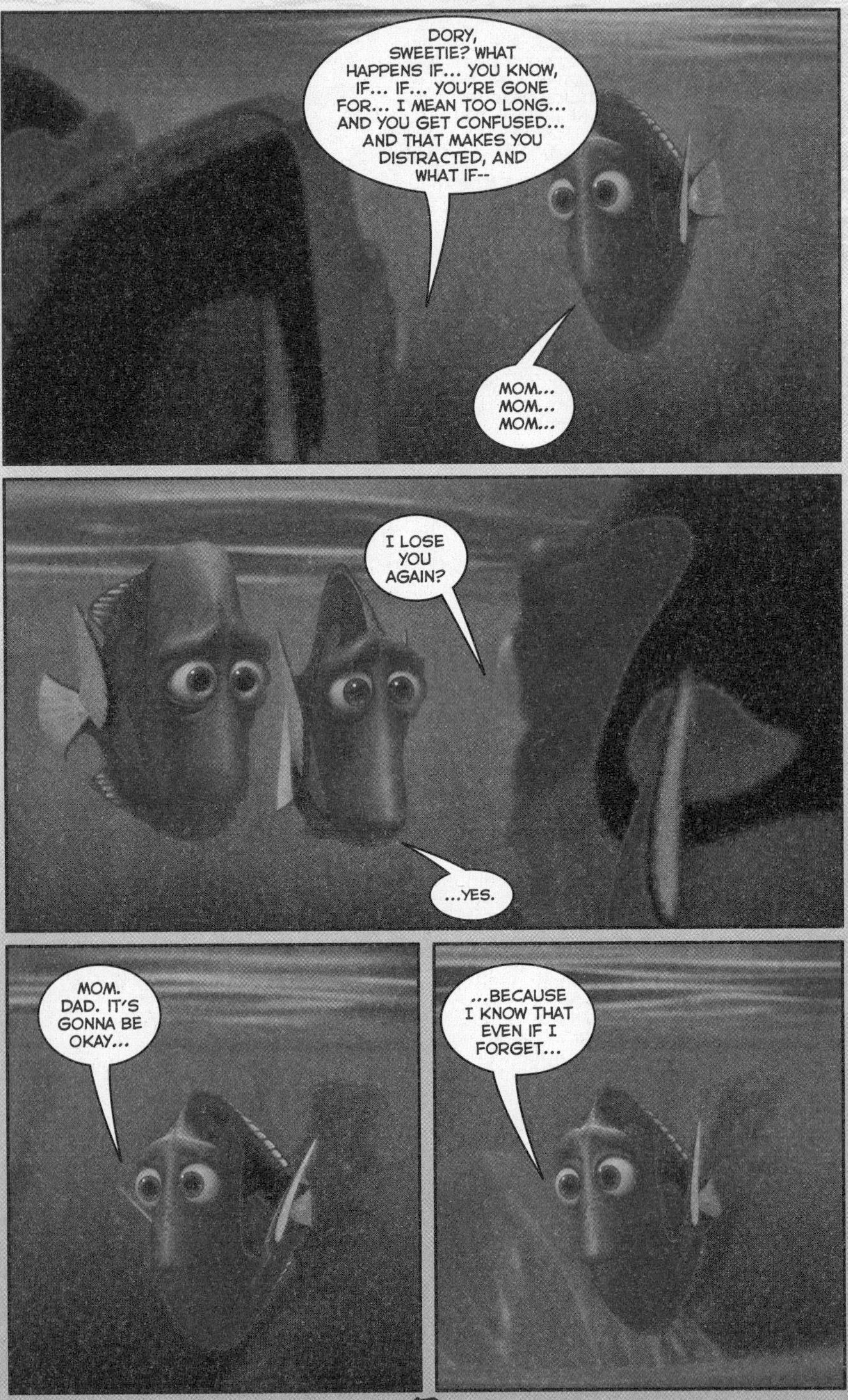
DORY, SWEETIE? WHAT HAPPENS IF... YOU KNOW, IF... IF... YOU'RE GONE FOR... I MEAN TOO LONG... AND YOU GET CONFUSED... AND THAT MAKES YOU DISTRACTED, AND WHAT IF--
MOM... MOM... MOM...
I LOSE YOU AGAIN?
...YES.
MOM. DAD. IT'S GONNA BE OKAY...
...BECAUSE I KNOW THAT EVEN IF I FORGET...

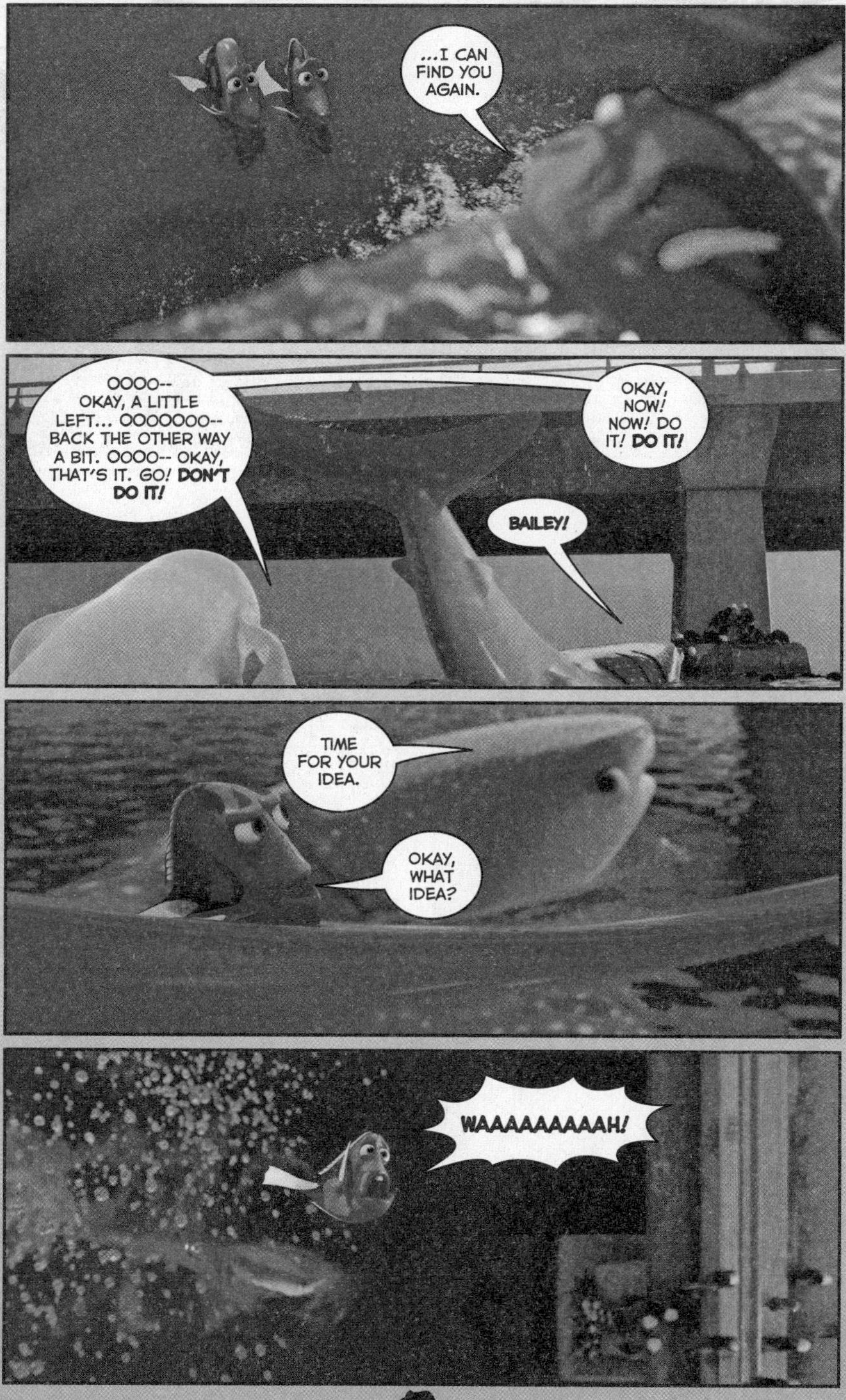
...I CAN FIND YOU AGAIN.
OOOO-- OKAY, A LITTLE LEFT... OOOOOOO-- BACK THE OTHER WAY A BIT. OOOO-- OKAY, THAT'S IT. GO! DON'T DO IT!
OKAY, NOW! NOW! DO IT! DO IT!
BAILEY!
TIME FOR YOUR IDEA.
OKAY, WHAT IDEA?
WAAAAAAAAAH!

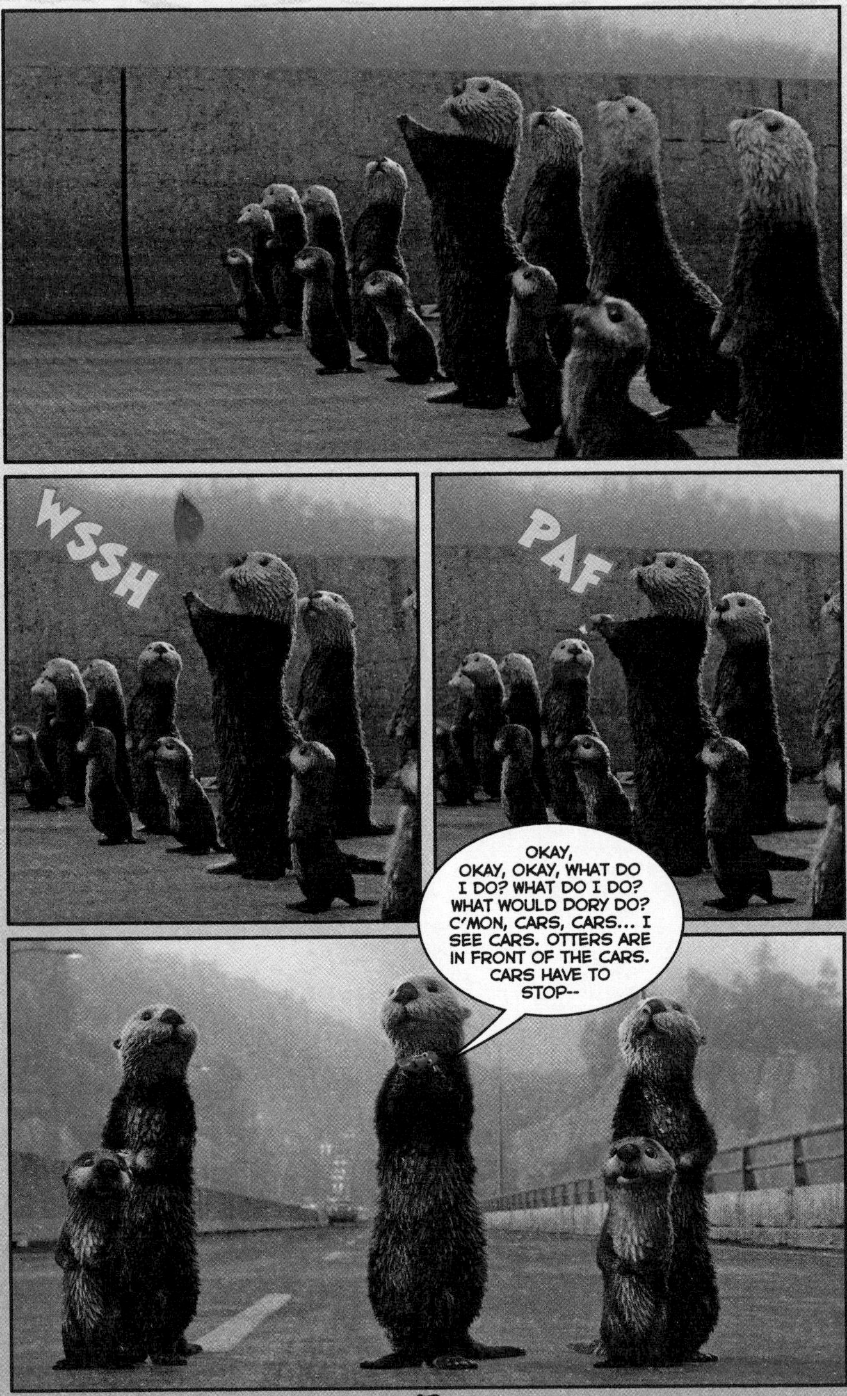
WSSH
PAF
OKAY, OKAY, OKAY, WHAT DO I DO? WHAT DO I DO? WHAT WOULD DORY DO? C'MON, CARS, CARS... I SEE CARS. OTTERS ARE IN FRONT OF THE CARS. CARS HAVE TO STOP--

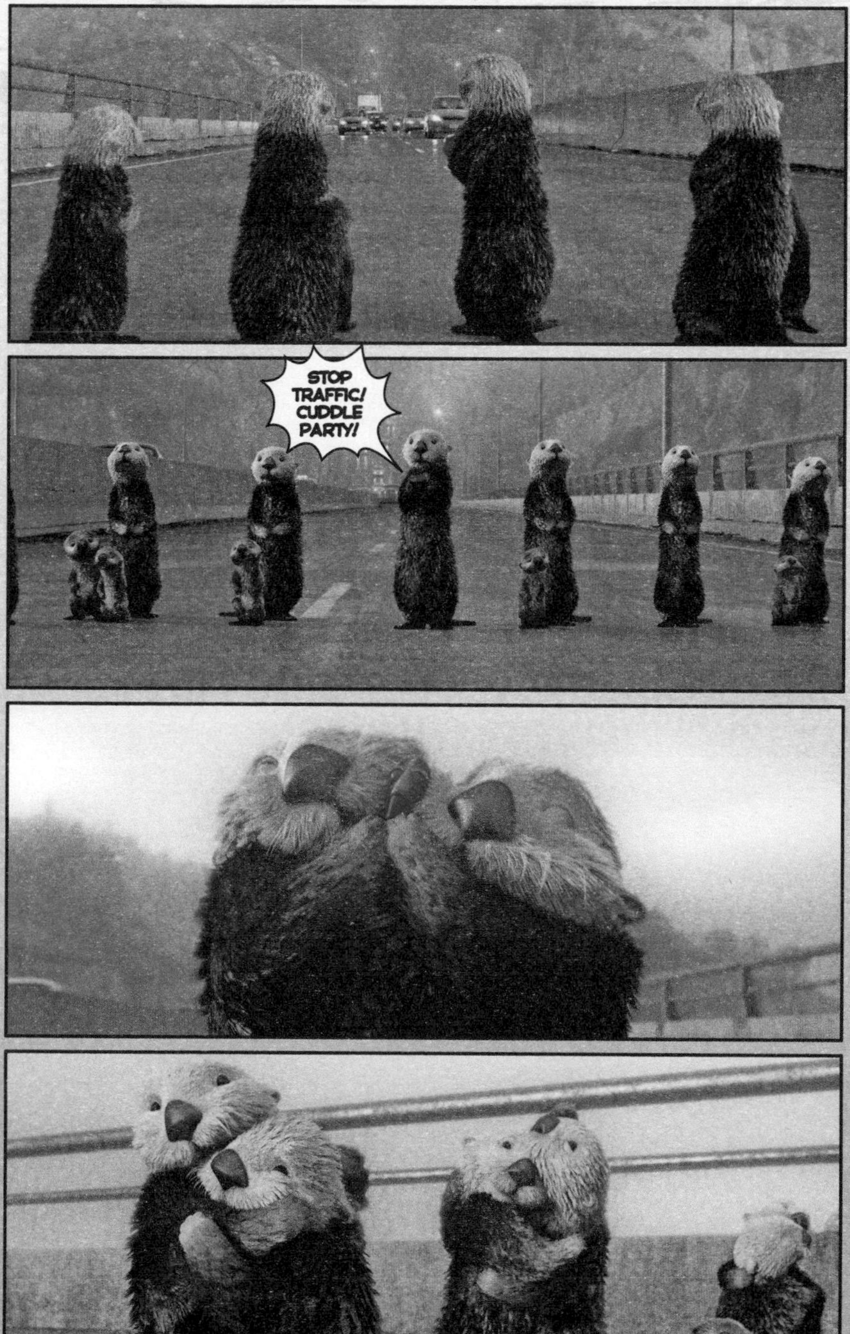
STOP TRAFFIC! CUDDLE PARTY!

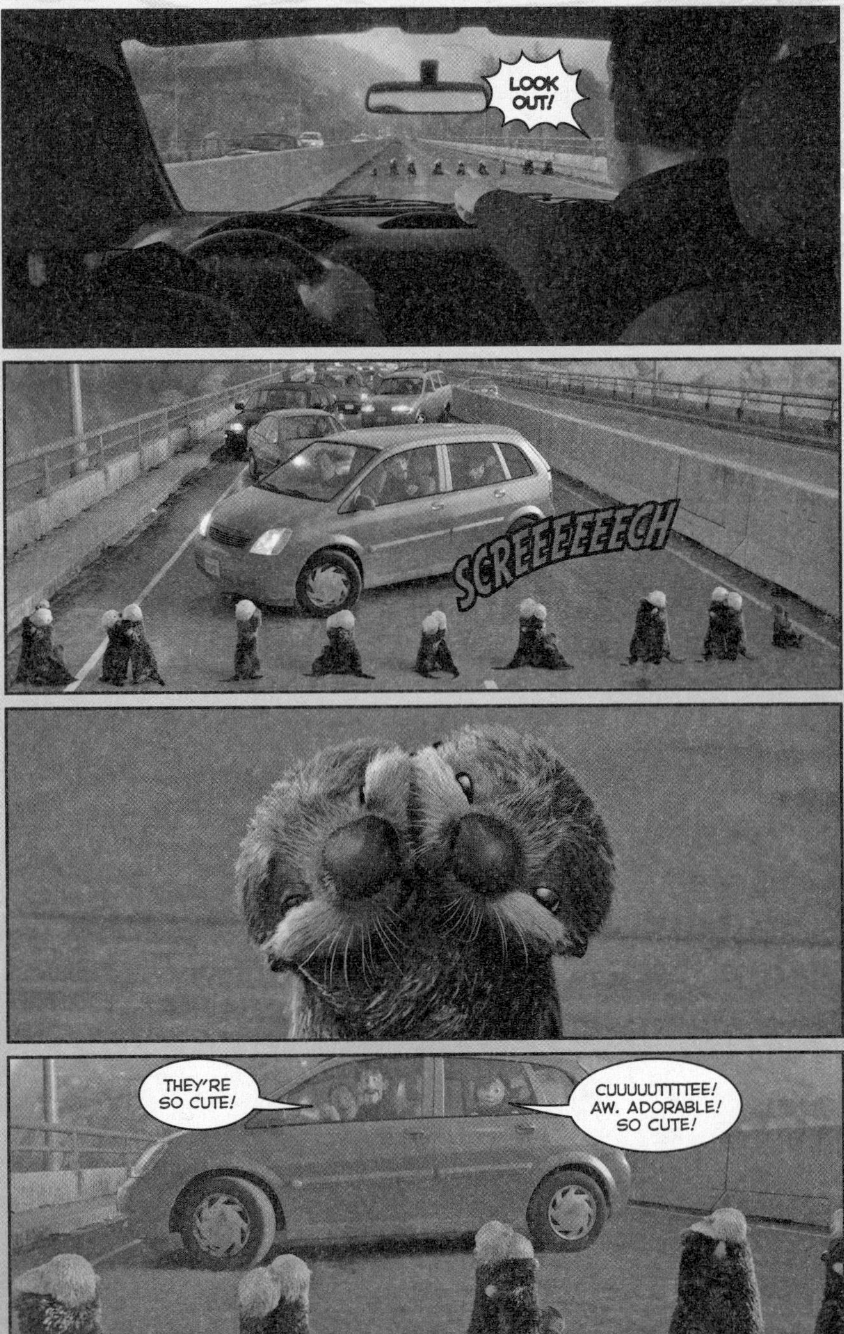
LOOK OUT!
SCREEEEEECH
THEY'RE SO CUTE!
CUUUUUTTTTEE! AW. ADORABLE! SO CUTE!

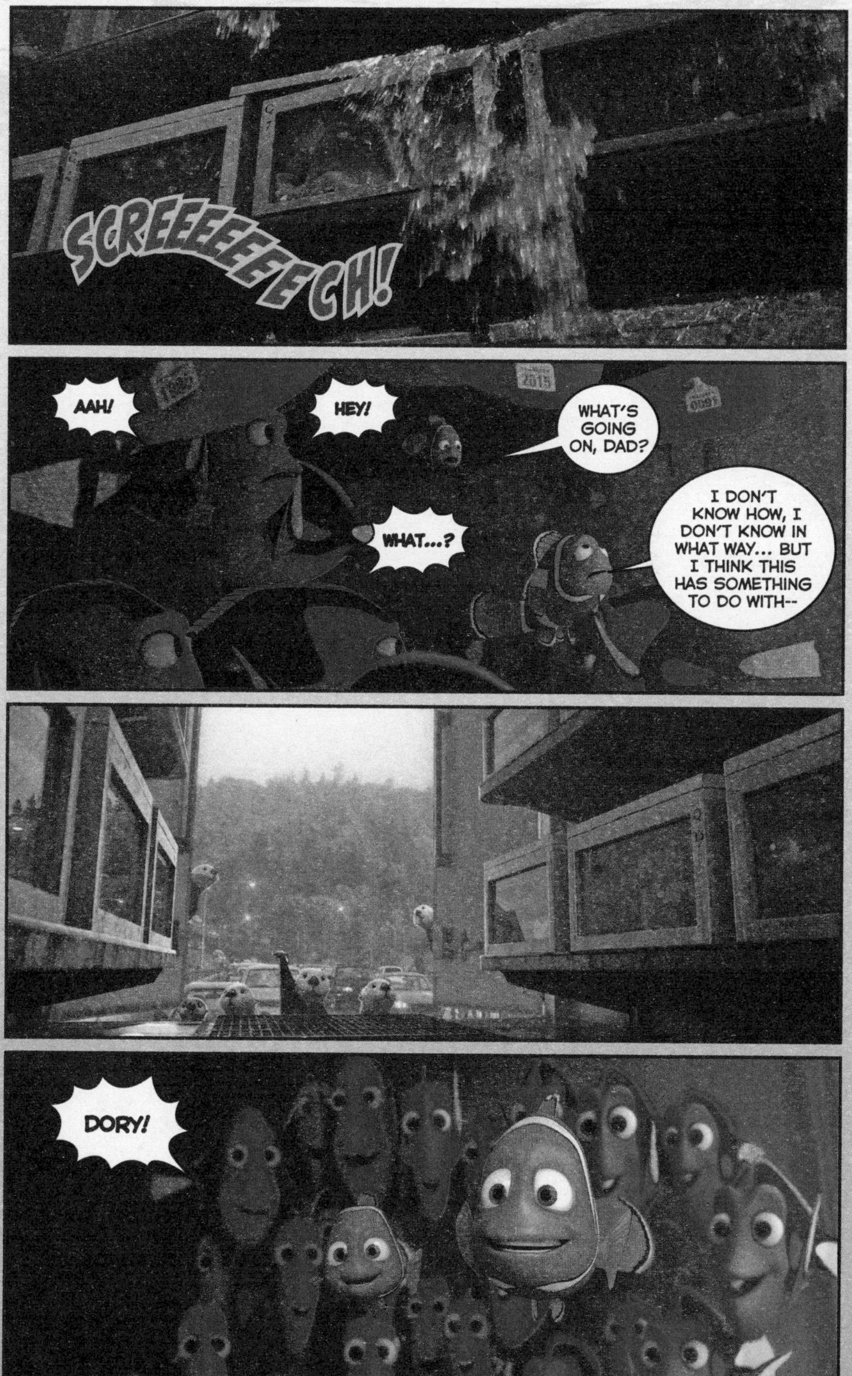
SCREEEEEEECH!
AAH!
HEY!
WHAT'S GOING ON, DAD?
WHAT...?
I DON'T KNOW HOW, I DON'T KNOW IN WHAT WAY... BUT I THINK THIS HAS SOMETHING TO DO WITH--
DORY!

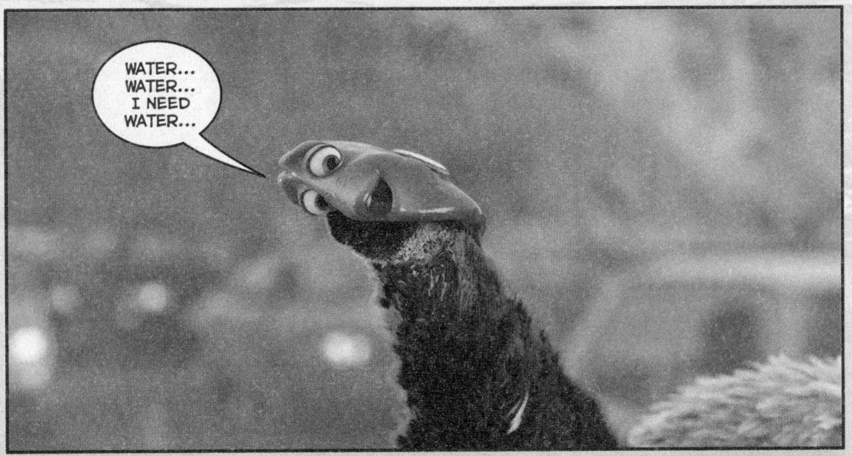
WATER... WATER... I NEED WATER...

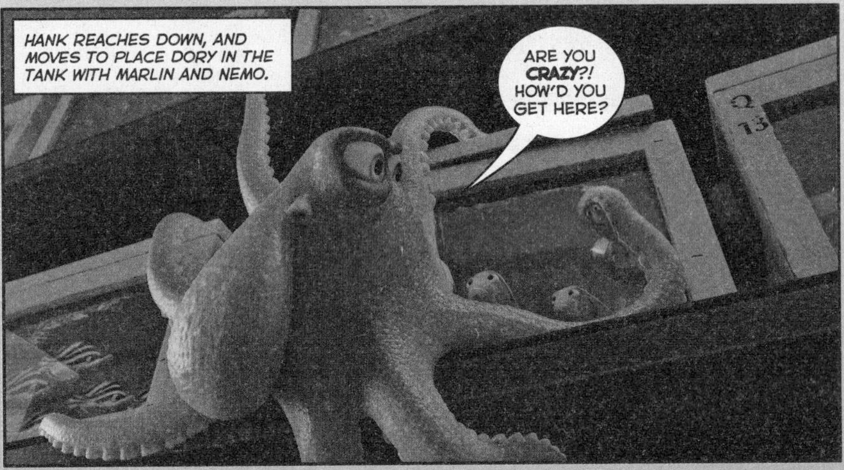
HANK REACHES DOWN, AND MOVES TO PLACE DORY IN THE TANK WITH MARLIN AND NEMO.
ARE YOU CRAZY?! HOW'D YOU GET HERE?

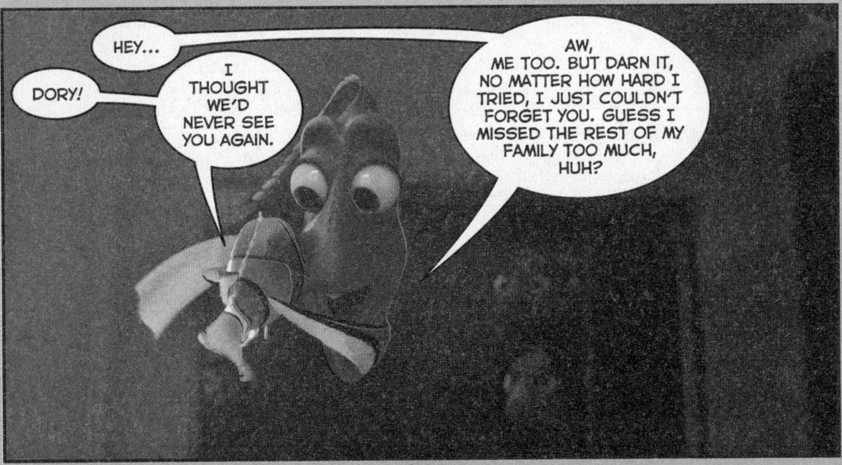
HEY...
DORY!
I THOUGHT WE'D NEVER SEE YOU AGAIN.
AW, ME TOO. BUT DARN IT, NO MATTER HOW HARD I TRIED, I JUST COULDN'T FORGET YOU. GUESS I MISSED THE REST OF MY FAMILY TOO MUCH, HUH?

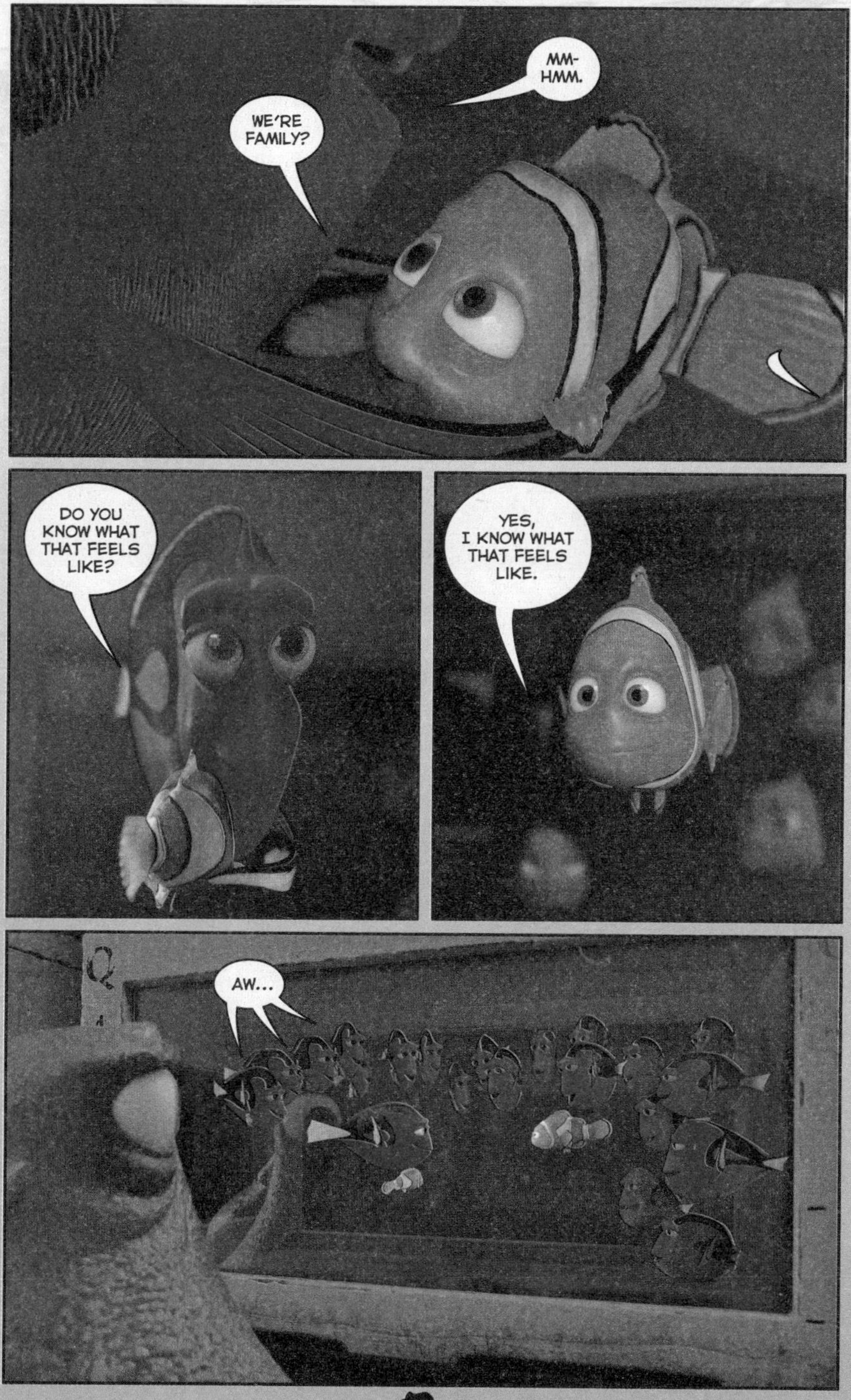
WE'RE FAMILY?
MM-HMM.
DO YOU KNOW WHAT THAT FEELS LIKE?
YES, I KNOW WHAT THAT FEELS LIKE.
AW...

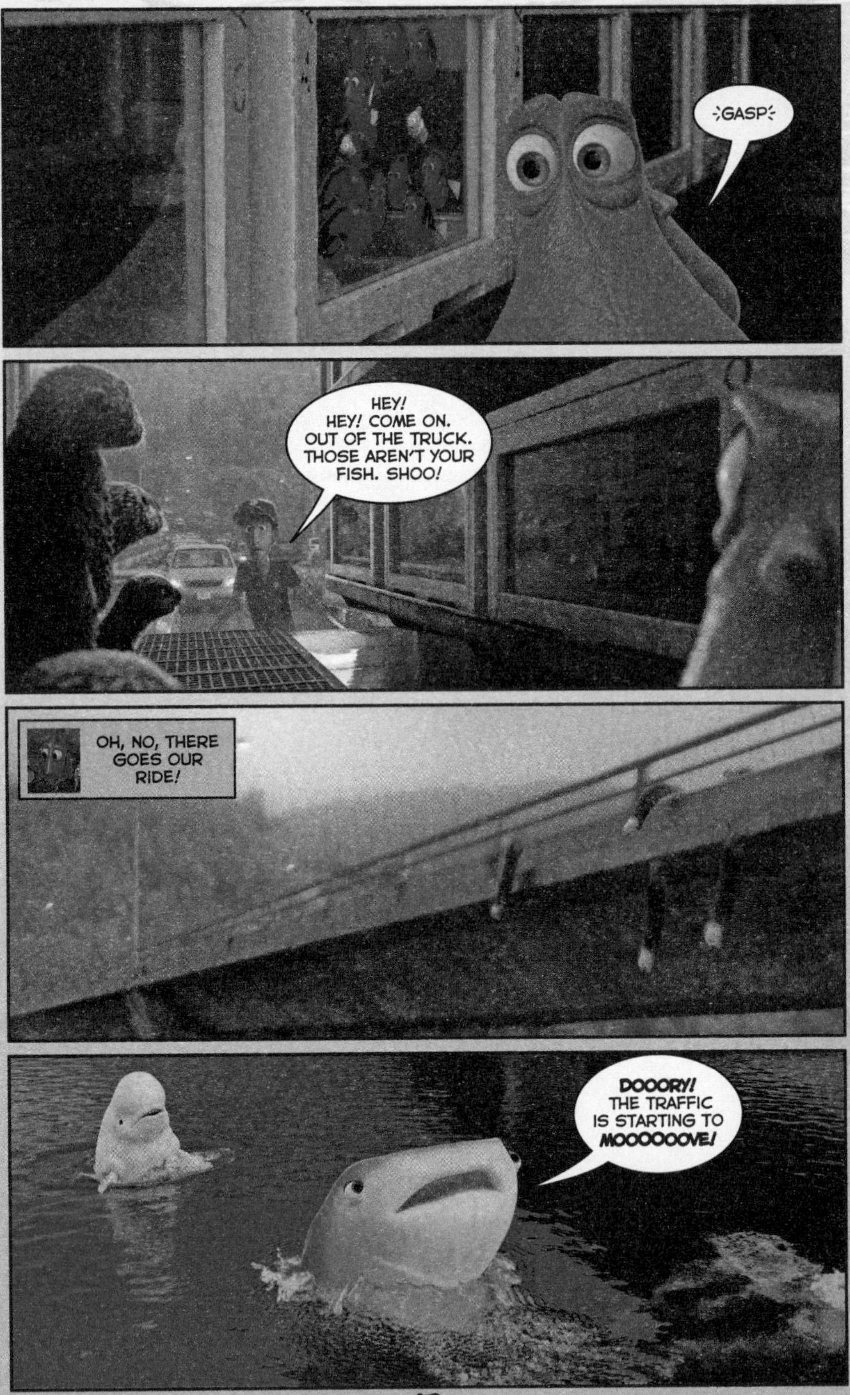
GASP
HEY! HEY! COME ON. OUT OF THE TRUCK. THOSE AREN'T YOUR FISH. SHOO!
OH, NO, THERE GOES OUR RIDE!
DOOORY! THE TRAFFIC IS STARTING TO MOOOOOOVE!

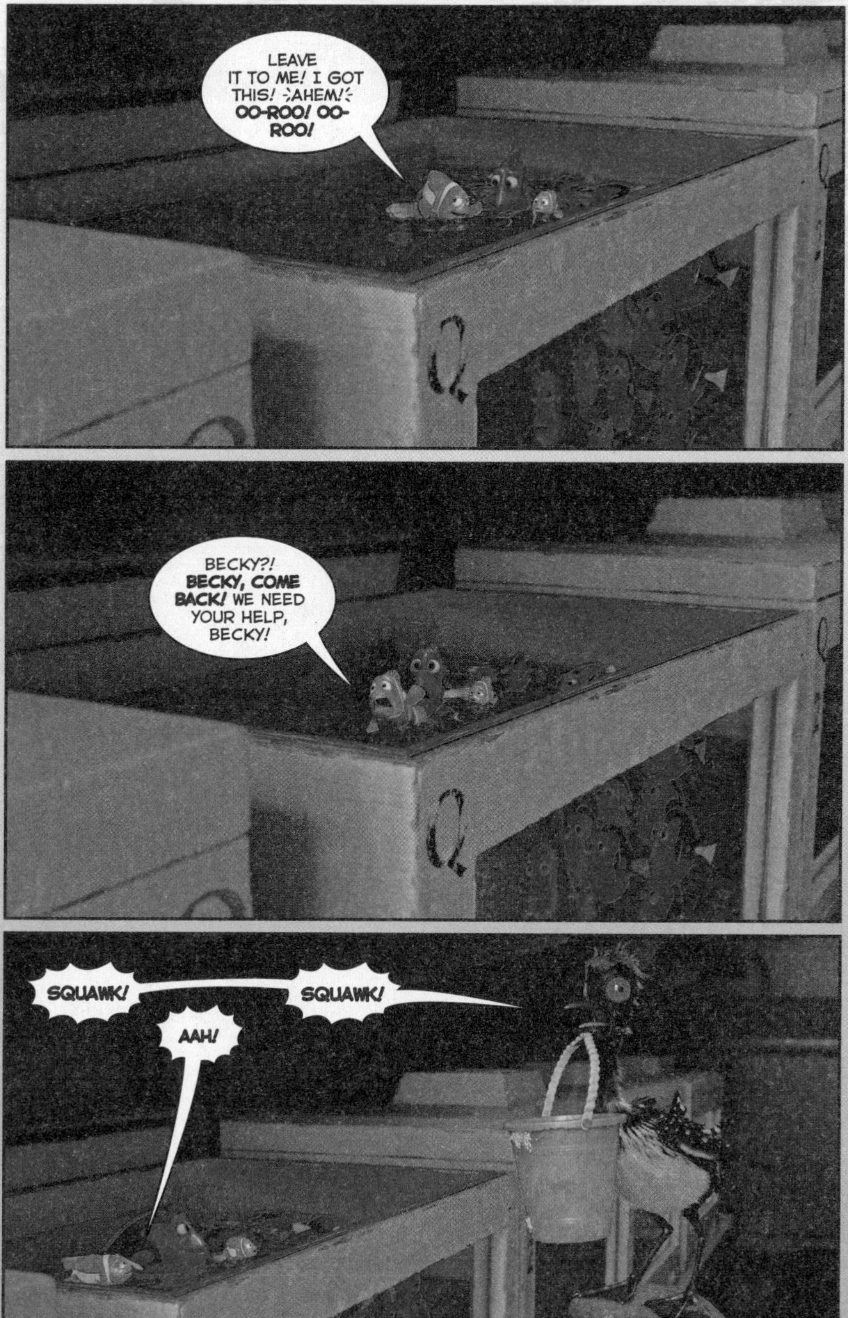
LEAVE IT TO ME! I GOT THIS! AHEM! OO-ROO! OO-ROO!
BECKY?! BECKY, COME BACK! WE NEED YOUR HELP, BECKY!
SQUAWK!
SQUAWK!
AAH!

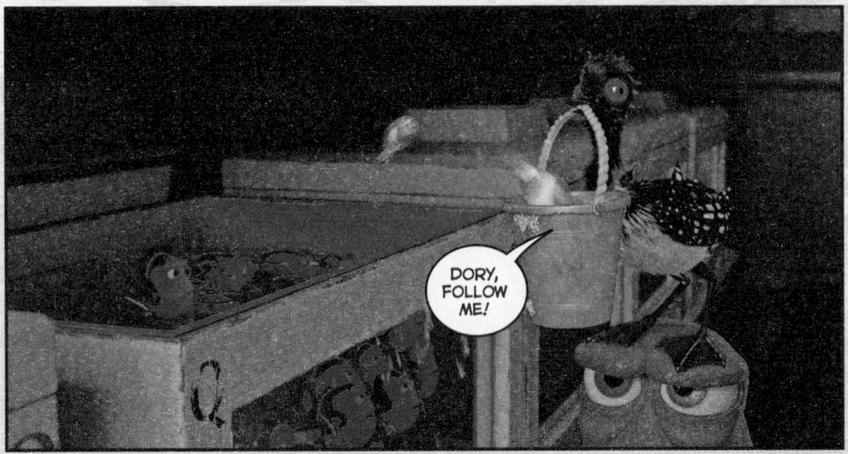
DORY, FOLLOW ME!

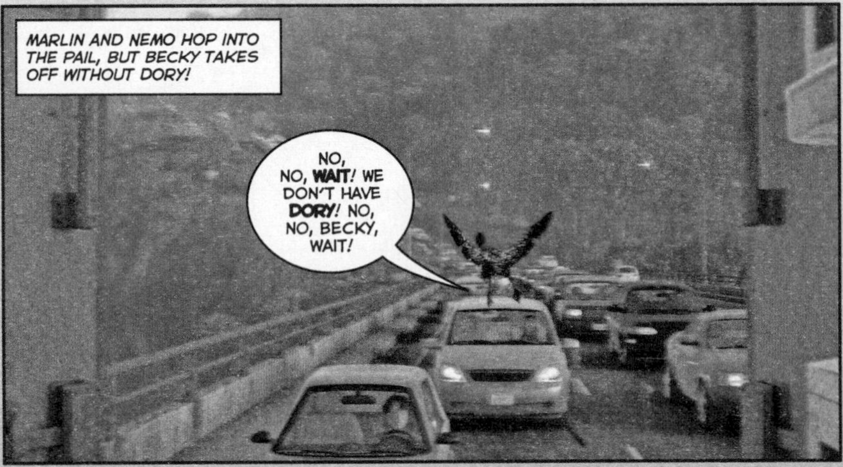
MARLIN AND NEMO HOP INTO THE PAIL, BUT BECKY TAKES OFF WITHOUT DORY!
NO, NO, **WAIT**! WE DON'T HAVE **DORY**! NO, NO, BECKY, WAIT!

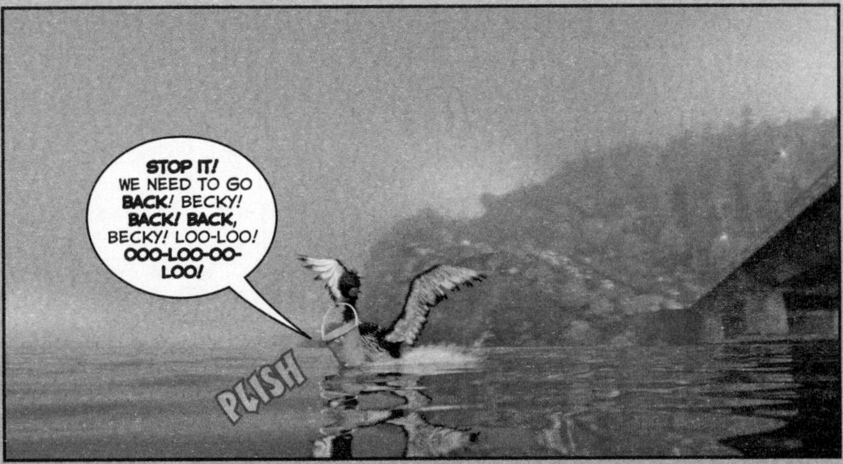
STOP IT! WE NEED TO GO **BACK**! BECKY! **BACK! BACK,** BECKY! LOO-LOO! **OOO-LOO-OO-LOO!**
PLISH

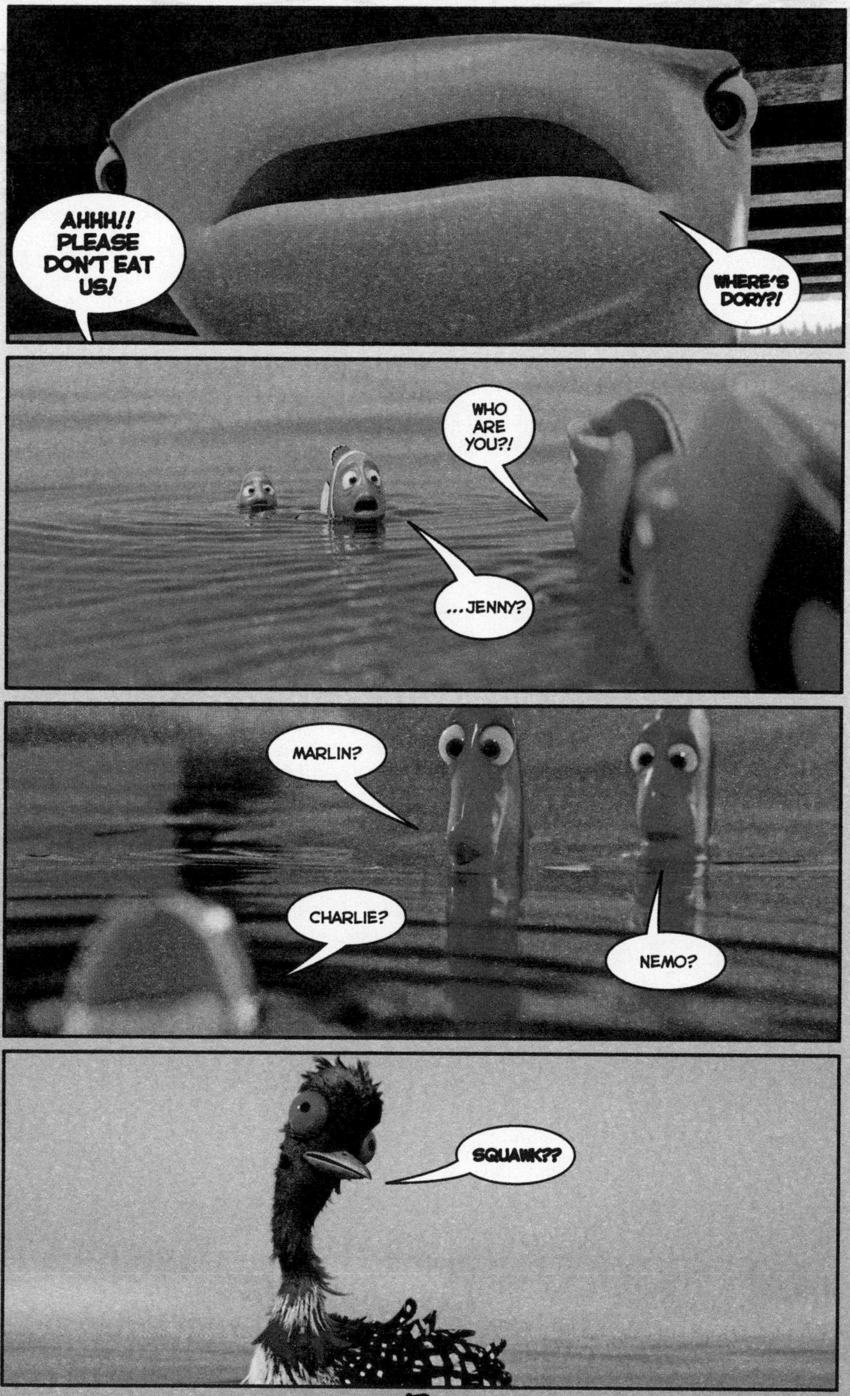
AHHH!! PLEASE DON'T EAT US!
WHERE'S DORY?!
WHO ARE YOU?!
...JENNY?
MARLIN?
CHARLIE?
NEMO?
SQUAWK??

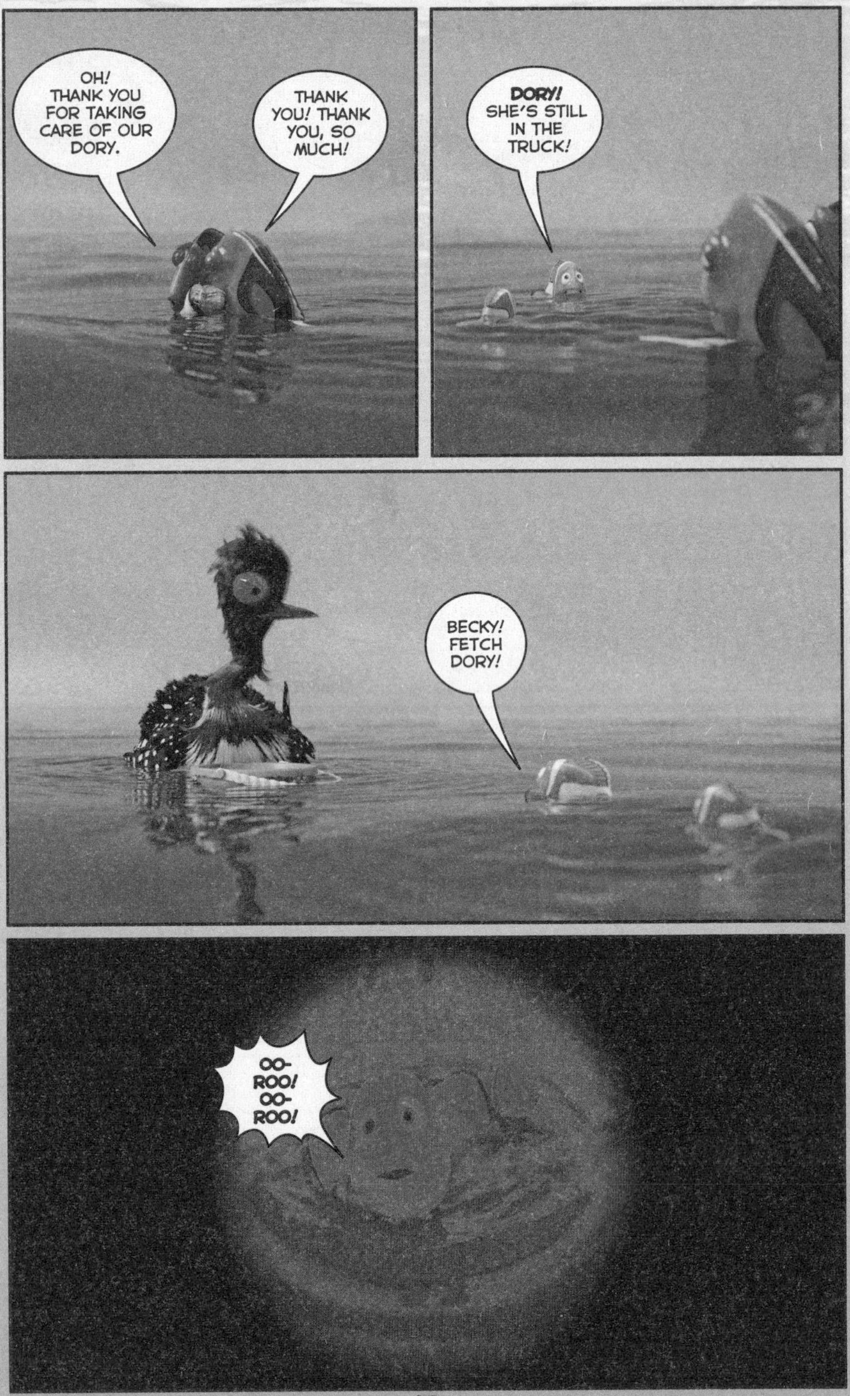
OH! THANK YOU FOR TAKING CARE OF OUR DORY.
THANK YOU! THANK YOU, SO MUCH!
DORY! SHE'S STILL IN THE TRUCK!
BECKY! FETCH DORY!
OO-ROO! OO-ROO!

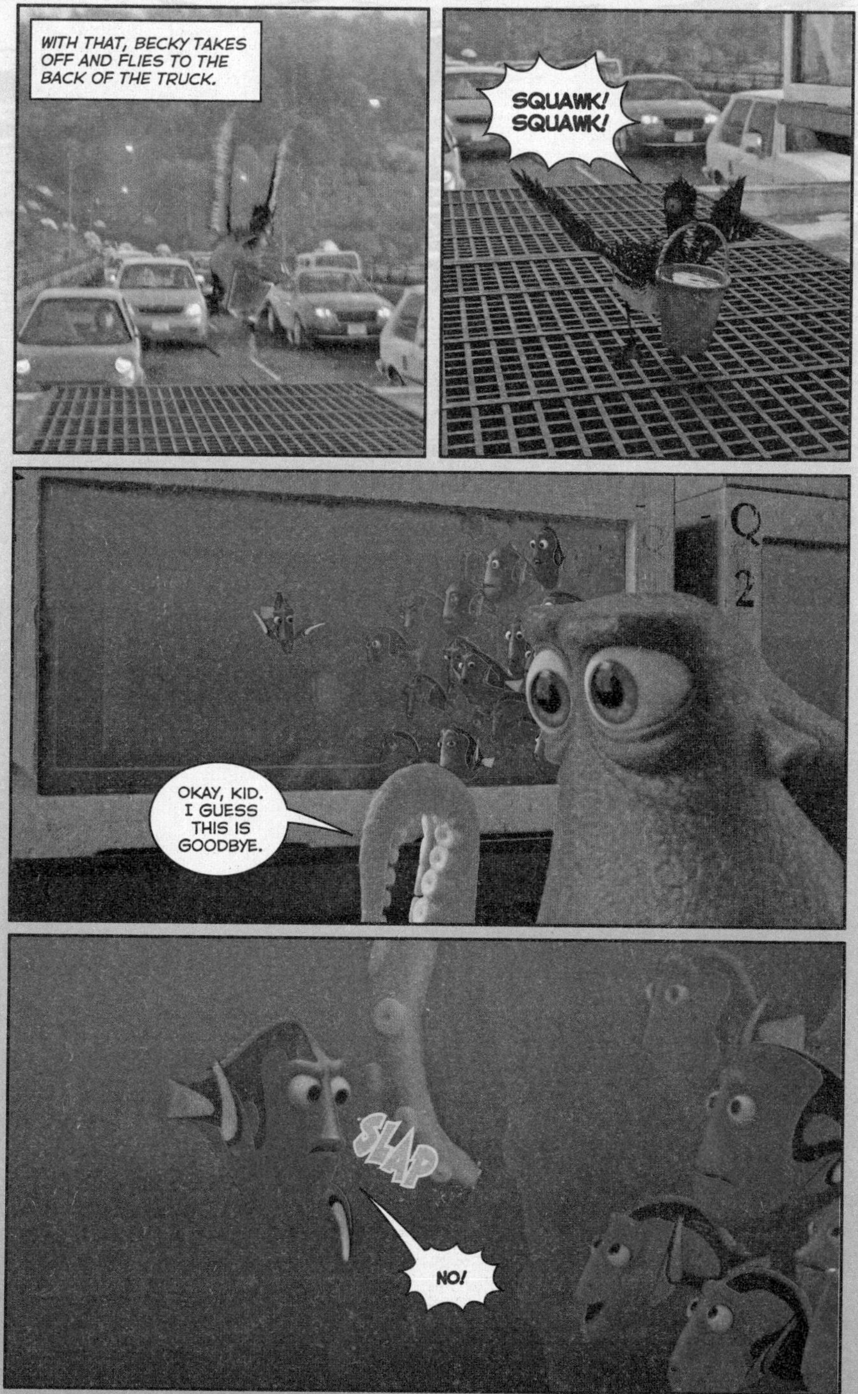
WITH THAT, BECKY TAKES OFF AND FLIES TO THE BACK OF THE TRUCK.
SQUAWK! SQUAWK!
Q
2
OKAY, KID. I GUESS THIS IS GOODBYE.
SLAP
NO!

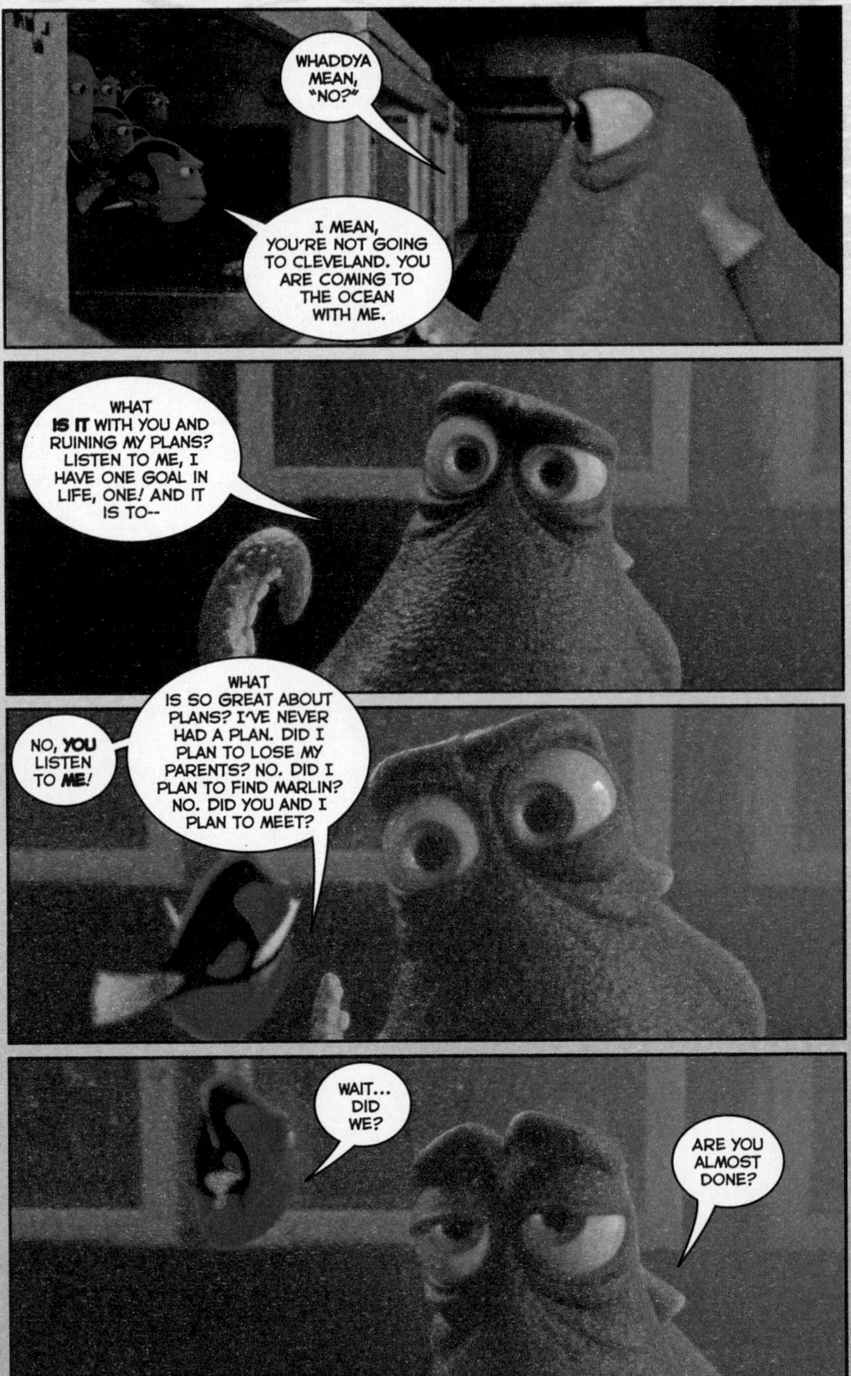
WHADDYA MEAN, "NO?"
I MEAN, YOU'RE NOT GOING TO CLEVELAND. YOU ARE COMING TO THE OCEAN WITH ME.
WHAT **IS IT** WITH YOU AND RUINING MY PLANS? LISTEN TO ME, I HAVE ONE GOAL IN LIFE, ONE! AND IT IS TO--
NO, **YOU** LISTEN TO **ME**!
WHAT IS SO GREAT ABOUT PLANS? I'VE NEVER HAD A PLAN. DID I PLAN TO LOSE MY PARENTS? NO. DID I PLAN TO FIND MARLIN? NO. DID YOU AND I PLAN TO MEET?
WAIT... DID WE?
ARE YOU ALMOST DONE?

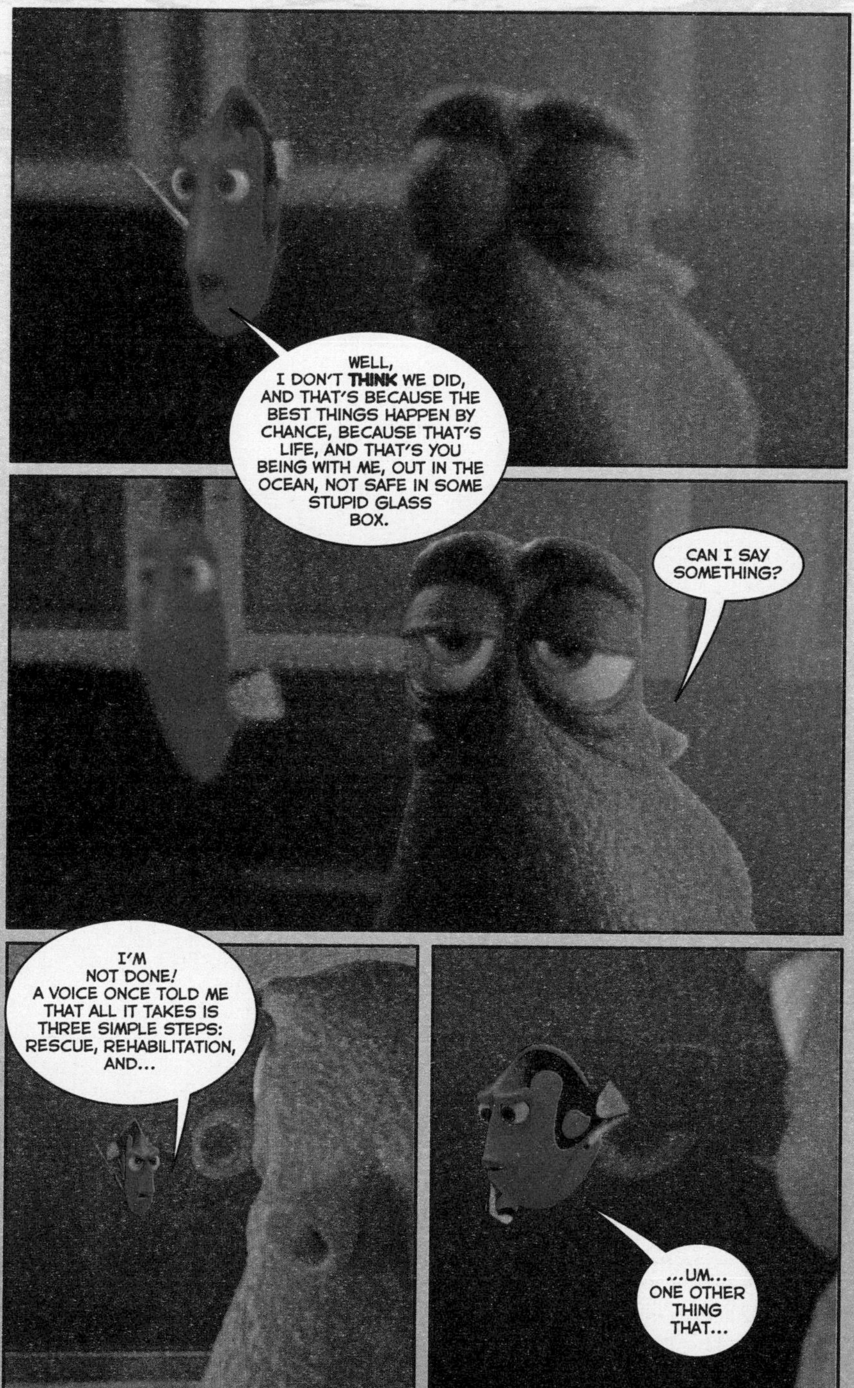
WELL, I DON'T **THINK** WE DID, AND THAT'S BECAUSE THE BEST THINGS HAPPEN BY CHANCE, BECAUSE THAT'S LIFE, AND THAT'S YOU BEING WITH ME, OUT IN THE OCEAN, NOT SAFE IN SOME STUPID GLASS BOX.
CAN I SAY SOMETHING?
I'M NOT DONE! A VOICE ONCE TOLD ME THAT ALL IT TAKES IS THREE SIMPLE STEPS: RESCUE, REHABILITATION, AND...
...UM... ONE OTHER THING THAT...

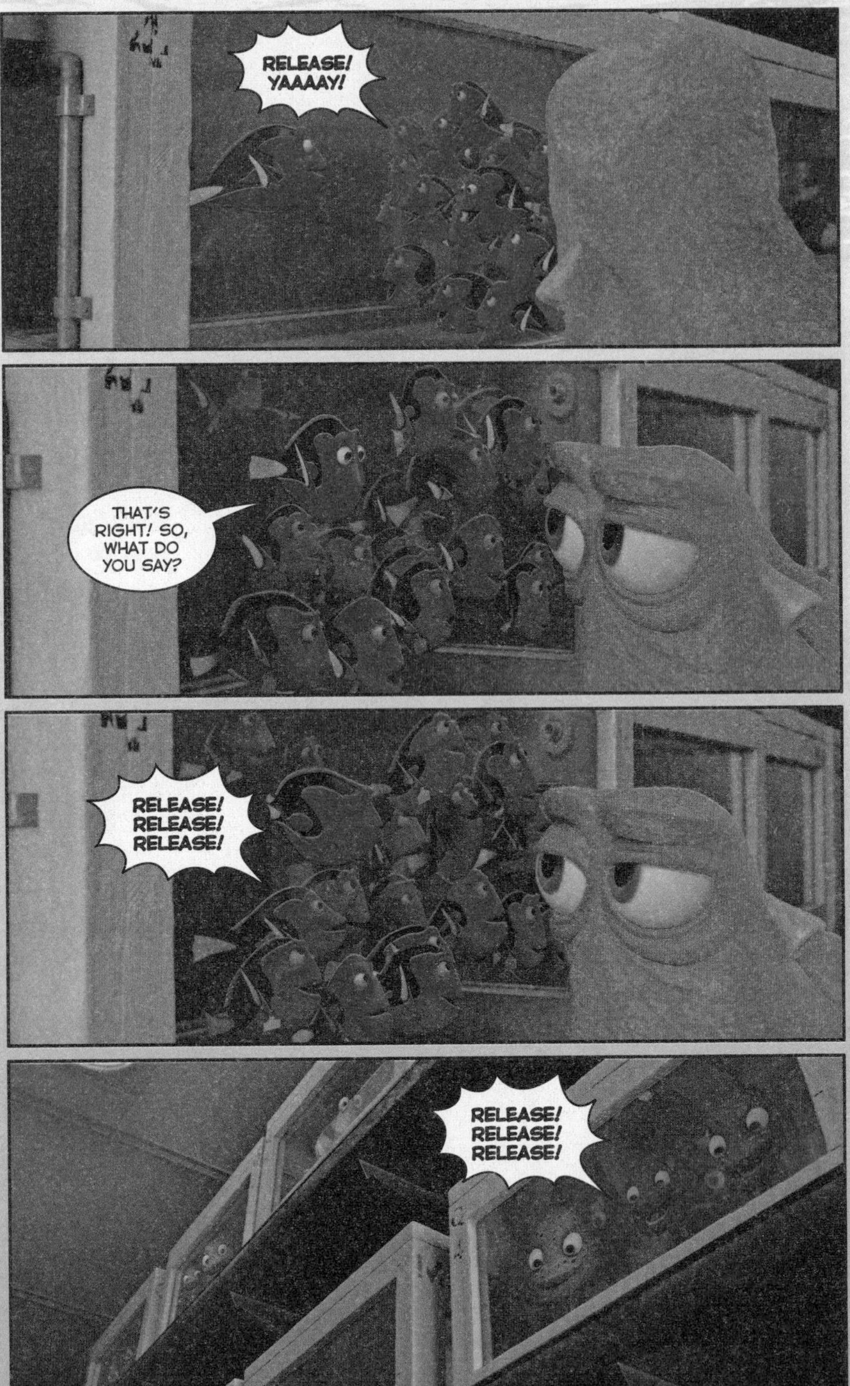
RELEASE! YAAAAY!
THAT'S RIGHT! SO, WHAT DO YOU SAY?
RELEASE! RELEASE! RELEASE!
RELEASE! RELEASE! RELEASE!

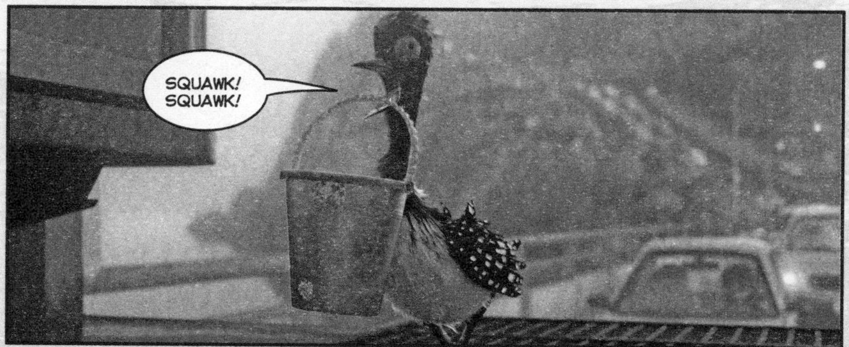
SQUAWK! SQUAWK!

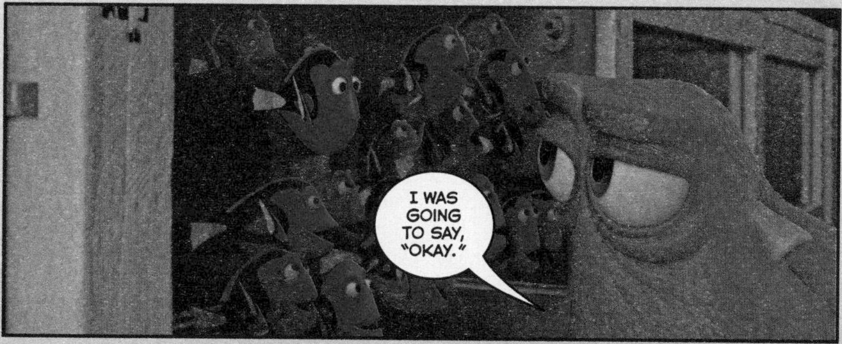
I WAS GOING TO SAY, "OKAY."

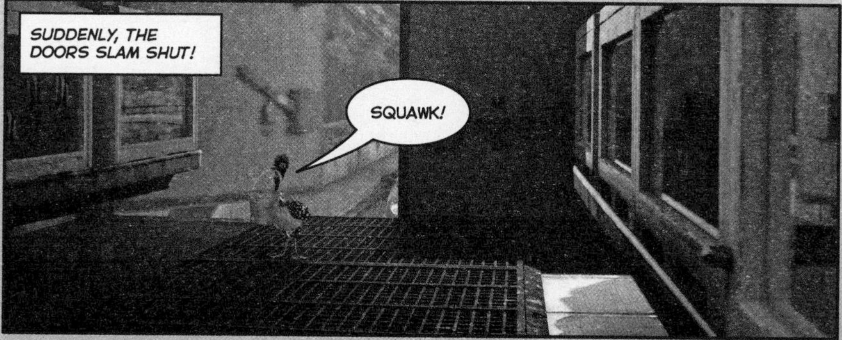
SUDDENLY, THE DOORS SLAM SHUT!
SQUAWK!

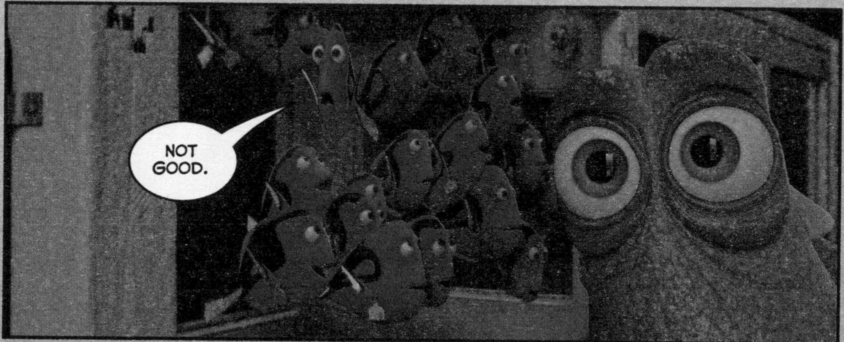
NOT GOOD.

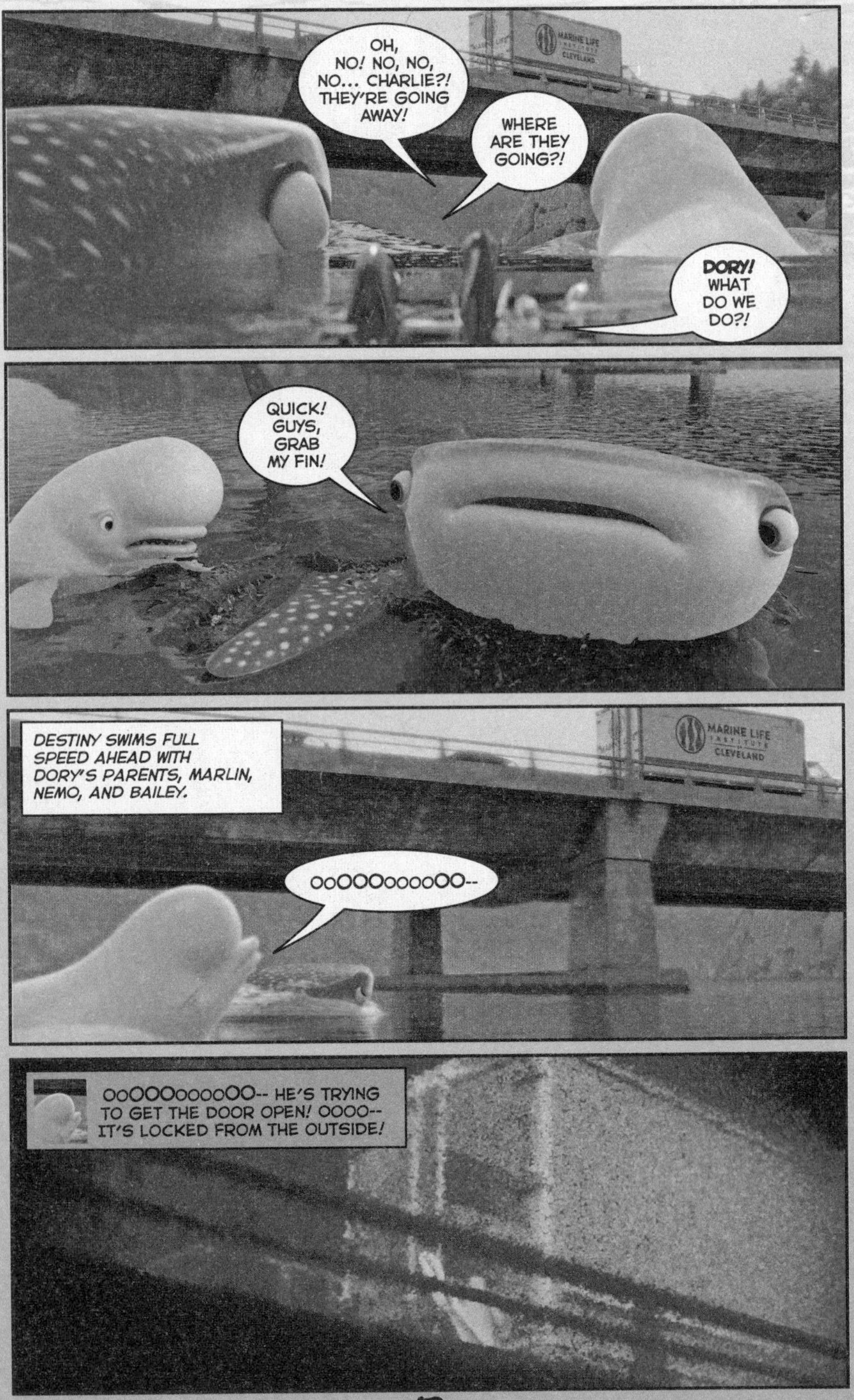
OH, NO! NO, NO, NO... CHARLIE?! THEY'RE GOING AWAY!
WHERE ARE THEY GOING?!
DORY! WHAT DO WE DO?!
QUICK! GUYS, GRAB MY FIN!
DESTINY SWIMS FULL SPEED AHEAD WITH DORY'S PARENTS, MARLIN, NEMO, AND BAILEY.
ooOOOooooOO--
ooOOOooooOO-- HE'S TRYING TO GET THE DOOR OPEN! OOOO-- IT'S LOCKED FROM THE OUTSIDE!

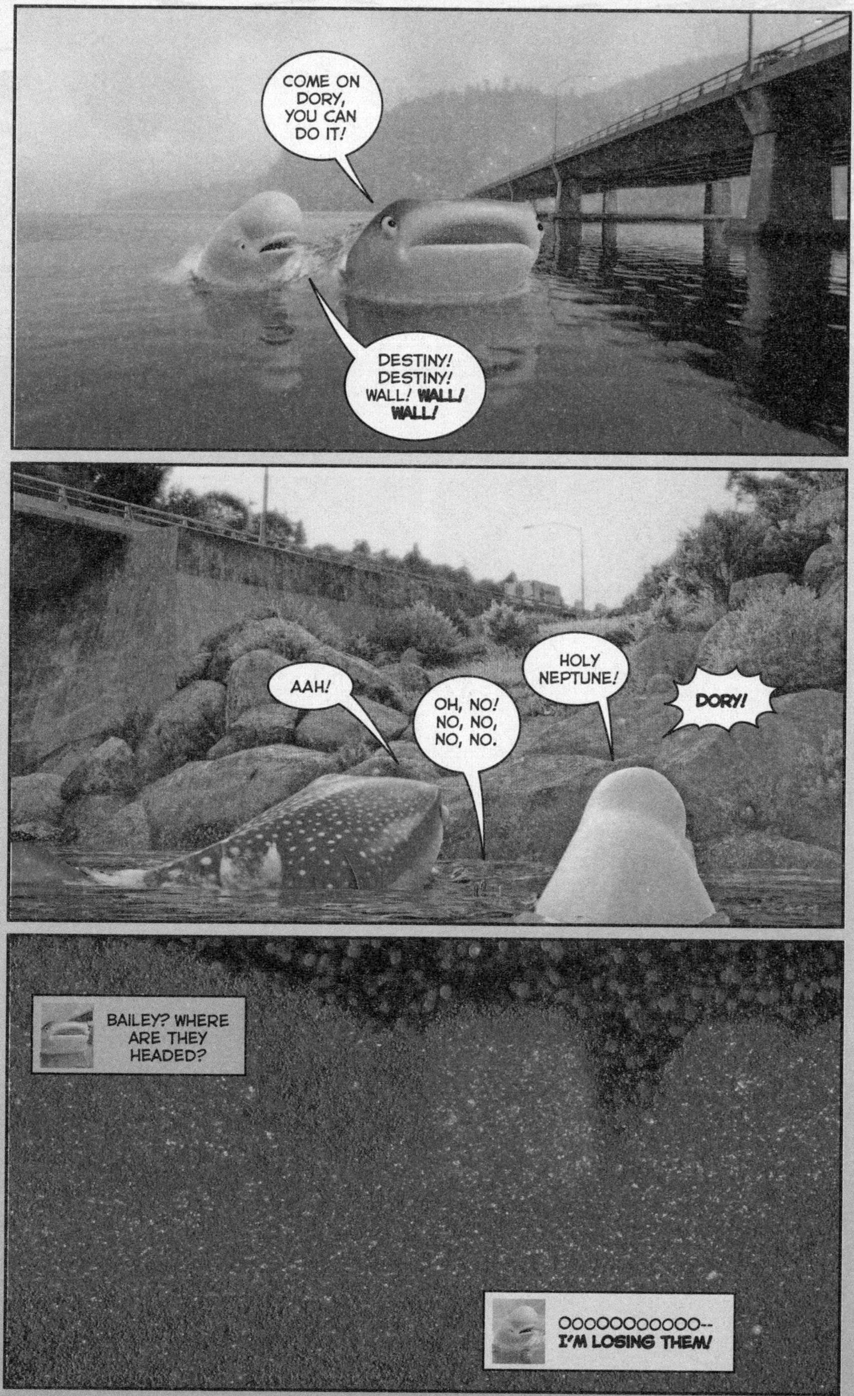
COME ON DORY, YOU CAN DO IT!
DESTINY! DESTINY! WALL! WALL! WALL!
AAH!
OH, NO! NO, NO, NO, NO.
HOLY NEPTUNE!
DORY!
BAILEY? WHERE ARE THEY HEADED?
OOOOOOOOOOO-- I'M LOSING THEM!

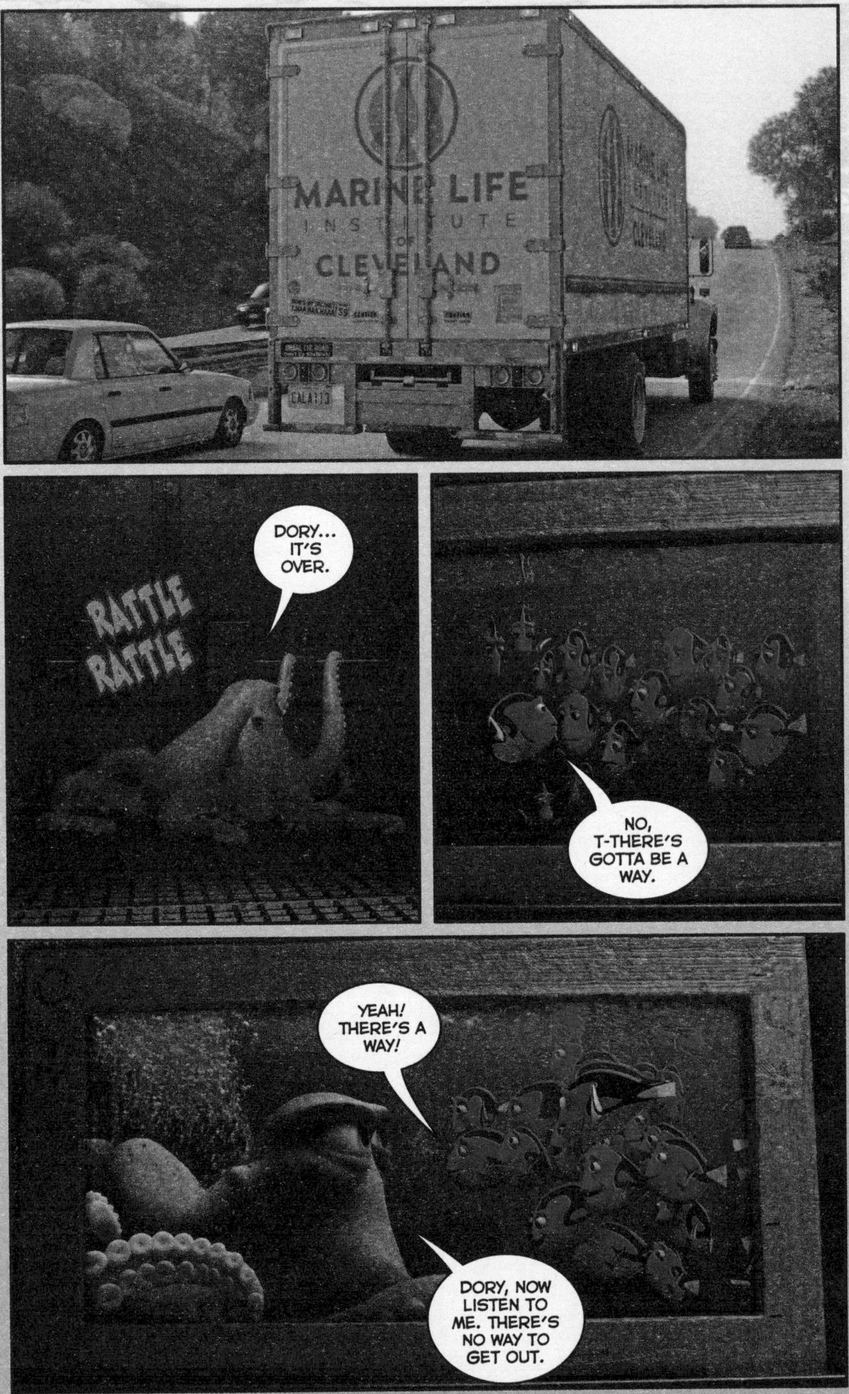
RATTLE RATTLE
DORY... IT'S OVER.
NO, T-THERE'S GOTTA BE A WAY.
YEAH! THERE'S A WAY!
DORY, NOW LISTEN TO ME. THERE'S NO WAY TO GET OUT.

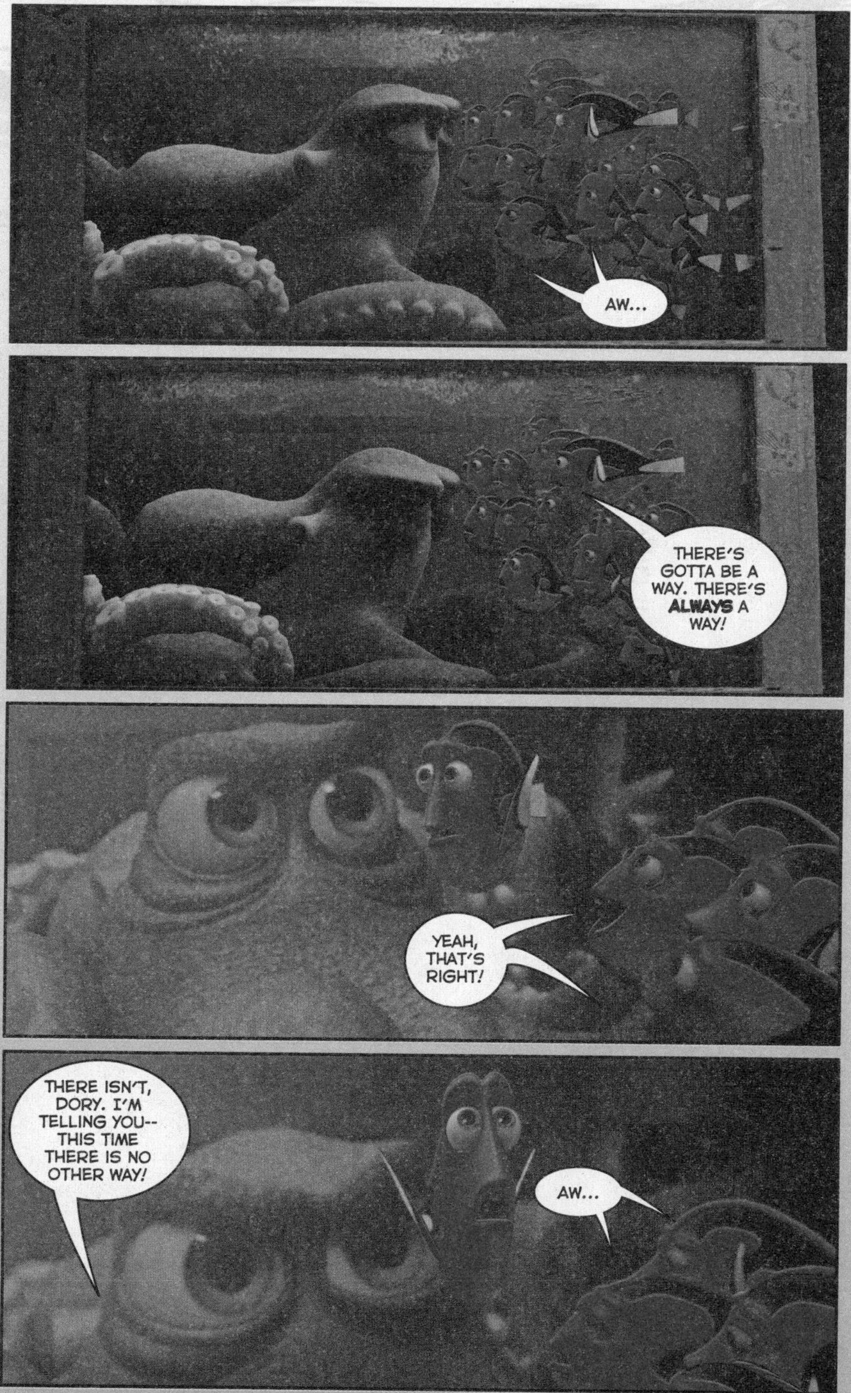
AW...
THERE'S GOTTA BE A WAY. THERE'S **ALWAYS** A WAY!
YEAH, THAT'S RIGHT!
THERE ISN'T, DORY. I'M TELLING YOU-- THIS TIME THERE IS NO OTHER WAY!
AW...

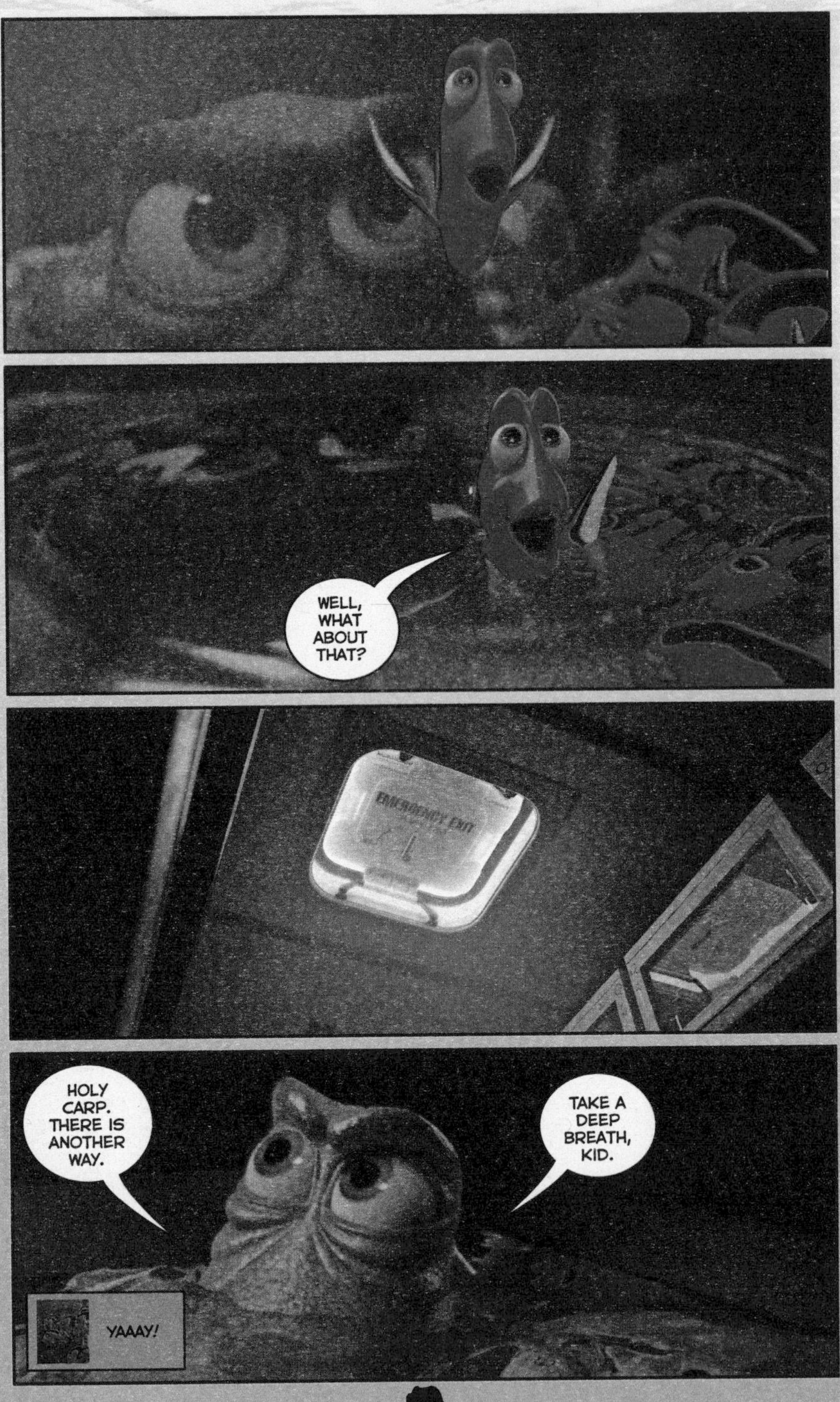
WELL, WHAT ABOUT THAT?
EMERGENCY EXIT
HOLY CARP. THERE IS ANOTHER WAY.
TAKE A DEEP BREATH, KID.
YAAAY!

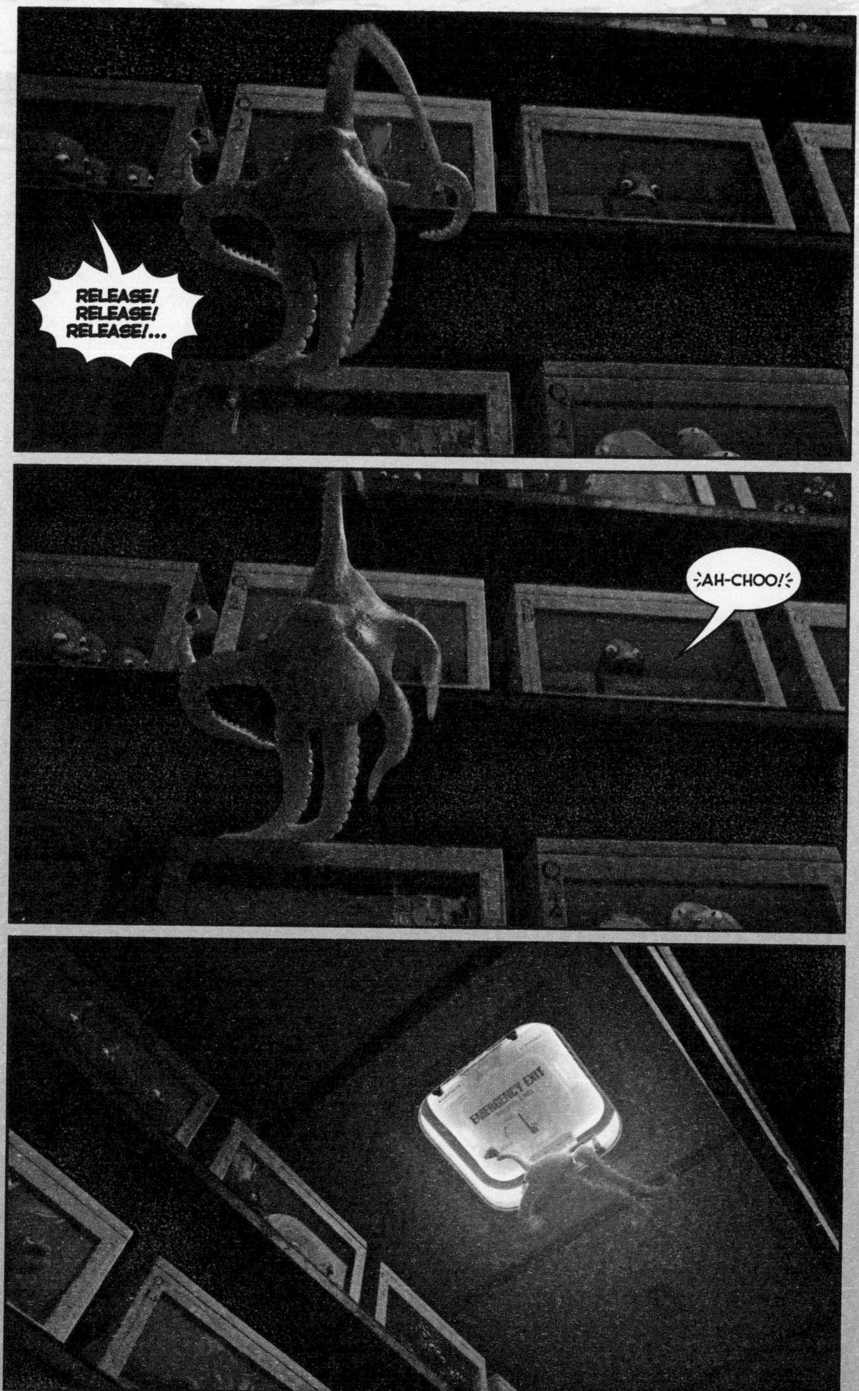
RELEASE!
RELEASE!
RELEASE!...
AH-CHOO!
EMERGENCY EXIT

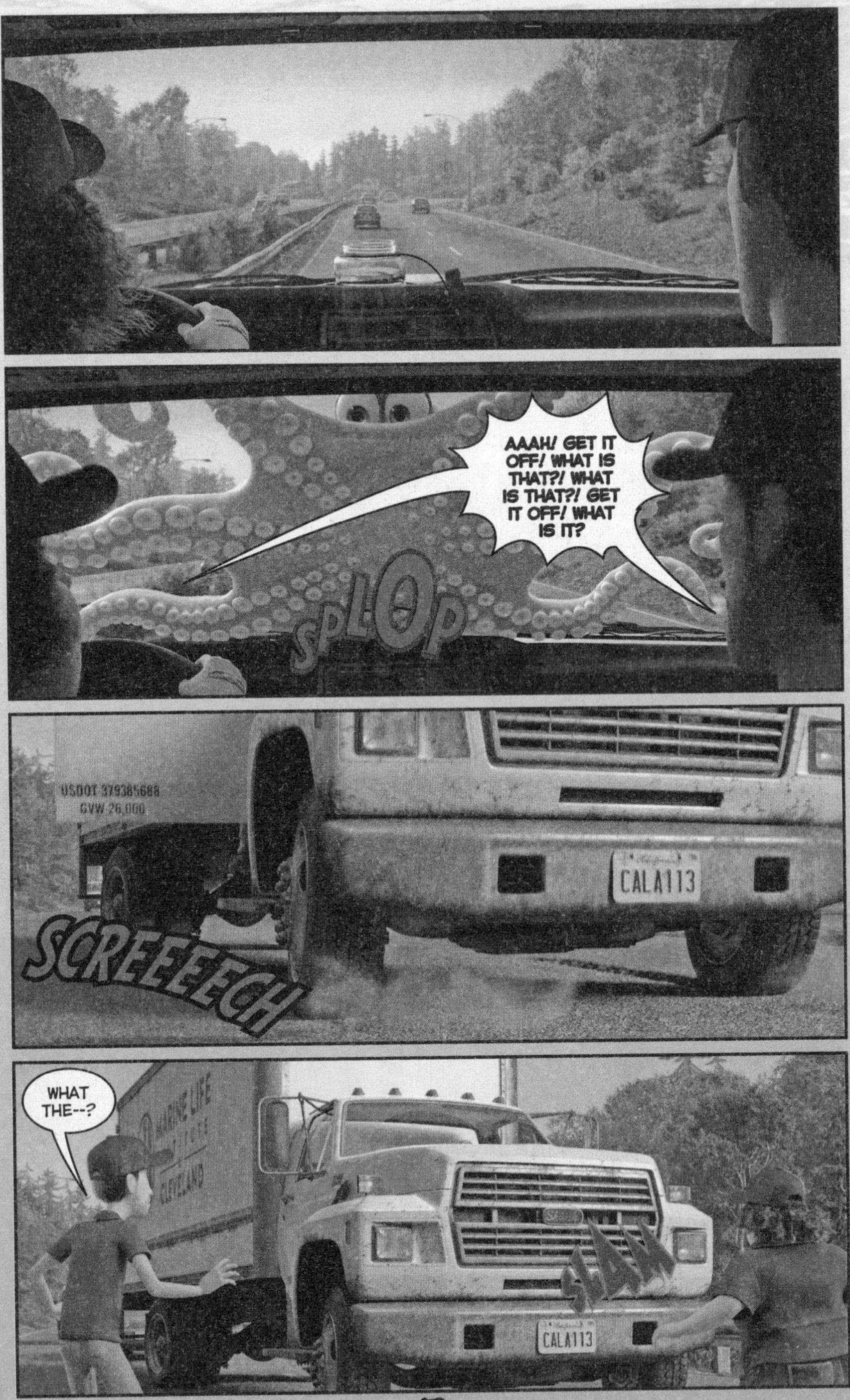
AAAH! GET IT OFF! WHAT IS THAT?! WHAT IS THAT?! GET IT OFF! WHAT IS IT?
SPLOP
CALA113
SCREEEECH
WHAT THE--?
CALA113

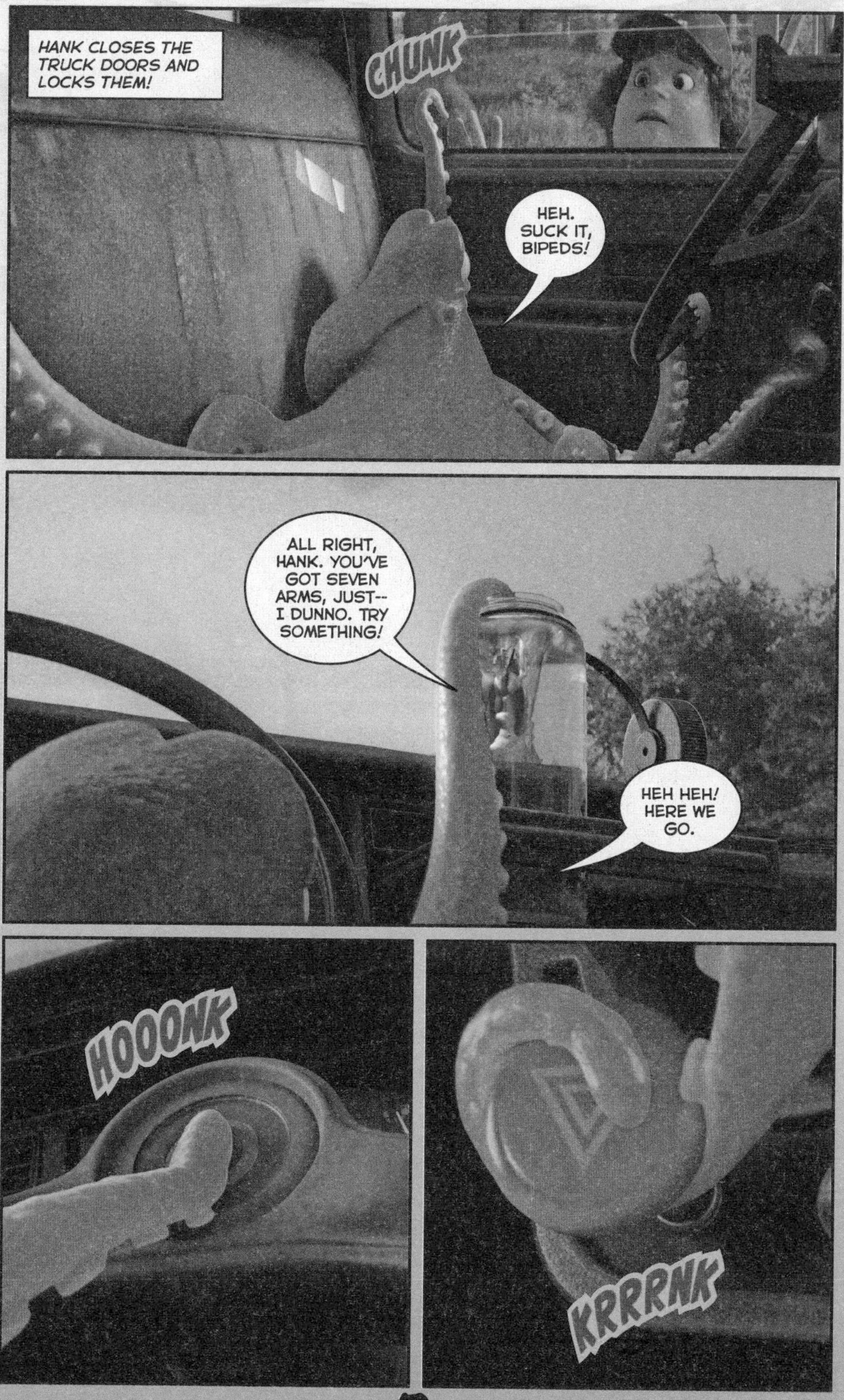
HANK CLOSES THE TRUCK DOORS AND LOCKS THEM!
CHUNK
HEH. SUCK IT, BIPEDS!
ALL RIGHT, HANK. YOU'VE GOT SEVEN ARMS, JUST-- I DUNNO. TRY SOMETHING!
HEH HEH! HERE WE GO.
HOOONK
KRRRNK

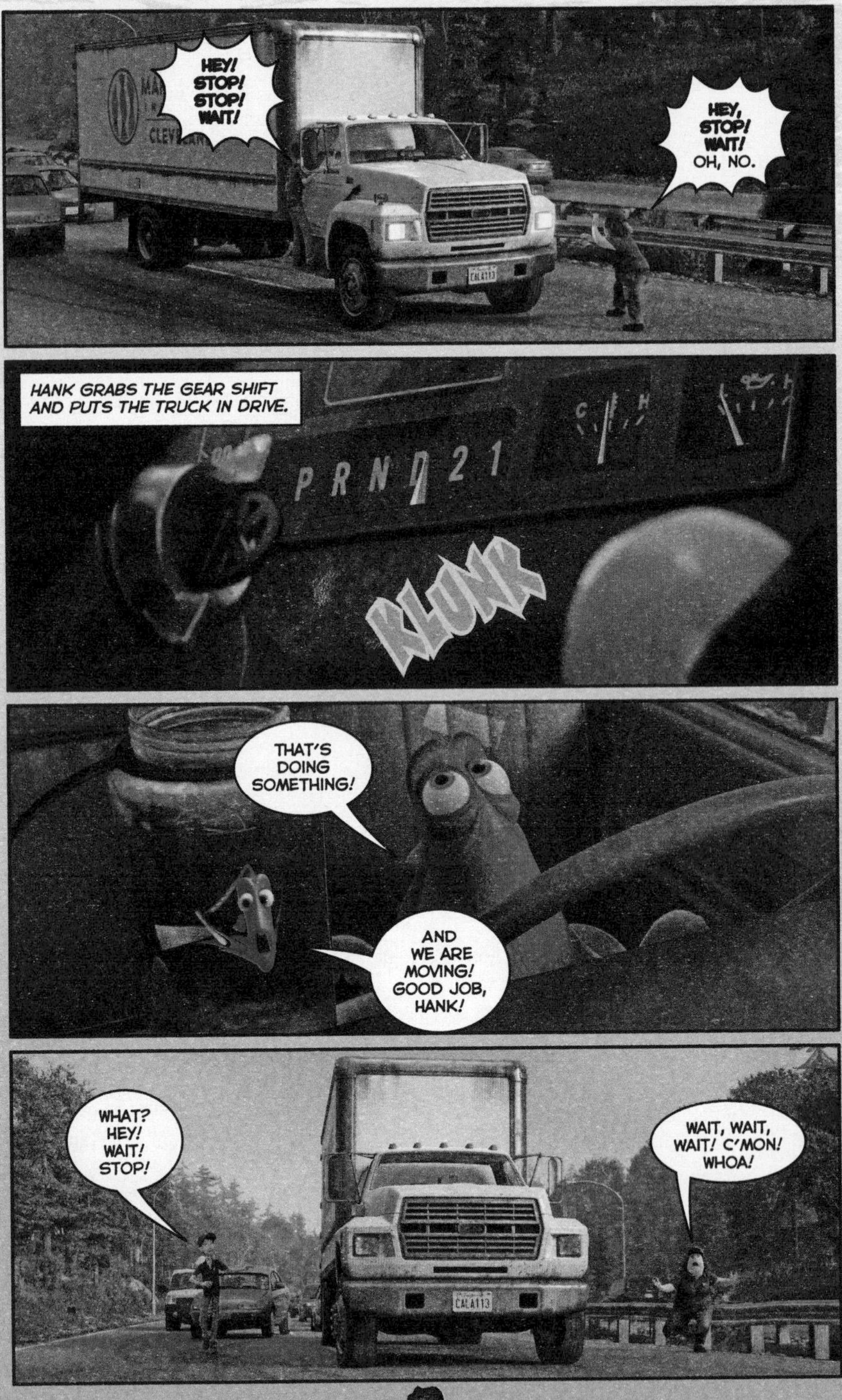
HEY! STOP! STOP! WAIT!
HEY, STOP! WAIT! OH, NO.
HANK GRABS THE GEAR SHIFT AND PUTS THE TRUCK IN DRIVE.
KLUNK
THAT'S DOING SOMETHING!
AND WE ARE MOVING! GOOD JOB, HANK!
WHAT? HEY! WAIT! STOP!
WAIT, WAIT, WAIT! C'MON! WHOA!

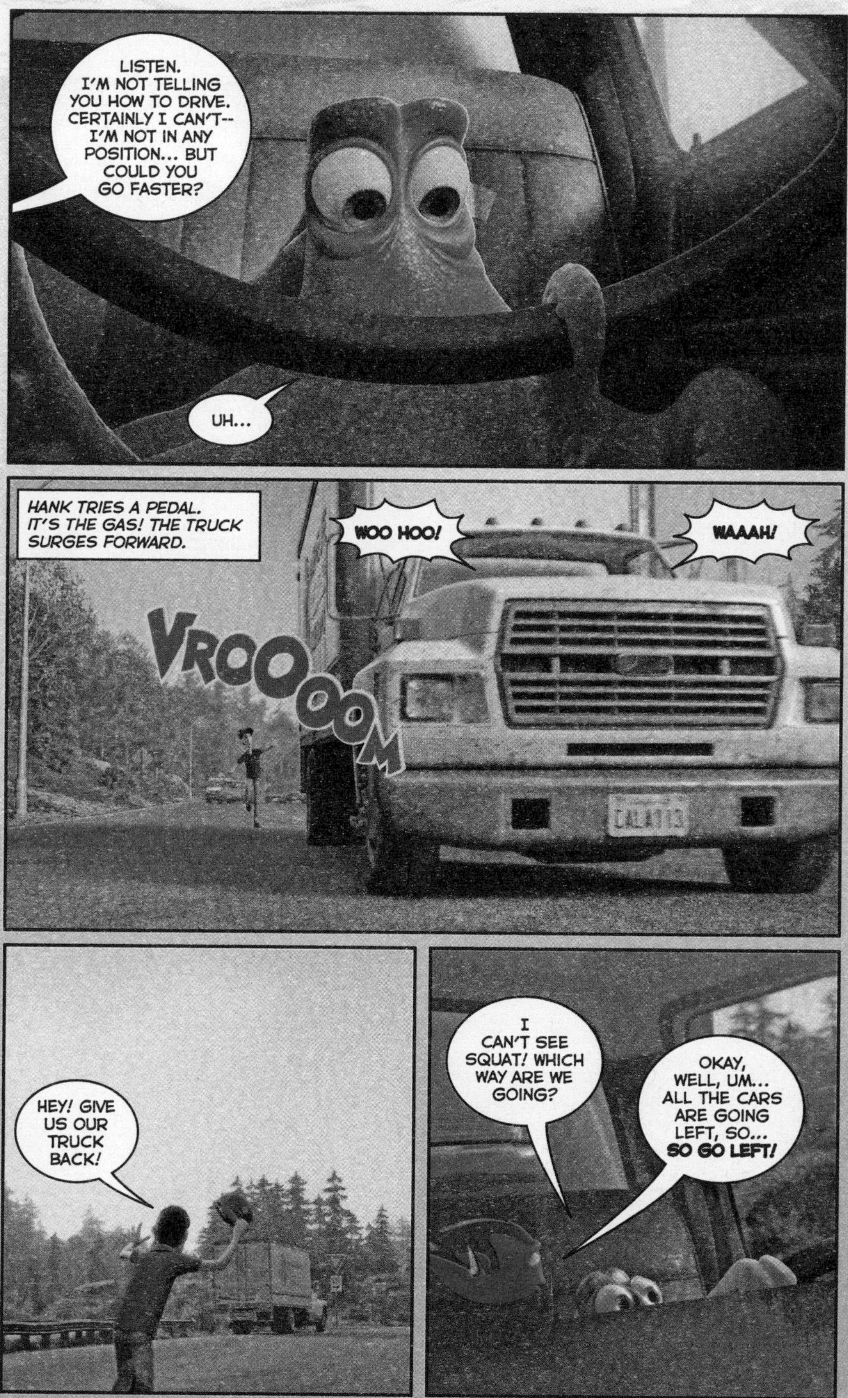
LISTEN. I'M NOT TELLING YOU HOW TO DRIVE. CERTAINLY I CAN'T-- I'M NOT IN ANY POSITION... BUT COULD YOU GO FASTER?
UH...
HANK TRIES A PEDAL. IT'S THE GAS! THE TRUCK SURGES FORWARD.
WOO HOO!
WAAAH!
VROOOOOM
HEY! GIVE US OUR TRUCK BACK!
I CAN'T SEE SQUAT! WHICH WAY ARE WE GOING?
OKAY, WELL, UM... ALL THE CARS ARE GOING LEFT, SO... **SO GO LEFT!**

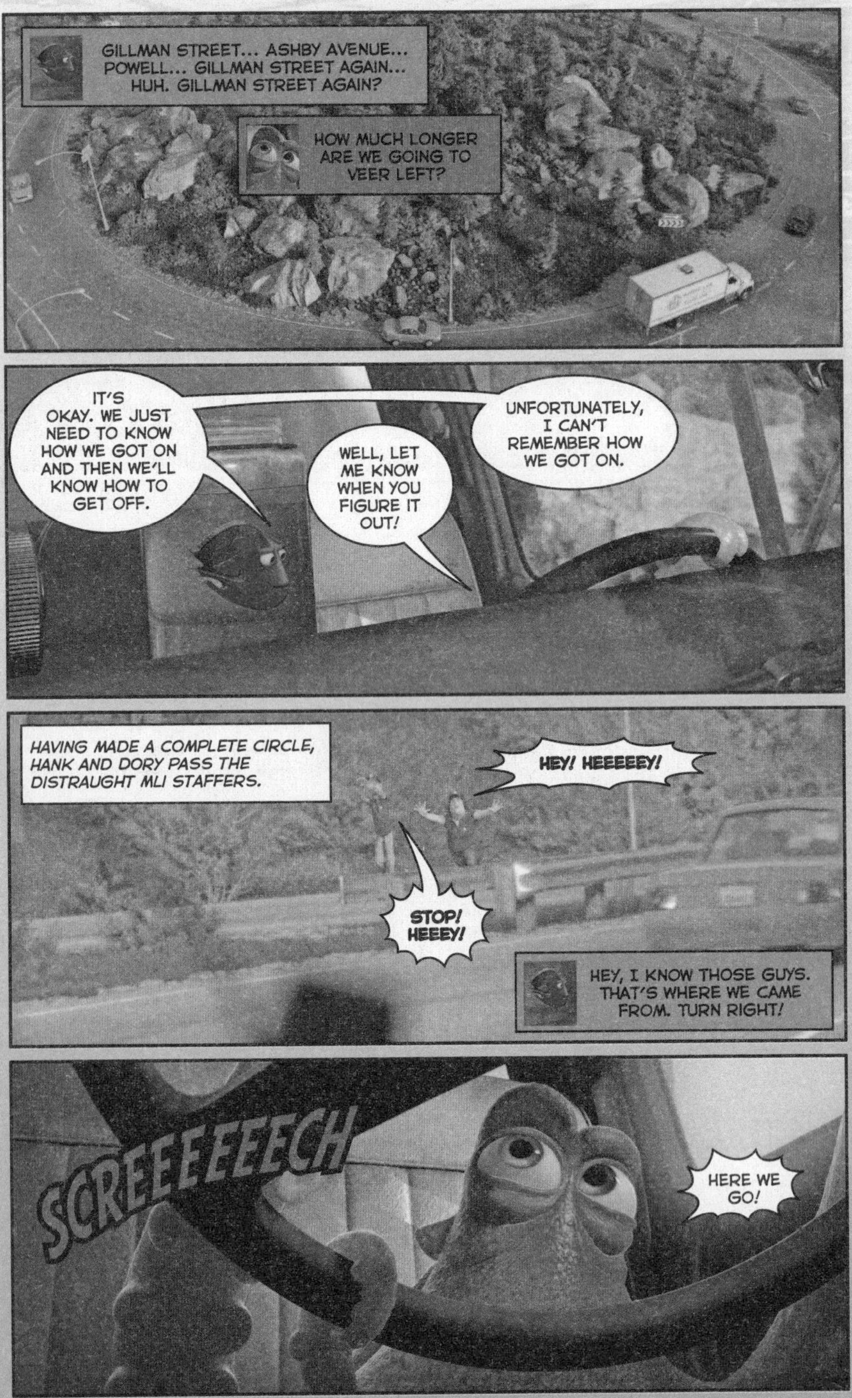
GILLMAN STREET... ASHBY AVENUE... POWELL... GILLMAN STREET AGAIN... HUH. GILLMAN STREET AGAIN?
HOW MUCH LONGER ARE WE GOING TO VEER LEFT?
IT'S OKAY. WE JUST NEED TO KNOW HOW WE GOT ON AND THEN WE'LL KNOW HOW TO GET OFF.
UNFORTUNATELY, I CAN'T REMEMBER HOW WE GOT ON.
WELL, LET ME KNOW WHEN YOU FIGURE IT OUT!
HAVING MADE A COMPLETE CIRCLE, HANK AND DORY PASS THE DISTRAUGHT MLI STAFFERS.
HEY! HEEEEEY!
STOP! HEEEY!
HEY, I KNOW THOSE GUYS. THAT'S WHERE WE CAME FROM. TURN RIGHT!
SCREEEEEECH
HERE WE GO!

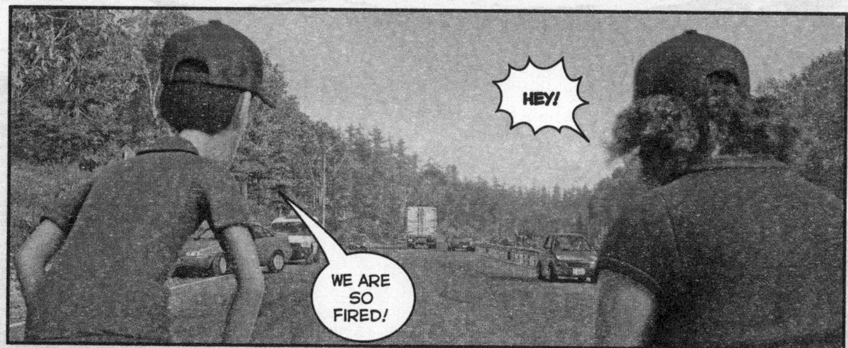
HEY!
WE ARE SO FIRED!

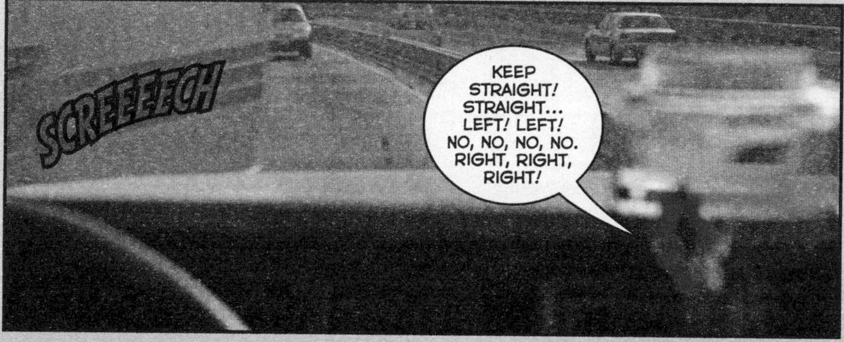
SCREEEECH
KEEP STRAIGHT! STRAIGHT... LEFT! LEFT! NO, NO, NO, NO. RIGHT, RIGHT, RIGHT!

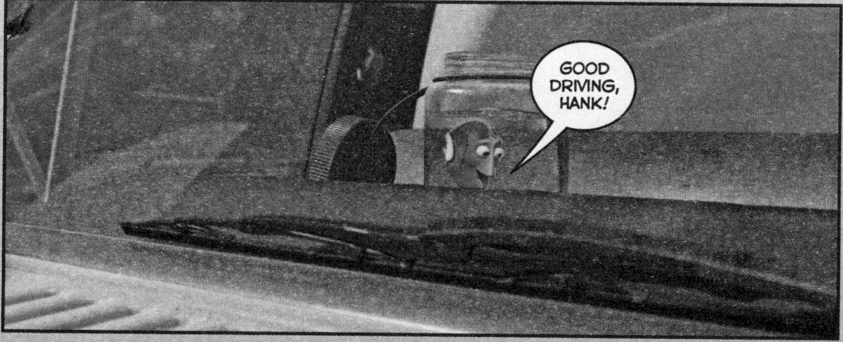
GOOD DRIVING, HANK!

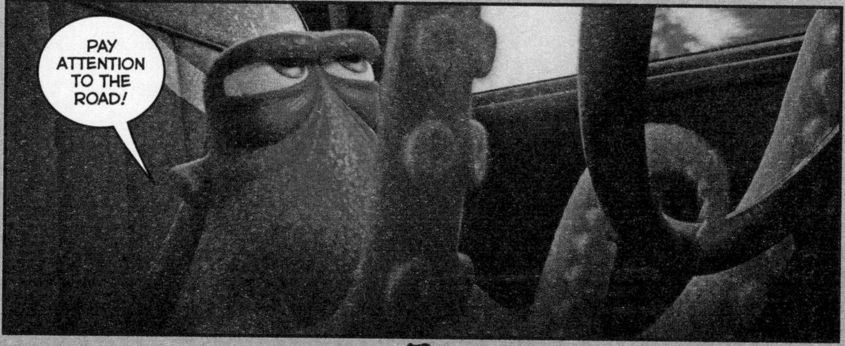
PAY ATTENTION TO THE ROAD!

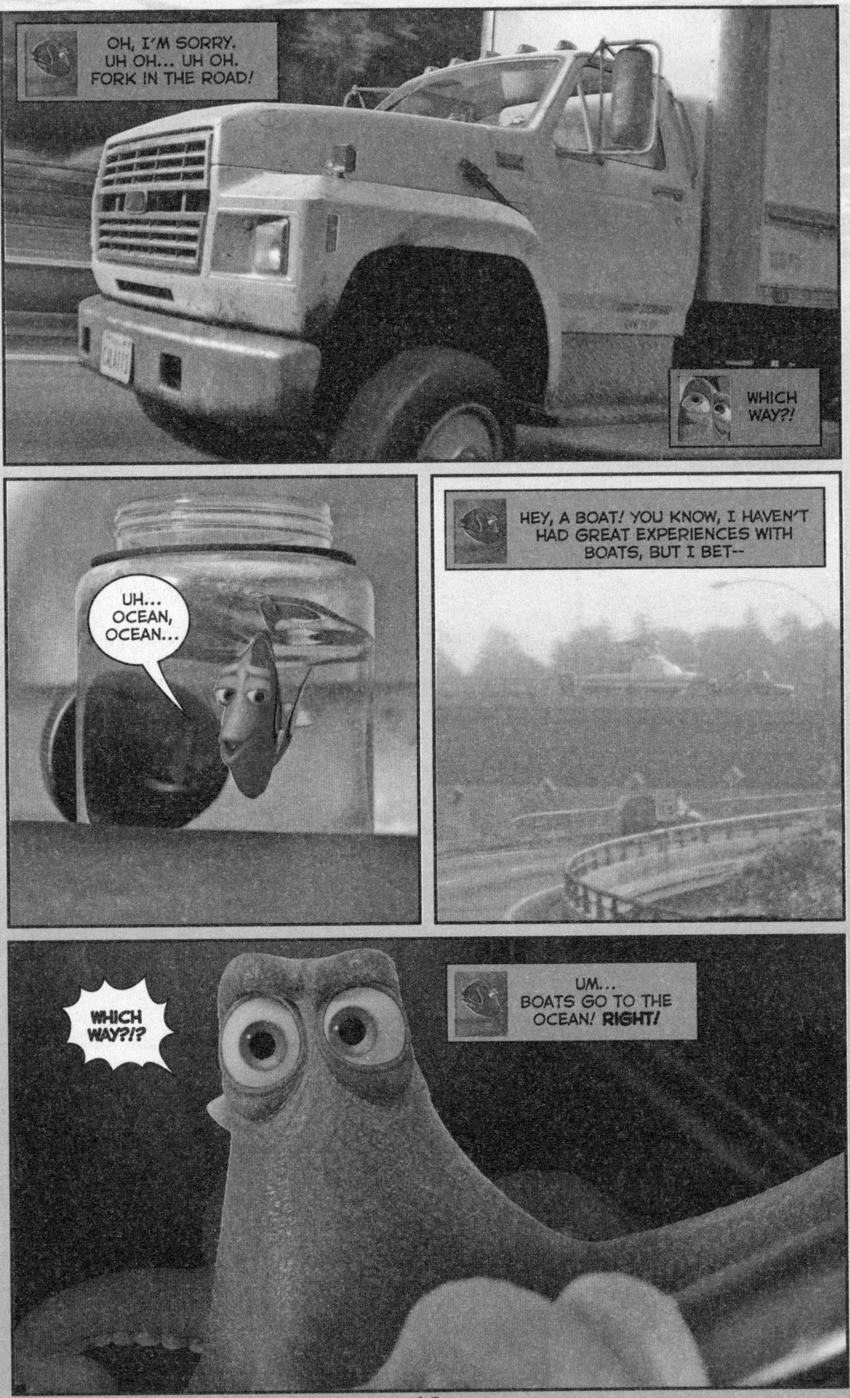
OH, I'M SORRY.
UH OH... UH OH.
FORK IN THE ROAD!
WHICH WAY?!
UH... OCEAN, OCEAN...
HEY, A BOAT! YOU KNOW, I HAVEN'T HAD GREAT EXPERIENCES WITH BOATS, BUT I BET--
WHICH WAY?!?
UM... BOATS GO TO THE OCEAN! RIGHT!

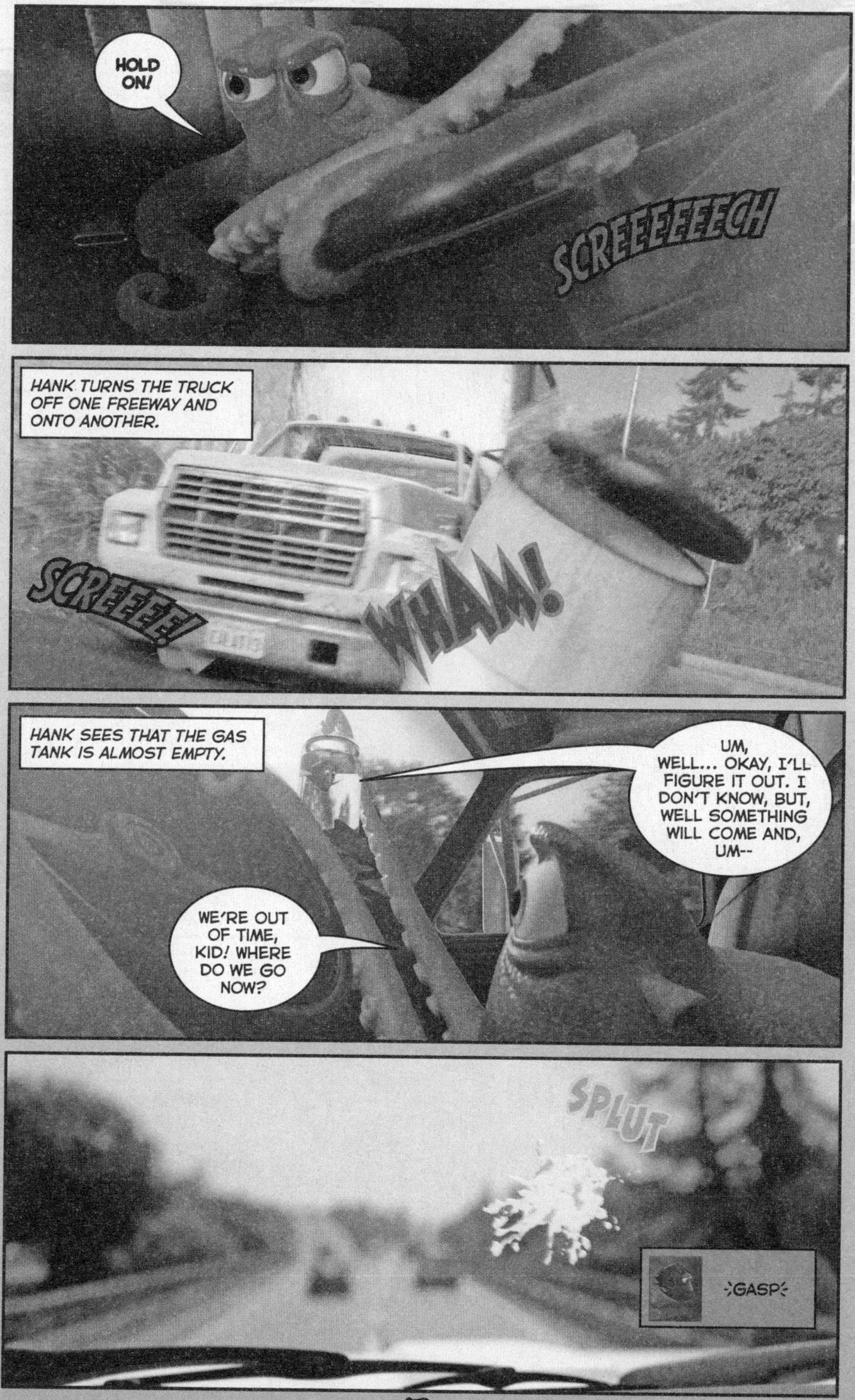
HOLD ON!
SCREEEEEECH
HANK TURNS THE TRUCK OFF ONE FREEWAY AND ONTO ANOTHER.
SCREEEEE!
WHAM!
HANK SEES THAT THE GAS TANK IS ALMOST EMPTY.
UM, WELL... OKAY, I'LL FIGURE IT OUT. I DON'T KNOW, BUT, WELL SOMETHING WILL COME AND, UM--
WE'RE OUT OF TIME, KID! WHERE DO WE GO NOW?
SPLUT
GASP

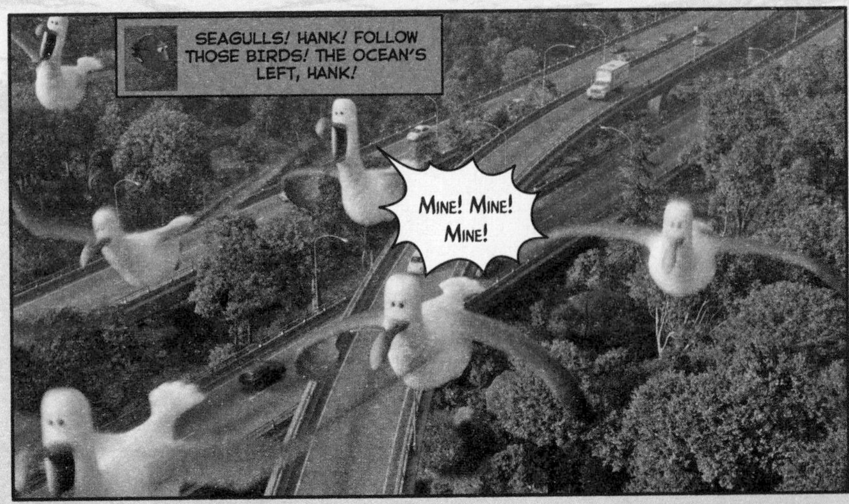
SEAGULLS! HANK! FOLLOW THOSE BIRDS! THE OCEAN'S LEFT, HANK!
MINE! MINE! MINE!

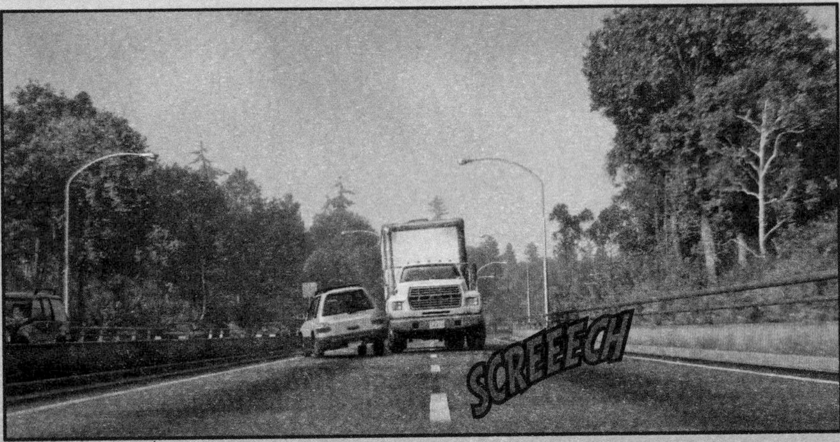
SCREEECH

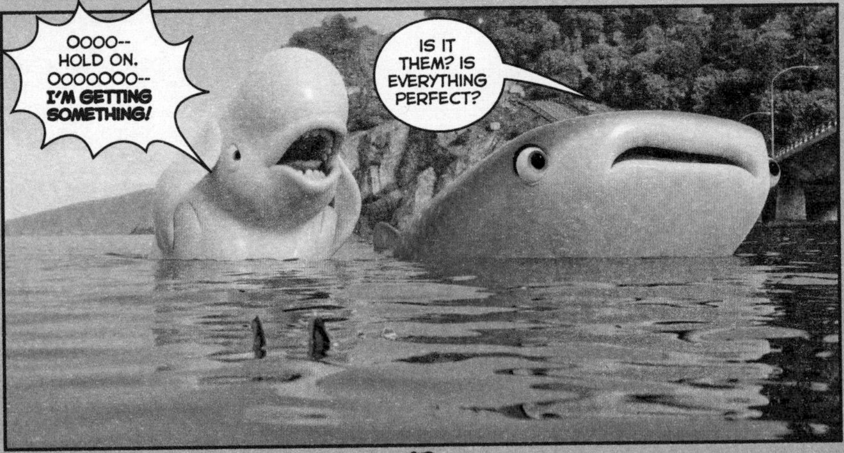
OOOO-- HOLD ON. OOOOOOO-- **I'M GETTING SOMETHING!**
IS IT THEM? IS EVERYTHING PERFECT?

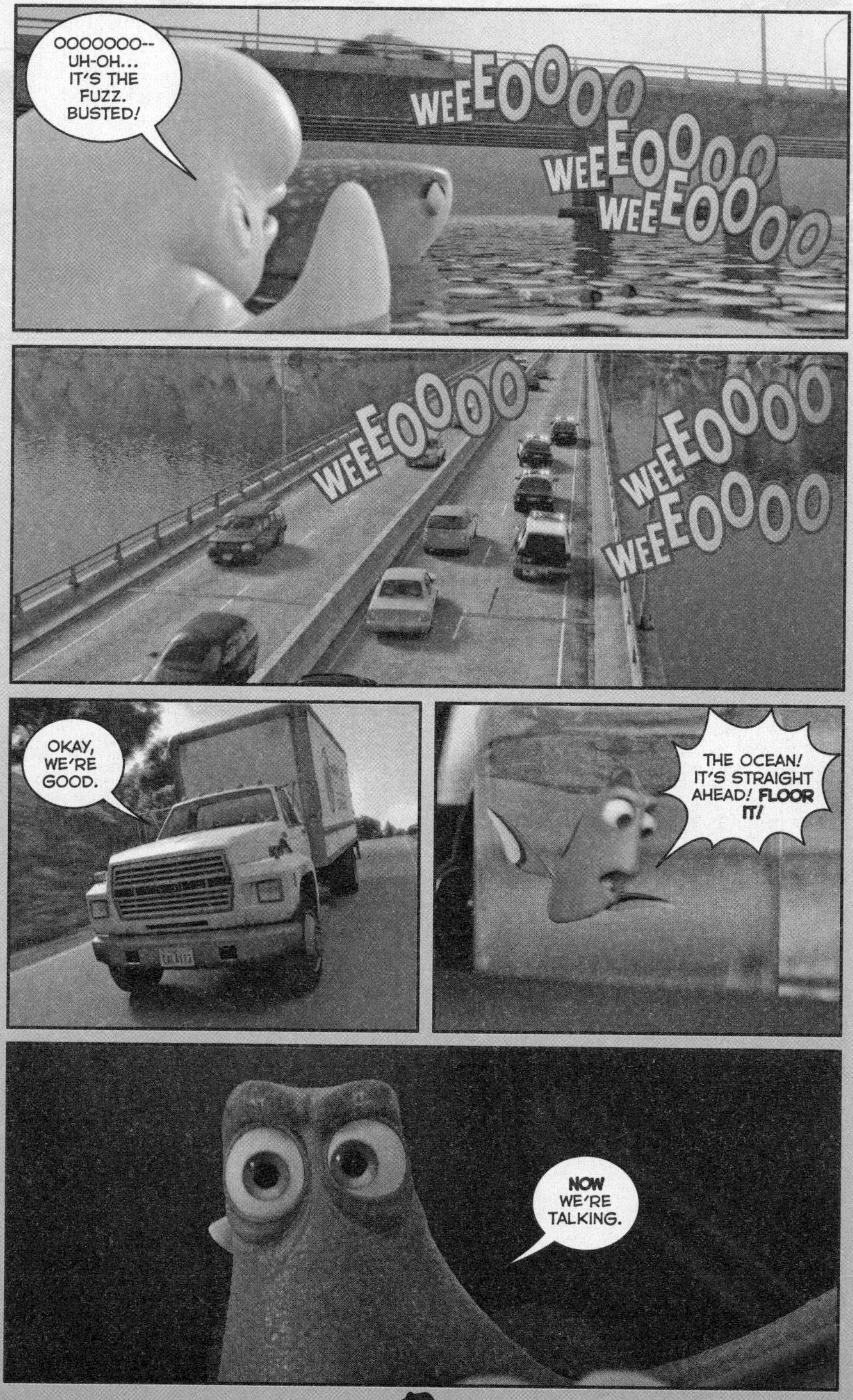
OOOOOOO-- UH-OH... IT'S THE FUZZ. BUSTED!
WEEEOOOO
WEEEOOOO
WEEEOOOO
WEEEOOOO
WEEEOOOO
WEEEOOOO
OKAY, WE'RE GOOD.
THE OCEAN! IT'S STRAIGHT AHEAD! **FLOOR IT!**
NOW WE'RE TALKING.

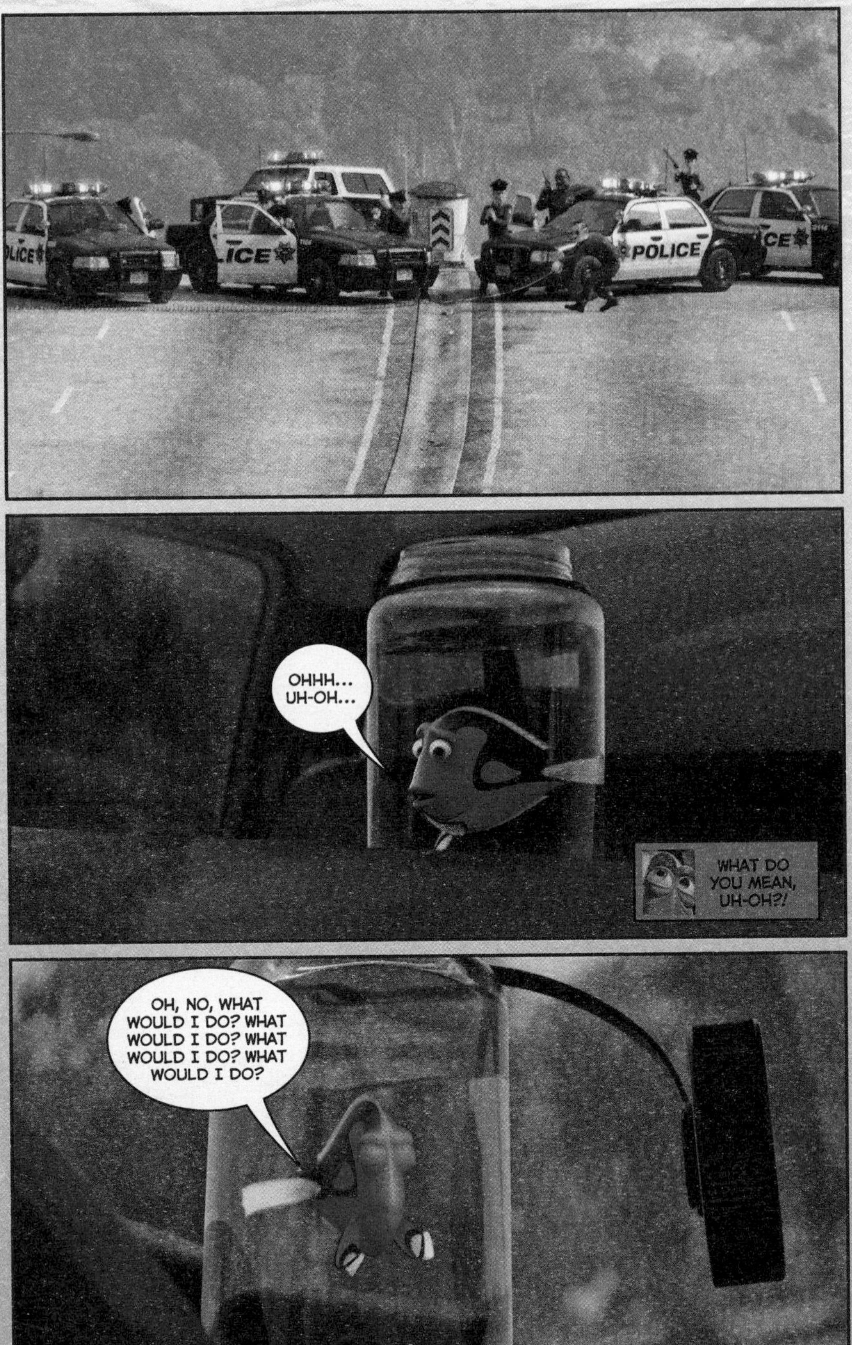
POLICE
OHHH... UH-OH...
WHAT DO YOU MEAN, UH-OH?!
OH, NO, WHAT WOULD I DO? WHAT WOULD I DO? WHAT WOULD I DO? WHAT WOULD I DO?

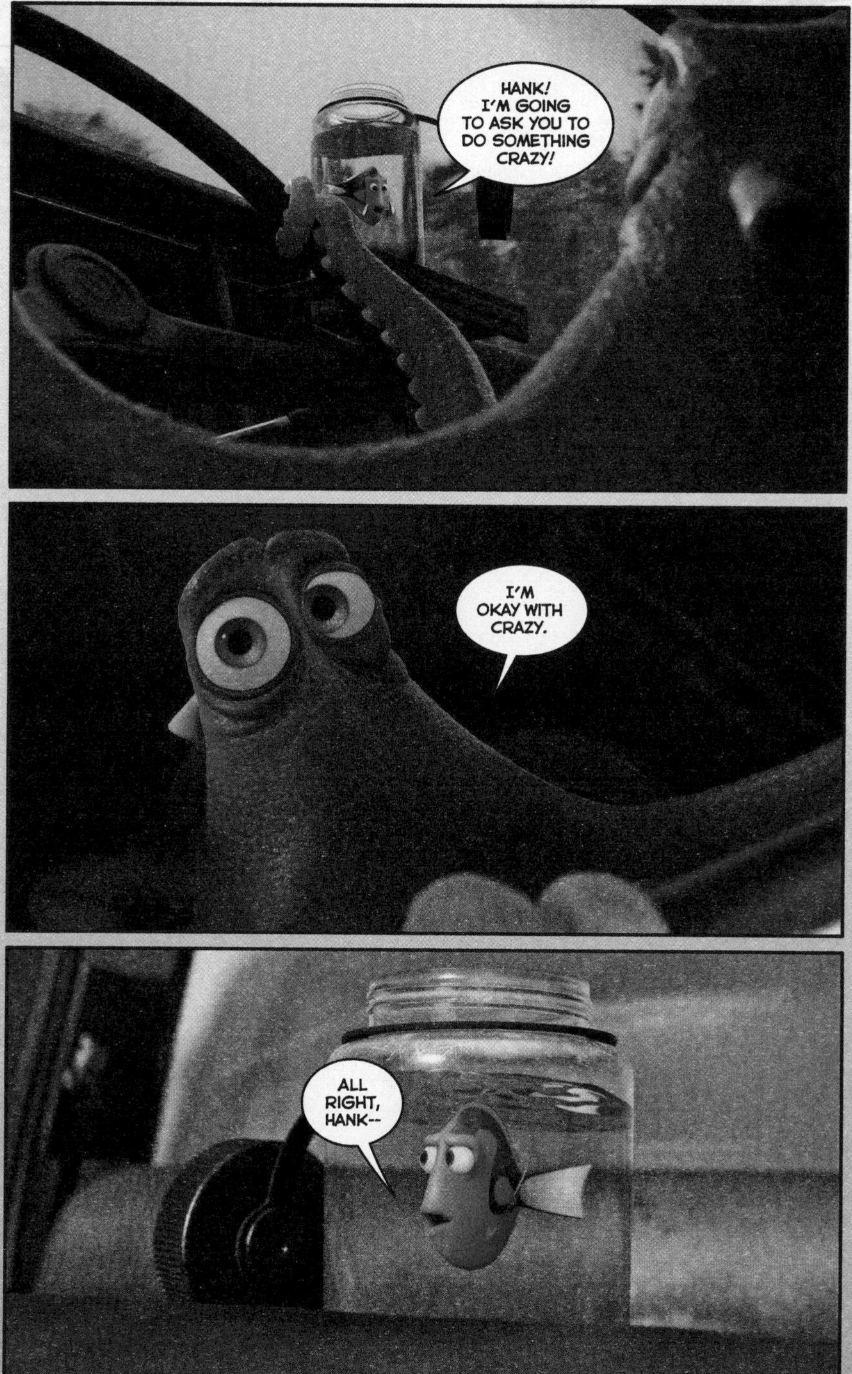
HANK! I'M GOING TO ASK YOU TO DO SOMETHING CRAZY!
I'M OKAY WITH CRAZY.
ALL RIGHT, HANK--

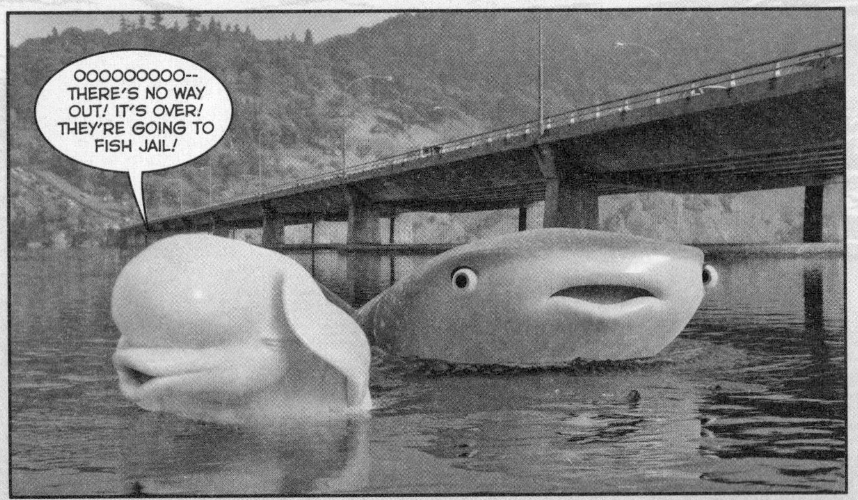
OOOOOOOOO-- THERE'S NO WAY OUT! IT'S OVER! THEY'RE GOING TO FISH JAIL!

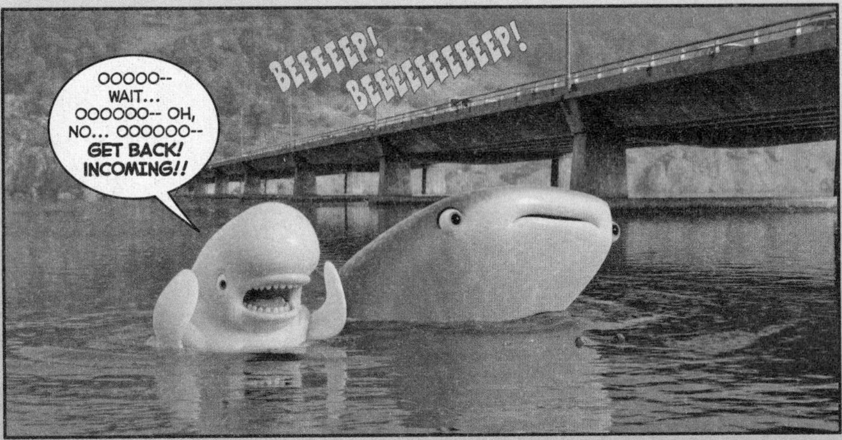
OOOOO-- WAIT... OOOOOO-- OH, NO... OOOOOO-- GET BACK! INCOMING!!
BEEEEEP! BEEEEEEEEEP!

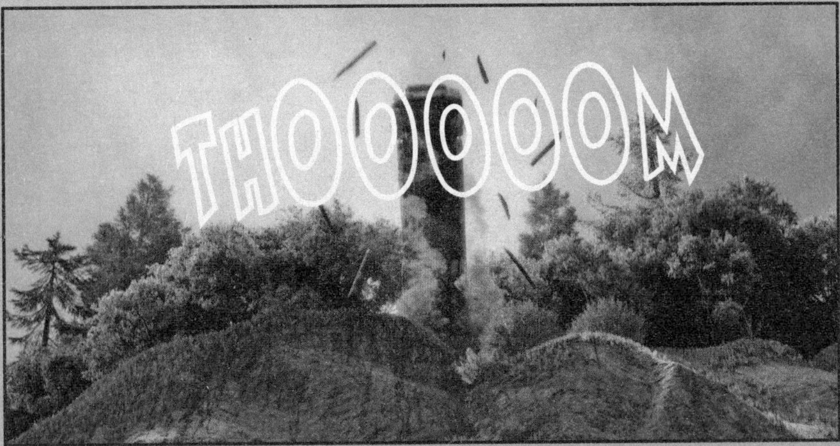
THOOOOOM

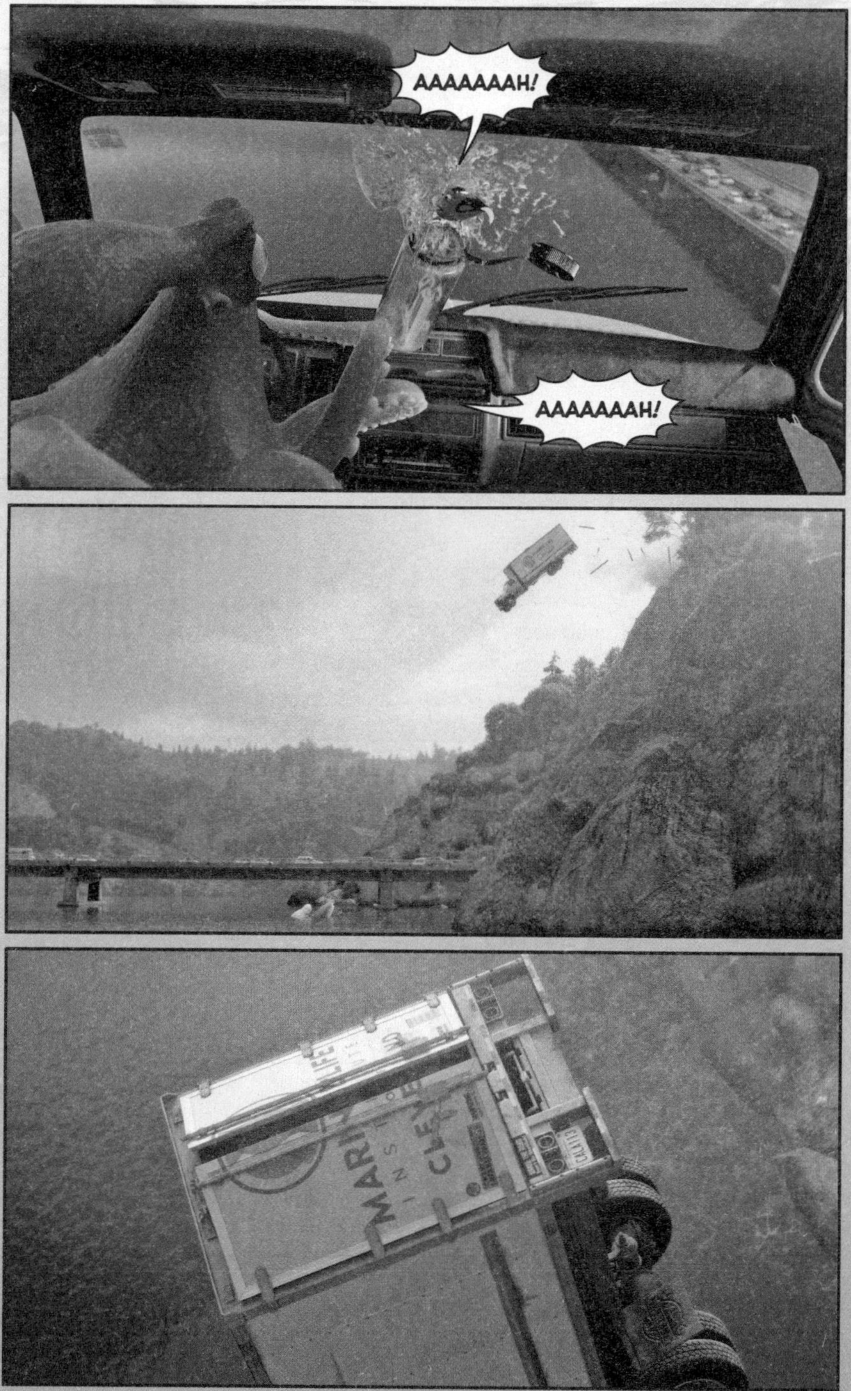
AAAAAAAH!
AAAAAAAH!

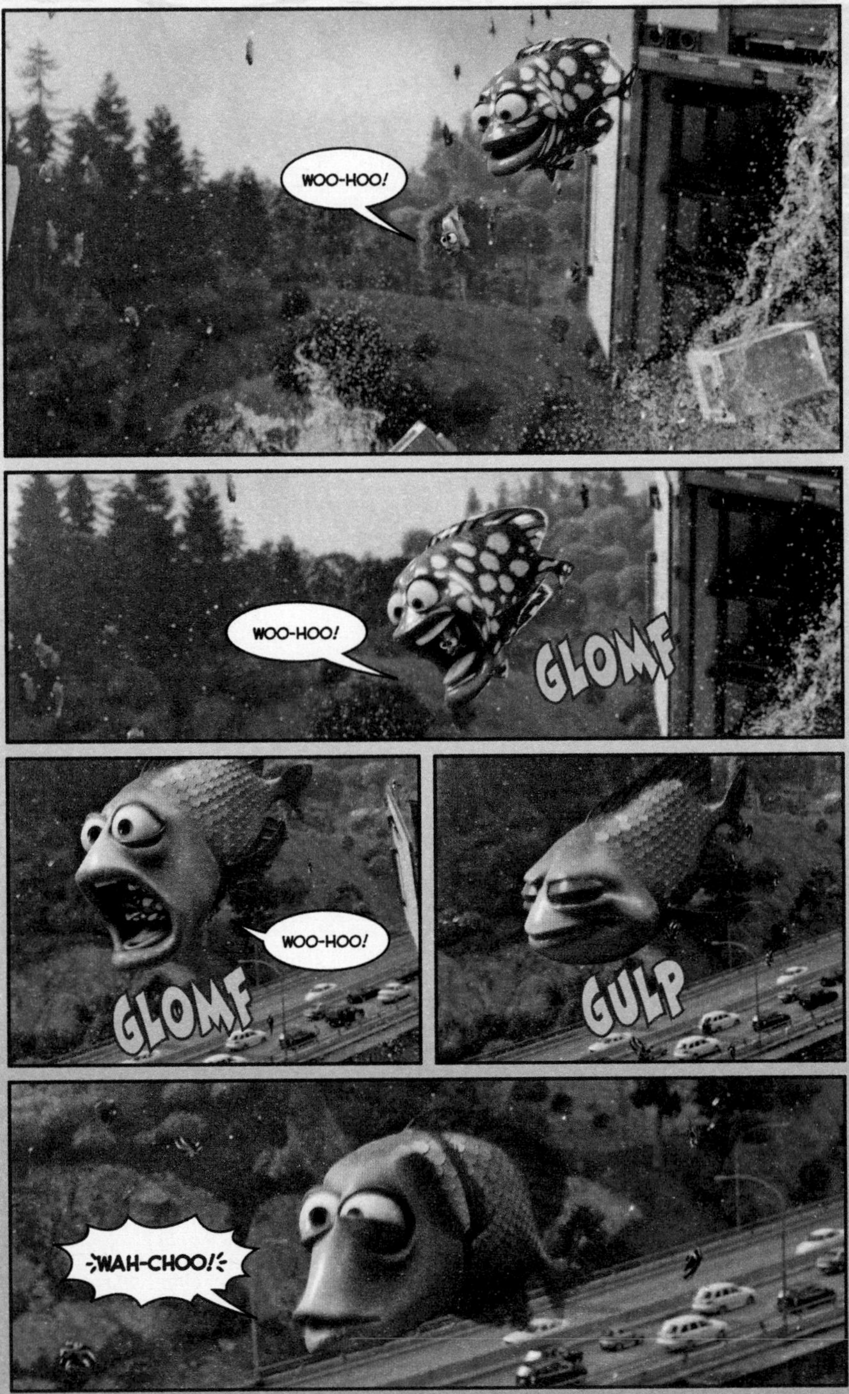
WOO-HOO!
WOO-HOO!
GLOMF
WOO-HOO!
GLOMF
GULP
WAH-CHOO!

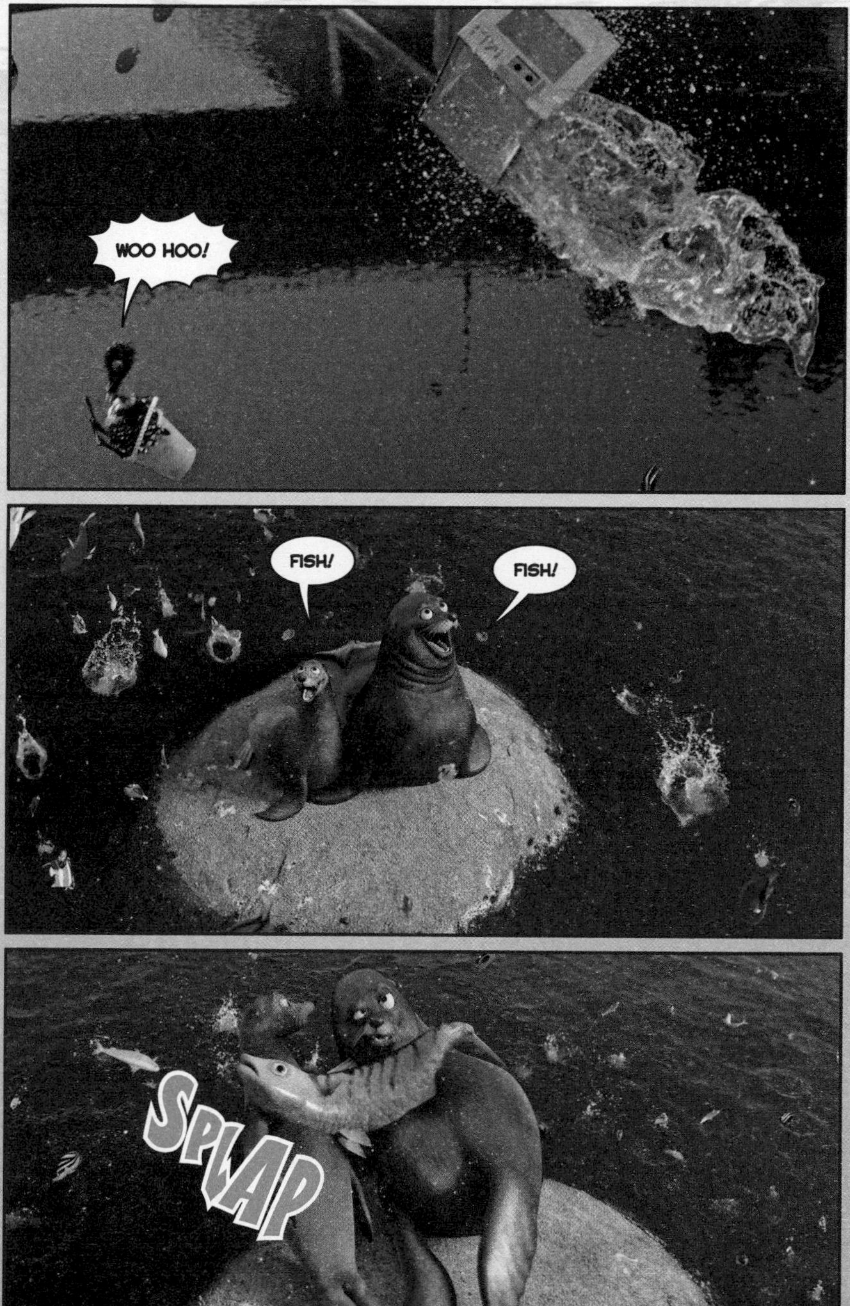
WOO HOO!
FISH!
FISH!
SPLAP

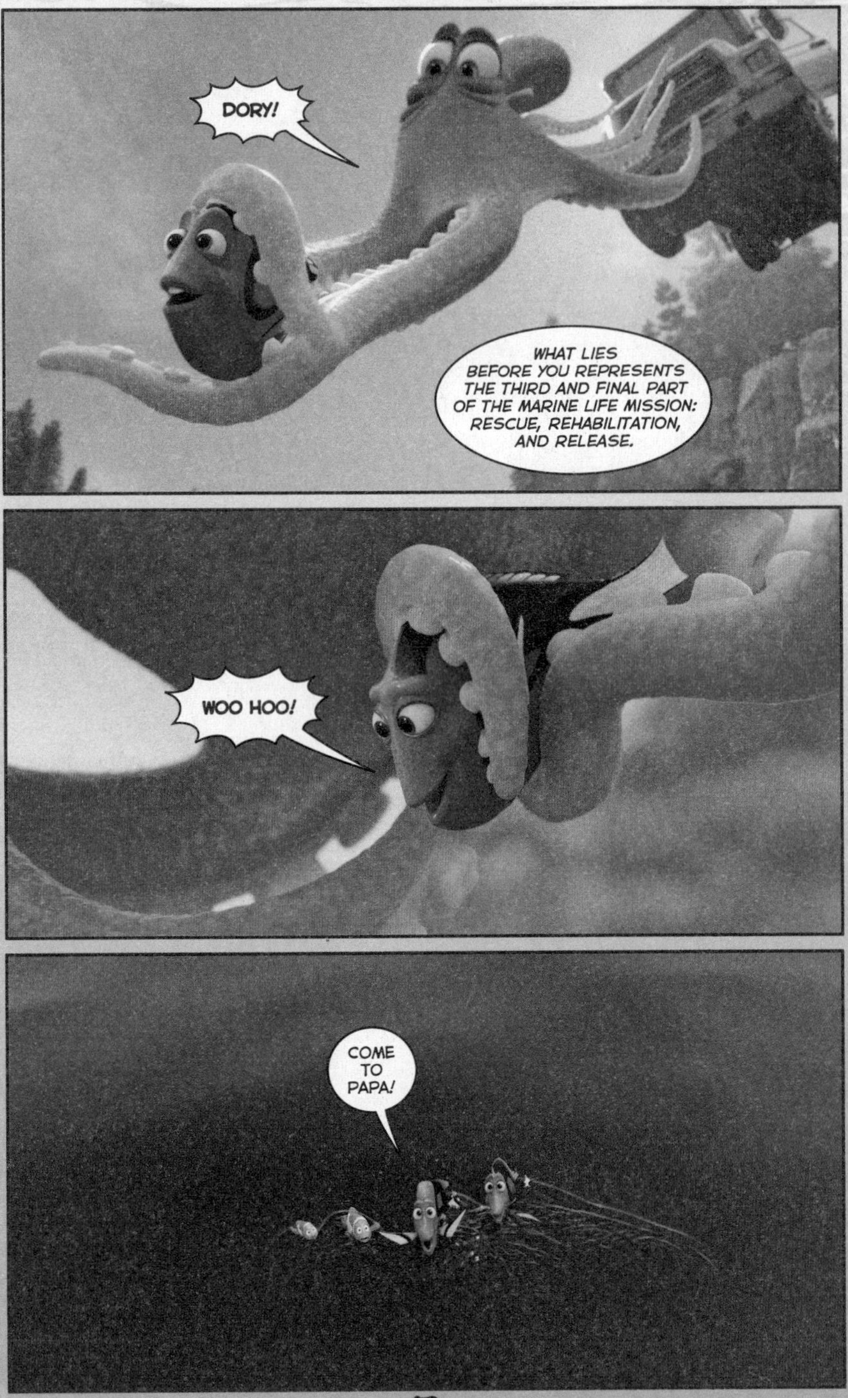
DORY!
WHAT LIES BEFORE YOU REPRESENTS THE THIRD AND FINAL PART OF THE MARINE LIFE MISSION: RESCUE, REHABILITATION, AND RELEASE.
WOO HOO!
COME TO PAPA!

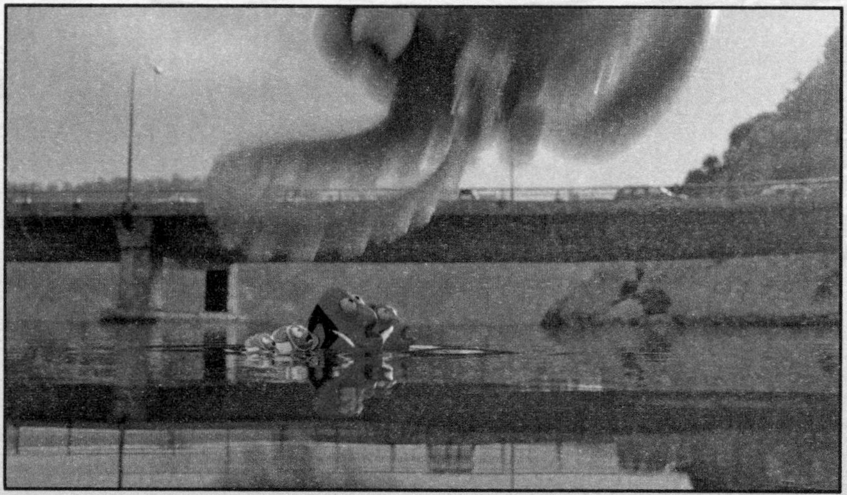

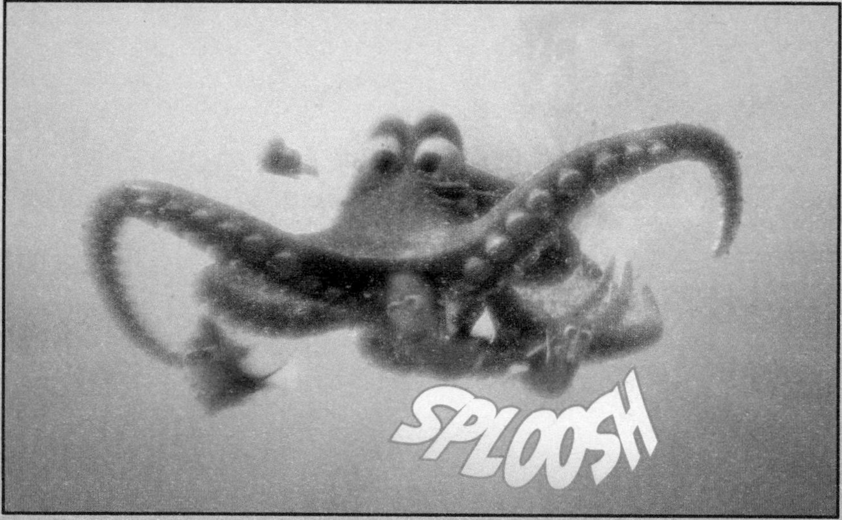
SPLOOSH

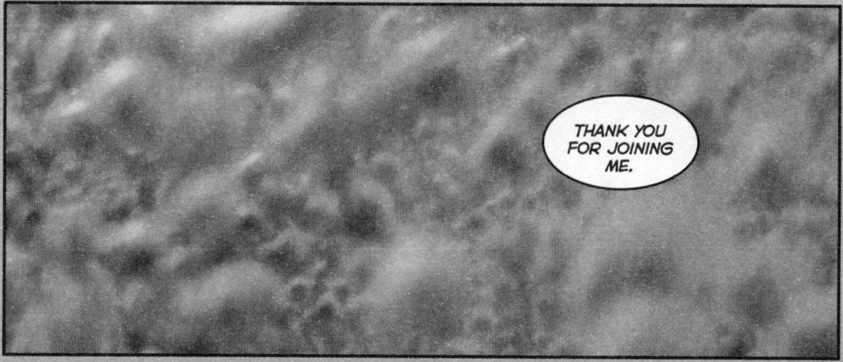
THANK YOU FOR JOINING ME.

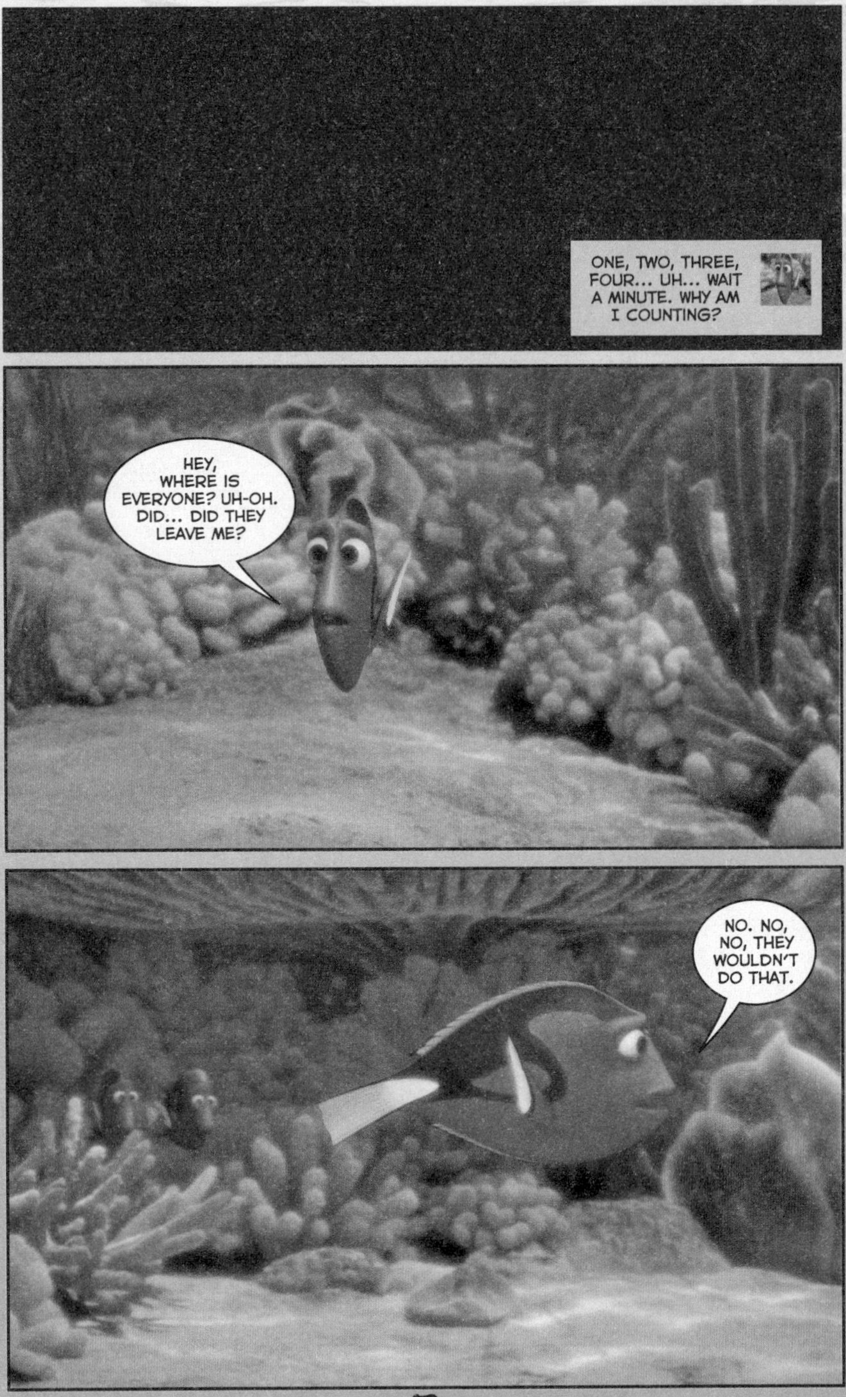
ONE, TWO, THREE, FOUR... UH... WAIT A MINUTE. WHY AM I COUNTING?
HEY, WHERE IS EVERYONE? UH-OH. DID... DID THEY LEAVE ME?
NO. NO, NO, THEY WOULDN'T DO THAT.

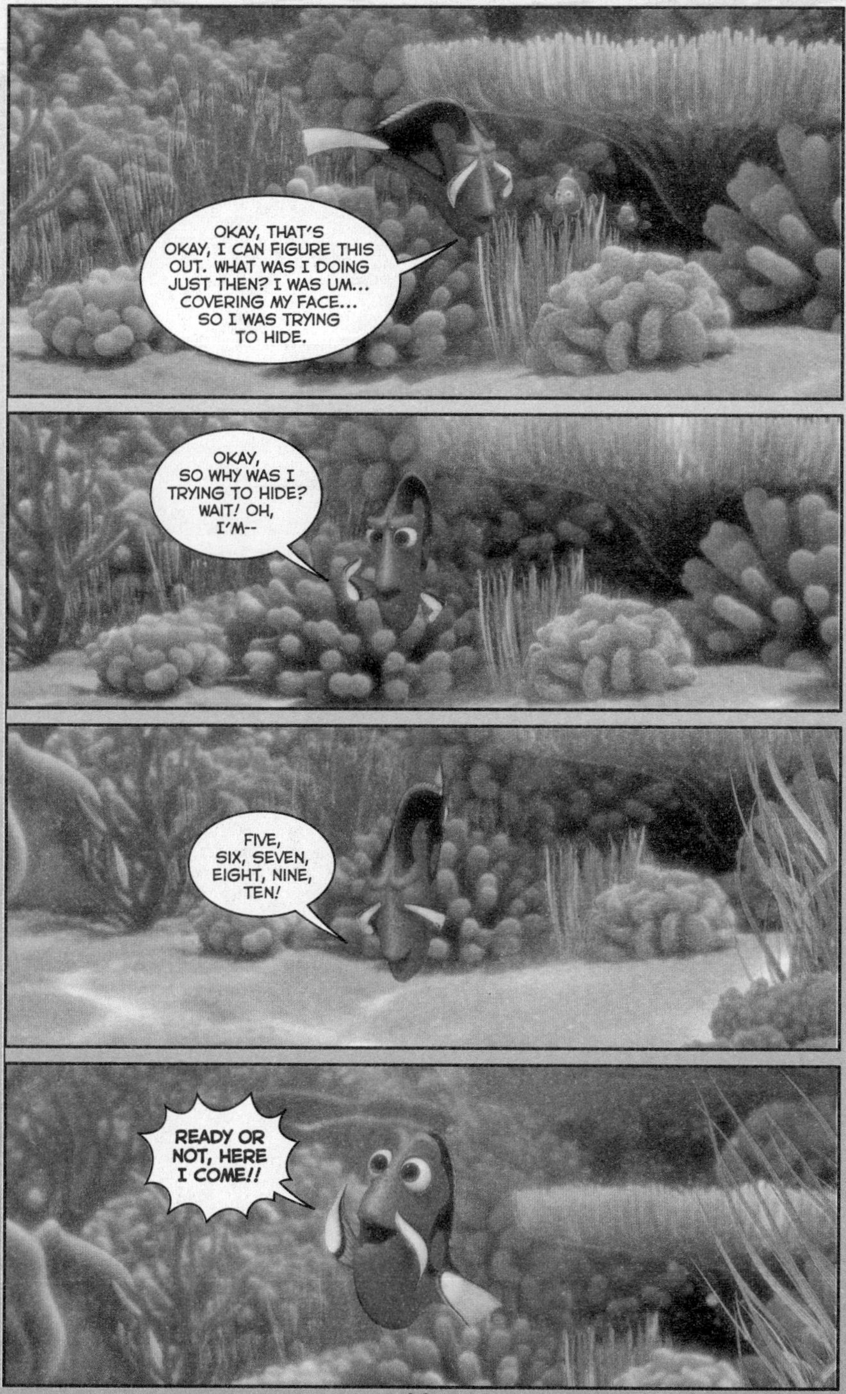
OKAY, THAT'S OKAY, I CAN FIGURE THIS OUT. WHAT WAS I DOING JUST THEN? I WAS UM... COVERING MY FACE... SO I WAS TRYING TO HIDE.
OKAY, SO WHY WAS I TRYING TO HIDE? WAIT! OH, I'M--
FIVE, SIX, SEVEN, EIGHT, NINE, TEN!
READY OR NOT, HERE I COME!!

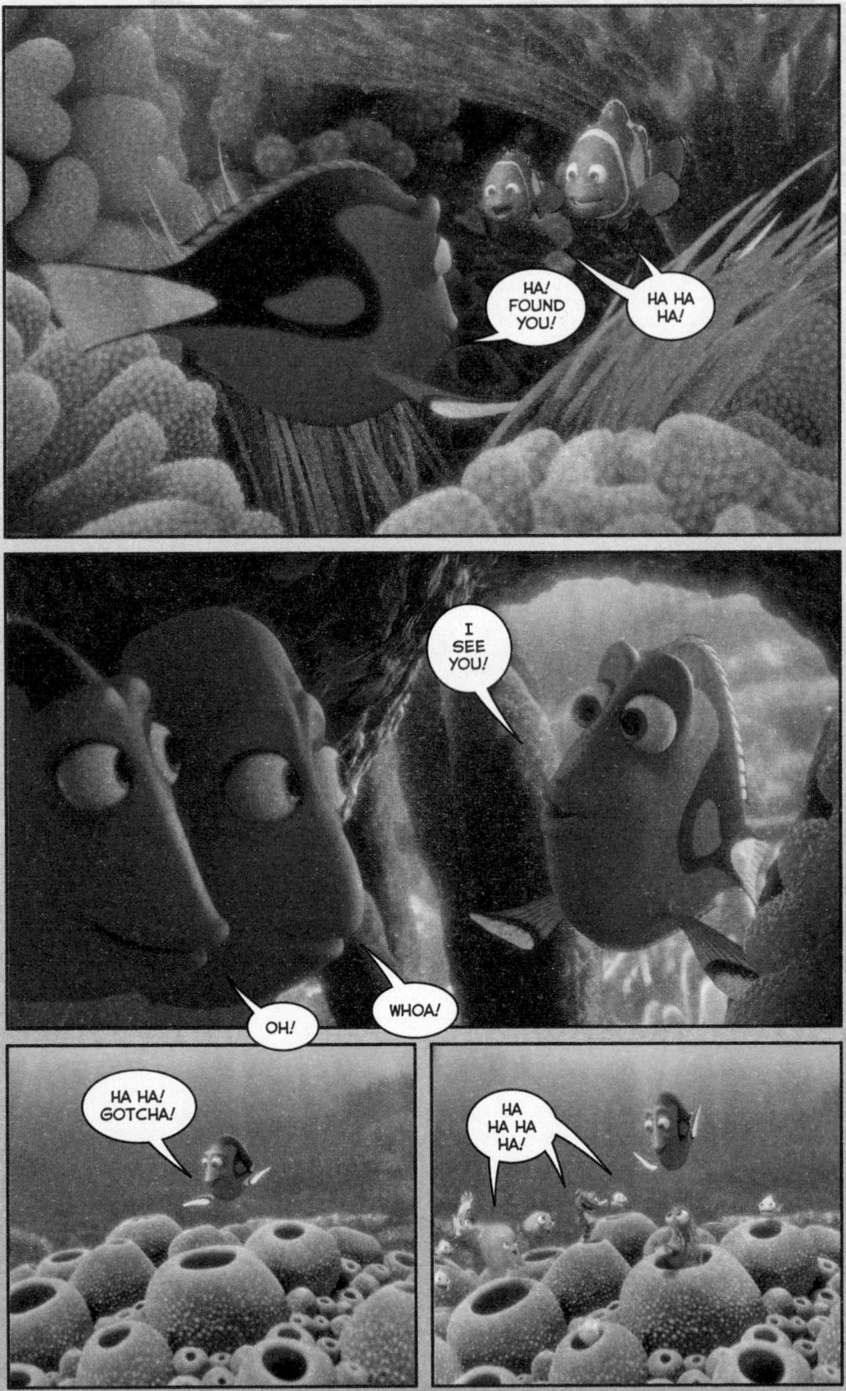
HA! FOUND YOU!
HA HA HA!
I SEE YOU!
OH!
WHOA!
HA HA! GOTCHA!
HA HA HA HA!

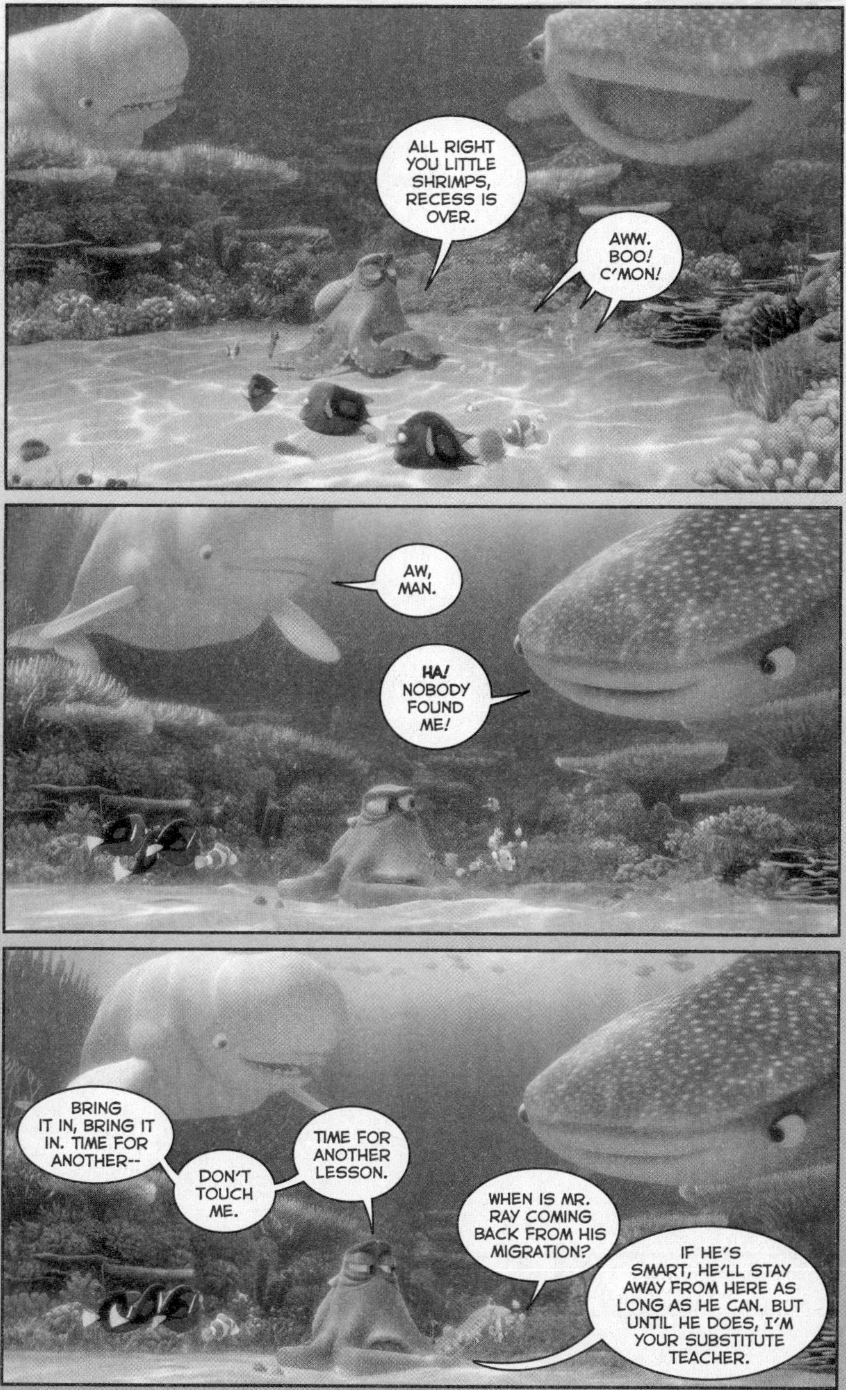
ALL RIGHT YOU LITTLE SHRIMPS, RECESS IS OVER.
AWW. BOO! C'MON!
AW, MAN.
HA! NOBODY FOUND ME!
BRING IT IN, BRING IT IN. TIME FOR ANOTHER--
DON'T TOUCH ME.
TIME FOR ANOTHER LESSON.
WHEN IS MR. RAY COMING BACK FROM HIS MIGRATION?
IF HE'S SMART, HE'LL STAY AWAY FROM HERE AS LONG AS HE CAN. BUT UNTIL HE DOES, I'M YOUR SUBSTITUTE TEACHER.

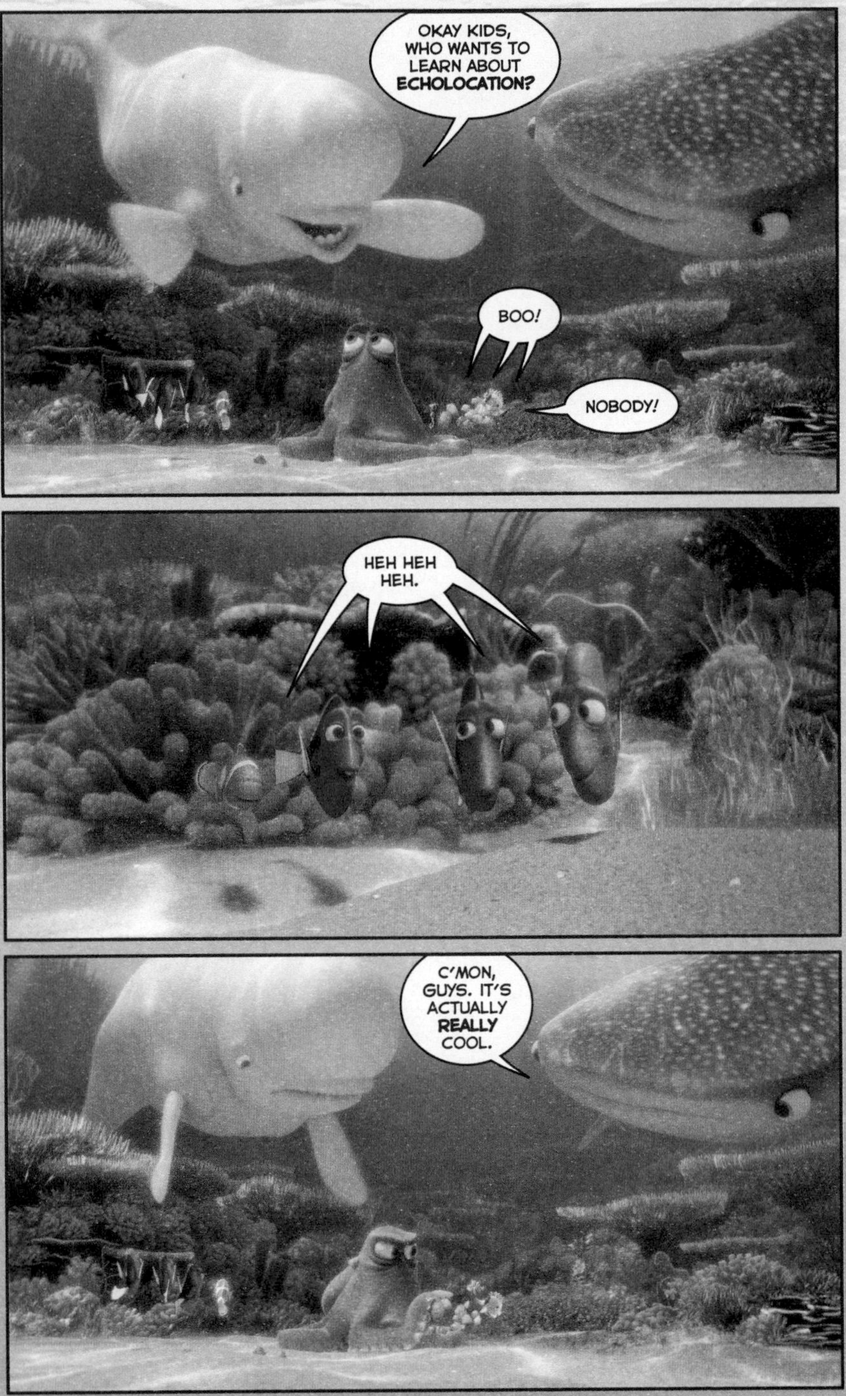
OKAY KIDS, WHO WANTS TO LEARN ABOUT ECHOLOCATION?
BOO!
NOBODY!
HEH HEH HEH.
C'MON, GUYS. IT'S ACTUALLY REALLY COOL.

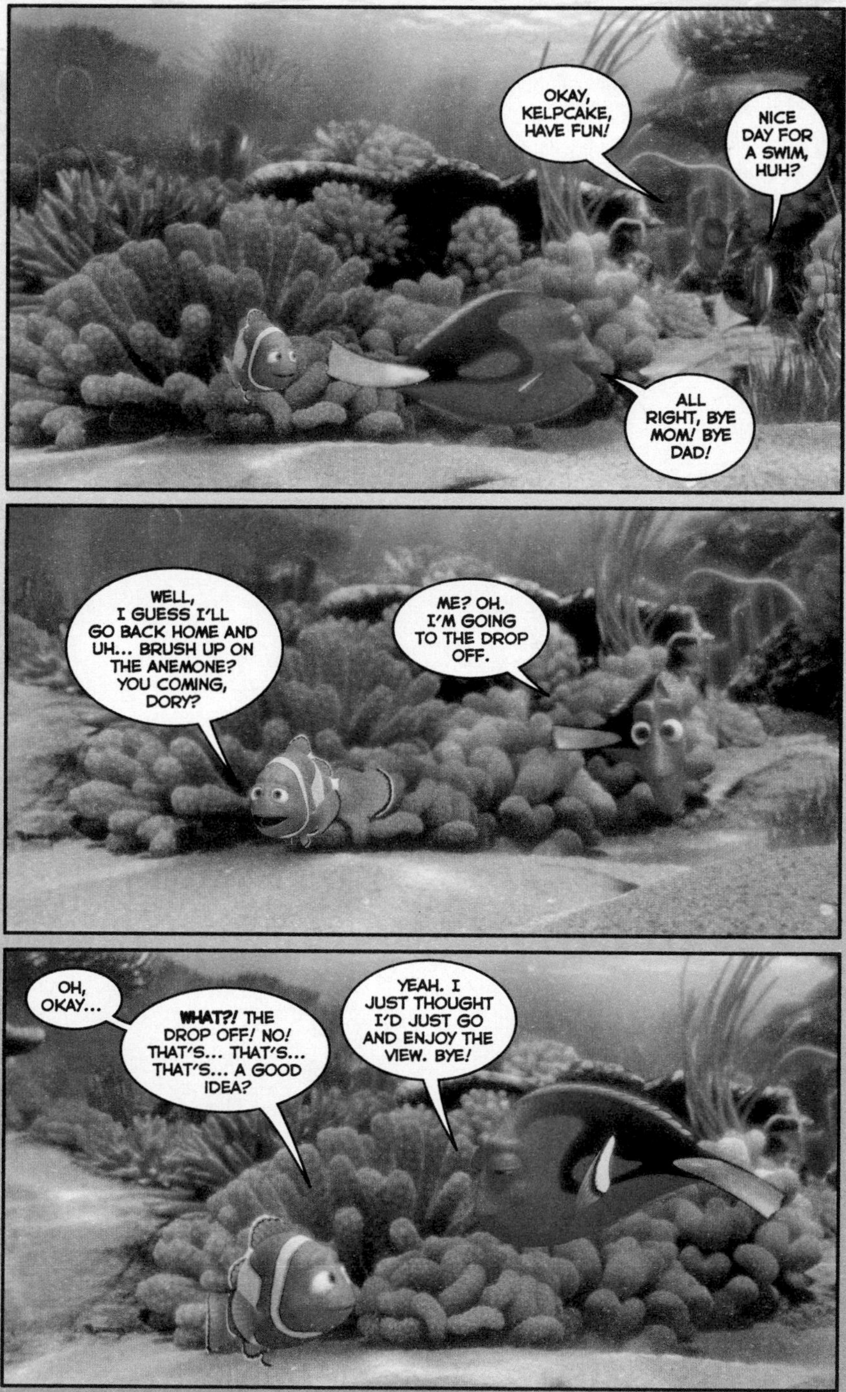
OKAY, KELPCAKE, HAVE FUN!
NICE DAY FOR A SWIM, HUH?
ALL RIGHT, BYE MOM! BYE DAD!
WELL, I GUESS I'LL GO BACK HOME AND UH... BRUSH UP ON THE ANEMONE? YOU COMING, DORY?
ME? OH. I'M GOING TO THE DROP OFF.
OH, OKAY...
WHAT?! THE DROP OFF! NO! THAT'S... THAT'S... THAT'S... A GOOD IDEA?
YEAH. I JUST THOUGHT I'D JUST GO AND ENJOY THE VIEW. BYE!

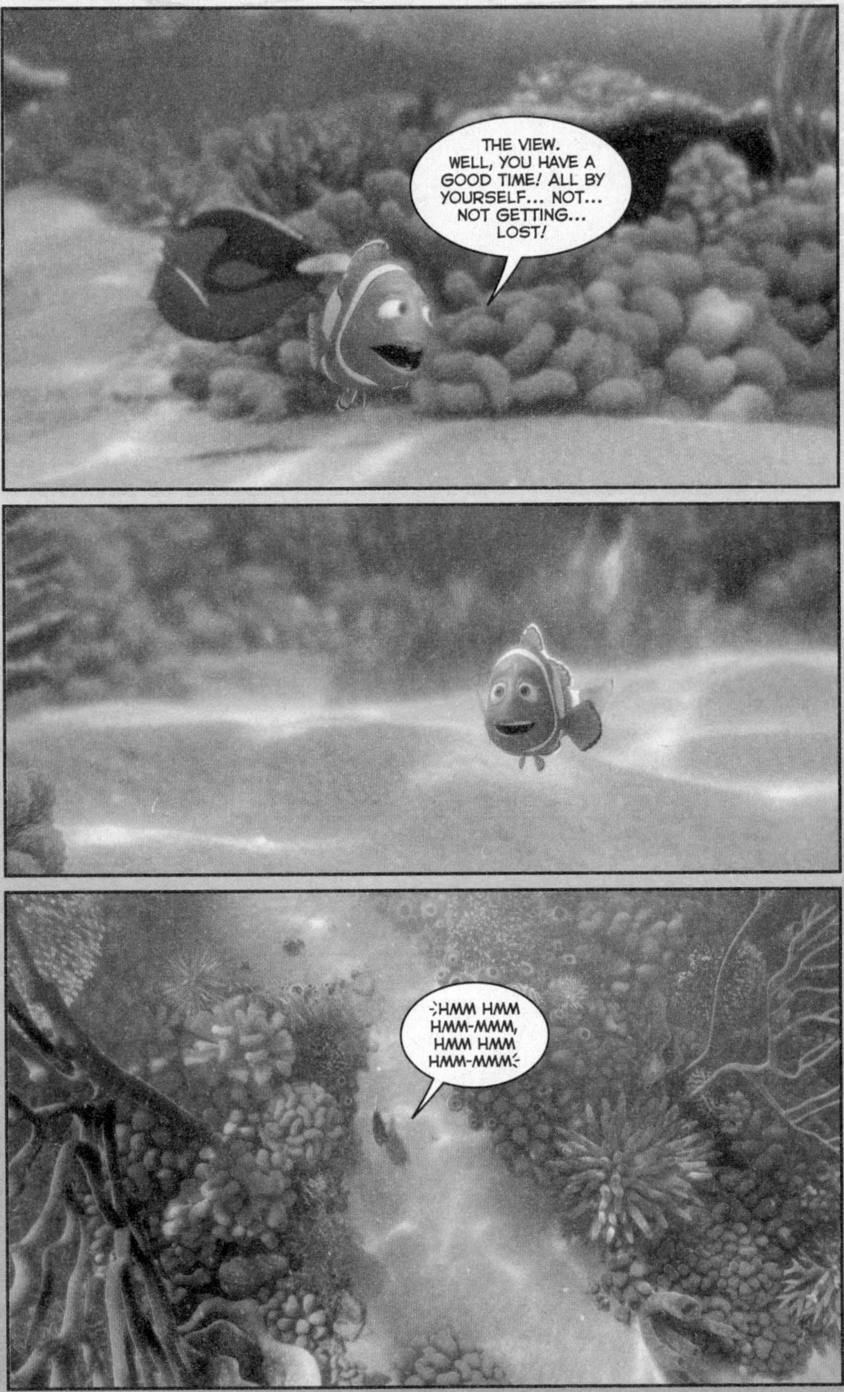
THE VIEW. WELL, YOU HAVE A GOOD TIME! ALL BY YOURSELF... NOT... NOT GETTING... LOST!
HMM HMM HMM-MMM, HMM HMM HMM-MMM

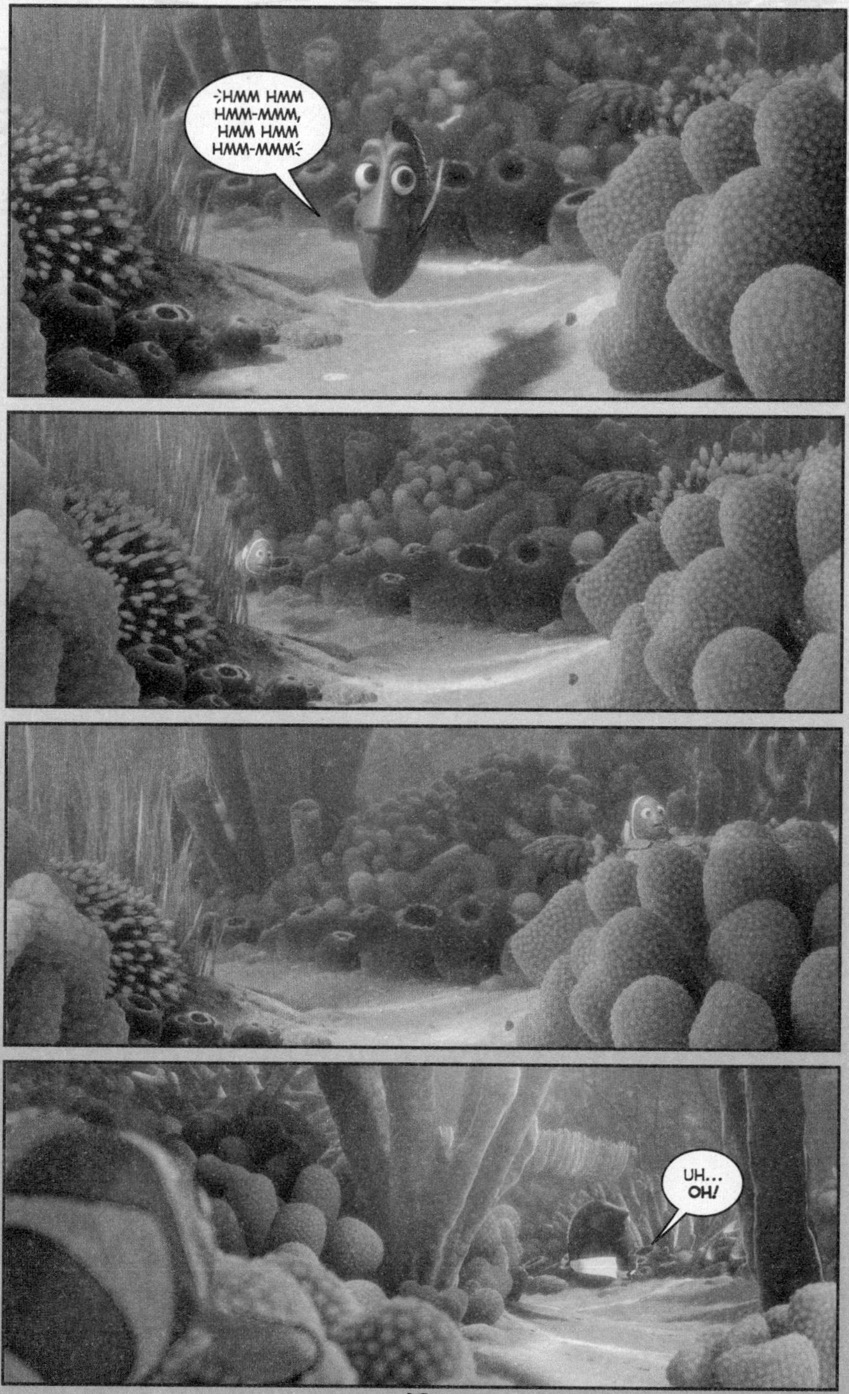
HMM HMM
HMM-MMM,
HMM HMM
HMM-MMM
UH...
OH!

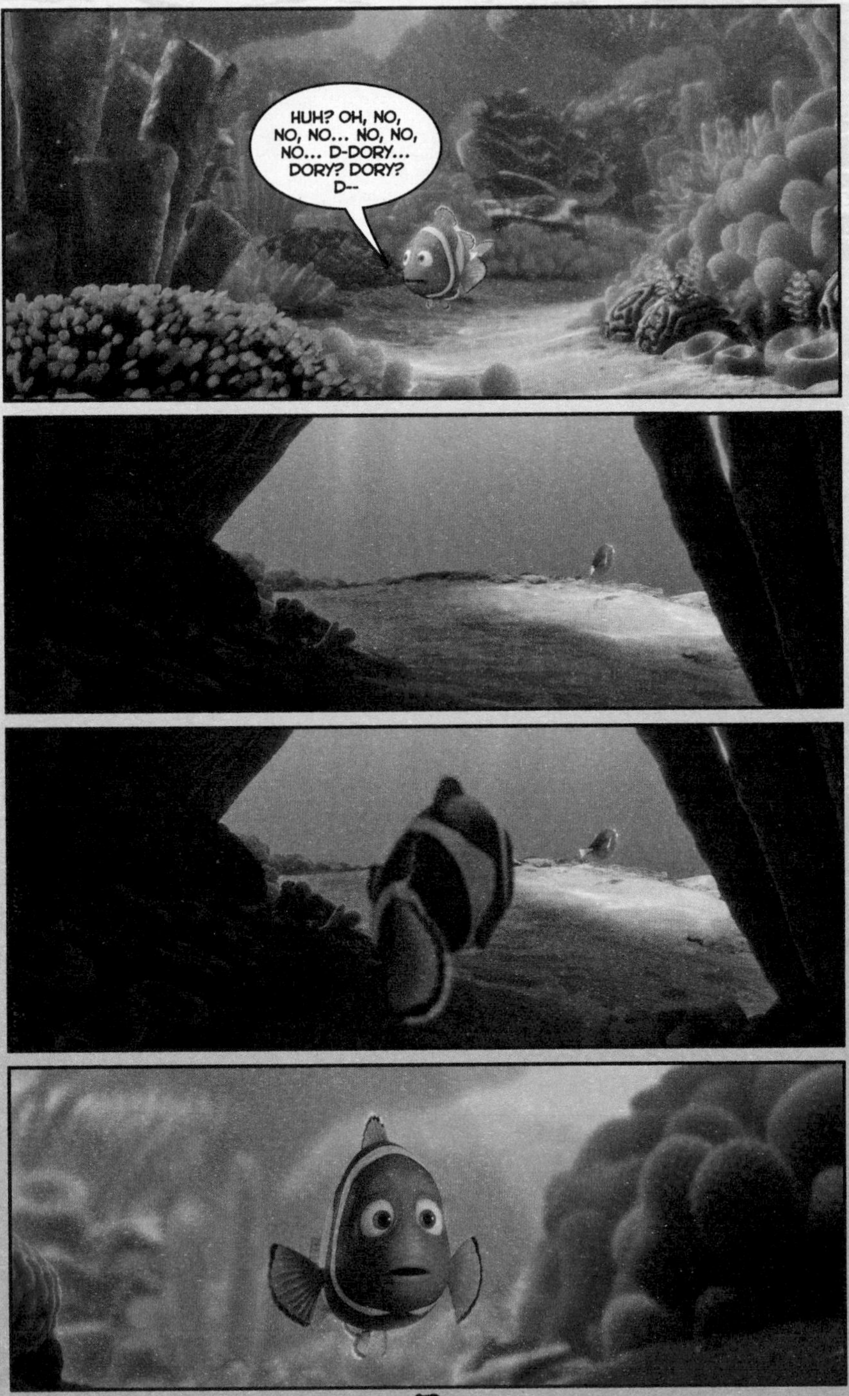
HUH? OH, NO, NO, NO... NO, NO, NO... D-DORY... DORY? DORY? D--

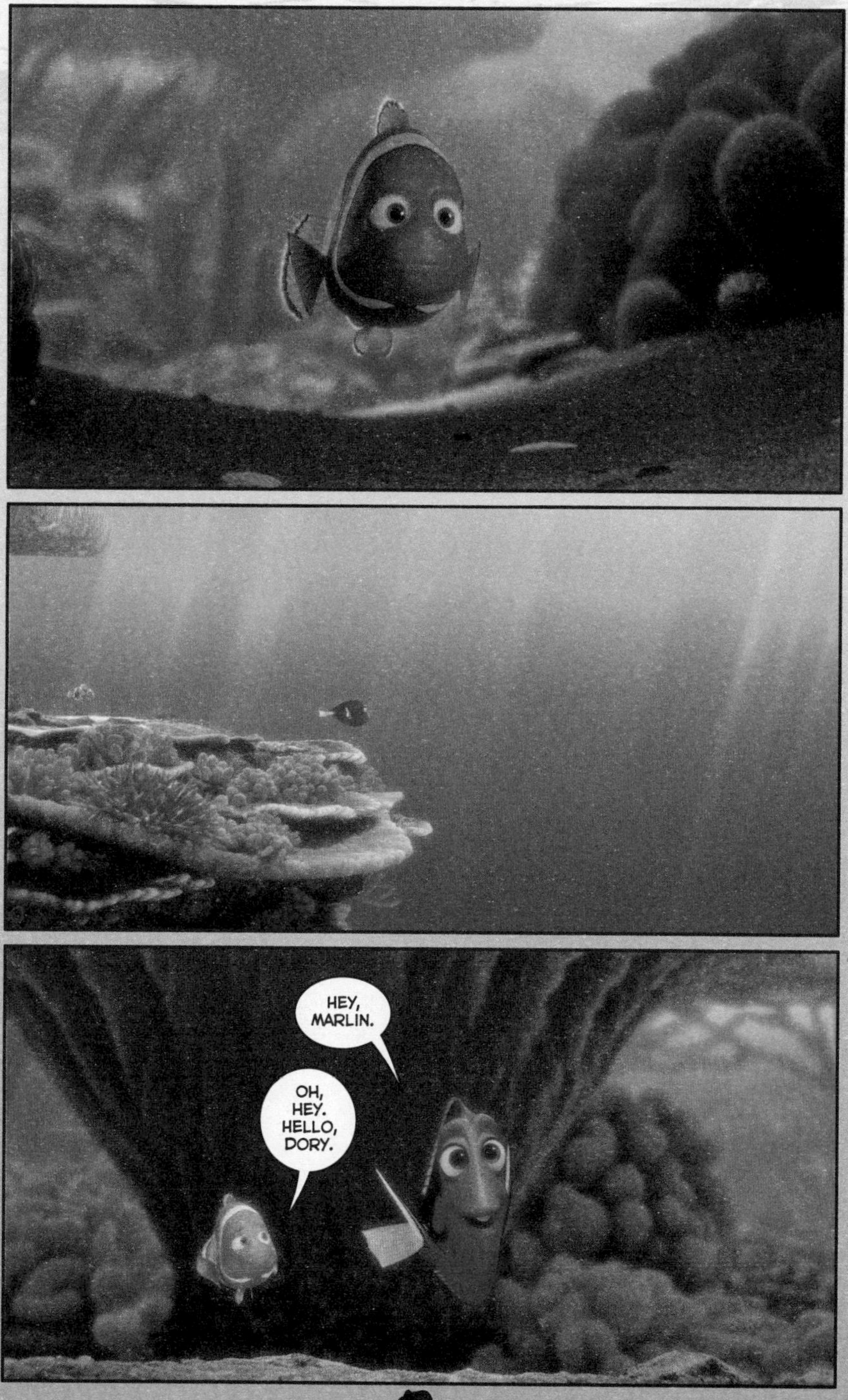
HEY, MARLIN.
OH, HEY. HELLO, DORY.

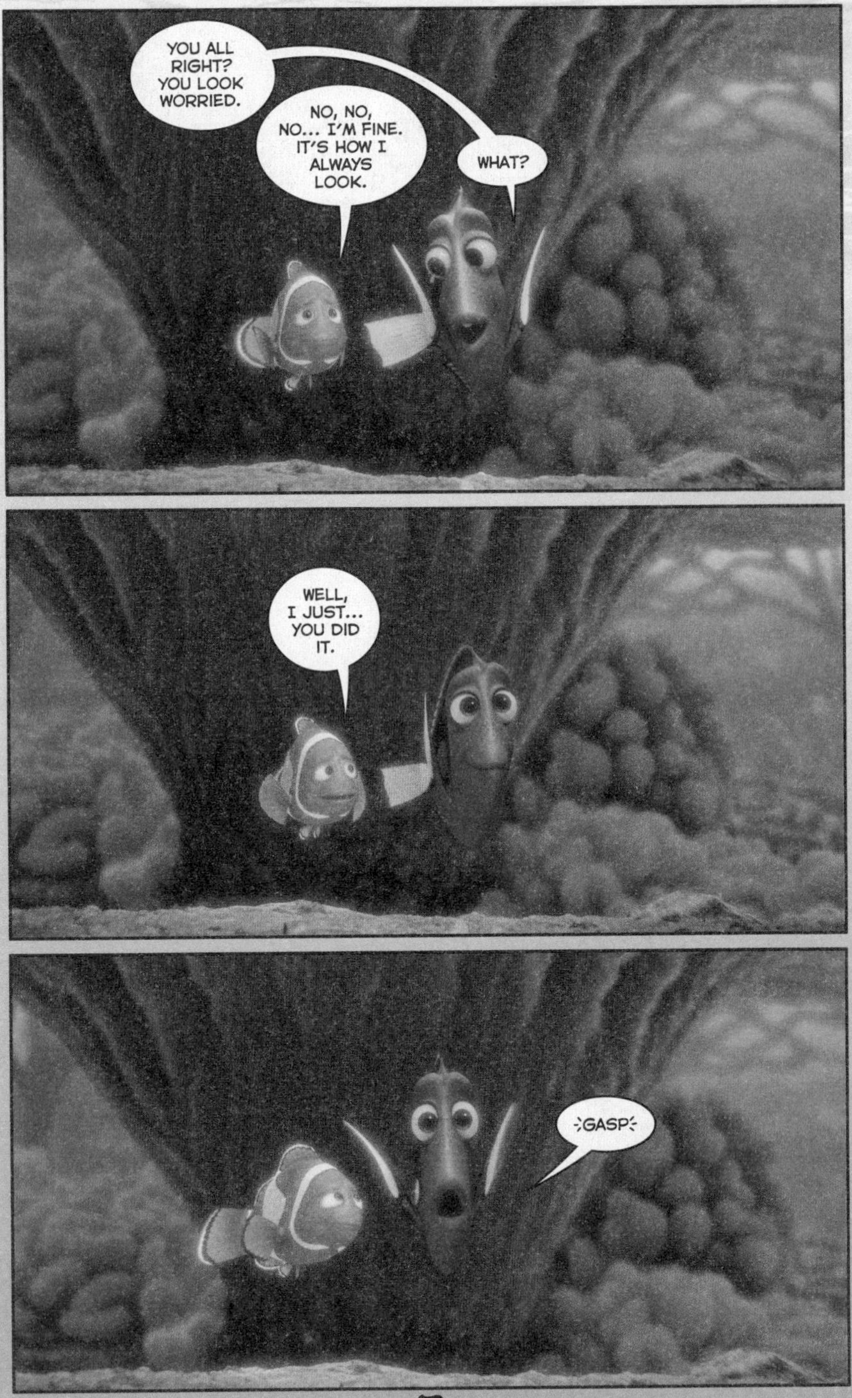
YOU ALL RIGHT? YOU LOOK WORRIED.
NO, NO, NO... I'M FINE. IT'S HOW I ALWAYS LOOK.
WHAT?
WELL, I JUST... YOU DID IT.
GASP

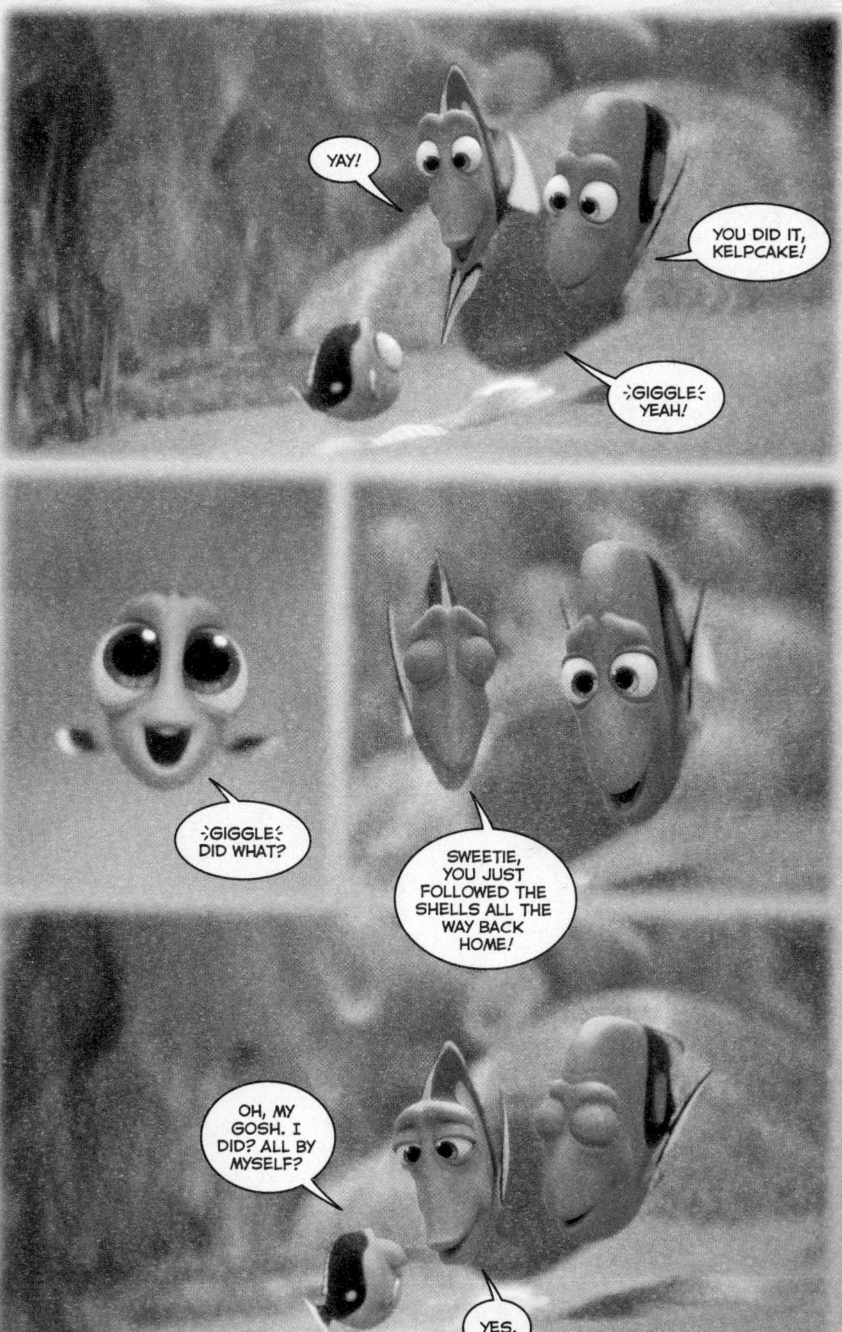
YAY!
YOU DID IT, KELPCAKE!
GIGGLE YEAH!
GIGGLE DID WHAT?
SWEETIE, YOU JUST FOLLOWED THE SHELLS ALL THE WAY BACK HOME!
OH, MY GOSH. I DID? ALL BY MYSELF?
YES.

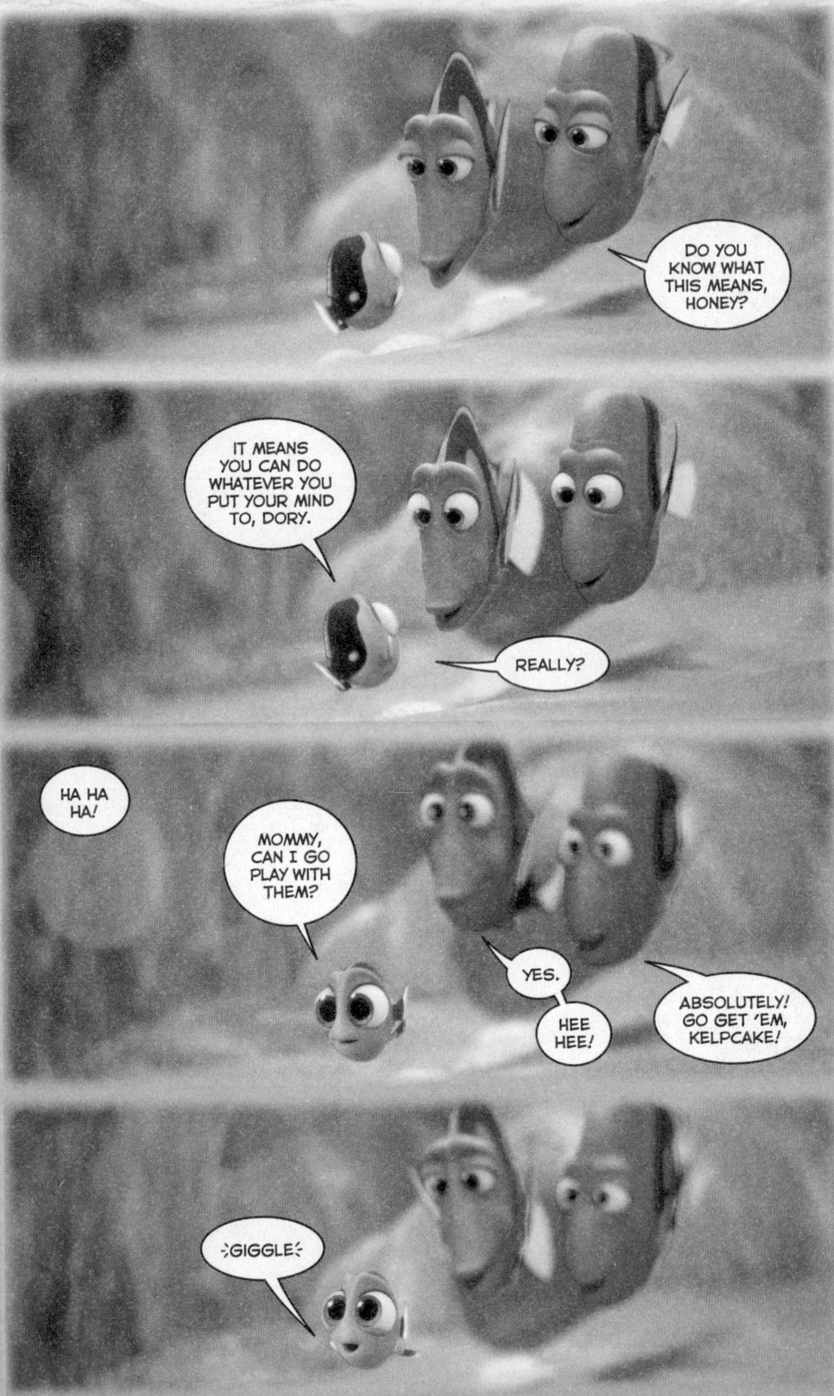
DO YOU KNOW WHAT THIS MEANS, HONEY?
IT MEANS YOU CAN DO WHATEVER YOU PUT YOUR MIND TO, DORY.
REALLY?
HA HA HA!
MOMMY, CAN I GO PLAY WITH THEM?
YES.
HEE HEE!
ABSOLUTELY! GO GET 'EM, KELPCAKE!
GIGGLE

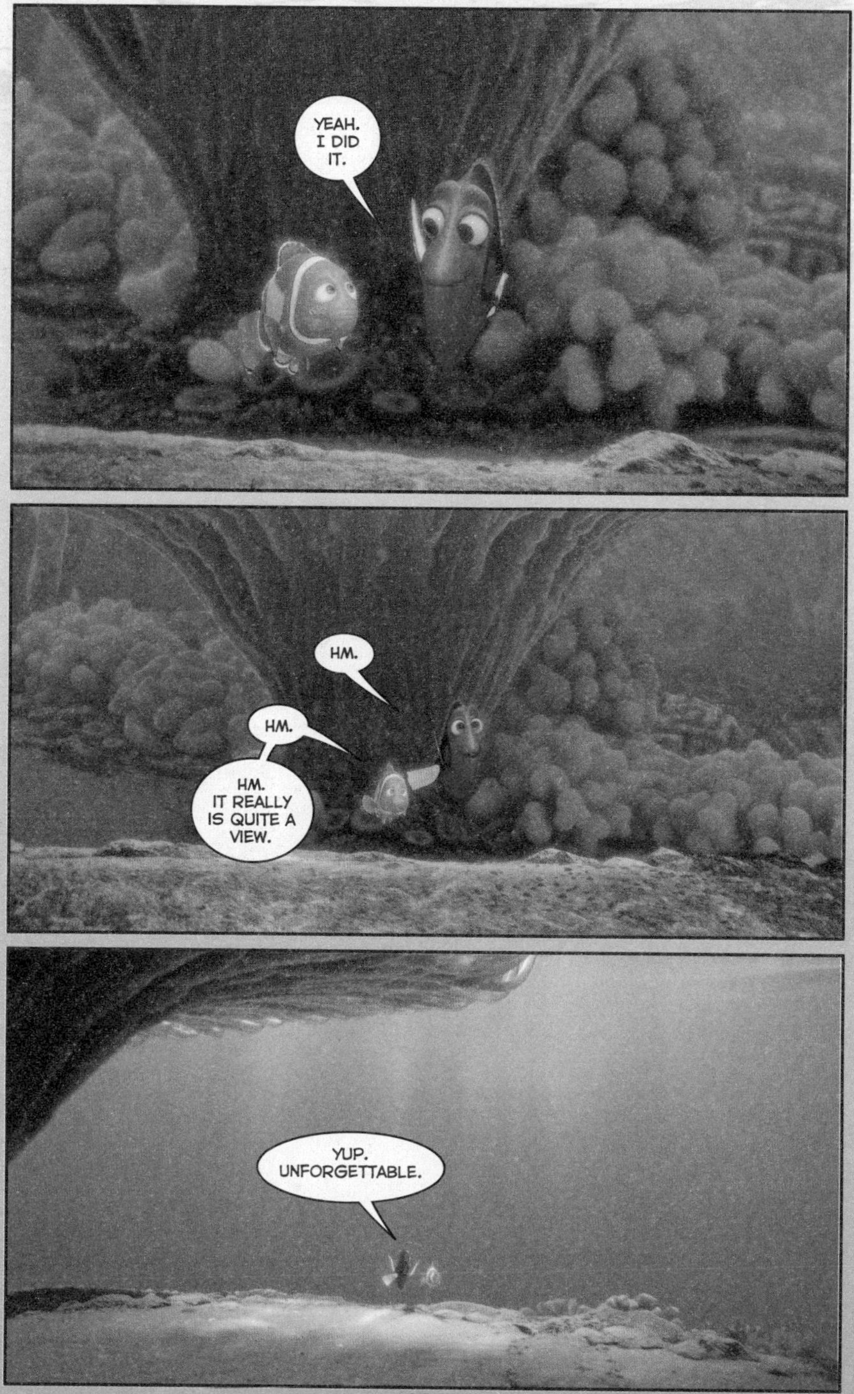
YEAH. I DID IT.
HM.
HM.
HM. IT REALLY IS QUITE A VIEW.
YUP. UNFORGETTABLE.

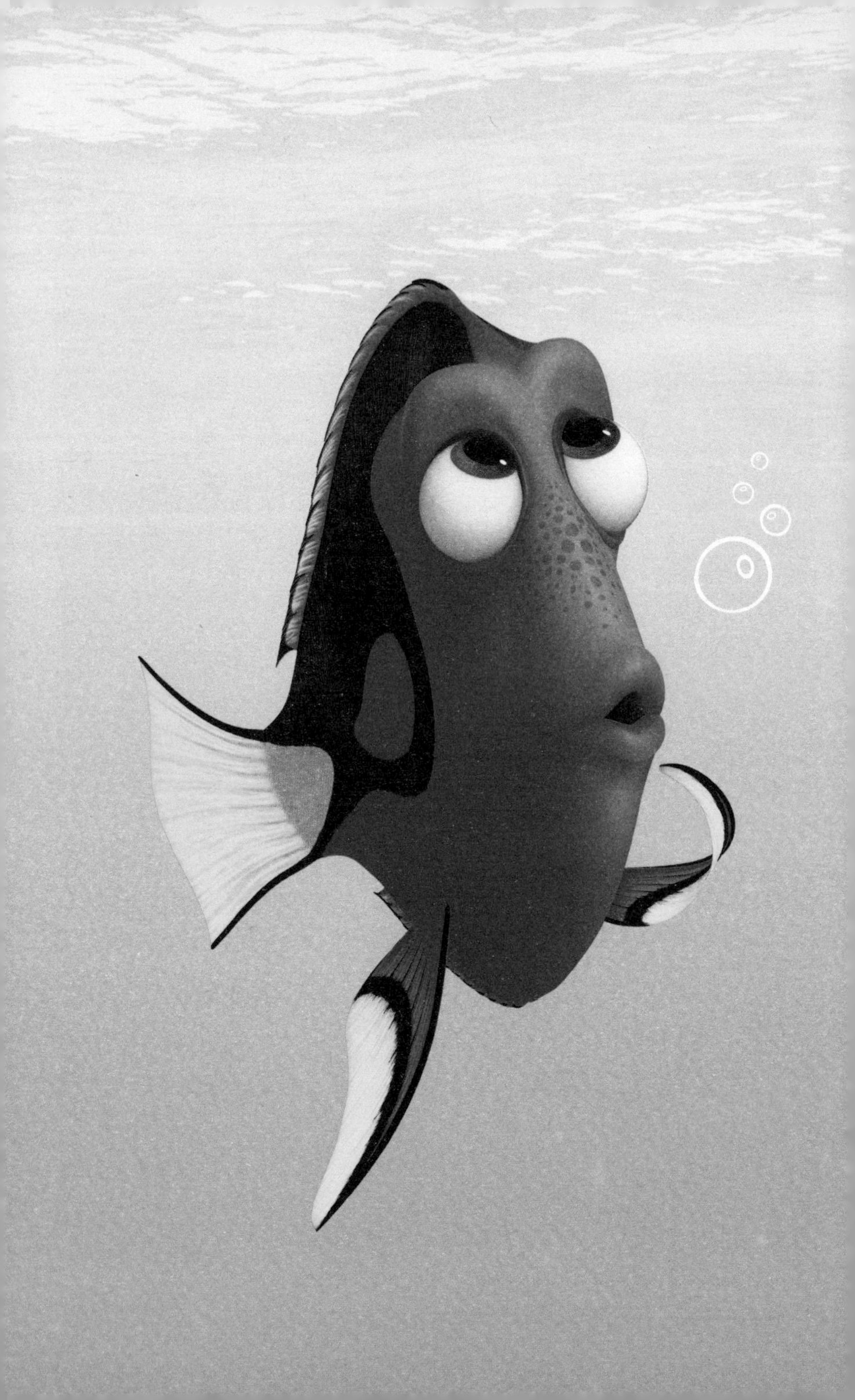

DIRECTOR
Andrew Stanton

CO-DIRECTOR
Angus MacLane

PRODUCER
Lindsey Collins

ORIGINAL STORY BY
Andrew Stanton

SCREENPLAY BY
Andrew Stanton
Victoria Strouse

ADDITIONAL SCREENPLAY MATERIAL BY
Bob Peterson

ADDITIONAL STORY MATERIAL BY
Angus MacLane

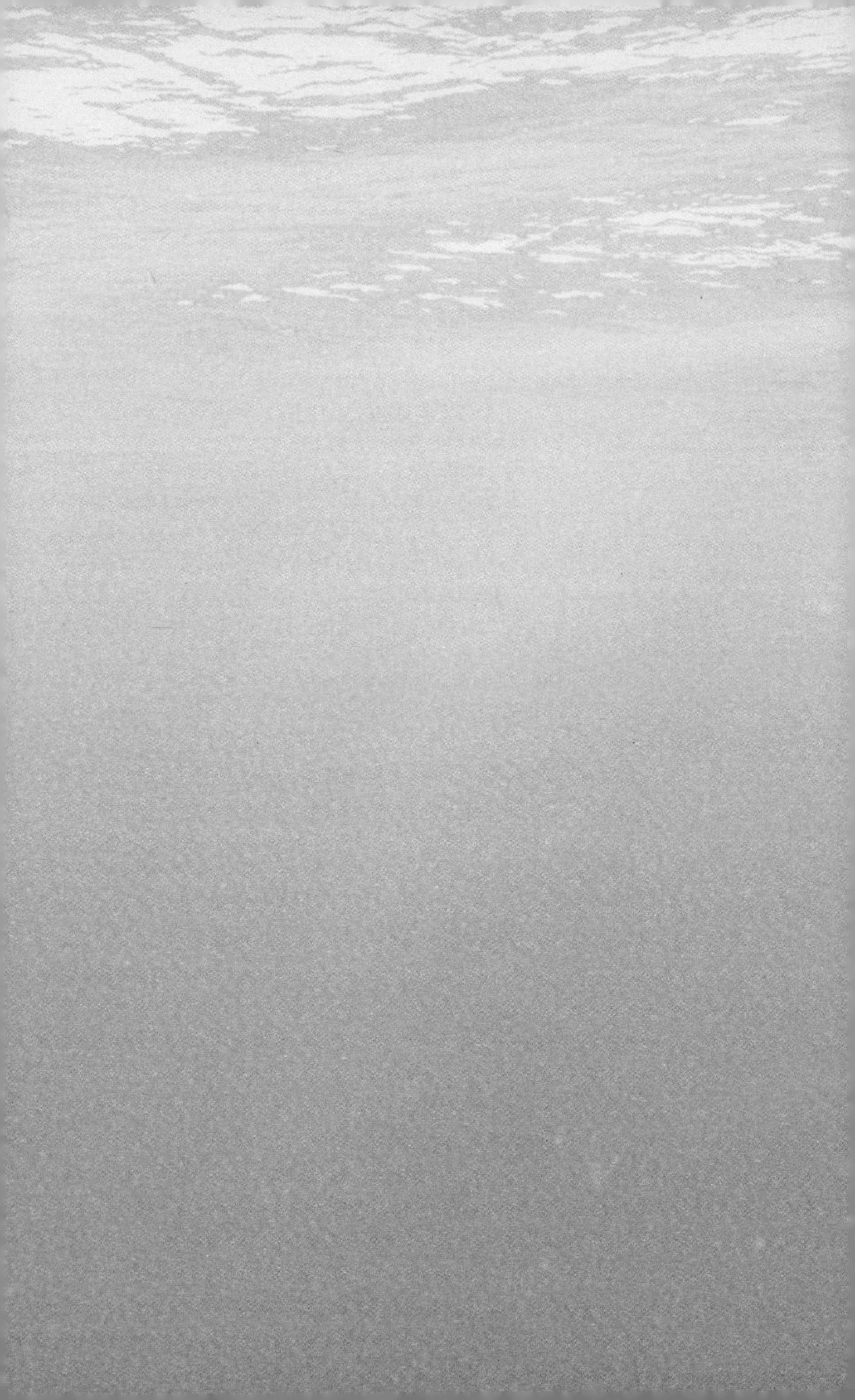

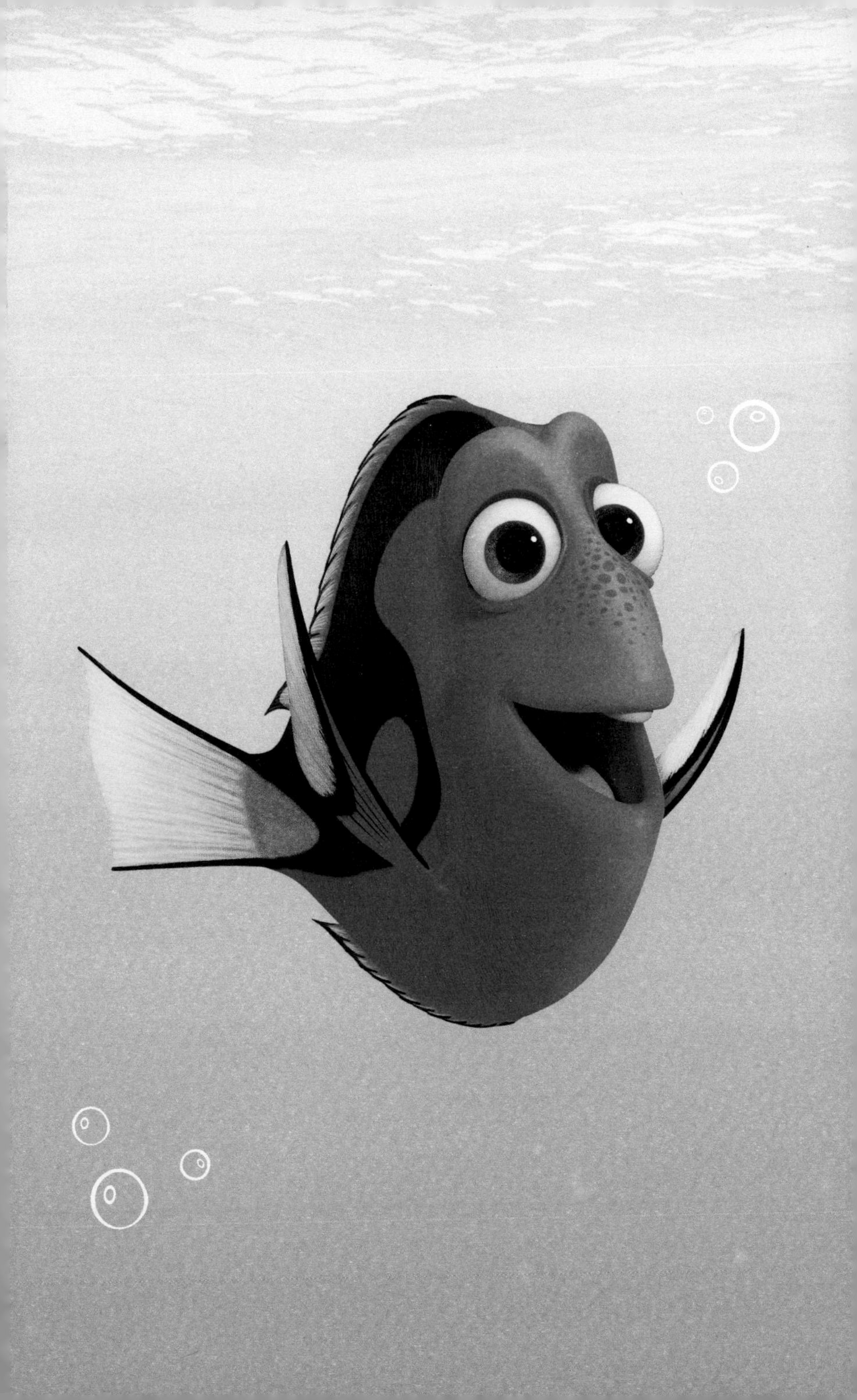